DAEMON
RISING

JOHN WILLIAM

ISBN 978-0-692-06161-9

RAMFIRAM

DAEMON RISING, BOOK ONE

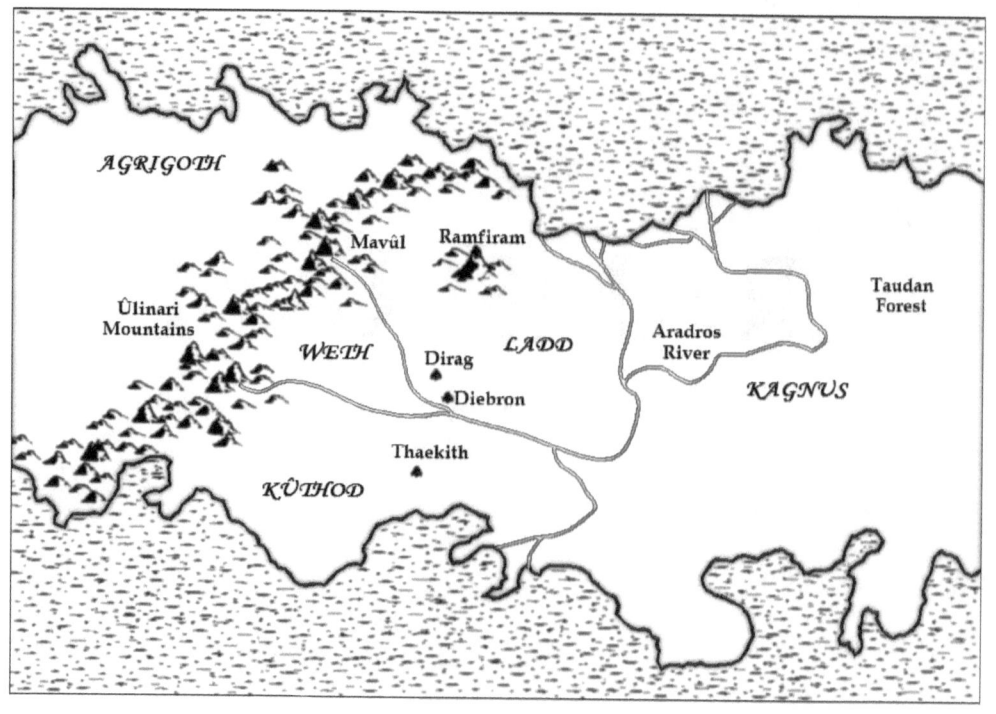

Prologue

For ages now it had tugged, growing ever stronger, at what used to be his mind. *Ages, years, days, hours*…his only indication of time was the schooling luminescent fish that made this black trench their lair. He hovered just off the murky bottom — watching, slowly revolving — with ghostly arms crossed about his naked, wispy frame. Hundreds of fathoms above, the myriad lights grouped and danced as a single entity, oblivious of his unblinking stare, perfecting a new variation in an endless evolution of darting, often explosive patterns. It was a dark beauty, this sanctuary of utter calm. A peace unknown to the world above.

Once there had been others with him. They'd formed a school of their own, each individual spirit drowned in the sea of collective consciousness: a pool of water heavy enough to stifle the *draw of life*. Those who could no longer feel that tug were lost, dispersed by the icy currents to which they took hold; yet his own throb had intensified with their departures, kicking and scratching a way free of the smothering veil. Lost memories started to return, features of his hazy form began to gather detail, and a steady fabrication of *weight* drew him down, closer and closer with every passing, until…

His feet touched the trench floor. He was the last of them all.

Thus he would roam the depths once more. He'd done so at first, aimlessly so, but each time found himself back at this place. The draw had been weaker then. No more than a nagging ache. A thing to fill the void left by the fleeing senses of his last life. Yet now it had become a pulsating beacon, summoning at fever pitch, and he moved forward to answer the call.

Eventually he escaped the submarine canyon and climbed onto the abyssal plains. Bottom feeders scuttled at the steps of his slow, gliding drudge, then turned back on him like insects attracted to light, threatening to swarm. Could they sense the draw, or was it his own aura that snared them? Shimmering eels slithered about like scouting vipers, grazing his smooth gray ankles. Crab steeds and anemone riders marched in single file behind — an army of glowing tentacles above shadowed claws — and wraithlike jellies formed a vanguard overhead. League upon league conjured thousands more, bolstering ranks and replacing deserters. *Hours, days, weeks*…they came and went untold in the blackness.

When next there came a change, it was a sense of rising…then his feet were treading over gravel instead of mired in silt…and finally he discerned, however faintly, some forms that didn't emit their own light. His maturing eyes adjusted to the hint almost at once, amplifying it a hundredfold, unlocking a sweeping panorama before him — and for a moment this thwarted his rigid advance, such was the unexpected wonder of the scene. Here too was a profusion of life: the multicolored coral fields below, teeming with endless tiny acts of symbiosis and predator taking prey, and the sleek, circling rays and roping schools above. But it was neither these nor the captivating probes of light blinking in and out about them that had immobilized him. It was the unmistakable walls and spires of a drowned city in the distance, skirting the farthest ridge.

Resuming his tireless stride, he veered towards the site and before long was passing between its toppled, mussel-laden gates. Long dark hair streamed about his head now, interfering with his sight, yet he could easily make out the familiar architecture of standing columns, portals, flights of steps, and crumbling arches. A paved road lay hidden beneath the sediment, he guessed — or remembered? — and he continued down it largely in solitude. His amassed creatural following shunned the ruins. Their legion was dispersed. Often a stray school looped past, or he nearly trampled a shuffling scavenger or shelled walker, but otherwise he was alone.

Or am I? he thought, craning his neck. A voice had tickled his consciousness. Reaching out with his mind, he spoke: *Come to me, child. I can free you of the ache!*

There was no response to this, so he pressed on beneath bridges connecting conical towers, over a ridge, through breaches in the rime-covered walls. *Whose city was this?* he struggled to recall. Images flashed: bronze-clad males patrolling battlements with long spears in hand; young females reclined in shaded grass, talking and giggling; children frolicking around a marble fountain. Theirs had been a proud race, he knew, ever strong until the catastrophic end. But with the forms came no faces. No names. A debris field of shattered brick and massive foundation stones lay at the heart of the place. All that remained of a once-lofty fortress. *Was I here when it fell?* he fought again to recall, pausing for the second time since his climb from the trench…

Then they were upon him.

You? sent one. *No, not you…* fired another, its tone oozing sarcasm. A third projected only insatiable hunger: a mind-rending sensation beyond words. Others bombarded him all at once, forcing him to raise the shield in his mind. Would he need to lift the sword as well?

A score, at least, penned him from all sides. Some appeared little different from the creatures they'd possessed, having been situated within plain sight of the intruder without drawing a second look. The nearest were two morays and an octopus with strangely human eyes. Still, he knew them less from the slight distortions of their forms than from the emotions hurled at his skull. The rest seemed to be something else. But they weren't. They were simply *advanced*. These had flung not only feelings — rage, sadness, wonder, desire — but clear thoughts as they slipped from behind the stones and into view. And these also displayed more than subtle human traits, with the proportion increasing by degrees up to one whose form was not far alien from his own.

The leader. Her slender limbs were humanoid, to be sure, yet longer than those sprouting from him and both finned along the calves and forearms and webbed at the fingers and toes. Coarse jade skin covered her entire frame, its tone lightening a shade about her tight stomach and pert breasts. She wore a motley garb of shells, corroded metal, and bones secured to belts of hide and clutched an impressive staff behind her back: the decorated tusk of a narwhale. Agitated by the resistance to their psychic lances, her pack began to circle and close. Yet, with one hand raised, she swam into their midst and subdued them all. And so he allowed her into his mind.

Welcome, Father, she said, coming to a halt within his reach. Her nose was broad and flat; lacking nostrils, it opened instead into a circular mouth beneath. Otherwise he found the face oddly pleasing to behold, especially its searching, sparkling eyes. Flowing black hair covered all but the tips of her finned ears, allowing only fleeting glimpses of the gills at her neck.

I'm not here by chance, he realized. *You have something I need.*

The key? She raised a hand to his cheek. A light touch to satisfy her guess. *But you're cold. Dead.*

As are you. None of us live. Not yet.

The hand withdrew, and her webbed feet propelled her back and away. *Nor is your task mine! But do you not wonder how I know of it? How I've become warden of the door? Do not fear...I won't keep the tool from you. I only ask this: why revive what shall surely fail again?*

He responded at once. *The seas are vast. The wayward innumerable. Yet though you dredged each and every league, making vassals of them all, you could not withhold the key. You are merely one who held on to her memories. I see now the face you wore before — but you hold no power here.*

The minion to the warden's left was a gray-scaled hybrid with hollow eyes and churning white locks extending from its scalp to a length twice its body's height. It must've read the arrival's thoughts in its mistress' mind, for no sooner had his reply ended than the creature lashed out. Its fists unfurled as groping claws, and its mouth gaped to reveal row after row of putrid, daggerlike teeth. It jetted within paces of the Father before the warden checked its attack. Snatching a handful of trailing hair as it lunged, she pulled and sent the monster's bulk crashing down. *It's no use, my pet. He says true...at least of the first.* She found the Father's eyes again and held them, attempting to mask her thoughts. Then, lowering her head, she connected. *Can you show it to me? My face? The one of old?*

Yes, he admitted. *But I won't. Much time remains to you in this place. Let go of memory. Do not seek to recall your name. Slough off this false skin and lose yourself — else you shall come to rue it.*

I have come to rue it, she said, projecting a true, deep sorrow. The servant she'd cast down, now back at her side, and many of the others mirrored her sentiment. She ceased treading water and sunk to her knees before him, her hands absently clawing the seabed. *I once reigned here, did I not? I knew it the moment I entered, so very long ago. And I found the key!...but we no longer feel the draw. You've stolen that from us all!* Gripping her staff tightly, she pointed it at him and cried: *Take the key as well...and leave this place!*

You shall walk dry land again, my sister, he proclaimed. *In time...*

She turned her face aside and entered her servants' minds. *Fetch me the ring!*

White spray crashed above the climbing terrace like ever-shifting clouds in a sky of magnificent cyan. The end of his dark oceanic trek. Alone once more, he gazed at the spectacle and yearned to find it reflected in the firmament beyond. Each step took him closer to the divide between water and air, and he could feel an absence of the latter substance as kindled flames in his chest. The undertow threatened to sweep him away, back to his watery grave. Yet he marched on.

Between the roll of one wave and the next he pierced the surface, spewing seawater and gasping for breath, and gloriously blinding light filled his eyes. The next wave lifted him, and in that instant he knew the moment of his first life's birth. The sandglass of mankind had become inverted. Its epoch was beginning anew. For a moment more he lingered, bobbing with the surf, eyes transfixed on a sight inland of the shore. Then his arms flailed and pulled his body forward. Soon his feet would drink the warmth of dry sand.

The stark-white tower rose amidst a pristine green of endless salt marsh, its pinnacle lost somewhere high in the ivory-clouded azure heavens. Crystal blue streams carved paths here and there through the rushes, and multitudes of screaming birds soared and swooped in flocks out to the farthest horizon. *The Earth is healed*, he thought. *And my haven stands.*

There were no eyes to observe the dripping, naked man emerging from the waves. There were no ears to hear his footfalls on the beach. He met the crest, started over dunes, and soon crossed into marsh grasses and cattails taller than his ample height, walking at times and wading at others. A colony of brown pelicans ceased squawking long enough to gawk from perches in an isolated stand of mangroves. An osprey lit down nearby, clutching a fresh kill. He left them behind.

The tower rose larger with each step—until at last he could make out the individual mortared stones that fashioned its four sides. All unblemished. All smooth, solid, and radiant as the day they were laid. At the base he found the structure's single entrance: its only portal save the windows he knew waited far above. The dimensions were scarcely enough to walk upright through, had the door stood open. But it was closed. There were no hinges nor bars. Only a thick slab of red-gold metal.

On the ring finger of his left hand was the key: a snake forged of the same material as the door, its head circling around to sink fangs in its own tail. *The end nourishes the beginning. The beginning births the end.* Coming within a step of the barrier, he hesitated, the warden's question swimming back to the forefront of his thoughts. *Why revive what shall surely fail again?*

But which is the true failure? *A collapse of bloodlines or a defeat of will?* The first would come indeed, this time as it had the last. And as it would the next. But as for the second... *Maybe this time will be different.* He raised his palm and placed it flat against the door.

What was another hour compared to the ages of his wait and the months of his journey? Yet now he felt time's passing as would his children to come. To them, each and every day would be precious. One moment wasted would be a thing forever lost, and the next could be the last. With each step on the spiral stair, another visage entered his mind. Faces of his firstborn. Those who once lived and might soon breathe again. He heard their voices in every touch of his hand on the unseen, guiding rail. He mouthed the words...then intoned them; and soon the tower's hollow belly echoed with a repeated song. At times it swam soft, almost a whisper. At others it dove deep to baritone. And between those bars it broke the chant to thrash wildly in a higher range, seething with emotion.

On and on he climbed in darkness until at last he reached the door overhead. It slid open easily, and once more he winced as light broke through the opening to attack his dilated eyes. Not two strides from his ascending form, positioned exactly at the center of the otherwise bare chamber, two objects sat in stillness: a waist-high rounded stone pedestal with a top carved to the likeness of a human hand and a tiny strongbox resting in its upturned palm. A sunbeam from one window fell on the support, illuminating its prize while leaving the rest of the room to shadows. The *draw of life* emanated from that spot—the beacon of his mystic lighthouse—yet he didn't go to it immediately. He had arrived. The throbbing in his mind had ceased, and nothing would start without him.

Framed by the northern window, the Father looked out over the waters from whence he'd come. He felt the wind on his face and smelled the salty air. He heard gulls screaming and waves roaring and the sounds of fish darting close to his head. He saw the warden passing through the tumbled city gates: ivory staff in hand, leaving her minions behind. He drank the chasm's deadly cold, caught a glimpse of dancing lights overhead...and quickly pulled away.

From the eastern window he saw the marsh, a great river, and the edge of a forest beyond. *The river Aradros.* His eyes scanned deep and came upon a lone deer emerging from a bramble thicket. He watched it pause, raise its head, and cautiously survey the trees for an enemy. He tasted the water it licked from a clear, icy stream. He smiled at the blue wildflowers about its hooves and at the red and golden butterflies flittering in the canopy above. The woods stretched unbroken ridge after ridge, past gullies and tangles and creeks and outcroppings, seemingly without end.

The southern portal revealed much the same lay of land; except now the river ran parallel to the seashore, cutting a path many leagues beyond it through the forest. A fog crept in and wrapped its misty tendrils about titanic trunks of oak and elm, hovering thickest just off the leaf-strewn floor as evening came on. Venomous spiders sat patiently in their webs amid branches that cluttered his mind's eye. The sight and faint sound of moisture dripping from a fern leaf, forming a little pool below, summoned to him an image alike yet discordant in its essence: hot blood trickling over a jutting rock to fall, strike, and soak deep, staining a wide crimson circle in the snow and ice below. *A loss endured and long forgotten…or a tragedy yet to come?* Whichever it was, the scene belonged to another place. *It's the West calling…*

The osprey he'd spied below greeted him at the final window, studying the Father with its keen, dark eyes between spurts of preening. Storm clouds were brewing outside. The bird made way for the view by clutching his arm tightly with its bloody talons, and he pulled it round so both of them could see. Away in the distance, beyond reach of the coming rain, past the great river's branches and tributaries and the unyielding wall of mountains, a serpent slid through the sea of sand that choked the plains of Agrigoth. The sun was set, the day's stored heat rapidly escaping, yet still he felt it burning through the snake's thin scales. The osprey screeched. *What part shall that land play, my friend?* It turned an eye on him and cocked its head to one side — as if considering the question — before gazing back at the night. Lightning flashed nearby, for an instant illuminating the marsh, and his sight withdrew from afar. A deafening boom followed. The bird screeched again.

Reaching out once more, closer now, he swept over hill and vale. Remote plumes of smoke drew near, a taste of sulfur permeated the air…and the fiery Womb came under his scrutiny. *You stir, Mother,* he projected, *…and so I come again.* Then he cut his eyes to his arm, spoke aloud: "Wait for me there!" — and hurled the osprey into the tumult.

An instant later he saw the bird aloft: an image caught in a flash of lightning. Satisfied, he backed away, turned, and walked to the pedestal. Thunder roared, and shadows danced about the chamber. He took in and let out a deep breath, reached for the undying hand of stone with a hand of immortal flesh…

And opened the box.

PART ONE

Dangling From Strings

TWELVE YEARS AGO

I awoke in darkness to the echoed howling of wolves. It was the first time since our departure that I could recall being conscious during the night, for a malignant fever had wracked my body from the onset, breaking me down at the end of each day's march. Yet sleep only exhausted me further now. Disturbing dreams gnawed at my mind where there'd once been tranquility, and the reality presented to me each morning was worse. At least I was no longer gagged with a foul bit, nor were my eyes covered, and the hunger inside to once again behold the daylight surely rivaled the cravings of my poor belly. The fever had broken. The weariness remained. I could feel my scrawny body wasting away from one moment to the next.

The moon shone dimly, but it was enough for me to picture my new situation. I'd been deposited on a narrow precipice overlooking a gorge, and I could hear water running swiftly far below. My arms were tied behind me to a gnarled juniper tree, and my weakness had taken away the ability to stave off the cold, making it seem as though my skullcap and Kûhric's coat were only preserving the frost that'd already found my core. I knew by smell that it was his clothing blanketing me—though another scent was beginning to choke out all others in the chasm's still air. Something dead and decaying lay nearby.

Unable to return to sleep or detect anything else in the dark, I was left alone with my thoughts. They began to torture me. Once more I saw my champion approach the sorcerer. Once again I saw the stones fall. I recalled how Kûhric had at first struggled to move and speak but had finally dropped his blade and stood silent. I saw a single tear well in his eye and run slowly down his cheek. Taloseth the Mage had waited patiently as all of this transpired. Then he'd approached Kûhric and buried his axe deep in the man's shoulder and chest.

And what about my mother? She'd fallen under the sorcerer's malice as well. Briefly I envisioned our dog feeding on their corpses, but my mind was too weak to sob over the thought. In truth, I didn't recall any proper mourning, for the inflictions wreaked upon me by Taloseth had left me in a perpetual daze. He'd hooded and gagged me on that first day soon after Kûhric's body hit the ground, then he'd marched off with me on a leash behind him. Over a week had passed since that day, I guessed, though time had become increasingly difficult to judge toward the end. The mage had yet to speak to me, nor had he brought me within earshot of anyone else…at least as far as I could tell.

Finally the sky began to lighten. Once more I tried my bonds to no avail and almost retched from the putrid stench enveloping me. With what material had he constrained me? I strove to see. It was my mother's braids.

"Sorcerer!" I screamed with all the strength left in my withered frame. "What did you do to my mother?" Tears had come at last. "What do you want from me?"

Soon as the echoes of my wrath expired, I heard a raven caw from the rim. Perched on a juniper of its own, it peered out over the divide as if it were some king surveying a dominion, paying no heed to my plight. I watched the bird intently as it shifted from side to side and croaked softly to itself. Then presently it fixated on the ledge directly above me, and I looked up to see what'd caught its eye.

There was no mistaking what I saw on that stone shelf in the early morning light. It'd been there all along, motionless as the rocks it was propped against. Kûhric's mangled corpse. My eyes jumped away from the awful thing as soon as they fell upon it, but my mind continued to peruse the image: a face hideously warped, the tongue protruding from a twisted mouth. I shivered in disgust. The skin around the axe's bite was crusted with black gore, and the rest was exposed as a mass of bluish-green blisters. It seemed the body had been handled only as much as was necessary to transport it to this place. But what'd driven the mage to leave it here? Had I not been tortured enough?

Gathering courage, I forced myself to take another look. Now I saw a broken collarbone protruding from the skin and bulbous eyes staring out into nothing. The raven saw them as well: morsels ripe for the picking. It cawed once again, flew straight toward the ledge where the body sat cross-legged, and perched on its rotting shoulder. I was certain I knew what would happen next…and I was just about to turn away from it when…

Kûhric's corpse slung up an arm at the bird!

My shriek met the raven's an instant after it was loosed. Kûhric had struck his target with a vigor surpassing that of living men. Feathers hung in the air as an iridescent black mass plunged to the river below. I longed to follow it. Yet stillness returned as abruptly as the violence had taken shape. Then I found myself wondering if it'd happened at all.

"Your mother's dead," came a sudden voice from the adjacent crag.

So my outburst hadn't gone unnoticed — but who was this to answer it? Now I saw the girl below me: not far to my left, standing inside a gaping mouth in the rock wall. Her right arm caressed one of its stony teeth. Her left hand clutched a slender staff crowned with a fox's skull. A narrow, treacherous path rounded the corner to join the opening's ledge, but it seemed she'd emerged from within.

She was cloaked but not hooded, and the encompassing garment was parted to reveal something of her delicate figure as well. That exposed skin, not unlike my own, had a reddish-brown hue to it. A rare trait among the woodland tribes. Uncommon too was the peculiar beauty I saw in her face. A seasoned charm, although I guessed she was no more than a few years my elder. Her hair was black as the feathers of her mantle, and for a moment I pondered whether she might be the spirit of that fallen raven. Had Kûhric reacted to her presence? I looked at the body. It was as I'd first seen it, locked in oblivion.

"You needn't worry about him," said my new warden as I met her eyes again. "His will is my own."

And what is *your will?* I thought but didn't ask her, having lost a struggle for composure. Cold and hunger crippled my body. The revelation of the undead baffled my mind. I stared and wept.

"Has our father mistreated you?" she grinned. "I thought he might. What's your name, brother?"

"I'm not your brother!"

The girl's smirk fell at my thundered reply, but she gave no other response than to back into the shadows, vanishing from sight.

"My name's Imlod, son of Nir," I said to her softly while finishing my bowl of honey-sweetened stew.

"See? That wasn't so hard now, was it? Imlod Nir: bastard son of the great mage!" Her grin had returned. "I'm your sister, Galfayan."

This girl who claimed to be my sibling was scrutinizing my every move, and although I was lost in gluttony, I couldn't keep myself from eyeing her between swallows. The shadows hid much of her body, but her striking face shone red in the firelight from where she knelt near the opposite wall. The entrance and the only window in the place were covered by skins. A water jug was within reach, and the stewpot and several utensils were on the fire. I could see little else.

We sat inside the main room of an ingenious clay brick dwelling situated in a natural recess in the limestone cliff. From afar, the adjoining cells looked like a stack of strongboxes — or so it had seemed to me as I was being led around the corner of Galfayan's crag. Few men would've expected to find such a marvel in this place, and fewer still could've contrived and built it.

Kûhric hadn't followed us.

"Where's the sorcerer?" I asked, setting an empty mug aside. Only then did I recoil from the vessel. A carved skull, grisly and raw. I suppose a grievous thirst takes no offense to such things.

"He speaks with his mistress in the valley below. We aren't his concern right now." The girl's oily, dark strands gleamed as they fell around her breasts. She wore a ring in her nose and a twisted leather cord about her neck: devices that amplified her odd charm.

"His mistress?"

"A daemon. The ancient ruler of this place." Her hand reached for something at her side. "Are you feeling better now?"

Not waiting for an answer, Galfayan turned her attention to the object she'd just retrieved. A small bone pipe. She placed it to her lips, fired the bowl with a lit splinter, and inhaled deeply.

I knew that smell. Maybe with her wits dulled and the sorcerer away, I could chance an escape. My mind should've been reeling with a multitude of plans, but it wasn't. I was entranced instead by the flame of her pipe and the gleam in her eyes. "My mother would've spoken of you," I blurted out at last. "Even if she was hiding something about him."

"Oh, I'm sure she would've babbled on and on about me!" Galfayan laughed. "You're right, Imlod. I'm only *half* your sister. But it's the good half." She put down the pipe, rose, and crossed the room to sit beside me. Her form was hazy. My heart was speeding.

"You've drugged me…" I slurred.

"Only to soothe you," she said as I became acutely aware of my drooping eyelids. Touching a hand to my forehead, she gently swept the hair from my eyes. "You need untroubled sleep."

My escape would have to wait.

The window was open. The light of noonday streamed in. With hunger, thirst, and drowsiness all sated, it was time to focus on my plight. Yet for the moment my thoughts lingered on Galfayan. Where was she?

I heard her in the next room even as I pushed aside the drape to enter it. Clothed as before, a moss-wicked candle within reach, my sister was filling a basket with various items from the table in front of her. She was preparing to leave.

"You're not needed now!" she barked as our eyes met. "Go back to sleep."

"What is this place? Why am I here?"

She picked up the basket and candle and moved toward the exit.

"Why won't you answer?" I demanded.

She paused and turned back to me.

"I could hurt you…"

"I think not," she said with a grin. "Walk with me."

We entered a passage that soon led to open air. The mouth of an earthen stairway awaited us, and she motioned for me to lead our descent. I took a few steps. The odor of death was returning.

"This is Mavûl Gorge," she said after a moment's reflection. "And you're here so I may continue to be."

"Speak plainly!" I growled, spinning to face her. "Or I won't go any further!"

She laughed and pushed me hard in the chest. My head struck the embedded log forming the next step down as I fell backwards, then I lay unmoving on one side with my face in the dirt. Someone took hold of my neck and arm and pulled me to my knees. I nearly retched at the stench.

It was Kûhric, of course, who'd been skulking behind the two enormous red rocks that bent the path at its opening. Though the sun shone directly overhead now, warming air, earth, and stone, the touch of those hands on my bare flesh was as the frost of a winter morning. Held firm and half-suspended above the ground, I could do no more than tilt my head to one side. There I saw a familiar serpent tattoo circling a withered finger, and that removed any doubt as to who had me. I didn't want him to turn me around, and he made no move to do so.

"Now that your nanny's here, you need go no further," Galfayan spoke as she rounded the bend.

"Let him be!" I cried, struggling in vain against the superhuman strength that held me.

"Let *him* be?" she scoffed. "You'd better start thinking of yourself, Imlod. The man you knew is no more. This thing is only his foul shell."

Once more the questions in my mind were suppressed by emotion, only now it was growing rage rather than grief and bewilderment. Galfayan stared at me for awhile, awaiting a response that didn't come; then she walked past my fixed line of sight, shaking her head in annoyance. "In a moment you'll be released — but don't run! He'll do more than bruise you for it!"

The sound of her footsteps soon faded, and Kûhric released his grip to step away from me. I wasn't prepared to observe his face yet, so I knelt and gazed at the clouds instead. I'd never seen them unobstructed by branches before — huge and looming bright in a wide-open sky — and the sight was beautiful and calming to me. Had it not been so, I might've attempted the rash escape that I'd just been warned against…or in my anger, sought to intercept and throttle my sister. Yet I looked on, trying to blot out the hatred and fear and disgust…

A bird of prey touched down in the brushwood topping the rocks overhead. *Another scavenger that he won't let near. But would he let me tend him? Am I strong enough to try?*

It was time to look into Kûhric's eyes. Time to see if any trace of my hero could be found in there. Would he smite me as he had the raven if I came too close? Maybe that would be for the best: to die by Kûhric's hands now rather than succumb to the torturous arts of Taloseth and his daughter.

Breathing through my mouth so as not to gag again at the smell, I pivoted on my hands and knees. Kûhric was crouching now, his back against the rock, and my movements didn't disturb him at all. I winced at the gruesome sight as before, yet this time I forced myself to stare until its horror lessened. Then slowly I moved toward him, holding my open hands out in front to show I meant no threat.

"Kûhric," I spoke sadly, quietly. "Can you hear me?"

The osprey screeched. There was no other sound or motion save the wind. I leaned in close to my guard's face. Fluids oozed from his nose and his gaping mouth. Insects crawled about in his disheveled black mane. I peered into his eyes, searching for a spark of life. But I saw only my reflection in those pools — and that image of me was, as my world had become, turned upside down.

PRESENT DAY

1

Standing knee-deep in the silt that supported her way of life, the girl said: "Don't come any closer."

"I didn't intend to..." the stranger replied. His face was lost to the startled young woman, hidden beneath his leather cowl, so he held up empty palms to her as a reassuring gesture. *She must stay calm*, he thought. *Where are you now?*

The water here is deep, came the answer, darting amid his own thoughts like a leaf caught up by the wind. *I won't be seen.*

Good, the man sent to his accomplice. Then he spoke aloud to the girl again: "I'm content to stare. You're a pretty one. Have they told you that?" Something in her eyes said he'd taken the right course. He drew back the cowl—revealing a slender face, hawklike nose, and dark braided hair—and smiled.

"No," she giggled, yet the tension hadn't wholly departed her. Looking back over her shoulder, she added: "They're too busy with the hogs to notice. Who are you?"

"My name's Megnus. I've come from Dirag to admire your dwellings. This one here's a marvel all its own," he said without directing her gaze to it, "...but I've heard there are even larger ones. Perhaps you could show one of those to me—at least from the shore? I'd be grateful indeed."

"I can take you to my father...or to the overseer," the girl began to explain, wringing her hands free of the icy muck in which she'd been digging for roots. With the arrival of winter at hand, she wouldn't be the only member of her clan scouring the lake bottom for sustenance. She'd alluded to a herd of pigs, and surely there were fish to be had; but such stores had to be properly managed, not foolishly exhausted at the first rumblings of one's belly. The rushes themselves were the true staple of these people. Their roots could be foraged year round and baked in ovens, the shoots and stems could be eaten fresh in the spring, and seeds would be harvested for flour in late summer. Megnus of Dirag considered all this as the girl babbled, till at last she came back to the point: "They'll be angry if I don't take you to them right away. We've few visitors besides the wolves."

A chill wind had arrived from the east while she spoke, rippling the surface of the lake, reminding the stranger of the task that his familiar should be near to completing. *What've you found?*

As you guessed. A breech in the wall. Only water guards their backs.

"Will you come with me or not?" the girl pressed, furrowing her brow at the man's introspection. She brushed a curl of thick auburn hair aside and awaited his response.

"Yes, of course," said Megnus, coming back to the moment. He took a step forward into the murk. The cloudless sky was growing dim.

The girl grinned and turned to lead the way, leaving her floating basket of roots behind. "If you like, I'll bring you something to eat. Mother has a stew in the pots, and the boys trapped a rabbit. They're not good for much else, but they know how to lay a snare." She was trudging along briskly, raising a ruckus with all the splashing, when suddenly she turned to ask: "Have you ever seen..."

The words died on her lips. The stranger was gone.

Tyth decided not to tell her father about the visitor. At first they were busy with the preparation of their meal, then they were busy partaking of it, then she told herself: *perhaps he's just a shy young man.* It was Tyth, not her clan's homes, whom this *Megnus of Dirag* was interested in seeing more of — or so she fancied. He'd all but admitted it, hadn't he? And he was handsome...

Most outsiders interested in their dwellings were traders, not wanderers who hid in the rushes and ogled girls. But she'd been to Dirag once herself and was aware of the contrast between her home and the modest huts of those woodland folk. Nearly a dozen men, women, and children made up her household — not to mention the smelly pigs that were sometimes kept inside — yet the large crannog held them all comfortably with room to spare. She still remembered her father and older brothers undertaking its construction: the stout piles they'd driven into the mud, the seemingly endless branches and stones used to build the mound, the bridge leading to the single gate, the thatched huts with their trimmings, and so on. *He probably was only curious about how we live,* she finally resolved. But she hoped differently.

The Land of Ladd, after all, was filled with possibility: for there were many rumors of change abroad. Old wars ended. Rivals thrown down. New pacts sealed in blood. But so far the words alone had reached Diebron. Theirs was a peaceful settlement separated from the center of grand design by league upon league of woodland — and their exclusion from such matters suited the lake folk well indeed. Warlords hadn't come to recruit their men. Raiding parties hadn't plundered their stores. They simply continued on as they had for generations: content with crannogs and boats and gales that bent the rushes beneath a clear azure sky. The elders made sacrifice to Mother Earth every day, never failing to voice thanks for what they'd received and never desiring anything more. Tyth was old enough to understand their meekness but too young for it to stifle her own curious nature. Traders' stories fascinated her; and any possibility of real change, be it for better or worse, seemed a thing worth wishing.

I should be asleep by now. Tossing in the pallet, shifting her fur blanket, she focused instead on the heavy breathing of her youngest brother. His bed was nearest hers for a reason. She'd once cared for this one as if he were her child, and their attachment had not yet broken. Her other siblings could be hateful at times — but not little Hadric. He was a sweet boy, always eager to help, always grinning. *I'll do something special for him this season. A boar's tooth necklace...or a bone flute...or I could beg papa to take us back to Ramfiram! Poor mama! She'd have one eye on us and the other on her baskets...*

Some time later Tyth woke with a start. The moon was still up, and Hadric's breathing was smooth and even. But something didn't feel right. Had she heard a noise coming from the yard?

She decided to go outside. Silver moonbeams rose from the lake's surface to greet her at the doorway, rushing in as her hands eased the flap aside, revealing the yard to her well-adjusted eyesight. *Did someone leave the gate unbarred?* She looked in that direction. A single cry would fetch her brothers.

"Did I wake you, child?" the old man glanced at Tyth and whispered as her gaze fell on him. This was the shaman Ediresh, a guest of her father for three seasons now: a silent, brooding elder who'd become like kin to her. He stood to her left in the palisade's gap, looking out over the lake. A withered hand drew the fur-lined folds of his weathered red cloak about his frame, barring the chill. His hot breath froze and billowed out over the water.

I worked myself up over nothing, she thought, moving to stand beside him. "I don't know. I just can't sleep."

"It must be something in the air," he replied, lightly stroking his gray-flecked beard.

Tyth's feet were freezing. The thought of returning inside occurred to her, followed by a strong desire to stir up dying embers, but there was something she wished to say first. Something she hoped would put her mind at ease before she lay down again. "Ediresh...can you keep a secret?"

"Keep a secret?" the shaman sighed, dark eyes wandering up from the water and out into the night sky. "Secrets can be dangerous." Meeting the girl's face again, though, he smiled and added: "But for you, my darling, I suppose I could handle one more."

The warm grin relaxed Tyth. "We had a visitor today."

The shaman's smile vanished. He grabbed the girl by her shoulders and bent to look her dead in the face: "Who was it? Why did you keep it from us?"

"Let go!" Tyth whined, still careful with her volume. Shoving the pawing hands aside, she added angrily: "He was harmless! A young man from Dirag. He didn't want to talk with papa! I thought you'd understand!" Ediresh was listening intently to her words, searching deep inside her eyes. Unable to endure the stare, she shied away. "I did nothing wrong!"

"You should've told us, Tyth!" The old man's voice was starting to rise. "Did you forget your place?" Suddenly he looked toward the gate, paused a moment, then returned to his speech: "What about your father's rules? This man could be more than he seemed!"

"But I told you he was just a traveler…and he spoke kindly to me…"

"Listen well, girl," came a sudden voice from above, drawing their faces to its source. "That man's no fool." Two metal blades shone atop the nearest hut like stars in the night—except their sky was a motionless figure cloaked in shadows. An intruder crouching with his hood drawn, watching. Waiting for the moment to strike.

Ediresh took a step back, gasping and clutching at his heart. The girl drew breath to scream…but nothing came save a sharp exhale of bewilderment and despair. A sound barely audible. She recalled the intruder's voice. It was her visitor, Megnus of Dirag.

"I won't shout," said the shaman, forcefully but in a lowered voice, motioning for Tyth to remain silent. "These people had no part in my actions. Do what you came for quickly—and be gone!"

"What's wrong, Ediresh?" someone called from a door beneath the intruder, followed by other sounds of stirring. *They'll all be out soon*, Tyth thought. *This can't be happening!*

"Stay inside, Esosh!" the old man implored. "They've come for me at last! It's no business of yours. Keep everyone inside!"

Now Tyth started to shake and cry. Her mother yelled for her to come, but she dared not move. Her father, Esosh, wouldn't cower inside. She heard him arming the men to storm the yard. *Oh Goddess, what've I done?*

The man above shifted slightly as if anticipating the onrush, but he said no more. And neither did Ediresh. At some point the shaman had dropped to his knees, and now his head was bowed with his eyes closed. Praying, perhaps.

Suddenly the men burst outside, shouting and brandishing their stone tools, skinning knives, and wooden spears as weapons. There were six in all. Fathers and sons. Lamentation joined the din, streaming from the women's hut. Little Hadric shirked his mother's grasp, dashed out, saw Tyth, and bravely ran to her side.

Tyth's father was the first to exit, leading the charge—and thus he was the first to fall. A leap from the roof, a knife in the eye, a deft roll aside, and Megnus of Dirag was on his feet again before Esosh's body hit the ground. The others came on without hesitation, fueled by rage at that loss and hoping to end the intruder's life just as rapidly.

But it would not be so.

Blackness rose up before them. A towering form wielding a cruel device. It swept over those who would impale its master, severing their limbs, silencing tongues, and smashing brains to a bloody pulp. Spears broke off in its flesh like snapped twigs underfoot. Blow after desperate blow fell dully upon its sides and back. Fallen men groaned. Filthy pigs squealed in answer from their pen, heralding the dead.

"Help!" shrieked Esosh's wife, running into the yard, her voice directed out over the lake. "Someone save us! Thayld Priregord! We're..." And then she too was put down, her slender fingers clawing in the dirt as her final breaths rasped free from a hilt of white bone.

Megnus had thrown that killing knife, and now he took up a fallen spear and slid it into the guts of the last attacker. The women's cries exuding from within plagued him as he bent to retrieve his knives—so he stalked into their dwelling, blades dripping gore.

"Did you think she'd forget?" asked the murderer when he returned. After wiping his knives clean with a swathe of leather, he looked for a moment to his servant—a lifeless monument raised amidst a moonlit field of carnage—before meeting the shaman's eyes. "Did you think you were *forgiven?*"

Ediresh shook his head woefully. "No. Only *no longer important.* That's what I'd hoped for after all these years."

"It was wise to change your name, Amasmir—but you should've become a fisherman," said Megnus, drawing closer to Tyth and her small protector. "Tell me: where are the others? Where have your Brethren burrowed?" He pointed a knife at Hadric's chest and waited.

The boy trembled but didn't shrink from his parents' slayer. "You can't have my sister!" Tyth heard him say, though she could barely comprehend the words. Her mind had cracked beneath waves of sorrow, and now the icy water drowned her from within. *If only I'd told them...*

"Have they not bled enough?" Ediresh shouted, his feeble body shaking now as well. "What kind of man are you? A killer of woman and child! A worm grown from the witch's spoor? You'd get nothing from me, dog, even if I'd the words to give!"

"My name is Imlod Nir. A name you've heard before. You can tell me now, or you can tell the queen when we return. Even death won't hold your tongue."

"No! I beg you...not that!" cried the shaman, crawling on hands and knees to grovel at his conqueror's feet. The realization of whom he was speaking to had instantly changed his attitude. "I know of another! I can lead you to him!"

"Is that so?" Imlod smirked. "Well then, it seems we must be going." Torches were fast approaching. Some could be seen as tiny points traversing the water in boats. Others circled the bank by foot. The overseer was apparently on his way, and a sizable host was coming with him.

Imlod pointed a knife at the gate, and Amasmir obediently turned to start for it. But even as he did so, he looked back at Tyth. "Stay where you are, children! Thayld will see to…"

Imlod Nir plunged a blade into Amasmir's heart in that instant, causing Tyth to cry out at last. The dark minion leapt forth immediately, seized the shaman's corpse, and heaved the dead weight onto its shoulder before running off with it. It reached the crannog's gate, threw the bolt aside, and became swallowed by the night.

"Look at me," said Imlod.

Tyth didn't want to. She didn't even want to breathe. But she had no choice. Her teary eyes flicked to his.

"The Queen of Earth commands us all, girl. There's another life beyond these waters. Seek it in Ramfiram!"

And with that, the assassin took his leave.

2

It was a day that chilled a man to the marrow of his bones. Winter was here, no doubt, but the forest tribes rarely had true relief from the cold. No, the frost that ate the villagers' hearts today was the pang of sorrow, for someone of great importance to them had died.

Imlod Nir stood among those gathered in the grove. Not because he felt the same as they did, but because every man, woman, and child of Dirag was there. Malbus Iryn had been their chieftain for as long as most could remember. He'd defined the essence of their clan. But now he was set to wander again, and it was their task to ensure his soul found the path. A stand of silver birch trees watched over the ritual with deference, waiting to extract through deep roots the power being given over to the black soil. Snowflakes fell lightly about the body and its retinue. A feeble elder wailed. A newborn baby cried.

"Here are your children, Mother," spoke a woman standing over the corpse, her voice and gaze directed earthward. "We give back what was given."

This was the priestess Sevos Let, a woman once revered throughout Ladd as an incarnation of their goddess. Her words still held power over these people; and though her solemn face was beginning to wrinkle with age, it yet radiated a rare beauty, with her carefully picked ornaments adding to the effect. Of these, the most striking were her twisted golden hoop earrings and the painted mussel shells woven into her dark locks.

"Malbus passed under the crescent moon," she went on, surveying the crowd, "...so we shall look for him among the lesser beasts and the brambles. He was a shrewd servant in this life. May he be equally keen in the next!"

Imlod's teeth ground tighter. This talk was afflicting the maiden beside him, and he knew without a glance that she'd soon be sobbing aloud. The crying of others had already discomfited him. What had these folk lost in one aged dolt that hadn't been taken tenfold from him? Men may say things of other men that are meant to warm hearts, yet all words are foreign to the foreigner. *Amasmir was easier than enduring this farce*, he mused, recalling his sister's pleasure as he'd led that rebel's animated corpse to her high seat. *But the priestess is the true prize.*

"Some of you have challenged my word on Malbus' death," said Sevos. She stepped aside as two gaunt figures came forth from behind. "You would have it a murder. But I tell you: it's not so! There wasn't a mark on him. His old heart gave out before his arms failed him, and that's all. We'll not spoil this day with such foolishness!"

The priestess' servants placed Malbus in a cist. One remained to arrange the body and receive its due, and the other quickly rejoined the throng. Both were bundled in heavy furs, but the soot tattoos on their necks and faces were clear to

Imlod's sight: markings, he recalled, like those his poor mother had borne in life. Yet unlike the venerated man these two attended, Nir had been denied a proper burial. Her body had been left where it fell on that terrible day in Imlod's past, and only woodland scavengers dwelled near his boyhood home. The woman's soul had been scattered with her bones, and if her son hadn't later summoned it to him, she might've walked the same dreary paths for seasons innumerable, forever haunting the lairs of beasts and men. *What choice did I have?*

She was there, of course. Beyond the rings of onlookers, just out of sight, her spirit drifted beneath the branches. Nir would alert or aid her son — her master — if need be, should anything go awry with his plans. More than once she'd saved his life, though he'd been unable to do the same for her. And the same could be said of Kûhric. He was lurking out there too. A twisted metal mask donned by an automaton of withered flesh and bones. No harm would come to Imlod this day or any other while they traveled with him. He need only reach out to them with his mind.

The priestess ended her speech, then Imlod fell in line with all those waiting to adorn Malbus' grave. So many goods passed into the hole that he was sure no soil would be needed to cover it. Some women brought elaborately incised clay vessels. Others cast in small charms or strings of teeth. Men handed over flint knives or antlers to the servant for proper arrangement, and after every offering the corpse was strewn with red ochre.

Yet when his turn arrived, Imlod Nir presented only empty hands.

"Don't touch him!" Sevos Let shouted. All eyes were on the scene unfolding there. A slender man kneeling at the grave's edge, his grasping arm frozen in mid reach like a hunter scented by prey. The horror smeared across Sevos' face. The tense and ready form of her snow-dusted servant.

"Why do you deny these people their chieftain, great priestess?" Imlod spoke in a loud voice then glanced back over one shoulder. This bit of blasphemy was clearly meant for the crowd. "Is it not in your power to..."

"Be silent!" Sevos screeched, drowning the provocation. "Grab him, Azilus! Shut his mouth!"

The servant reacted without hesitation. He yanked Imlod into the cist with him and clamped a hand over his captive's scowl. The other fist shot down and up again to produce a dagger: blade coming to rest across the interferer's throat.

The host inhaled gasps and loosed murmurs while Imlod scanned the trees. He questioned whether the whole of Dirag could withstand Kûhric if the minion suddenly bolted into the grove, but maybe he'd been a bit rash after all. Suppose Sevos would rather slice him open then and there than wait to learn what he was about. That would be unfortunate indeed.

His original plan hadn't included this course of action. The mission was to draw the priestess out of hiding and subdue her, not to bandy words with the woman before an entire village. But there was certainly more he'd intended to declare here before they stopped him, with the aim of raising his queen's true power above the lies of this renegade leader. He had to admit an appreciation for her quick decisiveness, though. She'd shut him down before barely a word had been spoken.

"Take him to your hut and bind him," Sevos told the servant.

Laughter flickered in Imlod's eyes as they shuffled him through the crowd. Behind the spot where the priestess stood, a shadowy form melded into the trees.

There was nothing odd about the stone apart from the runes carved into its surface. Yet it was more than it seemed. It was a doorway between two worlds. Now Imlod weighed it in the palm of his hand. He closed his fingers around it and took in a deep breath. *I'll find a better home for you, Mother,* he thought. *In time...I promise...when the Daemon's bidding is done...*

Such artifacts didn't have to be smooth pebbles collected from a creek bed. Nearly any object would do, so long as it wasn't a thing firmly implanted in the earth. But with multiple spirits at one's beck and call, an experienced sorcerer would consider portability to be the primary requisite for selection. A pouch of rocks could be easily carried and readily concealed, yet the stones themselves were durable enough to withstand rough handling and the drag of years. Imlod currently possessed only two of these stones: the shiny flat rock he held just now, used to control Nir, and the similar one stowed beneath his cloak that was tied to Kûhric. The runes were identifiers only, allowing him to tell the pair apart but lending nothing *magical* to the tools on which they'd been scrawled. Yet each tool itself, a fragment shorn from the great Goddess of Earth, contained enough binding power to raise up walls around a meeting place of souls.

His sister Galfayan, the queen, had only handed Kûhric's stone over to Imlod for a specific time and purpose—but Nir was *his*. He'd been the one to journey back into the Forest of Weth seeking her wayward spirit, and he'd been the one to carve her name into a stone after he'd found her. Why had he harvested his own mother? Was servitude better for her than endless wandering? Now that Kûhric was with him as well, the answer was clear. They were a family again.

It was a sickening thought, even to one such as himself—and he was a young man made old before his time, having been subjected to horrors one after another until little seemed sacred anymore. Not life. Not love. Not honor. To him there remained only vain pride, weak pity, and strict service. The queen, after all, was his family too. His only *living* family. He didn't hate her, despite her atrocities, despite the thing steadily corrupting her mind with each passing season. She'd granted him more than a beating heart when she'd spared his life all those years ago. She'd given him an opportunity. A chance to serve a greater purpose than what'd been intended for him. Still, these days it seemed Galfayan's continued elevation was the only purpose he'd ever have.

Maybe she'll finally allow Kûhric's release, once I finish these chores. Imlod's gaze crossed the servant's hut to the object of that thought. The minion seemed to be watching his master's work intently, his dark reddish-golden faceplate casting fiery shadows on the mud walls as Imlod coaxed a budding flame; yet nothing but utter night could be found behind the mask's curved eye slits and sinisterly grinning muzzle. Imlod could sense his old mentor's state well by now, though, so he knew Kûhric only looked *through* him into the netherworld: that damnable realm beyond the confines of normal sight and sound. The reek of bruised herbs lingered about the servant's flowing black fur and leather garments, and beneath those lurked a form that'd once been well built but was now long starved. Its thin arms were wrapped tight in hide save at the wrists and elbows, the joints held together by pegs and thong where tendons and ligaments had long rotted away. How the monstrosity could even move about remained miraculous to Imlod — trained though he was in the art that succored such abominations — and the supernatural strength it possessed was even more alarming. A great axe lay on Kûhric's lap, clutched by two crude plated gloves. His hood was drawn. Its studded skirts and tail fell loosely about shoulders dressed with metal scales.

I mean to raise this one, thought Imlod, projecting it to his minion. *We may need another if my plan runs ill.*

As you wish. I'll guard the entrance, Kûhric answered...yet he remained seated and motionless.

The body of Sevos Let's servant — the one she'd called Azilus — lay sprawled before Imlod, blood pooling beneath the head. Kûhric had suddenly appeared and bashed in the man's skull before he even knew his hut had been breached, and now guard lay dead while captive sat at ease: unbound and armed with his knives and a sword. It'd likely be hours before Sevos could pay a visit to Imlod or have him brought to her. The burial had been only the beginning of the day's ceremony, with sacrifices and feasting and dancing and so forth to follow...and the priestess would be at the head of it all, well into the night.

But for now the sun's shafts still pricked here and there through the canopy outside, and there was nothing to do but wait. A fire was made, and there was some food available to prepare an evening meal. Soon Imlod reclined and, still gazing at Kûhric's mask, began thinking about what he'd once glimpsed behind it. *Kûhric. Show me your face.*

Receiving the command, the minion raised his hands and unclasped the mask from its stained cords. The plate slid away and was set aside with his hood — and

Imlod studied the visage revealed. Brown plaster was caked now where Kûhric's flesh and dark hair had once thrived. Two pieces of white shell sat in the sockets that had before held living eyes, and only his mouth and raw chinbone remained exposed, the latter sporting etched swirling symbols dyed bluish green.

"Why does she do this to you?" Imlod mumbled to himself before sending it to Kûhric as well. He truly wanted an answer—but Kûhric didn't give him one. *Maybe he doesn't know.* There were other men for the witch to ensnare. Willing slaves, punished servants, chosen pets. So why did she put so much effort into this one? *Does his torment amuse her? Or is it mine?*

Why don't you feed like the others? Imlod pressed, feeling that much at least could be explained. But still there was no response. *Answer me! You're mine today. Not hers!*

If you command it, I will obey, came the reply at last—and Imlod felt a hint of emotion in it. Was Kûhric angry? As a rule, the undead remained mostly fixed in a dreamy, passive mood. Even in the midst of battle, with Kûhric giving and receiving terrible blows, the minion's thoughts were always calm and collected. Fighting was only another task for one built to serve.

Imlod decided to let it go for now. There was other business at hand. Setting his mother's stone aside, he took up a second object instead: the wing bone of a small bird, a thing Azilus had kept for a different purpose than what his killer had in mind. There was no need to scratch a rune in this makeshift talisman, as the planned minion's servitude would be short-lived. Imlod knelt and touched the bone to the corpse's brow. Firelight suddenly retreated into embers, and his exhaled breath came out in an icy plume. Drunk with need, drawn knowingly into the snare, he let the dirge of awakening slip into the mortal world...

...and there was Azilus weaving his way through the wood. Climbing where slender sprouts coiled into masses. Crawling under the arches of diving trunks grown thicker than the burliest man. The root-like vines were slick where they snaked under a gray, sullen sky: thirsting not, forever succored by wet, still air and rich, black earth. Dew ran and pooled now and again in the low places, hatching tiny springs of life amid an endless labyrinthine garden, and wingless beasts scurried about in horizon and wake, darting as he labored and lumbered. Eyes of chameleons and green serpents appraised his progress. A hint of smoke mingled with the pleasing scents of ivy and damp soil.

Long he strove but came no nearer to the encircling mountains. He paused at abandoned nests of men to finger their treasures and totems, but he took nothing from them and quickly passed on. The graven image of a tall being with arms stretched wide overhead frequented these dens, and though the woody stuff of each figure was smooth where a face should've been carved, a feeling of near recognition worried Azilus' thoughts.

Eventually his wandering took him to a high place. Topping the convoluted perch, he saw the source of smoke afar...and a wisp of human voices, dull and drear, traversed the void to find his ears. His only desire now was to reach that speck in the sea of tangle. A lizard crept to his shoulder from a hanging tendril and marked the spot with him. Then they set off for it.

Long again Azilus strove to tame the maze, yet now — guided by fumes and sound and a four-legged serpent — he won the mastery and reached his destination at last. Slipping under the final thick trunk, he found himself on the bank of a burning lake. Others peopled the rim: lingering statues with folded arms and downcast faces. Their dress and features differed from one to the next, yet all droned and chanted in perfect unison. At first, mesmerized by towering flames and unlearned of their rote, Azilus couldn't join them, though the urge to do so scratched at the door of his mind. Then the licking fire parted, and he beheld an ivory pillar rising high above the crimson water.

Upon it stood the Black Father. His arms were lifted, and his hooded gaze slowly scanned the shore as he led his children in song. After a time he let this pose fall and extended a hand to one of the fold instead, beckoning. The answer was immediate. A figure strode silently into the lake and was gone, and Azilus stepped forward to take its place in the ring. The dismal euphony penetrated his mind and streamed forth again from his mouth.

Night did not come. Day did not come. Men did not depart by the way they had come. The end of the song did not come.

But the lizard crawled down and darted beneath the vines.

3

The tyrant sat atop a stone dais in a seat of ornate wood and bone, drunk with wine, bloodshot eyes fixed intently on the writhing silhouette before him. Black smoke spiraled up from two censers, one on either side of the spectacle, to caress a slender, scantily-clad body on display. Now the woman's long hair caught the torchlight as she flailed about, moving in time with the shake of gourd rattles and the beat of skin drums. Now it hung still, gracing the small of her back as she slowly revolved for her master. Banded arms, ringed fingers, and wisps of haze reached out, came near his face...and pulled away. A flute played louder then faded. Waves of mirth rolled forth and crashed into silence.

Kordû mo Kar was a warlord of great proportions. He was first vassal of the peryton Kar: a horned daemon worshipped by the thousands in the Marshlands of Kagnus. Slaves, concubines, and armed guards flocked about this chamber of Thadda's temple in Ramfiram, over fifty leagues from the mire of their births, serving and dancing and carousing around the warlord's seat. And meanwhile in the heart of their homeland, a hundred priests prayed to the demigod Kar for Kordû's safe return—fasting and making burnt offerings and scarifying their bodies to prove their undying faith. Entire clans had been wiped out to bring this man's ascension. Bloodlines had been drained to secure it.

"Don't let this one steal your wits, lord." An old man with white hair and a trailing beard had just leaned over to whisper in Kordû's ear. The tyrant's chief minister, Gilal of Taudan. A curved nose jutted from the embroidered hood of the elder's rich woven apparel, and he held an oaken staff as long as he was tall. "Perhaps I should have the wine removed..."

"Perhaps you should," mumbled Kordû, certainly lost.

Gilal frowned in agitation then looked to the figure on Kordû's opposite side. As much as the solemn minister seemed out of place in these surroundings, the warlord's second attendant was an even stranger character. The marshal Cirad had lived among men all his life, but he was not a man himself. He was an elf. The pointed ears, long silver hair, and exceedingly fair, youthful face all gave it away. A sheathed blade hung at his side, and he also held a staff—though his, unlike Gilal's gnarled version, was straight as an arrow, a head taller than his own lofty height, and wrapped over and over with an intricate pattern of vines.

"A word, Cirad," said the minister, motioning for them to step aside and leave Kordû submerged in vice. "She'll summon us soon." Eyes from all corners of the chamber followed their movements.

Once more the parley would fall to this pair. It'd been the same when Ladd's queen had first arrived in Kagnus to woo their warlord and promise exorbitant aid for a mere trifle in return. And now with their arrangement nearly complete, the woman had summoned them here to ensure her reward's prompt fulfillment.

To watch them all bow before her: the *Queen of Earth*.

The minister's worried look told Cirad why he'd been pulled away. "We've discussed this before. I know you fear treachery—but Galfayan risked much to join us. She's honored her half of the bargain. We would've been shamed not to make this journey."

Gilal shook his head in earnest disagreement but managed to keep his voice low. "You still don't see it! All of Kagnus lay groaning at our feet. Our dream made living at last! But no sooner than we'd gained it, we scurried off like rats at the whims of this bewitching whore!"

"But if not for her, would our goal have ever been achieved? Would Kordû's visions—and our blades alone—have been enough to unite the realm?" Now it was the elf's turn to shake his head. "None shall rise against us now. Not while Kordû lives. Not while the tales are still fresh on our priests' lips!"

"It's not our absence that concerns me."

Cirad took a deep breath at that, then let it out in a sigh. "My days have yet to outstretch a life of your race, Gilal, but it takes no sage to read the witch's plans."

"So you have it all worked out, eh? How she means to make our master her pawn?" The minister grinned. "Any fool could see that, as you said. Certainly it's how you or I would play the game. But we deal with another sort here. The woman's gone mad! You should know that well by now."

"I do indeed..." said the marshal, distracted. His words trailed his green eyes as he surveyed the chamber's blackness. Years of service had taught Cirad never to engross himself in anything overlong. Familiar with his companion's habits, Gilal waited patiently until the elf's not-quite satisfied face returned. "Go on."

"There's nothing to go on about. I'm only warning you: we won't know what she intends till it's upon us. So you'd best be ready for anything!"

"Then let it come soon." Cirad sighed again and turned a thoughtful gaze on Kordû.

The warlord's head was slumped. A great laughter arose with the ceasing of drums.

Leaning in as he trudged forward, rigid against the cold, Imlod Nir might've been mistaken for one of the things following his orb of torchlight had they not been hidden in darkness. But he heard them clearly enough. The dead carrying the dead. No one had molested him so far, and already the deceased chieftain's dwelling was in sight. Sevos Let stood in its entrance, candle in hand, following his approach:

"Azilus? Is that you?"

Now, Mother, sent Imlod. Icy wind whipped into the clearing and found his face, sending his hair streaming. *We go inside.*

"Who's there?" the priestess demanded, her volume barely suppressed for the late hour. But even as she spoke there came a growl, low and menacing, from a few strides off to her left. She froze at the sound, likely debating whether to flee inside the hut or dash to the oncoming torch—be it that of servant or stranger.

The growling ceased, then Sevos' candle suddenly blinked out. Her shriek pierced the night as the hut flap burst inward, one dark form flailing backwards under the crushing force of another.

Moments later, crouched in a precarious haven between one of the dwelling's posts and its back wall, the priestess turned her gaze from Imlod to the kneeling form of Kûhric and the dirty corpse of Malbus Iryn sprawled before him. A huge wolf was there as well, resting silently with muzzle on paws, licking off them the dried blood of its evening prey. This was the beast that'd forced her inside: an animal possessed by the spirit of Nir. And the newly-risen minion Azilus stood watch outside, instructed to turn away any who might've been roused by Sevos' cry.

"Taloseth!" Sevos spat. "You bastard! You swore never to return!" Her fists were clenched in anger—but if she was afraid, she hid it well.

"Taloseth's long dead, priestess," Imlod replied, "...just as you were told. This one only wears his mask."

Sevos reached out to steady herself against the post. She still wore the fine clothing from earlier that day, though her ears and hair were no longer adorned. For a few breaths her jaw was slack with wonder, then finally she recovered. "I recognize you now! You're Galfayan's half-brother..."

"And you were once her mother."

That silenced her again. Perhaps some fond memory from her maternity had just been crushed. Kûhric stood during the pause and withdrew, batting the hut flap aside with his axe as he ducked through the portal. Imlod seated himself by the dead chieftain's head, pulled a fur pouch from inside his clothing, and began slowly withdrawing its contents.

"He took her away!" Sevos burst out, returning from secret thought. "Don't you understand? But she would've fared no better with me. I dared not claim her openly as my own. Bablak might've swayed the people..."

"Bablak?" snorted the unwanted guest. "The same fool who licks the dirt from Galfayan's feet? You'll see him again, priestess—and your son, Kirath, too. Soon as we're finished here."

"Worthless swine! What do you hope to gain? These people won't bend to your enchantments. Our strength comes from Mother Earth, and she alone rules our fate! All will see what you've done here come morning!"

"In the morning you'll proclaim Galfayan, *Queen of Earth,* to be your beloved daughter. And all will accept her sway."

"That's absurd! You've desecrated their chieftain's grave! You dare threaten me alone, with these wicked beasts at my hearth — but I wonder how you'll fare against my brother's warriors?"

"I've seen your brother Edohath and his men, boasting and bickering the days away. They're nothing." Rising, Imlod stepped to the hearthstone. Birch twig tea brewed there in a clay pot, and he stooped to pour some into a smaller vessel. With a nod and outstretched hand he offered some to Sevos. "Besides, I believe they're all away at the moment."

"Serve yourself!"

Imlod shrugged, took a sip, and looked above the priestess to a ceremonial mask dangling overhead. The thing's eyes had been set to roll and its beak to clack as its wearer danced. It reminded him of someone.

"You murdered Malbus, didn't you?" Sevos asked as Imlod looked on with impunity. "Speak! Tell me what he did to deserve this!"

"Would you have come at her command?" His eyes returned to the captive's face.

"So you flushed me out of my hole and into a trap. Innocent's blood for bait. How clever!" she mocked. "Are you enjoying the game? Who dies next?"

"That depends on you," said Imlod, and he returned to his appraisal of the raven.

4

"This way," the creature spoke with a surprisingly clear voice, and one of its sleek, short-furred arms swung back into the corridor from whence it'd come. It was obviously female: a fact exposed not only by its lack of clothing but by the sinuous way it moved and the womanly features yet retained in its hauntingly distorted face. For an instant the stifled cries and gasps of concubines and the shuffling feet of servants resounded in the chamber. Then all went still. A score of faces swept from the door to Kordû mo Kar's high seat.

Gilal of Taudan nudged his master awake then whispered something in the warlord's ear. After a moment of grumbling and shrugging off his attendants' offers of assistance, Kordû rose unsteadily, and the three lords from Kagnus left the chamber for the dark hallway. Their guide was a wolf that walked upright and reached out with human hands. A fell spirit peering out into the shadows through glazed white eyes. She wasn't the first beast of this kind they'd met, yet she was different from the others: those massive, shaggy brutes that opened their foaming maws not to speak but to devour the living and the dead alike, finding relief from their bitter agony by slashing the same into their foes. This female was serene and lithe and capable of converse beyond simple communication of her primal needs. Yet, as with her kindred, the curved fangs and ripping claws told of a capacity for quick and ruthless murder.

"She should've come to *you*, lord," whispered Cirad, treading beside Kordû, his eyes focused on the peryton tattooed across one half of the man's shaven head: Kar, horned and winged protector of Kagnus. "Since we arrived, we've been rounded up and put off…and now we're fetched to her like *slaves*."

"We're in her realm now, Cirad," Kordû slurred, one huge arm resting on the marshal's shoulder for support. The procession continued on this way until two successive turns revealed a stretch devoid of sconces, the torches replaced by a wide beam of light flooding in from one end of the portal. The rays were too weak for this door to be an exit, yet there had to be windows or an open roof in the chamber beyond.

"The queen awaits," said their guide. She turned back to meet the elf's face before examining the sword hanging from his belt. Neither pupil nor iris gave the look away, for she had none, yet those milky eyes rolled with the cock of her lupine skull. "Draw that blade in her presence, elf, and you'll feel my bite!"

The black circle's flames drank from its fiery coals, licked at its split logs, and belched thick smoke that billowed up and out of the ring of light mirrored above. It was as if they stood dwarfed beside the pit fire of a servant's hut, such was the feel and simple design of the temple's central chamber, yet over a hundred men could've stood in a line across the pebble-strewn floor. Dark faces glared at them from a bench along the far wall, none of their owners bothering to stand and welcome the queen's distinguished guests. Galfayan's eyes were locked on a gnarled black body raised before her ivory throne. The charred remains of an impaled man. Some poor soul who'd been brave or foolish enough to defy her.

"My lady, the lords of Kagnus have come at your bidding," the wolf-woman announced. But the witch didn't reply. Moments passed. The fire crackled, and the dark faces below her returned to the mesmerizing flames.

The scene's awe was lost on Kordû, though, besotted as he was. "Your tongue was looser in Kagnus, Galfayan! What's become of your manners?"

Gilal groaned at that. Cirad's hand slid reflexively to his weapon's hilt before a glance at their guide gave him pause.

"I've little time for them," said the queen at last. Not one of her servants had reacted to the insult. Just shy of a dozen, they filled one side of the stone bench from head to three quarters of its length. None were familiar to Kordû and his men except for Bablak Alnoor. Ramfiram's chieftain hadn't bothered to don a fine tunic or robe befitting his station or the presence of his lady and her guests. Instead he sat bare-chested and puffed up beneath a ridiculous war helm. A leathern bowl with two long copper horns jutting out and up slightly on either side. The breadth of his shoulders rivaled that of godlike Kordû standing before him, yet the stuff of Bablak's making had begun an inevitable fall from thick, tough muscle to luxurious flab. His round belly shook as he stood to speak:

"You cost me a gold torc, Kordû! They swore you'd live up to your vow, but I thought your old minister wiser!" He began rounding the table without leave, no doubt desiring to welcome the foreigners with clasping of wrists or jovial swats to their backs. He'd jested with these men before. The irritating grin beneath his braided black beard showed it plainly enough.

"Shut your mouth," said the queen, calmly, barely loud enough to be heard. Nevertheless, Bablak checked his advance at once and strode back to retake his seat. Galfayan's eyes were on Kordû now, taking him in. "Graumwen, show the lords to my table."

The wolf-woman did so, leading Kordû and his men to the first three stools at the table's right hand. Then, seeing everyone seated, she crossed the floor and warmed to her queen's side. As a young girl might imitate her mother's fashion, so was the slave Graumwen groomed and adorned. Both females sported thick tassels of oiled, black hair falling loosely over otherwise exposed breasts, pulled-back manes streaming to their hips, and golden hoops dangling from their ears. A bejeweled leather circlet and stained, patterned skirt were the only ornaments of the queen beyond those reflected on her pet.

"Does your *great lord* Kordû know the tale of our making, minister?" the witch began, stroking Graumwen behind the neck as if the creature were a dog. "The

Quenching of Thadda?"

"In some fashion, I'm sure, my lady," Gilal replied. He dipped his head in a slight bow of acknowledgement and respect for Galfayan's status, but his frown seemed to indicate displeasure at her not addressing the warlord directly.

"Well I believe it's time he heard it again." The queen scooped up a scroll of parchment from her lap then sent it soaring through the smoky air and skidding down the table to stop within her jilted lover's reach. "For with my return, the legends wake! All of you should know them well."

Kordû mo Kar leaned over, snatched up the document, and passed it on to his minister with haste, bored already with the inevitable blather to come. He rested a hand over his forehead and deep-set eyes for a moment before slowly pulling down along his face, ending with a tight grip on his coarse brown beard.

Gilal unfurled the scroll, his weathered eyes scanning the lines of curved and hatched runes laid down thereon. Then he stood, swept a gaze along the row of his audience across the table, cleared his throat, and began to read aloud:

"Like a king enthroned he was, even then, seated at our Mother's side in the stillness of the void. His desire for her was great, and it burned in him and grew and filled and overflowed, streaming into the darkness as a blinding radiance of light.

That light crossed the ocean of nothingness to spill upon our Mother, and her Womb was stirred. A dawn without end was begun, and beneath its rays of life there appeared Kamani, father of men, son of the Rising Sun.

From on high his gaze plunged and swam deep beneath the fires that licked then at the isle, and searching he found others who would heed the call. And these he brought forth and set upon the rim, and he sang to them in a speech near our own. And they looked up at him with awe and named him Ûl-Kamûn, the Sun Lord, and he smiled and named them Ûledrith, Lords of the Earth.

For an age they dwelt near the molten shores of Thadda, taming the land, spreading their seed, making sacrifices to the Goddess of Earth. Even then there was a *Ramfiram*, a 'Womb of the Mother' — a magnificent city of brick, metal, and stone. Even then there walked a priestess and her Brethren.

And whenever his people died, Kamani raised them anew, for he withered not, and he knew the art that opens Night's door.

But all ages wane.

On a time there came a tumult in the skies, and an orb thitherto unseen arose to blot out the Sun. Then came Rhanwŷr, first of the daemons, servant of the Night. Her power was terrible, and she slew a great host of the Ûledrith on her dark march to the Womb. There, triumphant, she waded in its fiery water, each step spawning a score of lesser daemons. Children of the Waxing Moon.

Atop a pillar at the very heart of the lake, Ûl-Kamûn drew forth the Mother's spirit to contest the Daemon. Yet even as Rhanwŷr stumbled and went down beneath a scarlet floe, the pillar cracked, and the Father fell with it down to his own black ruin. The whole of Thadda collapsed not long thereafter, spitting flames and lost souls to the heavens and belching choking poison across the land. Nigh all of mankind met doom there, at nightfall of that first long day. And so ended an age of unceasing light.

Yet the Night did not wholly reign, for the Moon also had fallen. And thus a truce was born: the balance of day and night and of life and death, a dance of the seasons, ever a waxing and waning, ever a rising and setting. The Black Father took up his court in the nether regions, never to return to the light from which he was birthed. Yet, in time, the Daemon's spirit arose to..."

"Enough!" spoke the queen, rising from her throne to embark on a casual stroll towards the fire. Graumwen stayed behind, following her mistress only with an eerie, longing stare. The witch's left arm lifted as she approached the table's end opposite her guests, and a delicate, golden-ringed finger bent to call forth the figure seated last of them all: a man, so it appeared, hidden beneath a weatherworn robe of the Brethren. He stood immediately and went to her side, the train of his once-crimson garb dragging the floor behind, smoothing the rocks displaced by his booted steps. The lower half of his face alone could be seen. A withered chin and jaw sporting a wiry, gray-flecked beard. "Skip to the end, Gilal," continued Galfayan, "...and tell us the scribe's name."

"Amasmir Dahsa," said the minister after a moment's pause, the tone of his voice conveying perplexity.

"What of it, woman?" Kordû exclaimed, having remained quiet as long as his inebriation would allow. "What do scrolls and scribes have to do with me? I've brought you my sword, but I've no ear for this blabbering! Is this a war council, or are we training as priests? Or fools?"

Bablak dared a short laugh, seconding Kordû's sentiment with a sharp hand slap to the table. He looked as if he'd begin railing as well. Then, meeting his queen's eyes, he quickly thought better of it.

"Fools, you say?" said the man at Galfayan's side. It was a low, rasping voice. "Surely you lack no training there, man of Kagnus." He allowed Kordû no time for outrage. "Our queen honors me with the reading of my own work. Yet you would rant and jest. Say we've no need of your sword—what then shall be done with you? Perhaps your marshal's blade will suffice..."

Galfayan grinned at the trailing implication.

Oblivious to the danger he was in, Kordû mo Kar stumbled up and kicked his wobbling stool aside. "It was Kordû—not Cirad—who heard Kar's voice! It was Kordû—not Bablak Alnoor—who led the thousands to battle!" He took one step toward the witch, his huge hands balled into hammers. "And it was Kordû — *not Galfayan* — who slew the Marsh King's champion and roared as he fled screaming from the fray!"

Cirad's hand touched his hilt again. Graumwen leapt up but stayed put, fur bristling, teeth bared.

"Today you lie in my den, warlord," said the witch, calmly but with the smirk of moments before supplanted by a tight frown. "As I bowed in your realm, so you must yield to me in mine. We waste time with your insolence." The flames behind Galfayan sizzled and popped, calling renewed attention to the scorched body above.

Kordû's pride wouldn't let him sit down. He stood firm, mouth agape with disbelief and rage, itching to take another step forward. He saw now how the witch baited him: an act of punishment on display, lackeys traipsing about with tongues unchecked, and the unspoken yet present irreverence towards his god. *She* wants *me to lash out*, he thought, struggling to clear his head. *It won't be murder then…*

Suddenly he realized she'd never let go of him, in life or in death — that if he didn't put her down now, he and his followers would never see Kagnus again. Frantically his eyes searched about for a thing that would be his weapon, found it in the overturned stool by his feet, then scanned the tense faces of both his retainers and hers. Bablak wouldn't interfere. Gilal would attempt to and most likely die. Cirad could keep the wolf off his back — *but for how long?* — and the rest would depend on Kar's favor and his own prowess. They might rip him apart afterwards, seeing their queen broken, or they might applaud and bend the knee. Kordû's crazed glare found his marshal's eyes and held them briefly, just long enough to ensure the elf's attentiveness. Then he signaled ever so slightly, calling for Cirad's blade to be drawn.

Without hesitation, Cirad nodded in return.

"Is there something else you wish to say?" the witch boomed. She was forcing the warlord's path, offering a line to be taken as either a final provocation or his last means of escape.

Kordû stooped to grasp a leg of his seat. It seemed he would right it, retaking his place with the others. That was what he ought to have done — but instead his mighty bulk swiveled back to Galfayan. Lifting the stool menacingly, he flared: "I'm the chosen ruler of Kar's multitudes, not a slave to some scheming conjurer!"

Then he lunged forward, igniting his marshal's leap from the table beside. They'd fought back-to-back before — had slain a hundred foes between them with little more than scratches in return. How was this different? What had they to fear? Exhilaration swept through Kordû, bathed him in unyielding strength, gorged him with an unquenchable fury…

...and was replaced by a sudden, intense pain. Not physical pain brought by the sword — the result of a quick, fluid motion that sliced clean through the back of his legs — nor that of the rocks that stung his arms and face as the force of his onrush sent him crashing to the ground. No, it was the pain of an *inconceivable betrayal* that drew Kordû's howl. A scream so loud it might've brought the chamber's dome crashing down on them all. A barrage of thoughts flew through his mind, threatening to render him dumb, attempting to strike from his reach the only thing he had left: the chance for an honorable demise. *On your back!* he demanded of himself. *Face whatever comes!*

She was already there, her impossible beauty looming above, as he heaved his sprawled frame about. The elf stepped easily to her side, lowered his blade, and placed his left arm about her waist. At this touch, Galfayan looked first to the warlord's face, ensuring she held his gaze, then turned hers to Cirad and kissed the elf deeply.

Tears came to Kordû's eyes. This last battle was the most difficult of his life. A battle that didn't require stoking his rage to win but rather pissing out those flames. The ache of his crippling wounds was nothing compared to the throb at his core: an anguish birthed from his efforts to stifle another insane cry.

"What's wrong, lord?" taunted Galfayan, frowning playfully as she turned back to him. "Do I have your ear now?" The elf's face said nothing at all.

At least not Gilal, thought Kordû as he glanced back over his shoulder. The minister was being held, both arms and mouth clamped tight, by the queen's servants. He'd have a choice to make soon. Serve a new master or perish with the old one. "If I'm to die, witch, then be done with it! Spare me your poison tongue!"

"Oh, you'll die, Kordû...but death is no longer an end. Just look around you. What of the scribe's name? What's it to do with you?" Galfayan bent low and cupped his chin with her palm. Moved her lips within a finger of his cheek. "It has everything to do with you! In the marsh you were a champion indeed — and so shall you remain. When the land falls to dust and the sea boils red with blood, so shall you remain. But I'll suffer no rivals. Neither alive and free, nor as earth-buried martyrs!"

5

"Children of Dirag!" Sevos Let shouted over the assembly. Those who hadn't managed to push their way into the clearing were lingering under its encircling branches. Few had bothered awaiting the priestess' arrival, and the majority of yesterday's offerings had already been reclaimed from Malbus' unearthed grave. Several knots of conspirators completed the mob, these having left behind shock and moved to debating action. The hands and teeth of some were clenched with stifled passions as they abided the speech of others. Others who couldn't help but burst, shaking fists and spitting freezing curses at the earth and sky in turn.

"Listen to me!" Sevos went on. She was perched atop a huge stone shelf with three hooded forms standing behind her. Two men holding forth long wooden staves on either side of a third. "Today I must beg your forgiveness!"

A hush fell. Why did this great woman need anyone's pardon?

"The man I seized yesterday is the half-brother of Galfayan—my daughter— who claims sovereignty over this land. His abuse could rouse her anger, should it be told...and for that I'm to blame! But fear not, my people, for the *Queen of Earth* summons you to Ramfiram! The Year of Conceiving is upon us, and she'd have the rites observed by every man, woman, and child! Those who answer her call won't be punished. No! You'll receive instead such gifts befitting honored guests, having leave to dwell by the sacred lake when the ceremonies are ended!"

In the Land of Ladd, every eighth year was known as the Year of Conceiving. In that year, bones of the deceased were disinterred from tombs scattered about the realm and carried on sacred treks to Lake Thadda in Ramfiram, the Womb, wherein they were redeposited in ritual fashion. White bones were the seed with which to impregnate Mother Earth, initiating a new cycle of rebirth in the living world—and thus for a devout Ûledrith not to participate in this ceremony was nearly inconceivable. Who could say whether their own departed kin might be among the next souls released?

Scattered murmurs and shouts rang out in the pause after Sevos' words; but most of the crowd said nothing, bewildered as they tried to work out why she was speaking of blessings at such a time of tragedy. The priestess stole a glance at her attendants—and Imlod Nir, the middle figure, read the struggle written on her face. He knew she believed few if any of the claims she'd just made, yet she'd delivered them all with flare. *A practiced skill.* He nodded his approval, and she turned back to the host:

"You've heard me speak against Galfayan before. I won't deny it. But now the queen's war in the marsh is over, and her eyes turn inward at last! We must accept her reign willingly—or else we'll be devoured by it!" She lingered here a moment with downcast eyes as if suddenly unsure of herself; but when her face rose, she placed a hand over her breast as if preparing to make a vow: "I've been shown the truth of her claim, my children! The Brethren were wrong to..."

"You lie!" someone cried from the throng, followed by more like outbursts. The crowd was losing focus. Yet just as it seemed the gathering might disperse, Sevos gave up her spot to one of the enshrouded figures behind her. The one to Imlod's left.

At first this man was still and silent. Few noticed there'd even been a change. Then suddenly all were aware of him, and their chatter died as his thick speech burst through the chill air: "Blasphemers! Sevos Let does not lie to her people! Behold!" He raised his hands and threw back his hood.

A woman near the pedestal shrieked but was quickly silenced. Awe spread and struck dumb all those in its wake. Many dropped to their knees, and some were incapable even of that. Seeing this, the revenant Malbus Iryn smiled and spoke again: "Have you already forgotten my words? The high priestess is to be revered and obeyed! Do you still doubt the powers of Earth? Would you bring disfavor to our home?" Some whispers and mumbles followed. Then the hush resumed.

Meanwhile to Imlod's right, the minion Azilus had begun to reek — and he wouldn't stop calling into his master's thoughts. *Am I to live next, Father?* he'd asked. *The serpent's gone!* Then, coming back to the waking world, he'd sent something more useful. *Beware the bald man — there, in the crowd. He conceals a blade.* Imlod was finding it hard to control so many undead servants at once.

"You *must* listen!" Sevos was pleading to the assembly. "I've seen to your needs in the past and taken your prayers to heart. Will you not hear me now?"

"Aye, lady," said a nearby woman. "Yes, priestess!" shouted another from further out. Other voices rushed in, most mirroring the willing sentiment.

Sevos nodded her thanks, looked once more with sad eyes at her old friend Malbus Iryn, then grasped his arm firmly and turned back to the crowd. "Look here upon the proof! By the queen's power, your chieftain's restored! Imagine what great miracles she might work for each and every one of you!" She paused to let that sink in. "When Galfayan returned to us in Ramfiram, years ago, the Brethren denied her. And though she was *my own daughter*, I stood with them. That was my folly! I defied the queen out of hatred for her cursed father — and because of my own vanity. Yet in that I did you all an injustice!"

"If she's really who she claims, then what've we to fear?" yelled the bald man with the hidden knife. "You spoke of punishment. For what? All of us worship the Goddess. We've done nothing to anger our Mother!" Several others echoed the instigator by sending like words down the ranks behind him or else hurling them at the priestess atop the stone.

This one had to be silenced quickly, Imlod knew — same as Sevos had muted him yesterday. It would be easier if Nir's spirit were here at the moment instead of with the wolf. The man would simply cease to speak as her soul possessed his body and smothered his will, with none the wiser of the cause. But she was off scouting now, so her son would need to handle this brazen malcontent himself. Yet even as Imlod took a step forward, Malbus surprised him by answering the man unbidden:

"Would it be the first time for Her to punish us, Gûnai? Remember the years of hunger, when deer fell dead where they stood? Did that not come from our offense?" He paused to scan the crowd with harsh eyes. "Must I retell the story?"

This frightened an elderly man close by—as surely it must have others who'd struggled with him through those bitter days—and he turned to Sevos: "But, my lady? You'll make a sacrifice? What must we do to appease the Goddess?"

"The high priestess has no time for this!" Malbus replied for her. "She's been recalled to her duties in Ramfiram and must depart at once. If you seek answers, then answer the summons of your queen!"

Darkness has been and shall ever be. Long after the substances that fuel heat and light have burned away—giving out at the end of a brief, fragile course—an everlasting night shall reign. Imlod Nir considered this as he watched the last tendrils of smoke from the evening's fire stream lazily into the night air. They mingled with black leaves under a low, moonlit canopy before melding into the consuming void.

He'd not slept much, if at all. Soon the sun would rise, its white rays creeping in through the thick foliage. Sitting motionless on a fallen, decaying trunk, Imlod pulled his gaze away from the smoke to check on the priestess yet again. Kûhric stood guard nearby, so he'd left her unbound, yet somehow he still felt anxious. Was she merely feigning sleep? Waiting for a chance to escape? *If she does bolt, she won't make it far.* He'd sent Malbus and Azilus out to sweep the forest ahead while Nir's wolf lagged behind to scare any would-be followers. Even if Sevos could outrun Kûhric at first, one of his tireless minions would soon retrieve her.

The wood's icy stillness had been with them for more than this evening. It'd wrapped around their journey like the shaggy coat hiding Imlod's thin frame. He drew the fur tighter, stood, and tried to form a conclusion to the sleepless night's ponderings. *What am I doing here?* Walking to the spot where Sevos lay curled up near their dying campfire, he stared down at her face illuminated by its glowing embers. She looked peaceful. Imlod used to gaze at times upon his slumbering mother this way, many years past in a diminutive hut beneath the branches of a seemingly boundless wood. *What does my sister intend for her own mother?* It was different with the Brethren. Those ousted priests meant nothing to him or to the queen, and they all knew what would happen if they were ever sought and found. But was Sevos Let to receive the Brethren's punishment too? He noticed the priestess' long lashes. They recalled to him an image of his lover: an acolyte in the temple of Thadda. *I just need to finish this, then I'll have a reprieve. I'm merely a tool. If not for me, Galfayan would've sent another in my place.*

"Why hover over me, vulture?" Sevos spoke suddenly, taking him aback. Her eyelids raised slowly, and she tilted her head toward him. "Were the others such easy prey?" She met Imlod's stare, and he read disgust in the look — but whether with him or herself, he couldn't say. "I heard about Osnom, but we guessed he'd merely fallen to those thieves he'd taken up with. Then Zigodus went missing as well. If only I'd put the two together..."

"I'd have found you anyway. None can elude me long."

Sevos pushed herself up to a sitting position. "Am I the last, then? What of Merogrin? Amasmir?"

Imlod nodded. "Taken. All four."

Sevos paused for reflection. "Are there more of you out there?"

"More hunters, you mean?"

"More vultures. More slinking puppets and baseborn cowards."

Imlod frowned. "If those are names you'd give your own son — then yes."

For an instant the priestess looked shocked. "I see."

Kirath, son of Sevos, had been Imlod's staunch companion since the very first day of his arrival in Ramfiram: an evening that seemed a lifetime away. The two were about the same height and age and were likeminded in most things as well; although Kirath, as the son of Bablak Alnoor, was more thickly built and more apt to fits of boisterousness and rage. His face was from his mother, however, as were his wits: facts that both delighted his paramours and irritated his father to no end. *She hasn't seen him in years,* Imlod considered. *She doesn't know what he's become.*

"Do those you found still live?" Sevos asked, pulling Imlod's thoughts back to the present. She was standing now and brushing off the leaves and dirt from her clothing.

"In a way. Even the one you buried deep in the wood. Renduil, was it?"

She drew in a sharp breath, and with its exhalation came a wash of red fury. "Vile bitch!" she snapped — and would've said more had Imlod's open hand not smacked the words back into her mouth.

She tried to return the slap, but he grabbed her tightly: one hand clamped to her arm and the other held over her mouth. "You'll be quiet," he whispered in her ear. "And never dare speak ill of the queen." He squeezed the arm, bringing a grunt of pain from her, then released it as he flung her aside. She stumbled and fell, ending right back where she'd lain for the night.

Imlod assumed she'd lash out again with her tongue, for Sevos was a proud woman: one not used to harsh treatment but unwilling to cower before it. But she remained silent instead, unmoving save to return to a sitting position. Her face turned away from his to stare into the moonlit forest.

"Look at me!" Imlod commanded. Was she crying? He stepped closer, took her by the chin, and spun her face back to his.

Not crying. The priestess was smiling...

A voice ran through Imlod's skull. It was Nir. *Beware! They come!*

Then he heard what Sevos had already made out. Far off, a baying of dogs.

6

Thayld Priregord pulled the ashen bow from his pack and strung it with practiced ease. It was a fine piece of craftsmanship that'd served him well on countless hunts over the years. *And Goddess willing, it will again this morning.*

Two days out from Diebron's crannogs, the overseer's meager cache of dried berries, acorns, and smoked fish was dwindling fast. Raiders had taken nearly everything his clan had in store; thus, in good conscience, he'd been more than spare with his packing. *The little ones need this food,* he'd thought the last time his hands went into the baskets. Then he'd put most of it back. Yet this lacking was of small consequence to a skilled hunter such as Thayld. He'd lose one day — two at the most, if he was unfortunate — then he'd have more meat than he could lug around. And besides, what mattered a few extra days when the clan had already delayed his trip for so long?

He'd awakened today before sunrise, just as he'd done most every day of his life. As a youth he would've better tolerated the wet, frosty ground on which he'd slept and the frigid air surrounding him, but the overseer had become an old man: hardy enough when called on, but now more used to the luxuries of roof and hearth. *'An overseer provides comfort for his people — not for himself!'* his father had said to him long ago, but Thayld wasn't quite so fanatical. He was thankful for the fresh clothing his wife had made for him. A solid outer leather skin to shed the water and cut the wind and an inner layer of fur to hold in his body's heat. It was the next best thing to having the old woman herself keeping him warm at night. *Still, it's good to be away again,* he concluded, notching shaft to string in near-blackness.

Yesterday afternoon's scouting had produced tracks beside a nearby creek, and those had led him to a trail of bent brush, some tufts of hair, and a pile of droppings. If the doe came that way again for a drink at dawn, Thayld would be waiting for her. If not…well, he'd have to stalk. Either way, it was time to go. His right hand moved to his neck unseen, yanked up the thin cord tied loosely about it, and brought the boar's tooth hunting charm to his lips for a ritual kiss. Then he set off, recounting the paces he'd ticked off last night during the walk back from his discovery. He did his best not to make noise as he fumbled from one trunk to the next, recalling the memorized order in reverse.

An hour or more passed before the hunter gave up the wait. Patches of soft light began to show about his feet, and he rose, wondering if he should fall back on his first plan — which was to fish the streams or trap smaller game to sustain him till he was nearly at Asalin's door, and only there bag a deer if he could. *I'd have a gift for him then. No, an offering,* he thought once again before remembering why the idea had been initially dismissed. *Too risky. He might judge me a poacher on his land.* Asalin of Kûthod, Thayld knew, was nothing if not just. Rumors of the monarch's laws and the penalties for breaking them crept far beyond the borders of his own realm. That was the reason for most of the crannog men's hesitation in reaching out to the man for aid.

The slaughter of Esosh's family had only marked the beginning of his clan's recent troubles. Twice more since that fateful day had fiends come in the night, dragging his people from the huts where they slept and taking whatever they pleased. Some of Diebron's men chose to pretend otherwise, but Thayld knew the truth: Esosh had been a warrior, but few of the others had ever even held a weapon, much less fought in battle. They'd grouped together and railed and plotted and vowed to be fully prepared for the next attack, if one should come. *And it'll come. Wolves don't leave a carcass to rot. They come back till it's stripped to the bones!* Thayld had tried to dissuade his people from that path, explaining the grisly end he foresaw if they showed the raiders any organized resistance. But they were beyond reasoning now, so he'd chosen this course on his own.

An owl's warning call brought his focus back to the hunt. He was moving again and, despite efforts against it, disturbing the wildlife in his vicinity. This thick-canopied forest of Kûthod was about as illuminated now as it was likely to be all day, yet Thayld drank in the faint light. He was entranced by the eerie, pristine beauty and the openness of the understory and floor. Not far ahead he spied a steep ridge and prepared for a climb, hoping to win a vantage point above some unsuspecting prey on the other side. He returned the bow to his pack frame and pulled the straps tight before starting up slowly, gently testing each root or stone he might grasp for support before committing to any move.

Halfway up he caught a whiff of smoke, then a moment later he was sure of it. Men, not deer, lay just beyond the ridge. His first thought was *relief.* He was a traveler in need of direction and news from the local woodsmen. Decent folk would also spare some food and maybe even a tough lad to guide him the rest of the way. But it was best to remain wary. The last thing he wanted to do was get himself killed in this venture.

Easing atop the ridge, the overseer found a good spot to kneel and gaze at the source of smoke. As he'd envisioned, an evening campfire now burned down to the coals, the fresh dark plume resulting from someone coaxing new flame using damp leaves. That someone was a young woman. Her face was lowered, but he could see clearly how she sat there partaking of her morning meal. She appeared to be alone; and Thayld thought that very strange, even for this alien land. After another moment spent watching her in silence, he stood and began descending. Careful, but not as slow and quiet as before. Trying as much to avoid a slip and fall as to not frighten the lass.

He didn't get far before she jumped up. "Who's there?" she cried, startled.

Thayld opened his mouth to respond but then, registering the voice and squinting to confirm something about the girl's face, snapped his jaw shut in anger and disbelief.

It was Tyth.

The barks and howls were at a fever pitch. The dogs would soon be on them.

Imlod had given ground. Not because he'd thought to elude his pursuers, but because he'd needed time to recover from shock. Yet now the sun was up, and he was no better off for it. *Backed into a gully*, he frowned, recalling a time from his childhood when he and Kûhric had faced a different pack of frothing hounds and barely lived to tell of it. His guardian had taken a nasty bite that day.

You're close?

I'm here, the dark servant replied.

Rustling leaves drew Imlod's gaze to the ridge above. *Come down. Quickly!* He pulled the back of his hand across his brow then turned to Sevos Let. The priestess wore a smirk. Drawing a knife, he approached and tightened his free hand about her neck.

The smile vanished. "Let go!"

Imlod only squeezed tighter, and she coughed and squirmed, punching him and digging her nails into his arm. "Don't think to run from me!" he warned as she flailed about.

Just as he loosened his grip enough to let Sevos draw air, Imlod heard Nir's voice in his mind again: *I can't draw them away, son. They run straight for you.*

Come, then. We'll fight!

Moments later she tore into the gully with red gore staining her muzzle. *I've stopped two, but there are more.* As he watched her limp to his side, Imlod noticed not all the blood was her prey's. A thick chunk of meat was exposed on her left haunch. One ear hung by a thread.

Seeing Kûhric standing nearby, Imlod spoke to the broken wolf and towering minion in turn: "Leave this form, Mother. Kûhric! Release her." Then, turning back to his captive: "I won't die easily, priestess—but if that's my fate, I'll drag your spirit down with me to the netherworld. I promise you that!"

The dogs' baying sounded out just beyond the ridge, and Imlod winced to hear it. He feared no man who harbored fear himself, but such animals as these could be devoid of fear. Bred for no purpose other than brutal killing. Edohath Let's men would likely loose arrows or spears from a distance or warily encircle to be picked off one-by-one by Kûhric's axe or his own blades—but the hounds would break into their midst and rip anything they found alive to shreds. He moved away from Sevos to scan the area for natural defenses, and she eyed him warily all the while. *What if I were to leave her and flee unburdened?* No, the dogs had the scent now and would run him down anyway. And to lose Galfayan's prize could be just as deadly…

A sharp yelp turned him about. The wolf was put down. Kûhric stood over the beast, one foot planted on its bloodstained hide as he wrenched his axe free. Sevos' eyes were averted from the grisly scene, but they continued following Imlod as he moved closer to it. The necromancer's apprentice hastily extracted a pouch from his clothing, spilled the contents into a cupped palm, selected one of the objects therein, and held it up in the other hand. Wordlessly, he knelt with eyes shut and touched the stone to the wolf's skull.

Now Sevos was aware of it: a sinking feeling, as when one fights sleep's pull too long and finds himself jerking out of a nod. She looked up wearily and saw her brother's dogs cresting the ridge. For an instant even their cacophony went silent and their relentless advance fell still. Then Imlod's eyes flicked open, and one of the hounds gave a low growl. There were five in sight: the huge Kagnian breed with short muzzles and cropped ears, all fitted with leather harnesses and spiked collars over sleek, white-speckled coats and rippling muscles. Recovering her senses, the priestess stiffened and appeared ready to run. But her captor had other plans. *They'll have to drag you off!* Imlod lashed out with a closed fist—and Sevos' world went dark.

Down the dogs came, barking and tumbling, followed by whisks and thuds of arrows streaking to earth, just as Imlod had imagined the ruinous dance would commence. Ducking behind a tree to avoid the barrage, he freed his knives and peeked up then back around to scan both ridges for attackers. *The hounds first, then the men above,* he thought as several faces met his glance from the north side alone. *They haven't crossed over!* he grinned. With no threat from behind, his odds were much improved.

Multiple arrows struck Kûhric as the lead dog reached bottom and lunged at him. This one took the axe deep in its skull; and as the archers saw their errant shafts fall within arm's length of the unconscious priestess, they wisely chose not to send another volley. But the hounds were undeterred. The four remaining beasts leapt as one, latching on to Kûhric with powerful jaws and dragging him down under their combined weight like the taking of a deer. Imlod had hoped for just this as he saw them barreling down: that they'd group together rather than split for separate targets and thus themselves be more easily targeted and dispatched. He gave up his oak trunk shield and fell upon the roiling mass in a blur, making use of both hands to slice quick before his victims could turn back on him. *One…two…three…*

Pain grabbed his shoulder and spun him around. A second shaft hissed by his head, and a third took the final dog indiscriminately in its spine, drawing a burst of gut-wrenching yelps as the animal's hindquarters plopped lifelessly to the ground. Then a young warrior was in Imlod's face, desperately hacking and slicing as if the impending kill would make a hero of the lad back home. It was all Imlod could do at first to draw his own weapon and avoid the blows, skilled as he was at swordplay, for the arrow in him burned and sapped his strength — and, for all he knew, wept out his very life as well. Fueled by their companion's bravado, the remaining warriors dropped their bows and rushed toward Imlod. Their whoops and cries rivaled the dogs' barking, but their killing prowess did not. Imlod knew this well and recalled it now, as he'd observed them sparring in Dirag before their departure. Thus, despite his wound, he took heart.

Within a few more strokes Imlod found a groove and stepped in, handing the assault back to his attacker. The young warrior's eyes went wide with disbelief, and he stumbled just before his brothers-in-arms could join the fray. Stumbled and died, his neck releasing a torrent of blood. That checked the wild onrush of the others. They fell into a wary circle with muscles tensed and blades pointed inward, debating whether to engage or give up the hunt and run.

Imlod held his sword low and loose in one hand and clinched his jaw against the fire in his opposite shoulder. He glanced over to where Kûhric had fallen — and found the minion stubbornly attempting to rise on mangled limbs with no success. *Lie still! You're only making it worse!*

"What're you waiting for?" came a harsh rebuke from beyond the circle. "He's wounded and outnumbered! Take him!"

Dressed in finery at odds with the motley pack under his command, Edohath Let appeared too princely a thing to be out leading a hunt. But Imlod knew his true worth: the only properly trained warrior here besides Kûhric and himself. The man had just been kneeling over his waking sister, but now he stood and set a hand on his sword's pommel.

Imlod's eyes returned to the ring of assailants. One of them, a fool wearing little more than a wolf's pelt with the animal's head resting atop his own, looked ready to hurl his spear from close range. "Scared to face me yourself, Edohath?" he shouted past this one.

His taunt's answer came from the ring of foes. As a living snare it collapsed on Imlod with teeth of stone and metal — yet it did so with some restraint, each man taking care not to strike down one of his own or to be the one accidentally struck. But now Imlod tasted their sweet caution, drank it deep, and spewed it back as a weapon upon them. Dodging a blow aimed at his side, he killed the man in wolf's clothing with a fake and slash then spun to deflect the thrust of a seeking spear. He dropped to his knees, sliced at a leg, and rolled aside as its owner shrieked and crumpled into a writhing mass on the ground. That near-amputating blow cost him his blade, though: for it lodged deep in bone. There was no time to regret it. Taking this foe's spear as it fell from the man's wound-clutching hand, Imlod rammed it through the nearest of the remaining attackers and, immediately releasing the shaft, grabbed the next warrior by the arm and hurled him over one shoulder—grunting as the body flew heavily to earth.

Then came the moment of Imlod's defeat. The instant where his last standing opponent saw an opening and took it. This one wielded a massive axe of wood and flaked rock; yet even as his crude weapon came pounding down, the man's sure victory was denied. A skull other than Imlod's suddenly appeared between him and his prey. A rotting ball sitting on the shoulders of a walking corpse. A head that didn't care if it were cleaved in two. And indeed it *was* sundered...all the way down to its gore-spewing neck. But the body remained erect.

Malbus. Better late than not at all! Imlod whirled to hammer a fist into the final assailant's jaw. The man's legs went to mush beneath him, and he crashed to the ground beside his companions. The other warrior Imlod had thrown was rising to flee, terror sweeping across his face as his one-legged comrade shrieked in agony. Imlod found his dropped knives then silenced them all just as he'd done the hounds. Clean sweeps across the neck.

Breathing heavily, Imlod scanned the carnage for what was next to come. He saw Kûhric crawling slowly toward him on his left and, further off to his right, the empty space where Sevos had lain moments before with her brother standing guard. *Craven!* he thought, summoning Edohath's face to mind. *I'll run you down like the fawn you are!*

But it didn't seem Imlod would, in fact, be doing any running just now. With each breath he took the adrenaline was wearing off, and anguish and exhaustion were taking hold. *Azilus!* he called into the nether plane—and without awaiting the answer, he grabbed at the arrow in his shoulder with both hands and pushed the shaft hard till its jagged tip exited the other side. Blackness flashed across his vision as he screamed in pain. He stumbled and fell to his knees. Took another deep breath, reached for the arrow again, and broke the shaft near its fletchings.

I'm near...

No! Imlod winced and moaned, squeezing his shoulder around the wounded area. *The priestess escapes! Kill her brother and bring her to me!* He fumbled for the pouch in his clothing and yanked it out once more. *My mother will guide you!*

Yes, master...

Nir's stone tumbled out of Imlod's palm as he collapsed to the ground. His eyelids were heavy, and blackness was creeping back to the edges of his sight. He was just about to surrender to it when he heard the sickening noises to his left. A snapping of bone and the rending of flesh. He rolled his head sideways to confirm his suspicion.

Kûhric was feeding off the dead.

7

For days now bitter pain had risen with the morning sun, leaving Marinya all but useless. Today that feeling was gone. Not because she'd found sustenance at last, but because she'd been without it for so long. The thought of food repulsed her now...and her baby must've entered a similar state, for this morning he'd yet to scream for her breast. She propped her head up and stared at the tiny bed of leaves with a crazed look in her eyes. The infant's skin was covered in dirt. *He knows too. Our end is near.*

She was still useless. The distraction of a groaning belly had been the cause before; but now she just no longer *cared* to move. The last thing she'd eaten was the meager remains of a spitted rabbit stolen at the village outskirts three nights ago—and she hadn't even been able to finish it all in one sitting. It was difficult to believe her stomach was actually shrinking with her abdomen so bloated. It looked almost as if she'd regressed to the days of her pregnancy. *If only that were true. If only I'd been satisfied with my duties in Ramfiram.*

With great effort, she managed a sitting position then a wobbly stance. She'd always been thin, but now her legs were little more than bones. After an absent bout of scratching at her flaky arms, she gently scooped up the baby and limped over to the ledge. She stuck a cupped palm into the chill stream roaring down the cliff. *So much water,* she thought. *And so far to the bottom.* Should she leave the child here and try to hunt again? She had no true weapon. No tools. Should she risk another beating in the next village? *Everywhere we go, they've already been told. They won't accept my child, no matter how much I beg! They'll barely even look at us.*

She heard the infant whine—a weak cry that slapped back to them from the walls of their tiny cave—but continued to stare at the cascade before her. In it, a vision of her queen was taking shape. A beautiful woman not far past Marinya's own years, Galfayan materialized now with her slim yet sensual body wrapped in a cloak of raven's feathers and a circlet of fresh ivy and vines woven into her black locks. She greeted her ill-favored servant with a look of disdain.

"Mistress," spoke Marinya meekly, bowing her head and lowering her eyes. She brushed her own dark hair from her face and waited.

"Look at me, girl." The queen's sweet voice seemed at odds with her initial expression.

"Yes, my lady. How may I serve?"

"Serve? I think not. You forget what you've done."

Not since the days of her childhood in Kûthod had Marinya felt this utterly powerless. King Asalin had seen to it then, justifying the overbearing control of his little princess by naming it *protection.* Her queen—no, her *goddess*—saw to it now, needing no justification at all. *I brought this upon myself,* Marinya sobbed on the inside. *I fled my father to come here! I begged to be placed beneath her!*

"I suppose you thought some strapping village lad would sweep you up at first sight," the queen continued. "A pretty wench with a tear-streaked face and rich robes to boot." Marinya remained quiet. Her mistress sighed and smirked. "The same ruse you conjured to snare my poor brother, was it not?"

That baited statement sparked another sort of conjuration within Marinya. It called up a wave of unchecked anger. "The only snare about Imlod is yours!"

"Is that so? Tell me, then: where's your hero now? This man for whose sake you earned my displeasure? Why's he not here to protect his woman and child? Do you imagine he's not misleading some other whore as we speak?"

There was some truth in Galfayan's speech, Marinya knew, and she felt that truth summoning tears. *Where are you, Imlod? You should be here. Why are you letting this happen to us?* She cried aloud now, too weak to hold back the flood any longer. "Why've you done this to me, mistress? What's the harm in loving your brother?"

Galfayan actually appeared to be moved. "Hush now. Be strong! The harm was in breaking trust. You're *mine* — not his. If you'd only come to me first with your desire, perhaps something might've been arranged. But you didn't, and so you had to be punished."

Hope sparkled in Marinya's eyes. "*Had* to be? Do you mean it's over now? Please, mistress, I'll do anything you ask! Just allow my baby to live. I'll never disappoint you again — I swear it!" Her lips quavered as she spoke. Tears ran down her cheeks. "I beg you!"

The witch considered this for a moment as Marinya continued to sob. "Yes, child. You've suffered enough. Come. Embrace me, and we'll start anew."

The girl was too relieved to answer, yet she managed to stifle the tears and don a pitiful smile. The queen returned a wide grin...and her eyes...they held her servant enthralled...they beckoned...

Marinya closed her own eyes and took one step forward. Water splashed the baby. He stirred and began to cry.

"Come to me!" Galfayan urged, extending open arms. "The end is near!"

Forgive me, Imlod. Marinya hugged the baby tight, took one more step...and fell. Her child's screams mixed with the raging water.

Marinya Layva stirred in her sleep and moved a hand to her ripe belly. Her unborn child was kicking softly inside. "Just a dream," she whispered. "You're safe, little one."

PART TWO

Breaking the Chain

TWELVE YEARS AGO

Soon I found myself free to move about, so long as my direction was opposite the one Galfayan had taken. A quick step toward her path had caused Kûhric to rise just as suddenly. I kept my motions slow and deliberate after that.

"I'll fetch water to clean you," I said to him, easing back into the passage, and for the second time in my presence he made a movement seemingly of his own will. One not strictly necessary to fulfill his mistress' instructions. He turned his head slightly as if to say: "Touch me and die."

That gave me hope.

Nevertheless, inside the cliff once more, shielded from both heat and stench, I lost the nerve to return to Kûhric. My feet made for a dark corner, and I sat there quietly, intending to study my own fate. Yet as I began rummaging idly through the piles of cryptic parchments stacked on either side of me, my mind eventually settled on Kûhric and my mother instead. On the events that'd taken them from me in the Forest of Weth...

The sun never shone fully on my face in those years. Blazing down from the primordial orb, multitudes of golden rays were devoured in a writhing canopy high above the ferns and lichen on which I tread. My waking moments were enveloped by a stillness and haze that permeated every crack and pore, yet I sensed the life beneath that seeming void of decay. Phantasms lurked behind monstrous trunks spiraled with emerald moss, and I drank from icy streams amidst the sounds of waterfalls stepping their way down to the great channel. Vipers lay twined about gnarled roots. Millipedes wound through sorrel stalks and spent leaves. The stifled incipient energy of the place nearly suffocated me.

The souls of my ancestors resided in the elder trees and swam in the greater waters, and in that time of my life I never dreaded the thought of joining them there. I was at peace. Young and artless. Only two distractions occupied my mind as the seasons passed: routine trips to the village of Elim and visits by Kûhric, my mother's lover. The latter pleased me best—and not only for the break in monotony. This man had taught me to hunt with a bow and to fish in the streams that fed the river Aradros, and once he even let me win a dagger from him in a game of chance. For many years he was the only father I knew.

That morning, as always, I'd emerged before the sun. The flaps of stitched hide that formed our dwelling's doorway swung back together in my wake, raising only the slightest rumor of my passing, and within a few quick steps I found myself standing before the slumbering coals of our evening fire. There I pulled on fur boots, tightened thick leather breeches, and rubbed the hunter's salve into my throat and bare chest. The frigid morning air was invigorating, and I sucked it readily into my lungs, absorbing a new day.

"Find my pack," came a whisper from close behind. Startled, I nearly leapt into the embers. After snorting lightly at his jest, Kûhric stepped in place beside me and added: "I'll stoke the fire."

I'd begun the morning quietly so as not to wake my mother, yet at Kûhric's order I began to scour noisily through things obscured by the night. There was a gift for me in his bundle, and I was anxious to have it. After confiscating a skin of wine and a half-empty bowl of mushrooms, I soon came across the prize.

"Bring it," he urged, sensing I had my greedy hands in the pack by now. I could see his face aglow as he leaned over the resuscitated flames: pale skin, dark hair, beard dangling from chin but missing from cheek and upper lip. Even when the man smiled his eyes looked grave to me, but he wasn't smiling now.

It was a small statue of the Goddess, carved in bone and painted with ochre, that Kûhric pulled from his deerskin pouch and thrust into the firelight. For my benefit, he began turning the thing slowly from front to back and around again, and my smile grew wider with each roll of his fingers. Then he placed the figure in my eager hands, grinned, stood, and returned to the warmth of my mother's slumbering body inside the hut. The fire had to suffice for me, so I lingered there awhile, staring at the Goddess as she submitted to my touch.

The Earth Mother was seated upon a beautifully engraved dais, her arms supported by the skulls of two huge wolves. Her belly swelled with mankind. Her breasts were ripe with its bounty. The smile she wore was a promise. The sharpness of her eyes was a warning.

My own throne was nothing more than a rotten stump. Ripped from the ground in some forgotten year, its reclining angle at least offered a degree of comfort. Huge ears of fungi grew from its sides, and my feet rested upon moss-covered roots while I leaned against the weathered base. I could walk the trail to it with only a hint of light for my guide, and there I'd often sit until faint shafts of light came forth to die on the cold earth. And so it was this particular morning. My head was filled with Kûhric's tales from the night before, leaving much to daydream about as I awaited dawn. I saw myself with him, wading through the midst of a glorious battle, winning praises that dwarfed the names of all other champions. Yet such high thoughts were soon replaced by earthly ones as the day came on. I reminded myself of my calling. My mother was a parchment maker, and I was her *procurer of skins* — and I was already behind in my rounds.

It didn't really matter. The traps lay untouched, and the thickets betrayed no movement. Neither did Kûhric's hound as I eventually stumbled upon it by the creek, and — annoyingly — it completely ignored my presence. Mud was smeared on its nose and left flank, covering the few white splotches normally visible on an otherwise black coat. I placed a hand on its wrinkled muzzle. It pulled away. Apparently my attentiveness was blocking some spectacular view, so for the first time I did more than glance in that direction.

A woman in rags stood facing us downstream. Exquisite blonde locks curled around her thin face, drawing attention to slightly parted lips. Her frame was lithe, and she held a magpie at her breast. This she looked upon with downcast eyes as the forest worshipped her loveliness in silence. Even the gentle trickling of the stream — timeless though it'd been a moment before — seemed irrevocably displaced by the lady's presence. It was a scene no man should see. Yet, caught in the same trance as the animal beside me, I was witnessing it. Who could say how much time passed before I broke free? Surely she'd heard me call the dog as I'd carelessly trampled into her reprieve, yet she seemed oblivious to it all. Why was she here, alone and half a day's walk from the nearest village?

At last I rose and took one step forward as if to call to her — only to feel my heart die as she looked up to show me the lidless sockets of what must've once been the fairest of eyes! The bird took wing and instantly vanished before her brow, and the golden and ivory hues of her hair and skin gave way to the gray dust of Earth. I swooned and staggered, dropping to one knee as the specter's mouth twisted to a longing gape that devoured my sanity. Then the sickening sound of my scream ripped me from the waking world as she approached.

Surely by the grace of some kindlier spirit, my head had become only partly submerged in the creek where I fell, my long brown hair flowing before my face in the current. I was alive, and the fiend was gone. Only one thought remained: *Run home!* So I did. The stupid dog barked and nipped at my heels the whole way.

"Speak," said Kûhric as I fell before his feet in exhaustion.

I couldn't tell him. Before that sprint I'd have done so, but now I was past the delirium. A warrior stood before me. A man I revered. A man who'd reproach me for such folly.

"I'll beat the life out of you, or you'll speak." His tone was callous.

"Where's my mother?" I asked, attempting to stall as much as discover her whereabouts.

No sooner than the words had departed my mouth, I saw her appear from behind a stretcher. Like the shade I'd just encountered, my mother was fair to behold and seemingly full of youth. Her hair was the color of mine, braided rather than free-flowing, and more of her body was tattooed with crescentic markings than not.

"Imlod's not yours to lay hands on, Kûhric," she said. "Return to your rabble if you can't control yourself here!"

Kûhric merely smirked as Nir ushered me toward the hut. She stopped only to light a small wick in the vat fire before we stepped inside.

Though it was a simple construction fashioned of saplings and branches, our dwelling was spacious enough for the two of us to move around freely within. Besides the furs we used for both mats and blankets, the only other objects inside were several baskets and an assortment of clay pots. From one of these vessels Nir poured animal fat into a shell then dropped the wick in after it. Placing the acrid candle between where we sat facing one another, she stared and sighed while I caught my breath.

"What've you done?" she asked in a lowered voice, indicating I should reply the same.

Even now I can't say which frightened me more: the specter's distorted mask or my mother's face as I described the encounter to her. I'd been expecting her to pronounce me ill or punish me for lying or maybe even humor me by pretending to acknowledge the story and conjuring up some meaning to it. But as I saw how she was *actually believing* my words, I found myself caught in her rising madness instead. Before the tale had rightly finished, she sprang from the hut and began spewing some babble about how *he* had returned. I ran out behind to find her clasped to Kûhric's knee. Her head was bowed low in supplication.

"Calm yourself!" the warrior commanded. He snatched up a handful of my mother's braids and pulled back on them, exposing her face to his.

"Take us with you!" she pleaded, tears beginning to trickle down both cheeks. "If not for me, then do it for the boy. I know you care for him!"

"What daemon's gotten into you, woman?"

"Didn't you hear me? The sorcerer's come back for Imlod!"

The plan was simple. Like a weasel caught unwittingly in one of my snares, the intruder's eagerness for bait would be his undoing. At least Kûhric believed it would be, and Nir was too distraught to go against him. I was to lie concealed in a thicket with the hound while my mother went about her work in plain view. Kûhric gave no indication of where he'd be, but I assumed his plan was to loose arrows from a hidden spot in the branches.

Soon I became dissatisfied with my appointed hiding place. Fear should've gripped my mind and frozen me there, but in fear's place came a succession of concern, curiosity, and boredom that eventually led me to stir as the afternoon waned. Leaving the dog where it'd settled down, I began crawling cautiously back towards the hut. I contemplated whether or not this would compromise

Kûhric's position. Perhaps he was watching Nir instead of me. Or maybe he'd deserted us both.

At least I could see her now as I peeked out from my new hiding spot behind a forked oak trunk. My mother was stirring the liquor bath with her back turned to me: a mundane image that helped ease my anxiety. She'd been forced to learn her trade while still a young slave girl in Ladd, and that skill was what'd drawn the sorcerer's attention. I knew little more of the man at the time, and before that day I'd never heard a reference to him inspire anything beyond a muttered curse or sarcastic remark. He'd purchased my mother and set her up in this place, and for a few years thereafter she'd made the parchment leaves he used for recording arcane knowledge.

Then one day he'd set her free, leaving as abruptly as he'd come.

I contemplated again what a sorcerer could possibly want with some boy he'd never seen. How could he even know of my existence? Nir's frantic comments had convinced me he did, yet I knew of no talents I possessed that might aid his cryptic designs. Certainly I could ply my mother's trade with some competency by now, but he could just take her for that.

Presently Nir left the vat and picked up a scraping knife. This step required the greatest skill, and I worried she might damage the pelt in her distressed state. For awhile I studied her trouble face as she progressed with the delicate work — until at last I glimpsed distant motion through the branches behind her.

A shrouded figure was traversing the uphill path. The crunch of its tread told of something more solid than another apparition, yet I'd never seen a living man so strangely clad. His headdress and tunic were neatly cut tanned leather rather than the stitched fur worn commonly by Weth's natives, and antlers protruded sickeningly from the hood as if the sacrificial beast had usurped and transformed its slayer. The fantastic plate mask concealing his face could've been forged in the very fires of the netherworld, and his left hand held the axe *Sacrosanct*: giver of both death and life. His right fist was closed tightly around the unknown.

Thus Taloseth the Mage arrived in the failing light. His former slave took one look in his direction and instantly fell to the ground as if dead. Then — as though he'd placed me there himself — he veered and began walking directly toward my position while the daemonic mask held me completely enthralled. All he had to do now was pluck me up and be off. I even walked out from behind the tree and presented myself to him.

"Back away, Imlod!" shouted Kûhric as he moved into the clearing, twenty strides or less behind his target. He'd discarded the sable coat that was like a second skin to him, leaving the sinewy strength of his youth exposed. His stark white chest accented the purple scars of warring years, and I feared a murderous lust beating inside it would overcome him at once. But for the moment he only paused and adjusted the grip on his drawn sword. It was a symmetrical blade, rounded at the tip, the tang buried in the marrow of a sinew-wrapped handle of bone. Before that day I'd thought it the most splendid of weapons, but...

Taloseth's axe had clearly been forged with some foreign skill. There was no blemish on the metal, and I could feel its sharpness with a sense beyond those serving my daily needs. The wooden haft boasted no ornamentation, yet the head was etched with dozens of elaborate symbols lost to my understanding. Any other man would've been foolish to bring such a treasure into Weth. But Taloseth was no ordinary man. Here was a man so confident—or possessed—that he failed to even acknowledge the threat of Kûhric's presence. The sorcerer continued his trudge toward me unchecked.

"You've lost your way, shaman!" hailed the warrior. "Night approaches, but you're not welcome by our fire!"

Again there was no response from my would-be abductor, and I remained mesmerized by the unseen gaze behind his metal visor.

"What've you done to Nir?" Kûhric pressed. "Turn and face me!" Obviously I'd been wrong to guess he'd turn to his bow. Arrows in a stranger's back would brand Kûhric an assassin, the lowest form of life in the eyes of his kin; so instead he'd just issued the challenge his sword-brothers praised, and now he meant to cut his opponent to pieces in their name.

Kûhric's words had finally drawn Taloseth's attention, for at last he turned from me to his assailant. As if suddenly loosed from a tight cord, I stumbled backward when the sorcerer's entrancing gaze left me, yet there was no visible effect on Kûhric when it fell upon him. He advanced on Taloseth with sword raised high. *Sacrosanct* remained low at the mage's side. When my defender came close enough for me to read the wild look in his blue eyes, I drew a breath and held it. Kûhric stopped abruptly, fanned out in a battle stance, and waited.

Then, calmly, the sorcerer opened his right hand and tossed two pebbles to the ground.

And so my life had been forever altered.

My mother had withheld much from me...but I didn't doubt her intentions. A seemingly harmless lie had been told and believed readily enough: my father had been one of Kûhric's brethren who'd perished in a past battle. Taloseth had been mentioned to me in some fashion, and that must've been good enough for her.

At last I decided to return to Kûhric, but not before examining the dwelling for another way out. Finding nothing but the sheer cliff walls, I took up a water jug and turned to leave. Yet a sudden idea stopped me short. *I'll have to fight.* In doing so, Kûhric had been utterly defeated, but he'd not known what he was up against. What he'd failed to achieve by force, I'd accomplish through stealth or surprise.

Still, I needed a weapon. Not some weighty implement with which to strike at Kûhric, but rather a blade or spike that could be easily concealed. I searched the rooms for such a thing. Nothing escaped my scrutiny, yet after a hundred curses had subsided, only a bone needle and a jagged stone shard were revealed. It occurred to me that Galfayan had likely performed the same search as I slept and deposited any items of potential in her damned basket.

Thus my fate had come to lie with a piece of rock. I hid it within my clothing, retrieved the water jug, and stepped outside.

PRESENT DAY

8

"They fear your name," said Kirath, son of Sevos, kneeling before his sister's throne. "But they still worship the world around them. The oak and the soil and such. None but their brigands and outcasts heed your call."

"Yet *they* are the same fools who'd slay a thousand men over a deer — and freeze to death before bruising a sapling!" Galfayan hissed. "Why must we live like animals? Scrounging and pissing and sleeping our lives away? We are masters of beast and brush and stone alike!"

"We are one with the Mother," Imlod objected from his customary place of audience: kneeling on Kirath's left, facing his queen's right hand.

"*We are not!*" she lashed out. "We're pricks in the veil of Night. Thousands upon thousands we are. But each is alone."

Two small panther cubs frolicked in Galfayan's lap, the latest gift to her from Bablak Alnoor in atonement for some ridiculous slight. The one on her left was dominant, pushing his brother aside for the lion's share of his adopted mother's affections, and now he mewed and hissed along with the queen, irritated at the withdrawal of her playful hand. The other cub fought back weakly whenever goaded but seemed more content to lie and stare. Imlod peered into that one's eyes as he spoke again:

"I made use of your mother's tongue to spread the summons in Dirag, and they still wouldn't listen. You have a great vision, sister. A new Ramfiram to rival the one of legend. But whom shall such magnificence serve? Me? Kirath? Or you alone? Your people won't love the things they're forced to build — nor the queen for whose sake their wives and children are enslaved." He glanced over at Kirath's face — and found a look of shock there — before turning accusing eyes on Galfayan. "Isn't that what you've done? Sent out raiding parties to spoil your own land?"

She took it surprisingly well. "And what of your own fine work, Imlod?" The queen picked up the submissive cub by the scruff of its neck and looked it in the face. "Have I won your hate too?" Her modest dress and the way she wore her hair today — the side-swept bangs, fresh braids resting on her bosom with clean, flowing tresses behind — lent her beauty a touch of innocence that was, at least of late, far from usual.

She knows I prefer her like this, thought Imlod. *Is it for my benefit? What does she want from me now?*

When he didn't reply, Galfayan turned stern eyes on him, and in that instant an image came to Imlod's mind: the goddess figurine, a gift from his childhood that he yet retained. *Those cats aren't her pets. You and I are, Kirath. Her hunters. We're already on all fours, so all we need to do is turn around to look the part.* He glanced at Kirath again. *You're even wearing a wolf's hide…like that fool I slew in the gully.* And indeed the man was. Its scalp was draped over the studded jerkin covering his chest; and a wicked mace dangled at his hip, its spikes sharper than a canine's bite. Twisting his braided goatee about the index finger of his right hand, Kirath appeared as if he were about to speak in Imlod's defense.

But Galfayan spoke first. "Why are you looking at *him*? Kirath can't help you. Not this time." She grinned at that—clearly amused at something about which Imlod was still in the dark—then settled back into a frowning stare.

Am I to be scolded now? For what? I brought the priestess back. My task is done! "I didn't intend to anger you—only to advise. Isn't that why we were called here today? To listen and give counsel?"

"I only desired to speak with you after your long absence, brother. Is that so strange? To reward your success…and to be the first to tell you the news." Her smirk returned as she allowed the last statement to settle in.

What news? Imlod's mind combed rapidly over everything since the struggle with Edohath's men. That'd been no more than six or seven days ago, and not long before then he'd been dawdling in Dirag, ears attuned to all rumors abroad. What of significance could've occurred between then and now? He lifted a hand to his shoulder. The puncture there was almost fully mended, as the arrow had touched nothing vital. Only a dull ache lingered.

That battle had been a close thing. In the end, drained and faint from tending to his wound…and averting his face from Kûhric as the minion forced himself to heal through consuming dead flesh…Imlod could do little more than lie and wait for unconsciousness. But Azilus and Nir hadn't failed at their task. They'd run Edohath down and dispatched him even as Sevos looked on—helpless to prevent her brother's demise.

"Look at him, Kirath," said Galfayan, pulling Imlod back to the present. "He'll be good for nothing until I've told him."

Kirath nodded, a knowing look on his face. "I'll wait outside."

When he was gone, Galfayan set the panther cubs down and rose from her throne. Imlod stood to meet her. Nearby torches flickered from the movement, and shadows grew on the wall behind. "Well, which do you want first? Gift or news?"

"News."

"Are you certain?" she toyed, her face coming to within a hand's breadth from her brother's. She raised a palm to his cheek. "You'll find the reward pleasing, I know. But the rest...I'm not so sure."

"As you wish."

Imlod's acquiescence had been immediate and sincere. Galfayan's head came to rest on his shoulder now, and her lovely arms wrapped about him. It was a rare moment, and he couldn't help being sucked in. Her hair was perfumed. Her breath felt warm on his neck.

"Does she embrace you like this?" she asked, her head still on his shoulder.

She means Marinya. "She once did, yes. But you're cruel to speak of it now." The tenderness, whether true or feigned on Galfayan's part, was over for him now. His body went slack in her arms. Pulling his head away from hers, he noticed something odd: strands of gray hair intermingled with her raven locks.

"Am I?" She let go of him then and retreated a few steps toward the column of morning light streaming down from the temple's dome. "I don't regret my command. That girl was cluttering your mind, and I needed it clear. Yet now we have a reprieve!" She turned back to him. "I'm preparing to travel again, Imlod. Will you come with me this time?"

While Imlod considered that, two servants approached. The first held out a golden tray brimming with fresh meats, dried fruits, and nuts. The other stood slightly behind with an earthen pitcher in hand. Galfayan selected a few morsels and gestured for Imlod to do the same. He waved this away but then accepted a cup of ale as two goblets were produced. After taking his first long drink, he spoke again: "So you're saying my reward is a trip with you to..."

"To our father's homeland. To Agrigoth!" She waited then, her eyes daring him to question it. He opened his mouth to do exactly that, but she came forth swiftly and touched his arm to shush him. "I'll explain later. But listen to me: Marinya shall come too! Unleashed from her vows and free to indulge in your affections. *That* is your reward."

And a sweet one it is. After staring into his sister's eyes a moment to ensure her sincerity, he leaned forward and kissed her softly on the cheek. "My thanks."

She smiled. "I was sure you'd be pleased. But brace yourself! Let's not forget the news."

Imlod's jaw tightened. He'd not seen Marinya for many months, and now their separation was coming to an end—unless these tidings would delay the reunion.

Galfayan's expression was unreadable. "Your woman's with child."

The house was eerily beautiful. Sitting morning-lit under an opening in the canopy far above, its dry-stacked stone walls were fenced only a few strides off by shadow and fog on all sides. A huge oak's roots and limbs reached out from an adjoining mound of earth as if to climb atop the structure from its leftmost wall, caressing the rocks beneath a shut round window and brushing against the thatch covering the roof halfway to its shifted, pointy summit. Smoke swirled lazily up from the chimney, and the wondrous smell of broiled meat floated in the air below. Purple winter flowers decorated the path leading up to an arched wooden door.

Thayld examined the metal door knocker before lifting and bringing it home twice, a boyish smile showing on his face as he did so. Then he stepped back to wait, arms folded across his chest. *This land suits him*, thought Tyth, frowning as she waited also a few steps behind. *And if he carries on like this around these people, they might not believe the hardships we've endured. I hope he doesn't forget our purpose here…*

She, at least, would certainly not. It'd been hard enough to pry herself away from little Hadric and catch up to Thayld after a delayed start — not to mention the tiring conversation to convince the old man of her uses on his quest. "I can't go home!" she'd told him, tears filling her eyes. "Not till I bring vengeance with me!" After the overseer's exhaustive correction, wherein he'd explained it was not *vengeance* but rather *justice* that Diebron sought, he'd finally consented and allowed her to tag along.

The sound of a latch drew Tyth's eyes to the now cracked-open door. There she met the face of a short, aging woman poking her head through the gap. At first the lady seemed wary, but the moment quickly passed.

"Greetings, miss." Her wrinkling face wore a big, kindly smile. She turned back to Thayld. "And to you, good man."

Thayld nodded his head in reply, and Tyth returned the greeting with like words. Then an awkward silence followed while the woman looked them both up and down. Finally she spoke again: "I wasn't expecting visitors today. You're from the lake — am I right?"

Thayld, apparently still bewitched with the place, only tilted his head again, so Tyth had to answer for him and return a courtesy.

"I thought so," said the woman, looking satisfied now with her would-be guests. "Well…come in and get warm!" She motioned inside. "The cooking's almost done."

The room felt hot to Tyth, bundled as she was in heavy furs, and immediately she began scanning for a spot to disrobe. There were no inner walls: just this main area and two draped partitions to her left. A tall young man stood inside the frame of the farthest. He greeted them with a curious frown and, although lowered, a drawn blade in hand.

"Forgive him, child," said the woman as she saw Tyth's eyes go wide. Then

Thayld noticed the blade too and tensed. "Pay him no mind," the woman urged again, touching her wizened guest lightly on the arm to soothe him. "Foul things have been seen in the woods of late, and Nendas here thought you were one of them!" She giggled a bit then, as if she held such reports of small consequence or didn't believe them at all.

"Who's to say they're not, Mother?" complained her boy, yet he grinned as he said it and promptly sheathed his sword. His wide smile and fair eyes lingered a moment on Tyth...then he moved to the room's bench table and gestured for the guests to sit with him. The house's back door was open, and the white rays encroaching from it fell upon the table's centerpiece of fronds while the hearth and several clay lamps provided the rest of the home's light and ambiance. "This is Oreldan's house," the lad began again, seating himself while Tyth worked to remove a layer of fur. "My father's away but should return soon. Come, let's eat. There's plenty for all."

And there was. Although she'd broken her fast with dried fish at dawn, Tyth blushed as she heard her growling belly competing with the crackling fire—and gratefully accepted a portion of each dish as it came around. The meat was rabbit flavored with a nutty paste, onions, and leaves, but the woman had also prepared seed cakes and a blood porridge. As they ate, Thayld found his voice and announced his name, title, and mission, ending with a few lines concerning what'd happened—and was likely to continue happening—in Diebron. He gave Tyth's name as well but avoided the specifics of her losses. *I suppose I should be thankful for that,* she thought, yet somehow her protector's conscious omission angered her. Even the admiring glances from their young host caused her to frown, though the lad named Nendas was certainly handsome with his chiseled face, creamy skin, and lean build. Not long ago she would've been flattered by the attention of such a comely youth, but a certain Megnus of Dirag had since frozen that sort of passion in her.

"I'm sorry for you both. And for your people as well," said Nendas when he perceived Thayld was done talking. Then, turning to Tyth, he added: "Did you see the fiends, my lady?"

"Yes," she spoke softly. *But I'll not speak of them here.*

It took only a moment more for her to realize she wouldn't have to, for the boy had simply been leading up to his own tale. With his eyes straying to the flames, Nendas spoke then of things that might've shocked her had she not just endured much greater terrors herself. A black bear found nearby with its throat torn out—and every drop of its blood drained with nothing more than a splash on the leaves to show for it. A red deer carcass discovered untouched save that its heart had been savagely removed.

"It's awful what happened to you!" the woman piped up as her son paused to sip his drink. "But you're safe now in the king's realm. Don't let Nendas scare you, girl. My husband sent word to Asalin, and soon his wardens will come and cleanse these woods—should there be anything but horrid *tricksters* to be found." Her eyes swept accusingly to her own son.

Nendas looked as if he'd offer a rebuttal, but Tyth spoke quicker: "Wardens?" Her confused look said the rest.

"Sacred guardians of Kûthod," Nendas answered. "I hope to join their order soon. You've not heard of them?"

Although the name *warden* sounded familiar—perhaps from a childhood tale or two—Tyth had to admit her present ignorance on the subject.

"It's been too long since the days of their glory…when their might was *truly* tested." Nendas sighed, set his cup down on the polished tabletop, and leaned forward. "Would you like to hear a verse, Tyth?"

At this his mother rose and left the house, mentioning the chores awaiting her outside; yet both guests indicated their desire for the young man to proceed.

So Nendas began:

The years of truce that birthed this age
Saw lords and daemons lay down blades
And elves sprang from their union

From mountain peaks to river's end
The Threefold host went hand in hand
Some spread by boat, others by land
And filled the trees with laughter

In time the ash of Mother's Womb
Was drowned in clearest water blue
And sated by that healing rain
The dust of Rhanwŷr merged anew
To summon home her children

To few her voice was rendered mute:
Fair nymphs and elves and centaurs hoofed
But most that heard her back did run
Their faces hidden from the Sun

To bow before the Daemon's throne
And sing for days of darkness

The hordes of Rhanwŷr, blades in hand
Stormed through the woods and hills and fens
"Resist!" the faithful Threefold cried
Till none of them were left save men:
A host of bloodied vassals

Yet, of these, one whom in his veins
Was mixed part elfin blood of fame
Defied the Daemon when she came
And with curved sword he slew her

Breladus was that hero's name
And from his youngest son's loins came
Kûthod's brave kings and wardens

"I have his blood in me," Nendas declared as the verse ended, eyes sparkling with pride. "I need only to prove my skills, then they'll take me on as prentice."

"I wish you success, lad," said Thayld.

"As do I," said Tyth. "But did all the elves truly perish? I once heard a man claim otherwise…"

The door had opened as she was talking, and in walked the master of the house. "Only those of the Faithful, young lady," he said as Tyth turned her eyes on him. "The elves beyond the mountains may be fair to behold, but their minds are twisted and perilous."

Thayld rose to greet the man.

"Please sit!" urged Oreldan. He looked an older version of his son. "We can discuss your business here later — but first we'll have a drink! And perhaps I'll recite a verse of my own for the pretty girl?" He winked at Tyth innocently then smiled at his son.

Oreldan proved to be a merry host. As the morning wore on toward midday, he and his guests still sat at the table, drinking and smiling and reliving legends of Kûthod and other lands besides. Tyth was especially grateful for the laughter, having needed it more than she'd realized. Yet although Oreldan's tales were as intoxicating as the spiced wine the man poured for her, Tyth tried hard to retain all that was said of Kûthod's monarch. Unlike the hero from whom he claimed direct descent, Asalin hadn't needed to win his throne through deeds of valor. He'd inherited the realm in a state of tranquility. Still, on the first day of his reign as a boy no older than Nendas Jush, the king had sworn a solemn oath to defend Kûthod's peace at any cost. And since that day he'd never failed to do so, most often through his orders and judgments — but also, at times, with his holy sword *Solitude* in hand. The very weapon Breladus had once used to slay the Daemon.

As for his family: Asalin's queen had been forced into seclusion by his own command many years ago, yet what the woman had done to earn his disfavor, Oreldan either didn't know or else considered it inappropriate to relate. Since the woman yet lived, however, the king couldn't remarry — although he kept a mistress — and to this day Kûthod's heir had remained his only surviving child by the estranged wife: a daughter named Marinya Layva. But it'd been years now since the princess had dwelt amongst her own people, for she'd traded in her inheritance for the cult of Ramfiram; and it was whispered that with each season since her desertion, her father withered ever more from pining. Despite the urgings of his court, Asalin had refused to name anyone else as heir in his daughter's stead, ever hoping that one day she'd repent and return to him.

When at last Oreldan rose to step outside, Tyth found she was in need of help to stand. *Too much wine. How shameful of me.*

Nendas extended her his arm and a mischievous smile. "Perhaps you should spend the night with us, Tyth. I don't believe walking would suit you just now!"

"She'll be fine," Thayld frowned, foiling the boy's design. "We must be going."

Having caught the boy's scheme also, Oreldan turned to Thayld: "As you can see, my friend, I'm sure Nendas would be glad to lead you to Asalin's seat. It lies three days from this hollow: in Thaekith, the City of Leaves."

9

She tried to imagine how it'd been—in ages past—to sit and survey the rim. Before the dangling baskets and tight cages and tiny boats and crude winches. Before the seamless rises and falls of dried brick dwellings and the babbles of men and bleats of penned beasts: an incessant cacophony that suppressed all but the loudest blasts of chill wind whipping through her free-flowing hair. In those ancient days this place must've been a haven of unsurpassed natural beauty and calm. Not that those attributes had wholly departed, but rather now one must seek them in the enormous bowl of pristine water far below. The only motion there was a dance of ripples across the leagues of Lake Thadda's surface, the colors shifting from azure to dark blue and every shade in between. There the two islands faced each other across the divide, as if the epic battle of Daemon and Father had been caught and frozen in time.

Strong gusts pummeled Marinya's face and sent fresh tears flowing sideways with her raven locks. The moisture matted some strands to her right cheek: the one facing the temple of Thadda. The white dirt on which she reclined no more than a single stride away from the steep drop stuck and marred the purity of her acolyte's dress, yet she paid it no mind. Looking past the gnarled trees clutching at life in the dry soil beside her, she gazed out to the Black Isle and wept. And though her silent cries beseeched each and every one, begging them all to awake and cast down the infernal den of hewn stone in their midst, the sparse tall pines of that shore remained still and unmoved.

They're all the same, the things that I cry for, thought Marinya, lifting a hand to sweep wet strands from her eyes. *A fatherless girl carrying a fatherless child in a fatherless land.*

Of old, the Ûledrith high priestess, her Brethren, and their chosen acolytes had been the only living souls allowed to enter or pass over the lake's sacred waters. Yet in the very moment of Galfayan's ascension to power in Ramfiram, that precept had ceased to exist. The queen had been rowed over to the temple that day in a skiff while showered with flowers and kisses from the rim above: a bastard girl with nothing more than a bastard brother at her side. But thereafter, for the first time in memory, the Womb had been opened to any man or woman who'd pray to the Mother's idol—and Marinya was one whose spirit had stirred upon hearing the decree.

Even the mighty Asalin couldn't keep me back for long, she sniffled, recalling her father's stern face. She tried to hold that picture in her head—just as she'd done on the day she left his world for this place—to make his scowl the archetype of repression. But it was no good. For years now that image had been unveiled for what it truly was: a caring rebuke that ended in a loving hug and smile.

Ironically, her father had been the one to nurture the love of Mother Earth in

Marinya. In those days, the only point that'd separated the religious practices of Ladd from those of her own people had been the Brethren's continued worship of the Father. Galfayan had since mended that division, though, by driving out the old régime. *How foolish of me to think her inspired! Our Mother Incarnate? The Queen of Earth?*

From her life's own voids — a lost father and lover — and the child growing in her womb, Marinya had finally come to accept reality. The Brethren were right. Whether raised on high in the days of legend or hidden now on the border of life and death, there must always be a Father. The balancing force of life. A hand to both rouse and soothe the fiery passions of Earth. Without him there was but a choice of deadly extremes. And by seeking to repress the Father, Galfayan had in truth not assumed the Mother's aspect, as she'd have her followers believe, but rather she'd fostered the spirit of Rhanwŷr the Daemon: a power that yearned to toss the world down into either an icy ruin or fiery chaos.

There was another void as well, less burning now than the others but no less significant. A mother she'd hardly known. Perhaps *the* Mother had become a substitute. Maybe the true reason she'd come to this place, beneath all her talk, was to join her mother in seclusion…

"He's here now!" yelled the winch man's daughter from behind, the tiny girl's sudden, high-pitched voice startling Marinya back to the present.

She wiped her eyes. "Please, child…help me stand." Now in the seventh month of pregnancy, she was having trouble getting around. Still, with one arm folded under her bulging belly and the other tugged by the girl, she managed to slowly rise and move away from the ledge.

The winch man, a slovenly brute named Lietan, stood waiting for her by the huge crank wheel that was his livelihood, one hairy hand gripping a spoke and the other a skin from which he was swigging. Seeing her, he set down the skin, smiled, wiped his mouth, and held out a palm for payment. His eyes went to her stomach: "Look here! What do you think, Thisill? Should I charge her for one or two?"

The child giggled as she danced over to him. "Two, Father!" Then another thought occurred to her: "No. A full measure…and a half!"

Lietan grinned, well pleased. "That's a good girl. So be it."

Surely he jests, thought Marinya, disgusted. Not so long ago, a man such as this would've dared ask only a blessing from her — and been happy if he got it. *These people have lost all reverence!*

Though she'd made the descent to the lake hundreds of times since arriving in Ramfiram, this was the first time she'd ventured to do so from here. At the spot frequented by the privileged few on their way to and from the temple, her acolyte's dress was payment enough. But she wasn't headed there today. It was the opposing isle she sought just now. The one she'd only rarely approached before by boat from the temple. The earlier visits had been in service to her queen, delivering sealed messages and receiving their answers for Galfayan. This time, however, she meant to beg an audience of her own...although she wasn't beyond using the temple's tokens to pay this sot for her passage.

"Clay?" spoke Lietan as she produced two imprinted discs — one smaller than the other — and silently dropped them in his palm. "I'd prefer the..."

"I have none," she interrupted him, too weary to endure his complaint. "The granary's scribes honor these tokens. Please...I must be going."

As she stepped into the basket and started down, Marinya's eyes lingered on the man turning the wheel. She thought how she'd come to share the sentiment behind his last words. *I'd prefer the grain.' Of course you would. To spare yourself a trip — and avoid dealing with Galfayan's vile, cheating worms.* Even the most ardent and persuasive proponent of such devices as the queen's tokens would become an object of ridicule or scorn in Marinya's homeland. Kûthod's citizens were hunters and gatherers, usually bartering with one another only to acquire goods of special craftsmanship. Yet in this great city, it seemed not a single man was left of that self-sufficient sort. Here farmers felled trees to raise hemp and barley and vegetables on plots about the rim. Here were pens where pigs and goats were raised solely for the knife. Where Kûthod shunned or even punished any who dared such breaks with nature, Galfayan's servants busied themselves with promoting them daily. The queen's *progress* had even spread far beyond the rim. Ramfiram was the center of a massive trading wheel, a hub about which the livelihoods of its surrounding villages revolved — and without which they could hardly survive.

Blown sideways by a gust of chill wind, the basket screeched and tipped a bit as it grazed the cliff. Marinya gripped the wood tightly and looked down. The ride was nearing its end.

Her hair was as blue as the lake's water, its long waves clinging wet to her delicate arms and naked bosom. There was no blemish to her snow-white skin save the crescent moon tattooed black on her brow, and her face and figure were near perfection. As she bent forward to touch the canvas, a beam of light caught and illuminated the flowers in her locks above one ear; then she turned to the window and narrowed her cool, azure eyes. A boat approached from the south. She recognized the oarsman at once but couldn't make out his passenger. The splash of her sister's dive ended the stillness outside, rousing a serpent's hiss and a fluttering of birds.

Her face returned to the canvas and, after a moment's reflection, below it to the shells and turtle carapaces that contained her paints. She dipped her index finger into the ivory paste—taking care not to touch it with the charcoal tipping the digit beside it—and brought it back to the picture taking shape. White filled the sky about a sun of yellow ochre, streaming out to meet a plane stained red by the Earth's maternal blood. But what did this union birth? A sea of blackness. Death. Yet the sun also touched the dark water, rising in splendor from it...

"It's beautiful," spoke Marinya Layva softly, peering in now from the open doorway behind.

"The end nourishes the beginning," the nymph Sigeya responded, "...and the beginning births the end." Her face swept around then to meet her visitor. "You came a different way this time. What have you brought us, Earth-daughter?"

"I'm here of my own accord today, my lady. I had a strange dream the other night—and I was hoping you might unravel it for me. May I come in?"

"I'll join you outside instead. Sienda should hear this too." Sigeya wiped her hands clean with oil from a nearby pitcher, uncoiled the lower half of her body from around the broken column on which she'd been resting, and—pushing off with her gorgeous blue-scaled, finned and fluked tail—began snaking toward the door.

They found the other nymph just emerged from a swim, her own fishlike tail dangling as yet below the water's surface. The rest of her dripping-wet body, a near mirror image of her sister's, lay atop one of the large smooth rocks lining the island's tight perimeter. She looked out over the crumbling two-story tower that was her shelter, peering up at the clouds. Beside her basked an emerald lizard— bigger than an average dog—whose crested head she stroked as if it were a pet. The approaching swishing and crunching of sand drew her eyes level with the shore. "Princess of Kûthod," Sienda greeted the visitor with a flat stare. "What does the witch want from us now?"

"She doesn't serve Galfayan today," Sigeya explained. "Yet she requires our lore all the same." Frowning, she added: "Few have ever come otherwise."

Sienda's eyes sparkled as her lips turned up in a smile. "You're too grave, sister!" Then, eyeing Marinya again: "It pains me to see you're still here, girl. Didn't I urge you to flee this place? Why do you linger?"

Marinya opened her mouth to spew excuses—her pregnancy, the wait for Imlod to return, a gnawing fear of the queen's reprisal—but then snapped it shut. Lowering her gaze instead, she shook her head from side to side, frustrated with her weakness. Then another thought came, and she looked up. "I could ask the same of you, my lady."

"Come sit with me. You shouldn't be standing long." Sienda motioned to a rock below the lizard's spot, and Sigeya took Marinya's arm to help her down to it. "As you can see, we're not the same as you, girl. Sigeya and I have been here since the first nightfall, and we'll never leave. We are Earth's adopted children, ever clinging to her breast, mirroring her moods in our bodies. In the beginning we were nagas of flame, as the Daemon spawned us. Then we were spirits of shadow, buried with Ûl-Kamûn beneath his black ash. And now we are long since risen anew, pure as the Mother's milk: the blue water that sustains us. But your home lies deep in Asalin's woods. Why remain here? Doesn't this decay sicken you?"

"It does," Marinya answered, looking across the waters to the Black Isle. "It plagues me now both day and night. Awake and in my dreams." She turned back to Sienda. "I'm afraid of the future, as I've never been before. Please, can you help me see what's to come? If not for my sake, then for my child's?"

As Sienda had said, she and her sister were truly connected to the Womb. Born from the Fire, their minds were radiant and their memories unquenchable, even after their first bodies had burned to smoldering embers. Yet the nymphs' great knowledge and wisdom weren't limited to their experiences alone. They'd dwelt in the netherworld for an age and needed no arcane art to gain information from the dead — for a part of their spirits still touched that gray, tangled plane. They'd outlived generations of rulers in Ramfiram since their rebirth. At times worshipped by commoners and magnates alike. At others, as was the present case, spared from a second death only for the cryptic gifts they could provide. As Galfayan hoarded the very words from their mouths, access to the sisters' cramped isle was granted to none but a few picked servants and acolytes well known by the boatmen. Yet the nymphs had no guards: for who would dare molest them, openly or in secret, and risk waking the Mother's wrath? Not even the *Queen of Earth* could do so. Not as long as she desired to keep up that farce of a title.

"Let's begin with your dream," Sigeya spoke after exchanging an unreadable look with her sister. "For sleep is akin to death…and in the netherworld, a soul's past, present, and future are one. Perhaps you glimpsed something of what lies ahead — or maybe it was but some ghost of days gone by, returned in a different guise to haunt you."

"And you'll know which it is?" asked Marinya. She was visibly relieved at the nymphs' willingness to help.

"As clearly as you can relay it to us, so can we divine and interpret for you."

Marinya did her best to recall everything. The cave and the waterfall. Her terrible hunger. Galfayan's harsh and soothing words. Her little boy's sad cry and dirty little feet and hands. She ended her recounting on the child — and suddenly she panicked, tears pooling in her eyes. "I can't see his face! Of all things to forget, with the rest so clear! What does it mean? What's wrong with me?" She sniffed and wiped a hand across her eyes. The sisters waited patiently as their visitor looked across the lake and attempted to compose herself. Finally she turned back and gave a weak but hopeful smile: "Can *you* see him? Is it truly a boy I carry?"

"Yes," Sigeya answered. "Your child is male indeed. But his face is hidden to us also."

The nymph glanced at her sister again—and something about the look this time made Marinya cringe.

It was Sienda's turn to speak. "The witch bade you be strong, and so shall I. You saw the baby's face. Now you cannot. It's because his future is uncertain. His life hangs on the choices you make."

Marinya's jaw dropped. "But...I thought you said..." The tears came back. *Stop crying! I shouldn't have come here...*

"I did," said Sigeya. "A spirit knows its future as well as its past—and if you manage to connect with it, a picture of days to come can be revealed. Yet it's just that. A *picture*. A finished painting, if you will, but one over which the painter still broods, able as yet to either mar the work or amend it. So a picture of your soul—or of others affected by you—depends upon the past to the very moment of your query, with every detail hinging on the prevailing course of your mind at the time."

"If that's true," said Marinya, sniffling, "...then what good comes from telling me this? To torture me?" She was too distraught at the moment to be angry, but otherwise she would've raged. "Some ill might befall my child, you say—yet my actions could hasten it as swiftly as avoid it?"

"You asked us to," Sienda replied flatly. "And why is it good? It rarely is." She paused to examine Marinya's face: perhaps to tailor her next words to what mood she found there. "Only those who catch a glimpse of the future may alter its path, Marinya. The blind man may row a boat, never knowing his direction, and the trip still take him somewhere—but the smith can shape many a thing from a metal whose secrets he knows. Wouldn't you rather be the smith?"

"Yes, my lady...so very much! Please forgive my doubts. Will you still aid me?"

"You alone of all the witch's messengers have never failed to revere us, so we will help you if we can. Shall we continue?"

Marinya nodded in thankful agreement before giving her attention to Sigeya.

"It's not true," the nymph began, "...that you could as easily toss your child into the net as cut him from it, for there were signs in your dream to guide you. But before I read the portents, I warn you: playing with fate can be a dangerous game for mortals. Perhaps you'll steer towards the desired outcome with eyes open wider than before, yet beware the ripples your oar strokes make! All souls and their fortunes are intertwined; so rock the boat of another, and for good or ill he may see you and set his course in your direction. Listen to my words and use them as you will—but tell no one else! Dip the oars lightly under cover of night, and maybe you'll cross the water unharmed. Do you understand?"

"I think so."

"Then know your dream's signs confirm the course Sienda urged you to take. To ensure your child's life, you must leave Ramfiram. Soon."

Confusion shown again on Marinya's face. "How can that be? In the dream it brought only ruin..."

Sienda grinned. "You've read it too simply, girl, as if the answers lie on the dream's surface. Tell her, Sigeya."

"There were only two souls connected in the dream," said the other nymph. "Yours and your unborn child's. The vision of Galfayan was not her at all. It was *you*. Does that help?"

Marinya frowned and shook her head '*no.*'

"You said she donned the black feathers of a bird, with vines running through her hair. Galfayan might indeed wear such garb in the waking world, but in your dream this was more than a reflection of her fancy. Black is the color of despair, the vines tell of a clinging to something, and the cave in which you met your dark half is a symbol of this very city: the Womb. So you hang on to your life here, though you love it no longer. That's no secret—but there's more. You spoke of feeling powerless before the witch and of being shunned by villagers, both revealing a loss of confidence in yourself. Your hunger in the dream is for food, yet what you truly starve for is praise and affection. You scold yourself for being attached to the witch's brother, fearing the man won't accept your child— still you defend him also, believing somehow you've caused him harm." Sigeya paused here, giving her listener a chance to digest the words.

After a moment, during which Marinya remained silent, the seer continued. "But these things speak only of the present and of you alone. The child's future is what concerns us. The boy was covered in dirt, you said. Gray is the color of death. The dust of Earth. If you remain in the cave...in Ramfiram...your son won't be born in this age. Yet there's hope! Though perhaps it felt wrong in the dream, you chose the right path. The cascade is the flow of your thoughts and emotions, and by joining your dark half there, you didn't meet your death—as it must've seemed then—but rather the end of a struggle within you. You faced the uncertainty of the future on that ledge...and cast yourself down into a pool of new life!"

A smile crept onto Marinya's face. "Yes...I see it now! His cry was so weak till we touched the water—then he screamed so loudly! And the water washed the dirt away!"

Sienda smiled as well. "Yes. Freeing him to be born."

"There's one last sign," Sigeya said, as if intent on spoiling the mirth. "Before the fall, you asked the son of Nir to forgive you, did you not?"

"I did." The acolyte's smile vanished. *What does this mean for us, Imlod?*

Sigeya looked to her sister again, then Sienda spoke: "Do you know why?"

Marinya lowered her eyes. *Because I must leave him behind.*

10

Once again Cirad stalked the temple's dim passageways, yet now with a different minister at his side. Having exchanged the tattered clothes of his ruined order for fresh ones of pure black, his bloodless face lacking even the stubble of what'd before been a spotted gray beard, Amasmir the Lich was hardly recognizable as the man of his past.

"And what of Gilal?" the elf directed to his ghoulish companion, resuming their conversation. "He was not to be harmed."

"The man doesn't lack for comfort," said the Lich, turning a chilling set of unblinking eyes on Cirad. "Do you wish to see him as well?"

Regardless of how many times he'd beheld undead since becoming involved with Galfayan, Cirad found this new henchman most disturbing. A hood had concealed the man's hair before, but Cirad had assumed that hair to be streaked like the now-shaven beard. Yet in contrast to his withered ivory face, Amasmir's mane was black as his robe—and long, straight, and flourishing. A silver circlet sat his brow, its amber stone resting just above the nose, and his voice was eerie as his stare.

"Not today," the elf replied at last. *I'm in no mood to be chastised.*

Despite Cirad's selfishness and shifting loyalties, he planned on honoring his debts to the minister from Taudan. Although his age in years actually rivaled Gilal's, the developmental period for an elf in proportion to the race's extended lifespan was much longer than a human child's. Thus it'd once been possible for Cirad to make a father figure of the man who'd freed him from bondage. The man who'd introduced him to then-rebel Kordû mo Kar, starting Cirad on his path to power—and to revenge. *I won't let the man rot in that cell, no matter the comforts made available. He'll travel with us to Agrigoth once he swears an oath to Galfayan.* At some point Cirad must suffer Gilal's condemnation of his betrayal, but other matters were presently at hand.

Soon a bolted door appeared before them, with the options of trying it or else turning left or right down adjoining halls. "Are you prepared?" asked the Lich, palm resting on the bolt. "Such sights can be unnerving to the inexperienced."

"More than staring at you?" the elf replied, undaunted.

Whether or not Amasmir took that response for the half-jest it was, he gave no indication. His hand slid the bolt aside, and the elf followed him into the chamber.

Cirad first noticed the room's lighting. Spilling out from the many lamps occupying recesses cut into the hewn stone walls, it filled the chamber with a sinister orange glow. Between each nook hung a perfectly centered, spotlessly cleaned cutting instrument—saws, axes, curved knives, two-handed swords—

their metallic blades flashing dully in the soft, flickering light; yet the elf knew this collection to be neither armory nor treasure hoard on display. One merely needed sniff the air and shift his gaze from the walls to the floor for proof.

Despite the drafts that brought in fresh air, threatening to extinguish the lamps, a powerful stench of death and decay invaded Cirad's nose as he looked upon its source. Nearest the far side of the room from where he and Amasmir stood, yet still within plain view, was a flat stone altar surrounded by a pool of blood. On that altar lay the headless body of a deer, its severed neck hanging over the foul basin into which every drop of its life had no doubt been drained. And in the pool—submerged to the torso, arms pulled up and out to the sides by thick chains secured to the floor—was the unmistakable hulking body of Cirad's former master. But where once a shaven and tattooed head had sat upon those broad shoulders, the antlered skull of the deer was now attached in its place.

As he followed Amasmir closer to the pool, Cirad saw that the motionless creature's head was slumped on its chest with its eyes closed. "Does he live?"

"Live?" the Lich replied. "No. Will he animate at my command? After this period of adjustment...most certainly. The queen said he loved the peryton more than he did her, and thus she ordered me to make him the image of his god—so they should never be parted again. He lacks only hooves and wings."

Animate at your *command?* Cirad mused. *But you're the same as him.* Ignoring the sick motive behind Galfayan's instructions to the Lich, he turned his puzzled face on Amasmir. "I hadn't thought it possible for one *servant* to control another."

"Most are unable," came the response, "...for they lack the needed degree of cognizance. Some, like the queen's furry shadow, are able enough but unsuited practically for it. But you will find, elf, that *I* am unlike all the others."

When he'd done speaking, Amasmir spread his arms wide and stepped into the bloody pool, careless of staining his new garb. *It seems he won't leave his order's color behind after all,* thought Cirad, leading himself to the spoken question: "How is it you perceive so much, Amasmir, but don't fight the control yourself?"

Wading within a step of the chained creature, the Lich stopped to one side of it and turned partially back to Cirad. "Because the servant who struggles with his master may find himself banished from this world, and there are things I mean to accomplish here first." Smiling wickedly, he turned his dark eyes back to the pool.

Things he *means to accomplish.* How bold were Amasmir's words! Was the queen aware of his behavior? Cirad sincerely hoped so, as although in name it would be Bablak Alnoor ruling the city in their upcoming absence, it was to be this servant truly left in charge.

"Ah...he wakes," the Lich reported, interrupting Cirad before his brooding could go on. The hybrid creature's wild eyes were open now, yet it appeared dazed, making no other movement. Amasmir cupped one hand beneath its jaw, lifted its drooping head, and turned the skull left and right in a quick appraisal before looking back at the elf. "Behold, Cirad. I give you Kordû, King of Beasts."

Marinya's puffy eyes betrayed a recent bout of crying, yet there were no tears of relief nor joy to welcome Imlod Nir home. "I thought you'd be happy to see me," he said from the room's single entrance.

"You're not allowed here!" she returned, her mouth agape and eyes wide. She looked more afraid than surprised. "Who let you in?"

"This did." Imlod raised an unfurled scroll that'd been dangling at his side. Marinya made to rise; but seeing her swollen belly for the first time, he frowned and gestured against it. "Don't get up. Let me bring it to you."

She studied him a moment longer before returning her gaze to the fire. "Slide the door behind you."

Imlod realized his visit had interrupted Marinya's evening meal preparations. It didn't matter that her small brick cell was grouped among at least two dozen more of the same: she and the other girls dwelling in the House of Acolytes were required to fend for themselves. There was no inner courtyard nor hall in which to mingle with the other off-duty servants or enjoy a communal feast; and there were no authority figures — besides guards stationed at the outer doors — to impose a schedule or rules of conduct. The complex itself reminded Imlod of his father's onetime abode in the cliffs of Mavûl Gorge. But that was a dead place, deserted long ago.

Crossing the room in a few steps, he dropped and sat cross-legged beside her. A slab of meat sizzled on a hot stone above the flames, but Marinya's attention was on the bowl beside it. She stirred its contents then licked a bit off the spoon. Apparently satisfied with the taste, she moved her clay lamp close and held out a hand for the scroll. Imlod gave it up with a smile, flipping the meat as Marinya began to read.

It didn't take her long. "But why? For your child's sake?"

Imlod opened his mouth to answer but was cut off...

"You knew before you came! Did the queen tell you?"

"Yes," he replied then paused, unsure how to handle his lover's queer mood. *Isn't it enough the ban's lifted?*

"What did she say about my son?" Marinya demanded.

"She said..." Imlod began but stopped, something registering in his mind. "Wait...your *son*?"

A flash of fear touched Marinya's eyes. "It's just a feeling — and what do you care, Imlod? You've been gone so long I hardly recognize you! You didn't plan for this child, but you did nothing to prevent it. And now I bear all the burden!"

"I didn't know! I'd have done everything I could to speed my return — even though she forced us apart! Not just for the child, but for *you*." His hand came up to touch her face. She pulled away from it reflexively, yet he saw his words and the gesture weren't without effect. She was beginning to calm.

After a few moments of staring at the far wall, Marinya turned at last and reached for Imlod's hand. "I *am* happy to see you." She showed him a weary grin. "It's just that...it's been a long, confusing day..."

Imlod reciprocated the grin, then both his thoughts and eyes gravitated to her belly.

She noticed this and pulled his hand inside her clothing to rest on it. "Keep it here. Maybe he'll kick for you."

As he sat there in silence, waiting for the first contact with his unborn child, Imlod turned his thoughts inward. What did becoming a father mean to him? Would life continue on as it had, just with an extra mouth to feed — or was this a turning point for him? *How can I be a father? I never knew my own...*

Suddenly the baby kicked hard. "I don't deserve this, Marinya." He yanked his hand away.

She must've thought his remark came from a sense of newfound happiness, for at first her smile grew even wider. Then she found his troubled face. "What do you mean?"

"You don't understand the things I've done...nor the things that've been done to me. How can I help raise a new life in this world, when all I've ever known is *death*?"

Though it would've done little to ease his mind, the solace he'd expected from Marinya didn't come. As if refusing to hear what he'd just said, she turned back to her cooking. "It's done. Will you eat with me?"

They returned to silence for the meal, leaving Imlod alone with his thoughts. If Marinya wouldn't speak in answer to his predicament, he'd have to reason it out himself.

The cycle of life, he mused. One's last breath escapes his earthly shell, then the soul begins its journey from this world to the next — there to wait upon a day of rebirth. Into the seed of a tree it might pass then...or an egg of some bird...or maybe even the womb of another human mother. That'd been the natural order of things since the time of Ûl-Kamûn's fall.

Yet there was another way. The one Imlod's mysterious father had sought but that Galfayan had actually achieved. A part of that *unlife* had touched Imlod as well; and although he hadn't asked to learn his sister's art thereafter, with all those sleepless nights spent under her harsh tutelage, he hadn't entirely spurned it. What else could've given him back those he'd lost? But things had changed now. Was it time to leave Kûhric to his fate and set his mother's soul free? To trade a ghostly family for one that could smile and laugh with him, feel the sun's warmth on their faces, and breathe in the fresh air?

He knew the answer, yet the question remained: *will Galfayan allow it?* With all the other pawns available to her, one might assume that she would. But this wasn't the first time Imlod had considered the prospect of his freedom, and now the obstacles to it came rushing back. Although the alien spirit within his sister's body might be imperishable, its hold over her mind was as yet incomplete. She was still *Galfayan* in part, however small, and that part—just like Imlod—craved a family of her own. It was he and Kirath who filled the void.

And there was the problem of Kûhric too. Why did she keep him enslaved still after all these years? Unlike the other minions, Kûhric didn't fawn over his mistress. He didn't even feed beyond that forced on him to keep his bones from rotting to dust. Was it she who punished him, or did he punish himself? The queen claimed the latter, but Imlod found that hard to believe. *Why would he do such a thing?* Was it possible, however slightly, that he could combat her will? And if Kûhric was still fighting, could Imlod leave him? Just walk away?

"Do you love me?" Marinya's soft voice came to tear Imlod from his reverie.

He realized she'd stopped eating to stare at him. *Could* he love her? She was the beautiful mother of his unborn child. A lost princess that'd somehow fallen for him. He should sacrifice daily to the Mother for providing him this fortune, but instead he answered: "I don't know how."

"Maybe so. But I could teach you." She smiled hopefully. "Do you *want* to love me?"

"I do…but…"

"But what?" she cut him off again, yet this time in calm urging rather than from brash anger. *"You don't understand the things I've done…*is that it? You're wrong. I know what you are—and how do you think I feel about myself? Every person in this city is her toy! You've killed for her, I know—maybe worse—but I've done little better."

"Is that so? In Diebron I slew a *woman!* She was no threat to me save for her cries for help—yet I took her life for them!" Marinya frowned at this, perhaps more at Imlod's rising tone than at the heinous deed revealed. But he went on: "Amasmir saw what I did and guessed I'd killed the other women and children too. That day I didn't…I only threatened to…but don't think me incapable of it!

One day I *shall* do such a thing—then no one will be safe from me."

"Galfayan killed that woman," said Marinya softly.

"You still don't see it!" Imlod shook his head. "He called me a monster, and now—because of me—that's exactly what he's become. Galfayan gave me the task, but I didn't have to do it. I could've run off and hid, never to return...or surrendered to those I hunted and let them judge me."

"But we *can* run!" said Marinya. "The Year of Conceiving is nearly upon us, and with all the commotion it'll bring to the rim, we might not be missed for some time."

"And where would we go?" Imlod sighed. "Escape is easy enough, but who can shield us from the hunt? They *will* come for us..."

"It's time for me to go home. Angry with me or not, my father won't let us be harmed. The borders of Kûthod are well protected. Our child would be a prince in Thaekith! Surely you'd rather him be there than cramped in this cell? In this infernal city?"

"He—or she—would hold the same status here," Imlod countered. "Your days in this house are at an end either way. You'll live with me from now on."

"That's not good enough! I must leave Ladd altogether. The baby won't be safe in this land!"

Imlod gritted his teeth. "I hadn't planned on telling you tonight, but it'll spare us this debate. We *are* leaving. Just not alone—and not for your father's realm."

"What are you saying?" Her face was scrunched up in confusion.

"It was the price to reunite us. We journey to the desert." Imlod paused for a response, but none came. Marinya was engrossed in thought. "Galfayan claims a desire to see the land of our father...but it's more than that. You can't speak a word of this to anyone. Do you understand?"

She nodded.

"The queen plans to seize power in Agrigoth."

"But...that's madness! Why would she risk such a thing, when she already rules in Ladd? She'll endanger us all!" Marinya grabbed his hand again, more firmly this time. "I must return to Kûthod—with or without you. Won't you come with me? Please don't separate us again!"

"I don't want that," he assured her. "It's just..." He drew a hand across tired eyes. "My father killed my mother, Marinya. And for what? Surely he must've cared for her once—even if it was little more than lust. So how did he become a heartless murderer? It was the Daemon that drove him, and it's the Daemon that haunts Galfayan now. She's my *sister*..."

"Promise me," Marinya said, moving her palm to Imlod's cheek. "Our boy will want his father. *I* want his father..."

Staring into her eyes, he leaned forward and kissed her tenderly.

11

It was a gate with no walls, a single stone archway amid the only barricade Thaekith had ever required: the trees of Kûthod. High above the understory where the forest's huge trunks narrowed, sunlight burst through the woods to touch the structure's summit, blinding rays throwing long shadows of the arch's sculptured truss along its angled slab sides. A dark path through tangled brush no wider than a deer trail ended just outside of it; and within lay a dense grove covered in green winter grass, strewn with the fallen leaves of red, orange, and yellow that'd earned the city its name so long ago.

Nendas and Thayld Priregord had moved on ahead, leaving Tyth to admire the arch alone. Standing directly beneath it now, she tilted her head skyward and gaped. "Who built this?"

"The founders of the city. In the days of Afendald, our first king." Nendas turned and began closing the distance to Tyth, causing his elder companion to halt and frown. But the lad wasn't concerned with Thayld. His bright eyes were locked on Tyth as he smiled. "His brothers took Ladd and Weth, but you'll soon see why Kûthod was the prize." Reaching for the girl's face with his right hand, Nendas gently raked a bit of stray hair from her eyes.

Tyth flinched at the touch but returned the grin.

"Come along, girl!" called Thayld. "We've not traveled this far to dawdle at the gate."

That made her angry—not at him, but at herself. *A few days ago I was prodding him on. Now look at me!* Moving past their young guide, Tyth walked quickly to the overseer's side. Nendas remained behind and frowned to himself a moment before retaking the group's lead.

They passed other spectacles smaller in size than the grand arch but no less awe-inspiring to the outsiders, and Tyth craned her neck at every one. A snake ready to strike, its curving body lifted from the ground in segments formed by three sculpted stones. A giant warrior freed from a sacrificed oak, standing proudly between two of its living kin. Then came the wonder of the citizens' houses. They were everywhere now, and Tyth needed no words from Nendas to confirm they were also remnants of a bygone era. At first glance one might've thought the dwellings had been erected about the sentinels of the grove, but on closer inspection it was plain that the trees had grown up around the stone brick residences. The thick roots of one specimen plunged to earth down the sides of the single-room structure beneath, caging the home in a gnarled hand with fingers partially obstructing the owner's view from his window. The trunk of another split and crawled for a space along a larger house's roof before turning up again to the sun. And there were many other variations: some even sporting newer marvels such as latticed hedges and enclosures, rooted chairs and tables, and living ladders climbing the walls of two- and three-story dwellings. Clearly the citizens of Thaekith took pride in their refuge.

But where are they? Tyth thought before posing it aloud. She'd once been told hundreds — perhaps *thousands* — of people called this city their home, but so far she'd seen only a few hurried passersby.

"Just follow the music," said Nendas; and only then did Tyth become fully aware of it, snapping out of a dreamlike state caused by the sights around her and allowing her other senses to take in the atmosphere. A beautiful harmony floated through the trees, growing louder with each step she took, and among the earthy, woody scents of the forest she smelled steaming food.

The head count of the inhabitants rose with the sounds and aromas till at last the trio reached the center of activity. The grove opened considerably here, allowing a clear view across to the area's far side, and again Tyth found herself enthralled by the sights. Nendas had been correct, for the multitude she'd been looking for was gathered in this place. A lavish banquet was in progress, with pipers and drummers, dancers and fighters, tricksters and adepts providing entertainment. Small children played about the bridges of a creek winding past their feasting parents, some groups apparently lost in fantastic worlds of their own making while others clearly mimicked the sport on display nearby. Within a circle bound by piled leaves swept from its interior, two men stalked a third, all bare-handed. For a moment this exhibition seemed little different from the poised dancing taking place around it — then suddenly it exploded in a blur of motion, followed by cheers from the spectators. In a few deft moves the prey had bested his attackers, sending both sailing hard to the ground; and now all three stood smiling in the center of the ring, expressing respect for one another with the clasping of wrists.

The savory foodstuffs were being prepared on and around a long trench fire just strides away from where the newcomers came to a halt: roasting boar and deer haunches, fish wrapped in leaves and laid in the coals, steamed mussels, and several large pots of soup or stew. Everything was being served freely in ample portions, and Tyth was just considering a sample herself when Nendas grabbed her by the arm.

"There's Asalin's throne," he said, pointing to a hill rising at the grove's center.

"Who can announce us to him?" asked Thayld after a pause spent squinting at the hill.

"A woman just told me what these festivities are about," said Nendas, "...and you'll be lucky to speak with him today at all. Emissaries from Weth have come, and the king holds this feast in their honor. But I'll take you to a warden I know. Maybe we can persuade him otherwise."

The warden Kaledric was a young man of considerable stature, handsome features, and a lean, muscular build. Free-flowing black hair fell straight to his shoulders, framing a clean-shaven face and blue eyes, and he was wearing thin scale armor with an ornate baldric running across the chest. Tyth found Nendas Jush comely enough, but this warrior's first grin her way had afflicted her with a racing heart and momentary loss of breath. *He's too good for you, silly girl. Misery is your only suitor now.*

By his simple nods and distracted glances, it seemed Kaledric was nearing the end of his present conversation with an elder citizen. Tyth stood patiently with her guardian and guide a few strides off to await the man's attention. Fearing to meet his eyes again, she moved her gaze instead to the spear he gripped then to the hand that gripped it. She leaned over and whispered to Nendas: "What's that tattoo circling his finger? A snake?"

Nendas nodded. "All wardens bear that mark from the day of initiation. A likeness of Asalin's ring, binding them to the king's service. Soon I'll have my own."

A few moments later Kaledric was done speaking with the elder. He turned to Nendas at last and was greeted with a slight bow in salute.

"What do we have here? Oreldan's lad, correct?"

"Yes, warden. Nendas Jush, if you recall..."

"I remember," Kaledric grinned. "And do you still desire to be my sword-brother?"

"Very much so! I've only to complete the trial. If one of you will vouch for me, that is."

"No need to fret over that, boy. I'll do it myself if need be." Kaledric's gaze moved on to Tyth then to Thayld. "But tell me, Nendas: who are these good folk with you?"

"Warden Kaledric," said Nendas, sweeping an arm back to his companions, "...I bring you Thayld Priregord, overseer of the settlement at Lake Diebron—and Tyth, the fairest maiden of his clan." He glanced over at Tyth and winked before continuing with the warden. "Their home's been ravaged by brigands, and they come seeking our aid."

"We've heard similar reports from others along our borders," Kaledric sighed. "Today we celebrate peace with Weth, but I fear it's only a prelude to war with Ladd. I'm sorry for your troubles, friends. What animals those men must be to prey on the weak and old!"

I'm not weak! Tyth wanted to scream, but instead a familiar wetness came to her eyes along with a pang in her gut—and she bit her tongue. *Hadric! I should be home with you now, not hiding with this old man!*

"One of them *was* an animal," Thayld Priregord replied. "A fell beast with a boar's head and a man's body! Never would I've believed such a thing could be, yet I saw it with my own eyes! They could've slain us all but took joy in our torture instead. They carried off some of our young and all but the dregs of our winter supplies..."

On the mention of the boar man, Kaledric had frowned as if unconvinced, and as Thayld finished speaking he let that subject lie. "I'll be glad to approach Asalin on your behalf, good man, though I can't guarantee an audience today. The king may delay a meeting with you till this feast is done...or charge me to deliver his answer instead."

"The lad here warned us of that," said Thayld. "I only ask you to tell him the urgency of our coming — and, if possible, that I'd like to speak with him myself."

"As you wish." Kaledric nodded to Thayld and smiled once more at Tyth in turn. Then he placed a hand on Nendas' shoulder. "You're coming with me, boy. The king should have a glimpse of his future warden."

Asalin of Kûthod sat his grassy hill alone. He seemed content to thoughtfully gaze at the darkening clouds while his people engaged in all sorts of merriment below. The embroidered buckskin robe he wore had slipped from one shoulder, revealing amber-jeweled necklaces resting atop a rayed, swirling bluish-green sun needled on his pale breast, and his hair was exceedingly long. Two jet locks of it fell over his shoulders down to his lap, with the excess swept back and tied up as a ball behind his head. The king's build was slight but not yet withered, and his chiseled face appeared timeless as the seat of engraved stone on which he sat. Living vines climbed and twisted about his ornate throne until they reached the pinnacle of its backrest: a bigger version of the red-gold metal band gracing the ring finger of his left hand. And clutching the wrist of that hand was a tiny gray owl.

They were almost sitting in the man's lap before his face left the heavens. "Welcome to Thaekith, guests. Kaledric told me your purpose here, and I share his sorrow for you." Rising from his seat, the king approached Tyth and, as she stirred to bow, waved her nervous notion away. He extended his left arm and watched as she looked up to admire the creature on his wrist. "His name is Skûlkī. Would you mind taking him for a walk, dear girl? He grows tired of brooding with me."

Must I go? Tyth thought, glancing first at the overseer then at Nendas and Kaledric for aid. *Surely Thayld wants me to stay. I can't leave this all to him!*

Thayld drew a breath and parted his lips as if to answer for her — but having sensed his young guest's trepidation, Asalin spoke again first:

"Rest assured, your plea hasn't fallen on deaf ears." Handing his pet over to a yet-stunned Tyth, Asalin turned aside and called a name: "Kedaynna!"

The woman who answered the king's summon was a flash of youth and beauty. With her smile beaming a good humor and an eagerness to serve, she approached the hill, ascended to Asalin's side, and slipped a thin left arm about his waist as she turned to consider the newcomers. She wore dangling earrings and a shoulder-less, embroidered green dress, and her hair was arranged in a fantail in the back—similar to Asalin's style. But it was clearly a striking female version of the warden Kaledric's face and grin that met Tyth's questioning eyes.

"I've a favor to ask, my love," said Asalin to the woman after introducing his guests. Then he turned his eyes on Tyth. "This young lady's taking Skûlkī for a stroll. I thought she might like a companion."

"Of course," said Kedaynna. "Say no more."

The king's mistress led Tyth away from the open grove until they reached a charming stone fountain that lay just beyond. "It's quieter here," she said. "Shall we stay and talk awhile?" Not waiting for a reply, she eased herself down on the fountain's ledge and studied Skûlkī for a moment before turning her gaze back to Tyth. "Asalin has always named his pets, but I think it's absurd! Names are for those who can speak them aloud. Come...sit beside me."

Tyth forced a polite smile in return but remained standing. The shock of being excluded from the men's discussion was wearing off, yet she promised herself not to cry. Not in front of this woman. *She couldn't possibly relate.* "My brother named a pig once. Are you Kaledric's sister, my lady?"

"Is it that obvious?" Kedaynna sighed. "I suppose our names do as little to hide it as our faces. Yes, between the king and the *prime warden* I'm well looked after. But you spoke of your own brother. Is he not here with you?"

"I had three brothers," said Tyth, "...but only one remains. That's why we're here. To beg Kûthod for justice."

Of course that caused the mistress to ask what'd happened to Tyth's siblings; and after all the tragedy she cared to reveal had been told, Tyth ended with a question of her own. "Do you think the king will send warriors to protect us?"

"Poor girl!" There was a genuine sadness in Kedaynna's voice. "Come here..."

Tyth did so—haltingly at first. But as Kedaynna took the owl from her, set it aside, and opened arms wide, beckoning, Tyth at last surrendered and let herself fall into the hug.

"For your sake I wish it wasn't so, Tyth, but you're not the first to ask for such a thing. I know what his answer will be. Only today, after many years of strife, does the king secure a formal end to the last battle he fought. He doesn't intend to wage war again. Not with Weth nor with Ladd nor with any other land. Not unless a war charges headlong into his domain. Asalin will offer your people protection here in Kûthod — as long as you abide by his laws — but he won't send a single man back with you to Diebron. If war is truly upon us, then we'll need all our strength here at home. He didn't send aid to your neighbors last month, so he mustn't send aid to you now. To do so would only breed hostility."

Although Tyth had prepared herself earlier for a refusal, it still hit hard. "So we came all this way for nothing? Please…can you ask him to speak with me alone? I have to convince him!"

Laying a calming hand on Tyth's shoulder, the mistress shook her head *no*. "Asalin's a man of reason, as all great leaders must be. He'll not be swayed by your emotion."

"But the monsters might've returned since I've been away!" Tyth complained, tears beginning to surface. "My little brother's not safe there!"

"Then stay with us and have him brought to you…" Kedaynna urged gently. "Beg your guardian to accept our protection and lead all your people here! What do you have left in Diebron except a plague of horrid memories?" Taking Tyth's silence to be consideration, she went on: "Here you could begin anew. You can even keep me company from time to time — and who knows what might happen next?" She ventured a sly grin. "Did you think I missed the way Oreldan's boy was staring at you?"

She's right, thought Tyth. *Forget about Nendas — but if I can't avenge my losses, I can at least protect what I have left.* "Thank you, my lady," she smiled a bit, sniffing back tears. "Maybe we'll do just that. Come, Skûlkī," she said to the owl. "Let's see if old Thayld and your master are done talking."

12

Only once before had his feet crunched prints into wet sand, on a white beach touching clear blue water under a cloudless sunny sky. But that alluring shore lay to the south, appearing to its seekers suddenly from the deepest woods of Kûthod, and this was another day on a vastly different shore. The sands of the northern sea were black as ash. Its water was murk. Its sky was a drear gray mist. Here a short space behind the weedy berm and dunes stood not a wall of dense forest but rather enormous cliffs of stone: the Ûlinari mountains. The hour was late. Night was poised to fall. Already the moon shone dimly through the haze overhead.

Imlod Nir walked the beach alone. When last he'd looked back for a gauge of distance from them, he'd found his companions mere specks to his sight. Those of Galfayan's servants not yet busy with preparing her evening meal or erecting her shelter would be searching for places to bed down and spreading pelts out beneath the open air with hands weary from the day's toil. Marinya had been provided a litter like the queen's in which to ride during each day's trek thus far; but even so, she'd been tired when Imlod left her. *She's likely asleep by now.* It'd been a hard thing to dash his lover's hopes of fleeing to Kûthod, and she was still upset with him. Their debate on the subject had been heated, its end coming only after he'd threatened to expose her plan to escape. "This is the safest path," he'd said in an effort to console her. "After the baby's born—when Galfayan's thoughts have turned from us—we'll find a way to leave then. I promise."

He decided to rid his mind of troubles for awhile, tuning his senses on the waves instead. Rushing inland, they groped at his feet; and the action was so soothing that he walked on and on leaving driftwood, shells, and rocks behind, not thinking of when to turn round, eyes locked on the spilling tide while night strove to devour his slow-moving form. Yet long as it may have seemed to an observer from the heights above, to Imlod this serenity proved all too brief: for soon a *presence* neared, reaching out to his mind from the breaking water. At first it was only a tingle. An indeterminable itch. Then—just as he recognized the surging feeling for what it truly was—a pair of cresting waves froze in their influx, rising to human height and assuming women's forms. Surprised but undaunted, Imlod stopped to peer at the arrivals in the fading light. *Why have you come?* he sent to them, a scowl coming to his face. *What does Galfayan want?*

Not your sister, answered one of the spirits, a hag with seaweed for hair and foam-white hands protruding from her streaming gray robe. Her eyes were pits of shadow. The other one looked the same, as if in life they might've been twins. *We were summoned by the nymphs of Thadda, and it's with them you speak. A grievous fate awaits your unborn son at the end of this journey, Imlod Nir—and they would steer you from it.*

Well...go on. Let's have it! Imlod demanded after a pause for consideration. Although he was aware of the nymphs' powers of divination — and he wouldn't have his child come to harm if knowledge could avert it — the sudden revelation of these creatures meddling in his affairs angered him. *But first you'll tell me how you know this and why you've bothered to warn me...and why I should trust you at all.* Something else flashed into his head. *And how does Marinya know the child's sex? You also seem sure of it.*

She didn't reveal her meeting with us? came the second hag's voice. *That was wise of her, yet she strayed from safety all the same. That was your doing, was it not? She faltered because of the love she holds for you. Or perhaps from* fear *of you...*

So it was you behind her wild urge to race home, Imlod frowned deeper still. *Did you have her fetched? Or did she come to you unbidden?*

Know this, mortal: your son is set to achieve wondrous deeds in his life — perhaps the greatest this age has known! Yet had Marinya not sought our aid, it's likely the child's importance would still be hidden. She had a troubling dream, and we helped decipher it.

What deeds? Imlod returned, the tone of his sending skeptical yet excited all the same. Nir's son was no hero. He hated what he'd become. But could it be that his child would rise above his own lot? If that were proven true, then his own existence would be justified in the end. As he watched the next wave pass through the hovering spirits, waiting for their reply, Imlod felt his pulse quicken from a surge of hope.

The prospect of the boy's ascension stirs you, Sienda observed through Imlod's connection with her ghostly avatar. *We've seen only glimpses of his future, but even those must be kept from you for now. Knowledge of one's fate allows the knower to alter it, and your child's destiny already walks a narrow ledge. One misstep, and maybe he'll not live to achieve it. Or worse, his deeds that would've succored your race might be twisted to works of untold evil against it! So for the moment we give you only what's needed to ensure his survival. The very same message we gave to Marinya. Deliver the boy to Kûthod! Leaving Ramfiram spared him from a death lurking there; yet because of your interference, we see that same fate — or one even more harmful — awaiting him now beyond the mountains. In the land of your father's birth there are those who'll act upon learning your son's heritage. Some for good, but others for ill. Thus we urge you: don't spend another day on this path!*

Let's say I believe all this, Imlod sent after another pause. *You must loathe my sister's reins on you — and it seems Marinya's placed her faith in your words. But tell me then: how do I accomplish your task? Galfayan won't grant us leave — unless I can deceive her somehow? Yet for me to dare that...there'd be no turning back...*

We don't walk the road with you, Imlod. It's up to you to find a way.

Wait, sister, said Sigeya. *There is a thing that may help him. We both saw it...*

Tell me! Imlod demanded again. *If I'm to attempt this folly, I'll need all the aid you can give!*

As the next wave rose flashing in the moonlight, the ghostly hags merged and crashed with it, vanishing beneath the watery blackness. *There's a prisoner in your camp. Release the old man, for in our vision he stood watch over your son. It seems their fates are intertwined.*

Wait! called Imlod just before their mental connection with him snapped, a thought popping into his head. Immediately the link was reestablished. *For the sake of my child, I'll do as you say. But first I ask a favor.*

What do you desire?

My mother's spirit doesn't belong with me here. You brought these souls up from the Black Land, didn't you? And now they return?

At mention of the spirits, they blinked again into view. *You would send her back with them?*

I'd have her find peace. Imlod dug a hand into his clothing then held out Nir's stone in an open palm. Images of his mother flooded his mind. Everything she'd done was for him. She'd been so beautiful and full of life, but she'd hid herself away with him in that wood against her own desires, wishing only to shelter him from the evil blood in his veins. Slowly he began to turn his palm down; yet the stone hung on, friction warring with gravity in the physical plane while another battle raged in his mind. *I thought we could be a family again, but it's not right! The art that brought her back is the same that took her from me. Please Mother, forgive me! For keeping you with me…and now for letting go…*

As that last thought trailed off, Imlod let the stone slip. It fell and hit the sand with a thud — and instantly Nir's ghostly form was there, hovering before him.

What is your command, my son?

You're beautiful still, Imlod mused as he gazed upon her wispy, emotionless face with watering eyes; yet he didn't send that thought nor respond to her at all. Turning his mind to the waves again, he addressed the hags instead. *What say you, sisters?*

The nymphs' answer didn't come to Imlod's mind this time. Instead the pair reached out with beckoning arms to Nir when she — following her son's gaze — turned to them as well.

No thought needed pass between Imlod and his mother for her to understand what was at hand. And no more tears nor loving hugs nor momentous, caring words would there be from her today than he'd received on their first parting in the year Taloseth the Mage slew her in the Forest of Weth — for death had long robbed Nir of what she'd once been.

Many waves washed up the beach before Imlod's thoughts broke away from his mother. How far had she traveled already while he lingered?

The stone that'd bound her lay at his feet in the blackness.

He picked it up and cast it into the waves.

It seemed he'd only just drifted off to sleep when a gentle hand woke him.

"Lord Cirad," the servant began quietly, removing her palm from his arm as he stirred. "Forgive me, but the queen's brother waits outside. He asks to speak with her at once."

"Then remove yourself and admit him." In the soft red light from the maid's candle, the elf noticed her eyes shift uneasily to the body beside him. Galfayan lay unmoving there, strands of her long, dark hair clinging to his pale chest and shoulder. "Go on. I'll wake her myself." He knew it would take more than a light touch and whisper to rouse the queen tonight, for the copious amount of wine she'd consumed was enough to drop a man twice her size. She wouldn't take this disturbance well. Still...it wouldn't do for Cirad to presume to speak for her, especially not to her brother. He'd learned that much from experience.

Imlod Nir's face appeared above their pallet just as Galfayan was rousing from a rough handling by the elf; and to Cirad's relief, the arrival found her displeasure in place of him. "What's this about, brother?" she slurred upon meeting Imlod's eyes. "Shouldn't you be cuddling with your bloated wench?"

"There's no time for this!" said Imlod. "Not if we're to catch them."

"Catch whom?" Cirad replied, brow furrowing at the thought of anything amiss. Anything for which he might've failed to plan. The elf was cold and calculating. He hated surprises.

"Someone's helped your old minister escape. They left his guard unconscious on the beach from a blow to the head."

Shoving his way past Imlod, the witch's lover was on his feet and nearly out the tent before she stayed him. "Where do you think you're going, Cirad? I'm not through with you!" The fur cover slipped from her bosom as she propped herself up to shout after him. She made no move to hide her nakedness.

Swinging back, Cirad lashed out: "Gilal's my charge! The ones who did this will find my blade as their reward!" Then checking himself, he added: "Don't trouble yourself with this, my queen. Give me leave. I'll have him back before dawn—along with the heads of those responsible!"

"I found the guard on my way back to camp," Imlod cut in. "Before the others came trampling over everything, there were only two sets of tracks leading off from the spot. Grant me the hunt instead. Sleep escapes me tonight, and you're both weary..."

"You're mistaken there, *boy*," Cirad spat, shooting an evil glance at Imlod.

"Dismiss us, Galfayan. He may come along if he likes."

She considered that a moment before laughing out loud. "You've gotten more of a rise out of him than I did, brother! No, my elf...you'll stay here and put that passion to work on me." She let herself plop back down on the pallet. "The task is yours, Imlod. Don't make me regret it."

Cirad drew a sharp breath to complain but quickly thought better of it.

Imlod could've followed the elf's example and left without a word, yet still he lingered. "May I take Kûhric, sister?"

"Surely you can handle one rogue yourself," she said with a sigh of agitation. "We'll wait one day here—no more. Away with you!"

Outside the tent, Imlod wiped cold sweat from his brow. He'd expected to find Cirad with the queen and guessed the elf's reaction, yet his nerves remained on edge. Cirad was an expert swordsman; and skilled as Imlod deemed himself with a blade, he'd avoid risking defeat at the hands of a seasoned master if he could. His plan would go easier now at the onset. *But soon as they think to check on Marinya...*

Fresh torch in hand, he called his lover's name softly as he passed through the dunes, eventually finding Marinya where he'd left her. "You see?" he whispered, bending to help her rise. "I know my sister. It went like I said it would."

Marinya's sigh said she remained unconvinced, but she let Imlod pull her up anyway. "Can't you see this is madness?" she whispered back. "Why run now? Why not when I begged you in the city, when we had time to prepare? How far do you think we'll get before..."

He clamped a hand over her mouth—and not too gently. "I won't argue with you. It's done now, and there's no turning back! We must hurry!"

So without another word the two set off, Imlod leading with the torch raised in one hand and the girl's slender arm clasped firmly by the other. There would be nothing near running, not with Marinya so far along in her pregnancy, and he was betting their lives on only his woodcraft and a weak head start. The straight path to Kûthod would have to wait a few days, for though Imlod could navigate the woods by day and night, he deemed only a perfectly executed feint would spare them.

A silent hour passed for the pair as they worked to undo the day's progress. This was the second such trek of the night for Imlod, and he felt sleep clamping down on him. *Not yet! We must get far into the wood!* Soon they'd reach the spot where the cliffs began to recede from the shore. The spot where the old minister from Taudan hopefully still awaited them.

PART THREE

Biting The Hand

TWELVE YEARS AGO

I chose to devote that afternoon to Kûhric. For each wipe at congealed blood and for every stitch needed to close his wound's gap, I asked myself a question and strove to answer it. The fear of having my head removed while pawing at my keeper was gone now, for surely I'd misjudged his glance. He didn't flinch while I probed exposed bone—crudely forcing it back inside before stitching—nor as I cleansed his face and hair. It felt like mending a garment or dressing a felled beast. I suppose it was both.

My labors had begun under the open sky and a parading sun, but as mid-afternoon approached I became aware of a sudden growing darkness. For an instant I thought Kûhric and I were being supernaturally transported back to the shadows of our home. Then I turned my face skyward to behold a thing just as unlikely. The moon was devouring the sun!

Kûhric sprang up and seized me then. I've endured many trials since that fateful day, yet never after have I felt a terror like the one gripping me with his icy hands. I believed the world was ending. That the deaths of my mother and foster-father had only been a prelude to what was coming. I realized I didn't want to die. I'd been taught that my soul was immortal, that death was merely sleep before rebirth, and that a part of me was interconnected with all living creatures on earth. But none of that would matter if the earth ceased to exist. If the life-giving rays of the sun were extinguished forever.

I hit, kicked, cursed, screamed, and bit like a wild animal in my attempts to break free of the juggernaut. Yet it was no use, for he simply dragged me by my hair through the dirt whenever my struggles threatened to impede our progress. It was clear where he was taking me, and I no longer wanted to go. But we did just that, and I was bruised and exhausted by the time we finally arrived.

"Bind his hands," Galfayan instructed Kûhric as I spit blood and earth from my mouth at her feet. That single red stain, harsh amidst the countless white stones of the valley floor, was the only offering I wished to present my father's daemon master, yet I knew something more would be required. An altar erected from those same stones, piled two cubits high, stood ominously on my left; and further off, Taloseth the Mage knelt with his back to me, engrossed with some bizarre markings on the rock wall before him. The absence of his bestial hood revealed mottled black hair, and the glorious axe *Sacrosanct* lay within his reach.

"Is it plain now, Imlod?" Galfayan gloated as Kûhric secured my wrists with cord. "The Daemon thirsts for our father's blood—and through *you* she'll have it!"

Then, as if mention of that thirst had suddenly roused her to it, the Lady of

Mavûl made her presence known. My thoughts became meshed with whispers of her hatred, and like waves of the foaming river nearby, crashing over and over against any obstacle, an undulating nausea attacked me. The resistance to my fate was broken. There would be no desperate stand with a puny rock shard, nor would there be answers to the mysteries burning my mind. It was all happening too fast. Galfayan fixed me to the deathbed, slashed open my side with a knife, then stood back — as I screamed in pain — to watch my lifeblood flow away.

The sun died as my head reeled, and stars arrived to escort my spirit to the netherworld. I was aware that my executioners were speaking, yet their words fell on deaf ears. I hearkened to the Daemon alone. Her spirit was weak from the drain of ages, bound to this place where her last body had fallen, but now she'd feed on my soul and walk the earth once more. Images from her previous lives flashed behind my eyes: the Waxing Moon battling the Rising Sun, a dark-haired beauty sitting on an ebony throne, a shepherd of strange aquatic beasts roaming beneath the waves. For a few moments more I felt her soul mingling with mine, overwhelming my senses. Then it was gone. Flung back into the scene about me, I saw my father again; yet now he was suspended above the ground under a seeming night sky. Kûhric's inescapable grip was at his neck, holding him aloft.

My hero had returned at last! If only I could free my hands to mimic the act unfolding before me and subdue my sister, then this nightmare would end. But the stubborn cord merely bit deeper as I struggled, and yanking at the stakes that bound me did no good. The wound in my side was bleeding freely. Taloseth's gasps and thrashings were growing louder. Where was Galfayan? Darkness was concealing her from me, or else she'd fled. My eyes darted nervously back and forth, and I expected any moment to lock on the image of a blade lunging at my throat. But it didn't come. Soon my father's struggling receded then ceased altogether.

The river's sound returned. All else was silent.

"We're free now!" came a sweet voice from behind me. The lips that'd formed those amazing words then proceeded to kiss my hands before seeking my cheek. Light was returning.

"Why?" was all I could manage in response. My head was still clouded. My body was numb.

"How much does it hurt?" Galfayan asked, turning her attention to the gash beneath my ribs. "I tried that cut on a fawn, but your skin's less tough. You've lost too much blood."

"You killed him…" I murmured while staring at my father's prostrate form.

"*We* killed him," she answered, a touch of anger in her tone. "You and I." Her hand was shaking as she wiped at my wound, but her voice held firm. Her eyes were clear but unconfident. "Isn't that what you wanted? Don't tell me it wasn't on your mind when you screamed at him from the ledge! He was cold. A man conquered by his own craft. He's always been dead to me—and he was nothing but a bane to you! Rest easy now. It's over."

"Untie me!" I demanded. Behind Galfayan's attempt at comforting words I sensed the blossoming of a power holding other motives. One who harbored enough hate and resolution to coldly murder her own father might not hesitate to dispatch another family member. I recalled my ill treatment by her thus far, but now wasn't the time to mention it. The rock shard was still hidden in my clothing. Kûhric was nowhere to be seen. I had a decision to make.

"Patience. Let me stitch this first," she answered, grinning. "Maybe I can best your work on my pet." Retrieving her basket, she began, and I felt as immune to the pain of that sewing as Kûhric had appeared to be during his. In the midst of my mender's labors, a thought suddenly occurred to me:

"Am I dead?"

"I'm sorry for putting you through this, Imlod, but I went to great trouble to ensure you *didn't* die. No, you're very much alive," she said, stroking my arm.

"And what of Kûhric? Is he alive, then?" I asked, not quite sure I believed her. My volume was rising.

"Kûhric? Was that his name? I told you his fate before."

"But our father only wanted *me!*" I shouted and squirmed, the exertion now rousing a sting from the last stitch. "Why did *they* have to die?"

"Because they stood in his way."

I let my head fall back against the stones and gazed out into the brightening void. Tears welled in my tired eyes, yet this time I was able to choke them back.

"Where's my mother's body?"

"Where it fell, I suppose. We raised the man you name *Kûhric* only."

"You were there?"

"No," she shook her head. "Enough questions for now. I've confused you. Let me finish. Then you must rest awhile."

"Untie me!" I screamed, earning an immediate slap to the side of the head. Not a gentle swat to merely grab my attention, but a forceful blow that brought sparks to my eyes and a ringing to my ear.

"I mean you no harm, brother. Truly, I swear it. But listen closely to me now and remember this for as long as you live: *Never will I answer to you.*"

She left me there that night to consider her statement. The slap had silenced me long enough for her to finish tending my wound, and Kûhric had appeared to strip down my father's corpse and haul it off. The sorcerer's robe was draped over me now in addition to my own coat, but I'd refused to eat any of the food offered. Darkness came at the usual time: a reminder of the marvel I'd witnessed only a few hours earlier. How could Taloseth have caused such a thing to occur? Perhaps it was the Daemon's doing. I'd just learned that demanding knowledge wouldn't benefit me, so before giving myself up to sleep I resolved to play along with Galfayan's delusions. At least till I received the answers I craved. Then I'd repay her for my injuries.

Sunrise brought with it the same enfeebling chill and hunger of the previous morning, so I had two more reasons to appear receptive to my sister when she arrived.

"Has the night cooled your temper?" she asked as our eyes met. She carried a smaller basket of interlaced vines now. Otherwise she was as I'd first seen her.

I nodded.

"Good," she continued, seating herself on the altar beside me. "I've brought some fruit. Shall we try this again?"

"You don't have to feed it to me. I'm calm now. Will you untie me?"

"Do you understand our arrangement?"

I nodded again.

"And you'll swear an oath that binds you to it?"

I thought about that for a moment. "Will you release Kûhric?"

"Perhaps," she said. "In time."

My anger was about to gush forth again at her callousness, yet somehow I held it in check. "You saved me."

"I spared you," she corrected. "What you owe me won't be easily repaid, but it needn't come between us. Here, eat something." She reached into the basket, removed a ripe berry, and held it before my face, entreating me with a playful smile. "Don't worry, they're mild."

I recalled the last time I'd accepted her hospitality. "Taste that one yourself. Then I'll eat."

"So you refuse to be fooled again, is that it?" she laughed and immediately grabbed up more of the fruit to make a show of slowly devouring them — as if savoring the ruinous concoction they obviously didn't contain. I watched and frowned.

"You must learn to trust me," she added after wiping her hands and mouth clean of juice. "There's no more need for deceit. We're free now, remember?"

"*You're* free," I said. "I'm in shackles."

Her face tightened momentarily at that, teeth grinding and fists clenched to stifle frustration. Then, with an audible sigh, she gave in and began removing my bonds. I could hear Kûhric's wooden steps approaching.

She finished and stepped away. I sat up and pumped my wrists and felt the blood return rapidly and painfully into my hands...and with that sensation came a fresh surge of rage. My earlier plan was forgotten, and all that remained was a burning desire to make Galfayan be the one in pain. I wouldn't wait any longer for the answers I sought. I would take them from her *now*.

"I'll swear on the Mother's image," I said, then reached inside my clothing for the figurine Kûhric had given me. Yet with it I seized something else, leapt from the altar, toppled my sister, and pressed the jagged shard to her throat.

But that didn't end my struggle. Galfayan's hands flew up to grab my wrist and arm, and my eyes went wide at the shock of her strength. Like me, she was young and tough from being raised in the wilds, so I hadn't expected to find her a weakling; but this was *unnatural*. Stubbornly I held on to my weapon even as her viselike left hand bore down on my arm and pulled it away from her neck — and as she slapped her right palm to the ground and rolled me over, reversing our positions. Apparently I'd just made a terrible error in judgment...and likely forfeited my second chance at life for it.

Rather than beating me senseless, though, Galfayan chose to squeeze my neck with her right hand and slowly choke me to death or submission. A triumphant smile grew wide on her face as her fingers constricted. My left arm was free now to claw or punch at her ineffectually till my consciousness slipped away — as she must've assumed I'd react — but instead I scooped up a handful of white pebbles and flung them at her eyes. She raised both hands to her face then with a curse, giving me only an instant of opportunity. And in that moment, heedless of any consequence, I postured up and shoved the rock blade straight into her throat.

Blood spewed out over the stone and my hand as Galfayan pulled away and jumped to her feet with a cry. Gurgling, she clasped the open wound, wobbled, stumbled, and dropped to the ground. Her body writhed once then went limp almost immediately, with her head falling to the side such that I was left staring into her savage, unblinking eyes. Something behind that death mask struck me with greater force than what had radiated from my father's visor in the Forest of Weth, and I was absolutely horrified by it.

Dazed and coughing for air, I rose on shaky legs of my own and took a few aimless steps forward before coming to my senses; then I dropped the drenched stone blade beside the figurine I'd snatched out with it and fell to my knees in supplication. The monster receiving my plea looked nothing like the warrior my mother had entreated mere days before, but now I sensed he finally understood our peril. His hand fell lightly on my shoulder, and for a moment it even seemed warm.

"Hold him tight!" came the raspy command from a once-severed windpipe that wasn't quite healed. Kûhric obeyed. His grip was ice once more, digging into me so hard I felt my bones might explode. Incredibly, Galfayan had risen, and now she stooped to pick up the shard and the figurine. The first she flung away in disgust. The second she admired in the same manner Kûhric had first displayed it to me. "It seems you misunderstood our arrangement, brother," she said, fixing her crazed stare on me. "*I'm* your goddess now."

PRESENT DAY

13

Cupping his hands together, Imlod raised the icy liquid and splashed it in his face. Then he leaned closer, dark hair dipping in the flow, and brought the next scoop to his eager mouth.

"You drove us hard, warrior," came a voice from behind. "A freed man can hardly complain, though my old bones ache. But the girl..."

"I knew the risk," said Imlod, glancing over his shoulder. He turned back to the stream.

"Yet the child's yours, she tells me," Gilal of Taudan continued, undaunted, using his gnarled staff as a crutch to close the distance. "Perhaps your heart lies elsewhere from them?"

A flurry of angry words nearly escaped Imlod's mouth—for what was his business to this man? But the minister's concern was valid, so he bit his tongue. Noon was fast approaching, and they'd been halted at this tranquil spot since dawn. But still...

"So she's awake? Then we should go."

"Ease yourself, friend," said Gilal, bending slightly to place a light hand on Imlod's shoulder. "Your ruse bought us some time, and now our footsteps are lost in the stream. I've given her some food. You and I may eat as we travel— but that's not wise for her. Let's rest here a bit longer." And at that, supporting his weight on Imlod's shoulder, the minister sat down on the bank.

Still gazing into the water, Imlod had just parted his lips to object when a familiar sensation gripped him. This shallow creek ran swift, and in that very moment, writhing in the stream's turbulent flow, the spirit of a deceased young woman came rushing down past him. He couldn't make out the girl's face, but somehow he felt he'd known her. *One of Galfayan's servants, perhaps? One who was supposed to be watching Marinya? Goddess!*

"What's wrong?" asked Gilal, noticing Imlod's reaction.

Imlod had caught only a glimpse of the ghost himself, but he knew the old man wouldn't have felt or seen anything. "It's a curse of my art. I saw a shade just now in the stream. Water seeks the low places of earth, so lost souls seek it in turn. To spill with it down to the realm denied them."

"Before we met your sister in Kagnus, I'd have doubted such words," said Gilal. "But no more." He paused to consider the water a moment himself before turning back to Imlod. "Why am I here, lad? What is it you want from me?"

"We mustn't linger here," said Imlod, standing to scan the area about them.

"But I'll explain what I can."

As Imlod relayed events to the minister, both he and Gilal ate sparingly from their supplies. But having barely slept at all, and now with a filling belly, Imlod soon found it hard to stay focused and cut the story short. "A fool, maybe," was the note on which he ended, "...to risk so much on muddy words."

"A fool?" said the minister. "I doubt that. I've not seen your nymphs myself, but their heritage is known in Kagnus. The great Kar himself — protector of my homeland — is akin to those sisters. It was no mistake to heed them, I believe."

Imlod ran a hand down his tired face. "There's a chance Galfayan would've just let me and Marinya go. But Cirad won't fail to hunt you."

Gilal frowned and stared off into the woods through which they'd arrived at this place. "You're right. We shouldn't linger here. I'll fetch her."

Until now the wooden beam barring exit had been lifted only once per day, signaling the delivery of the priestess' meager food and water rations and the removal of her waste. Light seeping through the cracks stung her eyes even before the door was flung wide; then — as a blurry figure wielding the sudden radiance stepped forward — she retreated once more to the shadows of her dark, stinking prison.

"Hello, Mother," the man's voice burst in, followed by echoes bouncing back into the cell from the maze of tunnels outside.

Immediately Sevos Let's pale, stricken face reentered the edge of candlelight. "Kirath? Is it really you?"

"It is."

Sevos peered at him from under her hand: a hand raised to shield weary eyes from intrusive light. "Praise the Goddess! Please tell me you've come to free me from this blackness!"

"I once served time in blackness," said Kirath Sevos, slowly approaching his estranged mother. He halted a step in front of her. "A blackness caused by *you*."

The prisoner's mood turned instantly from relief to anger. "If you've come to chastise me, Kirath, then leave at once! I don't need to justify my past to you — and don't pretend you've suffered here on my account! Bablak must worship the ground you walk upon!"

"Leave him out of this!" Kirath spat. "He does when he's allowed to. But he'd surer cut me to bits than anger Galfayan."

After studying his face a moment longer, Sevos suddenly reached forward, daring to wrap her arms about the child who'd been sundered from her so long. Tears pooled in her eyes. "Oh, my son! I've missed you so much! Why must we worry with these things now? You grew too much while I was away. Can't we spend what time I have left in happiness—or at least in truce? Won't you let me know the man my boy's become?"

But as soon as his mother had finished speaking, Kirath broke the one-sided embrace, pushing her away—and not too gently at that. "Don't try to deter me. I'm only here as the queen's messenger."

"No! Don't speak her judgment yet...I beg you!" Sevos fought back a sob, stopping herself just short of grasping her son again. "If there ever was a day you loved me as your mother, please hear me first!"

"Be quick about it," came the icy response, and Kirath dropped into a sitting position, half his face illuminated in red light and the other hidden in shadow.

The priestess let out a sigh that could've been either one of thanks or else of stifled belligerence toward Kirath's behavior. Wiping tears from her eyes, she knelt across from her son on the cell floor:

"I was abandoned too, Kirath. Not stripped from my mother, as you were, but separated all the same. Your grandmother Let was high priestess before me. She devoted her life to the Mother and her people and had time for little else...

Anyway, she died young. When I took her place in the temple, I swore never to bear any children of my own. Never to become a mother like *her*. But when I faltered—and I felt your sister stirring in my womb—I vowed then never to put duty above caring for my child. For just as the Goddess is our nurturing Mother, shall we not be the same to our own offspring? That's what I think Let, in all her wisdom, failed to see."

"Yet you failed as well," said Kirath. "Miserably so."

"Not by my choice! No matter what evil you've done for your sister over the years, son—or how I loathed your father even more than that damned sorcerer who gave me Galfayan—I'd never take back your births. *I love you*, Kirath! It wasn't my fault we were parted! Taloseth and Bablak took Galfayan from me— then *she* took *you!*"

"Not your fault? Maybe so...in the beginning. They drove you out, but that was many years ago. In all that time you couldn't have sent word or plotted to steal me away? It should've been you to care for me, but Galfayan was there for me instead. Can you blame me for my loyalty to her?"

"Of course not! But I did send messages in the beginning. At first the carriers returned to me foiled—then finally not at all. I couldn't bring myself to risk more lives. And if I'd actually tried to *steal you* away from here...you know I would've paid for that with my own!"

The look on Kirath's face told the priestess nothing, so she went on with her explanation. Justifications she'd earlier refused to give. "They would've had to go through every woodsman with an axe or spear to take me in the beginning. The villages were so outraged they threatened to gather and storm the city, but I'd seen enough blood spilt at the time — and they'd have been no match for your father's warriors and your sister's power. Galfayan knew it too and decided to let me go free. So tell me: what's changed? Why take me now, when my threat to her is less than ever before?"

Kirath remained silent but was suddenly unwilling to hold his mother's gaze. His eyes turned from her to stare at the candle between them.

"Answer me! Will she not speak with me herself? She hardly looked at me before the jailers dragged me off!"

"You're ready for her judgment, then?" Kirath took up the candle and stood. "I listened to what you had to say, Mother, but it changes nothing. I'm sure you find me less affectionate than you'd hoped, but I..."

"I find you *less*, indeed!" Sevos rose also and wiped a hand over teary cheeks. "Did you know they murdered your uncle Edohath? Have you no feelings at all? No? You're just another one of her monsters!"

"Now, now," scolded her son. "Say of me as you like, but Galfayan was born from your own transgression. How can you condemn the child you abandoned to a crazed sorcerer in the wilds?"

"He took her from me!" she shouted, thin hands darting up to claw her face in frustration. "How many times must I say it? Maybe I could've stopped it — but it was for *your* sake I didn't fight harder! Taloseth deceived me and shamed me! I didn't want you reminded of that every time you saw your bastard sister's face!"

"Less me than your red-robed lackeys, more like," Kirath replied with a snort. "The Brethren never looked kindly upon whores, they say..." His words ended with a sharp pain to the cheek. A slap he was either unprepared for or didn't bother to prevent.

Withdrawing the offending hand, Sevos stood there and said nothing more.

"Very well," spoke Kirath, fuming with his own stifled rage. "The queen's message to you is this: 'Your son's hand holds your only escape from this cell.'"

And with that he thrust a vial of poison into the light.

14

"A message from Ûlinari, great King," the manicured servant announced in a loud but nervous voice. The mere presence of Sanisar, Lord of Agrigoth, often afflicted people so.

"Read it," the Desert King replied nonchalantly, as if there weren't a thing in the world that need be reserved for his ears alone. All but his face—a gaunt visage with dark cosmetic about the eyes to mask the lines of his years—and his thin, veined hands were hidden beneath the folds of a brown-and-gold patterned robe. A chest-high lamp stood on one side of his ornate chair providing heat and light and the smell of burning incense, its support entangled from the floor up by a metallic snake. On the other side stood a man nearly twice as tall as the fire's support but hardly wider than it. This man was clothed in nothing but a wrap about his waist and a disturbing horned and bearded mask: a helm of sorts to conceal his entire head from view. He held a long, curved blade lowered in his right hand. Many other figures were also present, most sitting or reclining in the spacious chamber; yet besides the two voices heard just now, the room's silence rivaled that of the desert outside, stretching on and on for leagues under a chill, starry night.

Hearing his lord's command, the servant broke the missive's seal and began reading at once:

"To King Sanisar, Son of the Setting Sun. A caravan approaches your land from the East, my lord. Five score men and women, traveling the coast by day and reveling in their camp each night. There are none but a few warriors among them, yet I have seen the one they protect and have heard them speak her name. Galfayan, your brother Taloseth's daughter, queen of the woodland realms...and by rights, of this land as well..." Here the servant paused and swallowed hard as he realized the significance of what he'd just relayed. "Your servant by ill-made oath...Zamarian."

Silence fell again over the chamber as the Desert King pondered his response and the messenger stood wide-eyed, wringing his hands. Beneath the hanging fronds by a central pool, a little boy and his mother cut their eyes to the throne, obediently awaiting their master's speech as if any word from his mouth might be a command for them. Beyond this pair a trio resting on cushions lowered their cups and set tasty morsels down on serving trays, daring not partake of anything at the moment. And under a grand mural on one of the smooth stone walls, a row of elfin slaves stood and stole sheepish glances at one another as their overseer looked away.

Finally Sanisar responded: "Instruct Zamarian to greet my niece and lead her safely to the palace. She's to be treated with warmth and the proper respect. A single word she speaks otherwise will bring ruin to the offender. Understood?"

"Yes, great King," the servant nodded. "It shall be so." Then he swiftly rose and departed.

Soon the chamber's occupants returned to their previous attentions, most of them as if nothing were amiss — save the man at Sanisar's side, who leaned over to speak privately in the king's ear. "May I ask a question, lord?"

"Please do, Erathiel," Sanisar replied with a slight cock of his head. "I find your innocence refreshing."

"This *Zamarian*," the unexpectedly youthful voice issued again from behind the mask. "Why didn't you command his death just now? Surely his treasonous words displease you?"

"*Displease* me?" the king snorted, swiveling his head a bit more toward his questioner. "There was a time when I would've given my own life to see that man dead."

Here came another pause as the king's mind wandered back to those days, but at last he spoke again. "You're the finest warrior I've ever seen, boy. Some even boast you cut yourself free of your mother's womb, blade in hand! Yet all your days thus far have been spent training to *kill*. For you there is only *live* or *die*. *Succeed* or *fail*. Yet here at my side, young guardian, you will learn of paths that lie between."

"Please instruct me, lord."

"Very well," said the Desert King with a self-satisfied grin. His gaze was lost now in the flickering red of the brazier. "Then first consider this: why did you focus on Zamarian's *insolent words* and not the threat of which they told?"

"I...I understood the message, lord...but I didn't consider such a small band a threat. I thought you meant to see this pretender for yourself before you crushed her. Or that you desired to display her torture. Is that not so?"

"In part," said Sanisar. "But unlike you, I understand true power often lies beyond the number of blades at one's disposal. Can you not see Zamarian's intent? To force my hand against her. To awaken the same anger you thought would grip me. *Servant by ill-made oath*, he says — but tell me this: of Sanisar and Zamarian, which is the fool? The one whose teeth still grind at the thought of his vow...or the one who merely saw fit to accept it? Zamarian loved my brother and despised me, but his oath was to the throne. As long as I sit on it, he has no choice but to serve me well."

"I believe I see it now, lord," said Erathiel. "Zamarian believes this pretender could repel an initial attack...if ordered in haste with few spears behind it...and that word of her power might rally supporters to her cause..."

Peeling his eyes from the fire, Sanisar turned them on the masked warrior. "Good. And right on the mark save for one detail. It's not *her* power I fear, but my own. Whether she defeats my warriors or not hardly matters. Merely that I sent them against her would win support for the legitimacy of her claim. I must be certain of my opponent first, because Zamarian isn't the only old fool in these lands. Twice now you've named this *Galfayan* a pretender — yet I doubt that's so."

The young bodyguard nodded now as if fully answered then stood to resume his silent vigil — but his lord wasn't finished. Turning back to the flames, Sanisar spoke again:

"Our Father's power flows strong beneath this desert's sands, Erathiel…and many of us have learned to draw on it at will. Falirid won this throne by his arts, and he taught his sons in turn. But how long has it been since those days? How many years since I found my brother's spirit roaming the borderland? Even in death he fought our attempts to bind his soul…" The king drew a slow breath here and released it. "And do you know what Taloseth's spirit told me, boy, just before it broke free of our hold?"

"No, my lord."

"He bade me guard well this land I'd taken from him — lest the Daemon come and strip it from my grasp!"

Gathering up the folds of his robe, Sanisar rose and descended the dais.

Even Imlod agreed. Their pursuers — if there'd been any to begin with — had likely abandoned the chase by now.

He'd left Gilal and Marinya behind to explore the next grotto beyond their chosen camping space. It was a tight squeeze between the two moss-blanketed sandstone walls, but the anticipated wonder just ahead — previewed by a lone emerald trunk basking in cool sunbeams, its gnarled roots radiating over the stony floor — reached out like a gigantic hand to pull him into the scene. This place of gorge and roofless caverns they'd stumbled upon earlier had already improved his bleak mood greatly, for he'd rarely seen such natural beauty; and now he found himself giving in to the possibility of lingering here a day or two after the coming night. Marinya had been so brave in the beginning and done her best to keep up a steady pace. But she was long past needing an extended rest, and certainly they wouldn't find another area as defensible as this. With luck and skill, two men might hold the entrances to this particular chamber against an entire horde of foes without.

Since the start of their escape they hadn't remained in one spot beyond a single night, purposely shunning the dwellings of men, knowing a single word from a villager could set the most daunted pursuers on a renewed chase. Each time they'd happened on a village or a camp, Imlod had gone in alone to steal some food while the others slept; yet already their supplies dwindled again. *We need a fresh kill,* he thought, twisting out of the gap and stepping over roots to get to the tree they supported.

With one hand on the tree and the other on the stone wall, he pushed back his shoulders and stretched his neck to ease tension in his sore muscles, all the while peering down the rocky slope from this new vantage point. The next chamber was one of the few closed to sunlight from above, yet at its far end Imlod saw a tiny radiant portal in the encircling blackness. An exit from the winding network of grottos. The graveled streambed lay just steps beyond, and soon he was on his way down to it.

The noise of falling water that'd echoed within faded to a low murmur as he proceeded, and he winced as the loud crunch of his steps marred the tranquility outside. Squatting to sip from the stream, he noted the scenery here was just as odd yet appealing as that inside the cavern walls. A lush green moss seemed to cover all the stone and bark within sight here too, trees rose with roots wrapped about rocks rather than hidden deep in the soil, and feathery ferns dangled from every outcrop. Raising his eyes to the heights above, Imlod soon spied a hollow in the stone before him — one that might've made a perfect den for any predator able to scale the smooth, vertical wall up to its mouth — and this image brought another to his mind:

A skinny girl with hair black as her cloak of raven feathers, peering back at him from another such hole higher up in an imposing cliff wall. *Galfayan...am I free of your claws at last?*

"Another floating spirit?" came a half-expected voice from behind.

"You move fast for an old man," said Imlod with a grin. He stood and turned to see his smile mirrored by Gilal. "This current moves only silt and minnows." Wiping his hands dry on his breeches, he looked past the minister to the caverns. "We shouldn't leave Marinya alone."

"I'll return soon enough," said Gilal abruptly, detracting from the mirth that'd passed between them. Leaning on his staff, he began a slow descent to the bank.

"You've something to discuss with me?"

"I do indeed. I suppose you view yourself as my liberator, young man. And don't think me ungrateful for what you did! — regardless of your reason behind it. But forgive me if I still feel a prisoner."

"We've had this talk before." Frustration was plain on Imlod's face. "Once we deliver Marinya to her father, you'll be free to go as you please. You'd be no safer out there if you left us right now. The wisest thing would be to settle in Thaekith awhile and take a new name. Wait until we're sure they've given up on finding you before you set out again. How does *Megnus of Dirag* sound?"

Brushing off debris from a nearby fallen trunk, Gilal finally sat down. "That might work, if I were content to spend my days in obscurity." Catching the odd look on Imlod's face, Gilal sighed. "I can see why that confuses you. You've a lovely young woman with a child soon to arrive—and you want nothing more than to hide them away. To flee everything behind you. But it's not like that for me, Imlod. I must live so my actions shape my world! Gilal of Taudan was the prime advisor to Kagnus' rulers. But tell me—who shall this *Megnus* be? How long must I lurk in the shadows?"

"I can't speak for Asalin, but I promise you this: Marinya will say whatever's needed to win you his protection and favor. Perhaps he's in need of an advisor himself..."

Turning his eyes from Imlod to the stream, Gilal seemed to accept this as the only viable option at present. "I too had a child once. Not one of my loins, but one of my making nonetheless. I bled for him and freed him from slavery...and raised him to a rank no less than my own. But what did that get me? A knife in the back!" His face returned to Imlod's. "How did I not see it? Your sister's hook must've been in him from the start. Am I right, friend?"

"Just so."

The minister shook his head and sighed.

"You know the elf better than I do," said Imlod. "Galfayan possesses great beauty and power—but what is it Cirad hopes to gain from her? Surely a mere seat at the foot of her throne won't suit that one. He's too proud. I've seen how the submission pains him."

"Well...I suspect he's made a deal. What Cirad left behind in his homeland has tortured him ever since. Once your sister sits the desert's throne, he must believe she'll release all his kin from bondage." The minister yawned at the end of this; and as no reply came, his thoughts moved to something else. "On the day we were betrayed, they had me read a scroll of the elder age. Of the coming of the Daemon. I don't doubt Galfayan's powers, for I've witnessed them many times. But is she really what she claims? Is she truly *Rhanwŷr arisen?*"

"I was there when it happened," Imlod frowned, scooping up a handful of gravel and tossing it in the water, "...but I couldn't stop it. I wish no ill on my sister...only the thing inside her. Yet I fear there'll be no division left between them soon—and what am I to feel then? What else can I do but hide from her? From the day when there's nothing left but hate?"

"I should get back to the girl," said Gilal after an extended silence. "What will you do?"

"I'll set snares now, then hunt at dawn." Watching the old man begin to rise, Imlod stood with him. "Can you straighten a spear in the fire? Char a point?"

"I wasn't always an old, pampered man," the minister laughed. "How many do you need?"

"One for me, and one to keep with you. We're not safe yet." As Gilal nodded his agreement, Imlod moved to cross the shallow creek. Then a thought came to him, and he turned back. "I didn't tell Marinya about the child. About what the nymphs divined. Did you?"

The elder shook his head '*no*.'

"Good. We'll make it to Thaekith first, then I'll tell her. She doesn't need any distractions now." Scrambling atop a boulder, Imlod jumped from the far side and headed into the trees.

15

The rain had come before dawn, forcing a wet, groggy trio out of their open camp and back into the shelter of the grottos. They'd started a blazing fire then, and Marinya and Gilal yet waited out the storm there. But not Imlod. Though his plan to hunt had drowned with the torrent, he still had traps to check. Of all those he'd set yesterday, three had been located so far, and one had fortunately yielded a prize. An otter snared beside the water and dragged under by a rock, never to surface alive again.

The next trap was proving difficult to find. He recalled the general area well enough, but the poor visibility brought by the rain was sorely vexing him. Just moments ago he'd knelt in what he'd *thought* was the run, feeling around for the fencing he'd erected to guide a hapless creature towards its demise...yet all he'd found there was more mud on his boots and more water pummeling his back. After spending his entire childhood roaming a forest like this one, Imlod wasn't bothered much by freezing cold or soaking wetness alone; yet those conditions combined are enough to test the hardiest man. *If I don't find this snare soon, the deadfall will have to wait.*

Up ahead a thorny brush patch threatened a change in the trapper's direction; yet rather than a hindrance, this served him as a needed landmark to regain his bearings. Turning and grabbing hold, hand after hand, of the many smaller tree trunks about him for support, he pulled his way up to the adjacent hilltop—and there found the fallen, snapped-limbed evergreen leading down to the fenced run. It posed an even more treacherous descent than before with its loose bark now slick as well. Despite the icy wet misery surrounding him, Imlod laughed to himself as he carefully negotiated his footing and cursed his loss of bounds.

The decaying log crossed a narrow but deep gully rapidly filling with water below; and the rain came down much heavier through the natural crack in the canopy above, streaming from his drawn hood in a continual sheet before his face. He took the first step. *Fine.* The next. *Fine.* But as the weight of his third step came down, the bark beneath his foot gave way in a large chunk, causing Imlod to nearly plummet to the gully's bottom along with it. Gasping, he pulled his body up by the jagged limb he'd flailed for to save himself. Then, straddling the log, he sat to let his heart calm before proceeding.

But something was wrong now. Something to keep Imlod's life-giving organ thumping fast. Soundless black specks were flicking in and out of his narrowed peripheral vision. Feeling the urge to look up, he shielded his eyes, peered into the canopy overhead...and saw *bats*: hundreds of them circling, the whishing noise of their flight lost to the overbearing downpour. Lightning flashed in the distance, illuminating the spectacle. Thunder boomed and trailed away. Then the screeching began. In the space of a few breaths it climbed from eerily soft to steadily louder...to fever pitch...

To silence again, with not a single bat left in view.

That brief warning was all Imlod received before impact came. The crushing force of the blow sent him flying some distance outwards before he splashed into the debris-laden flow beneath. His assailant's impetus had fortunately sent the beast rolling off and away from him, but a sharp puncture to Imlod's side made him scream in agony. Spitting muck and leaves from his mouth, he defied the pain and sprang to his feet: for both senses and training told him that to delay an instant against this foe would bring death. He ripped the snapped branch from his body and angrily cast it aside...then replaced the stick with two drawn metal blades and stalked forward.

A head taller than Imlod, even with its thick, muscled legs bent slightly in a crouch, the werewolf standing opposite him would've instilled terror in nearly any other man; but Imlod was no stranger to the breed, having fought alongside such fiends as this in the past. Running on instinct and adrenaline and a deep, primal rage aimed at what was occurring, the wounded man appeared as savage as the nightmare he faced. Nevertheless, it was clear which side held the upper hand. The beast raised its frothing maw to howl into the storm — and two more wails joined with its cry from close above, followed by yet another loosed further in the distance.

"Marinya!" Imlod shouted to the sky in answer, chest out and neck bent back, sword and knife dangling at his sides. "Marinya!"

The werewolf in front and the one splashing down now to its side were huge males with long, furry arms, razor-sharp claws, and hands large enough to wrap about a human head and rip it from the shoulders. Their eyes were ivory orbs that pierced Imlod's body to glare at the soul within, and he knew their burning desire was to free that spirit by consuming its house of flesh. Yet they made no move forward. *They'll try not to kill me,* he reasoned, his mind grasping for how to capitalize on Galfayan's leniency. *But what of Marinya? What of our child?*

Water splashed again. This time from behind, its sound muffled somewhat by the noises of rising flood and downpour about him. With one blade held out front in a warding stance and his back to the earthen wall, Imlod cut his eyes and knife to the new threat. *Graumwen.* The brood's vile matron was crouching just out of harm's reach. Despite her smaller frame, this one possessed a canniness and greater agility that rendered her a deadlier foe to deal with than the others combined. And where another might stand overconfident before the prey under such favorable odds, the she-wolf bared her wicked teeth and appeared ready to pounce at an instant's warning. *Engage her first,* Imlod told himself. *Take her head while the others hesitate. It's my only chance...*

"Submit to us, brother!" bid Graumwen in her ominous, guttural voice. "Else perish and become one of *mine*. The queen has promised!"

With the lives of his lover and unborn son hanging in the balance, Imlod had no time to treat with this monster. His entire *being* cried out for her annihilation, as if anger alone might strike her down and burn her misshapen body to ash. Yet somehow he kept his wits. An inner flame burned in his eyes as he tossed back his hood and locked on the glazed spheres of his target. "I was there when they ran you through, Graumwen. Remember how you screamed and writhed? I'm warning you! Leave us be—or you'll feel that pain again!"

"Your blades can't harm me!" the hunter snarled back. Although they stood barely two paces apart, their words were shouts to be heard through the torrent.

"Even now you can't stand it!" Imlod ignored her to press on. "You stiffen at the very thought!" And with that slim hope of diversion—a harsh reminder of the fear and pain of *life* to a creature long devoid of it—he turned and lunged at the earthen wall. Appearing for an instant as if he meant to scramble up it and escape, the warrior kicked off and spun back just as Graumwen leapt forward, whirling his keen sword down to cleave through the hairy arm that would've grasped and hurled him to the ground. The fury in his heart burst free then, its power surging down his leg and into a straight kick that sent the she-wolf flying; and before the sprawling beast could even raise her head, Imlod's sword point came crashing through her open jaws, pinning that sleek, lupine skull beneath the flood.

One's demise is not as hard to accept in the face of such a quick and decisive victory, and even as he buried his weapon in Mother Earth, Imlod knew he was soon to follow. Whether he chose to turn and face it or not, his death was only a breath behind him. The jaws of the fastest male clamped into his neck and right shoulder, ripping at meat and bone, and the impact sent both man and monster whirling down next to Graumwen's vanquished corpse. Again and again and again Imlod's knife sank heavily into the male's eye and temple…till at last the massive weight went limp above the man and pressed his face under the water.

As consciousness began its final parting, Imlod imagined turning his face to meet Graumwen's beside him. His impaling sword was gone from her, and she looked back at him with a young girl's eyes: a beautiful maiden named Keshthe, returned from the days before the queen's jealousy had destroyed and corrupted her. The two faces smiled at one another…and the world around Imlod slowed and began to fade till all that remained was the girl's innocence. Her lips parted. She was trying to tell him something, but he couldn't quite make it out…

A violent jerk brought him back. Coughing and spewing up muck and blood, he felt his body lifted and flung over something solid that then set out at a rapid pace. His clouded eyes locked on the moving ground, making him nauseous, yet he felt no pain besides the burning in his side. His right arm was either missing or completely numb. His left hand, gore-smeared and hanging within sight, was being slowly cleansed by the rain. Each leap and landing threatened to bring the darkness upon him again, and at last he succumbed to its call.

Even with her body left behind, Keshthe awaited Imlod in his thoughts; save now the smile was gone, and as he gazed upon her with a frown of his own, he saw her face shift into another's visage. There were the lovely lips, harsh eyes, and raven locks now streaked with gray. *Galfayan!*

Yes, brother, her voice entered his mind. *This is no dream. Through Graumwen's released spirit I touch your own. You won't escape me so easily this time!*

Sister...please! sent Imlod. *Do with me as you wish...but Marinya served you well. Spare her and the child! I forced her into it. Don't punish them for what I've done!*

The face smirked at that. *You lie well, Imlod. But I didn't give you leave to speak. For years I've endured your preaching, hoping one day you'd prove an instrument worth my efforts. But no more! Your desertion was irritating — and now you've destroyed my favorite pet! So this is my judgment:*

Death is upon you, but your soul won't find rest! No...your corpse will be left here for the scavengers. Roam the wood like your mother before you! Marinya chose the same path and shall suffer the same fate. But the child is mine! Perhaps the son or daughter will prove a better student than the father...

Wake now and behold!

And wake he did...to the thud of his back hitting the rock floor and an ear-splitting screech nearby. "No!" he cried feebly as a huge wolfish shadow lunged across the wall towards its prey. As if he could prevent the heinous deed, Imlod thrust a hand into the air. But it was already done. Marinya's body collapsed in the circle of firelight: one protective arm still cradling her swollen belly and the other reaching out for him. Her eyes were horrible to look upon. Her face was deathly white. Blood began pooling beneath her at once.

He had to make it to her. Had to touch her one last time before the heat left her body forever. Had to let her know their child would survive. Clawing his way forward with the one good arm left to him, sobbing with each exertion, he was all but blind behind the growing mist of faintness and tears — and he paid no heed to Gilal's soothing words and touch found suddenly at his side. When his searching hand finally found Marinya's and gripped it, he felt her squeeze back. Weakly. Once only before letting go.

Gilal was still speaking to Imlod in a voice thick with emotion, but his words were lost on the fading young man. The minister stepped over Marinya, turned her over, and yanked away clothing to get at her womb. A knife gleamed in his hand.

Then Imlod died.

16

The Mother's eyes stared down at Sevos Let's upturned face without blinking: a lifeless gaze, one might say, with nothing else behind it save more of the cold, gray stone from which it'd been sculpted long ago. But the high priestess knew better. Even after years of daily ritual—wherein she'd knelt here just so, praying for her people's prosperity and the wisdom needed to guide them—the Goddess' idol could still hold her transfixed.

Yet today something more than awe and reverence for her deity had caused Sevos' own gaze to linger on the statue. *Personal thoughts* were distracting her, leading her mind astray from her purpose here...even while she retained a look of focused piety. Thoughts of *sin* with a man, no less—and a foreigner at that. A stranger who had no business here. A man whose religious beliefs were, at least in her estimation, only loosely aligned with her own. What was it about this man that had her thoughts always turning to him of late? That quickened her pulse whenever she heard him speak or saw him drawing near? She'd told herself it was only the mystery surrounding him—not the man himself—that intrigued her so...and that soon as he left Ramfiram her childish obsession would immediately depart with him. But was that the reality of the situation or merely a convenient lie? A pretense allowing her to further explore the mystery while ignoring the possibility of its lasting taint?

Suddenly she felt as if another set of eyes besides the Mother's was watching her; and, swiveling her neck to examine the space to her left, she found this to be true. The object of her musings stood still and silent beside one of the chamber's ornate columns, his dark-robed figure half-hidden in the shadows. *Taloseth.* He wasn't smiling at her—but his eyes were hungry, and she read in them exactly what he wanted. Rising, she grinned and began to move toward the man as he slowly backed away and melded with the darkness...

CLANG!

The noise startled Sevos awake. She must've dozed off while sitting propped against the wall of her black prison cell. They'd already come earlier to bring her daily rations. So why had they returned? She heard heavy footsteps descending the stairs. Heard the rattle of weapons and armor.

The door was unlocked and flung wide, and once more Sevos shielded her eyes against a burst of invasive light. The two guards entered and strode to her with immediate purpose, causing her to rise just as swiftly.

"What's this?" she challenged them.

"You've been summoned, priestess. Hand over the vial and come with us."

The poison. So they knew. Of course they did. Until they dragged her dead body from the cell or she tossed the vial out unused, the assumption was she still held onto it, debating the choice she'd been given. Should she unstopper it and gulp its contents before they could stop her? Would that be better than the fate awaiting her should she follow these curs out into the light?

"Now!" the other guard shouted in her face. "The Lich awaits!"

Was that fear in the man's cracking voice? The same fear that drove them to complete this task with all haste? If she tried to swallow the poison now, they'd act fast and simply dash it from her hand. Maybe even hurt her after. Better to surrender it and take her chances up above.

Digging into the rags she wore as clothes, she retrieved the vial then dropped it in the first guard's upturned palm. "The Lich? Where's your queen? What do they want with...*ah!*" Even as Sevos spoke, the second guard roughly snatched her by the arm and began pulling her toward the door.

"Silence!" he barked. "You can ask him yourself!"

She'd thought her eyes adjusted by the time they reached the temple's exit; but even on this chill winter day, the noontime sun shown bright outside in a clear blue sky, its rays reflecting off the mirror of Lake Thadda's calm surface to make her blink and squint yet again.

"Welcome, high priestess!" a raspy voice called to her from the water's edge.

Sevos thought she recognized that voice from her past. Then, as she tried to focus her gaze on the speaker, she thought she recognized the face staring back at her as well. Yet both had changed. Unnaturally so. The rogue Imlod Nir had forewarned her of this, yet it did little now to ease her shock. "Amasmir...?"

The Lich was just about to answer her when a noise to his left distracted the priestess and caused her to look in that direction; and there she saw Kirath, her son: gagged, bound at the wrists, and secured to a wooden post by a short rope about the neck. The young man was bruised and battered but appeared to have plenty of fight left in him. The sight of his mother had caused him to renew his thrashing and muffled shouts of protest.

At once Sevos cried Kirath's name then shrugged off her guard's grip to run to her child and fall on her knees before him. No matter that he'd resigned her to death not so long ago. No matter that he'd pronounced her a *whore*. She was his mother. It was her instinct to protect him.

The pair of guards behind her started forward to retrieve their prisoner, but the Lich waved off. "Don't worry, my old friend," he said to her. "We've not *permanently* harmed your boy."

Sevos pulled the gag from Kirath's mouth, and immediately he spat: "Look what they've done! They've murdered my father!" Tears of rage were fresh on the young man's face as his gaze locked on something behind the Lich — and his mother's jaw dropped as she turned to follow it. A massive stone slab had been rolled to within steps of the water, and it was now raised waist-high by a pile of the same logs that'd been used to transport it. There, with his eyes frozen open, mouth agape, and arms sprawled over the slab's sides, lay Ramfiram's chieftain, Bablak Alnoor: dead as the rock beneath him, a ceremonial dagger's hilt jutting up from his blood-streaked chest.

Next to this makeshift altar stood another figure similar to Amasmir, robed also in black from head to foot. This one's head was bowed with hood drawn, however, as it seemed to stare into a golden cup that it gripped with both hands; and the vessel's contents were made plain by several red lines streaking one side of it. Had this servant been Merogrin? Osnom? It didn't matter. Zigodus? Renduil? They were all the same. And as Sevos finally swept her gaze over the entire scene, she counted all of them present. But there was another minion here too. One whose appearance contrasted sharply with the others. As soon as she laid eyes on the thing, the priestess felt a fresh wave of horror displace her shock at the sight of Bablak's drained and bloated corpse. Gasping audibly, she fell back against her son, cringing in fear.

"Goddess, protect us!" she breathed out as Kordû mo Kar—sporting his new horned skull—began walking toward her. Although the creature's gargantuan frame exuded only calm confidence as he approached, his eyes were wild as those of a wounded animal surrounded by hunters. Stopping just in front of his master's captives, he bent and pulled Sevos off of Kirath, easy as a child picking up a beetle or plucking a blade of grass. Kirath opened his mouth again to object but received only a backhanded swat from Kordû in answer. A blow powerful enough to separate the young man from consciousness.

"Let go of me!" Sevos screamed at Amasmir as she writhed in Kordû's iron grasp. "Why've you done this, you *monster*?"

The Lich only grinned in response. Apparently the priestess' panic and tears were merely amusing him. Kordû carried the woman over and deposited her at his master's feet.

Sevos seemed surprised to be released—and was clearly struggling now not to collapse into a sobbing heap. "I demand to speak with my daughter! I know she can read your thoughts. Galfayan! Can you hear? Answer me!"

Amasmir's grin only widened at this. "Indeed that *was* true. But no more!" The Lich turned his head from side to side then raised both arms and held them wide in an encompassing gesture. "The Brethren have cast off the witch's yoke! This city now lies under *our* control—and *our control alone!*"

"But...how?"

Amasmir saw the priestess' face scrunched up in confusion—but instead of answering her directly, he turned his attention to one of his order. "Osnom!

Bring me the cup."

The servant that'd been staring into the vessel looked up from it immediately then turned to obey. Amasmir waited silently until the blood-streaked object was in his hand; then, reaching into the folds of his robe, he withdrew a pinch of some black powdery substance. Rubbing thumb and finger together to release the stuff, he let it fall into the cup.

"Do you know what this is, priestess?"

Sevos' body was trembling, and her jaw and fists were clenched tight from the effort of controlling her emotions.

"Not just the blood of Bablak Alnoor. Oh no." Still grinning, the Lich shook his head. "That fool's sacrifice was only the start. To provide sustenance for what I've mixed with it! To awaken the *true power* this dust contains! Do you have the answer now, Sevos Let?"

And soon as he said it, she did. "The Ash..." she mouthed in disbelief. "But we swore to take that knowledge to our graves!"

"And we *did*, priestess. All of us save you."

A sickness gripped Sevos at her core. Ûl-Kamûn's Ash was a holy substance whose existence had been kept secret by generations of Brethren: ever since the day of its recovery after the Fall. Not just a sacred relic, but reportedly one of the Father's own mystical possessions — or even, as some members of their order had interpreted, the very remains of his scorched flesh. "This is insane!" she shouted at Amasmir. "You don't know what will happen! This *sacrilege* could destroy us all!"

"Careful, woman, lest you suffer your husband's fate."

"You wouldn't dare!"

"Oh? And why not?" the Lich raised an eyebrow. "Perhaps you've forgotten, dear Sevos, how they cast you out of this city...then how you were returned in chains? Do you really think Ramfiram will rise against me in your name now, after all these years? Or in *his*?" Amasmir swept an arm back toward the altar and paused to let the last part sink in. They both knew more citizens would rejoice at the news of Bablak's death than would mourn the man...or at least wouldn't care enough to risk their lives to avenge him. "Galfayan still rules this city — as far as anyone but *we here* knows — and thus the people believe I'm still the instrument of her will. No, priestess..." he shook his head in denial, "...they won't rebel. And even if they did, we'd swiftly put them down!"

"Then why bring me here? Why not leave me in that cell, none the wiser of your crazy schemes? What is it you want from me, Amasmir, if not my death?"

The Lich sighed. "I'd hoped you might come to sympathize with us: your devoted followers in life. After all...your daughter's as much *your* enemy as she is mine. But I see this is too much for you all at once. Perhaps you're right, and I should return you to your cell for a while...to reconsider your position..."

At this point Amasmir turned from Sevos and found his attendant lingering nearby. Indicating that Osnom should retake the cup, he watched quietly as the servant slowly carried it to the lake and poured its contents into the water. Then, as Osnom made his way back to the altar to repeat the ritual, Amasmir gazed out over the lake and lifted his voice to the Mother:

"Goddess! Hear me! Hearken to your servant Amasmir Dahsa, First of the Order, faithful to you in both life and in death! Woe is upon us, Great Mother, for the Daemon walks among us again in deceit, clothing herself in your guise! The men of this city still name themselves *Ûledrith* — but this is not so! The true Lords of Earth held tight to your bosom. Not even death could pry them away! But these pitiful descendents won't heed you at all. And so I ask you, O Mother: how long must we endure? Look upon us! Behold what the witch has done to your children! I've been now to the land of our Father, and I've beseeched him, yet he but stands there idle, unwilling to respond, ignoring his promise to return to us in time of need. Thus I say to you: if Ûl-Kamûn will do nothing, then we must act in his stead! We must purge this land as it was purged before, and so bring about a new age!"

The cup — its lip dripping red — was soon offered up again. Amasmir reached into his robe once more to touch the source of his newfound freedom and power; then he smiled wide, appearing satisfied with the absolute silence surrounding him. A void bereft of any challenge to his designs.

"We warned you of this," spoke the elf, calmly as he could muster under the circumstances. "Even your traitorous brother said..."

"My brother's dead, Cirad!" Galfayan shouted at her lover from across the shelter, not bothering to turn and face him. "Just as you'll be if you don't hold your tongue! I'll have the answer soon enough. Now be silent or be gone!" She leaned over the fumes rising from her ritual fire, using both hands to waft them into her face and nostrils, and for the moment nothing more passed between the pair. Part of Cirad wanted to storm out of the tent and leave the witch to her vile craft, but the repercussions of this situation could be detrimental to his plans for Agrigoth — so he propped himself against a nearby post, folded his arms...and waited, his mind wandering back down the roads of life that had brought him to this time and place...

Like most other elves kept in the Desert King's palace, Cirad's parents hadn't been born into bondage, yet he was one of the rare few that had been. Most of his enslaved kin — loathe to bring children into the same bitter world they were forced daily to endure — not only shunned but often refused to breed in captivity, even under pain of torture or death. Nevertheless, Cirad's conception had been no mistake. "I can't explain what came over me," his mother Sûrdandî had once told him, "…but your father felt it strongly as well. Had either of us been unsure, you wouldn't be here with us today. It was as if your spirit called to us from the Black Land, begging to be born. We couldn't ignore your crying then, no more than we could ignore it after you'd arrived and lay helpless in your crib. There's something special about you, my son! Learn all you can of the world—for these walls won't bind you long."

At first these words had made Cirad feel special indeed. Yet even before the end of his first decade of mundane, often harsh, servitude—wherein each day he saw firsthand the stark contrast between the freedom enjoyed by human children and his own existence as an automaton—he'd already come to resent his parents' decision. *What's the point of living, if no choices are given to you?* he would ponder then: a sentiment that had never wholly left him since. Yet as his second decade in the palace came and went, the young elf had all but ceased to dwell on it.

Then one year they arrived: emissaries from Kagnus. Clearly amazed by the opulence of the palace and all the wonders contained within it, these men were soon fawning over then-king Falirid—Sanisar's father—as if he were a god rather than a mere mortal ruler; and the old monarch didn't fail to reward their display. As the foreigners prepared to return home, Falirid called for Cirad by name as one of the gifts to be sent with them. A bright specimen of youth plucked from an ever-dwindling breed. Recalling his mother's words, Cirad dared to embrace his departure as the start of a grand destiny, hoping there was truly some lofty purpose for which he'd been born. But exactly what that purpose was still lay hidden from him.

It was only after he'd arrived in Kagnus and befriended an influential advisor named Gilal that the elf's mission began to take shape in his mind. The Desert King's intention had been to merely transfer Cirad as a slave from one master to another, but the soon-to-be minister from Taudan managed to convince his ruler to let the elf serve of his own free will: to receive all the benefits and enjoy all the liberties fealty brings. At first the elf thought to take his newfound freedom and go at once to the aid of his kin; but fealty, however far removed from slavery, is not true freedom. Gilal wisely intervened, warning that only death or worse awaited Cirad if the elf ever set foot in Agrigoth again. And on that day he was right. Then was not the time to return.

But the years thereafter were exceedingly prosperous for the elf. With each passing cycle his abilities, determination, and station grew until once again fate's hand visited him, elevating him to a position amongst the three most powerful figures in all the marsh. That's when the dream of liberating his people moved into the realm of possibility, and every move he now made was focused on that goal. Would he ever see his parents again? Did they still live? It didn't matter.

This was beyond his family. This was for his entire race. Any who stood in his way would be cut down, just as he'd cut down Kordû. Achieving the goal was what mattered, and Cirad wasn't above any means that might propel him swiftly toward the desired outcome. From the instant he'd first seen her — even before he'd fully understood who she was — Cirad had seen in Galfayan a means, and now together they were so close to the end. *But will she honor her bargain when all's said and done?*

As if she'd read his thoughts about her, the witch stirred from her trance and began to speak…except she didn't turn to Cirad, for her words were no longer directed at him. Leaning back in the spot where she knelt, she stared into the coalescing vapors before her: "Show yourself to me, shade! I seek the power of far sight. Obey me, or else I'll bind you here forever, barring you from the pool of rebirth!"

For a moment it seemed nothing would change, then rapidly the gathering smoke took the shape of a tall man dressed in funereal garb. Many strings of beads, teeth, and claws adorned his neck and were draped also about his chest and waist; but if once they'd been stained in brilliant colors, they were now all but lost in his gray form. The specter's face was steeped in sadness. Its lips did not move, nor did any sound issue from it that Cirad could hear, yet the elf was certain — during the following silence in which Galfayan remained fixated on the hovering shade — that the pair indeed conversed. The longer the silence lasted, the more anxious he became to learn just what was being relayed…till at last he noticed the shade's form quavering as if it were agitated…then suddenly it was over. A sharp word and quick gesture from the witch, and only smoke remained where the spirit had been an instant before.

She stood abruptly and spun about. Her eyes were hazy, yet her manner and voice were sober and unaffected. "Curse this mortal shell!" she began ranting to herself before noticing her lover had chosen to remain. "Do they not know what dwells within me? Must I unleash it for them to learn?"

"Never speak that thought! Not even in anger or jest!" Cirad came forth and grabbed Galfayan by the arms as if to shake some sense into her; but, seeing her countenance turn feral in response, he slackened the grip immediately. "To rule these lands, yes. You shall be *Queen of All*. But the Daemon unchecked…there would be no subjects left! Surely you still see that?"

"Amasmir's discovered a substance of great power," she said, avoiding the elf's question by addressing their original conundrum. "One I must strip from his hands if I'm to regain control. The Brethren were wise to keep such a thing secret, yet how foolish they are to reveal it now!"

Cirad's hands fell away from her as she began to calm, and she headed for her couch to recline. "Then we must return at once," he sighed, his disappointment apparent. "Before our mission becomes known to Sanisar."

"He already knows." Galfayan was stretched out now, her skirt parting to reveal one long, bare leg that she let hang over the couch's side. "I've sensed his eyes on us."

"Why wasn't I told this at once?" Cirad's peeve had been set off again. "I must know everything that goes on here! His warriors could be setting a trap for us as we speak!"

"You overstep your bounds, elf," the witch frowned but didn't raise her voice to match his. "I no longer need you. Remember that. As long as you please me, I'll honor our agreement—but don't you dare school me again, lest you desire to rejoin Kordû!" She smirked at Cirad's shocked expression but didn't allow him a response just yet. "Imlod's loss pains me. I might've sent him and Kûhric to deal with Amasmir, allowing us both to continue on…"

"What do you mean? You intend to send me back instead?"

"You against the Lich?" she laughed aloud, summoning another look of anger and surprise to Cirad's face. "I think not. It'll take more than a sword to contest the Brethren now. Maybe Imlod's skills would've sufficed—or maybe not. It no longer matters. No, my love. That's not what I intend."

"Then it's settled," said the elf. "I'll order a strict watch till dawn, then we'll retrace our steps. Once you've dealt with this new threat…" He stopped short here. That threat wasn't what was really bothering him—nor was it yet another minor delay in his return to Agrigoth. It was a fear that Galfayan might choose to enter the desert *without him* that'd brought his outburst a moment ago. But now, staring into the queen's face, he suddenly realized she meant to do just the opposite: to send him on ahead while she returned home. And he saw that she knew he'd guessed it.

"Despite all your prating and your caution, Cirad, I've never known you to cringe from a task." She looked at him warmly, beckoning him to come recline with her. "So don't start that now. Go and look upon the faces of your kin and their masters, and let that feed the flame for when we return in strength. This time you'll only play the messenger. Keep your tongue in check and your blade sheathed, and no harm will come to you from it." Cirad sat down beside her with a thoughtful frown, his eyes focused on nothing in particular, and she leaned in and kissed his neck. "We'll speak no more of it tonight. And I won't leave here till Gilal returns with my prize!"

She reached for the elf's face with both hands and pulled his mouth to hers.

17

He didn't know when or where the plummet had begun or what awaited him below. The fall went on and on and on, with a perception of sinking all that was left to maintain his identity. All that was left to set him apart from the engulfing blackness. *Time* was not reckonable here. Moments or lifetimes passed — then it was done. His senses flashed awake as he plunged into the water. A deafening splash, an icy shock, and deep blue shade below a bright crystalline surface light. Then he was calm and floating upright, slowly revolving with his sight locked on the rippling barrier between water and air above.

Suddenly two splashes broke the divide; and two identical faces shot forward rapidly, propelled by sleek, fluked tails down within arm's length of his hovering form. For a moment the beautiful creatures encircled him, smiling and reaching out to touch him playfully; then they swam away to frolic with diving turtles and multicolored fish, although never completely out of sight. Yet as he continued to watch, admiring the wonder of the scene, he saw its perfection start to fade...till at last the clear blue backdrop had darkened to a rotting green, and the aquatic life about the sisters became a mat of bloated death floating on the surface above. The nymphs swam toward him again, but this time with the deliberate speed of frenzied predators darting in for the kill, their long black hair trailing as if blown by the wind. Their eyes were now glazed white orbs, and the skin of their cheeks split open to reveal mouths full of wicked teeth. The first to reach him checked herself just shy of collision, recoiling such that her body came up parallel with his own, hair billowing about her head from the abrupt change in momentum. As the other reined in beside her, the first one lifted an arm to point a finger at him. Then his world shifted...

Once more he found himself under the gloom, a mere speck moving beneath the encompassing dome of gray shadow serving this place as sky. His advance through the tangle was slow yet sure, for unlike the others he was no rambler here. He knew the way. The sense of it was like a shining beacon summoning him. But this time — in the jungle of vines fit for slithering serpents and flitting birds and scurrying rodents — Imlod Nir possessed no blade with which to cut a path, nor could he conjure the power to alter his spirit's form. This time he was forced to climb and crawl like the ones he'd guided here in the past.

It wasn't long before he came upon an abode: one of the nests constructed by new wanderers while they still retained thoughts of *possessions* and *home*. It was rare for him to find a soul lingering in one of these dwellings...yet here knelt one now, her eyes fixed on an ebony carving that she gripped with both hands. Over her head, dangling from the twisted, barren vines roofing her crude shelter, were strung the various goods that had accompanied her corpse to the grave.

"Why do you stare at him so?" Imlod asked presently, knowing well whom the carving represented. It was one like all the others in these dens. "You won't see his face in that statue."

From the woman's complete lack of reaction to his presence thus far, Imlod assumed his speech to be rhetorical. But just before he turned away, suddenly she sprang to her feet and ran to him with the idol held out so far in front that she nearly shoved the thing in his face. She said nothing and didn't need to, for the elation in her eyes told it all:

It's you, Father!

Imlod had seen his reflection often enough to confirm her unspoken thought as truth. Without a doubt, it was his own face etched on the carving.

Shocked by this sight, Imlod reflexively pushed the woman aside and set off again at a quickened pace. *Something's wrong here,* he mused, jumping atop then down from one of the gigantic, treelike vines. The woman's joy seemed terribly out of place to him in this dismal environment: a land growing darker now than he'd ever found it before. Its shadows lengthened before his eyes, seeming as if dusk were fast approaching. Yet he could do nothing but move forward. There was no turning back.

He passed more huts as he moved along…and more spirits staring at more statues before turning their excited attentions on him. Their faces appeared on either side of his path: some popping into view just as he reached them, while others were already there and waiting. Perhaps they all fell in line behind him, hoping to follow the Father's likeness to the lake of fire. But Imlod could only see ahead. There was no looking back.

After a time the rich, earthen smells of the tangle became masked by the scent of smoke; then billows of the stuff came into view above the next clump of trunks and vines. *The lake's just ahead…but I hear no song. What's this silence?* Only the crackling of fiery tongues licking black rock could be heard as Imlod set foot on the shore. And there indeed he found himself alone. A spirit singled out in the very spot where all identities came to meld. *But I'm no thief this time. I've run the natural course! What's wrong here? Am I to be turned away?*

A pillar rose from the lake directly ahead, and upon it stood Ûl-Kamûn, the Black Father himself, cloaked in shadow with a hood drawn to hide his face. He neither spoke nor moved; yet as Taloseth the Mage's hidden stare had once held Imlod enthralled, so now did the Father's gaze. For a moment it held him tight, banishing all other thought. Then it let go — and immediately his attention was drawn to the pillar's base. There he found the spirit of his lover, Marinya Layva, hovering above the flames: slender and pure again as the day he'd first met her. Her face was undeniably radiant, but even from a distance Imlod could read the deep sadness in her eyes. Something snapped in his mind. *Our child! I must go back!* He spun around swiftly…only to find himself facing the lake again.

"Son of Nir!" her voice came streaking to him through the fire. "How does it feel to be bound like those you enslaved? Visible to the Father...waiting for his call to a new life...yet cruelly chained upon the shore?"

"Marinya, please!" Imlod replied, falling on his knees, his gaze sweeping from his beloved to the Father and back to her again. "You *must* beg him! Tell him to let me go! Galfayan has our son. She'll raise him like me if I don't return!"

"Yes, that's true. She's already named him *Angaras*, meaning *'he who is birthed in death.'* But I tell you this, Imlod: our child won't endure that name long. Either he shall be delivered from that fate or quickly consumed by it." While speaking the last, Marinya's figure flickered in and out of Imlod's sight, as if her time here might be cut short at any moment.

"What pulls you? Is it *Him*? And where are the others? What's happening to this land?"

"Someone tampers with the Womb," said Marinya. "A ritual has begun. One that should've died with the Father. One that even your sister wouldn't yet dare. Soon all the Years of Conceiving shall be undone, and the bones of generations shall rise from the sacred water where they were laid to rest. The undead shall take up blades against the living, and ancestor shall drink descendant's blood on Thadda's slopes and in the forests beyond. And in the end, the Daemon shall be loosed once more, no longer held in check by Galfayan's flesh and will. Nothing can stop it now. With or without you, my love, this will surely come to pass."

"But who attempts this thing?" asked Imlod, bewildered. "Who but Galfayan has such knowledge? Such insanity?"

"One whose life you took for her. Amasmir the Lich."

Imlod frowned at that—then nodded as if he'd known the answer all along. "She wouldn't listen to me. But what's our son have to do with this madness? The nymphs said..."

"Does it matter what they said?" Marinya's form began to flicker again: worse now, as if her agitation was influencing the distortion. "Would you not still love him, regardless of his destiny? Would you not wish to return to him, even if he were to rise no further than the common man?"

"I never saw him..." Imlod sighed. "I never held him in my arms." Suddenly grief became anger. "Why doesn't *He* speak, Marinya? Why can't *He* stop what's happening? Has he lost all his power? Does he even care?"

"Don't you see? He *is* speaking. You and he...you're one and the same..."

On cue, the Father's hands raised to touch his hood. He pushed it back—and there revealed, incredibly, just like in the statues, was the exact likeness of Imlod Nir's face. Speechless, the clone on the shore locked eyes with his lofty double in amazement, and his jaw dropped as Marinya went on: "Did you think yourself a pawn in this game? Rhanwŷr knew better. That's why she sent your father after you long ago. All our hopes might've ended then, had Galfayan not interfered, yet still we lie just shy of the Daemon's grasp. Imlod, son of Nir: you shall return indeed! But this time you must take up the blade of Asalin and his forefathers — and with it, win back our son. And when at last you hold the baby in your arms, rid him of the hateful name he's been given. Name him anew: Eldasryn, 'heart of the tower.'

"Blade?" was all Imlod could manage in reply, for he was as yet thoroughly entranced. "Tower?"

"Don't fail me this time, my love—whatever the cost! For it's your son, not you, who can renew the world." Marinya's flickering finally ceased, only to be replaced now by a slow fade. She was leaving. "Go. We've wasted much time already. Go and do what must be done."

Even after her spirit had vanished and the dome above blackened to near pitch, still Imlod stood staring into the eyes of the Father. *My own eyes.* They glowed and flickered like the fire below.

At last Ûl-Kamûn extended one hand to him, and Imlod stepped forward.

He felt the woman's touch long before he ever saw her face. At times it was her hands on his neck and brow, checking him for fever. At others it was her ear against his chest as she assessed his shallow breathing. And now she raised his head, forced his lips to part, and poured water into his parched mouth. Now she spoke soothing words to him as he choked it down. But still he couldn't open his eyes. Still he couldn't thank her for the kindness.

When at last he did succeed in prying his lids apart, she wasn't there. Dim light from approaching dusk or dawn—he didn't know which—hardly entered the portal across from him before being consumed by the room's inner dark; yet to his long unused sight, its brightness was enough for him to raise a shielding hand against. Lifting the hand was also a thing not easily done, for just to bend the arm and raise it required much exertion. Some moments passed before his pupils were sufficiently adjusted. Then he began studying his surroundings.

He was still in the forest, it seemed, as evidenced by thick brush and trunks visible beyond a grassy clearing just outside the door. The grass failed abruptly at the building's entrance, replaced by a floor of smooth, bare stone slabs, and its walls were formed of blocks of the same whitish-gray rock. Thick furs blanketed his feeble body, and he smelled smoke, heard crackling, and felt the fire's warmth somewhere behind him. Presently he recalled his wounds and wondered how he'd moved his right arm at all—much less without searing pain. He craned his neck back and tilted his head sideways and down, straining to see the area where the savage bite had taken hold. The bite that had torn flesh, meat, and veins and surely crushed his collarbone. Moving his neck did bring a tinge of pain after all, and that—coupled with the stitched gape he observed on his shoulder—assured him the battle had been real. *The bone's mended...I can feel it. But how can that be? How long have I lain here?*

A quick inspection of the closed puncture to his side confirmed it: a talented healer had been tending him. Yet, although he'd once heard a rumor of shamans so skilled as to succeed in sewing damaged intestines and even in treating blows to the brain, he knew his hurts had been beyond mortal intervention. Then it all came flooding back to him: the carving, Marinya's ghost, his face mirrored above the flames...

He caught a sudden motion at the portal—and in rushed a large dog headed straight for him. But there was no need for alarm. The hound's tail was steadily wagging as it plopped its muzzle on the cot and began nudging and licking at his arm as if it'd known him for years.

"Come, Jaga!" called the woman from the doorway in a hushed voice. Then she realized her charge was watching her and spoke up. "Ah, you're awake at last! I apologize for the dog. He's grown quite fond of you."

"It's fine..." her patient responded in a weak voice cracking from disuse. He reached over to pet the dog between its ears. "Where am I? What is this place?"

"You lie within the Temple of Solitude, my friend. And I'm Layva Helir, the Keeper."

Can it be? Marinya's mother? Then I'm in... He nearly blurted this out before thinking better of it. *Careful. She may not know of her daughter's death, or she may question my role in it.* "My name is Imlod, son of Nir."

As she stepped inside and approached his bed, bending to pet the dog with him, he made a note of her face. Any doubt of her being Marinya's mother was removed. Without the silver ringlets falling from her woven head wrap and the obvious lines of age, she would've looked the image of her child. "Well, Imlod Nir, this is a tomb. The hero Breladus sleeps forever below you—and I must say, for a few days I thought you might be joining him. I was told you'd wake, yet it's still a marvel indeed!" Then, sighing over him, she added: "If only my daughter had received the same blessing..."

And there it was. She'd found Marinya's body as well. Imlod almost asked about the baby then; but he caught himself, knowing the child had been swept away by a foul beast to Galfayan's waiting arms. He focused on the woman's other words instead: "Told? By whom?"

"Patience." She lay a calming hand on his arm. "We've much to discuss. But first you must eat! All I've gotten in you so far is water and broth. Do you think you could stomach a bit of stew?"

Honestly, he didn't feel the least bit hungry at the moment, as it sometimes is with those who've gone too long without a meal. He felt only the weakness. Yet he replied that he would try whatever she had to offer.

"Good. Then lie still till I return." Withdrawing her touch once more, Layva Helir did her best to smile. "Jaga! Let's leave our friend to his rest."

The dog ran out at her prodding; and she followed, shutting the door behind.

As the near-darkness engulfed Imlod, so did a flood of mixed emotions. Part of him wanted to curl into a ball and wail and sob for Marinya until there were no tears left—then, refusing all sustenance, to huddle in a corner until his body failed utterly, freeing him to rejoin her in the netherworld as it should've been. Yet another feeling kept him from it. There was a *power* within him now. Slight at first beneath the dullness of infirmity, it suddenly grew stronger as he reached for it; and soon as he touched the source, he felt vigor return to both his muscles and his soul. The son of Nir was certainly no stranger to power: to those arts and abilities that knowledge and training had yielded to him over the years. But this was different. This was *quiet solidity*. This bordered on bliss. He hadn't been sent back here to fall apart, wallowing in sorrow and cursing the fate that'd once more bereft him of a family. He'd been sent back here to accomplish something.

The scream of bitter rage that'd been ready to smash through the walls inside him shrank back and fled away…and all that remained was his duty.

And revenge.

It started as a ripple in the mirror, as bubbles released from pockets of long-trapped air rushed up from the lake's bottom to pop on its glassy surface. Days and nights had passed since Amasmir drained the last of his cups into the water, yet the result of his ritual had finally begun. Moonlight flashed over the waves now as they radiated outward—first from a single point, then from another and another—until in the thousands they ran and crashed together beneath the black sky to make Thadda a boiling cauldron. And the stew to be served from that pot was a poison to man.

They didn't rise in unison like a deadly white wave foaming up to spill over the rim. Instead their muck-covered skulls broke the surface here and there, just as the bubbles had begun, more and more of their haggard bodies showing with each step taken towards the shore. They were neither completely skeletal nor completely whole; nor did all the bones of each come from the same source, but rather the summoned spirits had taken hold of whatever nearby parts fit as they labored to construct new frames. One arm or leg might be longer than the other, or the upper and lower bite might not align well, or any number of incongruities, subtle or horridly obvious, might be observed. Ligaments and tendons and even some muscle had grown rapidly to facilitate movement, but there was no need of skin or organs—for the animating force behind each minion was the parasitical soul within it. To look upon just one of their eyeless faces was enough to incite terror in any man, yet by the hundreds now they came forth.

Most wielded thighbone clubs or the like. Others even held shields formed of ribcages covered over by flesh. And for every mortal warrior's head soon to be bashed in by blunt bone, the dying hand would drop some pointy implement of wood, rock, or metal to be taken up readily by the slayer. For every hacked-off minion's limb there would be others, strewn all about, to choose from in its place.

Thus the undead army would keep on marching forward...until there was no one left to kill.

18

Imlod watched the man in front approach Layva and pause just out of reach. The Keeper had been expecting these two arrivals, yet something about the way she greeted them suggested trepidation. For a moment she stood there wrapped in the folds of her clothing, silently studying the lead man as he stared back at her with fists clenched at his sides...then she broke the spell by flinging herself at him with open arms.

Still no words passed between them; and as their embrace lingered, the other newcomer came over to stand opposite Imlod by the fire, the excited hound Jaga trailing him with a wagging tail. This one had to be Layva's warden, Darengar, whom she'd said had been dispatched as a messenger to the City of Leaves while Imlod yet lay unconscious. The man was middle-aged and quite rough-looking compared to his regal traveling companion. His oily dark hair was straight but cropped above the shoulders, and a wiry beard grew from his leathery face. His weapons were bow and quiver and a long, slender sword-staff — all of which he deposited within reach as he sat down, eyeing Imlod warily in the process.

"Where is she?" said the first man at last, loud enough for all of them to hear. There was no need to question this one's identity, for regardless of the Keeper's forewarning of whom she'd summoned and why, Imlod had been to Thaekith in the past and observed its ruler himself from a distance. Marinya's father, Asalin of Kûthod. "Take me to her," the king added without awaiting a reply. As their hug ended and Layva stepped back from him, he wiped a hand down both eyes and cheeks as if cleaning away fresh tears. Then she took his other hand in hers and turned to slowly lead him out of sight. She started speaking to him then as they walked, but their fading words were too soft to make out.

Imlod leaned forward to turn a spit. He and his host had been in the midst of preparing their evening meal when the others appeared. The mussel shells had already popped open on the heated rocks, and the fish were nearly done. Again he looked to the man across from him. "You're Darengar?"

The warden left off petting Jaga to meet Imlod's gaze. He nodded in answer, but his expression was one of perplexity and suspicion. "And you're a man who should still be in bed — or else in the ground." He shook his head slightly then, as if unconvinced what he was seeing was real. "When we found you, I took you for dead. But Layva said not."

Darengar paused here as if waiting for Imlod to offer some explanation for his miraculous recovery, but when none came he shifted his gaze to the food.

"There's plenty," said Imlod, eager to change the subject. "Have some."

They ate in silence awhile. Imlod guessed that, like himself, the warden was used to being alone more often than not — and that eventually made him think to ask: "No others returned with you?" Finished eating for the moment, he began wrapping up leftover food to save for Layva and Asalin. "None of the king's attendants?"

"Few know where this tomb lies, and Asalin would have its secret remain." Darengar glanced in the direction his lord and mistress had taken. "The Keeper's unharmed, I see—as much as I worried leaving her here with such *sorcery* afoot. You know who I am. So tell me: who are you? Why are you here?"

"My name is Imlod Nir, brother to the Queen of Ladd." Imlod watched as the warden's expression darkened, just as he'd assumed it would. "Marinya and I were…together. I was leading her home."

"When you were attacked."

Imlod nodded. His lover's final scream suddenly echoed in his head, and her blank eyes stared at him in accusation. He'd failed to protect her then, but now her spirit awaited him in the world below—and when he was done here, he'd be reunited with her again.

"I thought they'd set hounds on you," Darengar went on, "…till I found the tracks. It wasn't dogs. Only men—and something else. Did you see what they did to her?"

Imlod didn't respond immediately. His thoughts were still in another place. His eyes stared out into the forest at nothing.

"Answer me! Who was hunting you…and why?"

"It was her wish to leave," said Imlod at last, slowly returning his gaze to the warden. "We both knew the risk—but I didn't have to go along with it. It's my fault this happened. Galfayan didn't care about her. Only me."

"The witch came for you herself?"

Imlod shook his head '*no*.' "You saw the tracks of her beasts. And there was another man with us. They made him take the child."

"So you stood there and watched as they defiled my princess?" Darengar's tone was harsh again, and his hands had closed into white-knuckled fists. "One might question your part in that, Imlod Nir—*brother to the witch herself!* Am I wrong? How do I know those animals—whatever they are—aren't watching us as I speak? That this isn't some treacherous scheme to draw my lord into a trap?"

"Because the baby's *mine*. If those creatures weren't far away from this place by now, I wouldn't be sitting here talking to you. I'd be chasing them to reclaim my son!"

"But how could you know that…unless you're in league with them?" The warden glanced over at his weapons then, as if ensuring himself they were still present. "A boy, you say. You saw him, then—and heard him cry—but what makes you so sure he's still alive? Why would they slay the mother but spare the child?"

"Calm yourself, friend," said Imlod in a gentle tone. "I'll explain it all when your king returns. You wouldn't believe me now. Not without your Keeper's support."

Darengar considered these words while grinding his jaw. "Fair enough," he said at last. "It's not my place to judge you. Lord Asalin will see to that."

The sun was long set, and their fire burning low, before Layva and the king finally reappeared. Imlod had been resting and was nearly asleep when his eyes suddenly flicked open to find Darengar already standing with sword-staff at the ready, and he knew the warden wouldn't hesitate to use that weapon if ordered to do so. But it wasn't concern for his safety that worried Imlod about speaking with Asalin of Kûthod. Thousands of lives could depend on the ruler's decisions over the coming days — including that of the man's own grandson.

Imlod stood and gave a bow as Layva introduced him to the king by name.

"*Imlod Nir*," Asalin slowly repeated the Keeper's words. "A witch, then. Just like your sister." The man's tone was flat, and his expression was unreadable in the faint light.

Layva's mouth opened, and her hand shot up as if to grab Asalin's arm in reproach for his callousness — but she checked herself and showed Imlod an apologetic frown instead.

"I was, yes," said Imlod. "But no more."

"An easy thing to say." Asalin's eyes lingered on Imlod for a moment, then he broke the gaze and found a spot near the fire to sit. "Please..." he swept an arm over the area in a gesture that called for the others to join him.

They did so, with Imlod passing over some of the leftover food to Layva, who in turn passed some on to the king. The Keeper also produced an earthen pitcher and poured herself and each man a cup of currant wine. Asalin took a sip of his before continuing:

"What part did you play in my daughter's death, Imlod Nir? The truth only, now. Lies won't serve you here."

"I've nothing to hide from you, lord. Marinya was slain because of the choice I made."

Imlod then proceeded to relay everything of note from when he'd first begun courting Marinya through the day of her horrible slaughter and the abduction of his newborn child. And although it was clear by their intermittent frowns and glances at one another that both the king and Darengar were having trouble with parts of his story, they let him tell it without interruption. "Then I woke here in this place," Imlod ended, looking first to Layva before staring across the flames at Asalin. He assumed the barrage of questions would begin at this point, but the king just sat there eyeing him in return. So he went on: "I'm not the same man I was before. It wasn't just a dream. Marinya's spirit *did* speak to me. It must be hard for you to believe, but..."

"It's true." The Keeper had held her tongue long enough, it seemed. "I had a dream as well. A vision of the Father in the netherworld! He didn't speak to me with words—but there was no mistake. *It was him!* The pillar. The lake of fire. It was all there, and it felt so real! When I looked up at him, he showed me..." Her voice caught here with emotion, and she bit her lip, no doubt struggling with the image of her mutilated daughter conjured once more to mind. "He showed me what'd happened to Marinya. And he showed me this man and their son!"

The king shook his head as if unconvinced. "If Darengar hadn't led you there himself and found what you said you'd find, I'd call both you and your guest mad. I believe something took hold of you. Something that wanted you to find this man." The king's eyes flicked to Imlod again. "But was it really Ûl-Kamûn reaching out from the world beyond...or just a trick of sorcery? Maybe not from *Imlod Nir* here—for you say he was barely alive. But what of the witch? What if she sent some foul specter to haunt your mind as you slept? What if it's inside you even now, waiting for the moment to possess you again?"

"I would know it," said Imlod before Layva could respond. "I can sense such things..."

"Yet you just told us your days of *witchery* were done!" Asalin snapped back. "Why should I trust what you say? The only part of your story I believe without question is the part that condemns you!"

"Condemns *him?*" the Keeper interjected, a rising anger in her voice. "Really, Asalin? If there's anyone to condemn, then include Marinya too! For leaving us to begin with. For choosing to remain so long in that hellish place, when all her ties were here! This man nearly perished trying to free your daughter from the witch's yoke, when he could've chosen to remain loyal to his own kin. Can you not see they were in love? And love can't be denied—no matter what course *reason* would steer!" Suddenly a look of disgust came over her. "Wait. Maybe that's not right. Maybe he should've sent her away at the first sign of trouble—and not worried with her anymore. Wouldn't that have been wise, O great lord? It's what you did to me!"

"I'm not your jailer, woman," said the king. And though his expression was one of obvious displeasure, he chose to leave the Keeper's provocation otherwise unanswered. "What else did you see, Layva? What is it that makes you so eager to accept this man's outlandish claims? Would you have us all kneel before him now…and pledge our lives to *Kamani reborn*? To hand our ancestral blade over to the kin of our daughter's murderer? What proof do you have?"

At this point Imlod Nir rose and moved away from the fire, headed off in the direction of the temple. He might've excused himself first, but Layva's eyes were fixed on the king, and she was already firing back at the man:

"I saw the Tower! I've never been to Kagnus; but there it was, shining bright, its peak lost in the clouds high above the marsh! The Father's symbol pulsing on the door, beckoning me to enter!"

Asalin considered this briefly but shook his head again. "It's not enough…"

"No common man could've survived his wounds and then healed so quickly," Layva pressed on, her tone urging the king to reason. "Tell him, Darengar. You were there!"

Layva turned her face to the warden and saw him staring at the spot where their guest had vanished into the night. His hand was on his weapon, and he said nothing.

"More of the witch's sorcery, no doubt," Asalin replied instead. "Galfayan's a threat I've ignored too long. That much is clear. But my people will want more than another story of fiends in the woods, even if it comes from my own lips."

"But the witch killed our daughter! *Their princess!*"

The king sighed, and for a few moments no one spoke. Embers sizzled and popped. The drone of insects permeated the night air. Finally Asalin answered: "Marinya's been dead to them for years. The wardens go where I lead, but if I'm to believe this threat of an *undead army* marching on our realm, it will take more than them to defend us. Kûthod needs something beyond my own loss to rally behind. Something beyond your visions and this stranger's lies!"

Asalin indicated the place where Imlod had been sitting; and as if on cue, the man reentered the circle of firelight.

"Here's your proof." A leather sack was dangling from Imlod's left hand; and now he pulled it open and removed its grizzly contents for the others to see.

A wave of foul scent accompanied the severed head's withdrawal, and Layva shot a hand over her mouth and nose as it hit her. Startled, Darengar half-rose from his seat before checking himself. But Asalin sat perfectly still through the object's revealing: his only reaction a deepening frown.

The skull was obviously inhuman, but it wasn't wholly animal either. It was the head of some hybrid beast. A wolf, complete with fur and fangs — but with a shorter muzzle and iris-less white eyes. And Imlod was lifting it by a handful of long black hair.

Satisfied that Graumwen's image was now etched in his companions' minds, Imlod reopened the sack and began putting the horrid skull away. "I knew this woman before her change. She was young and beautiful like Marinya — but all it brought her in the end was Galfayan's jealousy. Yet in this form she became my sister's favorite servant." He finished tying off the sack then set it behind him. "Still…after I slew her in the gully, they didn't even bother dragging her off. A tool used and easily discarded. Same as me."

Imlod paused here to lock eyes with the king; but when Asalin said nothing, he went on: "Whether you believe everything I told you isn't important. I'm not sure I believe all of it myself. But if you wait too long, my lord, to believe *what's actually happening as we speak* — then you may find it's too late to avoid doom. Let me prove my worth to you. What've you to lose? Your people's respect, if I fail? There's more at stake here than that…"

"Indeed there is!" said Asalin. "Especially if you prove traitor."

"If this man were a traitor, we'd all be dead by now." Surprisingly this came from Darengar, who until that moment had chosen to remain aloof. The others' faces snapped to his as he spoke. "I'm not ashamed to admit it. Layva's right. Witchery or not, there's a power in him."

"And the courage to use it!" Layva added but said no more.

They were all waiting on the king now. Waiting for a decision or judgment that would move them beyond their present debate. When Asalin did speak again, he gestured behind Imlod, indicating the sack. "Before this season, such beasts as that lived only in our children's fantasies and in legends of ages past and of lands beyond the mountains and the sea. You must be a warrior of great skill and bravery not to have fled such foes. And greater still to have defeated one — if indeed that happened as you claim. And you've given me a grandson, you say. If that alone is true, and the child yet lives, then Kûthod *will not tolerate* its heir's abduction. Are you certain the boy survived? Where's he been taken?"

"He lives." Imlod knew this was so beyond doubt — and not only from the queen's words. He *felt* his son's life, faint but sure. "They would've delivered him to Galfayan…but after that I can only guess. She must know of the Lich's actions by now — yet Marinya's spirit made it seem Amasmir was acting of his own will. I can't imagine how…but if it's true, my sister would've abandoned the journey to Agrigoth. She'd need to return and deal with her rogue servant, one way or another. The only question is how she'll react to what he's begun. Will she try to regain control and command the undead horde herself — or will she seek to destroy it? Either way…if we're to free my son, I must confront her."

Asalin considered that. "Yes, she must be confronted. She must be taken and judged for what she's done. But it's late now. In the morning I'll visit Breladus' tomb to pray for his blessing — just as I've done many times before. But this time you'll go with me, Imlod. And we shall see if my ancestor finds you worthy."

19

Did you think yourself a pawn in this game? Rhanwŷr knew better. That's why she sent your father after you long ago...

Imlod knelt before the mound that was Marinya's grave and heard her words replay in his thoughts. It was early morning. The sun had barely risen, and he'd come alone.

...in the end, the Daemon shall be loosed once more...nothing can stop it now...

Was it all futile, then? Had he returned to the living world only to watch it fall? How could he *not* be a pawn if the future was already determined? Why should he even attempt this struggle, if there was no hope of ultimate victory? To hold off the darkness but a little longer? To blindly seek revenge, no matter the cost?

...it's your son, not you, who can renew the world...

There was an answer; but over the days since Imlod's resurrection, he'd come to realize how much simpler it was than that.

Would you not still love him, regardless of his destiny?

He didn't know how, when, or why — or even if — his son would change the world. But at this moment, none of it mattered. He only wanted to see his little boy. Hold the baby in his arms. *That* was the task he'd been charged with and the reason he'd been returned to this place. If he could make Galfayan pay for what she'd done...if he could ruin the Lich's designs and hers and spare the lives of thousands in the process...then he would. But first he must reclaim his own.

"There's a way to learn more about what's coming," Imlod spoke aloud now, rising to address the man who'd just arrived and was reverently waiting behind him. "But it requires the use of my art, and I'm afraid you'll brand me a *witch*."

"One who uses a witch's craft is a witch," Asalin said flatly as Imlod turned to face him. "What does a man who claims to be a god need with such sorcery?"

"Necromancy *is* the Father's power. Or at least the ability to draw from it."

"You mean the *Black Father*," the king corrected. "My people worship the Mother alone. We don't condone meddling with spirits of the deceased — and certainly not reawakening their corrupted bodies!"

"I understand that, lord. But if the Lich succeeded in what I was told, we've no time to waste. At least send Darengar into Ladd as your scout without delay! The undead don't sleep or rest on the march. If we linger here much longer, you may arrive home only to find your city already under attack!"

"I sent Darengar on to Thaekith ahead of us with a warning. He left before dawn." Asalin stepped closer and reached out to set a calming hand on Imlod's shoulder. "Come. We'll make haste as well — soon as we're done below."

The two men headed for the nearby temple and were soon passing inside. In the back near the ever-burning flame was a trapdoor that, once opened, revealed a staircase leading down. Asalin lit a torch in the fire before starting his descent. He motioned for Imlod to follow.

It wasn't far to the bottom, and the king moved immediately to begin lighting the chamber by firing several more torches ensconced at intervals about its walls. As the last one flared to life, Imlod stood in awe of the tomb's contents revealed: three distinct marvels on display in an otherwise unfurnished and unadorned room.

The first marvel was the sword; and soon as he saw it, Imlod recalled more of Marinya's message to him: "*...take up the blade of Asalin and his forefathers – and with it, win back our son.*" Mounted on the far wall, tip down, unsheathed and gleaming in torchlight, the ancient, mystical weapon needed no introduction from its owner. *Solitude.* Smoothly curved along most of its cutting edge on up to a wicked thrusting point, the metal was incised three times below this span and five times along the backing edge, reminding Imlod of a sharp-toothed leaf fallen on the autumn ground or – when the flickering light hit it just so – a wild, licking flame caught and frozen in time. The blade's flat was completely smooth, lacking embellishment and flaw alike; yet the guard was elaborately etched, and beneath the tightly-wrapped hilt was an impressive pommel shaped as a snake's head with ivory fangs and a pair of exquisite blue jewels for eyes. The serpent's tongue was a forked band that might be used to tie the weapon to its wielder's wrist.

The second marvel, its pieces affixed in proper arrangement to the adjacent wall, was a shield and set of armor unlike any Imlod had ever seen or imagined before. The metal-plated shield was rectangular except at the bottom where it curved to a tip and at the top where incised semicircles formed four sharpened blades. The single device, black-stained on its smooth, slightly convex surface, was the warden's serpent. Like *Solitude*, this shield appeared to be a cherished product of a bygone era that'd been meticulously maintained through the ages.

But not so with the armor set. Well-maintained, yes...but Imlod recognized its materials and craftsmanship at once as the work of a present-day master. All pieces were formed of beautiful bluish-silver scales – smoothed and shined to a mirror finish – with broad, raised pure silver lines around the borders and also running inward in intricate patterns unique to each piece's type. The set's magic was such that Imlod coveted it greatly upon first sight: even more so than he did the famous blade resting nearby. Childhood fantasies flashed through his mind, wherein he'd donned the armor and the shield and the blade – and no man could stand before him on the battlefield. But then those thoughts shifted as he slowly approached the armor's crowning piece.

The set's faceplate was unlike the beastly visor worn in turn by his true father Taloseth and his surrogate father Kûhric. That mask inspired fear. This was a mask of *fearlessness*. It had neither mouth nor nose but was shining and smooth where such holes might've been, yet the cut of the eye slits suggested a look of piercing, righteous indignation. This forward piece—of five total plates forming the helm, with the others wrapping around two to a side—was shaped similarly to the shield: square at its sides but coming down to a point at the bottom, with blades like two pairs of sharp horns jutting up and back from the top. For what seemed a long while Imlod stood lost in inner thought, staring into the visor's black eyes…until at last the king's own appraisal caught his attention. Then he moved to stand beside Asalin.

The last marvel was hardly less breathtaking than the others hanging above it. The hero Breladus' sarcophagus. Both visitors stood now at the coffin's foot, admiring its magnificently etched and painted stone that was—just as with the sword and the armor—free from any trace of dust or grime. Clearly the Keeper hadn't slacked in her duties.

"Do you know this here?" Asalin asked, pointing a finger at one of the many small symbols shooting out like a sun's rays from the stone lid's blank, circular center.

Imlod looked closely. It was a swirling, bluish-green mark like the ones he'd recently seen painted on Kûhric's exposed chinbone. "It's a simpler form of your wardens' serpent. It speaks of the regenerative powers of nature."

"Just so," said the king. "It's here…and on the sword and shield…and on my warden's fingers…and in many other places, both within Kûthod and without. It's seen so often these days that most people have ceased to contemplate it." He turned his troubled face to Imlod. "Do you think there'll come a time when its meaning is utterly forgotten? When men will take too much from Mother Earth without giving back—and the serpent grow too bloated to round on its tail?"

"I've already seen its use corrupted," said Imlod after another moment spent picturing Kûhric's patched face. "And yes…I believe that day will come. My sister's *progress* is nothing but a disease on this world. A way to spread control without even lifting a sword. Men who rely only on others to live will die when the others fail."

Asalin nodded in agreement then raised and displayed his left hand. "It's said this very ring is the symbol's source. Old as our first ancestors—or maybe even from an age before. Do you believe that, Imlod? That such a thing could endure for so long, unlost and unmarred? We've no metal like this in Kûthod."

"I believe what it represents here in your land—and so do your followers. And right now that gives it a power above any that might be locked within it." Imlod paused again to collect his thoughts. "You must've heard stories of my father, Taloseth…but I wasn't raised by him. Before Galfayan took me with her to Ladd, I lived with my mother in Weth, close to the border with Kûthod. One of your wardens visited us there often. Kûhric Besh. Do you remember him?"

The king frowned in thought. "Perhaps. There have been so many over the years…I'm not certain. But there's no one by that name currently in my service. What became of him?"

"His past isn't important now. He died — and he should've stayed dead. But Galfayan brought him back: just as she did the beasts that killed your daughter. And still he lingers on against his will, even after all these years." Imlod's eyes returned to the swirling symbol Asalin had asked him about, and he ran a finger along its curves. "That's what will happen to any who fall to the Lich's army, my lord. And that's what this symbol will become to them. Not the natural cycle of death and rebirth, but a wheel that rolls ever on to no end."

Asalin's frown deepened, and he shook his head as if to dispel the blasphemy from his skull. "And what of my grandson? Will the witch do the same to him?"

"No. She won't harm him — not unless we force her hand. She has other plans for Eldasryn. She thinks to put him in my place. To make of him what she failed to make of me."

"Eldasryn. A strong name…" The king sighed and nodded his acceptance of Imlod's words. "Then for now we must leave the boy to his fate and focus on my people's defense." Moving toward the hanging set of armor, he stared at it before turning back to his guest. "It's been years since I took *Solitude* from the temple — and even longer since I wore all of this. The time's come now to pass it on." He looked at Imlod appraisingly. "It should fit you well enough."

"No, lord…I can't accept. Marinya did speak of the sword, but I haven't come here to supplant you…"

Asalin raised a palm to stop Imlod there. Stepping over to *Solitude*, he pulled the weapon from the wall and held it up for the younger man to take. "There are some in Thaekith who'll covet the title of my champion and the privilege to wield this blade in battle; and under other circumstances, I'd say most of them deserve it more than you do. They won't understand at first. But I'm still their king, and they'll do what I say. I may have my doubts, but Layva believes in you, and she says Marinya loved you — which means she saw something in you too. You may not be *Kamani reborn*, but I believe you sired her child by her consent…and that makes you my son in all but blood."

Imlod stood with lips parted but lacking the words to respond. Unsure of the appropriate reply to the honor just bestowed.

"Go on," said the king. "Take it. Then we'll pray for Breladus' blessing."

Hesitantly Imlod raised a hand to the weapon…but it wasn't fear of a dead hero's rejection that gave him pause. Asalin didn't possess Imlod's art, so it was doubtful Breladus' spirit—wherever it was—had ever received a word of the king's prayers or was even aware of these rituals. No...if Marinya was correct, Imlod himself was a dead hero arisen. A fallen deity reborn. The moment he touched *Solitude*, he'd be accepting more than honors and blessings. He'd be accepting that he *was indeed* what she claimed him to be—and all the tasks and overwhelming responsibilities behind it.

He took a deep breath and released it, then slowly curled his fingers around the sword's hilt.

20

Kar...

The peryton's ears perked up as if his name had been called aloud. But only silence lay about him. He was the centerpiece of a snapshot in time: a motionless scene save for the subsiding ripples in the icy pool below him. The echoes of his lapping drink a moment before.

Brother...hear me...

And he did. Ears flickered then pointed forward in alarm. Feathered wings unfurled as powerful hindquarters stood him erect. His antlered head turned slowly from over one shoulder to the other, then his body began to turn also for a look behind.

No...come back! Stare into the water...

The nymph Sigeya grabbed her sister by the arm and pointed to a patch of darkening sky above Lake Thadda. "Look there!"

Now both their gazes were fixed on the heavens. If one stares at clouds long enough, eventually the viewer will let wind and imagination shape whatever he wants to see in them. But this was no daydreamer's fancy. This materialization was real. There, formed by the storm clouds, was the deer-like face with pointed ears and elongated muzzle, and the hollow nostrils and eyes were of the gray sky behind. And jutting from the head were the two beams with their many pointed tines.

"Do you see?" Sigeya pressed. "I've caught him at last!"

Sienda's face didn't reflect her sister's enthusiasm. She saw the wispy image above just the same, yet her memory overlaid it with Kar's true countenance: a bloodthirsty devil who'd slain her kin without remorse in the days of Rhanwŷr's second coming. "I warned you not to disturb him," she replied. "No good will come of this!"

"Nor will it from sitting idle. At least this is a chance." Sigeya reached for her sister's hand and took it, locking her slender fingers with their mirror image at her side. "Quickly! There's no time to argue. I'll channel." Even as she said this last, her eyes began to glaze and roll back in her head. "You know what needs to be said. Speak of that only — then we'll be rid of him!"

Up above, the dismal holes that were Kar's eyes flashed crimson once before returning to nothing. A sign that the link with his mind was firmly established. With hands still clasped, the sisters turned to one another; then Sigeya's eyelids flicked open, and the peryton began to speak through her mouth:

"*Witches!* Why must you plague me with your luring voices? For a hundred years I've been free of your coaxing and whining…yet I'd have had it a thousand more!"

"We don't act lightly in this," Sienda replied, fighting the urge to yank free of Sigeya's grip, "…for our love of you is no greater. But we've learned a thing you should hear. So remove your thought from harming my sister's mind, else I shall break this bond and leave you wanting."

"I've no need of your soothsaying."

"That's what drives us, yes," Sienda conceded. "But what I've to tell you lies in the present. Will you hear it or not?"

There was a brief pause before the answer. "Get on with it, witch."

The peryton's insolence was grating; but Sienda was anxious as he was to be done with this meeting, so she complied at once: "Your servant, Kordû, has been murdered."

Sigeya's grip tightened then — dreadfully so — enough to wrench a cry of pain from Sienda. "Did you think it beyond me to sense the loss of my *chosen*? I heard his dying breath rustle the leaves over this very pool, followed by the laughter of his betrayer! Why do you bring it back to me?"

"You're hurting me!" The grip hadn't relaxed yet, making it hard for Sienda to concentrate on anything else. "Let me go, Sigeya — or let *him* go! He won't listen to me!"

"She doesn't wish me gone yet." The pressure on Sienda's hand was relieved then without apology. "So…Kordû walks the Black Land. What of it?"

Sienda pulled her injured hand free and began rubbing it with the other. "I was trying to tell you. He's not *entirely* dead. She made him into a mockery of you." The nymph studied her sister's face and eyes, worried for Sigeya's safety should Kar's anger return. "Part man, part stag. You've seen such work of hers before, haven't you?"

A longer pause followed this time, and Sienda's fear was just starting to ease when…

"No!" Sigeya cried. Her open palms darted up to press against her temples, and her tail began to thrash in the sand. Her eyes cleared, clouded, then cleared again as she fought. "*Release me!*"

Sienda pulled her distressed twin into a hug, maintaining the tight embrace for as long as it took the other's spasms to subside. Overhead, the darks clouds were dissipating. The chance Sigeya had hoped for seemed gone.

Finally the pair separated, and Sienda spoke first: "Are you hurt? I told you. He cares for nothing but his precious forest!"

"No." Sigeya fell back into her sister's welcoming arms and lay her head on

Sienda's right shoulder. Her teary eyes gazed tiredly across the polluted gray water of the lake to the temple of her enemies; yet, at odds with her otherwise defeated features, her lips had formed a little smile. "There's another thing the beast cares for. The only thing strong enough to drive him from his den."

"What are you saying?" Sienda's own gaze trailed the storm as it marched off to the west. "Did he send more after? Words you didn't speak?"

Sigeya's smile grew wider. "Yes. He did."

For the dozenth time or more since first stowing it in his pack, the elf peeked in at Galfayan's message; and yes, it was still there: tightly rolled, seal unbroken. Should he reach in, grab the thing, tear it up, and stamp the pieces into the sand or let the cold sea breeze scatter them away? She'd left no undead servant with him, after all. No spy to listen in on him and intercede with her words should his speech to Sanisar go contrary to her design. The odds were against Cirad's survival, even without the brashness he knew the message contained. So should he play the game without it, relying on his wits alone? Or should he proceed as planned and hope the scroll's letters didn't spell his death?

Briefly he considered it once more. And once more he let the pack's flap fall.

Uncrossing his long, nimble legs, he stood and began brushing off the damp, dark grains that had come up with him. All the while his gaze and frown were directed at the stragglers: the needless, pitiful baggage that the witch had left in his charge when she deserted him. The gap of his considerable lead over these followers was closing at last; and as they approached him now, taking their time about it, he locked eyes with any who dared to meet his disdainful stare. Even the brave few who did shied away from it quickly, however, turning their faces to the sand at their feet or to the dismal gray water on their right. But presently one young man averted his eyes to the left instead—to the huge strewn rocks forming the many toes of the Ûlinari Mountains—and just before Cirad looked away, he noticed an unmistakable expression of surprise come over the lad.

Spinning to follow the boy's line of sight, Cirad saw it too: a lone figure atop the nearest rock, standing close enough to rain a stream of piss down on Cirad's perfect silver hair had he desired it. Elfish senses were supposedly sharper than a human's—yet how easily this man had crept up on him!

"Your kind don't roam freely in Agrigoth, elf," the stranger hailed from above. "Who gave you leave to do so? And who are these trespassers in our land?"

Suddenly some fifty spears arose behind him: shafts resting on stone and tips poking at sky. Their wielders—sporting thick leather armor on torso, shins, and forearms, with studded caps hugging shaven heads and short, curved blades at their sides—contrasted sharply with their unkempt leader. He was unarmored and unarmed, and long strands of a whitening mane blew freely along with his tattered clothing in the wind. Yet they all had one thing in common: their faces were grim.

Be calm! Cirad scolded himself, realizing his hand was on his weapon's hilt, itching to whip out the blade. *This was expected. Even desired.* A few servants behind him loosed shocked cries, though; and, glancing back, he found some of them frozen and clinging to each other for support, while all to be seen of the others were the footprints of their cowardly flights along the sand. *Let them run. I'm defenseless with or without them.*

"Well?" the stranger's voice came again. "Give me your master's name, and perhaps you'll be spared."

"I think you know it," Cirad replied confidently. He took his hand from his sword. "You've been watching us for some time."

"I asked you a question. Speak, slave!"

Slave. Hardly had Cirad returned to his homeland, yet here was that word for him already. *I'll see you die slowly, old bastard!* "My mistress is Galfayan, Queen of the East and the West. Who are you?"

"A bearer of words." And that was it. No outrage. Not even a question over Galfayan's claim to Agrigoth. "Bring her forth, then. She won't be harmed."

"She's no longer with us. I'm only a messenger as well."

The stranger's face grew tight, and he motioned to his warriors by raising one fist in the air.

Fifty spears leveled with the shore.

21

"Come sit with me, Imlod. She'll be done soon. You'll only get in the way."

Imlod glanced again at the spot where Layva knelt unpacking supplies. This was their first camp since departing the tomb, and he'd thought to aid the Keeper once more with her evening preparations. She'd already shooed Jaga away when the hound had come sniffing at her heels, though, and by the looks of her now — intensely focused on her work — Imlod had to agree with the king's assessment.

She'd wanted to stay behind, but Asalin had denied the request. It would be too dangerous for Layva to dwell alone in the forest over the coming days; and besides, most of her charges had come along with them. Imlod wore the sword *Solitude* strapped to his back, and the marvelous armor and shield were stowed in packs split between the trio to share its burden. Only the ancient hero's dust lay untouched beneath Breladus' temple.

Asalin's eyes followed Imlod's approach, remaining fixed on the young man as he settled down nearby. "I've been thinking about what you said," the king went on. "That it wasn't you, but Marinya's spirit, who named her son. *Eldasryn*: the *heart of the tower*. And not just any tower, according to Layva — but the oldest one of all. One that exists to us only in legend. The Tower of the Sun."

"It's no myth," said Imlod. "I've never seen it myself, but I've talked to some who have. The Kagnians say it rises above their northern coast, but they don't claim it part of their land. Instead they shun the place. There's no village within a dozen leagues of it."

"And why's that?"

"They don't share our beliefs. It's not a holy place for them, just a mysterious relic of a dead age. What they don't understand, they curse."

"*Our* beliefs?" Asalin raised an eyebrow.

"It doesn't matter." Imlod was in no mood to continue that debate with the king. "I'm not sure what the tower has to do with any of this...but we have to survive what's headed here first."

For a moment both men fell silent, staring into the woods as if they might see through the trees to the plains beyond. As if forming ghastly pictures in their minds of Amasmir's undead horde on the march. Then Imlod turned to Asalin again: "I feel Ûl-Kamûn's power flowing through me, lord — and that's no boast — but his mind is shut. I don't share his thoughts or his memories...and I don't understand the visions any more than you do. I *am not* 'one with the Father,' no matter what Marinya said. But I *did* fail her, and I'll do whatever it takes not to fail my son too."

"As your father failed you."

"You wish me to speak of my father?" There was anger now in Imlod's voice. "The man whose face I saw only once, on the same day he died? The same day he meant to sacrifice me to the Daemon? That bastard's the source of all this madness!" He looked away, shaking his head. "I've never heard of another man so possessed. Not even my sister's reached that height of insanity: where all the world around you is merely smoke and ash, as you go blind from staring into the flames of your single desire! To this day I wonder what would've happened had she not stopped him. If Rhanwŷr's soul had entered *him* instead. Would you all be dead by now? Or starving slaves mucking filth beneath the lash?"

"Is that why he left the desert from the start?" Asalin replied, ignoring Imlod's apocalyptic suggestions. "I heard he was once a prince there, but he gave up his birthright—just as Marinya did hers."

"What makes you so interested in him?"

Asalin sighed as if frustrated. "Because if you're really the son of Agrigoth's heir, then my grandson's a prince of two thrones."

Imlod hadn't considered that before. He'd enough to deal with besides. But the king had a point. *Maybe that's what's so special about Eldasryn. Maybe that's why the nymphs saw greatness in his future…*

"Galfayan claims it's true," Imlod finally responded to Asalin's question, "…as well as her elfin lover. Cirad told me he served Taloseth in his youth, when they both still dwelt in Falirid's court. And there were others who spoke to my father during his stay in Ramfiram. Before he caused the trouble there and left to hide in the wilds."

"When he lay with the priestess and got her with child."

Imlod nodded. "Then did the same to my mother…and left her behind too." Another pause for reflection. "She kept that secret till the day he returned and took me. She was trying to protect me from him. But Galfayan's since told me more about our father. She said he could read the heavens. That he knew the paths of the sun and moon so well he predicted exactly what would happen that day in Mavûl. A fleeting darkness when there should be light, in a spot haunted by Rhanwŷr's presence. The very time and place when the Father's hold over the Daemon would be at its weakest. She told me how Taloseth was seduced by the promise of immortality…and how she plotted to claim that power for herself…"

As Imlod was speaking this last, he felt an all-too-familiar sensation suddenly creep over him. *Not again!* It was slight, but it was there. *Should I tell Asalin? No need to concern him over a harmless lost soul, if that's all it is. I'll have a look first.* So after giving the excuse that he needed to relieve himself, he rose and headed off beneath the trees.

He hadn't gone far before he met a raven perched on a low branch. It was large for its breed and jet black—and soon as Imlod laid eyes on it, he knew it was undead.

"Follow me!" it croaked then spread its wings and flew further into the wood before lighting again, just within sight. "Follow me!"

Imlod hesitated. Reaching over his shoulder, he lay a hand on *Solitude*'s hilt and slowly drew the weapon. He considered the possibility of being lured away from the others so they could be more easily harmed...and he was just about to turn back to them when...

The shadows below the bird's new perch grew suddenly darker, and out from them stepped an imposing figure hooded and cloaked in black. The raven flew down and lit on this figure's shoulder, cawing excitedly before ducking its beak beneath a wing to preen.

"Who's there?" Imlod hailed, pointing his weapon at the approaching form. "Don't come any closer!"

But it did come closer—close enough to feel *Solitude*'s tip at its chest—before halting. Two mittened hands rose and drew back the hood. "Greetings, Imlod," came a voice known but long unheard.

Startled by the visage revealed, Imlod let his blade fall. *Kûhric!* Yet it was no longer a plastered skull staring back at him. It was the Kûhric of old. A face of flesh with piercing blue eyes. A face looking not to have aged a day from the last time Imlod beheld it in Weth, now so many years ago.

"Ah...I see you remember..."

"Yes, sister. I remember." Imlod knew he was actually communicating with Galfayan, not Kûhric. Kûhric's thoughts would be pushed aside by his mistress, alienated like some naughty boy banished to the corner of a room. "But why've you restored him now? You've never forced him this far before."

There was a pause here while Galfayan evidently considered her response—allowing a whirlwind of thoughts to pass through Imlod's mind. *Is Eldasryn safe? How did Galfayan find me? What does she know? Did she do this to Kûhric for the same reason she prettied herself for me before? To blind me with soothing images while feeding me lies? You killed Marinya, you bitch! You killed me! Forget the memories of this face before me! Kûhric's gone forever...and my sister too. I'm staring now into the very eyes of the Daemon!*

"Come now," Kûhric replied at last. "Why should I go on tormenting myself forever, as if I were a living man still? I'm greater than they are. As are you..."

Imlod took a step back and sheathed his blade. "Don't bother hiding behind Kûhric, Galfayan...or flattering one whose life you destroyed! Speak the truth—or *leave*. What is it you want?"

"Nor should you hide behind *Imlod, son of Nir*...for I know you've become something else." As Kûhric was delivering this reply, the raven on his shoulder grew restless and flew out of sight. "It's not too late for forgiveness, brother. I regret what happened. I was angry and felt betrayed, but it's my fault for giving the girl back to you too soon. *Come away!* Come and hold your boy! Only *I* can teach you to harness the power within you. Only *I* can..."

"No! Your words come from fear and confusion. You don't understand why I've returned. But when you do..."

Kûhric's expression revealed the queen's agitation at being seen through so easily, but she recovered well. "Your son Angaras has taken well to his nurse. He has a healthy appetite and was born free of illness or defect. It would be a shame if some untimely tragedy befell him now. Wouldn't you agree?"

"Spare me your threats. Nothing I say here will protect my son, if his death or torture suits you." Those were difficult words to speak — yet Imlod saw the truth in them. *She'd only hold him hostage, to force me to do her bidding again. I must trust in what I told Asalin...and in the prophecy of nymphs.*

"So you'll stand with these *tree-kissers* of Kûthod, then?"

Imlod nodded.

"I see," Galfayan replied through her minion. And that was all. Apparently she lacked the patience and humility needed for further persuasion. Directing Kûhric's rough grip at Imlod seemed her only other option, but that trial didn't appear to be coming. *Not yet.*

At last Kûhric spoke again. "Either way...we must make plans. The Lich's horde approaches."

"*We?*" Imlod hadn't expected that. *She proposes an alliance? What will she do if I refuse? Or if Asalin refuses?*

"You can't afford to refuse me. Would you have me join Amasmir instead?"

For a moment Imlod worried Galfayan could somehow read his mind. "No. I'd have you return to Ramfiram — to sit and wait till this is done. And if you won't give me my son now, then take him with you. At least he'll be safe in the temple."

"Oh no, brother. That won't do! Enough has gone awry in my absence." One corner of Kûhric's mouth turned up in a slight grin. "Besides...the decision's not yours to make. Why don't you run along and pose the question to your adopted king? He may see things differently."

"That's ridiculous!" Imlod scoffed. "Asalin would sooner join the Lich himself than side with you! You murdered his daughter!"

"Did I?" Kûhric's half-grin widened into a broad smile. "If you hadn't stolen her from me, she'd still be among us. Perhaps I meant to take her alive, but one of my hunters was overcome with bloodlust — and the deed was done before I could stop it. Perhaps if you hadn't resisted your capture, I'd have let the girl go in peace..."

"I didn't hide my part in what happened from Asalin, and he's no fool. If you hadn't intended Marinya's death, you'd have delivered his grandson to him in atonement."

"But it's not too late for that, either! Maybe he cares more for Angaras than you seem to. Maybe he'll be more willing to strike a deal for the boy, since he has no other score to settle with me. It's not *my* army marching on his land, after all. My plans were for the desert!"

Imlod shook his head '*no*.' "As I said: the king's no fool. Your shadow's crept into his borders, and he knows you won't pass him by forever. You don't have to be commanding his enemy for him to know you're responsible for it! He doesn't believe all I've told him...but he'll surely trust me over *you*."

Kûhric was frowning now, his eyes dangerously narrowed. "This is your last chance, brother! Return to me, and we'll rule this world together, side-by-side — or I'll even carve you a kingdom from it all your own! But deny me here, and there'll be no mercy. After I've dealt with you then, there'll be no coming back!"

But Imlod Nir had already dismissed the Daemon's boasts and temptations. Turning for his companions, he let Kûhric's voice ring out behind him without a word in answer or even a glance behind.

For a long time thereafter, the servant Kûhric stood motionless, staring at the spot where Imlod had passed from view. Then a strange thing happened. *Tears* began to pool in his newly-formed eyes.

And at last they spilled over, trickling down his ivory cheeks.

22

Tyth paused to tighten the cordage again. There was only one more line to impress with its twisted pattern in the clay; yet it was to be a single, unbroken wrap about the pot's entire circumference this time, and she must ensure both consistent depth and perfectly mating ends. Unconsciously holding her breath, she pressed an end to the clay and held it, began to guide the cord around…

And faltered. The wild yell that'd broken her concentration was followed by a mock version of it in a deeper voice, then the pair of hellions came flying past her—so close behind she might've flung out an arm to trip either one.

"Nendas!" she yelled angrily after them, stopping the one chasing the other in his tracks. The little boy simply ran on till he was out of sight, not bothering to look back. "I'm glad you've taken to Hadric—but you shouldn't get him worked up like that. You hear me?"

Nendas' eyes had yet to meet her own. With a wide smile still on his face, he was marking the spot where his playmate had scurried beneath the trees. "Come now, Tyth," he said, turning to her at last. "Shouldn't you be pleased he's happy, after all he's been through?"

"That's no excuse!" Tyth's face and hands returned to the pot to inspect it for damage. "See what your ruckus has done? Which one of you will fix this?"

Nendas chuckled at that. "Let the boy do it. Pottery's no work for a warden."

Tyth wanted to stay angry at him, but his warm, handsome smile melted the feeling away. She'd told herself not to let this young man get to her in that way, yet weeks had passed since she'd last put up a fight. In fact, Nendas Jush had barely left her side since she made the decision to remain in Kûthod. He'd said it was due to his upcoming test—and indeed he'd spent a large portion of each day training with the wardens—but she knew there was something else keeping him away from his own home. As he walked to her now and bent low for a kiss, she turned her cheek to him. "You're no warden yet, sir." She let a smile show then, patting the ground beside her.

He shrugged and sat down. "Soon enough."

She felt his hand run through her hair…and decided she'd better refocus his attention on her work. "Do you like the nose?" This one was a face pot. The ring nose was its handle.

Nendas grinned. "Who's it supposed to be? Not a pretty man, for certain."

Tyth considered it. "Looks a bit like old Thayld, don't you think? I guess it's all we'll be seeing of him now." Staring at the clay visage, she overlaid it with a memory of the overseer's face. *Why did so many choose to stay with you in Diebron, Thayld? You say the lake's your responsibility…but that's not right. The lake's people are your responsibility—yet you chose to keep most of them in danger. At least you sent*

Hadric to me. I'll have to be content with that. Nendas had slipped an arm around her waist while she was lost in thought. It felt right to be there. His closeness was comforting. "We'll be safe here...won't we?"

The young man peered into Tyth's eyes and began to speak — but his words were suddenly drowned by Hadric's excited shouting as the boy reentered the glade.

"Something's happening! They're calling everyone to the grove. Follow me!"

Everyone indeed. It seemed to Tyth that the whole of Thaekith had answered Asalin's summons. They were packed in a mass stretching from the foot of his hill to the grove's loose boundary and beyond. She and Nendas — and Hadric riding on Nendas' shoulders so the boy could see too — had arrived earlier than most, yet still the king and his attendants were hardly within earshot.

"Here's your proof!" Asalin was shouting. He stuck one hand in a box beside him and lifted its contents high for the crowd's inspection. Tyth didn't need him to explain what the object was. She could make it out well enough, even at this distance. A monster's severed head. Not a wolf's, but a *wolf-man's*. She'd seen others similar to it during the raids in Diebron.

"These *abominations* are meant to strike fear in us! To make us cower in our homes and pray for the evil to pass us by. To make us forget we're the sons and daughters of heroes!" Asalin turned his face to the werewolf's skull then; and as if disgusted by it, he unceremoniously tossed the gruesome thing back in its box with a thud. "You know I wanted peace. The peace we've all been celebrating! But this isn't a day for fear or for peace. War is upon us again, Kûthod! A war we've no choice but to fight. A battle we *must* win! If you fail to meet this enemy in the field and defeat them, there'll be no safe place for you to hide. If you break and run from *this enemy*, you'll be hunted down and slain to a man — then they'll enter our forest and do the same to every elder, woman, and child. Just like they murdered my daughter, Marinya!"

The host drew a collective breath as Asalin paused to let his message sink in; and directly after that, taking their lead from Kaledric, all the hill's wardens drew their swords and knelt with the weapons offered up to their king. Tyth guessed that no lengthy debate — like the ones back home presided over by Thayld — was forthcoming here. It seemed Nendas was correct. It *had* been too long since the might of Kûthod's wardens was last tested, for to say they appeared eager was an understatement. She noticed the feeling tug at Nendas too. His jaw dropped, and his eyes went wide. His hands snaked up as if he'd lift Hadric and set the boy down...but then it must've occurred to him that he was too far away and weaponless as well. His time for such a noble display would have to wait.

"No...not to me!" said Asalin, directing his gaze at Kaledric. "Not this time."

Then he turned to wave another man forth. An unassuming man whom Tyth hadn't noticed among the king's other retainers till now. "Our princess is gone, but she left us a child! A boy named Eldasryn: my grandson, and your heir! This man here is the baby's father—and so too my adopted son!" The king placed one hand on the man's shoulder and held his other arm out to the crowd. "Citizens of Thaekith! Here is your new prince and champion: Imlod Nir!"

Tyth was as surprised as most in attendance must've been by the unexpected elevation of a stranger to the second-highest authority in Asalin's realm, but there was something else about this *Imlod Nir* that'd caused her to fixate on him. The slender, dark-haired man didn't particularly look like either a champion or a prince at the moment, but he *did* resemble someone she'd met before...

Could it be? Tyth touched the arm of the woman in front of her and began to squeeze past. "Sorry...I need to get closer..."

"Tyth!" Nendas kept his voice low as he called to her back, clearly trying to avoid drawing more attention. "Where are you going?" But it was no use. She was already swallowed up by the crowd.

The king's announcement hadn't been met by resounding applause. Patches of mixed reactions followed the initial shocked silence then rapidly merged into an ocean of murmurs.

"Listen to me, people!" Asalin began again. "The Witch Queen of Ladd holds a power she can no longer control. A power we hoped would never rise again." He paused here for reflection, sweeping stern eyes over the quieting host. "But tomorrow we shall march out to meet that power—just as Breladus met it in the past! And with the very blade he used to slay the Daemon wielded now by your champion!" He looked once more to the man beside him and nodded a signal.

Imlod Nir returned the nod then swept his cloak aside to draw the fabled sword *Solitude* and thrust its tip into the air. The crowd gasped at the weapon's revealing, and warden Kaledric obediently turned his own offered blade from Asalin to the new prince.

"The king's wish is law!" Kaledric shouted, and the other wardens repeated it.

"No!" burst the desperate cry from Tyth's lungs, causing irritated faces on the hill to scan the sea of bodies in her direction. "Lord Asalin, beware! That man's your enemy!" The citizens around Tyth were either too surprised or offended by her bold interruption to make way for her, so she started forcefully wedging her body between them. "He's the witch's servant! He killed my parents!"

Kaledric rose at once with his blade ready but then hesitated, confused. Tyth stood with her mouth open as the warden's piercing blue eyes moved from hers to the imposter *Megnus of Dirag* then on to his king where they froze awaiting a signal to act.

"I'm afraid you're mistaken, girl," Asalin frowned. "And it's not your place to speak here. Kaledric! Please escort our guest to my home..."

"No...you can't do that again!" Tyth shouted as someone grabbed her by the biceps from behind. *Nendas.* "Let go of me! You must listen! He's not who..." Nendas' right hand shot up over Tyth's mouth to muffle her words, and his left arm wrapped around her torso, pinning her own arms against her body. She squirmed and tried to strike him for interfering, but his hold was too tight for her to break.

"*Not now!*" he barked in her ear, squeezing so hard that she winced in pain. "We'll speak to him after! Come on..."

Tyth began to sob as they took her away.

The king's mistress possessed a sweet, melodic voice which one might find at odds with the woman's regal bearing and chiseled looks. Humming the tune of a wordless song directed at the head resting in her lap, she ran a hand through its thick auburn hair and gently pushed a few stray locks behind the ear.

"I want to see Hadric," Tyth spoke again, interrupting Kedaynna in mid-note. But the words came softer this time. No longer a shouted demand but a request. Only the girl's lips moved. She kept her eyes locked on the room's door, waiting.

"Soon," Kedaynna replied. "I promise."

Today had started out so well. Tyth and her brother had made real progress toward moving on with their lives and leaving the nightmare of Diebron behind. But now *this* had happened, and it'd all come flooding back to her. Now she lay helpless while Kedaynna stroked her hair and tried to console her with soothing words; but all she could think of was how she wished it were her mother's touch and words instead of those of a heartless king's whore...and of how she wasn't a guest here but a prisoner confined to these quarters: likely awaiting punishment.

A silent moment passed in the room, then—just as Kedaynna began to hum again—there came a knock at the door. Tyth sat up immediately.

"Enter!" Kedaynna called.

The door opened, and King Asalin entered alone. After a pause to take in the scene before him, he walked to the bed as someone outside shut the door behind. He was still dressed as Tyth had seen him earlier, and he still looked at her with a frown.

"Hello, my love," Kedaynna greeted him. "Come sit with us." She indicated a nearby chair. "You must be tired..."

"Indeed." The king sighed. "Yet there's much more to do. I should be with them still...but I wanted to check on the young lady here. *Tyth,* I recall. Is that right?"

Tyth looked Asalin straight in the eyes and nodded, showing him a scowl of her own.

"I see you're still angry with me, Tyth: but you must understand our situation. You lost your family...and nothing I can say or do will change that. Yet now my people are in danger, too. Your *new family*, here in Kûthod. Now is not the time to sow doubt in their minds. We must all stand behind our champion."

"But he's deceived you!" Tyth suddenly cried out. "He's not what he pretends to be! He killed my family. He and some horrible monster like the ones you say come for us now!" Fresh tears began to form in her eyes. "I'll never forget his face. He admitted serving the Queen of Ladd—and even told me to go serve her myself! You must believe me! I've no reason to lie!"

"I do believe you. He freely admitted his guilt to me."

That shocked Tyth into astonished silence, but she recovered fast. "Then why haven't you put him in shackles, lord? Please, I beg you! You must act quickly— before he sets his daemon on us!"

The king shook his head. "As I said, girl...it's not so simple. We've all done things we'd change now if we could. As hard as it is to hear, what happened to your kin was only one of Imlod's many past crimes—but just like my wardens consider it their solemn duty to either kill or be killed at my word, he was only serving his ruler. The man's no sellsword or brigand. No thoughtless murderer who acts without remorse. It may've taken him too long to see clearly the error in his ways and break the witch's bonds, *but he has now*. Could you turn on your own little brother if he chose a life of evil some day? Could you take up a sword and strike him down, easier than you could slay a stranger? And how much harder to rebel against him were he your *king*—and if you'd taken an oath to obey his every command?" Asalin paused to let that sink in. "Perhaps you've forgotten how many others have suffered and fallen by Galfayan's will?"

"No, I remember!" Tyth's fists were balled now, and she felt her body shaking with rage. "All Kûthod rallies for a dead princess they hardly knew, but my loss means nothing at all! *Nothing!*"

Kedaynna reached for Tyth again to pull her into another consoling embrace. But Tyth wouldn't have it. It didn't matter if what King Asalin said made sense. It didn't matter whether this new *Imlod Nir* was legitimate or just another alias and role he was playing in some grand scheme of betrayal. She wanted the man dead either way. No...she wanted to see him tortured until he admitted his guilt before all of Thaekith and was then publicly executed for what he'd done. Only then would she be appeased. Only then would there be *justice*.

But Tyth was no fool. She could see justice would not be hers today. Instead of defiantly holding the king's gaze and waiting to see what impact her barbed words had on him, she slipped free of Kedaynna and threw herself down on the bed near its foot. Curling up in a protective ball, she fought the urge to sob.

For the space of a few breaths, Asalin and his mistress sat staring at Tyth's back before turning their eyes on each other. Kedaynna opened her mouth to speak first, but the king held up a hand to stop her. Shaking his head again, he simply rose and made to leave.

"She wants to see her brother," Kedaynna spoke to his retreating form.

"I'll send for him."

The door opened and was gently pressed shut.

23

The Queen of Ladd tore the last bit of meat from the bone, sucked it into her mouth, tossed the bone into the fire, then took a swig from her jug to wash the morsel down. Luxury was never far from Galfayan, even out here in the frigid wild. Spiced game, strong drink, warmth from furs and flame. All that seemed lacking was the presence of her elfin plaything.

He's probably dead by now, thought Gilal. The minister from Taudan gritted his teeth at that. His emotions were still mixed concerning Cirad. On the one hand, death seemed a fitting reward for the elf's betrayal; but on the other, it was hard to sever a bond that'd been so many years in the making. If not for Cirad, he'd probably be dead now himself. *Or worse.* The witch had already gloated to him about what'd become of his former lord Kordû. *She could've done the same to me.*

They hadn't bound him to the tree he sat propped against, but he remained a prisoner all the same. Galfayan had chosen to pitch her camp high on this ridge overlooking the snow-blanketed, sparsely-wooded field below: the plain where it seemed certain the armies of Kûthod and Amasmir the Lich would soon collide. For the moment she was making no effort to conceal her presence. Smoke from several cook fires snaked into the air, and unchecked noises rose from pockets of her followers huddled around them...and from her hybrid beasts occupied with some savage entertainment in the distance.

The sorceress' monsters were terrifying, no doubt, but their numbers would surely be dwarfed by those of either approaching army. Her small force sat here like a hornet's nest on a low branch, perilously close to being swatted down and crushed beneath the paws of two fighting bears. *If her plan's to observe from afar before choosing a side to aid, then she should have her minions hide in the woods till the moment for a surprise strike. And if she wishes to try joining a side before the armies even meet, then she should be marching either east or west right now.* It was as if the witch deemed herself an untouchable goddess on high, waiting to be amused by a display of mock combat on an insignificant stage below. A stage of puny actors who could do her no harm at all.

With this last thought lingering in his mind, Gilal scrutinized the witch again. She looked different now than she had before his failed escape. Her beauty was there — the youthful face and firm, slim body — but her eyes had a strange look to them, and her dark hair was heavily streaked with gray.

"Rista!" the witch called over her shoulder as Gilal continued to stare.

A young woman seated nearby looked up from the swaddled bundle in her arms as she heard her name shouted. Rista had been given the task of nursing Galfayan's newborn nephew Angaras: the baby whom Gilal had cut from poor Marinya's womb. The minister had observed this servant tending to the child earlier, and she appeared to him amenable enough to the job, if not quite happy to be performing it. *Maybe she lost her own baby.*

"Come here, girl," said Galfayan. But as the witch turned back around, she caught Gilal's gaze. "What is it, old man? You wish to speak?"

Do I? he thought. *Would it do any good if I did?* He held her eyes but didn't answer.

"Well? Let's hear it. What does the *famed minister* advise?"

Rista was at the queen's side now, but Galfayan paid her no mind. Gilal had stolen the witch's attention, and it wouldn't be wise for him to ignore her further.

"I've nothing to advise you, lady. You're supremely confident, just as Kordû was back home. I used to think him mad for ignoring my counsel, but in time I learned to bow to the higher power at work: for the *great Kar himself* was guiding my master. Perhaps you too see something I don't."

Galfayan frowned at Gilal's words but said nothing, and during the pause that followed, Rista sat down beside her mistress and offered up Angaras for inspection. The queen took a long look at the baby as his tiny arms moved and his little legs kicked beneath the blanket, but her expression never changed. At last she spoke again:

"You're no fool, Gilal. Kar is no god! He's not even the *protector* you claim. Who was he supposed to be protecting? Surely not the thousands who died fighting that war in his name. You and Kordû used Kar's name to control the masses; and all the while Kar was off wandering the dark woods, careless of your plots and schemes. Make no mistake, minister: *I* am the god...and Kar is but one of my children."

"So that's why you murdered Kordû and made him a mockery of our deity? To put *your child* in his place?" There was unchecked anger in Gilal's voice. "If you're so powerful, witch, then why lure him away from Kagnus before carrying out your treacherous deed? Why not strike him down then and there before the priests and declare yourself our ruler? I think I know the answer to that..."

"Shut your mouth, dog!" Galfayan's outburst was sudden and loud enough to startle Angaras; and as soon as Rista heard the baby begin to cry, she stood with him and moved away. Fortunately for Gilal, the queen kept her own seat. "If I'd wanted to remain with your barbaric scum any longer, I might've done just that. But your precious elf made me understand the real prize lies to the west, beyond the mountains. A civilized land, swarming with power. A land already mine by birthright, ripe for the taking. I don't need your pathetic savages, minister. Let them stay in the marsh and start killing each other all over again, for all I care. Let Cirad rot in a cell and curse me till I return to him and claim Agrigoth: then I'll laugh in his face as I sentence all his kin to death! I don't need any of them. I don't need anyone!"

"Hmm...are you sure? I'd say you're in dire need of an army of savages at the moment. And I think Cirad's blade will be sorely missed. Perhaps this *Lich* has grown too powerful for you to contest..."

Galfayan snorted at that and shook her head. "Amasmir surprised me, that's true. And now I must deal with Imlod as well. But I've something an old man like you doesn't. *Time.* All the time in the world! Let the pretender Sanisar stew on the desert throne a year longer...or two...or *ten.* Let his wondering when I'll return eat away at him till he dies of old age. Let Kagnus rise up and march on my realm for what I did to Kordû mo Kar, and they'll but spare me the trouble of fetching them! You just don't see it, Gilal. *I am immortal.* My flesh is a fortress all its own!"

Just as I thought. Gilal averted his eyes at last, staring out again at the snowy field below. *She'll heed nothing I say, no matter how convincing my arguments. Her pride's made her blind. But...perhaps I can use that to my advantage...*

"What?" said the witch after a moment of silence had passed. "You've nothing else clever to say?"

"No, my lady. As I said before: I'm no use to you here. You might as well let me go."

She released a peal of laughter at that. *"Let you go?* Why would I do that?"

"Why not?" The minister turned back to Galfayan, and his eyes held hers firm with no hint of fear. "What have I ever done to harm you, Queen of Ladd? And what could I ever do that would?"

He heard the noise again, faint and far off now, like the drone of a thousand distant insects on a calm spring evening. He felt as if he'd just been somewhere else, but already the memory escaped him. *A dream, perhaps, of another time and place.* His eyelids slowly peeled open. He was lying on his back in a dark room, staring up through a smoke-hole in a ceiling constructed of thick, tangled vines. The sky beyond was clear but drab gray. He was alone, it seemed, accompanied only by shadows.

Where am I? the man thought. A sense of near-recognition came to him — as if once more the memory or knowledge he needed lay just out of reach. Frustrated and disoriented, he sat up and swiveled his head from side to side in search of a door. *Maybe if I step outside...* It was too still and black in here to separate dream from reality. And the faraway voices...they were calling...

"Taloseth."

The sudden nearby speech startled the man. He'd not been alone in the room, after all. His head turned again, this time in the direction of the alien voice that'd spoken that name. The name he'd only then recalled as his own. "Who's there?"

he replied. Involuntarily retreating a few steps, he checked himself at the border of darkness and the circle of gray light.

A tall, slender man emerged from the shadows and crossed over the circle's edge on the opposite side of where Taloseth the Mage waited for him...but the stranger came no further. "Greetings, Father. I'm your son, Imlod Nir. Do you remember?"

The image of a young man bound to an altar of white stones flashed through Taloseth's mind — and immediately after, his fleeting *dream* of moments earlier came rushing back. He'd been there in Mavûl Gorge with the boy, reliving that fateful day. That hour of ritual toward which he'd fanatically devoted half his life to see completed: only to witness all his plans crumble to nothing in the end. Somehow Nir's son had followed him out of the dream into this place...but the boy was no longer a child. He nodded his head in answer to the man's question.

"I've watched you here before," Imlod continued, "...but never chose to reveal myself till now. Always you wake in this hut, right after Kûhric lets your corpse fall to the ground. Then you forget for a time. Isn't that so?"

Hesitantly, Taloseth nodded again. He recalled his own face then saw part of himself in the man before him — and part of the woman who'd birthed his son. A woman whom he'd slain before the child's eyes. And he would've slain the child too. *Should've* slain the child. Should've killed the boy that day in Mavûl — and the boy's sister long before then. But no...he'd failed...and it was *he* who'd been murdered. Betrayed by the girl whom he'd foolishly entrusted with power. And now the boy had returned as a man to face him in the Black Land, proving Imlod Nir was either dead himself or learned in the art as well. "Why have you come?" he said at last.

"You should've heeded the call long ago, Father. But you were too masterful in life. Too experienced and knowledgeable of this land to remain entranced for long. Once I saw you walk within sight of the fiery shore, only for that to be the moment of awareness. You don't *want* to be reborn. You don't *want* to forget who you were. And that's why you remain trapped in this endless loop, forever repeating that day."

Yes. Taloseth sensed no lie in Imlod's words, and part of him ached to learn more of what his son had to tell. Wanted desperately to make sense of it all. But the chanting rose louder as Imlod finished speaking, pulling at Taloseth strongly, compelling him to come join the other voices in song...and simply *forget*...

"At first I told myself you deserved it. That you were a madman who'd been corrupted by evil and received a fitting punishment. But as the years passed and the Daemon's hold on my sister tightened, I began to ponder what she'd told me of you. I started to wonder just how much of your evil was your own...and how much came from your meddling with Rhanwŷr's spirit...and why you'd begun meddling in the first place. It was strange how Galfayan avoided my questions. How she always said your motive was simply lust for power. For her, yes. But not you, I think. You were a scholar, and necromancy wasn't your only art. You studied the paths of the moon and the stars in the sky. You knew the sun would fail that very day in the gorge, didn't you? That very hour?"

Taloseth said nothing: only stood staring at his son with a blank expression. The lost memories roared past him in waves now, leaving Imlod's voice behind as a discarded catalyst on the shore. The hammer that broke the floodgate in his mind. The pull of the voices was fading as well…losing its hold on him…

Imlod shook his head at the lack of response. "It doesn't matter. I only want to know this: was it you or the Daemon who killed my mother?"

"Why did I go back for the girl?" said the mage, ignoring his son's question. "It was only *you* I needed. Even after all I taught her. Even though she knew what my failure would bring…" He bit off his words here, and his face went dark.

"Go on, tell me! What was your true purpose in Mavûl?"

Taloseth's gaze fell and locked on the circle of light at his feet…but otherwise he remained still and mute.

"Father?"

The mage's silence lingered…but finally he looked to his son again, confused. "To prevent Rhanwŷr's escape…"

Taloseth watched now as Imlod Nir fell speechless. The younger man's jaw dropped, and his face took on the expression of one completely mystified—even as the whirlwind in Taloseth's own mind was rapidly subsiding. *The girl deceived him too…*

Suddenly Imlod's head jerked to one side—and before the mage could even ponder what was happening, his son's spiritual body vanished.

A few moments passed, then Taloseth blinked and tilted his head to gaze up through the shelter's smoke-hole once again. Stillness had returned to the place, and he felt the weight of its shadows pressing in on him—but there would never be silence here. Never any relief from the incessant call. Sighing, he pulled his eyes from the hole and resumed his search for a door.

"Apologies, lord…"

Imlod jerked his head around and sat up straight, yanking both palms from the cold, wet earth. The sudden jump back from the netherworld left him dizzy, and for a moment he thought he might be sick. "I'm no lord, Kaledric," he finally spoke, then stood to face his visitor. "I may be a queen's brother and the father of a prince…but it takes more than that."

The prime warden hesitated before nodding his agreement. "Yet a man who knows this—and freely admits it—can't be too far removed, wouldn't you say?" The corners of Kaledric's mouth turned up in a grin…but as he watched Imlod and saw his smile go unreciprocated, he furrowed his brow and frowned. "Are you ill?"

Imlod sighed and shook his head. "What ails me will pass soon enough, one way or another." Cupping his hands, he raised them to his mouth, blew warm air into them, then rubbed them together briskly. "Asalin sent you to fetch me?"

Another nod. "Our scouts are returning. The enemy will be upon us soon, and the king would hear your counsel."

"I'm no marshal, either. I'm sure you've given him sound advice."

"I have indeed." Kaledric looked away now, training his sharp blue eyes on the opposing forest edge: far across the snow-laden field from where he stood. "But he's named *you* champion."

As that last word registered, Imlod felt keenly the weight of Asalin's armor, which he now wore, and of the legendary blade strapped to his back. "They're your men. We both know you should be leading this army instead of me. After this is done—if we survive—I'll gladly relinquish that title to you."

Kaledric turned his gaze back on Imlod. "Then why not do so from the start?" Notes of anger and frustration had suddenly come into his voice. "Asalin's word is law…but how are we to trust a stranger to lead us? A man we know nothing about and who's never fought with us before. A man they say wields the same dark power as his sorcerous sister! And as the unholy priest who's driving a horde of devils straight at us!"

Imlod's words had been meant to flatter and appease the warden, but now he realized too late they'd only served to pick at a festering wound. "I didn't want this. I even declined at first. But there's more to it than my humility and your pride, Kaledric. I'm not a leader who inspires others with words, yet I *am* a warrior—and today I'll lead by example. Galfayan lied to me from the start and manipulated me to do her bidding for all those years: but no more! Fate or not, I won't rest until my son's returned. That's what you can trust."

Kaledric gave no reply to this, and presently he turned away again, scanning the distant tree line. "I spoke to one of the scouts myself. A veteran blooded in battle before I was even weaned from my mother's breast. The look on his face when he told me what he saw out there…I've never seen him like that before…"

"That same fear will grip us all before this day's done." Imlod came forward now, stepping to the warden's side and following Kaledric's gaze out across the field. "But believe me when I tell you this, friend: those aren't devils heading for us. Amasmir himself might be mistaken for a daemon…yet the things he raised from the lake are only mindless drones. The Brethren found a powerful relic in Ramfiram, but their ritual was flawed. When your men see the creatures — when they watch them take a mortal wound and keep on coming — then their fear may turn to panic...then the panic to disorder...then some may look about them and think all is lost. But we can't let that happen. We must show them that even the undead can be hacked to bits and trampled to the ground. We must continue to rally them, no matter how many times we're driven back. No matter the cost..."

Kaledric tilted his head to study Imlod's face. "I don't pretend to understand all of this, lord, but the wardens of Kûthod aren't ones to abandon the defense of their home. We'll follow you today for as long as you hold true to your word — but either way, you can rest assured we won't leave this place till every last one of those damned creatures lies heaped in a mound!"

24

Imlod exhaled, his breath a plume of mist that swiftly vanished in the frigid air. The untrodden expanse of white still lay before him—yet behind him now stood the ordered ranks of Kûthod's brave fighters, comprised of both wardens and enlisted civilians alike. The war helm from Breladus' tomb lay cradled in his left arm, and his entire body from the neck down was covered in that gloriously shining armor: sleeved and sashed in deep blue-stained cloth. The prime warden had since moved off to the head of another contingent further down the line, but Asalin himself had appeared soon after to wait beside Imlod in Kaledric's stead. Although the aging king had made it clear that he wouldn't be leading his army today, the man was prepared to fight if the fight came to him. He was dressed in ornate scale plate with a tall, stout spear in hand.

The host was silent and still. Neither Asalin nor Imlod had addressed them after they'd formed ranks. No rousing words shouted over their heads aimed at bolstering their courage. No final instructions given on how to deal with their supernatural foes. Every man knew what was approaching. Every man knew what was at stake. All that remained to do was wait...then fight for their lives.

Before long, dots began to sprout from the opposing tree line. Asalin must've noticed this first, for even as Imlod became aware, the king was already pointing with his free hand across the field. "Look there! They come!"

And come they did. There was no order to their ranks. No lines. The first to exit the wood remained the first in the lead, with none halting for their cohorts to form up. They weren't running yet, but each creature moved inexorably forward without the slightest pause at the sight of Kûthod's army set like a bristling wall against them. If anything, the sight only caused them to pick up their pace.

"Prepare to march!"

As Imlod heard Kaledric's shout repeated down the line, he pulled the war helm from the crook of his arm and placed it on his head, securing the mask in place. The sounds of others readying their gear all at once rolled over him like a crashing wave from behind, and he set a hand to *Solitude's* hilt, unsheathing the weapon and holding its blade high for the host to mark.

"Take heart, Imlod!" Asalin raised his voice above the din. "Breladus' spirit fights at your side! Destroy these foul daemons—then we'll find Eldasryn and bring him home!"

Don't fail me this time, my love—whatever the cost! Marinya's cry reechoed in Imlod's mind at the tail of her father's words. *Go and do what must be done.*

In that moment it occurred to Imlod that all his days before had been spent hiding in the dark then slaying and running. *But today there will be no running!* He felt the eyes of the host on him now. A hush had returned as they awaited his command. Slowly he let *Solitude* fall, lowering its point level with the field. "Forward!" he shouted with all the strength of his lungs; then, hoisting his shield from where it'd been propped against one leg, he began the advance.

The enemy came at them from all directions: heedless of tactics, fearless and numb to pain. Kûthod's champion spun and slammed his shield into one's side, knocking its axe free from its skeletal hand and sending the fiend crashing to the ground; though hardly had the snow claimed this one's weapon before another scooped it up, and instead of stepping in to deliver an ending strike to the fallen, Imlod found himself on guard against yet another berserk attack. Nevertheless, the outcome of this encounter was the same as the dozens before it. *Solitude* rose and fell, thrust and swept, disarming the creature before swiftly hacking it down.

Their numbers seemed endless. How many had risen from the lake, and how many had the Brethren animated from the corpses of poor villagers slain along the way? Whatever the tally, it was clear some were either newly raised or had fed more often than others, their bodies ranging from near-raw bone to at least outwardly hale. But this wasn't the time to dwell on such things. It was time to avoid becoming one of them.

The mask of judgment turned this way and that as Imlod sought his next opponent, but when none immediately presented itself, he paused to survey the battlefield. His army seemed to be holding their own. He watched one of the formations threaten to break under the weight of sheer numbers thrown against it, yet at least for now there were enough able bodies to step in and replace the injured or slain. *But what if the dead don't stay down? Where's the Lich?* What if he—or Galfayan herself—appeared and started raising them? Kaledric's scouts had found signs of a camp on the ridge soon after they'd arrived, the embers of its extinguished fires still warm...but those who'd followed the tracks leading out of that camp hadn't returned. There'd been beastly footprints among those tracks. Many. The Queen of Ladd had been here, no doubt. And she was likely still out there somewhere, watching this battle unfold and waiting for the right time to engage.

"Imlod!"

The cry came from a distance, but Imlod heard and swiveled his head toward the sound. A man was pushing and slashing his way through the throng, clearly aimed at reaching Imlod's position. Imlod recognized him at once. It was Layva Helir's guardian, Darengar.

"Follow me!" the warden cried again when he saw he had Imlod's attention. "Kaledric needs aid!"

A moment later Imlod found himself sprinting in Darengar's wake, trailing but a few steps behind as the warden used his sword-staff to scythe a path for them through the fray. His head turned from side to side again as he ran, eyes appraising the action all around him...but it didn't take long for them to reach their destination and the source of Kaledric's troubles.

"There!" Darengar shouted as he slowed to halt, extending his weapon in the direction he wanted Imlod to look.

A wide circle had opened here in the midst of the general fighting. A circle it seemed the undead minions ringing it were trying hard to keep from collapsing: the only organized effort Imlod had seen from them since they'd shambled out of the trees onto this field. Bodies of many dead or dying wardens lay strewn in the circle, with only Kaledric and one other ally still on their feet. And at the center of the ring stood the focus of their attention: a huge, heavily muscled hybrid with a deer's antlered head and a half-naked body splashed and smeared all over with gore. Imlod recognized this warrior too. His sister had displayed the creature to him before they'd left Ramfiram for the desert. *The once-lord of the marsh.* Kordû mo Kar.

"Guard my back!" Imlod shouted then bolted for the circle, not waiting to see if Darengar was even in a position to follow. The undead were swarming thick in this area, and he knew a rally cry here would likely go unanswered. Holding his shield out in front like a battering ram, he smashed through the ring just in time to watch Kordû take the head clean off Kaledric's lone companion — with a swipe from an enormous double-bladed battleaxe — then deliver a thunderous kick to Kaledric's chest that sent the prime warden flying nearly out of the ring.

"Kordû!" Imlod yelled to distract the beast from Kaledric. The monster spun its red-spattered head around, locked a wild eye on him, then loosed a horrible bleating noise before charging.

Imlod leapt forward in answer, thrusting out his shield to meet Kordû's first attack. Seeing the wide arc of his foe's swing, he planned to drive in close after blocking the axe and impale the beast before it could launch a back swing...but when the impact actually came, the staggering power behind it nearly ripped the shield from his arm. Now it was Imlod thrown off balance instead, and he barely recovered in time to dodge the next swipe of Kordû's axe...and the next. Then a fourth swipe came that he caught with his blade. Again Imlod felt an unnatural strength behind the impact, and although he'd gripped *Solitude's* hilt with all his might in anticipation of it, he also nearly lost the sword — and only just managed to deflect the blow. How could a creature so big move so fast? How could Imlod mount an assault of his own when he could hardly counter the unrelenting flurry coming at him?

He thrust out his shield again to block the next wide swing with it...but the beast surprised him in that moment by varying its attack. Kordû raised the axe high overhead then sent it soaring straight down at Imlod's skull with a grunt of exertion; and this devastating strike—with both gravity and the monster's weight adding to the force propelling it—was more than Imlod could withstand. He got his shield up in time only to feel it crash into his faceplate: an explosion of power so potent it whipped his head back and sent the mind inside into blackness. His body fell then like a chopped tree, ending up spread-eagled in the snow.

Impact with the ground snapped Imlod awake just in time for him to see the axe jutting skyward once more: an instant removed from raining down on him like a searing bolt from the heavens. He no longer felt the weight of a shield on his arm with which to defend himself, and only *Solitude's* wrist cord had kept it too from being lost during the fall.

His armored fingers fumbled with the sword's hilt. The axe began to drop...

Desperately Imlod rolled to one side, hoping to hear only the crunch of snow behind as the axe blade missed its mark—but what he heard instead was another ear-splitting bleat coming from Kordû. Flipping onto his back again, he looked up to see the prime warden straining hard against a spear shaft protruding from the creature's gut.

"Die, daemon!" Kaledric screamed as he pushed forward, attempting to drive his weapon's point on through. That skewering would've brought the end of any mortal man, but Kordû mo Kar was no longer mortal. Dropping its battleaxe, the beast gripped Kaledric's spear with both hands, drew out the point from its flesh, then set its legs and twisted its torso with such force that Kaledric went flying off from the opposite end of the shaft: ending up right back at the circle's edge from which he'd charged just moments before.

Seeing a new opening to strike, Imlod stood and prepared to charge forward himself—but was surprised to find he couldn't. *Something* was holding him back, tugging him from behind...and suddenly he was being dragged off by unseen hands at incredible speed toward the forest edge, his feet kicking and arms flailing in a futile attempt to brake. Any bodies in his way were tossed aside as he shot like a hurled boulder through the throng, and the phantoms pulling him by his armor yanked at his blade too, seeking to strip *Solitude* from his grasp. But stubbornly Imlod wouldn't release the sword...doubtful as its use was where he was going.

To his sister or to the Lich. Neither was a welcome option.

Amasmir gazed once more at the man who'd murdered him, and his look was ice. Robed in black, he emerged from the shadows and stepped under branches laden near breaking with snow, face and hands pale as the frost about him; and similar figures appeared now on his left and right to form a half-ring about their master. *Vampires*...with starving eyes and wide smiles revealing the fangs they yearned to bury in hot flesh. And here at last was their prey, down on his knees in the snow. Paralyzed. His head lowered and strength sapped. His will surely broken.

The battlefield was still in sight beyond this clearing in the bordering wood where the Brethren had made their den, but the shouts and clangs of war were muted here as if the area were affected by a spell beyond the Lich's necromancy. And so Amasmir's words came clear, even as he spoke in a low, sinister voice:

"Ah...the son of Nir! All bedecked in finery ill-suited. Long have I awaited this moment. What was it you said to me, boy, on the day you ran me through?"

Engrossed with an inner struggle against the parasitic spirits crippling him, Imlod barely heard Amasmir's words, much less cared to respond.

"You said I should've become a *fisherman*." The Lich halted a single step away from the object of his malice. "Well perhaps I have after all. And look what a big fish I've caught! Laid out helpless on the shore. Unable to escape. Barely even able to breathe. All that remains is to scrape off these scales," he touched a piece of Asalin's armor with obvious distaste. "Then a bite of the meat beneath..."

Imlod was aware of the threat now and saw the other Brethren closing in. If he couldn't stall them, he'd soon be dead with his body sucked dry in the snow. But in his pride Amasmir had made a mistake. He'd failed to relieve the hero of his mystical weapon. "Perhaps you'll defeat us here, Lich...or maybe my death will only speed your end. But why've you done this? In revenge against me and my sister? And for that you'd punish *all*? Galfayan might be insane — but even with the Daemon inside her, she doesn't wish to *exterminate mankind!*"

"*Exterminate*?" said Amasmir, the corners of his mouth turning up in a slight grin. "No...you should've said *preserve* them. Your people's spirits are swaying like the rushes of Lake Diebron. Do you think they can withstand the storm that is *Rhanwŷr returned?* A whirlwind that will rip them from the Mother and leave them flat and rotting beneath stagnant water, bereft of all good use? Don't you see it, child? I merely bring an early harvest, and the next season of man will be stronger for it. If the Father won't rise from the Black Land to aid us, we'll all go down to him! Let the Daemon sit the throne of this world. Sit alone and starve!"

Madness, Imlod thought again but kept it inside this time. Inside where only he and perhaps his pair of leeches could discern it. These two threw curse after curse at him now, desperate to keep the warrior chained down; yet, one by one, Imlod met each assault and foiled it. They cast a shroud of fear over him, and he swept it away. They stuck a sickness into his gut like a poisoned, twisting knife, and he ripped it loose and angrily flung it aside. And the paralysis...

The Lich loosened and discarded Imlod's helm, and one of his hands yanked back on the warrior's dark hair, exposing the bare neck. "And now it's your turn, Imlod." His lips curled up, exposing two elongated incisors; and ever so slowly, as if time had slowed to a crawl, Amasmir leaned in for the kill. Behind him the arc of Brethren tightened, each one lusting for a share of hero's blood. "Perhaps we'll meet again…when my work in this world is done…"

The fangs were nearly touching Imlod's skin before he broke free—but then, all in a wordless moment, he banished the fell spirits from his mind and body, gripped his sword tightly, and thrust it into the Lich's belly with such force that it sliced clean through flesh and bone on its way out between the shoulders. The look on Amasmir's face, just before his pale visage went forever blank, was one of absolute shock. He'd wanted a drink of hot mortal blood, but *Solitude's* power drank his soul instead. And as their controlling master was suddenly gone, the remaining Brethren fell instantly on their faces in the snow, lifeless as stones.

The spell of silence was broken. Blasting through the trees into the clearing first came the savage bleating of what could only be Kordû mo Kar; yet its end came abruptly short of the final note as the beast's now masterless soul followed the Brethren's suit and fled swiftly from its grotesquely altered body: desperate to find the nearest path down to the netherworld. And immediately thereafter, sounding out from patches here and there until the battlefield was alive with it, came the exultant cries from the surviving warriors of Kûthod. Many of their foes had also fallen without having even received a blow.

For the moment—as Imlod returned to the field and wearily propped himself against the outermost tree—it seemed the living would actually triumph over the undead. But that moment was brief. Soon the sky darkened beneath the wings of Galfayan's bats, and wolf-men and boar-men and the like bulled hungrily into the fray, pouncing and charging and flashing cruel weapons of both man-forged metal and native claws, tusks, and teeth. Then those who should've stayed dead stood again under the witch's power, and warden faced warden, and the conflict sped toward its inevitable end.

The end of the Daemon's choosing.

25

"Stop!" cried the witch. "Your king is slain!"

Few were the surviving men of Kûthod who might've ignored that command: those who'd not yet fallen to the undead and become one of them. While Asalin had been among their number, they'd fought on bravely, heedless of the odds — but now the battle was over. Those within sight of the prime warden resisted a few moments longer, waiting to see if he'd wave a banner and shout his own cry to rally them. Yet there was no such call. Kaledric was alive, but there was no fight left in the man. On his knees in the snow. Sword tossed aside. Wide eyes locked on his defeated leader's body as tears welled and began streaming down his face.

"Drop your weapons, and you'll be spared!"

Galfayan's voice seemed to project unnaturally far and loud from her slightly elevated position above the host on an outcrop of stone. A lone island amidst a white sea strewn with carnage. There she stood with one booted foot on Asalin's corpse while raising the spear that'd skewered him overhead. The king's slack right arm was draped over the jutting rock's side, blood dripping from it to feed a growing red circle on the icy ground below.

Still some of Kûthod's warriors hesitated to comply, looking about them for a sign. Was there anyone left to lead them? Where was their champion? The man who'd been entrusted with Breladus' sword? The man who was supposed to use that sacred weapon to remove this foul sorceress' head from her shoulders? Had he stolen the blade and run off with it? Or was he lying somewhere among the heaps of lesser men, his skills no match for the great honor entrusted?

As if on cue, Imlod Nir appeared among them now…and *Solitude* was in his hand. But as with Kaledric, there was no call to arms. No defiant yell as the hero rushed into the scene, scything a path through any foes standing in his way. The man simply approached the outcrop at a slow walk, weapon held low at his side. He still wore Asalin's armor; but the helm was absent, making his identity plain. Dozens of Galfayan's beastly minions turned to eye his progress — as if itching to be loosed upon their enemy in force, to rip his body to pieces and feast on every morsel of his rent flesh and guts. But the witch saw Imlod coming too, and she held her servants back.

"You knew it would end like this, Imlod!" she hailed him, lowering her spear and removing her foot from Asalin's chest. "But you were a fool and chose the losing side! Look at them!" Her free hand swept out over the host, indicating the battered remains of Kûthod's army. "Rounded up like swine, ready to be herded into the pen!"

She paused here, no doubt waiting for Imlod to check his advance and reply to her taunts…but he continued his silent approach instead, unfazed, seeming as though he hadn't heard her. This made Galfayan frown in confusion. She turned her head this was and that, as if scanning the area for some hidden threat. As if concerned her brother knew something she didn't. "Rista!" she snapped. "Bring me the boy."

Eldasryn's nurse came forward hesitantly, head down as if afraid to look her mistress in the face. And one could hardly blame her. The sorceress' appearance had changed dramatically over the course of this battle. Perhaps Galfayan had drawn too much power as she swept in to ruin Kûthod's victory over the Lich, and this was the result of her controlling so many minions at once—or maybe at last Rhanwŷr had emerged from her unchecked. In any case, the witch's graying hair now shown pure silver, and her eyes were pure white: transformed into the same iris-less orbs of her undead creations. The woman's haunting beauty had melted from her, leaving behind a gaunt, sallow mask of horror in its place.

As Rista released her charge and backed away, the man who'd been guarding her then started into motion. Stepping to the outcrop's edge, he dropped to the ground and began a slow walk of his own, seeming as a mirror image to Imlod's approach: save it was a darker reflection heading out to meet the shining hero. A tall figure in spiked black armor, gripping a majestic axe to match the opposing legendary sword. *Sacrosanct* versus *Solitude*. Halting within arm's length of one another, the two warriors stood in silence for a moment. Then Kûhric removed Taloseth's beastly mask and tossed it aside.

The time had finally come.

Yet still the pair hesitated to engage, and Galfayan's frown deepened as Imlod shifted his gaze from her servant to the baby now resting in the crook of her arm. Had she given Kûhric an order to attack, only for it to be *ignored*? A clear look of doubt flashed across the witch's face, but instead of screaming at her minion to obey, she chose to feign control. Perhaps only to buy some time while she fought a mental battle of her own with Kûhric's spirit. Suddenly a dagger appeared in her right hand as she let go the spear, and she held its tip just over Eldasryn's tiny chest. The boy's arms moved beneath his blanket, but he made no sound of protest. "My thanks, brother, for dealing with the rogue Amasmir. You've saved me a bit of trouble…and once more proved your worth. For that, I'm willing to go back on my words and offer you mercy. To give you a choice. If you want Angaras to live, you'll have to defeat Kûhric to save him. And if you can do that, I'll spare you both and return you to a place at my side. Resist further, though— and I'll plunge this blade into the boy's heart!"

"Don't you miss yourself, Galfayan?" asked Imlod calmly, showing no sign of concern for Eldasryn's safety. "Look about you. You've become as the werebeasts you keep, white veils drawn over your gorgeous eyes. Your hair's turned silver, and your skin's pale as snow. What did you hope to achieve? Time and again I warned you of the cost, but you never heeded me. And now at last it's taken you fully, yet left you with *nothing at all...*"

"Nothing?" the witch scoffed, laughing aloud. "Have you taken a wound to the head? Or perhaps the Lich marred your eyes? Today your lectures to me cease. You'll speak no more like some wine-drunk priest of the Mother, ranting about the futility of power. Today I've united all lands east of Ûlinari! Even the heathens of Kagnus will come if I call." She paused a moment here, drawing in a deep breath of self-satisfaction. "Yet all I *shall* achieve is only just begun. A pity you'll not endure to its fulfillment."

"Time and again you've risen, Rhanwŷr," said the hero, "...only ever to be cast down. The next fall draws near. Open yourself to it! Let's end this now!"

Her pets' sudden restlessness betrayed Galfayan's agitation. Some growled and swatted at their battered captives. Others pinned the men already beneath them tighter to the ground. The witch herself touched her dagger's cold tip to Eldasryn's exposed skin. Yet still the baby gave no cry of complaint, snuggled warmly in his fur blanket and peering out with sleepy little eyes.

Imlod's gaze found his boy's face, and after staring at the child a moment he smiled and addressed his sister once more: "Of all the powers you might claim, Daemon — from lordship over the living and dead alike, from the strength to rip stone asunder, to the direction of the moon's course in the dark night sky — you possess no power that may harm *my Son*. His day shall rise on the morning after this Night: a dawn that will see you enthralled!"

Another wave of doubt swept over Galfayan's face, and she looked worriedly at both the blade in Imlod's hand and the baby in her arm. "Enough of this!" she screeched. "Step forth, Kûhric! Strike off this fool's head and let *Sacrosanct* drink his tainted soul!"

But her servant didn't step forth. Instead — as Imlod turned his face to look in his old mentor's eyes one last time — Kûhric parted his lips and spoke of his own accord: "Do you remember that day, Imlod? When the sorcerer came for you? We might've run, but I forbade it. How different our lives might've been, if not for my ignorant pride. None of your sister's torments have ever rivaled the pain of that memory. Will you forgive me, Father? Please...can you help me forget?"

"What are you saying?" the witch shouted at her servant, her fear no longer hidden. She might've stepped forward then herself — but what happened next held her fast.

Imlod chose to release *Solitude* in that moment, and now his feared weapon lay useless on the ground.

All eyes turned once more to him then. Most expected to see the great axe

Sacrosanct rise and fall upon the unarmed champion. But instead — though the effort of will to accomplish it must have been supreme, with the witch's potent screams raining down on him all the while — Kûhric disobeyed again...and his weapon joined *Solitude* in the snow.

Then the Father's hand came to rest on the minion's cheek, and he said softly: "I release you."

Instantly Kûhric's body slumped and hit the ground; and his soul fled away, forever gone beyond the reach of the witch's cruel arts. *'Enraged'* wouldn't have described her mood adequately as she beheld her power broken, and she wasted no time in retaliation:

"Attack! All of you! Tear him apart!"

Yet even as the witch shrieked her commands, her body became covered in shadow; and hardly had she noticed it before the impact came from above: an explosion of force that knocked her flat and sent the baby flying from her arms. Without hesitation Imlod rushed forward to scoop Eldasryn up from the snow where the boy had landed. At last the *'heart of the tower'* began to cry...and for the first time father held son protectively to his chest.

In Mavûl Gorge the boy Imlod Nir had set upon his sister with a stone shard held by a hand of mortal flesh, and on that day she'd proven not so easily killed. Yet today a demigod's teeth ripped open her silky neck as one of Rhanwŷr's own offspring crushed her fragile shell, eager to release his mother's maleficent spirit.

"Revenge!" came Kar's feverish voice as he rose from the kill: nose stained red, blood dripping from his mouth. "Revenge for Kordû, my *chosen!*" Suddenly the peryton became aware of the men and creatures around him and, spreading his feathered wings wide, assumed a threatening stance. Yet even as Galfayan's frothing horde lunged at the offender, one by one each fell short of the target — until in the space of a few breaths there remained not a single undead minion on the field. As the last tusked boar-man skidded to rest, the beast's fist slamming down just shy of Kar's hoofed feet, the shocked faces of all remaining mortals became locked above the peryton's head. There the very fabric of this world was coming apart, and from that rift spewed a mass of black smoke and shadows, swirling upwards to the height of a dozen men before revealing the towering shape behind it. A wave of heat washed over the onlookers, causing many to instinctually raise a warding arm in defense. The smell of brimstone permeated the air.

For but a moment only the image of Rhanwŷr's true form loomed, inspiring a paralyzing fear in any who dared gaze into its fiery eyes. Then Imlod raised his hand again — as if he could reach up and touch the Daemon's cheek just as he'd done to Kûhric before — and at once the hulking figure vanished, dissolving back into the gray mist from which it had materialized. Below, Kar — his wings still spread, chest pushed out now with his back bent and face uplifted — released a deafening cry as the coalescing spirit rained down on *and into* his body: settling rapidly into its new home.

"Beware Kagnus!" screamed Kar-Rhanwŷr as the flames that had lived in the Daemon's scorching glare now melted his eyes and spewed from his hollowed sockets. "Beware the Tower!" Then, quickly as he'd plummeted from the sky to change the course of history, the peryton took to the air again and was soon lost to sight. The trailing smoke of his departure pointed clearly toward the marsh.

The first face he met inside the palace was one of kinship: Almari, elf-maiden, waiting patiently just inside the colossal double-doors. They locked eyes for only a moment before duties pulled them apart. She to hurry forward with a pitcher of water for her red-skinned masters in need of cleansing and refreshment, and he to personally deliver Galfayan's letter to the Desert King. Still, several things passed unsaid between them in that one look. On her half there was immediate recognition of him, even after so many years gone by, and the shock of seeing someone whom she hadn't thought to see again. Her expression was a mixture of pleasure and pain, and he knew the reason for it. She was excited to find him alive and seemingly well but guessed that for him to take one more step within this building might alter one or both of those conditions. Bondage was all she'd ever known, yet *freedom* was no alien concept to her. Why would Cirad return here, foolishly risking the sweet gift of freedom she'd never have?

On his half there was also an immediate recognition of her, yet Cirad wasn't surprised to find Almari performing the same task she'd completed countless times before in their youths. He noticed her lingering discomposure after their shared glance — betrayed only by a slight shaking of her hand as she poured from the pitcher — and quickly checked his emotion. He wouldn't risk any hurt to this fair lady by letting her keepers see her effect on him, so on the outside he made himself as unyielding as the sandstone walls surrounding them.

"Move along..." said his gloomy escort, the one whose name Cirad had since learned was *Zamarian*. Indoors and at eye level, with a fresh cloak thrown over his shoulders, the man was significantly less wild and imposing than when he'd waylaid Galfayan's caravan. As soon as Cirad had heard Zamarian's name, he'd recalled the man from his days of servitude in this land. A man who'd once been a boyhood friend of Galfayan's father Taloseth: the elder prince and rightful heir. *I should try talking to him again. He may prove a supporter, and maybe there are others here too. But I must be careful. The risk is great...*

They were walking again now, having left behind all but two of the warriors who'd accompanied them inside. Cirad and Zamarian strode a few paces ahead of the other pair, affording them some privacy; so if something was going to be discussed before reaching Sanisar's throne, the time was at hand.

"May I speak, lord?"

Zamarian merely glanced at the elf sideways then looked away.

"Don't you remember me? I'm Sûrdandī's child."

"She's dead," Zamarian replied abruptly. And that was it. No details of her demise — or of his father's status or of anything else — seemed forthcoming.

Emotion washed over Cirad. He almost stopped then in his tracks, lost in the memory of his mother's ever kind but troubled face. Should he seek the closest weapon and wreak havoc on these monsters who called themselves *men*? Yet even as he was pondering this, he found himself stopped indeed, having arrived at the dais of Sanisar the Usurper with no recollection of the final stretch to reach it. The fronds and murals. The pools and cushions. His silent kin who shuttled serving trays or waited along the walls. He'd missed it all as sadness, rage, and despair had taken over his mind in turn.

Regaining his bearings, Cirad found a *creature* looming before him: a tall, thin young man wearing an animalistic mask. The youth's slender left arm was half-outstretched, and he waited with his palm upturned while staring at the elf with hidden eyes.

"The letter," came a flat voice from behind the mask. Yet still Cirad made no move to comply nor to utter a single word of greeting to the king. He took note of the naked blade gripped loosely in the lad's right hand compared to his own lacking; then — finally realizing how close he was to the edge of great insult — he reached into his clothing, pulled out Galfayan's missive, and handed it over. *So this is it. The bones are tossed.*

The masked swordsman spun on his heels and began a casual ascension to the throne; and with his gaze never straying from the messenger, Lord Sanisar calmly held out a hand until he felt the smooth parchment touch his skin. Then he snatched the scroll from his servant, broke the seal, and began devouring its contents with ravenous eyes.

Cirad studied the king's face then, ever so carefully, searching for a sign that might reveal evil intent towards him; and as he did so, he scanned the immediate area with other heightened senses, mapping out a sequence of swift retaliation should the worst come. There'd be no escape, he knew…yet a heaping platter of *vengeance* lay but a short leap and two rapid maneuvers away. *At least you'll die with me, Sanisar.* Zamarian was right next to him. The old man's weapon within Cirad's easy reach. And at Sanisar's side was most likely a brash youth untested by true skill, holding another blade that Cirad might make his own. Many other armed guards were present, but they were neither close enough nor standing at the ready. *The deed might be done before their spears even lower on me.*

"I've forgotten your name," said Sanisar, wearing a grin as he peeled his eyes from the letter to look its deliverer in the face.

Amused? How could he be? Cirad had rather expected a fit of rage as the king's reaction to Galfayan's unveiled claim to his kingdom. *Even if he puts no substance to it, shouldn't he still be incensed?*

"Is the elf mute, then, Zamarian? Or does he wish to be beaten?"

"My name is Cirad, lord," he responded at last, overloud, making no effort to disguise his anger at the king's crude threat. "I didn't expect you'd remember it. You were a young man when I left this place." *And now you're old and shriveling, before even your frail race's normal time, looking the very image of your wicked father in that seat.* "Many years have passed — and I have another master now. What say you to her words?"

Sanisar chuckled at that. "You don't know what's written here, do you? Your mistress speaks more like her grandfather than my brother." Suddenly his face went flat. "I'm impressed."

Cirad's confusion was evident, but before he could respond...

"Here." The king tossed the letter to him. "Read it yourself."

A moment passed with Cirad's eyes locked on Sanisar's deadpan stare, then the elf gave in and opened the scroll. Silently he read:

Greetings, Uncle. You must be displeased to have my words from parchment rather than from me in the flesh. I assure you this was not according to plan. We have many things to discuss, you and I. But alas, for now a pressing matter draws me back home. Prepare to receive me again soon! Until then, I imagine you shall find good use for the bearer of this letter. He was once an elf-slave. Surely he recalls his duties...

There were a few more lines beyond this point, but Cirad hardly registered them. *Deceiving whore! You think to toss me aside? Just like Kordû? To return me to a bondage worse than undeath?* Buying time to calm himself and focus on what he had to do now, he pretended to still be reading. Yet in the midst of finalizing his suicidal plot, another thought occurred to him. *What if she* wants *this? She knows I wouldn't throw my life away with a clear head. Think! Don't fall into her trap!*

Perhaps sensing Cirad's delay, Sanisar motioned for his guards to lay hands on the elf, and they approached their would-be prisoner without hesitation from three of four sides. There was but a single path open to Cirad beyond an armed escort to the slave quarters, and he had only an instant to decide his course. Up ahead the young attendant's bearded mask seemed almost to grin; but otherwise the lad didn't move. His blade still hung low as if there were no danger at all.

With a speed few mortals could ever hope to match, Cirad shot out a hand for

Zamarian's hilt, took the sword for his own, and sprang up the dais without a cry or word of warning. Twice the blades of Cirad and Erathiel met and parted there in a blur before the contest was done. Then the defeated elf tumbled back down the steps, coming to an abrupt stop beneath a ring of waiting spears. The deadly points closed within thumb's length of his body.

For a moment it appeared Cirad was either dead or stricken unconscious, but soon he turned his face from the stone floor to the throne with a look of shame and disbelief, one hand coming up to touch his bleeding lip: the only wound he seemed to have taken beyond a thunderous blow to his pride. Above, the victor assumed his previous stance, looking as if the brief duel had never occurred; and the king's cold eyes gazed down upon his new slave at the foot of the dais:

"So now you see, elf—just as my niece soon shall—that it's of no use to strive against the Desert. Whatever weapons you hurl will merely pass us by in vain, touching nothing but the wind of the sandstorm. Yet each grain of sand is bitter sharp…and the storm won't leave you unscathed!"

Zamarian, having retrieved his sword from the steps where it fell, bent and placed his hand on Cirad's arm to help the stunned elf rise. The guards on the left moved aside to clear the way towards Cirad's kin along the wall and to the door leading off to the slave quarters beyond them. Male and female. Young and old alike. All stood there still as statues with their thoughts locked on the scene before them but with their eyes averted from it. Cirad stared at them a moment, felt the old man's grip tighten on his arm, then turned his eyes back to Sanisar as Zamarian began leading him away. "This changes nothing, Usurper!" he lashed out with words alone, offering no further resistance to his fate. "You don't know what comes for you!" He was on his way to the door now, yelling back over one shoulder. "She'll have your heart on a plate! Drink your blood from a golden cup!"

Rising slowly from his chair, the Desert Lord lifted his voice for the benefit of all: "Go and rot in your elf-den, *slave*, as the storm blows the sands of Agrigoth into the East. We'll not wait for your queen to come!"

26

Imlod Nir stood off from the others on the mound, holding his son pressed to one shoulder and gently patting the baby's back. Not long removed from Rista's breast, Eldasryn would soon be asleep if not already. The tiny hands that'd been opening and closing moments ago had finally ceased their movement. The little chest rose and fell in an slow, steady rhythm.

Imlod turned his gaze again from the nestled child to the scene before him. Kaledric was at his sister's side now and had pulled Kedaynna into a consoling hug. The beautiful woman's eyes were filled with tears over the death of her king and lover — but to her credit, she hadn't lost composure. Asalin wouldn't have wanted that. They'd dressed their fallen ruler in finery and sat him on his vined throne one last time for all of Thaekith's citizens to gather and see. For a show of collective respect from those he'd governed and protected so long. *He wouldn't have wanted this either. But the dead rarely have their say.*

To Kaledric's right stood the Keeper, Layva Helir, staring at the corpse of the man who'd once called her his queen and given her a precious daughter only to later cast her aside. Her expression was also sad, but Imlod hadn't noticed any wetness in her eyes or on her cheeks. Perhaps the well of tears she'd once filled for Asalin had dried up long ago. Her warden Darengar had survived the battle and was standing beside her, though the man was heavily bandaged and leaning on his sword-staff for support.

Most of the others circling the throne were unknown to Imlod. Ministers or nobles or such. The time to make their acquaintances was coming soon. They would want to see their new boy-king and introduce themselves to the regent, his father. They'd want to make their positions heard, attempt to gain Imlod's favor…and perhaps resubmit petitions that'd been earlier declined, hoping for different outcomes. Some might even want to slip a knife into his gut instead: like the girl who'd called him a murderer in this very spot before the battle.

And it was true. *Today I'm a hero, but they'll always whisper of what I was before. Marinya was right. Only our son can flee Galfayan's shadow.* Glancing at Eldasryn again, Imlod noticed Asalin's ring on his own finger. Kaledric had presented it to him earlier without any speech or ceremony, but the gesture's meaning was understood. The prime warden — and thus all Kûthod's wardens — would obey Imlod's commands. There would be no challenge here to Eldasryn's legitimacy and right to future rule. For a time, the regent and his son would know peace.

Somehow it still felt strange to hold the baby close. To finally have a living and breathing family of his own like he'd imagined: even though it was missing its third member. He and Marinya had given their lives to see Eldasryn brought to this place of safety and solace…but Imlod knew this was only the start. The beginning of another story. One he'd been brought back to ensure would unfold as it was meant to unfold. How many more people would die before the tale was truly ended? When and where would the killing begin anew? Or could it be that Eldasryn was destined for something greater than war and death? Whatever the answers, Imlod's mission was as clear as the meaning behind the gift of Asalin's ring: no man, beast, or daemon would lay a hand on his son in harm till the boy was of age to steer his own fate. And even then Imlod would stay by Eldasryn's side...for as long as he was wanted and able.

Someone cleared a throat nearby, and Imlod swiveled his head to find Gilal standing there. The old minister from Taudan had somehow emerged from the battle unscathed and presented himself to the new regent in its aftermath, citing the link to Eldasryn and his debt to Imlod as reasons to remain in Kûthod—for now. As their eyes met, Gilal stepped close to whisper: "Kirath waits for you in the garden...along with another."

Another? Imlod raised an eyebrow quizzically, but the old man just pointed with his chin back over his shoulder, indicating the regent should accompany him from the grove. After sweeping his gaze around the area to check that he wasn't the focus of too much attention, Imlod nodded then looked to Rista and bade her follow them. The young nurse dutifully held out her arms to take the sleeping baby, but Imlod only grinned and shook his head 'no.' The strangeness of holding Eldasryn wouldn't subside by handing him over at every opportunity.

The three figures turned to depart, and Thaekith's citizens gave way as they passed through the crowd.

Kaledric had set wardens at intervals around the garden's hedged perimeter to dissuade uninvited guests: those citizens who hadn't heard the area was now closed to the public—or else who knew but would pry all the same. The lure of an evil sorceress' corpse alone would be enough to draw many to this place. To point and whisper and stare at a dead witch. But Galfayan had been much more to Thaekith than that. She'd been their enemy. The force behind the Lich and his invading undead army and the reason why so many of Kûthod's brave fighters had perished. The woman who'd put a spear through their beloved king's heart. Imlod guessed more would come with the intent to burn his sister's body than to merely gape at it. Men who desired to act on their unquenched hatred and fear of the supernatural. Those who held a justifiable belief that as long as Galfayan's flesh lay intact there was a risk of her return.

The wardens stationed at the main entrance saluted Imlod then bowed their heads in respect as he passed through carrying Eldasryn with Gilal and Rista in tow. Once inside, the party made their way to the spot where Imlod had earlier directed the bodies of his sister and Kûhric Besh to be laid out on the icy ground; and as they drew near, they met the faces of two figures seated on a stone bench beside the corpses. His friend Kirath Sevos — as Imlod had expected — joined by the same girl who'd been in his thoughts just before he left the grove. *Tyth.* The young woman whose family he and Kûhric had butchered in Diebron. She was looking right at him...eyes wide, mouth a straight line...as if she'd been caught off guard and wasn't sure how to react. She'd not been afraid to lash out on the day she'd denounced him before the host, but perhaps it would be different now without the crowd to shield her. Perhaps now...seeing Imlod up close again as she had that night on the crannog...

"So," Kirath spoke first, his focus also on Imlod, "...how was it?"

"As expected."

There was an awkward pause here. Kirath seemed to be aware of the tension between Imlod and the young lady beside him. He'd likely been talking with her since Gilal left to fetch Imlod until just a moment ago: long enough to have heard all her story...and perhaps to have shared his own losses with her. The warrior's face was still mottled with bruises from the beating he'd taken trying to save his father in Ramfiram, and now his only sibling lay dead at his feet. The Brethren had dragged him along on their unholy march from the Womb, naming him a hostage to ensure his mother — the high priestess Sevos Let — would continue to hold the city in Amasmir's name. But after the Lich had been dealt with and the battle won, Imlod had returned to the Brethren's grove to find not only corpses but his longtime friend gagged and bound to a nearby tree. They'd since spent some time catching up on everything that'd happened after their last meeting weeks before.

"Imlod...this is Tyth," Gilal announced at last. "We met her at the entrance earlier. She came seeking a chance to speak with you..."

"He knows me. He killed my family."

The girl's words had come out softly, matter-of-fact, and Imlod found that he had no answer. Maybe it would've been better had she jumped up and spit and cursed at him and slapped him in the face or beat at him with her fists. Perhaps his holding Eldasryn had restrained her from such behavior — or maybe it'd been something Kirath had said to her before his arrival. In any case, Imlod's lack of response brought another awkward pause, but this time it was Kirath who broke the silence:

"Easy, now." He turned to her and placed a comforting hand on her shoulder. "Remember what I said. Imlod and I've had kin stripped from us, too. We know what you've endured. The one who caused your pain lies there at our feet." He indicated Galfayan's corpse with a glance and a nod. "Yet she was *our sister,* and we mourn her all the same."

Tyth turned her head to stare at Galfayan then, causing the others present to do the same. Imlod couldn't guess what the girl was thinking, but as for himself, he marveled once more at the change in his sister's appearance that'd occurred soon after her death. A metamorphosis from the abominable creature that had hailed him from atop the stone in those final moments of conflict to her natural, youthful beauty. A similar reversion to what he'd first experienced with Kûhric some days prior to the battle. He'd already arranged to give Kûhric a warden's funeral here in Thaekith, but Galfayan didn't belong in this place. This wasn't her home, and Kûthod's people wouldn't suffer her burial here. He'd have to let them burn her to ash...or else take her away.

"Nothing I can say will erase your loss," Imlod finally addressed Tyth, "...yet I'm truly sorry for it. Galfayan gave the order to take Amasmir, that's true—but I should've found another way. I didn't have to kill those people."

She looked up at him then. "And that's why you should be judged for it."

"I should."

"That's enough," said Kirath, suddenly standing as if to leave, "...wouldn't you say, Imlod? The girl's no fool, and I've made the situation plain to her. It's time to bury the past with these bodies. She has a brother to look after, and you have your son." He found Tyth's eyes and spoke the last directly to her. "Her *king*..."

Gilal nodded his agreement. It didn't matter whether the regent had single-handedly butchered entire villages or cavorted with devils or whatever else in the past. Today he was the boy-king's father and guardian. The man who slew the Lich with Breladus' sword then called a winged beast down from the sky to destroy an evil sorceress. The reality behind the latter deed would mean as little now as would Imlod's earlier transgressions. There'd be no trial for Imlod Nir.

"He's not *my* king!" Tyth snapped at last.

"As long as you stay here, he is!" Kirath threw back.

Gilal stepped closer, touched Kirath's arm lightly to calm the man, then eased himself down beside Tyth in the same spot Kirath had just vacated. "Where are you from, young lady?"

"Lake Diebron...past the river, to the north. We've no king there. Only the overseer. We came here seeking aid."

"I see..." the minister pursed his lips and ran a hand down his white beard. "But perhaps now it's safe to return? Don't forget: the same man you condemn here made it so."

"Return to what? An empty home?" Tyth held the old man's gaze firmly, daring him to answer.

But Imlod replied instead. "No, she's right. She shouldn't go there. She needs a fresh start. If not here—because of me—then somewhere else new to her. The Womb, perhaps."

That seemed to pique the girl's interest. "Ramfiram?"

"That's right," said Gilal. "Kirath's mother rules there now. Have you been there before?"

A moment passed before Tyth replied. "Once." Her expression had changed. Frown fading. Eyes widening in consideration—maybe even with a glimmer of hope in them. "Hadric would like that...but..." She sighed and shook her head slowly as if debating something with herself, then bit her lip as if fighting back tears. "I don't know..."

"No need to answer right away," the minister spoke again. He glanced up at Imlod for approval and, receiving a nod in reply, looked back to Tyth. "Think on it tonight and tell us your decision in the morning. How does that sound?"

Tyth sniffled then wiped at her eyes with both hands. She took a deep breath and released it, and some of her tension seemed to float away. "It sounds good."

She rose then from the bench with a clear intention to depart, and the others standing before her stepped aside to let her pass. Imlod looked at Tyth with lips parted as if he might have something else to say; but she purposely avoided his gaze and kept her eyes fixed straight ahead.

"That one's strong," said Kirath after Tyth was out of hearing but while their eyes were still on her retreating form. "I wonder if it's wise to set her free on her own. Years and leagues might not dull her need for vengeance."

"They won't," said Imlod. Then, gently peeling Eldasryn from his chest and shoulder, he stared at the sleeping child's face and smiled.

Epilogue

Night was fast settling over the marsh, the last rays of day abandoning the five weary travelers who stood gazing out to a point in the distance. Soon they must turn back to their camp for the evening, yet for now the view's spell was too strong for them to break. Across a sea of reeds and grasses swaying in the breeze, past winding creeks and ponds dotting the flat landscape, a single stone structure stood tall near the horizon. Its summit pierced the sky like a spear.

The Tower of the Sun.

At last someone broke the silence: "We should light the fire now, Kirath," Gilal offered over his shoulder as he made for the spot they'd prepared earlier, "...while you can still find the tinder."

"We should go without," Kaledric interjected just as Kirath turned to comply. But the prime warden hadn't been speaking to Gilal. His face was fixed on Imlod instead. "There could be someone out there watching—even eyes from the tower itself."

Imlod sighed as if frustrated with Kaledric's concern, but he squinted at the tower all the same. *Were* there any portals up there, far above the ground? He knew the history of this place—how the Kagnians shunned it, leaving it uninhabited—but considering Kar-Rhanwŷr's cryptic warning to the host on the battlefield, he couldn't blame Kaledric for being cautious. "If anyone's here to see our fire, we'll meet them regardless. Either tonight or tomorrow. We'll set a watch till dawn, though...just in case."

A moment passed without answer from the warden, causing Imlod to turn his head. Kaledric was frowning as if not quite convinced, but he nodded all the same: "As you wish, lord." Then he strode off to assist the other men.

That left only Rista at Imlod's side with Eldasryn bundled and strapped to her breast. The regent looked her way now and received a weary smile in response. It reminded him of how Marinya had grinned at him in their final hour together in life. This young woman was also brave and strong and seemed to have taken to her charge as if the baby were her own—and there was a hint in her eyes that she might like to take the boy's father as her own too. *Someday, maybe. If we live through tomorrow, and the world remains unchanged.* Imlod reached out and rubbed Eldasryn's little bald head. "I'll take the first watch but come for him afterwards. You need to sleep."

"I'm fine, my lord. Really...it's fine." She glanced down at the drowsy child and gave him a peck on the forehead. "I'll feed him now, then we'll lie down for the night." Another grin. Wider this time.

Imlod reciprocated the smile and nodded his thanks before turning away. He let the men know his intention, gathered a few provisions, then moved off to find a spot that would afford him a good view of the camp once the moon and stars lit the sky. Spring had come at last, but the nights were still cold, so he draped his cloak about his shoulders before settling down in a new picked location.

The group had traveled swiftly to reach this final destination in Kagnus, the one exception being their stopover of a few days in Ramfiram; and as Imlod sat removed from the camp and watched Kirath building up the fire, he recalled his reunion with Sevos Let during that visit. His business in Ladd had been official, with him playing the role of ambassador come to secure peace between emerging régimes. It'd been risky to present himself to the high priestess in her reclaimed position of authority, regardless of his own new station, for not so long ago he'd been the woman's captor and the slayer of her followers and kin. Fortunately for him, though, Sevos' elevation had only reinforced her desire to place her people's welfare above any selfish vendetta. She'd spoken harsh words and threats at the beginning of their meeting, but by the end the priestess and regent had seen eye-to-eye.

Not so with her and Kirath. That pair still had some mending to do, for the memory of offered poison yet lingered between them. With the passing of one's father and sister and the transfer of power to the other, their fortunes had been reversed, and that'd left Kirath in a similar position to Imlod's as the two men approached Sevos' high seat in the temple.

This last image reminded Imlod of the times he and Kirath had knelt before Galfayan on that same dais awaiting instruction. Reaching into his clothing, he fished out a leather pouch then withdrew from it a remnant of his past. Holding the goddess figurine before his face and rolling it back and forth in appraisal — just as Kûhric had first shown it to him in Weth long ago — he considered the gift once more. No longer should he look upon this object and see his sister and her sibling hunters there: for at last those days were gone. But could he yet read in it again the true, intended symbolism? And if he were able, should he focus on the Mother's smile of promise or else the warning in her eyes?

Imlod Nir...

The regent's own eyes widened at the faint voice, and he froze, awaiting more words to come. Still gazing at the figurine, he thought for a moment that Mother Earth herself was calling; but soon as the voice repeated itself in his now-focused mind, he knew its true owner. *I hear you, Sigeya. Why have you found me? What's wrong?*

Wrong? the nymph sent back. *Nothing's wrong. Not here, at least. Sienda and I are well — as are those you left behind. The high priestess kept her word.*

Good. The ones Imlod had left behind were Tyth and her brother Hadric, and Sevos had promised to find the pair a proper home in the city. *What is it, then? Another foretelling?*

Not this time. A veil's been drawn before Eldasryn's future since you departed for Kagnus. Rhanwŷr's doing — or else the work of a thing more powerful still. Perhaps some primordial force emanating from the tower itself. No...what I've to tell lies closer to your heart. It's Marinya...

You found her? Surprise and excitement were conveyed with Imlod's sending. He'd discussed this topic with the nymphs face-to-face in Thadda, but he hadn't expected them to actually succeed where he'd already failed several times. His mastery of the netherworld should surpass any other's, after all. Was he not Ûl-Kamûn reborn? Owner of the door between this world and the next? In truth, though — despite having ascended another step towards oneness with the Father at the battle's end — Imlod remained only an augmented version of himself. He knew he could reach deep and draw upon Kamani's voice and power at will, yet with that strength didn't come the knowledge of a god. If he chose, he could see the Father's realm through the Father's eyes, but Kamani's thoughts hadn't mixed with his own. The sisters were ancient immortal beings, however, possessed of arcane wisdom and centuries' worth of practiced abilities. Why should he have ever doubted them?

Yes, Sigeya replied. *But not where you assume. Her spirit's left Kamani's realm. She's been reborn into this world.*

Imlod's immediate response to the revelation was to question *'where?'* and *'in what form?'* — but instead of sending it to the nymph, he paused as other thoughts followed. Even if Marinya had returned a human, she'd be a newborn younger than Eldasryn and would retain no knowledge of Imlod and her past life. No, he mustn't ask those questions. He had to face reality: Marinya was now lost to him forever.

Imlod? Are you there?

My thanks, Sigeya. But please...that's all I need to know. Do you understand?

I do.

Imlod's link to the nymph fell silent after that. He needed a moment to clear memories of his lost lover from his head. Should he say goodbye to Sigeya now, or was there something else to discuss? If there'd been no divination, then nothing had changed since he last spoke with the sisters on their isle. Absently he began returning the Goddess to her pouch; but in doing so, he noticed Asalin's ring on the hand that released the figurine. Was this heirloom indeed the key to unlock his son's future, as the nymphs had foretold in Thadda? What awaited Eldasryn in the tower's heart, and why had Kar-Rhanwŷr cried out to beware this place? Had it been the last warning of the being Kar *was*, a desire to protect the race of men from meddling with a force they might be unable to control? Or had it been simply a threat birthed from the Daemon's rage and fear? Would Kar-Rhanwŷr be there waiting for him tomorrow, eager to bring an end to unfinished business?

The regent's thoughts drifted then and at last—though he'd tried to avoid it—settled on Marinya once more. He saw her spirit hovering above the lake of fire. He heard her words to him: "...*it's your son, not you, who can renew the world.*" But what did the world have in store for them? What was there to renew? Galfayan was dead, yet the Daemon lived on, having passed into yet another host—and this time into the body of a lesser daemon: a true child of the Moon with innate powers of his own. Had the real battle against Rhanwŷr not yet even begun?

The silence lingered in Imlod's skull, and the only noises in the world around him were the buzz of insects and murmurs coming from his companions in the camp. A sudden series of loud pops from their fire pulled Imlod from his trance. How long had he sat lost in thought, brooding on the past and the days to come? At some point Sigeya must've realized he'd say no more, for their connection was broken. Imlod stared now at the campfire's licking flames. Someone was poking a stick in the hot coals to stir it. *Kirath.* Would his friend become reconciled with Sevos after this journey was over, and was Kirath ready to play warlord for the high priestess in Bablak's stead? Would Ladd be fit to act as a shield against the coming storm should it suddenly blow in from Kagnus, giving Kûthod time to revive?

An hour passed, then another...and at last Imlod heard Kaledric calling his name. He rose to meet the approaching figure, giving away his position as the warden scanned the area with a torch in hand. Having thus been relieved, the regent made his way back toward the dwindling campfire then on to the spot where he'd seen Rista bed down earlier. The woman didn't speak or stir as he drew near, so rather than risk waking her by plucking the baby from her arms, he settled for lying down beside them.

As sleep began to take hold, Imlod's fading thoughts summoned an image of Lake Thadda's vast dark water, and he saw himself drifting again on its smooth surface, alone in a two-oared boat. A covered bundle lay in the hull at his feet, and he stared at it now, reliving the scene just as it'd happened. In a moment his hand would grab the sheet and pull it away, revealing his sister's remains; then he'd gather up Galfayan's disjointed bones and drop them overboard, reverently depositing her in the Womb.

Morning came and went, and still the group labored hard to reach the tower. After spending hours trudging and wading through unaccommodating wetland, they were in the final stretch now, and they could see the red-gold slab barring entry to the structure. One might've expected an open portal with just a hint that a door had ever been in place: for as both Gilal and Imlod attested, clearly nature had reclaimed this area long ago—if it'd ever been inhabited at all. But instead the metal barricade facing the party looked as daunting to them as did the tower itself. Tiny by comparison, but unmarred and seemingly unyielding as the white stone embedding it, with no sign of hinge or bolt or any other feature that might be exploited to gain access.

Emerging one-by-one from the final grassy pond impeding their progress, the travelers gathered on dry land now, standing mere strides from their goal. Gilal was last to join them, breathing hard and leaning on his staff for support, but he hadn't voiced any complaint along the way. Imlod turned his eyes from the old man to Eldasryn as the baby wiggled in his arms. Rista had chosen to come too, but the regent hadn't allowed her to carry the burden of his child today.

"Look there," said Kaledric, drawing all eyes to the thing at which he pointed.

Halfway between the arrivals and the tower, an osprey had just landed. The bird stood watching them with its head cocked to one side quizzically, showing no sign of fear. The regent stared at the bird, and for a moment it held his gaze. Then it turned and glanced at the tower before looking to Imlod again. Almost as if saying 'what are you waiting for?'

With the child-king resting in the nook of his right arm, Imlod strode past the osprey to stand before the metal barrier. On the ring finger of his left hand was the key, its serpentine head circling round to sink fangs in its own tail.

He raised his palm and placed it flat against the door.

DOOMBRINGER

DAEMON RISING, BOOK TWO

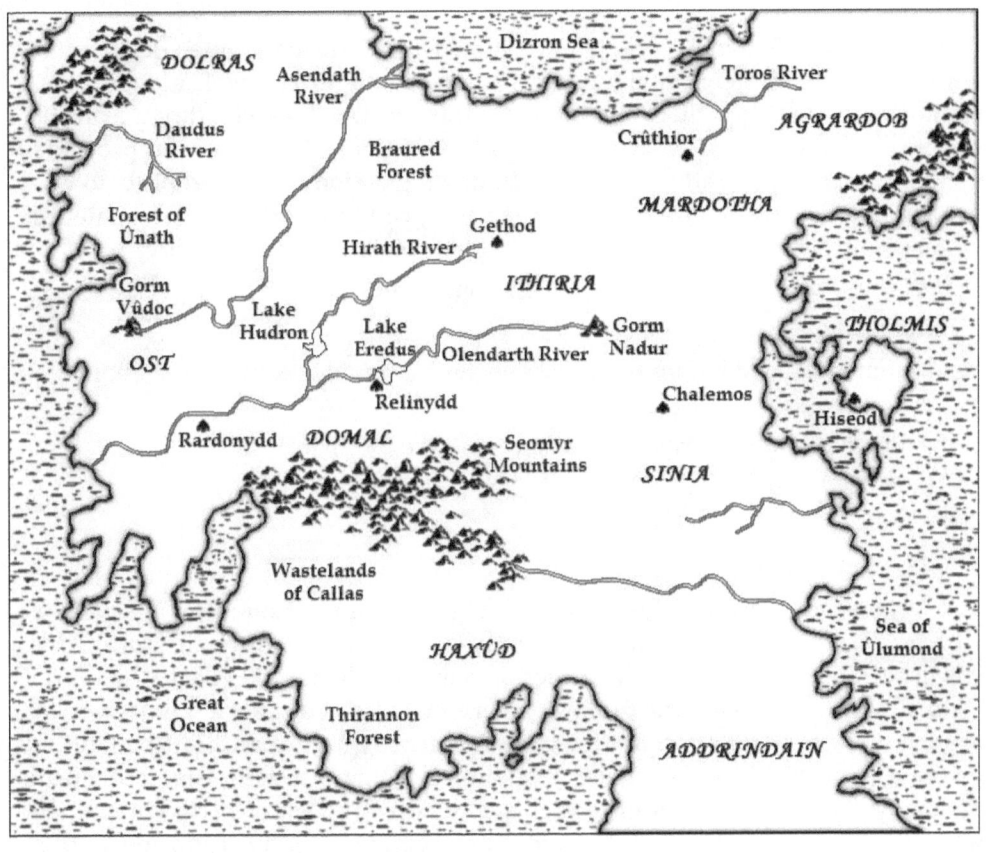

Prologue

"Who are you?"

"I'm Voret, son of Idra," Baeldrin lied. "And you are..."

"The librarian."

Baeldrin shuffled in his seat. Before him, across a dusty wooden desk, sat a withered figure, beaten down by time, bent over by age. His skeletal hands lay resting on the desktop, their bulging veins transporting blue blood past arthritic fingers and on into the sleeves of his dark brown cloak. His bald head protruded forward and hung slightly to one side, bestowing an inquisitive property to his person; but his pale green eyes exuded a condescending and oppressive intellect obtained only by traveling the long and bittersweet road of experience.

"As I see," said Baeldrin. "But what's your name?"

No response.

A moment lapsed before the visitor began again. "I've come to ask about ephemeral revelations."

"And what is an *ephemeral revelation*?" said the old man.

"I was told you knew."

"By whom?"

"That's of no consequence."

"Perhaps not," said the librarian, grinning, his laughter sounding more like a wheeze. The man's bony head oscillated back and forth, slightly, uncontrollably. His lips drew up, revealing a near-toothless mouth, then settled back down. "You already know what the thing is. Everyone does. But only a scholarly man has the capacity to question it." He gave Baeldrin a queer, disconcerting look before continuing. "An ephemeral revelation is ironic, you see? Greater than an epiphany, it encompasses your thoughts, emotions, and actions. A split moment when they all agree. It's a bolt of inspiration, cognition, enthusiasm, and genius. But it's profound! As soon as it comes to you...why, it's gone. Gone, I tell you, and the average man returns to his meaningless task and his mundane existence with thunderous confusion and dejection reverberating in his mind."

The librarian slowly retracted one unsteady hand, opened the topmost desk drawer, and pulled from it a long, narrow pipe. He stuck the tip to his dry lips. A flame touched the bowl, and the smell of spent tobacco was displaced by the soothing aroma of new-burning leaf. His head steadied as the small room filled with smoke. Baeldrin waited patiently until the elder began again:

"The wise man, however, pathetically clings to it, searches for it, pretends he understands it, and attempts to compose or act upon it — whatever *it* may be." He leaned back in his chair, musing, but then grimaced, returning to his original position. "And this afterthought is the measure of man."

The smoke hung dank and motionless from the ceiling, and the shadows in the room shifted as the sun's rays fell to earth unobstructed. The clouds outside had broken. The flat bars on the room's solitary window arrayed the bright light in a checkered pattern across the opposite wall.

"What if one could harness these revelations? Call upon them at will?" the visitor questioned. His countenance displayed not the slightest emotion.

"What? Ridiculous! Haven't you been listening?" A scowl came across the librarian's face. "No one even knows what they are..."

"The explanation you gave seems good enough."

"Just words, like all these." The old man's finger swung around, indicating the books that engulfed every square inch of solid wall. Most appeared as if they would disintegrate upon touch: a thick layer of dust was bedded on their jackets. "Besides, I gave you a *definition* — the best one that I could — not an *explanation*. Explanations are particular."

"You're truly wise," said the visitor, beginning to rise from his seat as if he were now fully answered and the brief discussion had reached its end.

"If you really believe that, then heed my advice," said the librarian. "Forget these occurrences and return to the mundane. Searching, groping, and obsessing over them will leave you trapped in the dark confines of your mind. Objectivity will strip the wonder from your life and empty your soul. The variegated world out there will become monochromic to you. Gray as your cloak and miserable as a storm cloud."

Baeldrin snorted at that, shaking his head slightly from side to side. And with the motion came a sudden change in his expression: a mocking sneer to replace the stone face he'd worn into the room along with the false name. "A wonder, then, that you've managed to endure so long." Looming over the desk, he moved a hand into the folds of his cloak, eyes gleaming with an unmistakable sinister intent.

The librarian stared at the man before him. "So," he spoke after a moment's pause. "My time's come at last..."

Baeldrin circled the desk and crouched beside the elder. Pulling his dagger free, he held it loosely downward with forearm resting on knee. "Yes. The time has come."

"And the ephemeral revelations?" the librarian asked, staring across the desk at the empty chair.

"The conversation served its purpose. I know what you're hiding here, old man. *Where are they?*"

The librarian slowly turned his head towards Baeldrin, and — with it framed in the incandescent window — his green eyes became black bulbs. Trembling, he spoke with contempt: "You already know."

"Indeed," said Baeldrin as he thrust the dagger hard into the victim's body just under the elder's rib cage. A sharp grunt and short, low moan escaped the librarian's lips. Then it was done. Straight to the heart.

Removing his bloody weapon with equal force, Baeldrin folded the corpse over on the desk and wiped the dagger across its back. His free hand gripped purposefully about the librarian's neck, found what it sought, and yanked loose his prize. The broken cord was threaded through a fur-lined leather pouch. He pinched this between thumb and forefinger, felt two small lumps inside, smiled, and closed his hand around it. Then, returning the blade to his cloak and pulling up his hood to hide his face, he left the room.

The streets were bustling with people. Baeldrin faded into the crowd.

PART ONE

1

It was nothing more than a prick in that fathomless black orb—the blazing globe of life caught and reflected in the corner of her pet's eye—yet its rays had given birth to the warm draft on which the great bird now hovered and soared. Waves of searing heat danced along the bare red walls beneath and beyond the divide, distorting all about her save the clear azure sky. Shrill cries ripped the air above, piercing her ears before rebounding from the cliffs down into the valley far below.

Motionless as the stone tower beneath her feet, the woman named Saedus of Ost followed from the rim the hawk's every circle and dive. Her eyes, gray as winter dawn, should've been shielded from the blinding sun by lovely white hands. But they weren't. They were opened wide instead, unblinking, staring at the cruel points of beak and talon, lost in the flutters of wingtip and fantail. And though indeed she looked upon these things, she didn't see them—for her spirit reached out and usurped the sight of her bird, making its keen, wide view her own.

"It walks the river," she spoke suddenly aloud then returned as swiftly to silence: her only welcome for the imposing figure approaching from behind. A man with flowing raven hair climbed the final steps of the tower's winding stair, his thick chest and broad shoulders hardly clearing the portal without causing a break in his kingly stride. A curved ebony horn hung at his waist, rim banded in etched gold, and his rich crimson-stained garments reeked of the black herb. His expression was calm.

"Such is the habit of restless shades, I'm told," said the man.

"Not a shade, Baeldrin," replied the sorceress, lowering her gaze. "A ghoul. And one of great power." The hawk circled high once more, screeched, and flew out of sight. Saedus turned as it did so, adding: "One with a hunger that can't be sated."

Baeldrin couldn't help noting the correlation. The captivating being before him was referred to in some circles as the *Spider,* and indeed she seemed akin to the widow spiders of the north: a species whose females devoured the males as soon as their usefulness was ended. Baeldrin no longer questioned that Saedus was using him. So long as his due was delivered, he'd serve the Daemon herself, even if that cost him his soul and more. But he'd not be consumed by this witch. There'd soon be a measure in place to ensure his protection.

"You'd hand over my glory to this wayward soul, then?" he said at last, turning his thoughts back to the present.

"I'll honor our arrangement." The sorceress narrowed her devilish eyes and fixed them on her guest. "*As shall you.*" Though the man eclipsed her by nearly a head and wore the countenance of an imperious monarch, it was clear who ruled here in the stone tower.

This wasn't Baeldrin's first visit to the *Spider's* kingdom as a result of their *arrangement*; nor would it be the last. Her barbaric realm shared a border with his native Domal — Ost's larger and more civilized neighbor to the south — and a journey here and back home again for him could be accomplished well within a week: easily concealed by the pretense of a hunting expedition or some other innocent jaunt to the backlands. Each time he made the trip he felt the witch's invisible threads constricting tighter about him, and again now he contemplated just how tangled in her web he'd become.

With her own mind wrapped around harvesting a new prize from the river below, Saedus had been swift to dismiss Baeldrin's concern regarding his role in their upcoming plans. Yet, moving now to descend the stair, she offered him a consolation in passing: "Remember this, prince. Your father's throne will be of little use to you, should you find yourself lying broken on the battlefield, trodden beneath enemy heels..."

Baeldrin watched the sorceress fade from view then strode from under the alcove to the parapet wall and gazed out over the Forest of Ûnath. Legend had it that in ages past, the Daemon had cut the river through those trees as a route for lost souls to navigate to the afterlife. The Asendath, it was named. A murky flow that snaked down to Gorm Vûdoc before spilling into a basin beneath the mountain's roots: a final stop for the damned before entering the underworld.

Tracing the river's path as a courier might scan a map before departure to a foreign land, Baeldrin finally settled his attention on Gorm Vûdoc. Snow-capped and barren, the mountain loomed ominously against the colorful backdrop of the world, lording over its surroundings, oppressing them with its mighty precipices and meaty knees. Staring outward, the prince felt his zeal subdued and thus retracted his gaze. "Witches and warlocks," he blew out in disgust while pulling two small round stones from his pocket. His eyes glowed with a lustful fervor as he looked upon what lay in his palm.

After a moment he closed his fist about the pebbles and, with a wicked grin, exited the balcony.

The sorceress stood waiting in the courtyard as the ghoul was being escorted in from the wilderness. Though armed, her imp servants kept well away from their captive: for his cooperation was no part their doing, and they were visibly frightened. More than one of the blue-skinned pygmies quailed at every turn of the ghoul's head, ready to cast down weapons and make a run for it; and the rest were hardly better, having enough courage only to prod the beast on by darting in and out from a distance. Each one's blade may have been raised high when he jumped forward in turn, but all of them looked as if they'd rather chop off their own hand than get within arm's reach of the prisoner.

Saedus approached the party with a regal gait and cast her intimidating gaze on the ghoul...whereupon the imps managed to suppress their fear long enough to kneel in fealty before her. The ghoul wasn't impressed with this production, however. Instead of following suit with his guards, he laughed brazenly: "What is this trap you've laid for me, sorceress? I go north and south, left and right, up and down, only to find I've returned to the gates of your lair. Release me from your web, witch, for I'm no shade. Do you not know my name?"

"Which name, beast?" replied Saedus, her tone a loom weaving mockery in with scolding. "The one of the knave you encroached upon, devouring his mind and twisting his shell? Or that of his usurper, a spirit ancient as the river?"

At this the ghoul drew his lips further back from the bloodstained fangs of a distorted, gaping mouth. Black drool fled this grin and trickled down, pooling about the mammoth chest that some poor man's frame had grown unnaturally to become. His eyes were two milky-white reservoirs of madness. His hands were murderous claws large enough to envelope a man's head and squeeze it to a pulp. The length of his arms alone nearly outstripped the tallest of the encircling imps, and he was naked save for a gilded belt from which hung hide strips stretching down to knobby knees.

"Yet it makes no difference," continued Saedus. "For now I name you anew. Henceforth you are G'nilbor, servant of the *Spider*, champion of my legions." She smiled as one satisfied, standing beautifully poised and confident before the face of chaos and destruction, the folds of her striking lavender robe rippling slightly in the wind. "Do you accept this charge? Or shall I return you to your stroll?"

The guards had little time to react. Faster than a deer pierced through, quick as an arrow bolting a wounded beast like lighting into a thicket, G'nilbor made his decision and presented it to the witch for the briefest of contemplations. The hulking form lunged, batted two imps aside as if they were mere wisps of smoke, and — with hardly a sound above the rush of his foul breath — stormed in for the kill.

Yet incredibly this savagery was checked. Instead of planting his huge, bare feet for one last leap that would've sent him slicing into Saedus of Ost, ripping the woman's delicate limbs away from her lithe, sensual body, G'nilbor abruptly went down on hands and knees in the dirt. The imps still standing hefted their weapons and made to run forward — but Saedus waved them away. She needed them no longer, for her banshees were present now. These five spirits began an undulating dance about the fallen ghoul, rising and falling in the air on which they hovered, circling, each one taking and shifting shape by summoning to her soul the gray dust of earth. Their noiseless cries found the mind of their captive, and they broke him...and he cursed and howled as if his bowels had just been sliced open or his manhood cleaved away.

"Stop them!" he roared, claws covering his ears as if the wails flung into his mind were audible. "I'm...yours...witch! Make them stop!"

The *Spider*'s smile returned as she gestured swiftly with a raised hand—and the banshees vanished at their mistress' dismissal, recalled to whatever talisman she used to bind and house them.

G'nilbor was spent. Although he'd been tormented for mere moments, the ghoul felt as if the ordeal had lasted for several days. His arms felt heavier than lead when he drew them up from the earth, and they hung lifelessly by his side as he arched his spine and tossed his head back to meet the sky. His chest was heaving. One eye squinted in pain. Yet presently he cupped his hands over his face and returned to a more erect posture. His breathing slowed. His fingers slid slowly down his face, claws reddening the pale skin underneath. He stared now at Saedus amenably...but not without loathing.

The woman gazed back at G'nilbor, looming over him like master above dog. She was tall and handsome and appeared ageless. Long black tresses framed her slender face before falling onto her shoulders, resting in the bony recess between neck, breast, and robe. She wore an impudent expression.

"I see you've grown powerful, sorceress," G'nilbor said with some effort. "Yet even Ûmrothsul Aldrotherin's throat was opened as he slept."

"The Red King was a fool!" she retorted. Her eyes were wild and beautiful. Then she laughed haughtily: "Did you think you'd be sharing my bed?"

G'nilbor's mouth turned down at the edges with rancor. He held his tongue, though, knowing further threats and taunts would be pointless.

"No?" said Saedus. "Yet you *are* mine—and shall evermore be. Your hunger is relentless. Your days of starvation unnumbered." Now the sorceress turned casually away from her new trophy, not even bothering to glance back with her parting words: "And unnumbered shall be the dead who lie on the field of war. They shall be your spoils, usurper."

G'nilbor was not altogether displeased at this prospect. His punishment, an insatiable appetite for flesh that gnawed his gut and distorted his mind, was one reserved for ghouls: those who'd once served the Daemon in life but been cursed by her in death for some failure or betrayal. These lost souls forever walked the earth in limbo, finding host after host, denied not only the release of rebirth but even the black sleep of hell.

As Saedus walked away, a man passed her on his way towards the beast. He wore a long black cloak haltered at the top around his chest, and a great pendant in the likeness of the moon hung about his neck. Sable nails and lanky fingers protruded through leather gauntlets, the ties crisscrossing up to the elbows. His head was bald and white as chalk. Pink eyes peered down on the monster.

"Welcome, ghoul," he began at once. "Do you need to be shackled? There's no escape, and any aggression towards me will leave you with something more intolerable than that famished belly of yours. I'm the *Spider*'s steward, and I am not without her—even when she's away. Do you understand?"

G'nilbor remained silent and expressionless. It was consent.

"Good," said the man. "I'm called Valreecius. Come, beast. First you shall feed, then we'll begin your training for war."

2

"The king requires your presence, Lord Dragan," said the soldier with all the authority he could summon; yet under the stony glare that was returned to him, his bravado withered like a blade of grass before the raging inferno. "That is...if you'd be so kind to oblige..." His voice trailed as he glanced over his shoulder — likely plotting an escape route should he need to turn and run for his life.

But instead of surging forward to throttle the frightened messenger where the man stood, Saedus' son merely sighed. Rising from the stump where he'd been seated, he wiped the dust from his thighs. "Mûran!" he called, removing the sword from his hip and handing it to that particular one of his red-skinned Haxûdī captains who was standing nearby. "Have your boy clean and oil my sword. And see to the camp. We've earned a rest tonight."

The Haxûdī nodded, and Dragan Saedus turned back to the soldier who'd come for him.

Relief washed over the man's face. "This way," he muttered then turned and set out across the camp.

Dragan followed detachedly as the soldier led him through the never ending array of tents that blanketed the field. Passing one, he passed a thousand...their campfires flickering to reveal the war-hardened faces of men: chiseled, sinewy, attenuated, grim as the gaze of the dying. Some tended their wounds, and others tended the dead, but all returned his stare. "That's him," they'd whisper. "The one who slew Agriretrim of Agrardob at the third wall." A handful murmured "*GrimHelm*" and "*DoomBringer*," but Dragan continued on behind the soldier and gave no heed to the cognomens.

Turning his gaze to the eastern horizon, he became ensnared by a vision of the Mardothan capital: its great black walls revealed in haunting silhouette by the enemy's funeral pyres. *Crûthior*. The focal point of this prolonged contest between the plainsmen of Sinia — his current allies, hailing from the south — and the warlords of this arid northern realm. Spirals of smoke intertwined high above the earth and shrouded the moon in a gray cloak. Horn blasts rang out intermittently, formally consigning the dead to the next life. It was a sound that carried to Dragan's ears supinely, oppressed in the dank summer air, amplifying his reverie so that much time passed of which he was unaware.

"Dragan!" boomed a voice born to conquer any trance. "Kiss the Daemon, men, your champion's returned!" This was Fedrin, son of Rae, the stoutest man-at-arms Dragan had ever known: a timeless figure sprung, it seemed, from the very pages of the *Book of Kings*.

"I might've yielded under a Mardothan hand, had I known you'd be the first to greet me," said Dragan, the slightest of grins battling for ground on his tired face. The bear was upon him now, slapping him on the back and grabbing him firmly by the arm, leading a trail of others who dared not do the same. "Where's Bronwyn, old man? *Hers* is the face I would see."

"I'm sure you would, my lord," laughed Fedrin, and the crude gesturing that followed found a special home in the minds of his lackeys. Some of them used the chorus of mirth to slip away, back to their own doings, yet most wouldn't be satisfied until they'd heard the account from Dragan's own lips. The Lion of Agrardob, after all, had been no craven.

Nevertheless, Dragan chose to courteously sidestep the men's request. What he wanted now was to forgo the ensuing revelry and instead seek his true spoils: Bronwyn, a meal, and a bed. He was forestalled in this by Fedrin, however, who confided that the woman had already been sent for and was coming to greet him. "Besides," Rae added less confidentially, "…you might wake a pace taller and a shoulder broader if you don't clear things up at once—and I don't believe there's room enough left in the world for more of you, brother!" Laughter erupted from the expanding throng like a spreading brush fire…and on top of every cry was another call for the tale. Yet just as Dragan was about to give in and relay the story after all, he was suddenly interrupted. A clamor had arisen deep in the crowd, followed by a mass shuffling of bodies.

As he stood watching this scene unfold, Dragan couldn't help but liken it to that of a growing storm: the ebb and flow of men shifting as if reacting to a great eye forming in their midst. So engrossed was he with this comparison, in fact, that the eye was almost upon him before he realized it…then Fedrin stepped out to clear the path's last hindrance, revealing two soldiers escorting the fairest being Dragan had ever gazed upon. The long, slender legs and that taut, curvy young body. The sleek blonde hair falling loosely over enticing shoulders. And that flawless face, searching his own with her luscious green eyes…

Yet before Dragan could move to embrace this perfect creature, he was once again checked: a subtle gesture from Bronwyn that told him *no*. "I too would hear your tale, *GrimHelm*, if it pleases you," she spoke with the merest arch of an eyebrow.

Dragan hesitated. Staring deep into her eyes, he read her thoughts—and she his. There'd be much to discuss later, but for now there was no escape. No reason to retire. He adjusted his contemplative gaze toward Crûthior, paused momentarily, then focused on his spectators. Stretching his arms out wide, he began to slowly revolve, exposing his silver breastplate to the crowd. With a mirror-like finish, the armor glowed red and brilliant in the firelight—and etched about its collar was the curse: *The head whose body bears this armor shall not be severed, but the bearer shall bring doom upon all his adversaries.* Dragan's long brown hair clung to cheek and neck, and sweat glistened on his shoulders and arms: all of it testament to the murky conditions summer brought to the inhabitants of the Realm of Mardotha…and now to its invaders as well.

"So you men would hear of the Lion's defeat?" the hero began, projecting his voice out over the heads of the audience. "Imagine the frenzy among our ranks, then, when the miners brought down the second wall! We needed to breach that gap to finish our foes—yet my men were engaged in a fierce struggle on the left flank that hindered our advance. Mardothans were pressing in on us from the eastern gate, intent on hurling their deadly missiles. Yet we managed to stunt this onset, and most of our forces passed through the breach unscathed."

"Yet in that hour a messenger brought to me grave tidings, proclaiming that my friend Camus Robi, fearless leader of our Ithirian allies, had been slain—and that a battle for his spoils had erupted beneath the third wall! Grief took hold of me then…yet I refused to let woe triumph. Instead I gathered my warriors about me and set out to put an end to the abomination. We waded through the masses, pushing and pulling. No man could deny us our path, so fever-pitched was the anger in our gazes!"

"Finally, after much toil, we reached the place where Robi had fallen. Seeing Camus' mangled corpse lying there, my mind went blank with rage—and I slew anyone my sword could reach. If I killed one, I killed fifty! And so it seemed we would salvage my friend indeed, for a circle opened up around his body to allow us access."

"Yet the enemy wasn't done—for in that moment Agriretrim of Agrardob, the one they named the Lion, strode into the circle and challenged me to single combat! You should know this: his golden mask and helmet, bushy blonde hair, and stout frame all resembled his namesake. Towering over the rest, he was the prize of that army, and one could sense the vigor return to those Mardothans who'd been on the verge of despair. The Lion pulled from his back a large mallet stained by the bludgeoning of countless men, put the hammer to the ground, and propped his weight against it. He thought he would kill me. But I knew I'd kill *him*."

"Yet before his death he would speak:

'So you're the *Bringer of Doom*? The *Bastard of Domal*? You must forgive me, but I don't see the first…'

'I've no time for banter,' I said. 'We've broken the pen, and now we must skewer the pigs before they flee squealing back into the wild! Give me the body, Lion, or you'll lie beside it!'"

At that, cries of approval engulfed Dragan, and he shouted back: "Enough! Be silent!"…to no effect. Bronwyn touched his arm lightly and held up a hand before the crowd. A hush fell.

"The Lion would've said more," continued Dragan, "...for golden mouths hide silver tongues. But my men were eager to be done. The circle wouldn't hold long. Enemy spears darted in and out, horns sounded, and a swarm of our own arrows bit through and felled my bearer! I had to be quick."

"Raising my blade, I charged the man head on — then faked and leapt aside, hoping to force a wide swing. But the Lion wasn't fooled. His hammer caught my wrist and sent my sword singing to the ground! And he left no time for me to miss it — curse him! — hurling that damned bolt aloft like their God of Gray Sky, raining blows upon me that would've broken a lesser man, denting my armor, bursting my lungs, crushing my very thoughts..."

It was Fedrin who'd taught him this next trick: the pause that reins them all in, the moment that raises a common man, lucky to have survived, to a hero of godlike proportions. All were silent, hanging on his every word. Satisfied, he took up a dreadful frown. Anger and pride were summoned forth and welled to overflowing. Then he shouted:

"But I am no lesser man! I am Dragan Saedus, captain of the Haxûdī, slayer of the White King and the Beast of Thirannon! How could this fair-haired kitten think to bleed *me*? Yet still he would boast, shouting to the sky as one gone mad:

'See now, Father! See how doom is averted! This man is weak! His race is weak! They'll all be ground to dust!'"

"Then I found my sword, and my sword split his haft, and my fist swatted his blood-smeared mask aside, cutting off his crazed words. The giant staggered back, stumbled over Camus' body, and crashed to the ground beside it."

"And there the great golden pride of Agrardob found the shadows at last, for my blade pierced his eyes on its path to Mother Earth!"

The crowd gave a final cheer that turned swiftly into a clamorous cacophony. The soldiers had been appeased by Dragan's tale, and — slowly dispersing — some of them began recounting their own feats of bravery while still more boasted of future exploits. One man seemed unmoved, however, remaining at the crowd's edge to stare at the hero from under his maroon cowl. A peculiar pendant hung loosely about his neck. Long thin forearms protruded from his cloak and rested in the crook of a tyberwood staff. Dragan became aware of him and returned his gaze. He'd seen those eyes before.

"Well done, lad!" said Fedrin as he clasped Dragan's shoulder, spinning the young warrior about-face. "I couldn't have done it better myself."

"What? The killing or the speech?" asked Dragan, annoyed. He looked back over his shoulder. The cloaked man was gone.

Taken aback, Fedrin gave a reproachful snort. "You're tired...and rightly so. The day is done."

"More than the day's done, my friend. Tell the king I won't be paying him a visit tonight."

Fedrin shook his head slowly, as if in fatherly disapproval. "You want me to tell *Deserus Oen* that you've refused his summons *yet again*? I run dry of excuses for you, son!" He paused here, expecting some sort of rebuttal from his brazen companion: but Dragan merely stared back in silence, gritting his teeth in further agitation.

"We'll take counsel in the morning, then," said Fedrin at last, shaking his head once more. "I'll send for you at daybreak."

Dragan nodded absently, for his thoughts had strayed inward. Watching Fedrin and the old man's entourage depart, he felt a hand caress his forearm.

Bronwyn. He turned to her, frowning: "Poltoros has come. He bears the Sun of Domal."

3

An hour passed...then half of another...and still Bronwyn paced about the tent or else sat nervously wringing her hands, unable to shake the image of the strange foreign messenger — nor the look on her lover's face as he'd announced the man's arrival. If only Dragan had never warned her this day might come. If only she'd remained ignorant of the sun pendant's meaning, then she might be relaxed enough to proceed with her nightly rituals. Brushing her hair, cleansing her skin with oil, applying perfume, and slipping into her silken nightclothes: everything wanted for presenting herself to Dragan when he finally retired to her from war's exertions. But as it stood now, she'd begun none of these things. All her thoughts hinged on what she'd see next in Dragan's eyes...and what the look would reveal of his plans before he even spoke.

At last the tent's flap parted, and in strode the hero of the day. A lesser man might've come shambling forth with shoulders hunched and head bowed after enduring Dragan's colossal labors, but not the mighty *DoomBringer* himself. He entered with a swagger, chin held high, seemingly reinvigorated.

Immediately Bronwyn moved to stand before him, locking her eyes with his. *"No..."* she began, grasping the man's thickly muscled arms as if she might try to shake some sense into him. "Please tell me its not true!"

Dragan placed his own hands on the woman in return, drawing her into an embrace. His hold on her was firm but not rough, and at first she made no effort to separate from him. Yet when it seemed this contact might be the only answer forthcoming, Bronwyn pushed off Dragan's armored chest to inspect his face once more. Even in her exasperated state she was magnificently gorgeous, green eyes glowing like emeralds against flustered cheeks.

"You can't leave us now!" she pressed, her voice rising with her agitation. "How could you even consider such a thing?"

Dragan broke free of Bronwyn's glare and brushed past her to create space between them. He began to pour himself a cup of watered wine from a nearby pitcher, then spoke over his shoulder:

"There's nothing to consider — just as I told you before. My men break camp as we speak."

Dragan's paramour was none other than the niece of Deserus Oen himself: king of Sinia and leader over all the allied forces encamped here on Crûthior's doorstep. Her royal father Torensus hadn't raised his daughter to be meek and mild, and Bronwyn always spoke her mind without fear of reprisal. Closing the distance to Dragan yet again, now she let her emotions fly. "You coward!" Her hands balled into fists and rose partway before she overrode the instinct to lash out with them. Tears were forming in the corners of her eyes. "Here we stand on the brink of triumph, and our greatest champion would *desert us* in the night? Can you not delay this madness till morning, at least? We can discuss it with the council. Surely they'll make you see reason, even if you won't hear it from me!"

"Is that really why you're so upset?" said Dragan after taking a drink from his cup and meeting Bronwyn's eyes again. "Or is it because of *us*?"

"It's both!" She shook her head as if disgusted by the question. "Did I really have to say it? They all told me not to fall for you, Dragan, but I wouldn't listen. Even your friend Camus, slain this very day—whose memory you'd dishonor by not attending his funeral pyre! He warned me that battle was your only bride. But now you shrink even from that, like some whipped dog slinking back to its master with tail between legs? What hold does your cursed mother have over you, that the mightiest warrior in the realms is cowed by her mere words?"

Dragan frowned deeply at this. He was used to his lover speaking her true thoughts; but if any besides her had uttered those words just now, that person would likely be vomiting blood. "You don't understand our arrangement…"

"Then by all means, enlighten me!"

The *DoomBringer* considered this a moment then shook his head *no*. "It's enough for you to know I'm bound to her service. The Sun of Domal is a token of that bond—and I *will* honor it, whether I like it or not. She bids me return to Ost with haste, and that's exactly what I mean to do." These words had been stated firmly to convey the surety of Dragan's intent, but now that they were out in the air, the warrior's expression and tone softened. "You must know I'll come back to you, Bronwyn—soon as whatever task mother's set for me is done. She's never held me long. It'll be no different this time." At this he set down his cup and reached to stroke her cheek with one hand, but she flinched from the touch:

"*Whatever task?* You mean that…creature…of hers didn't tell you what she wants of you? And still you go blindly to her summons?"

"He refused to say."

Bronwyn snorted at that. "*Refused?* What man would dare refuse you? You're not yourself, Dragan. I don't understand this at all." One eye's pool of tears broke and trickled down her cheek, and she jerked a hand up to wipe it clean. "You share a bed with me—but not your secrets? Not your *heart*. I see now what I am to you!"

This time when Dragan reached out and pulled Bronwyn close, he pressed her body tightly against his own. She pushed back at him feebly and bade him let her go, but he refused to relent before she herself did—and when she finally ceased squirming, the tears were flowing freely down both cheeks as she fought to control her sobs.

"My feelings for you are true," said Dragan, lifting her chin so he could meet her eyes. "I came here seeking only the glory of battle…just as Camus said…but I found something else in the bargain. Not a day shall pass that I won't see your face in my thoughts. Not a night that I won't long for your embrace. I'll find you again—even if I have to scrape like a beggar at your father's door, once this war is won and he's seen you safely home!" He showed her a smile then, hoping it to be reciprocated.

But it wasn't. The anger had drained from her with the tears, yet still she remained unappeased. "That day might not dawn at all, now that you forsake us."

A valid point. King Oen's war efforts in Mardotha hadn't been going in his favor when the *DoomBringer* had first arrived in the camp, many months past. The enemy warlords had the advantage of Crûthior's walls and a near-constant influx of reinforcements and provisions from their allies in Agrardob further east: a desert land that spawned hard men who were eager to test their might against all comers. Without aid from their own allies in neighboring Ithiria and the isle of Tholmis, the Sinians might've been expelled before Dragan had ever laid eyes on the black walls.

Yet all that had changed soon after he'd entered the campaign. He'd swiftly proven not only his individual superiority on the battlefield but also his ability to inspire others to great deeds of their own. And his Haxûdī followers were also masterful in the fray: many of whom might've been heroes in their own right, absent the star of Dragan Saedus burning brightest of all in their midst. Yet now, with those lights soon to be extinguished, could the Sinian alliance still maintain its forward momentum—or might the banished shadows of fear and doubt begin to creep back among their ranks?

"There are other champions at your uncle's disposal," Dragan replied at last.

"Yet none that could take your place." Bronwyn turned her cheek and laid her head against his chest, releasing a long sigh as she did so. "I can't stay here without you, Dragan. If you must go, then you'll have to take me with you."

"You know I can't do that…"

She peered up at him sharply. "Why not? You take the Haxûdī. Were they summoned as well?"

"Not directly. But I have a feeling they'll be of service. They've all sworn to protect me—Ûladriss, especially. I'd be hard pressed to keep them from trailing me without absolving them of their oaths. Oaths that were blessed by their own king as reward for my victory over the Beast of Thirannon. Besides, your father and uncle will be angry enough without my stealing you to boot. I'd likely find an army at my heels before I ever reached mother's gates."

Just as Bronwyn's lips parted to offer a rebuttal, another voice sounded over her, slightly muffled behind the tent's flap. "My lord. All is ready."

"Speak of the wolf, and he stands outside the door," murmured Dragan. Then, with volume raised: "A moment, Ûladriss."

"He's been out there the whole time, hasn't he?" said Oen's niece, once more attempting to push away.

Dragan frowned at her guess but ignored the question, pulling her back to him instead. Holding her eyes, he leaned in to give her a parting kiss.

"No!" she cried — and her hand flew up to slap the warrior's face.

He caught her wrist before impact and eased it back down; but then finally he let her separate.

"So you're really going to do this? Right now?" she said, anger flaring again. An anger mixed now with both sadness and shame. "Without giving anyone but me your farewell?"

Perhaps the attempted slap at his face had turned him suddenly cold to her, or maybe for the moment he could no longer deal with his own rising shame. In either case, Dragan turned from his lover then without further word, parting the tent flap to join his Haxûdī marshal without.

As he started off from the tent, Dragan expected to be pummeled by a steady stream of Bronwyn's curses aimed at his back. Yet the only parting gift from the woman, it seemed, would be a reflection of his own silence.

4

The finest pinpoint of white on the blackest canvas, and nothing else existed. Yet Astelidus Ny could feel his face parting thin air as his charger propelled him towards it. The steel hoops of Bellaroth's reins rapped gently against her bronze chanfron, generating a rhythmic knell in the warrior's ears. He strained to hear something else…anything else…but heard nothing. Not even hoof against earth. There was no earth.

It seemed an eternity before the point became a dot…and the dot a disc…and the disc a glowing sphere of yellowish-green flame. It was still far — too far — like the sun to the earth, yet now it cast the dimmest light on man and steed as they approached. Astelidus noticed something queer about his arms. They appeared sickly and shriveled: not the meaty limbs he'd known his entire life. He loosed the reins, lifted his palms close to his face, and immediately recoiled at what he saw. What skin remained was ghastly pale and splotched with corruption. The muscle underneath was diminished, exposing segments of chalky white bone in places. The putrid stench of death became recognizable.

Astelidus didn't remain perturbed long, though — for living or dead, his soul flamed with a passionate pride that couldn't be extinguished. He moved a bony hand to his side and, clasping the hilt of his bastard sword, excitedly drew blade from scabbard. The length of it burst magnificently into cool blue flames that pulsed to the beat of his heart and swayed to the rhythm of his breath. Bellaroth neighed. Two streaming balls of fire issued from her nostrils. Astelidus looked on with wide eyes. *The end of time.*

The sphere of light dilated until it loomed gigantically before man and beast. The horse slowed to a canter, then to a trot, and finally came to a complete halt. All was still in the void. Silence reigned. The man gazed at the spectacle before him: no longer a flame, but a glassy orb.

"What curse have you put on me, Daemon?" shouted Astelidus, his words whetted by the muteness of oblivion. "Where's my father, and his father, and my ancestors of old? Where's my dearest brother, Banlorest, whose death I couldn't prevent? Where is the river and the mountain?"

The warrior stared intently at the sphere, flame-brand clasped tightly in his right hand, reins held loosely in his other. He became aware of a faint slit in the orb's center running pole to pole. The breadth of this grew at its equator until a black ellipse developed. The eye of the serpent rotated, its pupil scrutinizing the visitor. A hiss came from somewhere in the nothingness:

"You're mistaken, Astelidus Ny. Soon you shall travel the river, but that time isn't now."

"But I'm dead. Rotting. Can't you see my flesh?" The warrior held up his forearm for the serpent to behold.

"Not dead, but dying. Poisoned."

"Poisoned? By what?"

"A snake in the grass."

The man knitted his brows. "Killed by a snake? Never! It was I who slew..."

"Fool!" spoke the serpent, its voice replete with contempt. "When the rats have been devoured, what then shall I eat?"

"What is this riddle?" replied the man, his agitation boiling over into rage. "I've no patience for your noxious words!"

"Indeed. Yet know this, warrior: your lack of patience shall be the death of you, as it was the death of your *dearest brother.*"

The malignant emphasis placed on those last words sent Astelidus spiraling into a blind fury. Bellaroth reared as he put his feet hard into her sides. Coming down, the warrior thrust his flaming brand deep into the serpent's eye. The pain-ridden shriek that followed burst his ears, racked his brain, sent blood pouring from his eyes and nose. Small gray tendrils issued from the wound, writhing up blade, hand, arm, shoulder...freezing his flesh and bone, choking his life away. When they reached his heart, he was dead. Blackness triumphed.

Yet there existed a light in the darkness, small and remote, once again before Astelidus' eyes. *The eye of the serpent?* he thought, disconcerted. *No, just a solitary star on a cloudy night.* The man sat up, bending his legs and resting his forearms across his knees. He'd chosen, as was his wont, to make his bed in a long, thin patch of woods on the outskirts of the Sinian encampment. Behind this grove, shear precipices of shale dropped some fifty fathoms down to the valley below.

He wiped the stray red locks from his face and peered into the valley. The air was fresher here, unpolluted by the smoke and dirt constantly circulating in the camp, and the scent of pine was more pleasant than the poignant perfumes his servants used to douse his linens. Although several wells had been tapped by the invading army, water was still a commodity that couldn't be wasted on washing sheets—even for a warrior as renowned as the son of Ny. There was hardly a trickle of stream between Crûthior and Gethod.

As he began wondering which of his servants was probably sleeping on his bed in the tent, he noticed far below a string of torches winding along the road, heading west. He stood, walked to the cliff's edge, and grasped a sturdy pine to steady himself. The column of fire coiled around as it followed the twisting road further down into the valley. *Too many snakes for one night,* he thought. Because of the telltale number and odd spacing of the lights, Astelidus correctly assumed this fiery serpent to be composed of his rival, Dragan Saedus, and the band of skilled Haxûdī that followed the upstart as if he were some god.

"Leaving on the eve of victory," the Sinian snorted. "Good riddance."

Astelidus had never liked the son of Saedus. Though he couldn't deny the foreigner's prowess on the battlefield, he disdained the man's lack of loyalty: an attribute that Astelidus himself held in high esteem. He found himself recalling how Dragan had dismissed him as if he were no more than a mere shield-bearer at their first encounter — and how the same man, upon arriving in Mardotha, had refused to kneel before the king of Sinia and pay homage.

If only he'd turned you away then, mused Astelidus, staring into the night, *...it would've been* me *today boasting of victory. I would fall upon my own sword at King Oen's command...but how could Bronwyn, so decent and fair, have taken up with the likes of you?*

He had no answer to that question. Any fool could see the foreigner was ruggedly handsome, but so was Astelidus Ny — as many a comely maiden had attested. And before the upstart's inglorious arrival, Astelidus had been on the path to becoming the prime Sinian champion himself, having achieved several spectacular feats of daring and prowess before stubble had ever cropped up on his chin. It may have been Banlorest, his father's eldest son, who was groomed for greatness, but every courtesy denied the younger brother he made up for in sheer determination. Could he wear the shoes his brother's feet were meant to fill? It was time for him to find out.

Astelidus broke his gaze away from the night and headed back to the camp. There he found a sentry and pulled the man aside, speaking in a whisper: "Who has departed?"

"*DoomBringer*, my lord," was the confirming answer. "He wouldn't tell us his destination." The guard looked worried, almost frightened, beneath the pale moonlight. "Could he mean not to return? What will happen to us then?"

"This war won't be decided by a single man, no matter how skilled others deem him to be," said Astelidus, somehow keeping his cool.

"As you say, lord...yet some believe he's invincible...that if not for him, the Mardothans would stream forth like ants from their gates!"

Astelidus frowned deeply. "We shall see. But let them come, I say. There are other heroes among us."

The sentry nodded, apparently unconvinced.

A queer mood struck Astelidus then, and he almost laughed in the sentry's face and berated the man as a witless cur. Instead he said simply: "Back to your post."

The yard rushed past. He could hardly contain himself, for now his time had finally come. Did Bronwyn know of Dragan's parting? If so, Astelidus would be there to comfort her. If not, Astelidus would be the one to tell her. Either way he must see her face now, no matter the hour. He must know how much this rogue truly affected her, before she had time to compose herself on the morrow. There would be guards about the tent where Bronwyn slept: most likely hers, now that Dragan's were gone...but Astelidus knew her men well. They might complain a bit at first, but in the end they'd admit him.

Where is the damned place? he silently cursed. He'd visited them before, most times on errand, although a few trips had come from invitation. As much as he secretly loathed the *GrimHelm*, Astelidus had surprisingly found Dragan to be somewhat fond of him. It seemed the man liked to hear stories of others' bold deeds nearly as well as boasting of his own. And Bronwyn had always smiled and spoken fair to him...

Cutting behind a makeshift smokehouse and a wagon laden with furs, he got his bearings at last. The entrance to Bronwyn's tent was straight ahead. *Here I am. I was headed right after all.*

But it wasn't right. The destination was correct, but *something else* was not. There were no guards here. Not at her tent, nor at the next...nor at any within view. Years of scouting had sharpened Astelidus' instincts, causing him to grasp hold immediately of the slightest thing out of place in a situation — and he did so now, dropping down quickly into the shadows and holding his breath. Ever so slowly he drew his sword, careful to keep steel out of moonlight. Someone else who shouldn't be here slinked nearby. He heard muffled footfalls. He could feel the tension in the air.

Should he call out? Should he go inside? Either one should suffice to ensure Bronwyn's safety — but neither would catch the lurker in the act, revealing his or her identity. A good thief, spy, or assassin could disappear in the blink of an eye, running and hiding or blending in with a gathering crowd. No, he'd wait longer and make certain of this person's intentions before bringing them to naught. *My timing must be perfect. Bronwyn must not be harmed.*

Agonizing moments passed in near silence. Maybe the supposed intruder's instincts were as honed as those of Ny's son — or perhaps even more so — and Astelidus' presence had been perceived as well. It could also be that something rather harmless was about. A scenario crossed his mind where the guards had been given leave for the night, and it was only some old drunkard wandering about, stumblingly lost — but sober enough not to risk waking anyone of note. *No. I know what I heard. I know what I felt.* And he still felt it: someone's presence not far off. Someone more patient than he was.

Still the long moments passed, and no one else came. Only the low drone of insects and distant snores broke the stillness of night. But at last he heard a faint slit of canvas ahead...then a shuffling sound...then he was on his feet, dashing for the entrance, batting the tent flap aside, sweeping his wide eyes about the dimly-lit interior, when...

A blinding cloud of dust struck him square in the face.

A woman's shriek and a coward's point pierced him simultaneously, one to announce his death and the other to secure it. Pain exploded in his chest, and a burning fire seared his eyes. He loosed a ragged groan as the murderer pushed him against something hard—a support—and prepared to make an end of him.

But the dirge for Astelidus Ny was not yet to be sung. In the shadows of the tent his attacker saw little more than he did, blinded though he was, and instinct again took over. He caught and slowed the next stab as it connected slightly off the intended spot—his heart—and instantly kicked off the beam to bowl over the assailant, sending both of them sprawling. It was indeed a man with whom he struggled briefly on the ground, Astelidus discerned quickly enough. A man of slight build yet surprisingly wiry strength. *But not strong enough, dog!* On his side now—behind the assassin—he bent back an arm, wrenched free the dagger, and stabbed again and again and again. Yet still his victim made no sound.

Someone entered the hut, yelling and darting about. Other voices followed, including Bronwyn's, and light suddenly penetrated the closed lids of Astelidus' throbbing, blurry eyes. They stood over the scene as he rolled off the dead man and rubbed at his dusty face. Bronwyn spoke his name in surprise; the others he barely heard at all. Concerned with his wound, they tried to pull him away, but he wouldn't have it. Not yet. He opened his eyes and moved close to the dead man's face.

But it wasn't a man, after all, whom Astelidus looked upon with impaired vision in the lamplight. Pointed ears, nose, and chin told the tale clearly enough. *A sand elf!*

5

Baeldrin recognized one of the three guards silently following his approach but had never bothered to learn the man's name. In his mind, the whole dirty lot could scarcely be called *men* at all, much less *soldiers*, and he'd never been shy of letting them know it. *They're all dense as the witch's pets,* he mused, *...and nearly as ugly. But imps don't play their masters false...nor speak unless spoken to...nor drink themselves into oblivion on the eve of battle...*

They continued to watch him intently, dark eyes sunk beneath the nasals of their leather and steel caps, until he vanished under the once-magnificent wall of his father's city: Rardonydd, fading jewel of Domal. For hundreds of years it had enjoyed its prestige as the dominant of the twin ruling cities: a stern but wise and protective big brother to Relinydd, the trading hub on the shores of Lake Eredus. At the height of its power — acknowledged by most scholars as some time during the reign of Baeldrin's great-grandfather, Caleb the Gazer — Rardonydd had been both the head and heart of a realm encompassing not only Domal's present-day borders but also half of Sinia, near three quarters of Ithiria, and the entirety of Ûnath and Ost.

Countless years and lives spent to win that territory and hold its borders, Baeldrin considered as he passed through the archway. *And only two generations of dotards to lose it. No, to give it all away!* The sun blasted the prince's face as he stepped out of the shadows that'd served as a brief reprieve from the searing heat. His right arm raised involuntarily to shield his eyes, then he moved on leisurely into the streets, sidestepping fallen chunks of wall and shattered paving stones as he did so. *They've ceased now to even clean up their mess, much less fix it. And why is that, I marvel? Could it be these wonderful urchins, whores, and driveling peddlers I'm passing are content to wallow in their own filth?* He'd meant this to amuse himself, but it served only to deepen his scowl. One of the merchants — a plump, balding man laying out bolts of gaudily dyed cloth — caught his eye, held it insolently, then returned the frown. *Dog! Does he not know his prince? Or perhaps he doesn't care at all. I suppose I'd not either in his place, with no consequences for breaking the laws.*

The uncommon scent of jasmine filled the air as he turned one corner to find himself in an even rarer scene of tender parenting, and he lingered for a moment to take it in. Tired hands ran across his face and on into his hair, pulling the long jet strands away from his shoulders. *I need sleep...but not yet. I must see him first.* The little girl, in the midst of having her shiny brown locks braided, kept smiling, even giggling, as her bright eyes caught a glimpse of the prince. And her comely young mother had a grin for Baeldrin as well — though one of a different sort, it seemed. Under other circumstances he might've returned the same, but today the suggestion only somewhat lessened his bitter frown. A hot breeze rushed by, and again light stung at his eyes as he glanced away, searching the promontory beyond. He resumed his tread.

It wasn't long before another sun came bearing down on Baeldrin's face: a round disc and three daggerlike rays — piercing north, south, and east — shallow-carved above the gargantuan double doors of his father's crumbling sandstone palace. "No mountain, river, wood, or fen can hold back the swords of Domal," Acomalath had said to both of his sons together once, before his own father's cravenness had been thoroughly passed on, "...but the Great Ocean shall spill forth from the West someday to wash over us all." Baeldrin no longer believed this — not so much the cataclysmic forecast as the sweeping boast.

"Welcome, my prince," rasped one of his father's honey-tongued retainers as the doors began to slowly arc inside. *You sicken me,* Baeldrin wanted to say, yet he only nodded and passed through. Thankfully, the inner court's cool fountains and ample shade made it a good deal more pleasant within than out in the street, and the huge beams of light streaming down from the dome's uncovered portals weren't so blinding. Others had come to call on the king as well, among them an aged soldier, a lady and her servant dressed in fine linen shifts, and a merchant trio with their silly hats and oiled, pointy beards. They'd have to wait, though. Rardonydd's heir didn't bother with the lists.

Acomalath sat with chin in the palm of his right hand, staring lustfully at the dainty maiden pouring his wine, as his firstborn passed through yet another set of double doors. "Am I to have another bastard brother?" said Baeldrin angrily as he approached the dais.

"I hadn't dreamed you loved the one so much as to desire another," spoke the king with a lazy smirk, his gaze still on the wench until she finished her task and strolled seductively out of view. Then his eyes swept to his legitimate son: "Or perhaps you and dear Dragan have made peace?" A bark of annoying laughter followed. "Where've you been, my son? They say your poor mother's sick with worry!"

Although he'd soiled it thoroughly from trekking the dusty roads, Baeldrin noted the extravagance of his own crimson garb as opposed to his father's plain sandals and tunic. "*They?* Perhaps if you dressed like the king she'd allow your presence."

"Enough of this banter!" snapped Acomalath, his brow furrowing. "Why are you here instead of waiting patiently in your quarters? I've hardly begun with the lists..."

Did I go too far, dear *Father?* "I'd know if the rumor is true. Has Relinydd betrayed us?"

The king looked wounded. "Betrayal? Are you mad? Dragan seeks glory in the north, so why should our Sister's strapping lads not also? Our own borders are secure — and all of Domal shall benefit from the veterans and spoils that must doubtless return. I'm surprised you're not here to ask leave yourself...to beg for a legion to take with you!"

"I am," said Baeldrin simply, though inside he struggled not to say more. There was no doubt Acomalath loved the bastard best, and Baeldrin yearned to strangle him for that fact alone if for nothing more. Yet at present his father — fool and coward that he was — was still of use. *He must freely give me what I need. The old man mustn't be harmed...at least for now...but it's past time he danced to my tune.*

"Truly?" spoke Acomalath, reaching for his cup. "Forgive me, lad, but now I'm confused..."

"Can you not see, Father, even now?" The serving girl reentered, preparing to offer the prince both food and wine. "Leave us!" he said, sternly but without raising his voice. She did so immediately. "We should be *aiding* the Mardothans, not helping Sinia — our ancient *enemy* — expand its swollen borders! I know you say we're at peace now with the Sinians...that we conceded to them only land that was first their own...but where's our own pride fled? What of the glory of Domal?"

"I've always admired your fervor, son. But our days of expansion through *warmongering* are done. The pride of Domal lies now in its culture and heritage and in the wealth that flows daily into our coffers. If Deserus Oen ever turns fool enough to set his eyes upon us, he'll rue it soon enough. Besides...hasn't he the right in this current bout of his?"

"If you consider a personal slight to Oen as just cause for full-scale invasion, then yes," the prince returned. "Mardothan warlords are never inclined to hold their tongues, as I'm sure you recall — especially not Argen Van."

"Come Baeldrin, it was more than that, was it not?" the king lightly scolded. He was distracted now, his fingers picking through the tray beside him for some particular morsel. "I was told that Oen's young daughter was abused — by none other than Van himself, on the eve of his departure from Chalemos. They say she wouldn't speak of it at first because he threatened her so. Poor thing. What if that girl had been one of your sisters? Wouldn't you have urged me to raise our own banners, as Deserus has done?"

"Perhaps she didn't speak till Van broke a tryst, for all I know — or care. And I've been *urging* you for years! One legion, Father. I should have a right to more, but that's all I require. *One legion.*"

"Do you assume me an imbecile?" the king snorted. "And what would you do with that legion?" He paused, waiting. "Answer me!"

"First I'll march on Relinydd and cease this new folly."

"Then somehow vault us into a position where I must grant another legion, and another, and another...till every man in the kingdom need take up a spear? I won't have you invite war to the walls of this city — nor any in homage to it!" Acomalath was visibly tiring of the conversation. His eyes scanned the chamber once then settled on the double doors as if looking for a guard to have the prince bodily removed.

Maybe he's not such a fool...but has there ever been another man so craven? "Calm yourself, lord." This pained Baeldrin infinitely to say, but the time for sweet talk was clearly at hand. "I understand your concerns. Yet all my life I've served you well and asked little in return." He dropped his gaze for a moment in feigned humility. "If I can't have the legion, then at least grant me a lesser boon. What I ask for now is no more than what the witch's son received on his last visit. And I'm your trueborn heir."

"You wish me to supply you with arms?" spoke the king, clearly puzzled. "You have no warriors, Baeldrin. Your brother won his through great deeds of prowess..."

The prince wasn't troubled by this. "I ask only for keys to the armory and a store twice the size of what Dragan was provided — and enough slaves and carts to haul it away. As for the warriors who'll don the gear...perhaps it's time I won some of my own."

A wicked grin jumped to Acomalath's lips and was as soon gone. He'd be rid of this son and the man's harping at last — for nothing more than a surplus of shields, helms, swords, and spears. "Madness, I say...but I suppose I do owe you that much. Summon my scribe, and you'll have your missive." Baeldrin merely nodded and turned to go. "What? No words of gratitude? I recall your brother being more appreciative of his gift."

"My thanks, lord," said Baeldrin with a curt bow, "...though your gift was somewhat less than desired."

"Don't despair!" the king spoke again after a moment's pause, addressing his son's retreating form. "The swords you take shall far outstrip the men willing to bear them for you."

You're wrong, old man, Baeldrin smiled. *Imps and goblins need no persuading.*

6

"Is this the path we must follow?"

Silence.

"My lord? Which road should we take?"

Ûladriss reined his steed closer to Dragan's courser and laid a hand upon his master's broad shoulder before repeating the question. Dragan broke his reverie and peered forward. A fork in the road.

"We must take the path south," he said. "The north road leads to Dolras and the ruins of Ûmrothsul Aldrotherin's kingdom."

"We'll be stretched thin either way," replied the Haxûdī chieftain, cocking his head to study the road. "One column. Perhaps six men abreast."

"There's no other way," said Dragan, "…unless we hack our way south and follow the Hirath to the mouth of Lake Hudron. But the forest is dense…and the riverbed no wider than this track."

"Are we in danger?" asked Ûladriss, a sly grin on his lips.

"Always, friend," Dragan laughed.

"Good. My blade itches to be unsheathed. All the same, I'd advise sending the scouts ahead again."

"See that it's done."

Ûladriss nodded, turned, and trotted back down the column.

Dragan took in a deep breath. This cut of the wood had a curious smell to it, both rotten and fresh at once, as if the earth still bled through wounds taken long years before. He recalled the northern practice of sacrificing elder trees in times of plenty: his mother's clan, among others, believed the act aided perpetuation of new life. Small, mysterious glades opened suddenly around bends in the path and closed as quickly behind Dragan's intruding band, their rime-encrusted grasses and clovers now covering ground where elm roots had once taken hold. The Haxûdī stooped or pushed aside branches of surviving specimens as they followed the road, no doubt wishing the ritual culling had included a widening of their present course as well.

Their trek thus far had been as bleak as the name of the forest sounded in Dragan's ears: Braured. Not a living man, bird, nor beast larger than a rodent had presented itself within his sight thus far, and already three days and nights were behind them. Yet there'd been signs. A boar carcass and a fired clay urn. The first, freshly slain, lay sprawled atop a huge man-worked stone in one of the glades, its throat cleanly slit and tusks removed. In the muck at the base of the altar someone had scrawled the ancient runes of sight and warding. The second message, however, was less clear. Set amidst the roots of a gnarled oak just off the path, the huge clay vessel was impressively ornate—with sculpted deer for handles and satyrs dancing gaily about its girth—yet its contents couldn't have been fouler. Black blood curdled about a floating half-stripped and shattered human skull. The stench was horrible.

Savages, thought Dragan as he contemplated this last spectacle, though an unbidden image of Ûladriss' face kept him from repeating it aloud. With that shoulder-length, greasy black hair, knotted beard, and wild look about his sharp brown eyes, the Haxûdī chieftain could've played the role of *savage* himself—as could have all the warriors following them into this cursed place. *Yet my men are different*, Dragan mused. They could be brutal, surely: a necessary trait that he too possessed and summoned forth at will. But they were also inflicted with the disease called *honor*. It'd shown its fair-seeming head countless times thus far during the days Dragan had spent among this band, beginning on the night he'd first traipsed into King Toldriss' hall, mad drunk and loose of tongue. Ûladriss had nearly slain him then, defending the honor of Haxûd's queen.

"You said to me once," began Dragan suddenly, breaking the lull of his ride, "…that a man may win glory even in defeat."

Ûladriss had reined in without a word a few moments before, retaking his customary position on his lord's right side. "Aye. This was so for me as I lay at your feet, spitting blood upon the king's paved floor. Don't you remember? It's one thing to face a trial with the end unseen—many fools throw the bones, eh? But to know the end before the beginning, *and yet submit yourself to it*…that's not the drink of every man, my friend."

"You speak like a wizened sage," Dragan laughed. "But tell me true, and it shall stay with me. None other shall hear it spoken." The mirth faded. "Surely you had a glint of hope? How could you have even lifted your blade if you were *certain* I'd shame you? I remember it well enough. You nearly took my arm off."

"My lord's missing the point again," the warrior smiled, showing off a bit of the gap Dragan had given him on that day, years in the past. "Shame would've wed me had I *not* lifted the blade. It was the other chiefs who found disgrace: Horga, Jesrim Greenboar, and the like. They saw only their deaths in your eyes. I looked beyond."

Dragan paused and shifted uncomfortably in his saddle. "What if I'd killed you? If I'd spat on your dead body and dragged it from Toldriss' hall, denying your gods their due? What then of disgrace?"

Ûladriss didn't hesitate: "Still, none would've named me *craven*." He held his head high, staring at nothing in particular. "What matters such things to you, *DoomBringer*? You're a man of no fear." He turned to his lord.

Dragan remained expressionless—yet these last words had cut to the quick. *She'd never name me* craven…*would she?* he thought, averting his gaze from the

Haxûdī. *Not my own mother...* The warrior's stare fixed him. Replication was expected. Unsure how to respond, he simply gave a curt nod.

The two didn't speak again until the sun had fallen well beneath the forest's canopy. With the band stretched thin, it took quite some time for Jedan Mûran to bring up the rear in preparation to camp—and the creeping pace of the baggage train only increased the duration further. Their cart mules were particularly and deliberately (so it seemed) laggardly: a hindrance ever since the departure from Mardotha. Spoils of war must be protected, though, so they'd been strategically placed in the middle of the column.

The *GrimHelm* ordained that camp would be made at the next large clearing, stating "...one's as good as the next." He sent Mûran's boy, Gavix, back down the path to relay the message. The lad turned his steed swiftly to canter off—but not before Dragan noticed the bloody bandage on the boy's left hand. Gavix had cut himself on Dragan's blade the night they'd broken camp in Mardotha, no doubt in a jittery attempt to clean and oil the blade as quickly as possible to avoid his father's heavy-handed wrath. Jedan had been all the more displeased to learn his son had been careless with the steel, and the boy would've been beaten if Dragan hadn't allayed the father's anger by offering him a swig of Tholmian liquor: most exquisite and rarest in the realm. The warrior had looked on the flask first with incredulity but then with a hearty laugh before taking a healthy swallow. And so the boy had been spared.

Eventually the woods opened into an oblong glade hugging the north side of a swooping bend. The men started pouring into the clearing like river into lake. Attendants immediately began erecting tents, tending horses, preparing meals. They ran this way and that, bumping into each other and shouting curses: a frantic race to accomplish their masters' commands before nightfall. Warriors unlucky enough not to have captured, purchased, or brought along a servant were left to do their work themselves. The rest congregated in circles to speak idly, awaiting supper. When Jedan finally brought up the rear, dusk lay heavy on the earth. His son strode beside him. Both were lanky yet becoming. Jedan wore a thick pointed goatee; his son sported the beginnings of one. Dragan and Ûladriss, still on horseback, greeted them:

"Hail, Jedan Mûran," said Ûladriss.

The man gave a courteous nod then looked aside to his son. "What're you doing, boy? See to your chores. The *DoomBringer* doesn't wait for food and comfort while we're bound to his service." Dejected, Gavix trotted off to do his father's biddings. Jedan addressed the two men:

"What news from the tongue of our snake?"

"No news," replied Dragan. "We sent four: two ahead, one north, one south. None have returned."

"One returned," Mûran corrected. "From the south. He claims he lost his bearings and got turned around. He was in full gallop when he came upon me. I should've gutted the fool! He was off hunting pig, I'd guess. Haxûdī don't get lost in the woods."

"Hunting. Scouting. Not much difference," Dragan mused.

Jedan gave him a reproachful look. Since Dragan laughed at death, he was often bored with strategy. The Haxûdī took matters more seriously.

"It's *we* who are hunted, Mûran," said Ûladriss. "Were the signs not enough for you?"

"Enough," said Dragan, stifling whatever response Jedan was about to make. "Hand me that flask."

7

Before exiting court, Baeldrin was given one of his father's more obsequious servants as his escort and general attendant during his stay in Rardonydd. This was a normal courtesy afforded to the members of the ruling house, aristocracy, and esteemed guests, but the prince had first refused the need for a chaperone in a city he'd known his entire life. His father had insisted, however, stating that no son of his would be seen about the city without proper accommodations, and went on to state that Martassin (the servant) would handle any administrative duties associated with the arms transfer. To Baeldrin it was all an act: the lanky attendant would spy his every move — and annoy him with incessant courtesies drawled out of his undersized mouth. But the prince had nevertheless relented with no further argument, not wishing to have his gift retracted on the account of such an inconvenience.

As the two men left the courtyard for the twilight without, Baeldrin halted in the portico beneath the Sun of Domal.

"Martassin," he said with all the pleasantness he could muster, "...who dines with my father tonight?"

"Lord, tonight his majesty will be accompanied by his council. It's the new moon."

"As I remember. I'll be attending, of course."

The servant faltered. Baeldrin, clearly agitated, continued:

"Forbid it that my father should perish — but if so, who then shall be king? Me, fool! Should I not tend to the kingdom's business?"

"Foolery. Yes, foolery it was, for me not to have realized this. I'll send word of your attendance."

"Good. My ride from the north was long and hard, and I'm spent. I must rest for an hour or two. Ensure that I'm roused in time for dinner. Farewell!"

The prince took a few quick, deliberate steps away from Martassin...but the servant immediately followed. They stopped again.

"What are you doing?" asked Baeldrin, though he knew the answer.

"Most gracious prince, it's my pleasure to escort you to your quarters in the keep."

"And what if I'm not going there?"

"I understood the young lord was in need of rest..." responded Martassin, a feigned smile growing beneath his straight but large nose.

Baeldrin reciprocated with his own sarcastic grin then looked back over his shoulder. The tower was no more than two hundred yards across the plaza, yet this insect would cling to him every inch of the way. *Will he also sleep with me, like some dog at my feet?* he thought as he turned and started toward the massive keep. Its black walls rose into the skyline. Smoke and steam billowed up from the top floor windows where cooks were no doubt preparing the night's dinner. The prince noted this and turned to his escort:

"Martassin," he said casually.

"Yes, lord?"

"Do you know why the engineers of old put the kitchens on the upper floors of the keep?"

"No, lord. But I've wondered. It seems very pointless to me. The hall is on the ground floor. All provisions must go up only to come back down. Very inefficient." The servant paused briefly before continuing. "It's funny you say this. No more than a week ago, the cooks put a complaint of this very nature on the king's lists. They requested to be moved to the first floor. "

"What did my father say?"

"He granted them their wish. They'll be relocated after the new year."

Acomalath's son snorted contemptuously, shaking his head slowly from side to side. *Fools...all fools,* he mused.

Martassin gazed perplexingly at the tower then back at the prince: "My lord? I don't understand."

Baeldrin made no reply, for his thoughts had turned inward. Seeing this, the servant didn't persist but kept at his master's heels, gazing up at the tower, the wheels of thought turning in his mind. Then...*ugh!*...he exhaled violently as he collided with his prince (who'd stopped abruptly two thirds of the way across the courtyard). The weakling felt like he'd hit a wall. He bent down, holding his stomach, trying to catch his breath: the breath he desperately needed to begin profusely apologizing for his incompetence.

"Lord...I'm...terribly sorry," he managed to get out — and, to his amazement, Baeldrin didn't thrash him or even scold him. In fact, the prince seemed not to have noticed. Baeldrin stood still with his head turned to the side, his eyes fixed on something in the distance. The servant followed his master's gaze into an alley where, just paces within, stood an imposing dark silhouette. Martassin squinted at the blackness, attempting to identify the stranger — and thus failed to notice the subtle hand sign tossed that way by the prince.

The man promptly turned and vanished. Baeldrin looked at his escort, who opened his mouth to question but was cut off. "Watch yourself," said the prince, his tone full of insinuation. Martassin, not a complete idiot, perceived the double entendre and said nothing. The two resumed their walk.

The pair of soldiers manning the oversized doors to the keep belonged to the City Guard, an estranged division of the army assigned to civil duties and police work within the city. In times of crisis they acted as bodyguards for the ruling family and aristocracy; and, consequently, their loyalty had to be unwavering — which meant they were highly overpaid. This of course didn't sit well with the general infantry, most of whom were dispersed along Domal's borders in small forts or villages where amenities of city life were non-existent. The adage *'first to get killed, last to get paid'* could be heard at any outpost from Gorm Nadur to the Great Ocean.

The soldiers' garb was moderately decorative: a crimson tunic underneath a leather breastplate underneath a vest of black iron chain. A sun-shaped clasp on each shoulder held a black velvet mantle that fell down past the knees, and plain black leather gloves and boots protected hands and feet. A solitary chevron on their sleeves indicated both men were of low rank. They held their steel crimson helmets at their left side: upright between forearm and hip. When Martassin and Baeldrin came between them, Baeldrin stopped and waited. Nothing happened. The prince looked at the leftmost guard.

"Last I checked, I was the king's son," he proclaimed.

The guard's gaze shifted to his comrade. The face remained expressionless — but those eyes revealed to Baeldrin that he no longer commanded respect or fear: at least not in Rardonydd. This fact distressed him greatly, but unlike the guard he didn't betray himself. The offenders turned in unison towards their prince, each threw up a rigid arm, palms outward, and let out a booming *HUMPH!* The newcomers continued through the doors into the keep. *The first two to dispose of,* thought Baeldrin. The impudent eyes of the guard vexed him such that he could think of nothing else. *The servants, the guards, my kin...don't they know my wrath will find them swiftly once I'm king?* Then a terrible thought entered his mind. His gut clinched. *Unless the old man intends to leave Domal to...* The thought was so repulsive that he couldn't finish the words, yet he knew they'd surface later to plague him. Thoughts of his half-brother always did.

In contrast to the lavishness of the palace, the lower level of the keep was all bare stone walls, smoky air, and dim light. In place of servants running up with heaping trays of food and brimming cups of wine there was but a washbasin and a pitcher of potable water at the entrance, and the only callers here were a filthy peddler and two girls of seemingly ill-repute. *Have they forgotten whose chambers lie above? Have I been gone so long?* Baeldrin's heated gaze swept the room. *Where is the steward? His head shall be next to roll!*

With her rear plopped in a fat guard's lap, one of the whores was first to see the prince. "Lord!" Squirming free of the hog, she nearly fell. The other guards and servants followed, rising to their feet swiftly with their eyes — and some jaws as well — open wide in surprise. Martassin's face betrayed his amusement at the spectacle, yet he valued his life too much to make a jest.

"Fetch Koras! Now!" Baeldrin stormed, sending a terrified lad flying up the spiral staircase. "The rest of you...out!"

At that, bodies scrambled from the hall by every conceivable exit, leaving the prince and his shadow alone once more. "Perhaps you'd like me to deal with the steward, my prince?" spoke Martassin presently. "If you still plan on joining the council this evening, you've not long to rest..."

"That won't be necessary," Baeldrin replied, calmer now. "You may go."

The spindly man frowned: "But..."

"You said you'd send word of my intention. Do you wish my presence there to be a surprise?" The prince smiled on the inside, knowing this put Martassin in a predicament: the servant must either take word himself, leaving Baeldrin alone, or risk blame for the upset caused by an unexpected guest. Either way Martassin would surely rouse the king's wrath.

Yet it seemed Baeldrin alone would be surprised, for Martassin had a way out: "Then I'll ask Koras for a runner. That boy who went to fetch him seemed quick enough."

It made no matter, however, for the delay here had been sufficient. By now the prince's personal servants — those who kept his secrets on pain of death — would've admitted his guest through one of the side doors, so he didn't care how long Martassin lingered outside his chambers. *Just don't let the worm eavesdrop at my door.*

Now that the fool had secured a stay, Baeldrin returned to the man's offer of dealing with Koras, accepted it, then headed off for the keep's third level. It was true that he had little time before he must reemerge — yet it wasn't sweet sleep he'd find in the interim. It was an informer and would-be accomplice awaiting him within: a man whom he'd known but a short while but whose ambitions supported his own.

Not only had Nephos Zera been admitted — the prince saw as he stepped into the room and bolted the door behind him — but the Mardothan had made himself quite at home. Reclined on the finest of Baeldrin's lush couches, the ambassador from Mardotha had already produced his etched bone pipe and was in the midst of a deep toke of herb. His newly shaven head glistened in the lamplight, yet his eyes were obscured both by the shade falling down from his jutting forehead and the jet black cosmetic applied liberally on their lids and at their corners. *At least he hasn't presumed to don one of my robes,* noted Baeldrin, finishing his appraisal with a glance at Zera's customary clothing.

Exhaling a plume of dark smoke, Nephos held the pipe out to his host and grinned. "Fair night, Prince Baeldrin. What's become of the dog I saw sniffing your tail?"

"Martassin?" replied Baeldrin, waving the pipe away. He needed his wits about him tonight, especially at dinner. "A dog indeed…but not one we need to trouble ourselves about. For the moment he's chained to Koras, and the maids shall keep an eye on him."

"Just so," said Zera. He set his pipe aside with a bejeweled hand. "And yet our walk has been delayed once more."

"I couldn't have gone with you anyway," said the prince, pouring himself a cup of wine. "I've invited myself to dine with the king's council." He took a sip before dropping wearily into the nearest chair.

"As much as your brazenness amuses me, Baeldrin, I must warn you: if you don't show your face to our coconspirators soon, it'll be more than my neck at stake. Ferried words mean nothing alone. You should be dining with *them*, my friend, to ease each one's fears with a smile and a firm slap on the back." The ambassador turned his head around to ensure the prince was listening. "From what little our comrades have heard from you recently, the whole scheme's starting to look like my own deluded invention."

Baeldrin began to raise his voice but then checked himself, fearing Martassin might be snooping about nearby. Yet his anger was apparent all the same: "You tell the old half-wits to sit tight! They can't threaten you nor me nor *anyone*…for if we're exposed, it shall be *all* our heads tarred and skewered atop the city walls! Today I secured the arms that Saedus requires…you look surprised!…so my stay here is a day or two at best. I must know you can handle these curs without me. Can you or not?"

"You make it hard for me, prince," the Mardothan sighed. He reached for the pipe again, lit it, and inhaled. "To save my land from the Sinian rodents," he exhaled, "…not only must I pretend to adore every word that spews from your father's lips, but now I must suffer his son's arrogance also. And as neither one of you are listening to me, maybe I should return home and take up a spear with my brothers. I had three of them when I left."

How much do I trust this man? Baeldrin thought. *Enough to tell him everything?* The answer to that was obvious. *Surely he can be told more, though. Enough to keep him here.*

And so he did.

8

Dragan's eyes watched rainwater pool in the cup formed by the palms of his hands...but his mind roamed far away, whisked over the leagues separating his warriors from their wives and homesteads by the honeyed tongue of a practiced bard. Lomion was the best Dragan had ever heard, capable of adopting the gruff demeanor of a boasting veteran as easily as the frivolous air of a courtly fool. At the moment—although most of them were soaked through to the bone from the evening's heavy downpour—the Haxûdī packed around the talented Sinian tagalong appeared to have the same opinion of the man. They laughed, hushed, and chimed in at all the right times, bright eyes and neat grins telling of the true pleasure each found in Lomion's wit and melodious voice.

"...and that's when your lovely queen found the bold warrior in her grasp!" finished the bard, his words booming across the sheltered campfire out into the night where Dragan sat alone. On cue, another round of boisterousness ensued.

The liquor was still hot within him. He needed to hear the tale Lomion was leading up to—needed *anything* to help validate his decision of leaving Bronwyn behind. He let the water slip through his fingers and looked up at the black sky. How many generations of mankind had done the same? How many thousands had pondered the courses of their tiny lives while perusing the vast, unyielding dome of Mother Earth? *Can I not foil even the claws of time?* he thought, absently cupping his hands again. *Will there be others like her to come?*

"Why do you stop, *whiteface*?" someone yelled. It sounded like Jedan. "Tell us of our lord's great deed!"

Dragan could picture the sly smile on Lomion's face—and that, coupled with the fickleness caused by his drunken state, made him grin wide in turn. His tired eyes closed...and he drifted...and then he found himself reliving the scene being shaped by the bard's words...

"Bring it now!" screamed Horga, red blood spurting freely from between the fingers clutched about his neck. The cry reached Dragan's ears, diluted by wails of the dying and the throbbing of his heart—a rhythm that beat in his mind like hammer on anvil, plaguing him with excruciating pain. *Thump! Thump! Thump!* The left side of his face was numb save his ear: it burnt with the fiery extremity of a white hot iron. The Beast had struck him there with such force that all who witnessed it thought him immediately dead...and left him so. Yet, prostrated by the wound, his face half-submerged in a pool of blood and bile, *he was still alive.* Two score bodies, brave Haxûdī all, were piled up in heaps around him. Their entrails stuck in his dark brown hair. Their blood and his own mixed within his mouth. He retched at the taste of it...then lifted his head slightly, slowly turning towards the voice. With his right eye blinded by guts, Dragan struggled to open his left, peeling the lids away from each other. What little of the woods revealed by the lanterns was a portrait of dark red: trunks, bushes, the ground, the Beast's shaggy coat—all spattered with the color of death. The monster tossed Horga's limp body aside like a doll, impaling him on the jagged tip of a broken sapling; then, clearly pained, it plucked arrows from its chest and stomach, drowning out the burly warrior's last feeble wheeze with a deafening roar.

Only one man remained standing: Ûladriss. His shadow danced like a flame to the swaying of the lanterns. In one hand he gripped the leather-bound hilt of his slender cutlass. The other held that which Horga so desperately wanted: the priest's talisman.

It'd been only two days since their party slipped past the shadowy barrier of Thirannon Forest to hunt the thing that'd plagued their lands for so many years. What few villagers yet daring to reside near the forest edge had come to mourn their departure. Some womenfolk fell at the warriors' feet, grabbing their ankles, pleading for them to avert doom by returning to King Toldriss' great hall. Their husbands, mostly farmers, eyed the passersby with foolish expressions. When one crone grabbed at Jesrim Greenboar's leg, he looked upon her with venomous spite:

"Every village, every face: the same thing. Why do you torture me, woman? Return to your home—and sow for me no more!"

Jesrim's words, spoken too loudly, did nothing but attenuate the company's waning moral. Nearly every face drooped with somber trepidation...yet there was one man who wore a tranquil grin that never left his lips. At the rear of the column Dragan Saedus strolled with a nonchalant gait, stopping occasionally to pick a flower for a weeping lady or child. One, a girl of no more than seventeen, stared at him with such perplexity that he burst into a fit of mirthful laughter. The sound was so incongruous with the villagers' lamentations that it brought the entire procession to a halt. They all looked on Dragan then with contempt, like a father on a child who'd dare make a mockery of his teachings.

"The northerner derides our expedition," declared Horga, speaking directly at Dragan but loud enough for all to hear. "I can endure his sneer no more!"

"Endure it you shall," spoke Ûladriss, his left eye still showing the slightest tint of yellow: the last remnants of the bruise he'd taken from Dragan's pommel. "As the queen wills, he'll remain in our company."

"Then we'll send him first," continued Horga vehemently, "...so at least I won't die before that smirk's been wiped from his lips!"

Toldriss' striking bride, Falchī of the Haxûdī, was younger sister to Saedus of Ost. Dragan had been sent to his aunt with a message intended for her alone— but the queen's cool words of welcome and the flowing ale had quickly stirred up one of her estranged nephew's arrogant bouts. At some point in the ensuing ruckus he'd blabbed the missive's contents before the entire court: "Though you sit atop a kingdom's throne, dear aunt, you're no less slave than I am. Or have you forgotten who lifted you to this dais? My mother demands a gift: a payment for all the troubles she endured for your sake..."

And so on this drear eve he stared at the titanic shell concealing his mother's would-be prize: the white bones of King Toldriss' eldest son, the cursed Beast of Thirannon. All mirth indeed, as Horga had willed it, was departed from Dragan now, sent far flying on the instant that grizzly paw had turned his face aside.

"Ûladriss! Fling down that damned *trinket* and come to me!" shouted Dragan frantically, spitting out more blood than words. He was sure that the creature's wounds were what warded it off for the moment—not some ugly rodent's skull wrapped in a crazed old man's chants and leather thong—and that the moment would soon be gone.

The warrior's head turned, and Dragan confirmed the fear he'd imagined would be swimming in the man's eyes. But then came a surprise. It wasn't the Beast causing Ûladriss' fear, Dragan discerned, but rather *himself*—the fact that he still lived after absorbing such a punishing blow.

The son of Saedus staggered to his feet and lurched forward, snatching up a spear and a wicked single-edged battleaxe in the process. There was no path for the fiend to avoid him now—had it the slightest notion to do so—for the Haxûdī had located the cave and fortified the area about its mouth while daylight yet lingered: aware the creature must show itself either upon a departure or return. None but Dragan had even considered venturing inside.

Their wait hadn't been long.

Surpassing in height some seven cubits above ground, the fallen prince stood before his attackers covered in thick black fur. His body was shaped as a man's, though the muscles of arm, chest, and leg were so heavily rippled that one might expect their mass to burst free at any moment from the sheathing skin. Dripping fangs curved down and back a hand's length from a skull that sang of both bear and wolf, and tufted ears twitched with every wild dart of two voracious glazed yellow eyes. Cruel talons writhed where once had been delicate hands, the nails sharp and strong as whetted steel.

With spear poised in hand, Dragan placed himself between the Beast and the Haxûdī. The usual keenness of Ûladriss had become dismantled by an extreme consternation. He eyed his future master obtusely, unable to comprehend what had just occurred—yet his feet began to move him forward, his prowess almost instinctual.

"Fool!" cried Dragan, quickly glancing over his shoulder. "Have your turn when I'm dead—but take one more step, *and I'll kill you myself!*"

The sincerity of the threat was conveyed by Dragan's eyes: two orbs of fiery passion that burned like the sun, as if a fire had consumed his skull. The word *doom* glowed about his neck, made prominent by the blood filling the shallow etching of his metal collar. Ûladriss was stayed. He'd known fear — but never cowardice. Yet whom here was his enemy? He was certain intervention would spell death. A death with no honor. So he backed away slowly and crouched behind an uprooted stump. Realizing his hand still clutched the priest's charm, he cast it down as if it were a venomous snake. His true talisman, he now knew, was standing before him.

Toldriss' lost heir plucked a final arrow from his thigh before turning an icy gaze on his opponent. He started...and hesitated, his visage betraying a glint of the same quandary that had afflicted Ûladriss. Though some thirty men lay as fallen leaves about him — each one alike, all nameless and faceless in defeat — the Beast seemed to recall the man now approaching as the first to have challenged him while the rest yet shrank in terror. Then the glint was gone. The creature arched its back and, in one violent motion, bent its torso groundward, flinging muscular arms outward to bellow an earsplitting roar. Protuberant teeth framed the black hole from which the sound radiated: a void so large it seemed likely to consume the world.

An instant later the Beast was airborne, leaping forward with cat-like agility. Dragan let fly his spear. The monster swatted at the missile but misjudged, and the dart's tip pierced through his claw. Folding in pain, his mass crashed down upon the enemy, sending Dragan tumbling through the nearby bushes. The son of Saedus scrambled to regain his footing — but the Beast was already upon him, mounting his back, a claw locked around his neck. The hero's outstretched arm reached desperately for the axe that lay just beyond his fingertips. *Too far*. The creature opened its pestilent mouth and thrust its head down, intent on ripping the foe to shreds.

To Ûladriss, lone observer and chronicler of the deed, the dire struggle that ensued was a rolling blur of bloody metal and fur. Yet even as he looked upon the chaotic scene, he still pictured the red gleam he'd found in Dragan's eyes. Had the glow been merely a trick of reflected lantern light, or was it a glimpse of a supernatural inner flame, yearning for release? Was it that flame fueling the hero's limbs as they suddenly exploded from writhing tangles to thickly muscled staves, propelling both man and monster erect? Could it be a thing greater than human strength that now lifted the behemoth in midair and slammed it heavily to the ground?

Dragan himself didn't ponder these things. He was acting on impulse — no thoughts, only action and reaction. From the dirt the Beast clamped its foaming jaws into its adversary's partially-armored calf, summoning forth a jet of crimson blood; in turn, Dragan dropped to one knee and dug fingers into his foe's oozing wounds, ripping two of the arrow-sized holes into gaping slits. Both opponents bellowed from their anguish and deadly rage. Then came another exchange, the creature rising once more to rake at the man or crush him beneath his besmeared silver breastplate — and the man attempting to get behind the creature, out of the reach of those deadly claws. But after one final, tumultuous slam to the ground, Dragan succeeded. The Beast of Thirannon loosed death throes that battered the man to the brink of his own demise, savagely parting stone from earth, bark from trunk, and flesh from body with every impact; but the hero's strangling right arm only sunk in tighter, choking and snapping and stealing life away. The roars and shouts ceased, replaced by sounds of carnage to both nature and combatants that intensified, reaching a nightmarish plateau...

Then it was done.

The victor rose slowly, favoring his bitten leg and undoubtedly broken ribs. He peered down at his work. Ûladriss joined him.

"*DoomBringer*," uttered the Haxûdī.

Dragan looked at his companion and grinned. "Give me your knife."

9

Baeldrin had thought a few cups of strong wine, a cleansing rubdown, and fresh clothing would be enough to conjure a second wind. But he'd been wrong. Then, to combat a nodding head at his father's table, he'd taken to drinking more wine to keep him occupied...and now...

He was quite drunk.

I should've accepted Zera's pipe after all, he mused with a frown, pretending to be caught up now in savoring his food, hoping not to outwardly reveal his state. *At least then I'd have one less headache come morning...*

For some reason this thought struck Baeldrin as funny, and a sharp snort of laughter escaped him unbidden. Immediately he cut his eyes left and right to the men sitting beside him — and thankfully found they hadn't noticed or didn't care about such foolishness. The next course of figs, dates, and a fowl in thin syrup was set before him, and he fell at once back into his gluttonous disguise.

About Acomalath's huge round feast table had been set enough cedar chairs for thirty subjects to dine comfortably in the presence of their lord. Yet not all of the seats were occupied tonight, as this was a meeting of council, and no wives or children — other than Baeldrin himself — were present. A brief formal welcome by the king had started the dinner, but the night's business wouldn't begin until everyone's stomach was full to bursting. Those not presently joining the prince in silent indulgence conversed at ease in scattered groups of two to three around the counter, while overhead the light from hundreds of curved fixtures cast a red glow down on huge wall tapestries, ornate vases, instruments of gold, and busts of polished stone. A hint of jasmine played background to a myriad smells from the sumptuous foodstuffs at hand, and tattooed servants worked fans of feathers behind each group of diners to whisk away the day's hot air.

As the last course was making its way around, Acomalath rose from his chair and, seeing his guests begin to follow suit, motioned for them to remain seated. *At last,* thought Baeldrin. *All I need do now is hold my eyes open and listen. No one will speak to me once their business begins...*

"My friends," the king was saying, "...the new moon rises, and so we gather once more. I take it you've found the food and drink satisfying?" A brief round of approval followed, some councilmen assenting with grunts rather than words due to their full mouths. Looking to the man at his immediate right, Acomalath spoke again: "Radovan, who addresses me first tonight?"

The spindly minister cleared his throat and replied in his usual high-pitched, droll voice: "My king, that would be Lord Tomisval. He tells me he brings news concerning your safety — and that is certainly of paramount importance to us all."

With a roll of his eyes and a loud sigh, Acomalath took his seat again. "What is it this time, Tomis? Another serving girl trying to poison my cup? Or perhaps a band of gremlins lurking about my bedchamber?" Even Baeldrin couldn't keep from joining the laughter following this last statement—although afterwards he chalked it up to the wine rather than to his father's wit.

"I'm afraid not," said Tomisval, standing as the king reclined, he perhaps the only man present besides the servants remaining composed. "Thus far it's but a rumor…or I'd have insisted on speaking to you immediately. Yet I fear the proof is soon to come. One of our previous informants took his own life this morning rather than speak a name to my men. There's a conspiracy against you at work, my lord. One that involves more than scorned wenches and fairies."

"Every week it seems there's some such news, yet nothing ever comes of it." Acomalath rested his chin lightly atop his raised index fingers, searching Lord Tomisval's eyes. The chamber was quiet again. "But if it will ease your mind, old friend, I'll indulge you. Exactly what is it that…"

A sharp clang resounded just then from across the wide table, cutting off the king in mid-sentence—and all eyes followed the noise to its source.

A moment later, as Baeldrin's sluggish mind realized the interruption had actually come from *him*, a jolt of terror struck the prince and manifested itself in the look on his face. Quickly he snatched from his plate the dinner knife that'd slipped from his shaking hand; but then, afraid to be seen holding any blade just now with talk of treachery—*his* treachery—hovering in the air, he as quickly set it down on the table and pushed it well away from him.

This should've been the end of the matter, with faces returning to the king as he resumed his reply to Tomisval. Instead, Baeldrin felt his father's gaze beating down on him, and the prince struggled to stifle old feelings of a child about to be severely scolded. Suddenly his mood shifted dramatically. What he should've said then was *nothing*—rather turning again to seeming diffidence. But what he actually said, in a near-booming voice thick with sarcasm, was: "Forgive my horrible clumsiness, Father! Have I broken your train of thought?"

"Tell me, son, is it not enough we've suffered you to dine here unbidden?" Acomalath's cheeks reddened as he fought to control his anger. "Your business with me today is done, is it not? Or has the wine cooled your *heroic aspirations*?"

Baeldrin's fists tightened at these words, and he looked as if he'd rise from his seat in a maddened rage; yet the king continued, undaunted:

"Leave us! I'll not have another word from you!"

A single thought had played over and over again as Baeldrin turned his back on the table and stormed from the room: *I'll strangle you myself.* Oh, how he'd longed to shout back…to curse the king for a coward and gold monger in front of the man's retainers…to boast of his own grand design for the throne and beyond. *Without their weapons at hand,* his swimming brain had even surmised, *I could've given them all a good thrashing.* But now, outside the palace again, his gait finally slowing to a weary trudge, the prince felt a welcome night breeze brush past his face to dishevel his dark mane…and the cooling air was beginning to bring some sense back to him. He recalled how soon he'd be departing for Ost, followed by plenty of time for plotting revenge on the way.

But all he really needed now was his bed. And he was well on his way to it.

10

The hour wasn't long past dawn, yet already the day's heat was building. A feeble wind joined the morning light streaming into King Deserus Oen's pavilion through many open flaps, providing for the moment a modicum of comfort; but Astelidus knew it wouldn't last. And though the air was fresh, it was too weak to sweep away the medicinal stench rising up to his nostrils from his bandaged chest.

Bronwyn sat to his left. How splendid it'd been, despite the horrid pain of his wounds, to have her so close over the past week. To Astelidus' surprise and lasting delight, she'd refused to hand him off to the healers, telling them that he was to remain where she could *personally* attend him — so thankful was she that he'd saved her life. Since then she'd hardly ceased fawning over him. *Touching him. I should strive to become a poorer fighter*, he mused, *...and be wounded more often.* Smiling from this frivolous thought, he turned his head to gaze at her. Dressed in an exquisite gown of yellow-gold and green that mirrored the colors of her hair and eyes, a bejeweled pendant resting between seductive breasts, the king's niece outstripped in magnificence all the tent's other treasures combined. And those spoils were neither base nor few — among them ornate coffers, painted vases, silver tripods, and weapons of elaborately etched steel.

Across from Bronwyn, fidgeting in his chair, sat Bastram Narohad: the man chosen just yesterday to succeed Camus Robi as the allied captain. The newness of his rank was evident, but Astelidus knew little, and perceived nothing else, of the man save his obvious warrior stature and frame. Under other circumstances the man might've been jesting with Fedrin Rae who held the seat immediately to Bastram's right; yet today the old man-at-arms seemed equally perturbed. He sat still as stone, frowning and gazing out of the pavilion to the yard — or perhaps to somewhere far beyond. *I should've known he'd behave like this today. Words shall be spoken he won't want to hear.*

Astelidus' gaze went next to Torensus Oen, brother to the king and father of the woman beside him...then on to King Deserus himself. Torensus, though in fact the younger of the two siblings, looked quite the elder today with his thin ivory hair and loose, wrinkled skin. In contrast, the king's face, though lined, was taut, and his eyes seemed yet filled with youthful vigor. Both were dressed in fine dyed tunics, their fingers and thumbs covered in rings and necks draped heavily with gold. Atop Deserus' thick curls rested Sinia's crown, and as he too sat quietly in his chair, watching and listening as a servant strummed the harp, one of his hands stroked his bushy gray beard.

Aware of Astelidus' appraisal, Torensus felt compelled to speak: "Son of Ny, why are you here among us this morning? You're fortunate to be alive. Surely our blathering won't speed your recovery..."

"He insisted, Father," Bronwyn returned, "...against my desire as well. Yet his station allows his presence. Besides...shouldn't you be praising rather than scolding him?"

To this, Torensus merely frowned and looked away, and the king seemed not to have heard the exchange.

Other captains of high rank, both native and allied, filled the common bench. A few whispered to one another, yet none of these would dare—as Torensus just now had nearly done—disturb the king's reverie. Astelidus knew them all well: so well that he might venture to predict each one's very words, or lack thereof, to come. But there was no time for such a game now, for the last council member had finally entered. As Galran of Tholmis took his place, the harp ceased, and all eyes turned to the king.

"What news has reached us since yesterday?" Deserus began, his deep voice cracking slightly from the period of disuse.

A lanky man shot up from the end of the bench and cleared his throat: "My lord, I'm pleased to inform you that, as I promised, my kinsman's warriors now march to your aid from Relinydd. Though overlong in its marshalling—as you know, and I much regret—the host is quite large: full of able young men eager to test their skills in battle."

"Eager to wrap their greedy fingers around spoils already won—that's more like it," someone announced loudly.

"Silence, Galran!" Deserus roared. "First you keep us waiting, and now you speak out of turn!" The king shook his head in disgust...then he began again in a lowered voice: "Any man willing to slay a Mardothan is a friend of mine, with or without a price." He looked at the captain from Domal. "Ramesh Anû. Though you've vexed me sorely these past months, in the end you proved true to your word. Remain with me this afternoon, and we'll discuss a suitable reward."

"My thanks, lord," said Ramesh with a smile—then seated himself as quickly as he'd stood.

With that over, Torensus leaned in close to his brother as if to confide in him. Yet he spoke so all could hear: "Perhaps these Domalin lads shall fill the void left by our fleeing Haxûdī, you suppose? Though I'm certain no man among them can match the *GrimHelm*'s might in arms..."

"My brother speaks truly," said the king. "Though Dragan forsook us in the end, we would not have won through the noon without him among us. No man can deny it. Thanks to his strength and courage, the enemy's great champions are no more—and only the third wall remains. So, my brethren, I ask now: who among you shall rise in his stead? The war's not yet won. Reinforcements yet buzz to Crûthior like flies to a rotting carcass. I need a new champion."

Silence fell within, amplifying the morning bustle of the camp without. Then several men stood all at once, though most appeared reluctant to do so. Bastram, Galran, and even Fedrin Rae were among them.

Astelidus frowned. *Can I stand without aid?* Frantic, he turned to Bronwyn — only to find her already staring at him. She shook her head *no*.

"Is this all?" asked Deserus.

"Lord Deserus…half the men present have risen," said Galran, exasperated. "Would you make heroes of us all?"

"You just received my warning, captain," the king spoke. "Has the Daemon devoured your wits?" He paused then sighed before adding: "Remove yourself from my sight."

Galran of Tholmis bowed then stormed from the tent, leaving the eyes of his peers wide.

"What arrogance!" Torensus snapped, his words followed immediately by a loud crash. A chair had overturned nearby, bringing a shattering end to one of King Oen's fine ceramics. Above the mess wobbled Astelidus — with Bronwyn's hug about his waist the only thing keeping him from tumbling as well.

Astelidus opened his mouth to beg pardon, but the king cut him off: "What have we here? See now, men? I asked for a hero…and here one stands. With no enemy within his grasp, he's settled for throttling my vase!"

Great laughter ensued from the men, for a jest had been sorely needed. Even Bronwyn chuckled as she fought to steady her ward. Realizing the king's call for a new champion had been contrived solely for such a display from Astelidus, the sniggling volunteers soon withdrew themselves. Even Fedrin sat down, though his broad, silver-bearded face had never moved from its awful scowl.

Despite the pain ripping at his chest, Astelidus managed a grin himself. "My lord, you're too cruel."

"Seriously, Ny," said Torensus, "…you shouldn't be here at all — much less showing off your balls." He saw Bronwyn's smile fade. "Forgive my vulgarity, daughter…but we all know it. Astelidus is a brave warrior, but his wounds are grievous. This war shall be long done before he retakes the field."

"He's right," spoke Bronwyn to her patient. "No one doubts your courage, Astelidus…but you've done enough. You need only rest now. Let's go…"

"In a moment, Bronwyn," said the king, catching her words. "First you must speak to us of the attack that left him in this state."

And so she did, relaying both what she herself had seen and what Astelidus had afterwards told her from his perspective. It didn't take long, and when she finished, Deserus spoke again:

"I'm eternally thankful that no harm befell you, niece—and thus to Astelidus, we're forever in debt. Yet I'm afraid we must hear more from you both: namely, what brought him to your tent in the dead of night?"

Neither Astelidus nor Bronwyn rushed to answer; but, surprisingly, Fedrin Rae stood then unbidden and addressed the king in their stead. His voice was uncharacteristically soft and meek:

"My lord...perhaps these things would be best discussed in private..."

"They have been, of course," Torensus cut in. "...but not to our satisfaction. These matters are of great importance—thus it's the king's wish that his council be informed as well. Bronwyn, you'll tell us what was last said between you and Dragan before his departure."

His daughter looked warmly upon Fedrin: "My thanks, friend, but I believe I can manage this." With a slight nod, the bear retook his seat. Then, after helping Astelidus back into his own, Bronwyn began:

"The answer to your question, Uncle, is easy enough. Astelidus says he saw the Haxûdī torches departing camp—and that he came to my tent seeking the reason behind it. Where does one find such a man as Dragan Saedus? A man of such unfathomable strength and skill, yet utterly devoid of both love and honor? He claimed that his love was true, oh yes—but how could it be? He deserted not only me, who cared for him deeply, but every one of us! And for what? Nothing more than his mother's whim. Can you believe that? And he claimed he had no choice in the matter. This from the man who refused to bow before the King of Sinia!"

As she paused to catch her breath, murmurs of agreement filled the void left by her voice. Yet her tirade wasn't done: "Curse Dragan Saedus! If he ever did love another besides himself, it must've been the witch who spit him from her thighs! He wouldn't even delay his retreat *one day* for the dirge of Camas Robi, a man whom he swore was his dear friend. I say this: let us speak the evil man's name no more among us. It'll bring nothing now save ill fortune." A loud round of approval ensued, but she waved it down then started over in a lowered tone. "You did well to cheer those words...yet you'll have no praise for what I say next. I'm no warrior. My presence here turns no tides. So perhaps you can forgive my weakness—for in the end, I begged the man to take me with him."

There was no initial response. Perhaps some of the men were too appalled to speak, yet those who had ever truly loved and lost were hushed not by shock but rather by their own bittersweet memories. Somehow Astelidus too understood, though the empathy did little to quench his anger. *You're mine now, Bronwyn,* he reassured himself, *...not his! Soon you'll beg only for me!*

After a moment Fedrin spoke again, still wearing his melancholy demeanor. "Long have I watched over you, girl. You're like my own daughter—if Torensus doesn't mind me saying it. So if you'd listen to me now, I swear to speak a truth: though I fear you'll not like my advice well, however much you need to hear it."

"Go on, Fedrin," spoke Bronwyn, her temper cooling. "I've never dismissed your guidance lightly."

The big man nodded, this time out of thanks instead of the earlier dismissal. "Nearly all you said of Dragan is true. As his friend, I'd deny it…but alas, I can not. Yet one thing I know to be certain: he loves you still. When your grief is no longer fresh, you'll see it too. Till then, to shun his name will only cause your thoughts to burn with him the more. Maybe a day will come when he'll return to us…and maybe not. But if ever it does, trust me — he'll not need our contempt to awaken his shame. He lives with it now."

"That's enough, Fedrin," Deserus interrupted. "Next you'd have us singing the man's praises again, and that I won't allow. Your point's taken, so let's move on. It seems more likely the assassin's blade was meant for Dragan than for my niece, but either way I fear many of us will sleep less soundly in the nights to come."

In the pause after these words, both Fedrin and Bronwyn retook their seats, and the king clapped for his servants.

11

The Haxûdī had awoken to a morning of muck and misery. The evening's rain had converted the path's loosely packed, leaf-strewn dirt into sucking mud, and their baggage carts were as bogged now in the road as their heads were in throbbing pains. One has little to do when the sky weeps so profusely save to hunker down with a woman or wineskin or both; and though only the memory of women — good or bad — had been there to distract the *GrimHelm* and his men when the torrent arrived, the wineskins had started full near to bursting. Now they were all but empty…left wanting…

Like my soul, mused Dragan as he dismounted to help Jedan Mûran's boy dig out a wheel. Gavix' effort had only worsened the predicament. "Go fetch me a plank." Dragan's look and tone were stern, befitting the mood of the day.

The lad ran off aimlessly, clearly more anxious to avoid chastisement than to fulfill the command.

Not bothering to wait, Dragan trudged into the muck and made ready to put his back into it, when…

"Allow me," said someone coming up from behind. The voice was thin and strangely dry.

Dragan turned in surprise.

"You've kept me waiting long enough," continued Poltoros, moving in as his mistress' son stepped aside. The eerie messenger appeared the same as when Dragan had last met with him before the gates of Crûthior — and without another word, he stepped forward and shoved the end of his tyberwood staff between the spokes, uttered an arcane phrase, and lifted gently. The wheel rose, slowly but without effort, and the mud below gasped as it collapsed back upon itself, losing its prize.

This wasn't the first such conjuration Dragan had witnessed — not even the first from this man — yet a wave of awe swept over him all the same. An image of the White King's myrmidons flashed across his mind. He heard again clearly, as if returned to the very moment, their bloodcurdling cries as wildfire streamed forth from Poltoros' staff to engulf their bodies: reducing them in mere seconds to ash and bones. He recalled how the servant beside him now, seemingly alive and whole today, had collapsed on that dark evening from the drain of sorcery and been ripped near to shreds by wicked claws and fangs…and how after his own tremendous feat, he'd wrapped the mutilated body for the journey home. Poltoros' face had looked different before he fell: tanned, full, and at least capable of subtle jest if not true mirth. Now it was as sallow and gaunt and detached as a talking corpse: for that was just what Poltoros had become. *He saved my life…but how he must despise me for the cost!*

"Your mother praises you highly," rasped the lich, withdrawing his staff from the wheel and turning to Dragan. "But I'm not impressed."

Dragan assumed Poltoros would elaborate, but instead the man merely stood and stared at him with cold, black eyes. It appeared he expected something from his onetime ward. But not knowing what that something was, the *DoomBringer* offered only: "How far ahead did you ride?" and, receiving no response to that, "Did you see the warnings?"

Poltoros cut his eyes over Dragan's right shoulder. A man was approaching on horseback. "Send him away."

"My lord," began Ûladriss, ignoring the stranger's dismissal. "If I may have a word..." He gestured to a more private spot just off the road. "It's urgent."

"In a moment," spoke his captain. "Wait there."

Ûladriss frowned, nodded, and yanked the reins, swinging his steed around.

Dragan watched the Haxûdī chieftain trot off before turning back to Poltoros with a frown of his own. "I'll dismiss my men as I choose, *servant*."

"He comes to report the death of a scout," said the lich, unmoved by Dragan's provocation. "The man's body lies in the road, not far ahead—his eyes gouged out and the lids sewn shut with twists of his own hair."

Dragan glanced to where Ûladriss awaited him and met the Haxûdī's eyes. *Yes, that's it.*

Poltoros was grinning now as if the scout's torture and murder amused him. "Two more there are, further on. Their conditions are similar."

"I jested with my marshal yesterday," said Dragan, indicating Ûladriss with a slight nod in that direction. "He saw to the necessary precautions, but we both laughed at the thought of an attack. What makes the wretched clans of Braured so bold? Has some leader united them? Or has lust for my spoils stricken every one of them dumb?" Not expecting an answer, he shook his head and went on. "They'll rue it. Each man with me has slain more foes than these *swine herders* have ever seen. Fools! Do they think we'll scare and flee...and leave our hard-won plunder behind?"

"No. They aim to kill you all. Did I see the warnings? Son of Saedus, I bring the only warning you need to concern yourself with, and it's one straight from your mother's lips. Quicken your pace—or forfeit your own precious gift. Must I say more?" The lich reached into his cloak, extracted something, and handed it over.

The Sun of Domal. Dragan studied the three golden rays and cursed the day of his birth. Then Gavix returned, daring to give his lord, the stranger, and the freed cart questioning looks. The *DoomBringer's* fist tightened on the pendant as his anger welled. *Damn her!* he thought, turning his icy gaze on the attendant.

"Where's that plank, boy? Tell me you've not returned empty-handed..."

"I...I...the men wouldn't listen," the lad stuttered and lied—his eyes in love with the ground—unable to withstand his master's stare.

"Go to your father and tell him you've failed me—and that your service is no longer required. Use those exact words and no others!"

Absolute terror seized the boy. He scrambled forward, fell on his hands and knees and groveled before his master, clasping the man's leg tight as if he never intended to let go. The pleading that ensued roused no sympathy from Dragan. With some exertion, he managed to kick Gavix from his boot. The boy landed face down in the mud then drew himself up slowly and limped away. He turned his head around to meet his lord's face.

Dragan marked the look as one of hate.

Realizing his anger had bested him only inflamed it more. He turned back to Poltoros, but the lich spoke first:

"I remember when you were but a child yourself, before foolish men called you by silly names. I read to you often—the *Book of Kings* being your favorite. You were most particularly fond of Nal'tanos Crimlore, the Golden King, a man methodical, astute, and wise in his resistance to impulse and anger. He placed a gold clasp shaped as a scale on his sheath, so that before he could draw his blade he must contemplate justice." A pause. "Yet it doesn't look to me that his color suits you now, *GrimHelm*." Special emphasis was placed on his last word.

Only those few who knew Dragan's past could so easily diminish his glory and toy with his emotions. This he hated above all. His anger faded to a dull rancor, then he spoke—less hotly now but with more spite:

"Be gone from my sight, *pigeon*. And don't return...unless you too wish to be flung face down in the mud."

"An empty threat," replied the messenger dryly. "Nevertheless, I hasten to be away. I've sent for..." The lich stopped short, reflecting. Then—with a sly smile—he spun and was on his way. Dragan watched him go before motioning to Ûladriss. The marshal trotted up:

"A friend of yours?"

Friend, or foe? A brief conversation ensued between Dragan and Ûladriss, yet the former would be unable to recall much of it later. His inner thoughts had drifted once again, touched off by his visitor...

The solitary torch shed enough light to reveal the two intruders' faces, but it couldn't uncloak the convulsing figure that lay at their feet. Dragan had crushed the young man's skull against the wet tunnel wall; and now he and his mother's steward stood over the body, waiting for the unfortunate youth's death: hoping it would come quickly. Every moan and twitch tormented them. Shame visited the killer, and pity tugged at the witness. Poltoros' blue eyes, brilliant as gems, glared harshly at the Bastard of Domal through the torchlight; yet though it took all his power, Dragan didn't shy away from the gaze. After a pause following the victim's final mewl, Poltoros released a quivering whisper as if he'd been holding his breath:

"What've you done? You've murdered this harmless man..."

Dragan's anger rose quickly, as if he'd anticipated such a chiding. "We're *here* to murder! Or have you forgotten?"

"Not the innocent!"

"What does that mean, steward? Didn't you hear Mother? Everyone in this realm is only an extension of *him*. They do *his* will. They're slaves to *his* power. Look...how many will we have to kill beyond there?" Dragan pointed ahead to where the tunnel necked down into another: one fit only for crawling. "Will they not have sons and daughters who'll mourn them once they're dead? Dead by *our* hands?"

Poltoros made no reply but dropped his torch to the ground, revealing the unhappy victim. A mass of black blood pooled around the poor youth's lifeless face. He'd died with his eyes open and mouth agape. A gruesome spectacle to behold.

"We had no choice!" Dragan pleaded, cooled by the sight of his work. "As soon as we were on our bellies he would've been off, fast as his legs could carry him, to tell someone. Anyone! It would've been our undoing!"

"For what price will our names be scribed in the *Book of Kings*?" the sorcerer mused, shaking his head as he stared intensely at the body below. "A price too great for me. The sight of blood has opened my eyes, child. We've no business here, so many miles from home. Let's leave the White King to his devices — and better yet, your mother also. Her mind's become twisted. I'll deny it no more. All who wish to be as gods will come to woe."

The portent didn't escape Dragan — and suddenly he became aware of the burden his new breastplate imposed on his body.

"I've been for you my entire life, old man," he started again. "Mother calls you *servant*, but I'd as soon call you *father*. You taught me so many things — but never spoke to me of men whose lives passed them by in mediocrity. Never of those who were birthed and died yet did nothing in between but toil in some field or beg on some corner. How many were there? What were their names? Had it been that they never lived, what difference would it have made? No, my friend, I won't fade into oblivion. The song of Dragan Saedus shall be sung long after

I'm gone. This is *my* time. I'm sorry."

Poltoros scowled. "And your mother?"

Dragan hesitated then pulled a small glass vial from his sleeve. The sorcerer peered at it through the torch's orange glow before shifting his eyes to its keeper. "Now you have my motive," Dragan answered, "...beyond fulfilling Mother's wishes. I've never cared to understand her grand plots and designs—but you know our mission here, and that should be enough for us both. This glass is to hold the White King's blood."

Heedless of their peril, Poltoros released a booming laugh that reverberated down the tunnel. "And you should beware, boy, of that curse etched about your neck." And with that he spun around and returned from whence they'd come. Dragan watched the torchlight wane until it was no more. There in the blackness he fought the urge to follow, but eventually he prostrated himself and snaked into the tiny burrow: entrance to the keep of Tiramas Vendhane, the White King and Lord of Addrindain.

12

Later in the day, after hours of uneventful trudging, a second report came as expected: another scout down. This one's ears were missing, and the ear canals had been filled with molten copper. Ûladriss, as he came upon the corpse, was clearly appalled. The first scout's body had been removed from the road before the company reached its spot, but Dragan had afterwards ordered anything else found to be left as it lay. "Every man of us shall look upon the work of our foe," he'd said. So it was done. And now a gap opened in the passing column about the second fallen scout as if the body were an area of impassable terrain, with only Dragan and his marshal lingering about it. They scanned their men's faces as each one surveyed the grisly scene and moved on.

"They're not afraid, lord," Ûladriss ensured, "...only shocked, as I am — and anxious to engage this pitiful enemy."

"I know, friend," Dragan replied. *"The Haxûdī laugh at fear.* And yet..." He paused, reached into his clothing, and brought out the Sun of Domal. "You see this? I wonder just how pitiful these woodsmen are..."

Ûladriss' expression showed he didn't understand.

Dragan smiled at the look then returned to serious thoughts. "It was once a thing I prized. A gift from my mother to her little boy." He ran his finger along one of the rays. "But it's since become a bane. A summons to her side. A token of my bondage. You say I'm a man without fear, Ûladriss, but it's not true. I'm afraid of *her.* Of what she might do. And I fear I may have led you into a trap."

"Let it come. Death has hung about us since the day we spoke our vows to you. The witch won't find us easy prey. But why, lord? Why would she turn on you?"

"Because she never gave me leave to depart? Because all my life I've handed over the spoils of my victories, but this time I wandered too far and long? Who knows her mind? The uncertainty is what scares me."

Ûladriss nodded. "No man may truly laugh at fear without ever having felt its grip — yet I've not seen you like this before. What's to stop us simply turning around? Don't mistake me: I ache to battle these vermin, trap or not. But for your sake..." He turned from Dragan and knelt over the dead scout. "I knew this man well. Corun, son of Vagris. He worshipped you and I as gods. If only he'd fallen before the black walls, slain by some valiant Mardothan."

"You don't understand," Dragan sighed. "No one regrets leaving more than I do, but there are things about me — things you must never know — that tie me to her. We must press on."

The end of the column drew near. Ûladriss stood, waved a retainer over to see to the corpse, mounted his steed, and rode angrily away.

Frowning, Dragan watched him go. *It saddens me to shut you out, friend. But would you still follow me if you knew? If you could read what's written on my collar?*

Rising slowly from bent knee, he extended his neck to peer over the trailing men. The vanguard was where he needed to be, but first he'd speak with Jedan. He tugged at the armhole of his breastplate as the rear guard approached: the hot air trapped inside was released, but only to be displaced by the tepid air of the atmosphere. The recurring downpours that were plagues to their travels seemed to have amplified the heat instead of stifling it, and the humidity was oppressive. Dragan wondered when the weather would give way.

It wasn't long before Mûran approached. He looked grave, as always, and that was well indeed — for this was no time for merriment. "Hail, *DoomBringer*."

"Hail."

"So…what do the woodsmen mean to do now?" asked the Haxûdī abruptly, looking askance at the mutilated body being carried from the road.

Dragan lowered his gaze to Gavix, who'd just come to his father's side. The boy's lower lip was busted, and one ear was as red as a beet — no doubt from the blows of a disappointed father. He stared at the dead man as well. Though it seemed to turn the lad's stomach, the sight must've been more inviting to him than the *GrimHelm's* eyes. "I'm told the intent is extermination," replied Dragan, looking back at Mûran.

Jedan's countenance didn't change. "Told by whom?"

He was about to answer *'a deceiver'* when another thought came to him. *'Did you see the warnings?'* Dragan's eyes were two pools of thought. If this clan was under Saedus' orders to assault his men, why were they waiting so long? Why all the warding signs? He saw now the folly in his last impulse of fear…

"Lord?" said Jedan, irritated by Dragan's pause.

"An old friend," his captain finally answered. The Haxûdī's frown curved even lower. Dragan set a hand on the man's shoulder: "Not all things can be explained now, for time is short. The wood's coming to its end — and if we're to be attacked, it'll come soon. Be ready. They may think to surround us."

Jedan nodded and turned to rally his troops.

The son of Saedus spoke again: "Another thing. Leave the boy with me."

13

As might well have been predicted after examining the other two bodies, the third downed scout's mouth had been sewn shut. Yet the final spectacle didn't lack a shock of its own, for this man wore the eyes of the first scout, the ears of the second, and his own removed tongue all threaded through by a cord around his neck.

Dragan could feel the eyes on him — and not just those of his column behind. The warriors of Braured were in the woods to either side of him now, he sensed: watching him contemplate their final warning. One more step forward might be all he was allowed before their missiles rained in, or a host several times the size of his own might be waiting patiently around the next bend...or most likely both. He wouldn't know for sure what was ahead till the moment his men faced it, for he'd sent no more scouts off to meet near-certain death.

" Gavix!" he summoned loudly without bothering to turn back, well aware of the futility of stealth.

"Yes, lord." The lad had been no more than a few steps away.

"My horse will only hinder me in this muck. Take him to the rear...then stay by your father's side."

"And mine too, boy," added Ûladriss, leading his charger up by the reins. "I doubt this enemy makes use of steeds."

Gavix nodded and was off with both horses in a flash, leaving his master disappointed. *He knows I mean to shield him from the brunt of battle, but he didn't have to accept it so easily.* The *DoomBringer* turned to Ûladriss: "What say you, marshal? Should we all press on, or should you and I go scouting ourselves?" *We won't fall as easily as the others, my friend...*

Before the Haxûdī could answer, however, a strange, whirring noise issued from far out in the woods. Both men tensed as it began, thinking at last to have heard the enemy's call to arms, but the sound merely continued a few moments more before ceasing as abruptly as it'd begun. Then silence fell again. Evening was fast approaching. Under other circumstances the rush to strike camp would soon be underway, but today Dragan had given his men a choice: "...either sleep under open sky atop this mud, with the last rays of sunlight falling upon your enemies' corpses — or else rest forever beneath it with them." That was how sure he'd been of an assault. Yet now...

"Why do you hesitate, men of Braured? We've seen your signs and haven't turned back! Is every one of you craven?" The *GrimHelm*'s shouts burst through the hot, still air of late afternoon, and every ear that heard them strained for an answer. The moment passed, and others came and went...

And nothing happened. Nothing at all.

Thoroughly disgusted, Dragan spit upon the earth before turning back to his marshal. "Order the column forward. We may even make it out of this damned forest before…"

"Look there!" yelled someone from behind. Dragan snapped his face around to the host then followed the speaker's gaze and pointing finger back to the path ahead. An old man with a tangled white beard, naked save for a loincloth and thong sandals, was just rounding the bend. He held a spear in one hand and led a young girl forward with the other.

The Haxûdī presence didn't surprise the man or his companion, yet the elder halted at a relatively safe distance from the column's head. Meeting the invading leader's eyes first to ensure attentiveness, he looked next at the child then spoke loud enough for all at the column's front to hear: "See, my queen? These desecrators heeded none of the signs you commanded us leave for them, and now our sacred wood nears its end. Will you let such boldness go unpunished?"

Although the *DoomBringer* was puzzled indeed by the odd scene before him, the elder's brazenness enraged him more: "No…you see *here*, old man! We care nothing for bloody altars and urns! You could've treated with us at any time — but instead your cowards slew my scouts!"

In response to the outburst, the elder simply let go the child's hand to extend an open palm: a rude gesture that said *shut your insolent mouth.* "My queen? We await your response. Shall we let them pass?"

Tugging nervously at one of her braids, staring at the *GrimHelm* through the eyes of a clearly spoiled child, the Queen of Braured pursed her lips to consider the question. "No," her high-pitched voice came at last, just before Dragan was about to rant again. "Kill them all."

No sooner had the girl's words permeated the trees than a volley of arrows, spears, and crazed war cries issued from them; yet this hail didn't find the famed Haxûdī cohort unprepared. Though some missiles indeed met with the intended fleshy marks, most of them clanged off armor or raised defenses to skid off into the brush on the path's opposing side, where no doubt more than a few friendly bodies caught the stray deadly shafts. Yet this was only the beginning. Incensed as he was at the old cur and brat of a monarch, Dragan turned his murderous gaze away from their scurrying bodies, allowing them to retreat as he focused on the axe-wielding berserkers charging around the bend in their place. *Daemon!* cursed Dragan to himself. *These men are stout!* So close did the frothing vermin resemble one another — with their thick, hairy bared chests, black manes, bushy beards, and crude fur boots and leggings — that he fancied them all having been pulled from the same mother's womb. *This is their elite. Slay them, and the rest shall flee.* Trusting the battle behind to his leaders of lesser rank, he shouted for Ûladriss to remain and rally the frontline against this charging swarm.

Amid the ensuing brutality, its owner ringed about by spattered gore, rabid howls of triumph, and groans of horrid death, a wicked smile built its home on the *DoomBringer's* lips. He'd not been disappointed after all. Killing was what he breathed for: the only thing he'd never betrayed. The next foe caught a swipe of Dragan's sword and left his forearm behind, loosing a terrible scream as blood jetted from the wound. Another savage charged to avenge his fallen comrade, only to have his head promptly removed by a magnificent swirl of the Haxûdī captain's blade.

It was a glorious slaughter.

But of whose side? Dragan indeed fared as well as any who knew him would expect, but as the last assailant within his reach ate mud, the *GrimHelm* swept his gaze about him...and felt a pang of doubt. The Haxûdī were fighting keenly — maintaining discipline, not backing down — but the enemy kept pouring in: wave after wave, slow but sure in its erosion of the defenders' human wall. More than a few piled bodies were now Dragan's own men. *This can't be!* he raged inside. *Too many already are slain here in this cursed wood!...all because of my own cowardice!* Suddenly his eyes fell on Ûladriss. It seemed the marshal had been pegged by the enemy as a key target, for no fewer than five towering brutes had somehow encircled him and — despite the Haxûdī's superior skill — were pressing the man to the brink with their coordinated efforts. Barging through the throng, Dragan arrived just in time to block a fatal blow aimed at the back of his friend's skull; then, as Ûladriss caught sight of his captain, the two warriors fell into a deadly dance, fighting side-by-side, engaging in joint maneuvers of their own against the multiple opponents. They ducked and twisted about one another, trading targets after each thrust or slash to confuse their foe and limit their own exposure. Each heedless of his partner's strokes — several of which came within thumb's width of friendly skin — the captain and marshal continued on in perfect sync, handing the assault back to their attackers...till at last none remained standing within their circle of defense save themselves and...

The Giant of Braured. Huge as he was — thick as an oak, dwarfing the tallest of his now-slain entourage by a head — the enemy champion appeared suddenly in the fray, slinging around his massive, double-bladed broadaxe as if it were no more cumbersome than a light staff or sword. This bastard rushed Ûladriss first upon entering the defenders' ring, catching the marshal unaware as the Haxûdī spun back from a final killing thrust. Then, from the corner of his eye, Dragan Saedus beheld a sight of utter horror: the collapse of his friend, Ûladriss Amaten, beneath the Giant's blow. The shock of that image was as intense as any pain his flesh had ever endured, but as he'd done with all those wounds of the past, now the *GrimHelm* set his jaw, imbibed the bitter drink that was his agony, and felt the brew stir up a fire of rage in his gut. *DIE!* he screamed inside at the Giant, over and over again, as he rushed forward to deal out his wrath.

His first cut was no feint this time, as otherwise it likely would've been. It was a sweeping arc that rained down with consummate fury; yet incredibly this assault was checked by the amazing strength and speed with which the enemy thug wielded his great axe. A counterblow even more swift and powerful barely missed Dragan as he recoiled in alarm. The Giant boomed with laughter at his adversary's surprise; and to make matters worse for Dragan — after the next few exchanges ended in him dodging both left and right to avoid the answers to his own strikes — he found himself back in the general melee: once more a target of multiple foes.

An instant later two of these were on him. Dragan leaned back just in time to avoid the pair of sabers cleaving air before his face and began a swirl of his own sword. The initial stroke of his counter took arm and blade from the assailant on the right, and the next was a sharp thrust through that one's throat. Then, almost simultaneously, the *DoomBringer* used his free hand to grab the left enemy by the neck and pull the man's body tight against his own. This one went into a frenzy, struggling wildly to break free...but Dragan merely withdrew his blade from the dead warrior's neck, shoved the struggling one aside, and — with a final sweep of his sword — opened a huge gash in the second man's unprotected back.

The Giant barreled forth again but now, having seen the quick dispatch of his fellows, without the previous mirth. Dragan tasted the man's growing doubt as the flurry came on, and not only did he manage to weather the storm, but with every returned stroke he seemed to gain more strength as his enemy waned. In a desperate attempt to regain control, the Giant stepped in close after a wide swing and thrust his axe's haft hard into the *GrimHelm*'s face. But...to the foe's dismay, the cracking of Dragan's cheekbone barely shook the young man, and as Saedus' son, enraged, answered the attack, the savage faltered and fell backwards over a corpse. Up came the axe held sideways to block the impending slash of Dragan's blade — yet haft and fingers were severed on impact.

"Wait!" gasped the Giant as Dragan prepared to administer the killing strike. "Hear me..." The brute's voice sounded strange...much different than it had at first during his cursing. Even his face was somehow *altered*.

I've seen those eyes before...

The *GrimHelm* sensed this change had neither come from the Giant fearing death nor the savage's vanquished pride — still he shrugged it off all the same. "Speak quickly!" he shook violently, fighting to restrain himself. Several Haxûdī ringed their captain now to offer him protection, yet he itched all the more to be away. *Ûladriss...*

"He summons you now to him," declared the Giant, cutting off Dragan's thought. "Go now by the swiftest road! Heed me not, and you'll suffer a fate much worse than mine. The witch shall inflict a never-ending torment upon you!"

"That *you've* already done," declared Dragan, his mind turning once more to the fallen marshal. "Now speak the name of your master!"

"Tiramas Vendhane," came the response. "The White King." And although those words seemed the last of the Giant of Braured, only as Dragan brought his death did the man's face and eyes again become his own.

Was he insane...or am I? The White King, after all, was long dead by Dragan's own hand. Again, he shoved such thoughts aside. *Ûladriss...*

Scanning the ground for his marshal's body, he came up short. *They drew me away. Damn them all!* And to make his heart sink even deeper, the struggle about Dragan rushed on toward what seemed an eminent rout of his men. "You'll not hear us mewl, rats!" his defiant roar boomed through the din. "Is this ragged ilk all Braured has to offer?"

What answered the *DoomBringer* this time was not a brash old man's grating voice but rather a single, clear blast from a hunting horn, filling the air above the noise of battle; and following that sharp note was the same whirring noise heard earlier: except it was much closer now, almost in their midst...growing steadily louder...and bringing with it the bitter day's final stroke.

Streaming into the fray came a host of disgusting little creatures, their blue, scale-like skin stretched over small but defined muscles, and their large heads sporting random clumps of filthy gray hair between spots of baldness. Every one of these dwarfish creatures wielded a square wooden buckler and a small but wicked hatchet, and they wore only a leather wrap around the groin for clothing. Their faces were disgusting to look upon. "Imps," breathed Dragan, mouth agape. *So my fear was grounded after all...*

The imps made their abodes in the gnarled roots of lesser oaks, deep in dark and barren Ûnath: the forest capping the northern expanse of Ost. The old tales claimed the creatures had once been dwarves but were banished by their own kind, cast from the great halls beneath Gorm Vûdoc for some treachery against the dwarven king, Ûlufund the Mighty. Denied passage to the south, the rebels were sent to starve in the region stretching between the mountain and the Realm of Dolras. Foreseeing their demise, some elected to retain what honor they could by taking their own lives; the others—either too craven or too in love with life for suicide—survived by dining on that yielded by the dirt and decomposition of the forest floor: worms, maggots, and the rotten flesh of rodents. They longed to chisel rock, to carve stone, to form marble into their likenesses—yet there was hardly even a pebble to be had, for only dirt, clay, and torment awaited them in the soft strata beneath the grade of the forest.

Dwarves have little skill in erecting dwellings from various resources, only in creating them by delving into that which already exists. So the outlaws turned to the trees to make their homes: the only things in the forest with strength, with a backbone. But they found the trunks of lesser oaks too small for domiciles, and thus the dwarves burrowed down into the earth and made their homes beneath the dome formed by the tangled tree roots. There they brooded in isolation and became a community of necessity only, having no great hall to fraternize within and no great deeds to recount. Over time, the dank ground, the darkness of the forest, the softness of the earth, and the inadequate food supply transformed the hearty dwarves into smaller, contemptible creatures. They lost their honor, their dignity, and their love for things of beauty — themselves becoming the antithesis of it.

Imps were unknown to most of the peoples between the Great Ocean and the Sea of Ûlumond, and those who did know of them disdained them utterly. Even the clans of Braured, uncouth as they were, would never treat with such. *Yet my mother does*, Dragan thought bitterly, *and myself by proxy, it seems. Perhaps it's best that my captains won't live to realize it.* Coming back to the moment, the Bastard of Domal spit blood and — sucking in a deep breath — opened his mouth to shout a command to his men.

But the order was never issued: for at that moment Poltoros, on a steed black as night, came charging headlong towards Dragan. The lich's face was shielded by a silver death mask — his own, ironically — and he wielded a flail in one hand: its morning star dangling by his horse's flank. His maroon cloak fluttered in the wind, shedding off from its edges what seemed as black flames...or perhaps the void of death. Dragan held his weapon parallel to the ground, bracing himself, intent on cutting the approaching animal's leg asunder. Yet just as the *GrimHelm* slashed at his target, the horse bounded over his blade. Poltoros swung the flail, sending its spiked ball soaring down...down...

...and smashing it into the skull of a Braured clansman whose dirk had been inches from Dragan's neck.

14

Dragan knelt beside Lomion. The bard was on his back, broken arrow shaft protruding from his stomach. The light in his eyes was fading as he repeatedly choked back the blood welling in his throat.

"A teller of good tales," said Dragan softly. His tone, however, was less than empathetic.

"And none greater than your own," the dying man responded, struggling to annunciate his words. "Yet here I am, laid waste...while you endure. It's not..." The bard coughed, spraying blood in the air. It rained back down on his face— then he was gone.

The stench of Lomion's loosed bowels hit Dragan's nose as he reached over to close the man's eyelids, and for a brief moment thereafter he contemplated his own demise. *Will it be as inglorious as this? Did Ûmrothsul Aldrotherin soil his pants when nevermore took him? A part that doesn't enter the poet's verse. Who would seek glory if it did?* His reverie was broken by footsteps drawing near. He looked up, the light of his torch revealing his caller. Jedan Mûran.

"Where is he?" spoke the *DoomBringer*.

"We've made a tent."

"Alive?"

Jedan nodded.

The two men headed down the line toward the tent that his men had erected hurriedly to care for Ûladriss and the other wounded Haxûdī. Hundreds of bodies lay strewn about the ground. Blood ran in a steady stream down gutters on both sides of the road. Dragan observed that most of the bodies belonged to the men of Braured and the imps of Ûnath; and this pleased him immensely, for although he knew it to be unwise, he'd grown to care for the warriors of Haxûd. He took great pride in their prowess and the renown they'd won together.

"How did your son fare?" asked Dragan as he stepped over the Giant of Braured's corpse, remembering with reservation the alien voice that'd usurped his enemy's tongue. *Whose eyes? Whose voice?*

Jedan looked at his captain with his usual stoic expression, then the corners of his lips slowly turned up in a grin. Dragan could remember seeing Mûran smile only once before—when he'd offered the man a swig of prized Tholmian liquor. "He took a captive," the Haxûdī finally spoke, obviously holding back the details to his pleasure.

Dragan's eyes widened in amazement. "You never told me you had an older son riding with you," he mused, playing along.

"Joke all you like, but you'll not be disappointed."

Seeing he'd extract no more information from Jedan at present, Dragan didn't press the warrior. Instead he turned his gaze back to the battleground. The imps were tending to their own dead and injured amidst the wood line. Many were scouring the deceased for spoils: a meager heap. The Haxûdī kept their distance from the imps. Some wore expressions of blatant repugnance...others of genuine amazement...but all let the creatures go about their own business, knowing it was they who'd turned the tide of the battle. Dragan observed one imp hacking feverishly at a woodsmen's finger that wouldn't relinquish its thin gold ring; and he noticed another dragging away a horse's hindquarter: no doubt to feast upon it days later in some lowly den. He felt his upper lip start to curl in disgust and was quickly aware that his men shared his distaste. He needed to locate the lich, who apparently controlled the vile lot, and send them away. *Only to be seen again at the gates of Ost.*

But Poltoros and his horde of imps would have to wait.

Dragan found Ûladriss unconscious on a cot in the muggy makeshift tent. A handful of wounded or dying warriors surrounded him. Some damned Haxûdī shaman who'd traveled with the band was dangling a talisman — much like the *rat stick* that'd been brought against the Beast of Thirannon — over his friend's swollen, bandaged brow, chanting an incantation that was lost to Dragan's ears.

"Take your trinket and be gone, soothsayer," spoke Saedus' son, never taking his eyes off Ûladriss.

"*Lord of Doom*...please...our brother here must be properly consigned to the afterlife. It's the way of our people."

"You'll be there to greet him if you don't leave my sight!" Dragan growled, shifting his icy cold gaze from his companion to the shaman.

The shaman grew pale, turning frightened eyes on Jedan, and the rearguard captain gave him a nod of dismissal. The man lowered his talisman and speedily exited the tent without another word.

After a moment, Mûran set one hand upon Ûladriss' cheek and neck. "A fire grows hot within him. I fear the shaman's right."

The *GrimHelm* opened his mouth to respond but was interrupted. A man had entered the opposite side of the tent, the maroon of his cloak barely visible in the dim light.

"Why is it when tribesmen speak figuratively we think it wise? Our love of poetry, perhaps?" said Poltoros — patronizingly as was his wont. "The man has a fever. His brain swells from the blow he received. He'll be dead by morning."

Jedan eyed his captain now, looking as if he expected the man to rip this stranger's heart from his chest. But to his surprise, the *DoomBringer* brooked no aggression. Instead, as if to a disaffected family member, Dragan spoke:

"Why must you plague me, sorcerer? Do you take me for a fool? I saw the blade lick his scalp."

"Then why do you linger? Your mother waits impatiently."

Dragan's brow furrowed. "Use your power, steward. Heal this man for me, and I'll tarry no more. We'll leave as soon as the dead have departed with escort to Haxûd—well before dawn, if that's your price."

"And if not?"

"Then we'll not leave this spot till all our wounded are dead or recovered. And after that…perhaps I'll find the need to wander the earth for a year or two, seeking absolution for the men I've laid low. Or maybe I'll find some wench in Hiseod, settle down, and become a goat farmer. I'm beginning to feel domestic."

"You wouldn't dare," spat the lich, but in his mind he was surely weighing the sincerity of the threat. He knew spite was a powerful form of pride and that some men would trade all they had for a taste of recompense against those who had wronged them. "I can't heal the savage," he continued, "…yet perhaps I can keep him alive until we reach Ost. Valreecius has tools to relieve the pressure in his skull."

Dragan nodded acceptance, seemingly lost in thought, before turning again to Jedan Mûran. "See that your fallen brothers are prepared for return to Haxûd according to your custom, but don't let the shaman protract the ceremony. The men are already exhausted, and we leave before daylight. The sylvans and the imps can rot." He started then for the tent's exit, parting the leather strapping before looking back at the Haxûdî. "But first…let's see this *captive*."

Jedan followed Dragan outside, and the two began another walk. Both were now silent. The sight of their wounded companion had stanched any notion of idle conversation between them—and Dragan's bruised face had begun to throb with pain besides. It wasn't long, however, before they found Gavix sitting atop a fallen tree trunk on the side of the road. The boy was oiling his father's blade. When he saw his master approaching, an expression of unease settled on his countenance. He looked around nervously. The two men loomed over him like towers.

"I was told you fared well this battle," said Dragan. "Not many men your age could claim such. Tell me whom you've captured."

The boy looked confusedly at Jedan, surprised his lord didn't already know.

"Your father wished to keep me in suspense."

Jedan frowned—for it must've seemed silly to him now to have played such a game—while Gavix fidgeted. "Your horse is…lost…my lord," the boy said at last with an effort.

It was Dragan's turn to frown at this, but he gave no other response. Jedan, on the other hand, snatched his son up by the throat as if the youth were a twig. "You shame me! Why didn't you tell me this?"

"I..." the boy was choking, "...you were...called away...before..."

Dragan laid a firm hand on the rearguard captain's shoulder: "Punish him as you see fit later. Time presses me."

Jedan loosed his grip. The boy slumped back onto the tree trunk, holding his neck and coughing. When he regained his voice, he continued:

"I was taking my lord's and the marshal's horses to the rear as bid...but as I rounded the first bend, fighting broke out all around. Chimaron took an arrow in the thigh and went mad! I loosed my grip on Allethion's reins to control him but was overpowered. He ripped his own reins from my hand and bolted for the woods...and Allethion followed. I ran after them — fast as I could! — until I could run no more."

"The woods were beginning to get thick, and I was about to turn back when I heard crying in the distance. I made my way to the sound and found an old man lying on the ground. Blood was running from his nose. A girl knelt beside him, weeping like a baby. When she saw me, she tried to run — but I caught her easily enough. She began struggling and shouting that she was *the Queen of the Forest* and would have me killed...so I pinned her down until she fell quiet. Later, after I'd brought her back to the column, I asked her how the old man had perished. She said a horse had trampled him."

"*Took a captive...*" mused Dragan with an affected grin, looking askance at Jedan.

The frown on Mûran's handsome red face grew deeper as he reprimanded himself internally.

The *GrimHelm* turned his gaze back on Gavix, who immediately broke the stare in favor of examining the ground. Yet before Dragan could speak, the lad suddenly looked up again and blurted: "I'm sorry about the horses — but I *did* bring you the Queen of Braured!"

"Have you forgotten who saddled Allethion before me, boy?"

"No, lord."

"Tiramas Vendhane. The White King. That horse is worth more to me than a hundred queens of this damned forest! You've made a great error in judgment. You're *my* retainer, not Ûladriss'. You're to serve me above all others. So why did you loose Allethion's reins to corral another's steed?"

The young man was speechless at first, then finally he mumbled: "I don't know. I wasn't thinking. It was instinct, I guess."

"Exactly. It was instinct for you to aid your own kind over another. Your sense of worth comes from your feelings, not your reason. And that's why you failed at your duty."

15

Astelidus returned the brush to the crude wooden table and took up the hoof pick again, this time talking to Bellaroth in a soothing voice before attempting to lift her foot. Under other circumstances he likely would've been successful in his first attempt, using a bit of gentle force if needed to get the task accomplished faster, but the son of Ny had not yet recovered his health. Of the pair of wounds he'd taken to the chest nearly two weeks past, only the deeper one still ached when he moved about—yet it wasn't this pain that vexed him so but rather the *weakness* from an extended time off his feet and away from drills and revelry and glorious battle. Luckily, however, his new calming approach with the horse was starting to have the desired effect, and therefore Astelidus kept up the soft praise as he set about the business of cleaning her hooves. *It's wicked enough that such a fine steed must endure this cramped, makeshift stable for so long*, thought the mare's master. *I must slack no more on your grooming.*

Horses of any breed or quality were no commodity in Mardotha—nor even in the flowing plains of Sinia, nor in any neighboring land besides—and as such the Sinians made little use of them in pitched battle. Thus, following from this fact, there'd been no erection of an organized, fully staffed and stocked stable complex in the camp. Each warrior in possession of a mount was responsible for tending to it on his own. To be certain, a good horse wasn't without its uses, outweighing in most cases the troubles in caring for one in this inhospitable realm; but typically those uses were limited to scouting and couriering and the occasional raid or skirmish. Bellaroth had seen her share of action in all of these areas since first arriving at the black walls of Crûthior, and now it occurred to Astelidus that she must be as anxious to return to the field as was he. *Oh, and how badly they need us, girl. How badly indeed...*

Since the departure of the so-called *DoomBringer*, the war effort hadn't been going well for the besieging army, and as Astelidus dwelt on this he remembered a sentry's words concerning Dragan: "*...if not for him, the Mardothans would stream forth like ants from their gates!*" The son of Ny frowned deeply. *How prophetic were that man's words! We should set him up as an oracle in one of King Oen's tents...then everyone's fortune might be known!* This sarcasm was not in the least aimed at self-amusement, for Astelidus knew the situation in the field to be grave. Frustration ruled his mind instead, for he knew himself to be the next true allied champion; and every day he strode not to battle another hero fell—or more ground they'd taken was reclaimed by the enemy. Yesterday's reports had told that the second wall's breach was now well under repair, the enemy's workers protected behind the shields of their new reinforcements: a fierce, heavily armed and armored war band said to be under the command of one Birakith the Baneful, close kinsman of the fallen Lion of Agrardob. A few days earlier Fedrin Rae had taken a wound to the thigh and was out of action as well; and still before that the Ithirian captain replacing the late Camus Robi—Bastram Narohad—had been slain during the very first sortie under his command. *And whom did they since name in place of him? I forget. Ah...what does it matter?...the poor man will likely join his predecessors within the week...*

Footsteps at the door turned his head.

"There you are!" came the voice that had grown sweetest of all in Astelidus' ears. "What in Daemon's name are you doing? Don't you have servants to tend your horse?"

"To keep her fed and watered...yes," replied Astelidus, unable to keep from smiling giddily at his unexpected visitor—although she, out of genuine concern for his well-being, wore an agitated scowl. "Yet I trust her grooming to no one but myself. It can be a delicate business."

"I hadn't thought you the delicate sort," said Bronwyn, her frown lessening a bit as she entered in and moved to Astelidus, watching closely as he went back to work on Bellaroth's hoof. Today Oen's niece was dressed in a tight-fitting bodice and breeches that would've suited a day of riding quite well, had that been her purpose in coming, and Ny's son could detect a hint of her fresh smell above the stable's mustiness. Her long, golden hair was pulled back in a single braid. "But there are many things about you I don't yet know." A moment later she placed a light hand on the warrior's shoulder. "Come...let's leave this work for another, and we can sit and talk awhile. Surely your retainer can handle this?"

"Retainer?" the red-haired man laughed...although he did lower the horse's foot and make to rise. "Lady...you're mistaking me again for another. There's a crone and a few silly little girls under her...you've seen them...who keep my tent clean and my belly full, but I'm not the *GrimHelm* with his pampering lackeys." Turning to meet her eyes again—and seeing her scowl return—Astelidus quickly added: "Forgive me...that was a poor jest. On the battlefield I may have a bearer assigned to me, indeed, but none dwell in my lodgings. That's not the way of..."

"No...you're right," said Bronwyn, cutting in to wave away his apology. "It was a slip. I do know *some* things about you and your clan." Then suddenly it was there: the smile Astelidus had been awaiting from her.

Saying goodbye to Bellaroth, the warrior took his guest by the hand and led her out into the sun. "One or another of my kin comes each day to exercise her," said Astelidus of the horse as they headed towards his tent. "She mustn't wither away as I have. You're welcome to ride her as well...whenever the mood strikes you."

"Perhaps I shall," his companion replied, "...but it won't be long before you mount her again, I think. You don't look so *withered* to me." Again the smile.

She's happy to have her hand in mine, thought Astelidus excitedly, his heartbeat quickening a step. It'd been a gamble to boldly grasp that soft, delicate hand, yet apparently the gesture had felt no more uncomfortable to her than it had to him. *Will this be the day for us?*

Upon entering the tent the pair were offered honeyed wine and a tray of nuts and dried fruits to take with them into the private sitting area; yet as soon as they were alone behind the drawn curtain, Astelidus quickly set all of this aside. His anticipation of greater affection was getting the better of him, and as Bronwyn politely asked her host for permission to sit, he dared reach for her again, hoping to lead her over to his feather-stuffed couch...

This time, however, the warrior had gone too far. Pulling her hand from his, she visibly blushed and said: "Over there will be fine."

Astelidus — although as disappointed by his presumption as her refusal — tried not to let that disappointment show. Recovering fast, he launched a new topic to dispel the awkwardness. "I hear our new *allies* from Domal will arrive soon."

"I'm not sure about that," said Bronwyn, retrieving her wine then taking a seat across from her guest, "...yet they're sorely wanted. Let's hope the rumor's true."

"Aren't you skeptical of these Domalins? If this day was in my grandsire's time, it would be their spears aimed at us — not them marching to our aid. I'm inclined to agree with Galran, myself."

"Galran lives to stir up trouble, and this day is *our* time. Domal's ruler may yet style himself *king*...but in truth the twin cities have long been severed at the hip. Have you forgotten how Relinydd's governor invited a contingent of our veterans into his city to aid in protecting our trade interests there? No, we shan't have trouble from the Domalins, I think — at least not while Acomalath draws breath. Uncle Oen knows this well, or else he'd not chance an alliance. But don't think he means to treat them as saviors, regardless of what aid they bring. Like you and Galran, part of him holds to old hates as well. The Domalins are to be seen as mercenaries. Nothing more. And I doubt their battle prowess will rise above that brand."

Astelidus smiled. "Once again I marvel at your insight, my lady...and that reminds me of something I've been meaning to ask you."

After taking a sip of her wine, Bronwyn returned the grin. "Go on then...ask me...but then you'll owe me an answer in return."

"As you wish. Tell me...why is it you left the comforts of Chalemos for this retched place? From how you cared for my wounds I might've mistaken you for a healer...but you're certainly too pretty for a warrior..."

Now her grin gave way to a cute little laugh at the flattery. "I didn't want to leave — if you can believe that — but father was afraid of what I'd do while he was away. Mother's been dead for years now...and he trusts his servants better than me to care for the household. Yet now that I'm here, I wouldn't have it any other way. Satisfied?"

Astelidus nodded and reached for his cup. "Now it's your turn, then. What do you want to know?"

"Well...to begin with...I'd like to know why you came to my tent the night you took those wounds. Not just what we told the council, but the truth. I didn't press when you first explained yourself, for your health was my only care...yet I could tell you were hiding something by the look on your face. Am I wrong?"

The son of Ny sighed. "No...you're right. I didn't lie to you, for I was indeed curious about Dragan's departure—just not enough so to risk rousing you in the dead of night. Don't you know by now how I feel about you, Bronwyn? *Daemon strike me,* but I wanted to know right then and there how much he'd hurt you by leaving...and I wanted to comfort you if he had...to let you know there's a better man waiting for you...one who could never abandon you as he did..."

"I don't wish to speak of him," she hissed, cutting her admirer's confession short. "And I'm not blind to your affection, Astelidus, but you'd do better not to be so forward with me. If your coming that night wouldn't have saved my life, I'd say you were foolish to dare such a thing. What makes you so confident?"

"A man without confidence lives a lonely life," said her host after a pause to recover from the harshness thrown at him. "As they say: better to have tried and failed than never to have attempted. It's your smile that makes me confident, my lady—and the gentle touch of your hand. Are my feelings not returned at all?"

"I'd best be going," said Bronwyn, flustered as she stood hurriedly to depart; but, before she reached the curtain, the warrior grabbed her wrist and pulled her into his arms. For an instant it seemed she might push off his chest and slap him, yet as his lips met hers he felt the struggle melt away. The kiss was passionate— yet for Astelidus over too soon. She peeled herself from him and turned again for the curtain, apparently wanting to leave their parting at that—and he knew this time he must let her go.

Yet even as the curtain still swayed from her passing, she paused at the tent's front opening to call back to him: "Rest and get well soon, warrior, for more than the thrill of battle awaits you now."

Leaning back against his couch, Astelidus Ny smiled at his good fortune. *If ever we see you again, DoomBringer, I'll be sure to thank you. Soon I'll have both your fame and your woman.*

PART TWO

16

This would be comical, thought Baeldrin, *if everything didn't depend on it.* The subject of his musing, an imp attempting to wield a sword as long as the little blue creature was tall, was obviously having a rough time of it. And, making it worse, the group of goblins nearest the scene—all decked in their new, more-than-slightly oversized gear—actually appeared to be admiring the imp's folly rather than scolding him (or at least ridiculing him) for it. If the prince had been closer to these fools just now he'd have issued severe reprimands, perhaps resorting even to violence to get his point across to the whole senseless lot. *The armor can't be helped...all must pick from the same cache...but those blades were set aside for the men of Ost. Why was I praising these creatures before? They're making it difficult now to remember.* From his perch atop the battlements, Baeldrin spied everything that moved through the wild grass below from the castle walls to the forest edge. The light of noonday fell unchecked upon him here, coercing sweat to bead upon his troubled brow—yet all that he felt inside was *ice*. As usual, the *Spider's* welcome on his return had been affected at best, and thus after handing over his haul he'd quickly sought this place of solitude. *Am I no different than the talking dead she keeps about her? Has she already laid some spell upon me? One from which there's no escape?*

After a final sigh and disapproving shake of the head, the prince managed to peel his eyes away from the imp's farce to command a broader view of the field. Scattered amidst the green and blue amalgam that was Saedus' creatural legion, appearing at a distance like little ant hills about which the insects were crawling, the crude pole tents of the goblins were nearly beyond count. Here and there the smoke from a cook fire plumed lazily into the air; now and again a burst of angry shouting or raucous cackling rose above the drone of barked orders and clanging metal from mass forced drills. Numbering perhaps less than one for every dozen imps and every score of goblins, the human warriors of Ost had wisely been split and relegated to the role of taskmasters rather than being retained as a separate unit: for certainly as combatants in their own right they couldn't be called elite. By day they mingled with those they'd been entrusted to arm and train, but by night most were allowed inside the walls to sleep or revel or worship in quarters set apart for their own. *Yes, worship,* Baeldrin recalled with yet another frown. *A more fanatical cult I've never seen—even amongst the slums of Rardonydd. I've seen the carven idols they keep of her...how they kiss the little wooden mouth...how they prick their skin to drizzle blood upon her. Could she have laid a spell on them as well? Each and every man of them?* Tonight—after the imps were departed for their dwellings in the black forest and the goblins settled into their gambling and carousing—the human priests would be at it again, leading the most devout in rituals and chants that could stretch on for hours.

But for now the drills carried on; and at their head, walking about like some starving beast pacing the floor of its cage, was the witch's champion. G'nilbor. Although this was but Baeldrin's second opportunity to appraise the ghoul since Saedus had dug it up from the Asendath, somehow the prince felt a strong sense of familiarity with the form and nature of his martial replacement. *See how they cringe and fall over themselves to get out of his path when he nears?* he questioned an anonymous third party in his head. *That's not merely because of his freakish size and mien. Mark my words: already this brute has slain and devoured not a few of those he plans to lead. And look there at Valreecius, even now still by the creature's side! Surely he must be grinning, like a dog wagging its tail, at his mistress' handiwork...*

At first Baeldrin had been angry with Saedus at what he took for a stripping of his soon-to-come glory on the field of battle—but it hadn't taken him long to accept the wisdom behind it. *Let this daemon do the killing, for all I care. He's suited well for it. Yet it shall be* me *who sits the throne...it shall be* me *who restores the great glory of Domal. Not G'nilbor. Not Dragan. Not Saedus of Ost. Me! I haven't cringed yet from any means to reach that goal...nor shall I start today. Let them play their parts. They'll all beg at my feet in the end!*

After several moments of observing the ghoul and its keeper, Baeldrin saw a man approach the latter to relay an unheard message. Then, without delay, the moon steward set off, leaving the field to G'nilbor.

Suddenly the ghoul ceased its pacing and stood still, turning its glazed white eyes upon the battlements, searching for something...someone...as if he'd just now read Baeldrin's earlier thoughts. For an instant the two locked gazes; then came a voice from behind, startling the prince and causing him to spin around:

"Have you not seen enough yet to satisfy?" spoke the sorceress through her sensual, black-painted lips, clearly agitated at Baeldrin's extended absence (likely more from mistrust in his free roaming than a desire for his company). Dressed in a low cut, embroidered gown of fine emerald-dyed silk, today she'd chosen to wear her hair up, and a single golden torc adorned each lovely white arm.

So beautiful, thought Baeldrin instantly, as he did each and every time he laid eyes on her in a new setting, the effect always difficult to shake regardless of her too-often spiteful words. *She must be older than my own mother, yet it doesn't show. Witchery it is!* And that word broke the spell. "I suppose it suffices for now," he replied at last. "This rabble has but one challenge to outlive. Yet the rest can't be achieved without initial success. Are there no more beasties you can conjure for us?"

"Your brother's arrived..." This change of subject—if indeed it was—came out casually as Saedus strode to the crenel adjacent Baeldrin's and rested hands aside the merlons to take in his previous view. "Are you not aching to see him?"

"Don't taunt me, woman! That man's no brother of mine!" Baeldrin had known a reunion with Dragan was soon to come, yet no amount of forewarning could subdue his expressions of hatred for the Bastard of Domal. Unconsciously he clenched his teeth and balled his hands into fists.

"That's odd. The two of you so favor one another." Her voice was flat and calm. "Look upon him and tell me he's not of your father's seed. You can not."

"I don't care what blood's in him. Acomalath's likely sired *droves* of bastards on the palace wenches over the years. Scores of them could be playing about his very feet without him even knowing it. What is it that makes Dragan so different from them? Why did my father not simply deny his claim? Tell me again, witch, if it pleases you...yet I'll never understand!"

"We've no time now for reminiscing. There are matters we must all discuss. Bore holes through Dragan with your eyes if you wish—but know when to hold your tongue! There'll be no *cock waving* in my presence, understand?" She was looking straight at him now, wild gray eyes begging him to object so she could stomp him even further into the ground.

"Oh, there's no need to worry about me. I wouldn't think of missing a single word from his mouth. Such proud boasts he always spews, yet one of them shall surely damn him before long—and I want to remember exactly which it was."

Despite the sweltering heat outside, Baeldrin felt the chamber uncomfortably cool and damp, and—although tallow candles sat the table and torches lined the walls— his eyes hadn't yet fully recovered from the absence of blazing sunlight. He wasn't so blind, however, as to fail in identifying the pair seated across from him as Dragan and the lich Poltoros...nor so naive as to assume either would rise to welcome him before he took his own seat. Thus, without a word spoken, he plopped down in the nearest chair, waiting for his senses to adjust. Saedus was but a few steps behind him, and now she seated herself at the table's head.

"Come now, Dragan...have you no greeting for your brother? Has it been so long you don't recognize him?"

"Longer still it should've been, had you not summoned me against my will. Baeldrin loves me no more than I do him...so let's get on with this, Mother. Tell me why I'm here." Indeed, it wasn't these words alone that revealed Dragan's urgency, for the man appeared as if he'd only just now leaped from horseback. His long brown hair a bit disheveled, and his precious silver breastplate covered in dust from the road, he'd either not had or cared not take the opportunity to wash and groom...or even merely to don a clean robe. A nasty bruise on his left cheek added to the effect.

"Patience...we'll come to it soon. You've traveled many days without that knowledge. A few moments more won't break you."

Baeldrin could see plainly the struggle on Dragan's face. *He wants to draw his blade and run you through, witch…right here and now. Yet he dares not. In that one thing we're alike, half-brother. Perhaps you may yet get the chance, though – if you survive long enough. Perhaps you'll destroy each other without my lifting a finger. How fitting that would be!*

Grinning at her control of Dragan, who'd not uttered any protest, Saedus now moved her attention to Poltoros. "Tell us, counselor, what you perceive to be our tasks at hand."

Rid now of the death mask with which he'd charged into Braured, the lich sat with cowl pulled back, revealing his grim countenance to those gathered in the chamber. Dry lips parted, and a raspy voice began:

"My mistress, long have you made your goal plain: to win the devotion of all men west of the desert, even as the men of Ost adore you now. It seems to me the most part of this is already achieved. Far to the south, in the land of Haxûd, your sister Falchī has been planted on the throne. She'll not hesitate to obey you. To the northeast, the Mardothan king Berac has found himself in league with us: not merely through necessity, as it shall first seem to our foes once revealed, but rather through years of your secret efforts toward that end. And – although it may appear the most recent accomplishment, but actually it being the longest in bringing to fruition – your assured alliance with Domal is of greatest importance. What kingdoms then remain, for now, outside your grasp? Dolras? Callas? They are ruins. Ûnath? Braured? Hardly worth mentioning as well, and you need but state your claim to make them ours. The isle of Tholmis will lie defenseless once its Sinian shield is removed, and lawless Addrindain must also yield or else be swiftly overrun by the neighboring Haxûdī. No, it is only Sinia and Ithiria that stand in our way."

"Thus we must focus now on the Ithiros, for they lie at our doorstep – yet not at the expense of procuring Domal. This is why Dragan and Baeldrin have been jointly summoned. To fulfill our plans, mistress, we must succeed on two fronts before Deserus Oen can react to either one."

"So you'd have me turn against those I've just bled for…is that it?" Dragan was clearly incensed. "To storm the walls of Gethod with your damned fiends at my back?"

"Why storm walls when you can walk right through the gate?" the sorceress posed, her face betraying self-satisfaction with her cunning.

Look at him, Baeldrin sneered inside. *It hasn't even sunk in yet. So preposterous it must seem to his mind.*

"No," Dragan answered. "Your plans can rot in hell! Is no treachery beyond you, Mother? You want me to grasp a man's arm in friendship with one hand while slipping a knife in his guts with the other? I've slain beast and mage-king and hordes of men for you, but this thing I won't do!"

"Please spare us, Dragan," Baeldrin chimed in with a snort of laughter. Then he turned his face aside: "Your son's spent too much time among the Haxûdī, Saedus. Now he fancies he's possessed of *honor*."

Dragan stood so forcefully that his chair toppled and crashed heavily to the floor. Absolute silence ensued. Leaning forward, he placed both his palms flat on the table to loom menacingly over his antagonist. A gaze hotter than the outdoor sun fell upon Domal's prince—and in a voice calm but drenched with threat, the *DoomBringer* spoke: "As long as I writhe about in the company of such snakes as you, then honor indeed shall ever escape me. Be that as it may. But listen to me well, my brother: if you wish to remain with us in the world above, don't ever suppose to make jest of me again."

Baeldrin's mouth opened immediately to lash out in response, but Saedus stopped him in mid-word: "Enough! I warned you both against such foolishness as this—yet I knew neither would obey. Baeldrin, you'll remain silent for now. We'll discuss your part at length, but for the moment it appears Dragan needs further *convincing*."

"What else would you say to me?" her son's face swung angrily to meet hers. "You plucked me from the very eve of glory in Mardotha—and in coming I bore casualties upon the road. Even now my marshal lies on the fence between life and death. All for what? You knew I'd refuse the deed, else why order Poltoros to keep the details from me? Why bring me all the way back here from Crûthior, with Gethod but a stone's throw from its walls?" For a moment he paused, as if actually expecting his mother to answer. But she merely stared at him with a deepening frown, and thus he continued: "So...now that I've come all this way, is there not some other task I might perform for you instead? Perhaps there's a rogue wizard about? Or a vicious dragon? Do the floors of your rooms need scrubbing?"

He's pushing it too far, even to be her son, thought Baeldrin, who actually would not have been surprised to see the Bastard suddenly catch fire and burn swiftly to ash—for such a blaze could now be seen in the sorceress' eyes. Yet Dragan didn't stop there:

"Answer me this: what's to stop me dispatching messengers this very hour to Gethod, warning my friends of your intentions?"

"What's to stop me clawing that breastplate from your chest? What would you be, O mighty *DoomBringer*, without that rhyme about your neck? What silly names could we devise then to replace your magnificent titles? Shall I give one a try? My son, we waste precious time. Accept it: you've no choice! For what I've given you, I demand the strictest obedience. You've known this from the start."

In what must've been among the greatest feats ever of self-control, Dragan quietly turned and strode to his toppled chair, set it upright, and pushed it back in place. A visibly trembling hand fumbled for something at his side, brought it forth, and set it gently down on the table. No one said a word. One by one he reached for and released the clasps of his breastplate; then he let the whole thing drop to crash mere inches from the sorceress' feet. Still no one spoke. After one final defiant stare into his mother's eyes, Saedus' son exited the chamber.

No sooner than Dragan was gone did Baeldrin reach for the object left on the table. *The Sun of Domal.* Then, after admiring this a moment, with a covetous eye he gazed upon the armor at Saedus' feet. *Ah, Dragan! Your secret's no more! Long have I wondered how the craven child became a warrior without peer. It's more sorcery after all. And now, weakling fool, you've left the power within my grasp!*

The sorceress guessed his thoughts and spoke quickly: "You've discovered a thing you weren't meant to learn, Baeldrin—and if you'd know more, you must ask Dragan himself. I give you only this warning: don't ever suppose to don the armor in his stead. It's not for you. To defy me on this shall bring a punishment most severe."

"I've no need of your baubles, whatever they are," the prince lied, laying the Sun down before meeting Saedus' stare.

"Good. For this I'm certain: Dragan will soon come back for it."

17

Dragan paused and drew a deep breath as he rested a hand on the iron latch of his chamber door. He'd been out of his mother's presence no longer than it took to climb the winding staircase to his aerial abode, and already a great swell of desire washed over his heart for the thing he'd forsaken. His head nodded slowly until his forehead gently contacted the heavy oaken door, and there he rested. His whole body seemed to slouch in weariness. *Shall I go back, like some shameless beggar, and plead for its return? Or have my days of glory come to an end?* He pulled the latch downward, pushed the door in, and passed the threshold of the room he'd called home for most of his youth.

The chamber was relatively modest with some ornate trimmings. Beneath a deeply stained cherry wood mantel, a brick fireplace was set in the wall adjacent from the bed, its oversized hearth stretching out to meet an impressive red and black Haxûdī rug that covered most of the oak-paneled floor. The rug was a gift from his aunt Falchī for his eighteenth birthday, and it'd taken a crew of men the better part of a day to maneuver it up the spiraling staircases. The bed itself held two sheep's wool mattresses and was framed inside four tall yet unadorned posts that nearly kissed the ceiling. There was no plaster on the walls, but an array of plain, monochromatic tapestries covered most of the bare stone and did a fine job holding in the fire's heat during the winter months. A large oaken chair with an oversized red cushion rested in the corner beside the fireplace. On the adjacent wall, one large window let light into the room and held the passage to a small balcony on which a few vines and plants grew.

Dragan removed his boots and sword and plopped down on his bed. Was he already weaker? More exhausted than he'd been an hour earlier? Less agile? He couldn't tell…but a growing panic was welling inside him which he tried desperately to suppress. His feats of glory flashed before his mind, jumbled together in a collage of blood, sweat, and steel. Moreover, he recalled the revels that'd always ensued afterwards, of which he was the sole luminary: a demigod, even. He saw the awestruck looks on the faces of common men in his presence and the contrived countenances of nobles and kings putting on their best acts not to grovel before his feet and plead for aid. He minded his independence of state, politics, and allegiances. He remembered the stench of the Beast of Thirannon, the sapphire eyes of the Lion of Agrardob, and the voice of the Giant of Braured. *The voice.* And with this last thought his eyes turned upon the trophy mounted above the fireplace mantel: the silver war mask of Tiramas Vendhane.

Dragan slid off the bed, made his way to the mantel, and—reaching with two hands—removed the helm from the wall. It reminded him of the death mask the lich wore but was more brilliant and detailed than that. Almost theatrical. Its face was gruesome to behold. Brows furrowed, eyes slanted, and mouth turned down in a huge semicircle. All features were exaggerated beyond proportion.

This was the *GrimHelm*. Dragan rubbed its right cheek absentmindedly with his thumb, his thoughts running back to a time before his name was synonymous with the thing he held...

There exist in the world some things from which a man can't easily avert his gaze. Fire is one of these things. Be it a candle's teardrop flame or the clawing blaze of a funeral pyre, it commands the rapt fascination of its onlookers. It's comforting as an old friend, deadly as the bitterest of enemies, and necessary as the air we breathe. It's entwined with the most primordial concerns of man: light and darkness, pleasure and pain, life and death.

It was these things the fire kindling in Dragan Saedus' eyes represented as he wrested a blade from the chest of Tiramas Vendhane and watched the limp body fall clumsily to the dais floor before the palace throne. The flame in his eyes was not like a roaring blaze nor even a flicker of fire: not superficial and palpable, but rather it glowed deep within him, like smoldering embers set within two pools of blackness. As if a blanket of nothingness had smothered the cool blue-green sea and blotted out the warm azure sky—the landscape of his eyes—and replaced it with things colder and hotter. Nor did the orbs revert as Dragan shifted his grim countenance up and looked from one scene of carnage to another.

The throne room of the White King was large and colonnaded, with massive pillars of fine-grained ivory marble that supported a cavernous vault running the entire length of the chamber. The sidewalls were intermittently recessed, inset with many statues of ancient heroes, beasts of the wild, and other mage-kings of old. Between the recesses there were wonderful prizes: armor displays, racks of polished weaponry, and magnificent paintings brought from faraway lands. The floor was granite tile with many embedded glass mosaics. One of these, a white tiger menacingly portrayed on its hind legs with front claws up, poised to strike, commanded the center of the floor. A chandelier in the likeness of an eagle hung above. Its feathers were crystal shards. Its beak and talons were solid gold.

An hour earlier this chamber would've been a spectacle of admiration for even the wealthiest king, but as Dragan's dark eyes surveyed it now he saw only decimation. Here were the charred bodies of the myrmidons, the elite cohort and guard of the White King, strewn about like leaves on a forest floor. He'd become trapped between them and their master—like an unrefined billet caught between hammer and anvil—and here he would've perished had Poltoros not come to his aid. Unlooked for, the steward had returned to save the bastard child whom he had helped raise from birth. Those guards closest to the sorcerer as he unleashed his wrath had been instantly vanquished, blown away in great clouds of ash by a jet of blindingly hot fire issuing from his staff; and the few surviving this attack had quickly found the tip of Dragan's sword as an alternate doom. Yet even as Dragan laid the last myrmidon low, so had the fate of enfeebled Poltoros been wrought.

The lore of the lands west of Agrardob holds that from mankind's beginning there has always walked a mage-king among them: a man possessed of an arcane power beyond his superlative wisdom and knowledge of the world. The Golden King, Nal'tanos Crimlore, for instance, if the need was dire, could call upon the heavens to rain down thunderbolts on his adversaries; and Tethramel Davin, the Green King, at the kiss of his staff could summon forth roots from the ground to drag his foes down into the bowels of the earth. Ûmrothsul Aldrotherin, the Red King — much like his descendent who lay now spent on the palace floor — could manipulate fire, setting his enemies ablaze at the wink of an eye.

Now the power of the White King was control over bird and beast: no animal was strong enough to resist his call. No sooner than the myrmidons' failure was secured did Tiramas Vendhane evoke his pet, a great white tiger, from its lurking place and, usurping its mind and body, set himself upon Poltoros. The steward gave no fight when the beast ripped into his flesh, tearing life away, for he was utterly exhausted from spell weaving. Yet, before darkness took him, he beheld Dragan charging headlong in his direction with sword aloft — a cry of anguish escaping the warrior's twisted lips.

What ensued afterwards is not accounted least amongst the deeds of Dragan Saedus. The slaying of Tiramas Vendhane lay in the slaying of his pet — for, like Poltoros, the White King had expended much energy in working his magic, and his life and the tiger's were bound so long as he stared through those yellow eyes but perceived with his own mind. The great beast, outweighing his opponent by threefold, at first gave ground to Dragan's reckless onslaught, warily backing off and leaping aside, forcing the man to waste his blows on the rending of marble columns and granite tile beneath paws and feet. Vendhane was biding his time, waiting for the warrior to tire, waiting for the opportune moment to strike; yet the flurry of his assailant's sword was relentless.

Dragan was fueled by pain and pride. The only person he perhaps had ever truly cared for had just fallen at his expense, and it was impossible to his mind that the steward's sacrifice might be in vain...that his own legend would be over before it even began...that the doom scrawled about his neck wasn't true...

Thus the frenzy of Dragan's blade so plagued the cat that it was backed into a corner. And there the son of Saedus hacked down his foe into a mire of blood.

Dragan turned the helmet over in his hands. He'd paid little attention to its construction in the past, but now he inspected every curve and buffed every imperfection like he was some damned tinker, all in a desperate attempt to distract himself from thinking about the thing he desired or the ramifications of what he must do to repossess it. He fought to keep his thoughts fallow, like an animal that has no capability for rumination, yet still the inevitability of choices that lay before him was too great to suppress. His mind was ablaze with torturous deliberation. The great dichotomy of his life was coming to a head, like a stream set out from high atop a mountainside but destined only to become engulfed by some lowly river. Little regard is given to the stream, pure as it might be, for it's just part of the whole: part of the murky waters into which it spills. So too would the legacy of Dragan Saedus be formed in the coming days, as what honor he still possessed would be lost in his life's river: that inexorable course wrought when he first placed his mother's gift upon his chest.

When Dragan, standing on the dais over Vendhane's lifeless body, had first seen his adversary's silver war mask hanging on the adjacent wall, his desire had been to don it: for its countenance reflected his mood, and he also desired to hide his face. To let the mask project outwardly what welled deep within. As it was now…standing on the hearth in his childhood abode…he found himself inclined to place the helm on his head once more; and, doing so, he sat down on the chair in the room's corner. For hours he remained there, motionless as a statue: even after his mother's servants entered the room, dismayed that he wouldn't answer their calls.

Still he wouldn't be stirred…and the servants grew horrified, much like the retinue of the White King had become when they found Dragan on their master's throne long ago. Those servants, knowing no other name to give him, had called him by that which he wore. *GrimHelm.*

18

Dragan found his brother in a derelict courtyard on the northwestern side of Saedus' tower. The prince was propped there against the ruined battlements of some long-forgotten fortress; yet, cold and lonely under a gray sky, the great alp Gorm Vûdoc dominated the scene, engulfing and diminishing Baeldrin's figure. Hundreds of deep, wine-dark crags appeared to roll from the peak's snow-laden shoulders as water over a fall, splashing down into a torrent of rent earth upon the various levels of the mountainside. The *DoomBringer* had always considered this a prospect of which the eyes could never tire—yet clearly at present Baeldrin was staring only at the rubble beneath his palms. *His kingdom, before it's all over,* Dragan mused as he approached. His mood was somber.

Marking his company, the prince turned while dusting his hands against one another. "Come to say farewell?" The greeting was unpleasant.

Dragan retrieved an object from his cloak and, moving in closer, pressed it to Baeldrin's chest—firmly but without affront. "Take this, half-brother, and relieve me of half my burden."

Baeldrin took the mass into his hand and, peering down, saw what had been gifted. The Sun of Domal. Looking back up, he noticed a glint of silver under his rival's cloak—and understood then the meaning of the Bastard's words. "What burden did this place on you?" he replied, holding the pendant aloft. "Were you foolish enough to think such a trinket would prevail over blood? It entitled you to nothing. And now you gift it to me as if I were some beggar."

"Say what you will. Yet the light in your eyes could've lit Mother's hall when I set it on the table."

Baeldrin turned his head, puckering his lips in agitation and embarrassment. "And the enchantment beneath your cloak isn't lost to me," he replied in a voice laden with mockery. "This is the price of your vanity? A dog on a leash..."

"Tread carefully, brother, lest your hypocrisy run wild."

At these words Baeldrin marked an ominous glow ripen deep in his sibling's eyes, and suddenly he was frightened indeed—yet somehow he managed not to reveal or succumb to it. "Hypocrisy? You compare personal glory to the fate of nations? Your exploits are the petty stuff of bards. Stories told to the young and idiotic to keep them dreamy and complacent. You've no idea what it takes to turn the gears of the world. To manipulate the course of history!"

Dragan's brows furrowed. "Taunt me a third time, and it will go ill for you, Prince of Domal."

In his pride and agitation, Baeldrin opened his mouth to say: *would that your prize donned my chest, bastard, then threats wouldn't fall so readily from your tongue;* but he shut his lips without speaking, unwilling to test the fidelity of the haughty words.

"I didn't come here for this," Dragan went on. "Whether you admit it or not, the man who possesses that pendant—freely given by the king—is by tradition heir to Domal's throne. And though you're correct in that a trinket alone can't bestow its bearer the crown, not possessing it would only serve to create doubt and incredulity within your court. My fame doesn't lie in the ruling of others. So take it...and speak no more of your spite to me."

Fame or infamy? asked the prince inwardly, but he said no more. He placed the Sun of Domal within the folds of his red tunic then turned to resume his position amid the ruins. He made no gesture when Dragan exited the courtyard with parting words—yet the final say resounded in his thoughts as he gazed out to the horizon: *keep my secret, keep your head.*

19

Beneath the archway a mounted man, crestfallen, walked his new steed. On another day such as this in his past, on the back of another horse, he might've been already at a trot or even a canter…or perhaps he would've charged ahead in full gallop, only to sweep back through the lines of his brave Haxûdī, goading them on toward great deeds ahead. His mood would've been light at the least, if not outright ecstatic or even fey, at the outset of such an expedition. His armor would've gleamed all over in the sun as he wore it openly, the merest sight of him enough to instill courage into the most craven of followers.

But not this day. This day the son of Saedus hung his head in shame, hid his armor in shame, rode a horse of which he was secretly ashamed, and headed out on a mission that was sure to make his name — and also the names of those riding out with him — synonymous with shame. His path was the road to betrayal. His price was the retention of vanity.

He'd caved in so easily. There'd never been any real doubt he'd go back for the armor, for he had no identity apart from it. Not anymore. He could barely breathe without it nearby, much less ride to battle without it, naked to the stings of cruel fates that swarm about men of common ilk. No, he must do his mother's latest bidding, as he'd always done before, regardless of the consequences. That was the man he truly was beneath the juggernaut's shell. *A heartless coward.*

On the horse walked, and his men came up behind him, most either infected with their lord's sullen mood or keenly mindful of it. Dragan paid them little or no heed at all.

"So…this is the *Spider*'s offspring?" a bestial voice boomed on Dragan's left, yanking him swiftly from his trance. "He doesn't look it."

The gloom about Dragan evaporated, and — snapping his head up and to the side, attacking the scorner with rays of sheer hatred streaming from his eyes — he said: "And you're my mother's dung and fodder, looking every bit the part."

At this the ghoul growled low in his throat, and suddenly Dragan was aware of a circle of goblins closing in around him. Some of the Haxûdī nearby reached for their weapons…but their lord lifted a hand as he saw this, like a dog's master pulling tighter on the leash. His men relaxed then — if but a little — before hearing the ghoul's next words:

"Come now." The bulk that was G'nilbor stepped closer, daring to place his grotesque claw upon the reins of Dragan's steed. "Step down from this animal, and we'll see who plays the fodder. My belly grumbles. Perhaps I'll crack open your skull…make a meal of your brains…"

For the first time since his magical breastplate had fully proved its worth to him, Dragan considered its power and found doubt in his mind. Would it truly never fail to save him, even if his own strength waned? He didn't feel powerful today. Already some of the gloom that'd surrounded him moments ago was returning. Presently he found the ghoul's unearthly stare unbearable, so he was forced to break from it and look away.

G'nilbor smiled then, savoring the doubt he'd just tasted in Dragan as much as he'd enjoy gnawing the man's bones. "I thought not," was all he said, and he released the reins, stepping out of the *GrimHelm's* path.

Although he didn't feel up to it, Dragan had his reputation to uphold. His men's eyes were affixed to him, studying his every movement. He couldn't let this fiend have the last word. For him to actually engage the beast here would be folly for them both, regardless of the outcome, for such a thing wouldn't sit well with their mistress. But...

"If ever I see you, beast, beyond the hills of Ost, you'll have your chance at my skull. Yet beware. Some would-be meals are poisonous." And with these words Dragan kicked his horse and rode swiftly ahead, pushing through the ring of goblins to leave their enraged commander cursing him loudly behind.

He kept up a canter until they reached the wood line — but once the trees had swallowed him and his warriors, the branches hanging low on either side of the road, almost in the men's faces, he slowed them back to a walk. His head hung low again. The brief spar of words with G'nilbor had reminded him of his battle with the Giant of Braured...and that in turn had brought his thoughts back to the White King. *He summons you now to him*, he heard the toppled giant speak again in a voice unlike the man's own. *Go now by the swiftest road*. What did it mean? Could the spirit of Tiramas Vendhane actually still inhabit the world above? *Where would I find him if it did? In the same spot where I slew him? In Addrindain? That's much too far. There must be another way...*

"My lord?" came a familiar voice. *Jedan*. The rearguard captain had pulled his steed alongside Dragan's at some point and was now occupying himself with a worried stare at his master. "You don't seem well..."

"I'm not," the *GrimHelm* frowned.

Mûran waited a moment to see if anything more would be forthcoming; but as soon as it became obvious he'd have to pry, he wasted no more time. "Where are we headed now, lord? My men would like to know. And..." He hesitated.

"And what?"

"Is it Ûladriss that's troubling you? The albino told us not to worry...that he would recover in time. Did you leave instructions for him?"

"Valreecius is no more an albino than he is a healer, Jedan. He looks and acts the parts, but he's...something else."

At this Mûran only frowned a moment before nodding. There were already unanswered questions on the table, and he chose to add no more.

This wasn't lost on the *DoomBringer*, and thus he came to the point: "Tell the men we're headed for long-earned leisure in the halls of our Ithirian friends. In Gethod we'll grow fat, drunk, and weak to their women's wiles!"

Jedan was clearly taken aback. This wasn't like his master at all. Yet still he waited patiently for the next answer.

"As for Ûladriss..." Dragan sighed. *Thank the gods he's not coming with us. I wouldn't share my shame with any of you, brave warriors, if it could be done otherwise. But Ûladriss, most of all, I'd spare from disgrace.* "He'll stay put until we return or I send for him. Those are his orders. Do you disagree?"

"No, my lord," Jedan responded immediately, but then a long silence passed between them. The sun broke through the branches above, bringing a fresh burst of heat to the already sweltering day. Below was the sound of hooves crunching dry earth. At last Mûran spoke again. "I'll repay you for the horse. The price may be steep, but I'll find a way. Apologies don't suffice. That damned boy..."

"Speaking of the boy," said Dragan, ignoring the comment on his lost steed, "...how's he enjoying his captive?"

Mûran looked as if he'd roll his eyes but thought better of it. "It's fitting we should keep the girl as our hostage, but...forgive me...wouldn't it be wiser for a veteran to guard her? Dealing with her may seem punishment for Gavix at first—she *is* quite feisty—but you know how such things tend to go. He needs no distractions of that sort. He should be..." Jedan tugged at his black goatee as he considered something. "He should be out scouring the countryside for your steed...that's what he should be about! And I should go with him. Leisure isn't for those men who've failed in their duties."

"Nonsense!" Dragan waved this offer away, knowing success to be unlikely after the amount of time Allethion had been lost to them. But just then a thought struck him like a bolt of lightning. *Allethion! If the White King's spirit haunts those woods, wouldn't Allethion be drawn to it? That horse wasn't bred for mortals. It held a bond with Vendhane!*

The rearguard captain, ever observant, caught the quick change of Dragan's expression, and—anxious for a chance to regain his perceived loss of honor—he then pressed on: "The animal may've returned to linger near the site of the battle, for all we know. It may not be too late..."

"Are you certain you want to do this?" asked Dragan, turning at last to look the man straight in the eye. "The girl could be useful as a guide, but even with your knife pressed to their little queen's neck...if they come upon you in numbers..."

"I accept the risk," Jedan sat up proudly in his saddle. "Either Gavix and I shall learn the fate of Allethion and return to you — or in Braured we'll meet our end. This I promise."

"Very well. You have my leave. But, Jedan…"

"Yes, lord?"

"I have a request concerning the horse. It may seem strange to you."

"Name it, and it shall be done."

"If you do happen to find Allethion alive, I wouldn't have you retake him at once. I'd have you observe his movements instead — at least for a day or so. If he's alone and shows no sign of deliberate travel after that, then you may bring him back to me. Otherwise I'd have you follow him for as long as you dare…or until he finds the thing he seems to be searching for. You must do this without knowing the reason behind it. Is this clear?"

"Yes, my lord. We'll depart within the hour." If Jedan indeed thought his master's request strange, he didn't show it. Pulling the reins of his mount, he made to turn away.

Looking over his shoulder at Mûran as the man fell behind, Dragan nodded along with his parting words. "Captain. Good fortune to you."

20

Jedan Mûran pulled the leather reins up and to the left. His steed responded by coming to a stop — but not before making a quick circle that might've been a playful strut. Gavix soon came up beside with his captive grasping his waist from behind. She had a look of both fear and exhilaration on her face and — even after the lad's mount slowed to a halt — clutched him as tightly as if they were at a full gallop. Mûran reckoned she'd never ridden a horse; and he was correct, for these beasts were alien to her people and the forest they inhabited.

Now the small party had returned to her home, having drawn up before the entrance to Braured Forest. A swarm of vultures could be seen far off above its dense canopy, circling over the rotting dead along the road from the battle that'd taken place here earlier. They might even have smelled the stench of corruption had they been closer and had the wind been blowing in the right direction; but it wasn't blowing at all. The sky was cloudless. The sun was at high noon and had been glaring at them relentlessly since their departure from Ost. Their canteens and horses already needed water.

"The river to the north is less than a furlong from here," Jedan said, pointing a slender finger in that direction. "We'll water the horses there then make our way back south around the forest's perimeter. The albino says we'll eventually find a great lake and a river that feeds it from the east — and if we follow it till it bends southward again, we should be close to where the battle was had. And we'll have the carrion birds to guide us. From there we'll see what we will."

"Son," Jedan soon spoke again in a more serious tone (if that were possible), and Gavix met his father's gaze — only to find it locked on the girl still gripping him tightly from behind. "I'm not the *DoomBringer*," Mûran continued, his stern eyes returning to the boy. "Be proud your father has reaped his own share of glory and renown amongst our people — but I can't defeat ten men at once, nor will arrows part from their course to my heart. We ride here in great peril, even though we take pains to circumvent the northern forest. We must be stealthy in all we do. Understand? The girl's your responsibility. If she opens her mouth, even so much as a whimper — or if she tries to hinder us in any way — I won't hesitate to cut her throat." Jedan animated the last words with a finger running across his neck. "Bind her hands together and to the saddle."

"Father!" the son protested. "Look at her. She's terrified as it is. She won't go anywhere."

The rearguard captain let out a long sigh and pinched the bridge of his nose, shaking his head slightly with eyes momentarily closed. They flicked back open: "Are you stupid, boy? She's the *queen* of this wretched forest. What would *you* risk to have the world again at your fingertips if it'd been wrenched away?" He paused, partly expecting an answer; but his son appeared nonplussed, so Jedan chided him again. "I've a mind to gag her…and you also, lest more foolishness fall from your tongue!"

The boy racked his brain then for some clever rebuke—or any kind, for that matter. Unexpectedly one came to him, and as soon as it entered his mind it left his lips. "Will you gag the horses? They may neigh…and they don't understand what *this* means," he said, running a finger along his throat, careful not to show too much impudence in his mockery.

The man stared at his son harshly for a time, thinking to beat Gavix right there—but he couldn't bring himself to do it. The boy had made a valid point. He turned his eyes on the forest instead. "We'd not fair well without horses in this wood…on a mission of unknown duration with a child of little endurance." Jedan took another long look at the girl as his thoughts turned inward. "Bind her," he finally added in a voice indicating more backtalk wouldn't be tolerated. Gavix reached into one side of the satchel astride his horse and removed a length of rope. With some difficulty, he wrested the girl's arms from his waist and, twisting his torso around, began tying her hands together. Her eyes filled with tears as the rope bit into flesh. She began sniffling as her sorrows were loosed. Gavix placed a vertical finger to his lips, gave her a sympathetic *shush*, then tied the free end of the rope to a metal ring sewn into the saddle.

All the while Jedan watched impassively until satisfied with his son's work; then he nodded and, turning his charger northwards, set off for the muddy river Asendath. Son and captive followed close behind.

21

It was a dreary night in the Vale of Eredus. On the banks of the swollen river Olendarth, the great sister city Relinydd solemnly defied the deluge issuing with violent ferocity down upon her stone shoulders. On some other eve, the lights of the metropolis might've been misconstrued by a remote and weary traveler as innumerable and brilliant stars against the black backdrop of the night sky. But on this night, from the same vista, the city likely could've been mistaken for no more than a meager outpost. Not a living thing stirred in the open places within the confines of its heavy walls, and all lights save those permeating faintly from a few buildings had been extinguished by the storm. The majesty of the spectacle was diminished.

Within a small room of the northwestern guard tower, two soldiers sat facing one another, hunched over a little table that rested uneasily on the floor beneath their feet. The tower formed one cornerstone of the city's meaty wall, and both men had sought refuge there from the storm, unable or unwilling to stand guard amidst the sheets of torrential rain blowing wrathfully high atop the parapet. *It's too dark,* they must've told themselves. *Pitch black! What good's standing guard if you can't see your hand in front of your face?* This seemed justification enough for abandoning their post.

Each man had placed his betting funds for the night on the table. Unlike his partner — a native Domalin who seemed to be content with his money disorderly strewn about — the Sinian had meticulously stacked his coins into three equal but squat columns. In the board's middle were piled enough coppers to make half a silver: a considerable wager for two grunts. The Domalin nervously reordered the six rigid cards he held fanned out under his nose. "Well," he said at length, "...I hope for your sake you're not bluffing."

The Sinian grinned slyly then spread his cards out face-up on the table. "I never bluff. Two tall men and two crowns."

The Domalin peered down at his opponent's cards with wide eyes — then his mind began scrambling for some new sequence within his own that could trump his companion's. But eventually he conceded, angrily slamming his fist down on the table. "If I'd had *just one* of them damn crowns of yours..."

"Betting on coming, huh? That's risky," said the Sinian as he raked the pot to his side of the table. Immediately he began forming a fourth money tower.

"That's why it's called gambling, right?"

"Right," replied the winner, smiling inwardly at the prospect of a prosperous night as he scooted his chair away from the table and stood, stretching his arms wide. He stepped close to the room's only window: an array of translucent glass bricks set permanently into the tower, not large enough for a man to fit through.

Wiping the condensate and dust from the smooth surface to feign at peering out into utter blackness, suddenly he recoiled when a bright flash lit the murky glass.

"I'm definitely not going out now!" he exclaimed as the inevitable crack and boom of thunder found their ears.

"It won't let up all night," said his companion. "You know what that means, don't you?"

"What?"

"It means Captain won't be bringing his lazy ass out here to check on us." The Domalin reached in the satchel stowed under his chair and pulled out a bottle of whiskey and two bronze shooters. "So what do you say? Let's have a drink."

The Sinian rubbed his chin's whiskers contemplatively before returning to his seat. "So it looks like we'll gamble on more than just cards tonight. A month is a long time in the jug for a jig of liquor." Then he smiled. "But Daemon...I'll take that bet!"

The other soldier nodded happily and quickly filled the tiny cups. Both men then promptly tossed back the booze, fighting to suppress looks of distaste as the cheap alcohol burned its way to their bellies. Another flash of light burst in the window. The pair silently awaited the thunder as if they could do nothing else until it came—as though if it never came they'd be frozen there for eternity. But it did arrive a moment later, shaking with it all loose things in the room. The Sinian's eyes danced around to verify nothing had fallen; then he shuffled the cards and doled out six per person for another round. The Domalin drew his up and fanned them out, once again, beneath his nose. *Three whores. Ha! Beat that, plainsman,* he mused as he dropped four coppers into the pot. "Word from the northern outpost is a fog blew in from the west a couple weeks ago and settled over Lake Hudron so thick you couldn't see three fathoms in front of your face. Stayed like that for *four days,* they say. Wonder what could've caused a thing like that?"

"I don't know," responded the Sinian, matching the native's bet, "...but the forest's been foggy for the past few days. Maybe it's the same one. Some folks say a dragon came down the river and moved in."

"I noticed," said the other, indicating that he wanted two replacement cards. "Maybe this rain will be the end of it."

"I doubt it. Probably make it worse...with the moisture and all." The soldier from Sinia took three cards for himself and tossed a few more coins on the pile.

The native counted out an equivalent amount and pushed them into the pot. Topping off their cups with another two jigs of the good stuff, he held his shooter in the air for a toast. "Here's to the dragon of the forest. If I see him, I'll shove my sword up his butt!"

Both men laughed and tossed back their liquor as another low, thunderous rumbling found their ears. The Domalin furrowed his brows in curiosity, staring at the window. "Didn't see lightning that time..."

The Sinian shrugged his shoulders.

His partner laid down the three whores, one at a time, never taking his eyes off his opponent. The soldier from Sinia didn't seem perturbed — but he took one more long look at his cards before saying: "Can't beat that, I guess."

The Domalin clapped his hands and began to collect his winnings. "I was still a little nervous, the way your luck's been tonight." Then he stood and threw his cloak over his shoulders. "I need to piss." Drawing the cloak's cowl over his head, he warned: "You know, having you plainsmen around hasn't been all that bad...but don't think I won't box your ears if any of my money's missing when I get back."

"How would you know?" laughed the Sinian, indicating the jumbled mess of coins on the native's side of the table.

The Domalin grinned, unlatching the steel reinforced wooden door leading directly onto the parapet atop the city wall. Rain and wind burst into the modest room like an unwanted guest as he opened and slid through the crack he'd made, man cursing weather all the while.

The Sinian shuffled the cards a few times before setting the stack neatly back on the table then turned his attention to the window. Gazing into the blackness, he consciously didn't blink in anticipation of the next thunderbolt. Soon enough, the black void of glass was filled with a brilliant white light, and immediately he perked his ears, awaiting the primal rumbling that inevitably would follow...but instead he heard only a loud crash as his companion burst through the door — so frantically that the man stumbled and fell, smashing his head against the table. Money, cards, and whiskey bottle were sent airborne, scattering and shattering respectively as they rained upon the hard floor. The Domalin rabidly fought to gain his footing, crying in a fear-laden voice: "Sound the goddamn horn! Sound the goddamn horn, you idiot!" Then he was gone: a madman dashing out the opposite side of the room and up the spiraling staircase that terminated atop the tower roof.

The Sinian shouted after him for an explanation, but none came. Heedless of the weather, he jerked the tower door open and leapt onto the parapet. Shielding his eyes from the rain, he strained to see into the darkness — and at that moment another lightning bolt lit the world for a split second, causing the soldier's heart to freeze in his chest.

No more than a stone's throw from the city, serried in the field like ants on a mound, a multitudinous army approached.

22

The Mardothan's head flew upwards, cleaved asunder from its body. The awkward mass fell with a thud upon the damp earth at Astelidus' feet as he searched for his next victim. But who else was brash enough to contend with Sinia's champion? Recently it seemed every avenue pursued by the son of Ny beneath Crûthior's walls was devoid of glory, as if the battle ebbed as he flowed: as if King Berac's sole strategy was to mitigate Astelidus' mayhem in despair of eliminating it. Still the young warrior was a plague on the Mardothans, directly or indirectly, as Deserus Oen and his council took every advantage of the fear their new hero inspired in their adversaries' minds.

Yet again — and despite all his glories compiled upon returning to the fray — Astelidus still didn't produce a presence on the battlefield equivalent to that of the *GrimHelm*. The Mardothans remained emboldened by Dragan's departure and were issuing forth from their iron gates more frequently, even so far as to harass and burn the outermost Sinian camps. Crûthior's second wall was all but rebuilt, and the Toros River was reclaimed, with the latter of these allowing the Mardothans to accept much-needed food and provisions from Agrardob. But above all this, a new hero was treading Mardotha's plains. Birakith the Baneful, a man who wreaked comparable havoc upon the Sinians as Astelidus did upon his enemies. The two had yet to meet, however — intentionally, it seemed, as if the Mardothan warlords were hesitant to wager on a victory. They'd no other heroes to replace Birakith. The *DoomBringer* had killed them all.

And although Bronwyn had since come to share his bed and also his hand in public, Astelidus sensed a hesitation in her affection: a reluctance to his love. He contributed this to a number of things (including his own paranoia), suppressing the overwhelming urge to contribute it to any lingering feelings she might have for the defector, Dragan Saedus. *How could she love one who loves only himself, who laughs at others' misfortunes, who wanders the earth as a mercenary of fame?* Such as this he'd think...then always dismiss the notion to folly, blinded by the love he bore for her. Yet it irked him nonetheless.

But this day was different. The fighting around Astelidus had waxed along with the sun, and for every body he laid low there was another to take its place. The toil of his labors had drenched him with sweat, although he'd yet to fatigue under his armor's weight or the travail of his bastard sword. Today his task was to drive a wedge into the Mardothan forces — the apex of which would culminate at the rebuilt portion of the second wall — for with this achieved, miners would hurriedly tunnel beneath and collapse the weakened section, just as they'd done not so long ago. Yet from atop his rook high on the parapets of the city's tallest tower, King Berac and his council had descried the plot; and so, seeing no end to the destruction Astelidus waged against the mediocre of Crûthior, they'd at last summoned Birakith to vie with Sinia's champion.

Baneful was the man's cognomen: and rightly so, for his product was woe. A gladiator hardened through years of drudgery and combat, Birakith had risen to command a company of his own sort: resilient, brazen, and ignorantly steadfast. Unlike his kinsman Agriretrim, he was lowborn; yet, although smaller in stature, he was brawnier and more resourceful than the Lion. He'd traveled to Crûthior after hearing the tale of how a warrior known as the *DoomBringer* had felled his great cousin — and he was intent on discovering for himself the prowess of this Sinian *hireling*. Yet to his confusion and dismay, he'd found on arrival only that Dragan Saedus had since departed Mardotha like some craven in the night. But after witnessing firsthand the fresh destruction effectuated by the rogues of Sinia, he'd chosen to remain and fight.

Now Birakith and his soldiers strode through the city gates as a spectacle of steel. The product of their might…the plume of victories past…was their armor. Each man's possession was heavy and imposing: black, cold, contoured sheets of metal sat firmly atop breasts, shoulders, thighs, and shins of the hearty warriors. Most gripped a shield, tall and rectangular, in one hand and a short sword in the other. Birakith wielded only a two-handed longsword and further distinguished himself by wearing upon his great helm a crest of brilliant red horsehair that ran transverse across the scalp. The sea of rabble gave way to this mass of iron as it marched forth to meet Astelidus Ny. Seeing his target, the Mardothan captain bellowed in the voice of ten men: "Son of Ny, hear my words. Parley!" Then he commanded his troops to pull the other Mardothans away from their adversaries and shield them from the fray — until a half moon was formed on the battlefield, shaded by the cool brick of the city's second wall.

After hearing Birakith's words, Astelidus ordered the same of his men until a circular section of the battlefield was void of the living but full of the dead. Birakith the Baneful stepped into this ring to speak the first challenge:

"Astelidus Ny! Now that I lay eyes upon you, I marvel at why Berac held me back. I came here for revenge against the man who slew my kinsman — yet all I find is you: a freckled-faced boy whose glory lies in slaying farmhands! The ones this *DoomBringer* pitied enough not to kill while he remained! But a Mardothan is a Mardothan, and their deaths won't go unanswered. What say you then, Ny, here on the eve of your demise?"

"You speak to me as the child!" the Sinian bellowed in reply, stepping also into the impromptu arena. "But it was *your* leader who hid you from my sight! Great must be the wisdom of Berac! For I am the son of Silinveran Uel, who — like my father before me and his father before him — has dined with kings, lain with their daughters, and counseled their enterprises. Yet *you* would dishonor me? An ignoramus born in a pigsty to a whore on the outreaches of civilization, come to flex the muscles of this gang of brutish lackeys? We'll see how you fare without the iron curtain at your side!"

The Mardothan slowly reached behind his head, grabbed the hilt of his huge blade, and loosed it from its leather bindings. Bringing it round to his free hand, he held the weapon at an angle, tip pointing low to the earth. The matte black of his plate shimmered in the sun's rays falling on his broad shoulders from overtop Crûthior's high walls. "I need no aid in this fight," he replied coldly and with no dramatics — as if the words of Ny had nettled him. Looking askance at his troops so they understood, he began slowing approaching his adversary.

"Don't interfere unless there's foul play," Astelidus quickly told his captain, then he strode forth to determine the day's lot.

For tense moments the two champions circled, each sizing up the other. The man from Agrardob, gripping his sword's long hilt tightly with both hands, let the blade's tip trail in the dust to one side as heavily-muscled legs carried him in a wary stance along the circuit. The young Sinian — similarly poised to strike or defend at an instant's notice — stalked with a thick-bossed, round shield raised beneath his line of sight and his hand-and-a-half blade held overhead: the tip pointed straight up as if plunged into the belly of the sky. From the ring about them began now a deep, primal music, taken up spontaneously by both sides, effectuated by instruments that were swords bashing against shields and the guttural, staccato roars from their bearers. And to this savage ballad the heroes timed their deadly dance.

Birakith was the first to strike. Suddenly the longsword rose from its trail in the dirt and was swung toward Astelidus in a wide arc parallel to the ground...its wielder spinning with the weapon into position for his next maneuver; and with this, whether the *Baneful* had intentionally caused it or not, the slice brought up a cascade of dirt flung straight at his opponent's face. The follow-up strike was a brutal overhead cut that pummeled the nearly-blinded Sinian even beneath his warding shield, knocking him back a pace on unsteady legs before he could offer any counter.

The shield's metal boss had taken and deflected that fierce blow — yet for a moment Astelidus' arm felt totally numb, as if instead his limb had been struck clean and cleaved asunder. *Daemon, he's strong!* But there was no time to think further. The crowd roared once longer and louder. Another attack was coming.

This time Birakith crouched low with his swing, attempting to take the foe's legs off at the knees — and barely did Astelidus' jump avoid it. The longsword's tip drew a bloody line on his right leg just above the armored shin. Another overhead cut appeared to be following, so Astelidus raised his shield again in anticipation...only to have it crushed into his face and chest as Birakith feinted, giving up the perceived chop to send his entire bulk, shoulder first, barreling into the Sinian champion instead. The *Baneful* was not so quick with this move, however, to take Astelidus completely off guard, and rather than crashing to the ground, the young hero pushed off his assailant, using the force to help spin his body in a half-revolution — then bashed his shield into the enemy's back as he came about.

Birakith's partially-checked momentum, aided by the slam from behind, was enough to send the Mardothan sprawling in the dirt...yet he never let go his hilt. As Astelidus sprang to make an end from behind, his opponent rolled to one side and poked the longsword straight at the threat: whereupon Ny wisely checked his lunge to avoid being skewered himself.

"Up, bug!" goaded Astelidus, suddenly remembering his honor. "Up before I squish out the guts beneath your black beetle shell!"

A near-deafening roar issued from the Sinian half of the circle. Defying the pain in his cut leg and still-tingling arm, Astelidus grinned at his prowess and his jest alike. But Birakith the Baneful was not conquered. Already returned to his feet to again initiate the pair's wary circling, he answered: "You fools are the insects, boy! Flies swarming near an open mouth. Get too close, and in one bite we'll devour you all!"

Another burst of Mardothan aggression followed that Astelidus found hard to repel, but at some point during the next several exchanges he found a groove and started to exploit the more cumbersome swings of his opponent. More than one of his swift cuts would've ended the contest had Birakith's armor not met and turned them aside. *He's pressing too hard. He'll wear down before me.* Yet that wasn't how Astelidus wanted this to end. Sinia's young warriors had their eyes fixed on him. He must do more than feint and counter.

But just then a vicious blow struck Astelidus' shield, catching it right on the edge and cleaving it down to the boss — and both longsword and buckler were cast uselessly aside. Once more the end seemed at hand. Instantly the Sinian leapt forward with seeking blade...but was foiled again, for as if from thin air a curved knife appeared in the Mardothan's hand. Birakith dodged the thrust and slipped into stabbing range, whereupon the two men gripped one another and began to grapple for control. *Not again!* Astelidus recalled the sand elf's earlier attack even as he desperately fought to avert another sting — until his thoughts were jarred by a hard butt to the head.

The beatings of sword on shield and roaring ceased as Birakith's knife struck out toward the dazed Sinian's midsection, and likely every man observing this held his breath. But then something unexpected happened. Instead of promptly crumpling over and spitting up his death blood (as it seemed certain he would), in a fluid series of motions Astelidus swatted the knife aside, reached behind the Mardothan's head, pulled back on the crested helm, slammed his sword's hilt up into Birakith's nose, let the enemy's then-limp body drop, and stepped back into a ready stance with blade raised high.

The fighting men of Sinia released their breaths. Their new champion's glory was secure.

Suddenly Astelidus glared at the jet-plated figures and fancied their black armor leaking a thick crimson blood. From somewhere behind them a coward's arrow shrieked forth and grazed his arm—yet he hardly felt it at all. Bloodlust had taken hold. With an animalistic cry, he leveled his blade at the Mardothans and charged.

23

The younger boy barely skipped a beat when he saw the girl, merely voicing a curt, overloud greeting before returning to his sport. He had a long, thin vine wrapped at one end around his little finger and a tiny, hopping frog bound to the other, and the amusement he was deriving from this left him all but oblivious to the rest of the world. This tot's sole companion, however, was on the border of leaving childhood innocence behind; and thus, although he'd been laughing just a moment before also — with his own amphibian tied to his hand — the elder boy stopped in his tracks at the stranger's sudden appearance. His jaw slackened as he stared quite unknowingly at his own abducted monarch. He let his vine fall at his side.

"Don't be frightened..." said the girl. Her voice was sweet but at odds with her troubled face. Her eyes flicked to the smaller of the pair who'd just loosed another cackle of glee as he continued to play nearby. "Your brother?"

"Where'd you come from?" the older lad finally spoke, ignoring the question posed for one of his own. Someone had trained him well enough. "Who's with you?" Nervously he swept his gaze over the immediate vicinity. He'd rightly assumed a girl no older than himself — and not of his own village — wouldn't be wandering out here alone; yet his scan turned up no sign of others, nor did the Queen of Braured make any sign to give her captors away.

"No one. My name's Cat — and I go where I please." She took a step closer, forcing a smile. "What's your name?"

"Come, Righa!" the lad yelled suddenly in the direction of his charge before turning back on Cataya of Braured. "I'm Orum. You're from Adach?"

"Adach...yes." The girl frowned as she said this — but then her face took on a curious, eager expression. "Have you heard the tale, Orum?"

"What tale?"

Brushing a stray lock of black hair from her face, Cataya put her back against the nearest tree and slid down into a cross-legged sitting position at its base; and, after one more glance aside to ensure Righa was obeying his command, the elder boy warily followed her lead. As soon as his eyes were on her again, she lost no time in beginning...

"What's she telling him?" whispered Jedan, his face less than a hand's length from Gavix' right ear.

"She says what was planned."

"And nothing more?" Jedan pressed, ignoring the quick, agitated glance that had accompanied Gavix' response. The pair were on their knees, peering over a fallen trunk within earshot of Cataya's meeting but well hidden by foliage from view. "I can't see her hands...or her eyes. She could be..."

The woodland boy had just spoken again — rather excitedly — causing Mûran to cut short his voiced concern. The Haxûdī noted a smile on his son's face then: one which instantly conjured over him a shower of relief. Clearly Allethion had been seen, and this child was telling the girl all he knew about it.

And for the captain, success came not a moment too soon.

Despite his promise to Dragan, for the past few days Jedan had been on the verge of abandoning his quest. Already in this wood he'd resorted to stealing provisions from the locals; yet what he'd taken was proving barely adequate to support himself and the children, much less their poor, starving horses. And already he'd drawn his blade and ended one life...though the second man had gotten away. But the worst part of the ordeal had been, until its ending just now, that not a clue of Dragan's steed had been discovered. First they'd sought and eventually come upon the spot where Gavix had last seen Allethion, only to find nothing new. Then they'd scoured the forest around that area, still with no luck at all. Even after eventually being detected, however — and although he could hardly take a step forward now without looking behind, expecting any moment to see the brush part and spears come flying at him — Mûran had been reluctant to attempt Gavix' plan involving the girl. Yet he was too encouraged to curse his overcautiousness at present. Too proud of his increasingly resourceful son.

"She'll return to the horses now," Gavix whispered again after awhile to his father. Cataya was in the process of standing and wiping her hands clean of debris, apparently at discussion's end with her unknowing subject.

Jedan's expression fell sour again. No doubt he was concerned about letting the girl out of his sight, even for a brief period; but having held to the plan so far without deviation, he held his tongue and waited for her to wave goodbye and walk off — and for the native children to depart in the opposite direction — before stirring. "Quickly, boy!" he snapped then, seeming to have forgotten the high regard he'd held for his son but a few moments earlier. "It's your hide if we lose her!"

And at that, Gavix set off at once after the Queen of Braured at breakneck speed; yet no chastisement from his father could wipe the silly grin from his face.

24

It was raining again. Otherwise Dragan would've beheld the grassy knoll, distant as he remembered it being from the forest's edge. And the farmlands, rolling to the horizon, far as one's eyes could see.

All summer long, this rain's hounded me. Like a shadow constantly threatening, growing closer each day, until it settles in and becomes your world. A world you can't escape.

Dragan's hands rose to brush back his long brown hair. Soaked and under failing light, it was black. That suited his mood. A space of calm arrived where only the steady downpour could be heard about them. Then...

Thunder roared, announcing doom at Ithiria's door. But for now that doom merely lingered, not a single foot having stepped from this bit of shelter beneath the eaves. Here they were to stop and wait their contact's return. The youngest and eldest of their band had been left at the camp of three days ago; and another group, carrying both their own blades and the blades of those lingering behind, had split off early yesterday, heading silently north through the trees.

Haxûdī emotions on the venture were mixed. This act of few against many, of stealth, of cunning, of blindingly quick sweeps and thrusts of blades — would it win them great honor above all their peers? Those who believed that smiled, even now, despite the miserable weather. Or would this become what the others believed? What gut reaction made it seem?

"Disgrace," came a voice on Dragan's right. This was Ashkelī, a man seeking to fill the void left by his betters. "Forgive me, lord...but there's still time..."

"Don't presume to advise me, Ashkelī, as I might've allowed Mûran or Ûladriss. You haven't earned that right."

"As you wish..." The Haxûdī frowned — yet only for a moment, as if he'd known such an answer was forthcoming. After pausing briefly to stroke the side of Dragan's horse (this likely being nothing more than a show to hide his prompt dismissal from watchful brothers-in-arms), the man was gone, leaving the son of Saedus with his thoughts.

How long has it been since I was last here? he pondered, reaching for his steed's mane, taking up the attentions Ashkelī had begun and abruptly left wanting. *It was before the Haxûdī. Four years? Five? Old Mehdurin will likely be the same. The man has nothing left to fail him save more of his mind — hoary, bent, and stick-thin as he was already when I met him. His grandson will be a man now, though — and that needs considering. I need no bristling young prince asking too many questions. I need the old dotard and the men I befriended. I need the name of Camus Robi to pass my lips...soon and often.* At the remembrance of that name he shook his head. *Ah, Camus...it's good you didn't live to witness this day!*

Drenched to the bone, Dragan recalled then an afternoon of fairer weather: a walk up the paved road from Gethod's civilian settlement ringing the hill below to its ancient fortress situated a hundred fathoms or so above. The conversation between him and Robi that day...he could no longer recall...but the sights they'd passed along the path were returning to his mind. The last few houses of bricks, logs, and straw giving way to nature for a stretch. Azalea shrubs in full bloom of spring on either side of the road, welcoming the pair at the onset of their climb. The way wide to their going, even as the sentinel trees grew thick about them, its air heavy with the scents of flowers and rich soil and pine. Then suddenly came the wall, rising twice a man's height before them as the wood failed: at least four cubits thick and so old that grass had long taken root along the top. And here was the gate beneath the bulwark. The single entrance to the fortress at ground level.

Wide open.

Why storm walls when you can walk right through the gate? he heard his mother say...and with an effort pushed her words aside, refocusing on the images of his reverie.

Inside the fortress now, his mind's eye scanned left to right, pausing on each structure a moment before moving on to the next: a tall watch tower (indeed, the only tower besides the central keep); a huge tank for holding rainwater; the huts and pavilions of the soldiers, storehouses, an octagonal, thatch-roofed corral, two feasting halls...

And the sanctuary. That's where Mehdurin had greeted him. *Where his reign must end. I've no other choice.* Again Dragan recalled his friend Camus and saw the soldier's grinning face as they jested over something in the past. Then it was gone, replaced by a different smiling visage: the perfect features of another who would be disgusted by his present course. *Bronwyn.* Now all other thoughts and visions gave way to his lost love. He'd left her, disgraced himself; and if he ever saw her again, would he even have enough courage to meet her eyes? *GrimHelm, DoomBringer,* greatest of men...brought low by shame? Rendered impotent by that piercing emerald gaze?

Someone had spoken just now. Ashkelī again. Still half in a dream, Dragan asked the warrior to repeat.

"A rider, my lord. See there? And another besides."

The dream ended. Riders there were indeed: two silhouettes emerging from thick sheets of rain, growing and taking firmer shape as they approached. In but a few moments more their steeds' splashing hoofbeats could be heard...then they were coming to a halt before Dragan and his men. The one on the left—the same who'd ridden ahead to announce their presence—remained ahorse, his face all but lost behind the water streaming from his leather cowl; and he sat there still, having no further words for the foreigners.

The other man, however, dismounted quickly, pushing his steed's reins into the hand of the nearest Haxûdī. With a fist resting on his sword's pommel, his hood thrown back, Gethod's guard captain strode forth — almost threateningly — until Dragan was well within blade's reach. Then he stopped.

And knelt.

"Rise," spoke the *GrimHelm* simply...but what he thought was different. *On your feet, fool! You show me honor undeserved!*

The captain rose immediately and thrust out his hand.

Dragan took it. "I remember you, Captain. Irenys...is that it?"

"Indeed," the man nodded and, visibly troubled by the rain, put one hand to his brow, looking beyond Dragan to the trees.

Dragan placed a hand on the man's shoulder, and the Haxûdī made way as he led Garim Irenys beneath the branches to a spot of decent cover.

"Welcome back, Prince of Ost," said the man after wiping at his face. "I'd hoped we'd see you again sooner."

"A shortage of feasts of late, then, eh?" Dragan tested the waters with this jest. *A man who falls honestly and eagerly into mirth is a man without suspicion.*

A booming smile appeared at this, followed by a snort of laughter. "My men would say so...but come, I must ask you a thing now — then we need speak no more till we've left this foul weather for the comforts of hall. Forgive me, but these are Prince Kalen's own words. Will your men disarm before the gate?"

"They'll do as I bid...each and every one of them. But no man but me may touch my own blade." Dragan kept his gaze stern for this last statement, letting the Ithirian captain know a rebuttal wouldn't be allowed.

"I see. Will you ride ahead with me, then? Or wait here with the rest till the rain slackens?"

"No. We'll move now."

25

Release me!

A bead of sweat formed to trickle down Baeldrin's brow. The steadiness of his hands, normally unwavering, faltered suddenly under the strain.

The voice hissed again in his head, full of malice. *You weaken, mortal. Free me of your own accord, and I shall leave this world with you unharmed. Do not, and...*

No! the will of the master lashed out. *You must obey. You've no choice.* With a great effort he forced his hands still, wiped at the perspiration on his face, and continued the exercise, wide eyes returning to a tiny pebble over which he knelt. The folds of his fresh, crimson silk robe crawled the floor about him like a pool of spreading blood. A few strands of dark, slightly curling hair were matted to his face. His stare at the object of focus was intense.

Baeldrin had acquired this small stone and its mate from the librarian — yet there'd been a thing painfully lacking from that deadly transaction: knowledge of how to use them without succumbing in the process. Thus today (and not for the first time) he'd gambled with his very life in a venomous spirit's presence, armed only with what insights he'd gleaned from observing the sorceress' control of her own incorporeal minions...and caution...and, hopefully, an ocean of luck. Each time he released one of his pair — and only one, for to do otherwise at this point would be a monumental folly — he held it a bit longer than before and became a bit more comfortable with the invader of his mind. It was but a matter of time. *Soon*, he told himself, having learned by trial and error how to separate private thought from a sending. *Soon you'll cease to squirm. Both of you. Then my security will be complete.*

In the end you shall fail, the alien voice came again, unbidden.

Had the specter heard him after all? *A hole in my shielding?* Baeldrin's stare shifted to the wispy form before him. He knew it'd taken shape from dust in the air: drawn and shaped by the soul to a likeness of the flesh that'd once housed it. The figure's appearance was that of a young man, naked, slender on the verge of emaciation. Unblinking, otherworldly eyes narrowed angrily as the prince's gaze found them. The thing's mouth was fixed in a scowl. Its arms were folded about its chest, hugging itself as if the room were somehow frigid.

There came a knock at the door.

"I said no disturbances!" shouted Baeldrin, not daring to take his eyes from the spirit. A break in concentration here could be lethal.

After a moment's delay, the posted guard returned some near-unintelligible response, and Baeldrin thought that might be the end of the potential intrusion. It wasn't.

"I've traveled too fast and too far, prince," came another voice then, loud, on the border of anger itself, "...to be detained. Don't you agree?"

Nephos Zera. The Mardothan ambassador. Expected, but not this early. *Fast indeed.* "One moment."

Baeldrin focused all his thought on the focus object. Cold sweat threatened a return to his brow. Then somehow, all of a sudden, it was done. The phantom was banished again to the stone, and the stone was snatched up and concealed. Relinydd's self-proclaimed liberator stood and, releasing a long breath, faced the door, trying to summon a measure of composure. "You may enter."

Zera did at once, the double doors turning in to give way. He stopped but a few paces from Baeldrin to give his perfunctory bow; then the guard shut the doors, leaving the pair to study one another. Nephos with his usually shaven head showing stubble from the road, but otherwise appearing clean, as if he'd at least quickly washed and put on fresh clothing; the prince with his wet brow and face uncharacteristically pale. "Are you ill?" the Mardothan finally spoke at what he saw, appearing genuinely worried about Baeldrin's not-so-well-hidden state.

"No...a late night is all," the prince lied, waving off the Mardothan's concern. "There's much here that needs doing."

"I see. For a moment I thought you might've taken a wound in battle."

"Me?" Baeldrin laughed, attempting to put some emotion behind it. "I never drew my sword. The witch's pets did the bleeding for me. I can't risk combat at present. Far too much depends on my health, eh?" Reaching for his guest's shoulder, he smiled and clamped down a greeting. "Let's have a drink to it, shall we?"

Nephos appeared to like that idea. Following Baeldrin to a nearby table, he took up the decanter and offered to pour for them both. When that was done, he lifted his cup: "Baeldrin, Lord of Relinydd. Heir of Domal. To your health!" He drained his glass swiftly and set it down. If the liquor had burned his mouth, he made no sign of it.

The prince took only a sip from his cup before lowering it and moving away. The drapes to the balcony had been drawn until now, fighting against the room's single source of sunlight, but as Baeldrin arrived at that spot he let the rays win. "Come, Nephos," he cast a glance behind him before stepping out. "See the first fruits of our labors."

Baeldrin had commandeered this tower room from Ranod Lorege: governor of Relinydd for many years before the battle of a few days past. In name, at least, Ranod was governor still, but he'd no longer be allowed to rule this city as a king unto his own right, parted from Rardonydd in all but the titles of tradition. The man's life was safe—Baeldrin had pretenses to uphold as part of his plans—but that didn't mean Lorege was entitled to sit at ease in his old apartments, living it up with his gracious conquerors. No, he was currently in the dungeon, and that was where he'd stay until Baeldrin made ready to leave. On that day of parting, Ranod would be the one to stand above the crowd in the square below this very balcony — facing the dual spires of Ophim Nuarin that'd stood there since the day of Relinydd's birth, symbolizing the relationship between the twin cities — and there loudly proclaim the follies of himself *and King Acomalath*, declaring the time long overdue for a return to that original relationship in the strictest sense. What the king would do when he heard of this, or what plans he already had in motion to deal with the new power in Relinydd, Baeldrin hardly cared. *Whatever your decision, Father, wise or not, your council will delay you too long in its deciding. Zera has seen to that. Our secret friends shall play their part.*

The Mardothan was at his side now. "I must admit, prince...and forgive me for it...that your design for this city's taking seemed to me nigh folly. Yet I don't think I've ever been so glad to have been wrong. My congratulations to you on a brilliant victory!"

Baeldrin mused on those last two words a moment, lifting his cup again for a sip. "You should've been here, friend. Our fists were on the barred gates before they ever saw us. And their fear...Daemon, it was glorious to behold! Imps and goblins...ha! Fairytales come to life before their eyes! I'm surprised they didn't just open the gates and surrender then and there." Another sip. "If the damned Sinians hadn't been here, they probably would've."

Zera spat at the mention of his hated foes. "And what of the plainsmen? I trust you've made an example."

"Oh yes. One thing I must give them: they're not cowards. They could've fled easily enough, leaving the natives to their own — but they didn't. A runner or two perhaps, to bring tidings to their king. Otherwise most died, with but a few of their wounded left for us to corral. Saedus' ghoul alone must've slain two score of their best, just while my gaze fell on him. He's quite the savage."

Nephos frowned. His question wasn't fully answered. "So what was done to the captives?" The Mardothan's hatred of Sinia ran deep.

"Those who could stand? Stripped and beaten in the square. Like dogs."

A smile. "Fitting indeed! And the natives who resisted?"

"Already released. *Freed*, if you will, from the taint of those foreigners. Our propaganda shall be fetters enough for them, at least for some time. And Lorege will remain faithful after we've gone. Valreecius shall see to that."

"I'm impressed."

Baeldrin looked as if he'd speak again — but suddenly his face turned to the sky, and he fell silent.

"What bothers you?" asked Zera after a moment, conscious of the change in his host.

"Saedus, Argen Van, Dragan…what's there not to trouble me?" He pulled his eyes and thoughts from the clouds, focusing once more on his guest. "We have control over our part in this, Nephos. But the others…" He left the rest unsaid, keeping his sideways gaze locked on the shorter man beside him.

The Mardothan thought on that for a few breaths. "I can't speak as to your kin, but I'll venture it of Van. He's no stranger to deception, surely—you and your patroness have greatly profited from that. But I've known Argen half my life…"

"You misunderstand," said Baeldrin, cutting off the Mardothan's argument before it'd rightly begun. "Not treachery. *Idleness and incompetence*…these are the things I fear now. Van presented us an opportunity by forcing himself on King Oen's daughter—but that was an act to your people's disliking, however much pride prevents them from admitting it. Berac didn't want war with Sinia, even from the start. And certainly not now. Am I wrong?"

"You only state what I myself have told you."

"But what's the man done for us since? The *Spider* talks to Argen now and again, so she says, through some damned sorcery she thrust on him years ago. But to my knowledge they aren't *doing* anything. Berac still reigns…and Berac's not under our control. I've only his words of faith, brought to me through lips not his own. The man should be removed…"

"Berac won't turn on you. That's foolishness. Anything to drive Sinia from his doorstep, he'll do. Gladly."

"I hope you're right."

"And your brother? It's his incompetence you fear? Forgive me once more, prince, but the *DoomBringer* is much renowned, sorely hated though he is among my people. Surely his task isn't beyond him?"

"If it were a trial of arms alone, he should prevail—as he always does. But I've seen a new thing in him now, and it's not to my liking." The prince's eyes moved back to the clouds.

As nothing more on this seemed forthcoming, Zera decided it best to change the subject. "What toll did the battle take on your army?"

"With the best and brightest of Relinydd off seeking glory in your homeland, I feel somewhat shamed to report any loss at all. But as I said, the city's veterans and the Sinian reserve made a brave showing. Casualties were considerable, but little more than we envisioned. Saedus' monsters have served their purpose, and soon I'll tolerate them no more."

When the prince's eyes came down from the sky this time, Zera saw in them that today's meeting was at its end. The cup that Baeldrin had been nursing was suddenly taken up in earnest and drained, then its bearer turned to move back indoors. "Make yourself at home here, friend. My servants are yours — but for now I must attend to other matters."

"Very well, prince. I take my leave…yet perhaps I can delay your troubles a bit longer." The ambassador from Mardotha strode then to the chamber's double doors, opened them wide, gestured to someone without, and stepped aside — and in walked a comely young woman with short, curly auburn hair. Her nose and mouth were veiled. Her body was hidden beneath a flowing black robe.

The Mardothan grinned at Baeldrin's reaction then promptly passed through the doors and shut them behind.

The black robe slipped to the floor.

26

Dragan held the loaf tightly as he took a bite, squeezing as if it were the arm of a misbehaving child. His other hand slid forth from the table's edge, pushing the basket on to the guard captain, Garim Irenys, sitting beside him.

This was the bigger of the two feasting halls: large enough to hold all of the off-duty soldiers stationed here plus their guests of this evening. All, with room to spare. Twelve long tables there were, with benches instead of chairs, and rows of oaken pillars ran between them and along the strangely bare walls. Lesser doors were spaced at regular intervals to either side, but the main entrance was a huge set of doors in front, and a smaller pair opened directly into a sanctuary behind. As was his long custom, old King Mehdurin had excused himself earlier to that sanctuary after a few opening words to the crowd.

Thus it fell to Gethod's heir to entertain the *DoomBringer's* men. And so far, at least, he was having a merry time of it. *Too merry*, thought Dragan, clamping down on the bread even tighter for the next bite.

"And this fine fellow, here…" Prince Kalen was saying, his volume steadily rising and speech beginning to slur from the drink as he made a casual round about Dragan's table with his leeches — every one of them grinning like asses — in tow. Having stopped behind the object of his words, he locked a comradely grip on the Haxûdî's shoulder.

Dragan couldn't remember the name of this man of his at the moment — but as he caught the warrior's eyes, he sensed the tenseness that Kalen had no doubt just felt.

"Daemon!" laughed the prince, patting the Haxûdî's shoulder once — like he might pet his dog — before removing his hand altogether. Leaving off from what he'd intended to say next, he swept his eyes across the table instead. "If I didn't know better, Saedus, I'd wonder if you were mistreating these men." At this he leaned in quickly with smiling face, attempting to catch the Haxûdî's eyes for a reaction. When none was forthcoming, however, he looked back to the warrior's captain. "Why so somber, lord? Is there some entertainment lacking? A song, perhaps?" He cut a glance to one of the girls serving ale further down the table. "Or maybe the songstress?"

A burst of laughter issued from the prince's standing companions, yet it was from them alone. Dragan opened his mouth to respond — but Irenys beat him to it. "It's the foul weather, prince. You can get under roof quickly enough, but the mood's harder to shake." He looked to the *GrimHelm* beside him. "Especially if you've refused dry clothing…"

"You did well to offer us that, Garim," Dragan jumped in, "…but we're yet fresh from the wild. Already you spoil us with hot bread and wine." He made a supreme effort to smile. "Just be glad my men are famous for their honor, else you might find *all* your girls wooed from their duties before morning."

Another round of laughter. And, at a barely perceptible nod from Dragan to Kalen's Haxûdī of interest, the seated warrior looked back over his shoulder and smiled for the prince's benefit. *That should suffice for now,* thought Dragan, trying to maintain a sincere grin.

"Well in that case," spoke Kalen as the laughter died down, "...I'd best be off to get a head start on you!" Another look down the table and a parting grip to the Haxûdī's arm and—as quickly as he'd come—the prince moved on his way with his entourage chatting and chuckling behind.

The scene about the table that'd been before Kalen's arrival now resumed, with Dragan and Garim focused on the meal while their men ate silently also or spoke each to his own kind. *I'm searching for faults I won't find,* Dragan realized after a few moments staring at his empty cup. *Even Kalen...unjustifiably arrogant, but not mean-spirited. There've been worse princes. And this man* (he glanced over at Irenys) *reminds me too much of Camus. There's nothing here to make the deed easier! Nothing at all...*

"More wine, my lords?" came a soft female voice at Dragan's right shoulder, and both he and the guard captain turned towards it, startled each from his own reverie. Dragan declined after brief consideration, but Garim wouldn't have it:

"One more, friend." He gestured for the girl to fill Dragan's cup first. "The night's barely begun. We've yet to give you a proper welcome!"

Dragan didn't much like the sound of that, but he let the girl pour for him nonetheless. After Garim's cup had been filled also, the guard captain rose from the bench, cleared a space of table before him, climbed atop it, and raised his cup and voice high:

"Brothers and guests!" It took two louder repeats of these words to spread silence over all dozen tables, but presently he had the hall's attention. "I salute you! Will you hear more?"

A rumble of consent followed.

"Then lift your drinks, men of Gethod, and cheer for those with honors due!"

Instantly the cups of the Ithiros were raised. Some of the Haxûdī raised theirs as well and kept them up; others lifted theirs but then, thinking differently of it, set them back down; yet the most seasoned of Haxûd in such affairs never reached for their vessels, suspecting well what was to come.

"To the dead! To our men who marched on Crûthior, never to return, and to their valiant leaders. To Bastram Narohad! To Camus Robi!" Irenys lowered his cup to his mouth, drank from it, and raised it again.

To Narohad! came the booming reply from a hundred lips and more. *To Robi!*

"To our guests here tonight: the fierce warriors of Haxûd! Men some say can turn a battle at its bleakest hour. Men some say are born with blade already in hand, carving themselves free of their mothers' wombs! To the Haxûdî!"

To the Haxûdî!

"To our king and our prince. To our sons and our women. Let them rule the course of our lives, and let us lay our lives down for them in need. To Mehdurin! To Kalen! To all Ithiria!"

ITHIRIA! ITHIRIA!

And now Irenys drained his cup and handed it off to a fellow as if the speech were done. But it wasn't. Instead of retaking his seat, he swooped down upon Dragan and grasped the man's arm with both his hands — and others came from behind the *GrimHelm* to prod their guest along.

Before Dragan rightly knew what was happening, he found himself standing atop the table beside the guard captain, his arm held tight in friendship. The hall fell silent once more.

"And finally...to this man here beside me. A man whose deeds would seem myths — tales of fancy to put heart into our little ones — were we not living in the days of his accomplishments. We must praise the man who pulled our brother's body from the enemy's clutches...who slew the feared Lion of Agrardob in single combat — and that amongst the lesser of his feats! Mightier than Garlmorgot who toppled the Blue King's tower, I say this hero must be. *GrimHelm! DoomBringer! Champion's Bane!* To Dragan Saedus, peerless as a god amongst men!"

Dragan didn't hear the roar that followed. The sound entered his ears and died there. A sharp pain touched his stomach...made him want to retch...and it worked its way to his chest...found his heart...clamped down tightly. No letting go. *They honor me above king and country! I can't do this! I won't do this!*

Panic overwhelmed him. A vision came, unbidden, of his warriors as mere shadows beneath the thunderstorm sky, lightly scaling the walls and dropping to the grounds below. He saw a guard fall with barely a sound — an arrow taken in the eye. Then lightning flashed, revealing drawn blades...

Is it too late to stop this madness? Trading imagination for his own eyesight, he began then to scan the faces of his warriors...to search beyond those nearby for a check of the side doors. There they were: his men spread out among their hosts, watching the exits as had been planned — but he couldn't discern whether these were only those warriors who'd entered with him. His mind slipped back into the vision, and he pictured others arriving: wet, cloaked figures stepping silently to the sides of their brethren — extra weapons stealthily passing from one hand to another. Had this already occurred?

"I'm deeply honored, Irenys," Dragan managed before lifting his own cup to the crowd then stepping quickly down from the table, all but rudely yanking his arm free in the effort to get away. "But you must excuse me..."

"Wait! Dragan!"

The guard captain's voice pelted him from behind as he hurried between the long tables...and he ignored it. However, just as he was clearing the lane's end, suddenly there came a call he couldn't ignore. *The king's herald.* Mehdurin had reentered the hall and was preparing to speak. All talk and traffic came almost immediately to a standstill. The nearest exit from Dragan was barely ten strides off—but he dared not run for it...dared not set things in motion that way, while perhaps there was still time. *Once he starts speaking, I'll move slowly...*

Yet the news brought by the old king's hoarse, cracking voice held Dragan in check. It nailed his feet to the floor such that no few men could've dragged him away. Baeldrin. Relinydd taken with hardly a fight. Sinians stripped naked and beaten to death in the streets.

His brother had succeeded easily. What would Saedus do if Dragan did not?

Damn her! Damn her to hell! His feet started again for the door...

And faltered. In the corner of his eye came the glimmer of drawn steel.

"No!" he shouted in vain. "NO!" It was too late after all. His visions were materializing. In the next instant he witnessed Prince Kalen's last smile on earth: an amused, inebriated grin aimed at the sudden outburst. Then it was gone, replaced by a mask of terror as Ashkelī's sword slid into the heir's back and out through his gut.

Chaos erupted in the hall, and the *Bringer of Doom* had no choice.

He played his part.

27

Astelidus woke suddenly, legs kicking down linens and right hand searching frantically and futilely for the sword that wasn't there. He didn't make it to standing, however, before the realization hit him. *Another dream is all. It wasn't real.* Yet for more than a fleeting moment thereafter the horrid image still hung in his mind, floating behind his wide-open eyes. His breathing was heavy, and his red hair was nearly soaked through with sweat.

A soft hand touched his arm. "What's wrong?"

The moon peeked in from an open flap in the tent above, but its light wasn't enough for the warrior to fully make out Bronwyn's face — so instead the son of Ny turned his gaze back to the darkness. "I'm fine," he said. "Go back to sleep."

She gave no response, yet Astelidus sensed his lover still listened: waiting patiently for him to come clean. If he were to comply with her unspoken urge, though, he must hurry, for already the nightmare's details were fading fast.

"It was Ban," he spoke again presently in a near whisper, his face still turned away. "Just as I last saw him — before the pyre. *Gods*…there was so much blood. The damned cowards slit his belly and left him to rot…" Here he paused a moment for reflection, and a second soothing touch from Bronwyn's hand confirmed her attentiveness. "His last breath couldn't have been more than an hour before we arrived. One hour…after nearly a week's chase…*one damned hour!*"

"Don't do this, Astelidus…" Bronwyn sat up and wrapped her slender arms about him. She lay her head against his neck and shoulder. "You know it's not your fault. You tried to warn him…"

"*I tried to go with him!*" the warrior lashed out angrily, though he knew it was misplaced. Shrugging off her tender embrace, he turned, planted his feet on the ground, and stood, unwilling to let the woman's body distract him as her words sought to excuse his blame. "They'd never have taken us then."

"You don't know that," Bronwyn tried again, though her voice held a tinge of anger from the rude break. "Who knows how many Kedran there were?"

"Eight ahorse. Three dozen afoot. I scouted the tracks myself."

"You're missing the point…"

"What point?" Astelidus' voice moved with him away from the bed; he bent after a few paces, feeling on the ground for his clothing. "That he should've been more patient? Should've awaited all the reports before mounting up? That was never his style — nor is it mine. Rarely does restraint win glory."

"And rarely does glory come without a great price. Your deeds of late have all but won this war, Astelidus. Crûthior's shell is finally broken — and at daybreak we'll spoon up the soft meat inside. But still I beg you: have a care! Don't let your brother's pride take you as well!"

"What's this, now?" spoke the warrior in a sarcastic tone. "Another daemon come to foretell my fate? I thought I'd woken from that nightmare...but perhaps I'm yet dreaming after all." He pulled his shirt over his head. "Or maybe you've confused me with Dragan Saedus: a slave to signs and portents."

Astelidus paused after this last bit, half-expecting to hear Bronwyn rise and storm from the tent at the ill mention of her last lover. But she chose instead to stay and fall silent.

What am I doing? he thought. *I should be thankful she's concerned for my safety.* Returning to the bed, he sat down, twisted at the waist, and reached back to touch her reclined form. It was her smooth, bare arm that his hand met, and he began to stroke it lightly. "Forgive me."

For awhile longer Bronwyn remained quiet, letting her arm be caressed. Not until the warrior removed his hand and, still clothed, lay down once more beside her did she speak again:

"What else did you see? You woke with such a start..."

Astelidus considered that a moment. "I can't remember it all now...but the dream was different from real life. There were these...*things*...with Ban when I found him. Their bodies shifted as they danced around his corpse, cackling like madmen. And their eyes! One looked at me...and it felt as if my bones turned to dust..."

"You're scaring me." Torensus' daughter moved closer and lay her head on her lover's torso, ear over his beating heart.

"You wanted to know."

"And now I do. But that's enough. I want no such terrors finding their way into my sleep."

Bronwyn's tone revealed she'd said this not quite all in jest—so Astelidus didn't react to it as such. Instead of a short laugh or added quip, he gave her a light kiss on the shoulder before rising from the bed again. Then, with thoughts turning toward the morrow, he stood and looked up at the moon.

Across the dark plain flowing east from the Sinian encampment, behind the three breached walls of Crûthior—each one black as the death that'd found them all at last—another set of eyes rested on the night's orb, and another mind deeply contemplated the day to come. Berac, king of Mardotha. He stood alone on the balcony of his bedchamber, high in a tower of the citadel, one hand on the rock before him and the other with its index finger wrapped up in his long, braided goatee (a habit of his while in thought). Tall and slender—hair black and skin reddish-brown as typical of Crûthior's natives — he was shirtless in the hot, still night air, donning only breeches to cover his nakedness. Asleep atop his feather-stuffed cushions in the room behind, their presence revealed in soft, unwavering candlelight, lay two scantily-clad women. One of his own race, and the other a striking specimen of the sand elves. And seated across the chamber from this pair, at the table where Berac often took his morning meal, was Argen Van.

In contrast to the king (his half-cousin), Argen was beardless and — though hardly shorter — noticeably broader in arm and chest. Fully clothed, he sat with his comely face fixed on a myna bird that was pecking seeds from one upturned, cupped palm. Now and again he'd speak to the bird, and in turn it would mimic parts of his speech before dipping its head back down.

"*I once kissed a maid under moon,*" began Van poetically, his lowered voice yet traveling clearly to Berac's ears, "*...hidden by the tall grass from all eyes...*"

"Hidden eyes," croaked the bird.

"*And such tears she did shed at my parting...*"

"*And such trouble's since come from her lies.*"

"Trouble's come."

"*If ever chance brings me to meet her, once more beneath starry black sky...*"

"*I'll make certain this time not to leave her...*"

"*Till carrion birds circle nigh.*"

"Time's nigh."

Silence filled the room after this, during which even the faint night sounds of the city seemed momentarily hushed. One of the females rolled over on her side, her cheek coming to rest against the bare arm of the other, and the myna turned its bill on one wing to preen.

"Do you suppose I should find that clever?" spoke Berac presently. Turning away from the balcony, he strode to the table where Argen sat and pulled up a chair. "Should inspiration strike you again tonight, it best be a dirge oozing from your mouth."

Van merely snorted at this threat and turned his eyes back on the bird. But that was a mistake. A sudden loud noise — a balled fist striking the table hard — startled Argen such that he spilled most of the handful of seeds.

Leaning in, lowering the volume if not the intensity of his voice, Mardotha's ruler then added menacingly: "You weary me beyond weariness, fool. All these years of your pompous prating. All the days I've nearly wretched at the sight of your face. Curse Garmorin the Slaver! — and my grandfather for not keeping his prick out of the merchandise." Here he paused for a moment of contemplation, then began again: "Oh, the vultures come indeed, Argen, but not for Oen's bitch daughter. Without my protection, it's *your* eyes that may soon be plucked out. *Your* hide they'll hang first from the wall!"

If Berac's outburst had disturbed the slumbering women, they wisely didn't complain of it; and the little myna remained at hand, also seemingly unaffected. But Argen didn't take it so well:

"I don't have to be here," he threw back. "Even now I could slip away…run back to Agrardob—like the coward you think I am."

"Coward," said the bird.

"But ask me why I won't, Berac. Ask me why I choose to endure *your* face."

There came no response from opposite the table—other than a deepening of the ruler's scowl. Thus Van went on:

"A thousand times would I accept death most horrible—even stripped alive of my flesh by Erdramon's red glare!—if it would secure me a seat at your fall." Now it was Argen's turn to lean in, boldly looking his fuming king in the eyes as if Berac were the Flame God himself, about to deliver said torture. "To see you bow down before Sinia. To bask in your groveling at Deserus' feet…"

This time Berac's fist found his abuser's face—and instantly he sprang to his feet, ready should Van dare retaliate in kind. But instead came only a guffaw…

"Yes, lord!" exclaimed Argen with the laughter still in his eyes. He wiped a hand across his bruised jaw and went on: "Strike me down! Kick in my ribs and skull and leave me a bloodied sack on your floor!" He stood now himself and leaned in even further over the table, arms spread wide and chin held high, begging to be struck again. The myna flittered up to his shoulder and started to chuckle: a sickly musical pattern, repeated over and over and over…

"You're insane…" muttered Berac as he took a single step back, mouth open and brows raised high in disbelief. Suddenly he didn't feel safe occupying the same room as this madman, though he'd never felt threatened by Argen before. "Leena!" he snapped at one of the women—no doubt to send her for the nearest guard—but as he turned to the cushions, the command died in his throat. The elf-woman held Leena tight against her own body: a dagger pressed against the human girl's throat.

"Insane?" repeated Argen, a knife much larger than the elf's now appearing in his hand. "Perhaps I am. For not acting till now." Warily he began to round the table. "My little bird told me your secret, Berac. It told me you plan to *flee*." He paused to let the accusation settle between them. "After you berated me as a cringing dog—then swore you'd strike a deal with Oen on my behalf?"

The Lord of Mardotha raised both arms in a warding gesture, took two more steps backwards, and darted a glance behind, having no doubt just considered a plummet from the wall as a very real alternative to the danger before him. "You won't make it out of here alive if you harm me! Put down that blade, cousin. *I'll take you with me...*"

But Van had already pounced. Berac managed to lunge aside, avoiding the brunt of the assault—yet the maneuver cost him his balance. He landed flat on his back.

Instantly Argen was atop the fallen king, threatening Berac's jugular with a prick of his weapon's tip. "Didn't you hear me? I don't want to kill you—but I'll be damned if I let you slip away in the dead of night. You'll stand before Oen, bastard!" Argen dug in his shirt with his left hand and produced a short coil of rope—presumably with which to bind Berac's wrists. "You'll..."

A fluttering of wings interrupted Van's words, and as he screamed and flung the hand with the rope before his face, frantically trying to shield his eyes, he left Berac free to reach for the knife. Swiftly grabbing Argen's wrist with both hands, the king twisted the offending blade to aim at his attacker's chest—then pushed with all his strength.

Blood gushed out and washed over Berac's face. Letting the corpse pitch to one side, he rose at once with Argen's knife in hand, ready to defend against the elf. But the elf wasn't there...only Leena, with one hand to her neck and her face a picture of bewilderment.

Realms away, the *Spider* spoke her thought aloud: "Tomorrow you lose your city, Berac...but it shall be yours again, soon enough."

And, back in Crûthior, the myna repeated her.

PART THREE

28

It was a thing coarse when set against her perfect curls, her head of dark hair so soft and full and lustrous that it was the very picture of youthful beauty. Yet the hand stroking it gently just now — large but no longer meaty, with liver spots and raised veins leading up to its gaudily ringed fingers — summoned a different image indeed. This was the quivering claw of a corpse not quite deceased, feebly scraping at the black soil raining down upon its body. This was a rake that could never quite collect all the leaves.

Though even as she gazed at her reflection in the polished metal held before her...and saw the dreadful thing creeping, threatening to sap her loveliness...the king's youngest daughter smiled. "Do you like this dress, Father? It was Jirra's, but Mother says it fits me best."

"It's lovely, my child."

And that was it. Silence returned to the chamber for a spell. Outside the sun raced along its path towards the noontime zenith — yet only a sleepy warmth had thus far found its way within.

The double doors to the throne room suddenly burst inward. "He's here, my lord! Free inside the wall!" The messenger gulped up air before rushing to kneel before the dais, his long, flowing robe nearly tripping him in the process. It was Martassin. Behind him, remaining just outside the doorway, were three more of Acomalath's personal servants, a few soldiers, and Lord Tomisval. Martassin glanced back at this last man — a habitual announcer of dark plots against the throne — before locking eyes with his master. "And they don't know how!"

"*Who* is here, servant?" Acomalath yanked his hand from the girl's hair to spin his body around.

The kneeling man opened his tiny mouth to respond, but Tomisval beat him to it: "Baeldrin! The entire city crowds about him in the streets!"

"*What?*" The king clearly hadn't expected such a thing. His dropped jaw and wide eyes confirmed it. "How's that possible? Why haven't you seized him? *He* should be here at my feet, groveling in Martassin's stead!"

Tomisval walked inside, slowly but not hesitantly. The look on his face was odd, as if many emotions were at war there. "I tried to warn you, old fool."

The king's eyes went even wider at this, but for the moment he said nothing to his suddenly irreverent vassal. Instead he turned to the maidservants present, commanding them to remove his daughter from the chamber. Only after a side door had closed behind her did he speak again, his voice now lower and calmer: "You're not yourself, Tomis. Never would I've thought to hear such words from your mouth. Are we in peril? Has my son brought an army against us?"

"That much we would've seen, long before its arrival. Yet one man is harder to spy. As far as we know, the prince returned alone—but he's not alone now." And here the man actually laughed, for it seemed one of the conflicting emotions had won out at last: the one of a man who'd surveyed the day ahead, judged it devoid of hope, and thus tossed his wits to the wind. "Are we in peril, you ask? *Are we in peril?*" The crazed laugh came again...then nothing more.

Acomalath was afraid now. His heart was beating fast. "Speak! I command you!" Desperately he aimed his voice at the doorway, hoping to find an answer there...it mattered no more from whom. "What's he saying to them? Where's the City Guard? Why hasn't he been restrained?"

The servants outside could no longer endure the situation, and off they ran. One of the soldiers managed to respond, however: "We would've come sooner, lord, but the doors were held against us. My king...*there is no more Guard*. He's disbanded them."

There came then an angry shout from farther beyond...followed by more of the same...and the soldiers turned to the noise with weapons drawn.

"What's happening?" shouted Acomalath. "Martassin!" He looked down to see his only remaining servant fully prostrate and squirming. "*Martassin!*" Lord Tomisval turned and began to withdraw as slowly as he'd approached. "Tomis! Where are you going? Stop, I say! Stop!"

"They come," was all the departing man said, never breaking stride until he was out of sight.

"We must flee!" rasped Martassin at last, coming to both his senses and his feet at once. "I know a way that won't be watched. Come quickly..." he started off immediately then checked himself, noticing the king hadn't moved. "Now, my lord! There's little time..."

Still Rardonydd's potentate didn't move, seemingly unwilling to abandon his throne without considering other options. His hands gripped the armrests so tightly that his knuckles went pale. Outside the shouts were joined momentarily by clanging metal; then that sound was supplanted by a scream of agony.

Martassin's franticness returned. "Please, lord, I beg you! You know what he'll do if he finds us..."

"Go then. I release you."

The servant started to object, but his master's booming voice drowned it out: *"Be gone from my sight!"*

The finality of this was obvious to Martassin...and so, gathering up the folds of his robe so as to move at a quicker pace, he bowed out of habit then sped away. As his light footsteps faded behind the throne, a chorus of heavier ones drew closer...closer...until the men who made them appeared at the double doors: doors that should've been closed and sealed but weren't. Apparently the soldiers who'd just moments before drawn blades to defend their king had had second thoughts.

Now utterly alone in the chamber, frozen to his high chair, Acomalath sat and looked upon the crew that filled the doorway then began passing within. Perhaps it would've been easier for him to swallow had they been warriors of some proud, foreign host, all bedecked in shining mail and glory—or even if they'd been a band of the darkest, foulest devils ever dreamt of come bursting in to devour his soul without a single word spoken. As it was, however, the king felt his innards lurch at the sight. Here were soldiers dressed in the garb of his city's defenders, hands and armor splattered with blood from the killing of their own. Then came something even worse: to him a revelation more shocking and distasteful than any other of his long life thus far. Entering the room now were not a few members of his own court and council. Most of these wouldn't meet his gaze…yet forward they all came, each fanning to one side or the other of the room, making way for what was yet to arrive. Instantly many things made sense to the king, and curses welled inside him—yet he fought hard to reserve all these for the one he knew to be the ringleader.

As if on cue, in stepped Prince Baeldrin, dressed in his characteristic crimson; yet his garb was finer than any Acomalath had ever seen him wear before. His dark hair, normally free-flowing, was pulled back and secured—and on his brow sat none other than the Diadem of the Gazer: a remnant of Domal's expansionist past that Acomalath himself had removed from the public eye and placed under lock and key. Also donned by the prince was the most insolent, self-predicating grin one could ever imagine. After striding halfway from the doors to the dais, he came to a halt. "*Mad* you called me, Father, when last we met in this chamber. Perhaps you were right about that—yet *madness* brings results, good or bad, one way or another. Lounging about this palace doesn't."

As Baeldrin had been speaking, another familiar face approached on his left: the ambassador from Mardotha, *Nephos Zera*. This man's name had come up several times on the lists…and each time he'd left dissatisfied. Another piece of the puzzle was now answered.

But that piece wasn't nearly as surprising as the one to follow.

Before the king could respond to his son's opening words, there was a *change* in the room. The same figures were there, looking the same; the same smells and sounds were in the air; and the air held the same warmth. But indeed something had changed, and whatever it was sent a chill down his spine.

"It's time to step down, Acomalath," came a voice the king hadn't heard in over a decade. Yet it was a voice instantly recognizable. Saedus of Ost.

Acomalath hadn't seen or spoken to this woman since their son had passed into adulthood, yet he remembered how beautiful she'd been back then and his passion for her. Thus, despite his current plight and what she'd just said to him, the king couldn't help but drink in that beauty once again as she traipsed lightly into the room: purposefully sweeping appraising eyes over everything in it but him. It was a beauty that shocked him thoroughly, for it appeared she hadn't aged a day past his last memory of her…and that shock must've been plain on his face, for Prince Baeldrin laughed at it aloud.

"Oh how your mind must be torn, old man! So lovely, is she not? More than all your little whores combined. And yet so deadly…"

"Be silent!" Acomalath was digging deeply now, searching for courage that hadn't been required since the days of his youth. He'd succumbed to luxury long ago, with too many years come and gone since his last thoughts of dying any other way than pleasantly in his sleep, preferably with a belly full of choice food and wine and a pretty lass at his side. His son knew him well. But for him not to have fled with Martassin like a scared kitten amazed even himself. Perhaps here, at the end, he might at least expire with dignity. Perhaps his spirit wouldn't be entirely forsaken by his ancestors. "I see what you have in store for me, my son, and long have I known that desire to be in you. But for this moment, at least, it's still Acomalath sitting on Domal's throne, so you'll keep your mouth shut till I've had my say."

The prince's smile vanished, and his hands curled into fists — yet Saedus was at his side now, and quickly she spoke for him: "As you will. We're not pressed." This last was aimed at easing Baeldrin's mind, and she added a soothing touch to his arm with it. Then she looked to the throne again: "But I warn you: be mindful of the situation…and have a care with your words."

"Perhaps you weren't listening carefully, witch, for I was addressing my son, not you." Quickly the king swallowed and went on, hoping not to have pushed too far already: "You've no rights over Baeldrin as you do with Dragan, though I see now you've claimed them both. How long has he been pinned beneath your talons, woman? How much of this treachery is his own…and how much of it is yours?" He paused a moment, knowing these questions wouldn't be answered. Not wanting them to be. "And you, friends…" His eyes swept over his advisors gathered within. "What shall I say to you? Shall I congratulate you all for your wondrous acting? How long has *each one of you* smiled while sitting at my table, eating my food and drinking my wine, all the while with this treason in your hearts? Do any of you know this woman?" He pointed at Saedus. "Have you any idea what you've placed yourself in league with? How easily you made me doubt the report of foul creatures in Relinydd, saying it was nothing more than the attackers playing on hysteria, dressing themselves up in the dark of night as fell beasts. But that's not true, is it? Have you all given your souls over to the Daemon, that you'd condone this witch's *abominations* and *perversions*?"

"That's enough!" snapped Saedus as last, no doubt regretting her allowance.

"No...let him finish," said Baeldrin. "It tickles me."

"Does it now?" Acomalath's entire body was shaking as he leaned forward to bellow this response. "Then perhaps you'd like to spread the amusement, son, by asking the witch to pull your strings — and make you do a little puppet dance for us!"

The odd feeling from when Saedus had first appeared suddenly redoubled — then in the blink of an eye it was multiplied by an untold factor, leaving the king completely debilitated. His body sunk back into the chair, and his head slumped to one side.

Baeldrin turned a frown on Saedus as soft gasps and murmurs issued from the walls and doorway behind. "That wasn't necessary..."

"I've entertained this farce long enough." As she spoke, her slender white hand dug into the leather pouch at her side and came out holding a small copper vial. This she thrust at the prince without explanation, for he knew its purpose as well as she did.

After but a short pause, Baeldrin reached for this object, took it, stared at it a moment, then faced his conspirators, lifting it high for all to see. "A coward in life deserves a coward's death!" he announced loudly — then turned once more to begin his ascent to the throne.

As his son stepped beside him, Acomalath seemed to regain a bit of strength. His head straightened, and his hands once more gripped at the armrests — yet for the moment he spoke no words, and his stare seemed to pass through the bodies and sandstone walls ahead of him, focused instead on something that lay farther beyond.

"Look at me," said the prince, squatting below eye level of his seated father and speaking directly up at the man's ear.

Slowly Acomalath's head turned, and the pair locked gazes. Tears welled in the king's eyes...and in the king's eyes alone.

"I've something to show you." Baeldrin's upturned palm came into view. An object rested on it — but it wasn't the copper vial.

The Sun of Domal.

"Surprised?" Baeldrin had to ask the question rather than read its answer in the face before him, for the king's expression had become locked in weary grief.

Yet, even through that despondent mask, the man could still speak: "Promise me your mother and sisters won't be mistreated. Let your hatred end here..."

"You change the subject," Baeldrin spat. "But have no fear. I've nothing but love for my mother and my *true* siblings." Sweeping his eyes back over those gathered below as if addressing some of them, he raised his voice: "Yet all the bastards beware!" More boasts in this vein were about to spill from his lips — until he met Saedus' stare. One of those bastards was her son. Turning back to the throne, Baeldrin lowered his volume and lifted his open palm for inspection again. "Do you know what your *precious* Dragan said when he gave this to me? He said he's no love for you at all. Never has. None!" The prince's earlier smile returned and, if it were possible, spread wider than before. "No, Father…don't suppose you'll be avenged by him. Don't suppose *anyone* shall ever wrest from me what's *mine*."

"*She* will." One of the king's index fingers pointed weakly at Saedus before curling back into his grip on the armrest, then immediately he added: "Your spite is wasted on me. My love for your brother is unconditional — even now as it is for you. Get on with what you came here to do, boy…then go and live with what you've done."

Frowning, the prince stood and withdrew from sight the symbol of his once-dominate nation, replacing it with the vial he believed would usher in a new era. He unstoppered the thing and held it before his father's face. "So be it."

Slowly, the king's shaky hand rose to receive the drink of death — yet, just as he would've touched the poison's container, suddenly vigor returned to his arm. Through the air and down the steps bounced the vial, swatted from Baeldrin's fingertips. Dark liquid splashed onto the prince's garb. "Peace is not cowardice!" shouted the doomed king.

Acomalath's next cry was unintelligible, however, as his enraged son buried a knife to its hilt in his lung.

29

Light diffused through the dusty atmosphere: a light too feeble to overcome the piercing radiance of the brighter stars yet strong enough to deny the weaker audience. The sun had long been swallowed by the western horizon, and now the hour of twilight was upon Gethod. Darkness would soon engulf all that firelight couldn't stave off — and all that the uncorrupted heart couldn't defend against.

The streets were empty. The shops were closed. Whether the citizens had fled to the countryside after the coup or had barricaded themselves within their homes, Dragan knew not. Nor did he care. He was sick at heart; and worst of all, the thing that was gnawing at his soul — the heavy feeling at the end of his throat — was unidentifiable to him. Was it guilt? Remorse? Shame? There'd been a time when infamy and fame were as indistinguishable to the *DoomBringer* as right and wrong…when all that mattered to him was that his name would outlive his mortal self…that his legend would endure the test of time. Whom hadn't he betrayed, abandoned, or killed in that endeavor? What was different on this occasion?

He contemplated these questions as he stood alone, peering into the failing light atop the guard tower, high above the settlement below. The wind blew strands of dark hair across his chiseled face, and he reached over and pulled his cloak's cowl closer to his neck. There was something new in the air this night. It had an alien smell. A distinctive taste. He felt it on his skin and within his chest.

Fall was approaching. *And soon the winter after,* he mused — but that thought went beyond merely the weather.

Two birds were perched atop the palisade beneath him. They sang a sad song — or so Dragan fancied as he strained to hear it over howling winds rushing through the lonesome streets. *Streets that will soon be filled again.* He recalled the report from this morning. "Tomorrow or the next at latest," Ashkelī had brought the news to his captain, "…we'll be under siege. The remnants of the Ithiros in Mardotha have returned, and their ranks are now bolstered by militia from all corners of this land. Yet there's still time to withdraw, lord. Not all routes are cut off…"

Dragan had known all along this would happen, but the flight that Ashkelī had made no qualms of suggesting wasn't even an option — not if they were to hold true to his mother's plans. Indeed, the main purpose of this mission was a distraction. Saedus desired Deserus Oen's Ithirian allies removed and elsewhere occupied, making it easier to pit her army against the Sinians. At first this aim had been somewhat of a relief to Dragan: at least hiding behind these walls was better than her demanding him to take up arms against his former companions on the battlefield. But was *not* being there to protect them from her any better than cutting them down himself? And sitting idle for any length of time was certainly not his forte. Already a great restlessness was upon him. His entire being ached to heed Ashkelī's advice and lead the Haxûdī swiftly away.

Yet he couldn't do it. Now wasn't the time to falter. Before he'd led his men into the fortress and accepted the cup of friendship from Garim Irenys…before he'd given the nod that'd ordered old King Mehdurin and his retainers dragged away…that should've been the time. He'd almost halted the wheels of motion then, but he'd been too late. What good was it to stop now? Would it erase that image of Garim's body sprawled before Mehdurin's chair? Could the winds that bore abroad the word of the *DoomBringer's* latest treachery simply fail and turn back without the tidings relayed?

No. I must see this through to the bitter end. Then perhaps I might slip away…to a faraway realm…or to some godforsaken land beneath her desire. Take the armor with me, but leave my name behind. That's the only way out.

Having forced at least enough resolution to his troubled thoughts to get him through another night in this cursed butcher's den, Dragan performed a final scan of the streets below then made ready to descend. Hardly had he turned away, though, before he caught a glimpse of motion from the corner of his eye. Riders. Three mounted solo and two mounted as a pair, with a riderless steed led behind. At first sight they were unidentifiable to him: silhouettes in twilight that rounded the wall to come at the fortress gate. Yet before they could reach it he'd made them all out.

Hathrad was at their lead: the only one of the group whom Dragan wasn't surprised to see. This man had been with the *GrimHelm* at Gethod's taking and had been acting as a scout ever since. No doubt he'd come upon the others at some point on the road or in the wilderness and offered to escort them in. But directly behind Hathrad rode Velyn and Woryn Scath, the same brothers who'd been left to watch over Ûladriss back in Ost; and with them, alive and seemingly hale, rode Ûladriss Amaten himself. Still, the surprise didn't end there. On the same horse as Ûladriss, looking quite the opposite of the marshal—bent over the reins, exhausted and perhaps wounded—sat Gavix. And the unmounted steed behind them was Allethion.

So the boy accomplished his task…but what of his father?

Hathrad would be let in with no order from the tower needed; so rather than hailing the group from above, Dragan turned and hurried down to meet them in the yard. Yet by the time he reached the gate, he found the arrivals already being swarmed over by their Haxûdī cohorts. After the *DoomBringer*, Ûladriss was the most respected and highest ranked of the entire company, and all were as eager to learn how this man fared as their captain was not to appear so himself. While Dragan had begun the tower's descent nearly leaping down its stairs to get at the friend he'd come close to losing forever, before touching the ground he'd composed himself and decided on the reaction he must show instead. Ûladriss had defied a direct order by coming here unbidden—and everyone present knew it, whether it'd dawned on them yet or not.

The crowd made way for their captain, and Ûladriss, now dismounted, was first of his band to meet Dragan's glare. A wicked scar ran across the marshal's brow, courtesy of the Giant of Braured. "Stay your anger, lord." He raised a warding palm with his words, perhaps fearing the *GrimHelm* might actually lay rough hands on him. "I've disobeyed you...but don't be wroth with the sons of Scath. I gave them little choice: kill me or let me go."

Dragan cut his eyes to the brothers. Velyn was down on one knee before a seated Gavix, coaxing the weary youth to drink something from a proffered bowl. He didn't even look up at the mention of his name. Woryn, on the other hand, suddenly felt the need to go relieve himself.

"Where's Jedan Mûran?" Dragan demanded.

Ûladriss glanced back at Gavix to find the lad's attention turned on him— then quickly closed the distance to his captain, even daring to take Dragan by the arm as if he'd lead the hero away. "Jedan's dead, lord...but we shouldn't speak of it here..."

Ripping his arm from the marshal's light grip, Dragan shoved past Ûladriss to approach his retainer; and Velyn—acknowledging the captain's presence at last—stepped aside, leaving a void through which Gavix could see his master. Looming over the boy, the *DoomBringer* said nothing at first. Instead he crossed his arms and, frowning deeply, met the lad's stare.

Gavix was somehow altered since Dragan had last beheld him. Up close he didn't seem to be wounded, after all—yet he appeared now more as a haggard veteran than a fledgling recruit. A wiry beard covered his cheeks, and he was even thinner than usual: stick-thin, nearly. His face sagged, and his eyes were beyond tired. Yet these changes were both temporary and superficial. The real difference, Dragan sensed, was inside him. *Not wounded in body but in heart and mind. Wounds that won't easily mend...*

"There's the horse," Gavix spoke in a soft but angry voice. A raised finger indicated the spot where Hathrad was waiting to hand Allethion over to his captain. Ûladriss remained standing where Dragan had left him, but most of the crowd, including Velyn, were starting to wander off now. It was clear from the *GrimHelm*'s foul mood that there'd be no call to celebration resounding through the yard at present. "My father's dead because of that cursed animal," Gavix went on, his volume rising. "Take him—then release me from your service."

For an instant Dragan's composure nearly slipped. Perhaps with so few left to observe the scene, it wouldn't have mattered anyway. Yet, steeling himself against the urge to lift up the young man into a comforting embrace, the captain instead issued frank words of his own. "Jedan's fall is regrettable, boy — but he knew the risk well, even pressing the task against my initial dismissal. I'm not inclined to lose another man under present circumstances — whether to death or desertion — and certainly not at the insolent command of an inferior." At this Gavix' face became a mask of shock mixed with fury, and Dragan noticed that the youth's hands were now balled into white-knuckled fists. "Furthermore, you misspoke concerning Allethion. It's not the beast's fault…but your own…that he was lost at the start. And tell me this: how is it you still live when your father doesn't? Were you not with him when the fighting commenced — or did you flee from it, deserting him? We'll have no words of praise for you till the story's full told. Rise now and…"

"Gods, Dragan!" Ûladriss stepped forward once more, coming swiftly to Gavix' side. "Slay me where I stand if you must, but I can't let you go on like this. Can't you see the boy's *fey*? Do you want him to take a knife to your guts while you sleep?"

"My thanks for providing him with such a foolish idea." After turning stern eyes on Gavix again for a moment — perhaps to impress upon him the futility of Ûladriss' suggestion — Dragan finally gave in to the marshal and walked away. Taking the reins of Allethion from Hathrad, he began to calmly stroke the horse's mane while the stares of the other two drilled holes in his back. But no sooner than he'd begun to do so, the steed's eye opened wide to catch his attention; and as Dragan fixated on it, a series of visions flashed through his mind. These came and went with such a rapid ferocity that their parting left him disoriented and weak in the knees; yet thereafter he found he could recall each one to mind in vivid detail.

First came the child queen of Braured. Seated with her back to a tree in her native forest, she was engaged in questioning one of her people concerning the whereabouts of a magnificent white horse. Her rehearsed speech came out in an easy voice…yet all the while she was busily giving away the concealed position and number of her nearby captors — and indicating her true identity and plight — with mouthed words, hand gestures, and crude pictures sketched in the dirt.

The next vision jumped forward in time and space…and there was Allethion, rearing before a circle of ambushers. Jedan was mounted on the horse, his blade drawn and raised threateningly overhead. The child queen cackled with delight as she dismounted and ran to her compatriots; yet the slack-jawed Gavix froze atop his steed, unable to come to terms with the girl's betrayal. Then someone put a spear in Mûran's back as he swung his sword down upon another foe's skull — and Allethion bolted as the stricken rearguard captain keeled over in the saddle.

Another shift. A now riderless, bloodstained Allethion sauntered into a wooded grove and up to a white-robed figure awaiting him there. The person's back was turned on Dragan's mind's eye. Clearly the horse knew this man and was glad for the reunion, for right away he began to nuzzle the figure's shoulder and neck. In the backdrop could be seen Gavix' ashen face poking from behind a tree. The robed man's arm reached to stroke Allethion's mane, and...

Dragan jerked his hand away from it. Ûladriss had spoken to him just now, but the words hadn't registered. Still half in a daze, the son of Saedus looked to his marshal. "What did you say?"

"I said let's go inside, lord. Please...there's much to discuss."

30

Dragan led Ûladriss down the central aisle of the larger hall then on into the sanctuary. Not a word was spoken during the walk, for Dragan was far away, contemplating the visions that'd entered his mind as he'd peered into Allethion's black eye. And there was also the voice of the Giant of Braured: the voice that'd come from that grisly man's mouth but wasn't his own. *He summons me*, Dragan thought. *Why? Is a trap being set?* He needed his companion to shed light on the subject by recounting Jedan Mûran's fate.

The pair took seats across from one another at the long rectangular table that was the room's centerpiece. Thick slabs of oak formed the top on which Dragan propped his meaty forearms. A candle burned between the men, the shadows it cast under the Haxûdî's cheekbones making his gaunt countenance appear even more pronounced — almost skeletal. Dragan was reminded of Poltoros...and his heart nearly failed him. Had Ûladriss, in his absence, succumbed to the lich's fate? He struggled to recall what the marshal had looked like outside moments before, but he couldn't conjure the image.

"Are you recovered?" the *GrimHelm* spoke at last.

Ûladriss took in a deep breath. "In body, yes. But..." His eyes flicked away from Dragan to the table. "There's another wound that festers in me now, lord. A thought that was before unthinkable."

"And what is this thought, marshal?"

"To break the oath I swore to you."

Dragan didn't respond. The sick feeling had returned, stronger and clearer than before. It was all shame now. He felt as if he no longer knew what it was to be the *DoomBringer*.

"It seems there are titles worse yet than *craven*," continued Ûladriss. "Oath breaker...and..." The marshal's eyes returned to Dragan as his mouth struggled to form the epithet that would defame his lord.

"I won't hear it!" snapped Dragan, suppressing a sudden rage within. "You won't name me thus."

"No, I won't. Yet the Ithiros return, and by tomorrow's eve I'll have named myself either one or the other. I know this is why you ordered my stay in Ost — and why you sent Jedan to tarry in the woods. But what of my other kinsmen? I've come here to share their fate, at least...if not decide it for them."

"By tomorrow's eve," echoed Dragan slowly. "But not at this moment." A long pause. The wind had died with the sunlight, and an eerie quiet prevailed. "About Jedan..." he continued. "Tell me what you know."

"Perhaps the boy should speak it," responded Ûladriss, visibly uneasy.

"No. I won't see him again just yet."

"As you wish, then. Yet I hardly believe all he said."

"Go on."

"He claims they devised a ploy to discover Allethion's whereabouts from the locals—but the girl betrayed them. They were waylaid as they recovered your steed, and Jedan was speared in the back. Gavix managed to escape but was pursued to the point of certain capture or death…when he claims a great fog materialized and disoriented the sylvans. They lost his trail, but he became lost as well and—in shock, no doubt—allowed his horse to take him where it would. When the fog lifted, he found himself on the outskirts of a small grove. Within were Allethion and a man draped in white robes." Here Ûladriss hesitated.

"And?" urged Dragan again, his expression curious and attentive.

"The boy said the man wore a dark mask beneath his hood, making it appear as if he'd no face at all…and that he never removed it."

"No face…" repeated Dragan, dreamily now.

Ûladriss was clearly finding it more and more difficult to relay the account—and he must've been taken even further aback by Dragan showing no signs yet of incredulity. "This man bid Gavix come forth from the wood, assuring the boy that he was friend not foe. But the lad was too frightened to enter or flee and so remained frozen where he stood. Then a great black cat appeared in the grove, dragging Jedan's corpse with it. It handled the body gently, like it would a cub, and set it down at the robed man's feet before returning from whence it'd come. Seeing his father's body, Gavix was overcome. He forgot his fears and raced into the grove."

"He doesn't remember how long he wept over his father, but eventually the man in white prodded him to action. They traveled north with Jedan's body in tow, crossed the river into the wastes, and buried him there. Then the stranger handed Allethion over to Gavix and told the boy to return to you."

"What exactly did he say?" asked Dragan, his brow furrowing.

"He said, 'Tell your master to seek the Red King's keep. There he'll learn the truth of himself.'"

"Vendhane," muttered the *DoomBringer*. "How can it be?"

"You believe this tale?"

"I do…yet…" Dragan shook his head. "The White King of Addrindain could indeed command bird and beast…and Allethion was once his own. But he died years ago…"

"Yes," said Ûladriss simply. The story was well known to him.

Dragan leaned back and, removing his arms from the table, ran both hands through his hair. Then he froze, staring at Ûladriss. He could see his marshal was dying on the inside. He'd put the man in an impossible situation: having to ask Dragan to release him from his oath was the same, if not worse, than him breaking it outright.

"Ease yourself, old friend," he spoke at last, following the words with a tired but reassuring smile. "And forget my poor welcome in the yard. I'm not wroth with you…nor am I a stranger to your burden. Your choice between undesirable paths. Not a morning passes that my eyes don't open to such a choice: my mind already churning it over, trailing from the night's dreams. I've but to turn my head to gaze upon it—because it's always with me, never far from my side." A pause…then Dragan leaned over the table to lay a firm grip on Ûladriss' resting, extended forearm. "It's time for me to come clean with you, marshal. Look here at my neck." Dragan gestured with his other hand to the ancient writing etched around his collar. "*The head whose body bears this armor shall not be severed, but the bearer shall bring doom upon all his adversaries.* That's what it says. Now do you understand, Ûladriss? That it was no man who bested you in Toldriss' hall? No godlike hero to which you all swore allegiance—but an ordinary bastard hiding beneath some magic relic dug up from the past? And you and your warriors are the armor's slaves as well, by proxy. Slaves to the witch who thrust this cursed thing upon me!" Releasing the marshal's arm, he brought both hands up to the breastplate, tensing as if he'd latch on to the hateful object and strip it away. But no sooner had his clawing fingers touched the shining metal did they relax to smoothing palms, then—with a heavy sigh—the *GrimHelm* melted back into his chair.

For a few moments the Haxûdī merely sat in silence, staring back at his lord with sunken, weary eyes.

Dragan wasn't certain how he wanted Ûladriss to react. If the *DoomBringer* had been the one to receive this revelation instead, he likely would've jumped up and angrily challenged the charlatan to a rematch of their original duel. Even just a bit of color returning to the marshal's face at the news would've been an improvement, he thought. But this was Ûladriss. If he were preparing to slit your throat, he'd either matter-of-factly tell you so—or just do it. "Well? Say something, damn it!"

"So you'd have me believe you're some *weakling dog*? That without this plate strapped on, you'd have neither the strength nor cunning to even lift your blade? Is that what you're telling me?"

Dragan frowned deeply but held his tongue.

"If the armor's truly magical, as you say, then yes…it was trickery. And yes, you might not have defeated me without its aid. I see that its hold on you is real enough, in any event, and that it's led us to this impasse. But Dragan, you must understand me: ever before today, wither we went—no matter what was before us—you always led us well! That breastplate didn't inspire us to great deeds. You did. It was wrong to keep the secret from me…yet still you remain leagues above the common man…"

"No," said the *DoomBringer*, shaking his head. "It's not enough. Until I can prove I'm my own master, I'll play no more at master over you nor anyone else. You're the better man, Ûladriss. We both know it. I'll give the Haxûdī one final command, after which you're absolved of your oaths. Depart this place at once, while there's still time. Return to Haxûd."

Again Ûladriss' mouth opened but had trouble forming the words. Finally he gave up, simply nodding in reply. Then another thought occurred to him: "And what will you do, lord? Surely you don't mean to ride north—straight into the snare that's been laid for you?"

The *GrimHelm* rose from the table in a way that indicated the marshal should follow suit—and that their brief reunion was at its end. Dragan stuck out an arm to the Haxûdī in friendship, and each man gripped the other firmly behind the wrist. Neither seemed eager to let go.

"Tell the boy…" said Dragan at last, reluctantly withdrawing his hand, "…to hold his chin high. His father was a valiant man who died an honorable death. Tell him he has the freedom he asked for—but that it's for him to make the most of it. He did well in returning the horse. Jedan would be proud. Tell him…*I'm* proud."

31

Astelidus drained the gem-encrusted goblet and dashed it to the ground. Laughing heartily, he pulled the Mardothan wench closer. His companions cheered and egged him on.

He was drunk. She, his captive, wasn't. Yet despite the fear still written on her face—which was certainly lost on her captor—she did nothing to resist him. No, she returned each new kiss with a bit more vigor than the last, and between these less-than-tender moments her eyes began to fall more and more often upon the bounty spread before her. Soon she'd be gorging herself with all the rest of them.

One girl among countless spoils plundered from the broken city of Crûthior. That's all she was. But the son of Ny was a conquering hero. Now he tore off another leg of roast pheasant and brought it to his mouth for a huge, ripping bite, looking every bit the part of a barbaric chieftain of old.

"Lords of the Plains," came a sudden, heavily accented voice from across the feasting benches, not more than a half dozen paces off to Astelidus' right. "May we entertain you?" The speaker was a short, bald-headed male specimen of race unfamiliar to the Sinian. He had yellow-tinted skin and piercing blue eyes and was dressed in a garishly dyed shirt and striped trousers. His face betrayed not the least bit of trepidation as he smiled wide, bowed slightly before his would-be audience, and gestured with a sweep of his left arm toward the small troupe of performers standing at attention behind him. These were slender, comely young women of race and clothing identical to that of their leader—though instead of shaven heads they wore their jet-black hair pinned up in unusual arrangements. Two of them pressed odd wrapped bundles to their bosoms as they smiled shyly before Crûthior's new masters. The rest were musicians: a flute and various bells and drums were among the instruments in their possession.

The men along the benches turned their eyes on Astelidus, deferring to their inebriated champion for a response to this brazen little foreigner's request. Yet at first Astelidus merely stared at the stranger. He sucked another ample chunk of meat into his mouth and made a show of slowly chewing it.

Darkness had descended over Mardotha a few hours ago, though gone now for the triumphant Sinians were the evenings spent hunkered around campfires outside the walls. Tonight they dined in luxury within the city proper…and the open courtyard in which they sat at ease was illuminated by a myriad of oil-on-water lamps strung on crisscrossed lines overhead. The night air was cool. The food and drink were in unending supply. Somewhere within the citadel behind them, Deserus Oen no doubt met with his council to plot on days to come—yet down here nothing was left to be done but carouse. Why not let the insects fawn at their feet? Hadn't Astelidus and his men won this right with superior strength of arms?

Finally he gave the foreigner a nod to proceed, and immediately the troupe's bundles were set down and unpacked. In the space of a few moments a white cloth screen was erected, lit from behind to reveal the backdrop of a colonnaded throne room. The two girls who'd held the bundles ducked behind this screen while the musicians began to play a regal, introductory tune. Then the opening characters appeared: shadows of flat puppets manipulated by moving thin sticks attached to their joints...

A king and queen sat waiting upon a dais as a man came forth to bow before their thrones. Rising, the arrival then presented a gift directly to the queen, who received it with unchecked elation—even going so far as to rise herself, embrace the bearer, and plant a kiss upon his brow. The king was visibly displeased by this occurrence...yet, nonetheless, he allowed the man to depart unrestrained.

Presently the painted chamber backdrop was replaced with one of a garden, and the music took on a seductive flair. Here the gift-bearer and queen walked alone, and this time their embrace lingered beyond a mere peck on the forehead. So a tryst it was, then—and at this point Astelidus guessed correctly what would happen next. He'd heard this story before. The queen was Nishi, first wife of King Toldriss of Haxûd, and her paramour was said to be a warlock come down from the Wastelands of Callas. Perhaps the queen's gift had been a love charm of sorts—as one version of the tale suggested—or perhaps the man's own charms and the queen's appetite had been enough. Either way, Nishi was soon caught in the forbidden act by her eldest son, Rayas.

The musicians picked up tempo. Drumbeats raced with the prince's heart as he drew his blade and advanced on the warlock with murderous intent. Yet just before Rayas' thrust hit home, the queen screamed and threw herself before her unarmed lover—and was herself run through in his place. Seizing advantage of the prince's shock, the warlock began his escape...but Nishi's shriek had alerted others, and soon rough hands were laid upon the man. Prince Rayas, however, horrified by what he'd done, had already turned and fled like a madman into the wilds.

Now the backdrop returned to King Toldriss' hall. The warlock was brought forth in bonds and flung down before the throne, whereupon he was sentenced to death by the enraged monarch. Yet before this judgment could be performed, the doomed prisoner cried out, cursing both king and prince (as the puppeteers played out his words in unfolding images above the man's head). He warned Toldriss that, even at the moment of his own death, his freed dark spirit would summon a powerful magic and unleash it on the prince, transforming Rayas into a terrible monster that would plague the king's land. Still, whether disbelieving of the threat or beyond caring in his anger, Toldriss didn't hesitate in giving the order to proceed—and the warlock was promptly beheaded on the dais steps.

At this point even Astelidus' sluggish mind was able to pass beyond a mere prediction of the play's remaining scenes and rather consider the consequences of what they'd likely reveal. Were the performers about to display a puppet of Dragan Saedus as the hunt for the Beast of Thirannon commenced? The same man who'd first deserted the Sinians in an hour of need then—as they'd recently discovered—betrayed and murdered their Ithirian allies in Gethod? Surely only an ignorant fool or a man with a death wish would chance such an act under the present circumstances. Yet, even as Ny was still debating whether or not to stop the play short, up indeed came the exaggeratedly imposing shadow on the white cloth.

DoomBringer.

Suddenly the entire screen imploded under the weight of some object hurled from the benches, and the music ceased in mid-note. "How dare you glorify that traitor?" Astelidus was standing now with a hand on his blade. "Get out of my sight—lest I slay you all!"

The startled troupe leader opened his mouth to question Astelidus...but, seeing the fury in the warrior's eyes, he promptly clamped his jaw shut and started helping the performers quickly gather up their belongings. Some of the girls began to cry as they scurried off, but Astelidus was unfazed. He glared at the troupe until the last of them was out of sight then spat on the ground—as if expelling the entire matter as a poison from his body—before returning to the feast. Just before retaking his seat, however, he caught a glimpse of someone unexpected. She stood facing him at the edge of a nearby congregation...and was staring at him with a scowl no less brutal than the one he'd presented to the foreigners. He wondered how long she'd been watching him; and, in hopes it'd been only briefly, he remained standing aloof from the wench at his side.

"Greetings," hailed Bronwyn as she approached the benches. This night her dress was an uncharacteristic crimson, and her hair was done up in a loose bun. As the lustful eyes of Ny's companions began to lock on her, she forced a smile for their benefit...yet her own eyes remained fixed on their champion. "Will you walk with me, my love?"

Astelidus wasn't fooled. On a different occasion he might've jumped at that offer; but right now he could still read the anger in her gaze, and it was sobering him fast. "What are you doing out here? I thought you were up there with your father and uncle..."

"I was," she said simply, holding out a hand for him to take. "Shall we?"

For Astelidus to decline her invitation now would be a clear slight witnessed by the many onlookers. Bronwyn was the king's niece, after all—not some tramp Ny could publicly ignore or verbally smack around. Defeated, he begrudgingly shuffled around the bench…and the pair set out at once, hand-in-hand, headed for the bright yard's exit into Crûthior's dimly lit streets.

"The courtyard's one thing, Bronwyn," spoke Astelidus as soon as it became plain where she was leading him. "But I don't think Torensus would be pleased to hear about you roaming the alleys. We've not rounded up all the natives and put each and every one of them to the sword, now have we? There could still be hostile gangs about…"

"And what manner of fools would dare assault me with the *famed Sinian champion* by my side?" Again, under other circumstances, this might've been taken as a compliment. But just now Bronwyn had made no effort to disguise the sarcasm in her tone.

"You saw me with the girl—is that why you're angry?" Astelidus needed to get to the bottom of Bronwyn's dark mood fast…whether he dug himself deeper into the hole by doing so or not. This little interlude was raining hard on what'd started out to be a fine evening for him, so it was time to get everything out in the open and settled. Perhaps if he worked it right, events might even turn in his favor—with Bronwyn ending up in his bed in place of the Mardothan whore. "She means nothing. An amusement at the table only…to uphold my reputation among the men. I'd no mind at all to…"

"Oh, *please* spare me!" Bronwyn interrupted, scornful laughter mixed in with her words. She yanked her hand from his grip and turned to face him, bringing their stroll to a halt in the middle of the street. Astelidus noticed a few passersby glance their way at the developing scene, but Bronwyn paid them no mind. "Do you really think I give a damn about your hussy? You flatter yourself, indeed! I came down here looking for a warrior's advice—but instead I found a whining brat slinging dishes at innocent girls!" Astelidus would get a word in at this, but she quickly raised a palm and shook her head to deny him. "No, I don't care how drunk you are. That's no excuse. You just preached to me on what's proper and not, so I'll return the favor. A celebration is one thing, Astelidus…but *that* was hardly above an orgy!"

Now Astelidus' anger returned in full force, and his voice rose with it. "So you'd have me cheer at the sight of my enemy? Bang a cup on the table and call for more tales of his *heroic* deeds? Pray tell me this, woman: what is it that so binds you to Dragan Saedus, that even were he to *murder your own kin* you'd still cling to his knee? No matter how many champions I lay low nor how gallantly I woo you, will I never live up to that knave in your eyes? You're sick to love such a man, Bronwyn. Sick!"

Barely had the hateful word left his mouth when she slapped him hard across the face—and just as swiftly did he grab her by the arms, practically carry her across the street, and pin her to a wall. To her credit, Bronwyn didn't scream; but her eyes did go wide at this unexpected reaction...and even more so when Astelidus raised his own hand above her in a fist, readying to strike her down.

Luckily for them both, however, the return blow never came. A small crowd had gathered in the area — and, now with witnesses involved, Astelidus realized he might very well pay the ultimate price for letting such impulse go unchecked. Letting his hands fall, he took a few steps back and glanced over his shoulder at the onlookers. His scowl bid them to disperse — and they did, albeit some slower about it than others.

"You're right..." said Bronwyn presently in a soft voice, taking Ny off guard. Tears welled in her eyes and were beginning to trickle down both cheeks. "I *am* sick...of a great many things. And you were right about the Mardothan girl, too. It *did* hurt me to see you kissing and fondling her — though I tried to tell myself otherwise." Here she sniffled and wiped a sleeve across her eyes; and Astelidus, terribly regretting how he'd just behaved, stepped forward as if to pull her into a tender embrace. But she wouldn't have it. She showed no further aggression but simply held the warrior off with a light push away.

"Bronwyn...I'm sorry..."

"Don't you dare speak to me! And don't follow me when I leave. Go back to your revel, Astelidus. But when you wake tomorrow, think on this: Dragan *is* a deserter and a traitor and a slave to his own vanity; but of the last of these, *so are you*."

32

"Apparently your father's...parting words...had an unexpected effect on the council, lord," spoke the menial, nervously wringing his hands. "Some of them had a change of heart! Even now their propaganda swarms through the..."

"I can see that, you imbecile!"

The fragile servant's knees went weak at this sudden outburst, and he almost fell back down the steps he'd recently ascended. When he found Baeldrin's face again — wincing from his new cherished position as a filthy dog groveling before its master — his pallor was a definite shade whiter. "Please...don't harm me, lord. It's just that..."

"Out with it!"

"They mean to supplant you with a...a governor...like the one they have in Relinydd!"

A pause. The ever-present noise floating up from the streets suddenly rose a notch and quickly fell again.

"And to whom, should I guess, might the traitorous crones have this *governor* report? Themselves?" Baeldrin snorted, clearly disgusted. "A few more names for the list — along with all the others yet to be punished for insulting me. That's all it is." Looking over at the tower's portly, balding steward to grab the man's attention, he nodded then at the wiry servant underfoot: "Add this one's name as well."

But before the steward could acknowledge the command or the servant spit out his next frantic plea, a third voice rose from the tower's stair and spilled out onto the open top floor. "Perhaps you should've made an effort to hide it from them."

"*It*, Zera?" replied Baeldrin indifferently, recognizing the familiar voice. His attention had already returned to the streets below.

"The truth. That you're exactly what your father said you were. A puppet dangling from the witch's strings." The Mardothan ambassador walked brazenly to Baeldrin's side and gripped the man's shoulder; but the king was too lost in his own troubled thoughts to register Zera's goading for what it was and didn't even flinch in response. For a moment both men stood staring down from the tower at the riotous insects packed in Rardonydd's slums, then Nephos faced Baeldrin: "Yet he who struggles in the web merely gets stuck tighter. Is it not so?" A tiny smile came to his lips as he stole a glance over his shoulder.

Enemy... Betrayer...

The voices were twined with Baeldrin's thoughts. Slowly the king reached into his robe and closed a fist about the stones he'd concealed there, heeding the spectral warnings. "So it's *you*," he replied at last, rotating his head to meet the ambassador's gaze; and as he did so, he caught the kneeling menial's confirming nod from the corner of his eye.

For an instant Nephos actually appeared hurt by the accusation...then his smile resurfaced wider than before. "You made a mistake, friend, in supposing those you turned traitor would unlearn treachery on their own. What terrible fear did you set in their bones, that they'd rather take their own lives than risk you hurt? Or what unshakable loyalty did you win from them through your noble deeds and charm?" The Mardothan chuckled his derision. "You were so consumed with your own goal that you gave no mind to the tools that helped elevate you. Did you not think it would show?"

Baeldrin's face had grown hot now with rage, but somehow for the present he held violence in check. There can be times in a man's life when pride swells so high that it even wars against the basic instinct to survive. Baeldrin felt the noose swiftly tightening around his neck, yet he wouldn't be denied a final say: "And still the old fools mean nothing! They've no power of their own. I always knew Saedus would cross me, Zera—so the only mistake I made was trusting *you*!" Suddenly he shoved Nephos with such force that the man fell backwards and landed sprawled out before a band of soldiers just beginning to fan out from the stairs. Malicious intent was plain on their faces. No doubt begging whatever god he worshipped to let him go unmolested but a moment longer, the quivering servant was last seen crawling off behind—and the tower's steward had already vanished.

"I'll not be the witch's scapegoat!" said Baeldrin, offering the newcomers his deepest scowl. Extending an open palm, he turned it sideways, letting the two pebbles spill out. "Come forth, if you dare!"

Two of the mercenaries did so without further ado, naked blades gleaming in the afternoon sun. They were a fairly imposing pair, each rivaling the king in stature if not quite in girth—yet their advance lasted but a single step. Dropping to their knees, each man cast his sword aside. Their eyes began to bulge as hands clawed at necks in their frantic efforts just to breathe.

Mesmerized by what was befalling their unfortunate companions, the rest of the soldiers instantly sprouted roots where they stood—till the first of the loosed spirits took visible shape before them. The nightmarish horror of the visage this one donned, coupled with the terrible wailing sound that issued from it, was too much for the hired help to take. Nearly all at once they turned and fled, crashing into each other like bungling dolts as they hit the staircase. At least one slipped or was pushed and took a screaming tumble down. Yet that did little to impede the others.

"Hold!" shouted Zera, having scrambled to his feet. "He can't stop us...*ah!*" A spirit was on him, and he began to gasp and claw at his neck like the now face-down, unmoving pair had done. Laughing, Baeldrin advanced on him, pausing only to scoop up the closest of his two stones and a fallen soldier's blade. Clearly he meant to run Nephos through with the latter, but as soon as he came in stride with the spirit that was holding his prey, it turned its ghastly face on him and shrieked:

Get ye back! This flesh is mine!

"Fine! Take him!" It was hard enough for Baeldrin to keep from loosing his bowels as the wave of fear washed over — yet he needed to do much more than that. The enemy was down, but he was far from safe. Two spirits were free, and he was having trouble with just this one. Where was the other? He reached out for it with his mind. No response.

I taste your fear, mortal. With Baeldrin's thoughts momentarily elsewhere, the spirit gripping Zera had loosed its hold on the ambassador; and now the king found himself penned against the tower wall. Panicked, he lashed out with his blade — only to have it snatched away. Another shriek even more awful than the first wracked his brain, and unseen fingers, cold as ice, began to constrict about his neck. Slowly. Agonizingly so. Recalling at last the one pebble returned to his grip — and heedless of whether it was the correct one to spare him from this unfortunate predicament — Baeldrin croaked out the words of banishment.

Immediately the frosty tendrils failed. The tormenting spirit retreated a few paces, allowing its spurned master a moment to believe his command had done the trick. Then, ripping forward like a blast of hurricane wind, it swooped the king up and hurled him straight out from the tower's ledge. Screaming wildly, Baeldrin flailed his arms as if he might actually fly away from impending doom, while directly below — as if all eyes there had been eagerly locked on the events above — a space opened up in the crowd of bodies: a gaping maw eager to receive him.

But instead of greeting death in that dusty circle of earth, the king found himself standing in the midst of everyone, heart pounding but otherwise totally unharmed. Whether his savior had been the other spirit yet under his dominion, reacting tardily to the earlier unanswered summons — or merely the first specter intent on toying with him further before ending the game — he had little time to consider. Not three strides away an angry simpleton had just tipped off the mob, pointing his chubby finger at Baeldrin's face; and now there was nothing to be done but *flee*.

An elder pushed down. A young mother, swaddled babe in arm, carelessly shoved aside. The king paid no heed to anyone as he barreled his way through the throng. Thus far the shouts of "usurper!" and "murderer!" and the like were only on his heels. Yet if he slowed, and the news passed him by...well...the first obstacle to halt his reckless advance would be the last.

"This way, lord!"

Baeldrin's eyes turned instantly on the speaker: a hooded figure standing in an open doorway just up ahead, his thin arm beckoning to the shadows within. The voice sounded familiar...and under present circumstances, Baeldrin thought that good enough. Grabbing a young man by the shoulders and brutally hurling him into another to cause a distraction, he bulled through the stretch to the portal and flung himself inside.

The door slammed shut behind, immediately followed by the sound of a bolt being drawn. Angry shouts pummeled the heavy oaken barrier — then shoulders and fists.

Suddenly light flooded the passage. The candle's holder doffed his hood to meet Baeldrin's eyes.

"Martassin?" gasped the king. "But..." Something much heavier than a fist struck the door just then, threatening to rip it from the hinges.

"No time now," spat the servant, his nerves clearly rattled. "Follow me!"

33

The beast lifted his red-smeared face from the body to sniff at the air. His lip curled in disgust as the sound of footsteps behind joined with a familiar scent on the breeze. Yet otherwise he remained nonaggressive: eyes glazed, staring out at nothing as if he were entranced.

"Time draws nigh, G'nilbor." Valreecius' words broke the spell on the ghoul, and he spun on the moon steward with wicked fangs showing and every muscle of his rippling bulk tensed. Still Valreecius stood calmly before the creature—as if nothing in the world had ever frightened him. "No more cravings. No more bondage. Your spirit free to roam where it will. Or you may remain leashed and starved till the sun's light fails and the world becomes as ice. It's up to you."

"I need no witch's lies to prod me, thin man," spoke the ghoul. "Her son has insulted me…and for that I'll gladly destroy him!"

The steward sighed, shook his bald white head, then continued in a tone one might use to instruct a clueless child: "Were the task as easy as that boast, she might've set some lesser vassal to it. You're not the first to dismiss Dragan so easily. Do you believe yourself cleverer than Tiramas Vendhane? Stronger than Haxûd's cursed prince? You'll need more than both to defeat the *DoomBringer*. Yet…if you care to listen, perhaps I can instruct you…"

Attempting to feign disinterest, G'nilbor turned his eyes again beneath him. A claw reached down, latched onto one of the corpse's wrists, and pulled up on the limb with a loud crack. "The man's no god. I smelled his fear in Ost."

Valreecius nodded. "Indeed. But you must do more than *out-threaten* him to prevail. The key lies with his armor. Take that away from him, and he'll all but defeat himself."

"I'm no thief, lurking in shadows. I win my spoils in battle." Returning his gaze to the steward, G'nilbor brought the severed arm to his mouth, bit down on the flesh, and tore a large chunk away. No sooner than he'd begun to chew on this morsel, however, did a ragged pair of goblins dart out from behind a nearby boulder to grovel at his feet. They looked as if they'd not eaten in days. The ghoul swallowed, took another bite as the starving pair eyed him with drool on their lips, then tossed the limb carelessly away. Instantly the goblins set off for their prize, pushing and clawing and falling over each other to be the first to set hands on it. "Where did the witch unearth this armor?" G'nilbor added at last, paying no heed to the grisly scene playing out on his right. "What is the source of its power?"

Similarly unaffected, Valreecius replied: "She hasn't revealed that secret to me. But wait and ask it of her yourself, if you wish. Even now she prepares to empty Rardonydd. Her force will join itself to ours within the week."

To this G'nilbor only grunted in response, and it appeared that the steward was done with the ghoul for now and would take his leave. Yet he had one final comment to make:

"Our mistress tells me her son will soon lay down the armor willingly. This she has divined. But until you see Dragan without it strapped to his breast, turn your eyes upon any other man afield save him. Surely there'll be no shortage of Sinians for you to slay."

34

"Why aid me, Martassin? What's in this for you?"

"It's as you said, lord," huffed the frail servant in reply, pressing his free hand against the damp passage wall for support. He bent slightly to catch his breath. "Acomalath's dead. And that makes you my master—no matter how it came to pass."

Baeldrin grinned, beginning to understand now. "Your father served also."

"And his father as well." Recovered a bit, Martassin gathered up the folds of his robe and made forward once more. "How would I survive without a patron? This life is all I've known."

"Indeed." Baeldrin turned to follow the candlelight. "But I'm not convinced I should trust you. I'd not be spared from that mob only to be delivered as a gift to her doorstep."

"The witch? I've no more desire to see her than you do."

Baeldrin released a snort of laughter at that statement, its echo bouncing back to them from somewhere ahead in the blackness. "You misunderstand me then, servant," he continued, well above a whisper. "Oh, I'd see her again. Her and that treacherous worm, Zera...if he yet lives. But it must wait for another day. I'll prepare a surprise for them—same as she did for me—save for her there'll be no escape!"

Martassin's only response to Baeldrin's outburst was a quieting gesture, and so the pair walked on in silence for a spell. It wasn't long, however, before they turned a corner, coming to a stop before a heavy iron door.

As he watched his thin guide fumbling with a ring of keys the man had fished from his robe, a new thought suddenly came to Baeldrin, and his eyes narrowed again in suspicion. "How did you chance to be at that door? You couldn't have known I'd be fighting my way through the street..."

"No," the servant agreed. "But I'd been watching you from below for some time, hoping to catch your attention when you departed—if it wasn't too late to warn of what was to come. I'd not thought the departure would be so...hmm, *dramatic*...but I was ready all the same!" Having decided on the key to use and turned it in the lock, Martassin put his shoulder against the barrier and began to push.

First to cross the threshold, one hand raised against the torches illuminating the incommodious cellar within, Baeldrin cursed aloud. "How much longer till we emerge from these ratholes?" His eyes swept the room, glancing at the casks stacked against its side walls before coming to rest on a lone, central table. "And who's this lout?"

The servant entered and swiftly locked the door behind him before answering his master's question. "Your *Master of Ale*, my king."

Sprawled over the table, a spilled mug of his own craft just out of reach, the inebriated brewer shifted slightly at the influx of noise — raising his head slightly to turn a long-bearded face away from the intruders — but he wasn't fully roused from stupor. Within the space of three breaths he began to snore loudly, causing Baeldrin's frown to deepen.

"As much as I could use a drink," the fallen king announced, looking again to Martassin, "...for your sake, I hope there's more to this."

"Of course there is, my lord. This man knows the tunnels like the back of his hand. He can lead us all the way out of the city from down here."

Baeldrin considered this briefly, then nodded and started across the room for the opposite door. "Then wake the fool, and let's depart!"

35

A star-filled sky was somewhere overhead, yet it made no difference under the canopy of Braured Forest. An occasional lightning flash was the only beacon for the blackness within — save for a small, glowing hemisphere produced by the party's campfire. The two light sources were in sharp contrast: one silhouetting a thousand trees in the briefest spectacle of achromatic luminosity, and the other saturating the bark of a few of them with a red-orange luster painted on in many coats throughout the evening. Rain hung heavy in the air, yearning for release from its gassy prison. The cold winds that'd blown down from the Dizron Sea would likely play redeemer, for already a few drops had escaped to guide the way for their ensnared companions.

Ten Braured warriors, one wench, and a boy of twelve hunkered around the fire in silence, yet silence didn't prevail in their world. Already heavy raindrops made pitter-patter on leaf and earth, and thunder boomed and rolled with every successive bolt. The wind howled as it broke about mighty tree trunks. The fire crackled in delight whenever it received another dead limb or was stoked by a sword. And there were other sounds too. Sounds that wreak disquiet on the mind and strain in the muscles. Sounds almost imperceptible but unable to be ignored: the snapping of a twig, the distant baying of wild dogs, the rustling of leaves...

Even a fool could've discerned the heavens would release their lot tonight, thus long before twilight's creeping tendrils had overtaken the sun's last rays, the company had prepared cots by hanging thick hides from tree to tree above. All that remained was to wait the onslaught of weariness following their meal of hog liver before most of them would be crawling into their makeshift beds. A few drooping eyelids indicated this time was fast approaching; and perceiving it so, Darak — the man who fancied himself the group's leader — broke the muteness:

"If our travel goes well, by tomorrow evening we'll be back in the Queen's presence. And what will she say when we arrive without beast or boy?"

"You mean the *bones* of beast and boy..." said another. He was a stout man with a scar running from forehead to cheek through his left eye. "They jumped into the river and drowned. Or worse — they crossed into the wastes where only spirits dwell. No track evades the eyes of Betha'ta. You know this." He looked askance at the woman. Her eyes were closed in sleep or deep meditation.

"Will that be enough to satisfy her?" asked Darak, noticeably agitated.

"Afraid she'll strip you of your prize?" the scar-faced man laughed. "Any of our spears could've felled the red man just the same."

At this, Darak looked down in admiration on a finely-crafted sword lying sheathed at his feet. Its hilt was simply but adeptly wrapped in stained leather with a solitary emerald inset at its base, and the pommel was a two-pronged fork of polished steel. By comparison it made the other nine warriors' blades seem but machetes stamped from a single plate of rusty iron. If only the sylvan knew how many greater men than himself this sword had so easily been run through. The blade of Jedan Mûran.

"You're an idiot," Darak replied. "Who can make sense of Betha'ta and her ramblings? They fled north. We saw that much with our own eyes, didn't we? The boy atop the animal. What did she call it? A *horse*? But to return and claim the man's body, only to head north again? Why back north?" Then he lowered his voice and spoke solemnly: "The Queen wanted the red man left to rot like our kin did alongside the muddy road. She'll not be pleased to hear it otherwise..."

"Makes sense to me," spoke a different warrior. "North then follow the river south to the witch's lair. That's what I'd have done. That's where Cataya said the one called *Bringer of Doom* led those men — where she was held prisoner. Only I think the boy grew weary of the southern side of the river and crossed...or else drowned trying. Either way, he's dead now."

"She'll still be angry," spoke Darak after a crack of thunder initially cut him short. "Seems she fancied the lad. *Bleh!* Why else would she scream so awfully when your spear went for the boy's belly? We've not been out here for this long because she wanted a *head* — but because she wanted a *toy!*"

Most of the men chuckled at Darak's words, but the boy of twelve looked up with a scowl. He'd become obsessed with the Queen of Braured since meeting her in the forest. It was his ears that'd heard Gavix' fabricated tale — and his eyes that'd seen Cataya's desperate cry for help scrawled in the dirt. He was her true avenger. Why hadn't she given *him* the man's sword? For now, he must be satisfied with his new post in this rugged cohort, although it seemed more of a punishment than a reward. It didn't disappoint him that they'd failed in their mission: for he saw the truth behind Darak's not-so-deftly executed allusion.

The biggest man of the company — a brute of nearly twenty stones — let out a massive yawn and struggled to his feet. Gripping his bulbous head as if it were in a vise, he spun his jaw upward in one swift motion, releasing a cracking sound to rival the thunder above. Taking two steps forward and holding his hands to the fire, he began: "That little..." But his voice suddenly died — as an arrow sang from somewhere in the darkness, piercing the back of his neck. The broadhead exited just below the warrior's chin and stopped, protruding enough for him to see it. Blood spewed from his mouth as he choked to find his last breath, and his hands clawed at the shaft as he fell prostrate onto the fire. His bulk extinguished the flames as he crashed down upon them, sending embers of all sizes flying in every direction. These rained down until thousands lay strewn about the camp, each one pulsing to the rhythm of the harsh wind...and with their rapid fading departed both warmth and light.

The nine other men, the boy, and the woman Betha'ta leapt to their feet and scrambled to grab whatever weapon they could find; then they huddled together with their backs to an uprooted tree trunk, facing the direction from which the arrow had issued. Tense moments passed as they strained to see into the gloom without. Finally someone yelled: "Look!"

Beyond the camp's circle, two eyes stared back at them through the darkness. Eyes glowing like a wolf's — but not yellow. Red. Unblinking.

"You'll pay for that, coward!" screamed Darak, but his voice was as hollow as his threat. "Show yourself!" He perceived that — despite all those clutched about him — the eyes in the woods seemed to peer at him alone, and he wondered if he were indeed the sole object of the glare's malice. He was frightened but wouldn't name it to himself. Couldn't name it. He was the leader of this band. Mustering his courage, he took one small step forward and halted. The eyes vanished.

For what seemed like an eternity, the warriors, wench, and boy stood frozen like statues. Their weapons were poised to strike, and their gazes were fixed on the point in space where they'd last seen those eyes. Rooted in place...unable to think...unable to speak...unable to act. The winds howled, and thunder rolled as rain finally began coming down in thick sheets upon their heads. The sound was deafening, and its onslaught stirred Darak from his trance. He took another step forward...then a few more. The sylvan stopped at the invisible barrier where he imagined their camp ended and, craning his neck, broke its plane. He clutched Jedan Mûran's sword tightly in his left hand.

Nothing.

He retracted his head and, with a side step to ensure his back was to a tree, turned to his companions. Now he was regaining sense. He must prod them to action. He must lead them either against or away from this foe. He opened his mouth to speak — but his voice and heart failed him. In that moment, a bolt of lightning illuminated the forest, and for an instant he beheld an intruder perched atop the woody tendrils of the uprooted tree trunk above his men.

Darak clutched his mangled, half-severed left hand as he stumbled and fell just outside the campsite: now a death ground filled with the maimed bodies of his companions. Enfeebled by his wound and the terror that seized his mind, he made no attempt to regain his footing...but began crawling frantically, elbow to knee, further into the woods. Leaves and muck clung to his bloody appendage, briars lacerated his face, and bent limbs and twigs sprang back to batter his body in recompense as he rooted through the compost and underbrush. Close behind was his assailant, pursuing Darak at a leisurely gait. The sylvan couldn't see it, but the man held the spear of a Braured warrior in one hand and the reclaimed sword of Jedan Mûran in the other. Crisscrossed on his back were his own blade and bow.

It wasn't long before Darak had utterly exhausted himself in navigating the forest floor; and thus, rolling over, he conceded to the stalker…*waiting*, his face smeared with blood, rainwater, and tears. Then a heavy boot came down on his heaving chest, confounding his breathing. He gripped its toe with his right hand and stared at the indistinct figure looming above. Fear swam in his lonely eyes, but he knew *his* eyes couldn't be seen in the dark — and this vexed him, for pity was his last and only hope.

Little did he know that pity was a concept foreign to the *DoomBringer*.

"So, dog, you think yourself worthy to wield the blade of Jedan Mûran, most valiant of Haxûdī?"

"I…*please*…" groaned Darak, squirming under the pressure of Dragan's heel.

"And did you think it wise to hunt the retainer of Dragan Saedus, as a fawn without its mother?"

"No!" huffed the warrior.

"You don't *now*," continued the *GrimHelm*. "Mûran was worth a hundred of you lice. But eleven will have to do…for today."

Uneducated as the sylvan was, he could count past ten — and no sooner had the connection been made did he feel the spear bite through his belly. Screaming in bitter agony, he groped at the shaft that'd skewered him.

How long it took Darak to die, only he knew…for Dragan was off, the howls of death trailing him ever more faintly through the darkness.

36

The soldiers jeered at their black-robed captive as they pushed and dragged her along; yet, although her eyes and scowl spoke of a murderous fury at the abuse, not once did the elf-woman lash out against it. Her demeanor suggested to Berac that she'd given herself up voluntarily to his host's men rather than been caught unawares — but when dealing with her kind, it was never wise to let one's guard down. With a casual glance over his shoulder, the ousted king summoned a pair of spearmen to his side; then, draining the last drops from his wine cup, he pretended to ignore the parade until it came to a sudden, silent halt no more than three strides from him.

"Well, Fashra?" spoke Berac after a moment spent staring into the elf's eyes. "Can you give me a reason why I shouldn't have you spitted on sight?"

But the woman wasn't fazed by his threat. She neither fearfully blurted a prepared response nor dumbly stammered in search of one. She dropped to a knee and bowed before her master — yet the movement was so coolly executed that it could've been taken as an affront. "I was willing to watch you handed over to the Sinians, but not to strike at you myself. I could've finished you off when Argen failed to restrain you, yet all I did was keep Leena from screaming."

"Am I supposed to be grateful? Flattered? *Bah!*" Berac flung his empty cup at the elf then, purposely aiming short of her kneeling form by at least a hand's breadth. It bounced off the ground before striking her shin, dulling the force of the impact if not the venom behind the toss. "Answer the question!"

Fashra rose swiftly and stepped back, nearly returning to the rough grips of the soldiers behind her. Even now she seemed not to be rattled — just unwilling to remain a downed target. For all she knew, Berac might snatch up a spear to hurl her way next. "I'll give you two reasons, then. One: because you yet desire the comforts of my body." At this she flashed Berac a knowing grin and reached down, briefly parting her robe below the waist to reveal a sleek, bare thigh. Her long, straight silver hair gleamed under the midday sun. "And two: because I've gathered some information for you."

Seconds passed as Berac stared on, stroking his goatee in thought. Fashra's little exhibition had succeeded in distracting and temporarily calming him. The lust in his eyes was far from hidden. Yet at last he regained his senses, scowling: "You'll not be slithering under my sheets anytime soon, girl. And why should I believe any report from you…assuming you've one worth hearing?"

Fashra's eyes narrowed. "It was you who sent my brother to his death in the Sinian camp…but he knew the risk yet didn't begrudge the task. If any of his slayers' plans are foiled by what I've to tell you, then I'll consider it revenge for Ashyd's fall. Your enemies are mine also. *Listen to me*…and if you're pleased with what I've to say, then perhaps you'll retake me into service."

Berac wondered when he'd last heard a thing that truly pleased him. This exile in the wilderness wasn't such a far cry from his palace life of ease: he had ample supplies of food and drink, servants, and entertainments provided by his desert allies. Yet each day passed outside of Crûthior saw him slip further into depression. It was even worse on him now than in the hours leading to the city's inevitable fall—for at least then he didn't have this dreadful shame of desertion to bear. Yes, here in his cousin Hatrakori's camp on the fertile banks of the Toros River, leagues from the black walls, he'd little to do but sit and sulk, awaiting the instructions of his cursed foreign mistress. Sit and rot from a poisonous rage in his guts. A rage for which there was presently no outlet.

"My lord?"

"Go on, then."

Even having pressed him so, Fashra paused now, her face turning to the tent behind Berac. The elf's slender mouth parted but snapped shut before the words came. The futility of requesting a private conversation inside had likely dawned on her. Thus, resetting herself, she began: "Doubtless you thought I'd fled the citadel after you last saw me...yet I kept hidden there till but a few days ago, passing unseen in the invaders' shadows. I thought if I remained behind long enough I might catch a scrap concerning my brother's fate, but I heard nothing of him in all the soldiers' babblings. Eventually I discovered King Oen's niece—the rumored lover of that warrior my brother was sent to kill—and it came into my mind that I should abduct her: for if any besides the *DoomBringer* himself knew what'd befallen Ashyd, surely it would be her. Yet before I could lay hands on the woman, the strain on me grew. My presence...or that of others like me...had been discovered. The guard was suddenly increased. I'd no time left for anything save a fast escape." Here she stopped, scowling. Berac had turned his face away from her disinterestedly, motioning for a nearby servant to fill him a new cup of wine.

"So you failed. Hardly surprising. Seems to run in the family, wouldn't you agree?"

With supreme effort, Fashra stifled an immediate outburst. The men behind her stepped forward in anticipation of the opposite, hands moving closer to hilts. At last she unclenched her teeth and replied: "Under present circumstances, that remark coming from you seems a bit unfair..."

In delivering these words, the elf had just gambled with her life. Now hands were *on* hilts, and a near-dead silence had fallen over the scene. The only noise was that of the river babbling off at a distance to her left. She was used to being treated like a dog by Berac, the soldiers...by all the human usurpers of this waste that had centuries before flourished under the care of her ancient kin. She could tolerate a personal insult, a reprimand, or even a moderate beating. But what she could never take from them in silence was such idiotic comments concerning the inferiority of her family or her race. So few of her people remained to toil in this parcel of the world. Here the elfin line would soon fail—but never their pride.

Luckily for Fashra, however, the king chose to laugh her response away. "I'll let that one go…for the courage it took to speak it. But that one only. Now get to the point! I don't care about your misadventures, elf…nor did I need another picture of the Sinian bastards lounging in my chambers and roaming about my halls."

"Very well," she nodded…and the soldiers relaxed. "There are some within Oen's council who, seeing the king's revenge achieved, urge him to withdraw at once, letting his warriors take only such spoils as they can shoulder for the march home—and leaving not a single man behind to be slaughtered upon your return. They lost men defending Relinydd from the Domalin prince's sudden assault and, hearing rumors of a greater upheaval in the West, now fear to leave their homeland undefended. Chalemos is well fortified, they say—but should the Domalins seize an opportunity to burn their way south through the villages of Sinia, Oen's force would likely starve before it could lift a siege. Gethod is in chaos. Scarcely can they depend on aid from the Ithiros, neither for supplies nor men-at-arms. And what few of their allies from Relinydd who didn't race home at the news of that city's taking have since been recalled without reason given, adding to suspicions. What? Why are you grinning so?"

"Because you've told me nothing I've not already guessed and well planned for—and thus have placed yourself back in a precarious position. I return to my original question…"

"Oh, but I'm not finished yet, lord. They say Oen had a look at Van's corpse before its burning…and that he was furious to find Argen dead before he could judge the man himself. He doesn't desire to leave behind the city that so many of his people fought and died over, regardless of how much loot they could carry out of it—not on little more than a whim that Domal has its eye on a conquest of Sinia. Thus the plan is to split his forces, leading the majority south…yet leaving enough behind in an attempt to hold the city until he can manage a return."

"Ha! The fool!" Berac suddenly leaned forward in his seat, eyes wide. She had his attention now. "He'll spread himself too thin and so be defeated on both fronts! No sooner than he sets foot out of Crûthior will we storm the weakened sections of the walls. Our scouts report they've hardly begun repairing the outer breach yet. The dogs are too besotted with my wine and women to lift a finger, no doubt, foolishly thinking any resistance left to be scattered and broken. This is much better than striding through the open gates into a city stripped bare! We'll regain much of what was dashed from our hands…and flay the offenders alive!"

As he spoke these last words, a hint of madness gleamed in his eyes — and Fashra thought it best to let his boast hover in the air a moment before deflating it with what she had left to say. Picking up on this in the woman's expression, Berac faltered. His smile vanished, and his brows furrowed as he addressed her again: "Is there something more?"

"If only it were that simple. Oen won't leave until Crûthior's fortifications are again sound. And with you currently sitting here idle, it won't hold him up long."

Berac's frown deepened. He could see where this was going, and he didn't like it at all.

"Furthermore, he's taken to giving out spoils to your commoners still living in the city in exchange for their aid in mending the wall — and, if necessary, even in defense of the city against you. Those who come before Oen but don't accept this, he plans to turn loose once the defenses are restored. Till that day, he'll let none out that can't find a way themselves. Yet I doubt even then you'll see many wandering here." She raised a warding palm before Berac could retort. "Take no offense, lord! You're not a hated king in the eyes of most. But neither are you loved enough for them to risk striking out into the wilds, when the alternative is to keep their homes and come into a bit of wealth to boot. The Sinian hoard will be significantly diminished by this…but lust for plunder isn't what started this war. Despite the rumbling of some of Oen's captains, their own shares will likely not be cut too deeply. Most of it will come from the king's own pile, no doubt."

Berac was still fuming, but Fashra sensed his anger was no longer directed at her. He sat there in silence, scowling while twisting a finger in his black goatee, his mind turning over the information given.

Her plan had succeeded. At least for the present, she'd regained the man's confidence.

At last Berac reclined in his chair, taking another sip of wine. "So, Fashra — assuming all this can be verified — what would you suggest I do?"

"You should cease lounging here, awaiting a sign from that foreign witch — or else you won't be walking through the gates anytime soon. *Force Oen's hand!* Make him see the wisdom of his opponents in the council. Attack now, with all the strength you can muster!"

37

Three environs flirted with one another at the hinterlands of the Dizron Sea, the spot where the northernmost finger of Braured Forest was separated from the wastelands of Dolras by the murky river Asendath. On its eastern bank was the woodland, with damp topsoil and illimitable spikelets of grass jutting through the leafy decomposition that lay strewn about the earth. The leaflets swayed in unison to the conduct of cool marine winds underneath the thick canopy of the tree vein. But across the river were the barrens, with cracked earth, arid climate, and dust flurries that spawned as sporadically and rapidly as they disseminated. A burnt red sky stretched on infinitely into the northern expanse, and dark gray clouds blandly hung forever there, void of the hope of release. To the north was the sea, sapphire and cold. Vast but passive. Its northern limits were unknown to men.

Thus the great steed displaced leaf, soil, and sand with the stamping of its massive hoofs as its rider drew it up before the river mouth at the inlet of the sea. The man wore a thin, travel-worn cloak that appeared gray as a storm cloud as it flowed carelessly below his bent knees. Its cowl covered his face so that his visage wasn't betrayed, yet the shadow it made couldn't lessen the brilliance of the man's eyes: fugitive red turned a striking blue. His feet were set within two black iron stirrups and sheathed by muddy leather boots that rose nearly to the knees. His hands were exposed. A silver ring encircled his right thumb.

The rider turned his mount towards the setting sun and followed the river for many miles till he came to a narrow bend in the waterway. Telltale signs of crossing were present there: the semblance of an old road through the trees, a truncated bank, and a rotting post that still found its footing midway across the river — an old indication of depth for the wary traveler. The man took note and then guided his horse into the cool water. The gradient of the river bottom was steady but acute, and soon the opaque waters rose up his steed's flank, causing it to struggle against the current. But the rider maintained control, comforting the animal, and eventually both man and beast reached the river's far side, drawing themselves from the water and climbing the embankment up to the arid plateau.

The man dug into his saddlebag, withdrew a waterskin, and took a drink — preemptively, so it seemed — as he surveyed the desolate landscape. But the next drink was stopped in mid-motion, vessel halfway to his mouth. Nearly a furlong away was an anomaly. An oak tree, proud but lonely, had grown tall amidst the cracked earth where nothing else would grow at all. It held no shadow, for the entire dome of sky seemed to be the sun: one monochromatic blanket of burnt red above the land. Lowering the waterskin, the man steered his charger toward the tree.

As he came beneath the spreading branches of the oak, the rider saw a small barrow and an accompanying inscription carved into the trunk above; yet he'd no need for its words, knowing this to be the epitaph of Jedan Mûran, rearguard captain of the steadfast Haxûdī horde. Dismounting, the man patted his horse's neck before kneeling over the grave. Dust particles danced before his eyes. He placed one hand atop the mound then, slowly retracting it, reached in his cloak to pull something from its folds: a talisman like the one Ûladriss had clutched as he stood diminished in the flickering firelight before the Beast of Thirannon years ago. Setting this thing on the mound almost ceremoniously, the man drew back his hood. His face was grim, and his eyes were reminiscent as he turned them to the north.

His final destination lay somewhere across that distance: the ruins of the Red Castle and the ancient keep of Ûmrothsul Aldrotherin.

Returning to the folds of his cloak, he retrieved his flask of Tholmian liquor and — thinking of the smile it'd once conjured on Jedan's face — allowed a grin to show briefly on his own. After taking a swig, he lay the flask beside the talisman and rose to his feet. "Mûran, if your gods will grant me your ear, farewell! And if you sued for vengeance in the halls of the dead, know that your prayer's been answered. I leave these things here as a token of our brotherhood — and the other shall be an heirloom for your son." As he spoke the last words, Dragan glanced at the Haxûdī's sword strapped to his steed's back. Then, leaping into the saddle, he galloped away.

38

The horn blared again much closer now, causing Ranod Lorege, governor of Relinydd, to begin nervously wringing his hands. He'd resisted the urge to flock with the others to the gate, opting instead to vainly hold on to a semblance of authority — as if he meant more to Saedus of Ost than one of the slaves carrying her litter down the wide, paved street. Already he could make out the palanquin and its bearers as they approached the square, for the sorceress had chosen to lead her procession rather than build expectation through bringing up its rear. Beside the fidgeting governor stood Valreecius, motionless as a rock by contrast, in his characteristic garb.

"I warn you again, steward," said Lorege, suddenly breaking the lull in their conversation. "It wasn't so hard a task to remind the citizens of ancient law yet standing, pacifying them to Rardonydd's blood heir. But *this*..." He cut himself short, gesturing at Saedus' outlandish procession to let the scene speak for itself. "There'll be riots, at least. Perhaps worse. I can't be blamed for their actions..." He turned his face then on Valreecius expectantly but was met with no response. The steward's mouth was a thin, straight line, yet his pink eyes were locked on Saedus' litter with an unmistakable mesmerized glee. Spiderlike fingers clutched the moon hanging from his neck, holding the thing slightly off his sunken chest; and these bony features of the man's body, coupled with his smooth ivory skull, reminded the governor of a skeleton pulled straight from some unearthed tomb. Presently — as Ranod stared on, somewhat enthralled now himself — Valreecius smiled as if an amusing thought had come to mind or someone had whispered something to his liking in his ear. Had the steward always been like this? This *creature*? Or how and when had the transformation begun? Was this what lay in store for Ranod as well, should he survive long enough in the witch's service? At the moment he felt not so far removed from that fate.

For a man well beyond his middle years, the governor of Relinydd had long maintained an appearance of youth and vigor — yet the whirlwind of the past few weeks had left him far from unscathed. His face had grown pale and gaunt, his hair seemed to be thinning and graying by the hour, and new lines of age crept up about weary, doleful eyes. He'd been defeated, jailed, thoroughly abased, and even manhandled by the usurping prince all within a brief span of days; and now, in little more than a fortnight from his fall, he was about to endure another changing of the guard. No matter if Saedus had been pulling Baeldrin's strings all along: with the prince out of the picture now, she might have vastly different thoughts on Ranod's usefulness as a puppet dictator under her rule. He was but another fly caught in the *Spider*'s web, awaiting his turn to be sucked dry. And he knew it well.

"Greetings, brother," came an eerie, unanticipated voice from directly in front of Lorege—and the jittery governor flinched at the sound. Turning his gaze from the steward to fix wide eyes on the scene before him, Ranod quickly realized that he wasn't the only one startled. Spears were half leveled. Mouths were frozen partially into shouts of alarm. In the midst of his guards stood a maroon-cloaked man with a hooded face aimed at Valreecius; yet Valreecius didn't appear rattled by the intruder having seemingly materialized from thin air, and his lack of reaction was likely the only thing still keeping Ranod's soldiers at bay.

"Poltoros," replied the moon steward. "Welcome, old friend."

The release of tension was almost tangible. Mouths closed. Grips slackened. A few of the more diligent guards remained facing the newcomer, but most lost interest immediately in favor of the ever-nearing parade. Minus the shock of his stealthy approach, Poltoros was to them but one more mysterious, robed servant: hardly anything at all when set against the bizarre grandeur now on display. Of the marvel of imps and goblins alone the soldiers might've had their fill—for there were more of these creatures already inside the city than there were fresh ones streaming in through the gate—yet new wonders and opulence were afoot.

The procession's head was almost upon them, so they could easily make out the bodies flanking and falling behind Saedus' palanquin. Here came the chanting priests swinging incense burners at their sides, women strewing petals on the road, and even a few acrobats juggling or tumbling their way in and out of the throng. Half-naked, painted-bodied dancers stepped and spun in time with the beating of drums. Long lines of slaves pulled a wagon bearing a stone altar heaped with burning elm branches, and a smaller group pulled a cart laden with casks from which serving girls were dispensing wine, mead, and beer into cups and doling them out to anyone holding forth an eager hand. The sorceress must've been in a generous mood when she opened Acomalath's coffers, for all but her lowliest slave was bedecked in strings of pearls, torcs of precious metals, and other adornments fit for Rardonydd's upper crust...and some lesser coins and trinkets were even being tossed out by the fistful to the roaring crowd. And while these things were going on, the priests' acolytes were busily reminding everyone of who'd made this entertainment possible. Reaching into their bags again and again, they brought out tiny carven idols of their mistress, kissing the wooden mouth of each one before passing it on to the next awestruck citizen.

Most of the witch's army would remain without, busily striking a temporary encampment. There wasn't enough room in the city to house them all, had an occupation been Saedus' desire—yet Ranod was aware that their stay would be brief at best. Enough time to remarshal and resupply, then the combined force would be swiftly away, marching off to wage war on the plains. Yet here were a chosen few Domalin captains whom the *Spider* would flaunt before the crowd, prancing in on steeds draped in the same finery as their blazoned riders. In the lead came their supreme military commander—the general Sorec, whom Ranod had met twice before—answerable now only to Saedus herself. His horse was dressed in full silver-plated barding and covered with a black caparison. The man himself wore a cape of the same color, yet his armor and crested helm were shone in both silver and gold. Six chevrons were stitched on the baldric slung across his chest, indicating the highest military rank a Domalin soldier might dream to attain.

And above his captains' heads waved Domal's banners: the standard crimson discs and rays dancing on fields of jet black.

"You look surprised, governor," said Poltoros, pulling Ranod from his study. "Has Valreecius not been forthcoming with you?"

"He's said enough." Lorege turned his gaze on the lich and frowned. "Save to explain why you're here instead of riding in her lap."

That was a mistake. Poltoros gripped his tyberwood staff and tilted it toward Ranod, ever so slightly, mumbling under his breath—yet the effect of this action was anything but slight. Suddenly the governor felt as if a hive of agitated bees was trying to sting its way free from his belly. Gasping, he doubled over in pain, nearly falling to his knees before the sensation passed. Cold sweat beaded on his forehead. One or two of the soldiers swallowed hard and gripped shafts tighter at Ranod's obvious discomfort...but that was the extent of their response.

The lich glanced at Valreecius. "You've been allowing such impudence from this pawn, brother? I'm disappointed."

"He's been civil enough till now," said the moon steward. "But, yes, it seems the queen's reception has run contrary to the one he envisioned...and I'm afraid it's jostled his mind. Prepare him swiftly. She's upon us."

At these words all eyes turned to Saedus' litter, catching it just as her tattooed slaves were setting the thing down. It wasn't a large affair, allowing room for but one person to recline comfortably within. But what it lacked in size, it made up for in its ornateness: carved ivory posts, silk curtains, and a painted metallic canopy. Ranod could see the curtains weren't drawn, although his view wasn't such that he could make out the witch within...and apparently she wasn't in a hurry to exit. The bearers loosed the poles, stepped aside with arms folded, and waited as the rest of the procession began to grind to a halt behind them.

"Come," said Poltoros, sweeping a robed arm toward the litter, beckoning the nauseated governor to lead the way. The tone of his voice made it perfectly clear that this wasn't a suggestion but a command. "Stand up straight and play your part. You should know it well by now."

True enough. But this wasn't the same as when Baeldrin had strode through the gate. There'd been no such fanfare then. At least not at the onset. Slowly Lorege started forward, forcing his chin high and his hands to his sides. He was rightfully anxious yet perversely desirous as well: eager to look upon the woman whose unnatural beauty he'd only heard told of before this day. He wondered if he should kneel and kiss her hand...or curtly bow...or fall before her feet, fully prostrating himself. All eyes were on him, a hush having descended over the crowd. He came within a few steps of the litter where he could see its occupant plainly within – and hesitated, fighting against the urge to just stand there and gawk at her like the dumbfounded fool that he was.

"Offer her your hand," spoke Poltoros as he breezed past Ranod, pushing his staff onto the nearest acolyte. Then – without so much as meeting his mistress' eye – the lich approached the palanquin, lifted from it a polished oaken box, and stepped swiftly aside to let the governor retain the spotlight.

Winning control of himself, Lorege closed the distance, whereupon Saedus of Ost took his hand and rose from the litter. She was nearly as tall as the governor, standing regally before him in an indigo-dyed silhouette dress with the skirt slit up to mid-thigh. Ranod drew a deep breath, scanning the curves of the witch's body before lighting his gaze above her slender ivory shoulders. Her long, black hair was pulled away from that perfect face, falling in a tail down her back, and her charcoal-painted lips were locked in a wicked smile to accompany the crazed gleam in her eyes: eyes that Ranod met and held with his own for but an instant only, melting under her piercing stare. As he'd already released her hand, the governor settled for a bow instead of a light kiss in greeting. Then, knowing not what else to do, he took a step back from her and turned to the lich, awaiting the next prompt.

Now Saedus raised a hand to the masses in a greeting of her own, turning her head slowly from side to side, taking them in. For a brief moment of uncertainty the stillness lingered – then suddenly a rush of beating drums, clashing cymbals, and reporting horns was struck up by the assembled players, followed by a near-deafening outburst of applause from the throng. The priests and acolytes began to raise their arms presently, motioning for the crowd to calm; then Saedus and her entourage – including Ranod – were on the move again, heading for the steps to the platform beneath the spires of Ophim Nuarin.

Poltoros stepped in line with the governor, caught Ranod's eyes, and directed them to the box he was carrying. "The Diadem of the Gazer," he said, spreading a palm out, almost caressingly, over the wooden surface. "Your queen shall see Domal's golden age renewed, governor. Do as you're instructed – and perhaps you'll retain your place in the new regime."

Lorege turned his face from the lich to Saedus, frowning at the sorceress' back as she took the steps before him. A tingle in his gut reminded him to be careful with his responses, yet he doubted at this point – with all eyes upon them – that he'd be afflicted again. "This farce will last no longer than Baeldrin's," he spoke for Poltoros' ears alone. "She hasn't even the blood to back it! Another will rise up and remove her soon enough...if she doesn't fall to the Sinians first." Ranod cringed as the last of the words left his mouth, but this time the lich didn't seem offended.

"Through blood born or blood spilled, it makes no difference. She'll wear this crown for as long as she desires it. And you'll be the one to set it on her brow."

39

Unquiet pierced the *DoomBringer* like an arrow as he sat ahorse, studying the towers of the Red King. It was a feeling like none other since his departure from Mardotha. Not shame, regret, nor guilt. Not love, hate, nor rage. No…this was different. It occurred to him that the journey to Dolras was an action of *his* will, not his mother's — and that he couldn't easily recall another time when this was so. The once mighty walls of the castle perimeter lay broken in heaps all about him, the jagged edges of their crumbled stones long smoothed by the west winds blowing in from the sea. Carefully he swept his eyes over the rubble. A steady stream of debris evanesced from it like smoke from a flame, sending dust clouds dancing east across the sky.

A marble-clad archway that had once supported the massive city gatehouse still stood defiantly intact among the ruins. The arch remained, but the barbican was destroyed; and the iron bars of the gate had long been looted, most likely by some forgotten horde of raiders desperate for armor and weapons. The gateway was huge. Twenty men could pass its span abreast, and engines of war could roll with ease beneath its lofty rise. Many reliefs and inscriptions were carved into the marble cladding. The largest one was situated above the keystone at the crown, and — though eroded and fragmented — the words could yet be discerned:

From the Womb to the Pyre
The First, the Last, the Fury is the Fire

Dragan mouthed the words softly as he urged Allethion on beneath the arch. *The Fury is* Desire, he mused, recalling a common saying passed down through the ages: one that'd originated in mockery of the Red King's death but had since evolved into a universal maxim. A saying to which he could surely relate…for desire had burned hot within him for as long as he could remember.

Passing now into the outer city, the *DoomBringer* surveyed his surroundings while his mind wandered back over all he'd ever learned of the place's history. Aldrotherin had been the castle's last permanent inhabitant. What'd been a mere stronghold and watchtower prior to his coming, he'd transformed into a bustling, opulent city. Rasyrethra, *Sun beneath the Sun*, he'd named it anew. During the city's springtime it'd rivaled Rardonydd and even ancient Hiseod in population and power: for at that time, the climate was milder, the ground was fertile, and the sky was only red at day's end. Bourgs and farms sprouted from the earth like crops outside the city walls as far as the Asendath to the south and the Daudus to the west. The Red King had beckoned, and the masses had heard his call: for the freedom, wealth, and protection he'd promised them was indeed secured in the flowering of that golden age. Yet as the happy years marched on, the people's debt to Ûmrothsul was steadily accruing. And sadly, they knew it not.

The streets and alleys making up the outer city's grid were, for the most part, still unobstructed. Brick half-walls and stone foundations remained, but it was a mystery now what buildings they'd once supported. Dragan could tell a few by their layouts. A buttery. A smithy. An inn. The rest, however, were little more than shapes in the dirt. He passed by them all slowly and cautiously, navigating the eastern road as it wound its way up to the keep.

The inner court was contained by a curtain wall, which had been the original castle wall before Aldrotherin's arrival. This wall too was crumbled, although in places it still retained its full height. The demure archway of the gatehouse stood in sharp contrast to that of the outer. It was made from ashlar, modestly sized and with no inscriptions. Its gate was missing also. A large column more than a yard in diameter lay toppled before the entrance. The *GrimHelm* dismounted, tied Allethion to the remains of a nearby statue, scaled the column, and entered.

The ward was as barren as the outer city, and he wasted no time traversing its length. His eyes hadn't lit on a single ingot of metal since entering the city, but now the keep's massive ironclad doors loomed over him, barring his passage to the hall within. Dragan rubbed his palm lengthwise down the door. Here the vandalism had stopped. Not a trace of wear or defacement could be found on the smooth metal surface. All the hardware was intact. The stones and wooden beams that comprised the vaulted forebuilding were undamaged. *What is this?* he thought dubiously, peering momentarily back over his shoulder to survey the ruins a final time before recalling his gaze. Two mighty loops of black steel hung heavy before him, inviting his pull...but as he reached to grasp them, the doors creaked open involuntarily. The gap formed allowed the red-orange haze of the sky to paint a narrow welcome path on the dark floor within. He hesitated, his mind running through potential traps. Yet soon this began to chafe him; and so, gripping the hilt of his sword, he took a step forward and entered.

It took a moment for his cool blue eyes to regain their sight within the dimly lit chamber, but as his vision waxed, the *DoomBringer* perceived a figure perched on the high throne at the great hall's far end. The being was draped all in white, and his face was hidden behind a featureless black mask. *Must all men who vex me wear masks?* thought Dragan, recalling the lich Poltoros. He didn't consider how many men *he'd* vexed in his past while donning his own.

"Name yourself!" he spoke, holding his position by the entrance. "Friend or foe?"

"Neither," came the answer reverberating down the length of the hall. The voice was clear and loud as the tolling of a bell. And as ominous.

The response irritated Dragan. His fist clinched tighter around the hilt of his sword. "Who's summoned me here? And why?"

"Come, *Master of Doom*, and know."

Dragan couldn't tell from the distance whether the resonating voice actually belonged to the stranger before him or if it'd emanated instead from elsewhere in the chamber. The masked man remained motionless with his gloved hands on the throne's armrests, and his white raiment fell in a pool before him on the dais. The light from a few score candles illuminated the area directly about the throne, yet it was too weak to reach out and reveal the hall's breadth. Two columns of opposing statues set atop tall stone pedestals ran lengthwise from door to throne: full-scale likenesses of all the mage-kings of ages past. Only darkness lay behind them.

"What beasts lurk in the shadows for me this time, Tiramas?" said Dragan. "What set of eyes do you peer at me from?"

"Approach and learn the truth of yourself," replied the voice.

For a moment Saedus' son turned to peer back through the open door to the desert outside…then he started forward again, closing the gap to his summoner. As the statues nearest the throne became visible, he began to recognize some of them from their portraits in Poltoros' *Book of Kings*, and his thoughts raced back to Vendhane's chamber in Addrindain where he'd once looked upon much the same. Each pedestal held a stone placard with its king's words inscribed.

There was Nal'tanos Crimlore, the Golden King, with his square-cut jaw and shrewd gaze. He held a sword in one hand and an open book in the other. His words read: *Let Justice be Done, Lest the Heavens Fall.*

There was Tethramel Davin, the Green King, his legs metamorphosing into tree trunks whose roots spread atop the stone pedestal. He wore a great beard on his face, and his hand gripped a gnarled staff. *Return to the Earth* were his words.

And there was the Blue King, Orkayl Deigan, called the *Chronomancer*. His heavy eyelids drooped beneath bushy brows, and his hooked nose protruded above a wispy beard that fell to his belly. An hourglass rested in the cup of his upturned palms. His words read: *All Things Doth Time Conquer.*

The last two statues were the Red King and, unexpectedly, the White King. Dragan wondered how the latter had come to be. Tiramas Vendhane had dwelt in Addrindain—never in Dolras, at least to his knowledge—and Rasyrethra had withered long ago with the death of Ûmrothsul Aldrotherin. Their words read: *The Fury is the Fire* and *Hearken to my Call.*

Here the *GrimHelm* stopped, some twenty feet before the throne. "I've traveled many leagues to reach this place," he began again, "…and now that I'm here, I rue it. So give me your tricks or your words, Vendhane—or whoever you are—but either way, be quick about it!"

The man seated on the throne gave no response; yet in place of one, Dragan caught movement from the corner of his eye. In one fluid motion he unsheathed his blade and set its tip between himself and the White King's statue…then took an involuntary step back as he watched the marble become a substrate to some new and ever-shifting presence. Ethereality swathed the figure like mist hanging over a lake at dawn, yet this vapor flowed over the cold, white surfaces of the stone, vanishing in places and materializing in others. At the statue's head it coalesced into a face: a living phantasm overlaying the inanimate guise of the marble beneath. And set within that face…those eyes…

Late is your arrival, son of Saedus, the words of Vendhane's spirit crashed into the *DoomBringer's* unguarded mind. The telepathic invasion was so abrupt and forceful that Dragan flinched and nearly dropped his weapon. Yet before he could level the blade again on the specter he faced, he saw another statue flash awake behind—not unlike a candlewick bursting into flame—causing him to spin about on…

Ûmrothsul Aldrotherin himself. *And coarse is your impudent tongue! You've not earned the privilege to make demands of us. Not yet!*

Perhaps never. The Blue King was slowly forming beside the Red. *The hour of your ascension is fleeting, child. Another seeks to corrupt the line. To take your rightful place.*

Dragan was suddenly aware that *all* the statues within view had awakened, though at present only these three had permeated his thoughts. The pause after the *Chronomancer's* words lingered now…for so long that Dragan wondered if he might be imagining things. Yet there were the forms hovering before him. They were waiting for him to speak. Allowing him time to recover from shock.

"My right to what?" he responded at last. "This broken throne? I left one of those behind in Addrindain. And who's the man to keep it from me, should the seat be my desire? This masked enchanter dawdling upon it?" Only after he'd spit this out did he realize it was an answer to words unspoken aloud—but the man of flesh before him didn't question the outburst. Had he heard the voices as well?

Have you forgotten my words to you in Braured? returned Tiramas after a briefer pause than the last. *No, Erroth is my servant: one whose term has lingered well beyond its time. You may question him when we're done. For now, you need know only that he dons the white to show his current allegiance…yet he hides behind the faceless mask until his identity can be reborn under a new master. And the color of that master is black…*

Do you take me for an idiot? Dragan forced a telepathic response. *This servant, as you call him, hid his face from me because he knew I'd not come otherwise. Clearly he holds some power of his own, yet I'm no stranger to magic.* Considering the last piece further, Dragan returned his eyes to the throne and spoke again aloud: "How do I know this isn't just some parlor trick of yours, wizard? What do you want with me? A chance to finish what the real Vendhane could not?"

As I said, slayer: you are not a King yet. Not until you break free of your mother's grasp can you ascend. Aldrotherin got straight back to his point with these words, glossing over the end of Dragan's reply about tricks and ulterior motives as if the hero were a toddler speaking gibberish. *It is she who would usurp your power, just as she's leeched from others in the past. You know of what I speak.*

The servant on the throne remained mute, and so Dragan decided to give up speaking directly to him. If all these distinct voices were indeed coming from the stranger, he wasn't only a wizard but also a talented impressionist. Dragan was beginning to doubt his initial skepticism. *Blood and bones. Yes, I know of what you speak. She would've hidden all of it from me, no doubt, could she have managed it — but I had to be told enough to play my part.* He turned his face and thoughts then from the Red King to the White. *You, Vendhane…and the Beast of Thirannon…and the very soul of the Daemon herself, for all I know — or care to understand. It takes more than a hedge witch's potions to bring a mutilated corpse back to life and to summon up devils from the forest depths and the bowels of the earth. But if this is truly your spirit, Tiramas, reaching out to me from beyond, then tell me this: why would you aid me? Mother may have ordered it, but it was my hand that took your life…*

Because your destiny is more important than any petty revenge. A new voice had joined the others now: cold, emotionless, but laden with power. Its tone sounded just as Dragan remembered Poltoros delivering it to him from the *Book of Kings*, all those years ago. The voice of the Golden King, Nal'tanos Crimlore. *Tiramas knew his reign was drawing to an end, Dragan, before you ever entered his domain; and it was your hand that claimed the succession — exactly as it was meant to be. The line of Kings is not governed by good or evil. Some of us were more righteous than others in life, it's true, but all of us were our own masters. What is your excuse?*

The mere presence of his boyhood idol was enough to leave Dragan for the moment speechless — never mind Crimlore's affirmation of his preordainment as mankind's next mage-king. The Golden King, it was recorded, did not lie. And yet…something wasn't adding up. *My excuse? You see many things, Kings of old, so surely you know the true source of my power. Mother gifted it to me — so why would she want it back now, when she could've recalled it so many times before? Little time's passed since I cast it down at her feet. If she wanted me dead, why didn't she do it then and there? She could've sent her pet Baeldrin to my room while I sat helpless, pondering the course of my wretched life…*

Helpless? This was Vendhane again. *Far from it. We indeed know the source of your power, warrior — yet until today you did not. That breastplate you wear, while of impeccable craftsmanship, holds no magic of its own. You have been sorely deceived.*

"What?" Dragan cried out as he stumbled, nearly crashing into the nearest pedestal before he regained control of his limbs. Instinctively he raised his blade and waved it as if warding off an impending blow from nowhere—and his other hand darted to his chest, clutching at the armor to ensure it was still there. "You lie! It can't be..." *Why would she... No! The curse...*

Silent until now, the Green King chose this point to intercede. *Not a curse, but rather the boast of an ancient armorer whose peerless skills followed him to the grave. A man of my time, he was. All things were brighter in those days.*

No. Dragan slowly shook his head. *I don't believe it. All this is but a ruse. You would have me lay down my defense, then unleash your minions upon me...*

Awaken, fool! boomed the Red King's voice. *Your witch-mother communicates with spirits from the underworld. She knows your fate as well as we do!*

She always knew this day would come, added Orkayl Deigan. *The day when your eyes would be opened. She used the armor as a leash to hold on to you for as long as she could...to channel your growing power to further her own gains. Yet now she's made her final move, and she discards all tools – all* rivals *– no longer needed. Your father is dead. Your half-brother deposed. The Mardothans have been abandoned as fodder in the north. And now that you've completed your final task...*

Once more Dragan felt his knees weaken. He set the tip of his sword upon the floor, leaning upon the hilt as if it were a crutch. *They...murdered Acomalath? They said he wouldn't be harmed...that he'd only be forced to retire to his estate.* Now Baeldrin's last words to him stung as they ran back through his head: *"You've no idea what it takes to turn the gears of the world..."*

Your power lies within you, said the White King, drawing the hero's gaze once more to the specter's haunting eyes. *It's been there since the day you laid me low. Yet the sources that fuel your mother's devilry are fast running dry, and her hold on you is slipping. She'll take your life now, if she can, then harvest your blood as she did mine. But if she succeeds in this, she'll not stop there. She will raise you from the dead. Bind you forever to her will!*

The image of Poltoros' disjointed corpse suddenly flashed in Dragan's mind; then, just like that, something snapped in him. His time here was done. What more could the voices reveal to him if he stayed on another hour—another day, another *year*—that could set him any clearer down the path to what he must do. He felt his grip tighten on his sword's hilt. His strength was returned, and now it pulsed through his limbs with the beating of a raging heart. *The bitch shall die!* he shouted at the unwanted guests in his head, desiring them banished to the abyss from which they'd come. Then, without so much as a parting word, he spun on his heels and began storming from the hall.

"Wait!" cried Erroth, startled by Dragan's sudden retreat. Leaning forward, he reached out with an open hand—as if he could pull his would-be master back with it.

But the *Master of Doom* kept on walking until he reached the doors…then he was gone.

The servant dropped his head and hand and fell back into silence.

40

The tent's flap opened suddenly, jolting Fashra from peaceful slumber. Her eyes flicked open, and her slender muscles went instantly taut: yet she remained perfectly still, using the dark to hide her wakefulness. With even keen elfin sight of no use, she reached out with her other heightened senses to uncloak the scene about her. The warm breath on her shoulder revealed that it wasn't Berac returning from a trip to relieve himself, although the feel and smell of a gentle inrush of night air confirmed the flap had indeed been parted. A light footstep. Another. Then came a sound like a small metal hinge creaking—and she sprang into action just as a soft red light illuminated the tent. In one smooth sequence of motion, the elf rolled from her lord's bed, grasped some object from the floor to serve as her weapon, wheeled on the figure holding the lamp, lunged…

And was tossed aside like a limp doll, her body striking with a *thump* against one of the thick poles near the tent's rear. There she hung in midair—unable to speak or move—as if invisible hands had clamped down on her neck and all four limbs and pinned her to the support.

The combination of light and noise was enough to finally stir Berac. Shifting, he propped himself up on one elbow, groaned, and brought up a hand to shield his bleary eyes from the bright onslaught. Instantly he felt the tip of a cold steel blade touch his neck beneath the beard.

"Don't cry out, friend," came the intruder's hushed, imploring words. "I'm not here to harm you. Only to speak."

"You…" replied Berac in a voice raspy from disuse. "But…how?" Slowly he lowered his hand to the bed. Squinting eyes darted about the tent, seeking and swiftly finding the incapacitated elf-woman. His lids opened wider at the sight of Fashra's supernatural predicament—but his astonished gaze didn't dwell on her long. Turning his attention back to the intruder, he added: "What's going on here? Why have you come?"

"Nothing's amiss outside, I assure you, other than a few guards pried from their posts and detained. In a moment I'll lower my blade as well; but first look again at your woman, Berac, and realize what you're dealing with here. You and I aren't strangers, and I'd keep the peace between us. Yet don't doubt who holds the power here and now. Raise an alarm, and I'll run you through, crush the life from this elf, then fade into the night. Nothing gained but nothing lost from the venture. Understand?"

Berac glanced at the helpless Fashra as instructed and, apparently convinced, nodded his reluctant acceptance.

Baeldrin withdrew his sword but didn't retreat from the blade's reach. Rather, he hung the lantern on a hook and sat down at the bed's edge, letting the point of his weapon touch the ground as he rested one hand on its pommel.

A soft moan—almost a whimper—escaped from Fashra, and the men's faces returned to her. She was clothed only from the waist down, and her sleek arms had been pulled behind her, causing her chest to jut out. "You've a fine kitten there," Baeldrin mused. "But I don't think I'll release her yet. I suspect she has sharp teeth and claws. Am I right?"

The Mardothan king nodded again. "This is...the witch's magic?"

Baeldrin frowned, briefly puzzled. "I see you haven't heard. What of Van's bird, then? She said it passed over to you."

"I'm afraid the *kitten* here pounced on it, once she convinced me to sever ties with Saedus. It would've been too dangerous to keep around at that point, with stray ears open to its wiles. What is it I've missed?"

"Good girl!" Baeldrin grinned, sidestepping Berac's question to study Fashra again in a different light. "I should rethink your treatment, now...since you've clearly begun my work, even before my arrival. If I'd known I had such an ally here beforehand, I wouldn't have ridden two horses to death in my haste. I might've even dared to give myself over to your master's guards instead of staging this little production. But no matter. Nod if you agree to back down once I let you go."

The elf did so—and almost immediately she visibly relaxed, her body sliding down the pole to crumple into a squatting position. One arm came up to cover her breasts...but otherwise she honored the agreement, remaining still. The look in her eyes was murderous, yet somehow she held herself in check.

"So you've rebelled against her also?" spoke Berac, anxious to bring Baeldrin to the point.

The Domalin prince chuckled at that. "Not by choice, in my case. Yet the result's the same. We're dethroned outcasts, you and I. Used and discarded. I always knew she'd betray me, but I didn't think it would come when it did. Not so soon after my triumph. She almost caught me unprepared. *Almost.*"

"You confronted her?" said Berac, a hint of amazement in his voice.

"No. She underestimated me. Sent her dog Zera to do me in. He failed."

"I see. It doesn't surprise me—of Nephos, I mean. He tried to hide it behind love of his land and kin, but there was always that *hunger* in his eyes. I was glad to send him away." A pause. "Is he dead then?"

"Perhaps. If not, he soon shall be. I swear it."

Taking advantage of the silence that followed this statement, Fashra began to rise. Slowly this time. No sign of threat. "May I retrieve my clothing?"

Baeldrin looked her way and nodded.

Both men waited without speaking while the elf-woman found her robe and donned it; then Berac motioned her over to sit beside him. As she did so, he eyed her appraisingly for a moment, running a hand through her silver hair. Clearly he was beginning to relax somewhat. With an audible sigh, he turned back to his uninvited guest. "You came here alone?"

"I fled from Rardonydd with a single servant in tow."

Now it was Fashra who spoke: "But…the guards…how did you…"

Baeldrin waved a gesture that stopped her short. "The secrets of my power are my own. As I said, I've slain no one. I'll release them all once we're done."

"Done with *what*, Baeldrin?" said Berac, irritation plain in his voice. "If you're merely in need of refuge…"

"No. That's not it." The prince ran a hand across his tired brow. "Let me get to the point."

"Please do."

"As I see it, Berac, I'm still Lord of Domal, you're still Lord of Mardotha, and we're still allies. Only now our enemy's changed. We can sit here by the river and attempt to drown our sorrows in women and wine, cursing old enemies and ill fates — or we can set sniveling aside and regain control of our lives. Yet time's of the essence. We must be decisive if we're to stand a chance against the witch. We've only a small window of opportunity — and if we fail to take it, she'll move quickly beyond *anyone's* reach. Once that happens, then who'll have won? Not you. Not me. Not the Sinians. In the end, she'd crush us all."

The Mardothan considered this a moment. "The same as you'd do, were it still within your grasp. Don't deny it."

"I won't. But you're right: it's no longer within my grasp. She's seen to that. Whether we concede to her rule or unite and cast her down, my empire dreams have been shattered. At best, I hope to regain my rightful throne in Domal. At worst, I'll lose my life in the attempt. But for now what I crave is *revenge*. Don't you desire it too? Surely you know who's ultimately responsible for your loss. Turn the hatred in your mind's eye from Deserus Oen's face. See who's looking over his shoulder? With that goddamned smirk on her face?"

Berac frowned but remained silent.

"Yet we must get past the foe in front to get at the one hiding behind," said Fashra. "I've also urged him to action — and nearly succeeded, had it not been for *Hatrakori*." She spat their host's name as if it were a mouthful of piss but dared not add an expletive to it. "That man would have us dawdle here for the rest of our days!"

Her master gave her a disapproving glance. He hadn't even blinked at her innocent question of moments before, but now she'd planted herself firmly in the midst of the men's conversation. She did raise a good point, however, so Berac decided to let it go. Besides, Baeldrin surely wouldn't allow him to send her off at this point. Since she was going to hear it all regardless, she might as well be allowed to participate.

"And by the time you're done wrestling with the dog before you — assuming you can tame it at all — the bitch behind will have set an entire pack of starving wolves against you both. What strength would you have left then to stop her?" Baeldrin shook his head slightly. "Perhaps I've given you too much credit, elf. Why beat the dog into submission — or even try to step around it — when you can simply toss it a bone? Why not give it a nice pat on the head, then sick it on the bitch behind? The Sinians must face Saedus now, regardless. Will you aid her cause by nipping the dog from behind, or will you march instead beside your last hope of defense?"

"Our *defense*?" Berac scoffed. "Those bastards booted us out of our city after killing droves of my people. Are you suggesting I kiss Deserus Oen's feet? Have you gone stark mad?"

"And you killed droves of his men in turn!" Baeldrin's voice rose to meet the challenge. "They didn't take Crûthior easily. However much they might boast the opposite, you know they must truly view Mardothans as worthy adversaries. Swallow your pride, Berac, and make a deal with Oen! Aid him now to remove the threat to us all, and leave him indebted to you in return. Only then will you safely reclaim what was yours."

Berac opened his mouth to rage again but instead bit back his words with a muttered curse and a sigh. When he spoke again, his voice was calmer. "Your argument might be convincing, were it not all founded on assumption."

"You forget that I was much closer in counsel with the witch than you ever were. I know *exactly* what she has planned for you once she's done with Oen — and believe me, it's far from what you were told. That knowledge was supposed to die with me. Yet here I am, delivering you this warning. I suggest you heed it well."

"And if I don't? As you see, I've already been criticized for delaying another assault on the walls. Even should Deserus and I come to some agreement, what makes you think our warriors won't turn on each other like rabid dogs at the first jibe hurled the other's way? And who's to keep the city while we all go traipsing down the plains?"

"I *could* force you to do it." A pause to let this sink in. "But neither one of us wants that."

"You overestimate your power."

Baeldrin shook his head. "Don't test me, Berac. You've just seen me render your woman paralyzed — and I can just as easily usurp your mind. I'd have your mouth spewing my commands with the fervor of a zealot, although your private thoughts screamed against them helplessly from some tiny corner of your skull. Please…I beg you…let's not go there."

At this Berac turned to Fashra for some measure of support, but the defeated look she returned him was clear. The Domalin prince wasn't bluffing, it seemed. It would be in both their best interests, at least for now, to play along.

Baeldrin correctly took their silence for the response he sought. "Excellent." Without further ado, he stood and sheathed his blade. "Tomorrow we go before Deserus with our plans. You'll offer him aid in crushing Saedus' armies; and in exchange he'll return Crûthior — along with a portion of its spoils, I presume — to you once the safety of his beloved capital is again secured. A city for a city. It's as simple as that."

41

The girl shut her eyes, spread arms wide, and let herself fall backwards into the waiting sea of green grass. A sigh of contentment escaped her as she struck the cushioned ground, and for a moment she lay perfectly still, smiling at secret thoughts, lids drawn as shields against the shining heavens above. Then slowly her chest rose and fell as she took in a breath of cool mountain air and released it.

The wind stirred, whipping the forest of emerald blades into a frenzy about her spread dark curls...and with it came the piercing screech of a bird of prey. Her eyes snapped open at the sound, and she sat up in time for a glimpse at the creature's descent—a majestic osprey swooping down on her from the slopes of Gorm Vûdoc—before it suddenly vanished, leaving in its wake a man standing no further than two strides away. He was tall, slender, and handsome, staring at her with grinning eyes.

"What is your name, fairest daughter of Earth?" spoke Kamani in the flesh. His voice was a gentle breeze that calmed the wind.

The girl swept a stray lock from her brow and returned her caller's smile. "I am your loving servant, Father. Name me what you will."

Without hesitation, the man went down on one knee, running his eyes over a patch of wildflowers growing at his feet. Reaching for the stem of his choice, he delicately plucked a flower from the ground—then stood and presented it to the girl. "Your name is but my first gift to you, Issalzon. Take this blossom from my hand...and feel life quicken in your womb. Our son shall be a king of men."

Tears of joy pooled in her eyes as the woman named Issalzon reached out to accept the Creator's offer...yet hers and his weren't the only eyes focused on the symbol of their union. The Asendath's banks were but a stone's throw away; and there, perched on a gnarled limb just outside the cave where the river meets the mountain, a lone raven brooded. Up to this point it'd been watching the pair in silence; yet soon as the girl's fingers touched the flower, the bird gave a caw of protest, took wing, and retreated swiftly into the cave. Issalzon took no note of this, for now tears streamed down her face as the Father incarnate closed his hand on her own. But the disturbance wasn't lost on Kamani. For the briefest moment the corners of his mouth turned down, and his eyes fell cold as they followed the raven into darkness. Then the smile won out over the frown, just as that darkness streamed forth and swallowed the world about him, fading his scene to utter black...

Time leapt forward, and the setting returned. There was Issalzon alone once more on the mountainside, now relaxing her swollen feet in the river. One hand rested on her ripe belly as she sang a lullaby to her unborn son, and she laughed to herself when he kicked her in response. Yet this happy moment seemed already at its end—for slithering toward her through the weeds was a venomous snake. The woman neither saw the serpent nor did anything unknowingly that might've provoked it…yet soon as the creature came within range it reared its head and lashed out, sinking dripping fangs deep into her stomach. Issalzon let go a scream of agony as poison spewed out to fill her womb; but even as the cry resounded, the scene dissolved and reset itself again, her terrible note ending on a darker picture still…

Blood-smeared and broken, a filthy naked woman knelt in the failing light at the cave's entrance, holding a strange bundle at arm's length out over the river's black water. At first it seemed she might drop the thing in, consigning it forever to Asendath's embrace, then suddenly she yanked the object back to her heaving breast, releasing instead a string of sobs that rapidly degenerated into a maniacal fit of laughter. "Why do you hide from me, coward?" spat Issalzon at the ceiling, and her hateful words bounced from the walls to race off into fathomless depths beneath the mountain. In the shadows her crazed, sunken eyes were dreadful to behold. "Could the all-powerful One not spare his own child from death?"

Oh yes, hissed a voice in immediate answer. Not Kamani's soothing tones, but rather a sinister whisper creeping into her skull from somewhere out in the gloom. *Indeed he could, woman — if he truly cared for you at all. But your* Father *has the mind of a child: a naughty lad who never cleans up his toys. Your son is yesterday's trinket to him, easily tossed aside for the jewels of a new day. Don't be deceived by his false promises! I am here with you now. Hearken to* me *instead…*

Taken aback by the sudden alien voice mixed in with her thoughts, Issalzon pulled her stillborn baby tighter to her bosom — as if the infant weren't already beyond protection. Her gaze darted to and fro, seeking the source of the words but finding nothing. "Who are you?" she shouted…and for an instant it seemed she might regain her senses and flee. But the voice returned just then, stronger than before:

You know me! We've spoken before…if only in your dreams. Kamani won't restore your son to life, Earth-daughter — but I can fulfill that desire and more. All you need to do is renounce his claim to you. Curse your Father's name, and bind your soul forever to the Night!

For a few moments thereafter Issalzon wavered as the insistent voice drew in its net about her, but in the end she found nothing from her former life to sway her against its persuasions. Following instructions given, she held her child out again above the Asendath…yet instead of releasing him to the river as originally planned, she lowered her prize beneath the frigid water, gripping it tightly as she cried aloud once more: "May the darkness consume you, Kamani! I'm your slave no longer!" Then she raised the tiny body from the sluggish flow, and the scene ended with a different cry than the one that had begun it: the birthing wail of her resurrected son…

Now the images came and went at a quickened pace, with no time for words and no sound at all. There was the Daemon's half-breed child as an adolescent: the first King scowling upon a massive ebony throne with his fiendish mother by his side. At their feet knelt the foul men and beasts who worshipped the boy as a god, and on his lap lay a withered black flower. A creature without eyes stood and raised a blood-filled goblet in salute to his master and mistress — then turned and drained the vessel's dark contents in a single long draught...

Next stood a solitary figure at the edge of a high sea cliff, the folds of his gray robe billowing in the wind as he observed a fleet of warships approaching over the choppy waves below. Presently this man held out a warding palm — and the ships stopped abruptly in mid-pitch or lunge, all held fast by the water beneath that was now a plain of solid ice...

A falling tower. A field of strangling vines. The Red King's throat slit by his lover in the depths of night. These all streamed past in the blink of an eye. Then at last came a vision of Tiramas Vendhane as he reached out to stroke his steed's ivory neck. Sound returned at the man's touch, and the horse snorted loudly...

...pulling Dragan suddenly awake. Instinctively he snatched up his sword, thrusting the steel out before him while he waited for his sight to focus in on...

The servant from the keep — Erroth — with one palm resting on Allethion and that black mask of his trained on the *DoomBringer's* face.

"Step away!" barked Dragan as he rose groggily, wiping sleep from his eyes with the back of a fist.

Slowly Erroth untangled his gloved fingers from the horse's mane and let the hand fall — but otherwise he made no move to comply with his host's command. Allethion nickered and nudged the servant playfully, craving more of the man's attention. "I didn't wish to startle you," replied the visitor in an unthreatening tone. "There's no need for that blade."

It took Dragan another moment or so to regain his bearings...yet fortunately for him it seemed Erroth was fully aware of — and sensitive to — his addled state, waiting patiently as Dragan reordered his jumbled thoughts. It was all coming back now, however. After bolting from the keep, he'd nearly mounted Allethion then and there to ride off into the failing light, so anxious had he been to set his hands about his mother's neck and squeeze the life from her. But good sense had prevailed before he could gather up the reins, and instead he'd led the horse to this very spot among the ruins to settle down for the night. He'd struck up a fire then to drive off the chill; yet even as he sat staring at the flames with the heat working its way into his flesh, his rage had steadily cooled to the point where he began to question the oath he'd just made. *The bitch shall die...* Was it really that simple? Slay his own mother on the grounds of rumors whispered in his mind by a pack of phantasms? Throw down his cherished armor without even testing the validity of their claim? He must've dozed off in the midst of those thoughts, then the visions had come. He couldn't recall ever dreaming so vividly before. "Why are you here?" he managed at last.

"Perhaps you've forgotten. My master said you might question me after you and he were done."

By now it'd become fairly clear to Dragan that this man wasn't out to cast some horrible spell on him, thus he sat back down, laying his sword across his lap. "So you *did* hear it all. In that case, sit...and take off that mask. If we're to speak openly, I'd have it be face-to-face."

At this invitation Erroth strode to a fallen pillar across the fire from Dragan and sat—but he didn't remove the mask. "That I won't do willingly," he said as he smoothed out his robe. "Another detail you might've missed?"

"I remember enough. Something about saving yourself for your new master, is that right?"

Although he could see nothing but black beneath the servant's drawn hood, Dragan felt Erroth's frown as surely as the sky was dark.

"Scoff if you like, son of Saedus, but know that I'm not bound to you *yet*. If your aim is to mistreat me, I'll return at once..."

"No!" said Dragan, surprising himself with the intensity of his response. It had just dawned on him that he *did* have some questions that needed answering. "Wait a moment. I meant no offense."

Erroth didn't reply to indicate he'd accepted this apology...but the man was still sitting there, and for Dragan that was enough to move on. "I'll respect your ritual. If only my own mask was not as infamous as the name it won me, I might well hide behind it from now till the day I die. But at least tell me how you came to serve Vendhane."

The visitor continued to sit in thought for a few breaths before replying with a question of his own. "You had an unusual dream just now, didn't you?"

It was all Dragan could do not to let his jaw drop at this—but somehow he kept his composure and simply nodded in return.

"Before you say I planted it in your head, hear me out. That's how it started with me. Not the exact dream as yours, mind you...yet it came from the same source. The Kings are men selected by Kamani himself, not some line of fools riding a birthright down the ages. And so it is also for their stewards. The blood of sorcery may flow through my veins...but without his mark on me, I'm little more than a charmer—just as you claimed."

"You had no choice, then."

"There's always a choice. Even for the Kings themselves. You can't give back your power once it's blossomed…but whether you use it for good or for evil—or even at all, for that matter—is entirely up to you. I chose to embrace my calling. The question is: will you?"

Dragan wasn't ready to go down that path at the moment, thus he quickly changed the subject. "Was it you who carved the White King's statue?"

The black mask dipped in a nod. "And I'll add his tale to a new *Book of Kings* as well. Yet in such works I'm but my lord's tool. His spirit guides my mind."

"And still you'd convince me not to be my mother's pawn." The *GrimHelm* shook his head then as if something weren't quite adding up. "I may owe you thanks, *steward*, for delivering my retainer from the sylvans and sending him back to me in one piece—but should I learn you've been playing me false…"

"I was there when you killed him," the servant cut in unexpectedly, seeming to gloss over Dragan's implication with his admission. "We were the first to find you seated upon his throne. You weren't ready to rule us then…and when you fled, you left us with nothing but chaos and civil war. Few men would judge me ill were I to play you false, slayer; yet—just as Nal'tanos told you—this goes well beyond revenge."

"Alright," said Dragan, setting his blade aside and reaching for a waterskin in its place. "You've made your point." He drank from the bladder and held it out to Erroth. The steward shook his head *no*, so Dragan shrugged and took another swig himself. Suddenly he frowned deep. "How do you know what I dreamt? Can you read my thoughts even now?"

"Only when your mind already lies open. The visions came to you from my master—if not from Kamani himself. Again, I am but an instrument. You've nothing to fear from me."

"I'm afraid of no man, wizard or not." As soon as the words left his mouth, however, Dragan knew they were no longer true. It was an automatic response that'd come from the many years of him actually believing it so. *But now?* He'd already admitted to Ûladriss that he feared his mother…and her pet G'nilbor had unnerved him as well. Today he'd been led to believe his armor held no magic: that the power had been inside him all along. A revelation that should embolden him all the more. So why did he feel the opposite, like any old fool could strike him down with hardly a fight?

In any case, Erroth passed over Dragan's bravado, continuing on as if he'd not even heard the hero's boast. "What do you recall from the dream?"

Dragan's hand rose to his chin as he gave this some thought. "No more than a few images now—though it seemed so real at the time. Some of it I recognize from the *Book of Kings*. The rest…I'm not sure."

"The trial of Issalzon…" sighed Erroth, his words coming out barely above a whisper.

The steward's question had been unnecessary, then. He'd seen all of it—or at least the greater part. "That's right," Dragan nodded, setting the waterskin down. "But what do such legends have to do with me?"

"They've everything to do with you—for whether you choose to believe it yet or not, *you* are next in line. The cycle's starting over. The age of the Black King is poised to begin anew. Will you follow in the footsteps of the first and become your mother's soulless puppet: a champion of the Daemon? Or will you accept the truth of the dream and nurture your gift as if tending the Creator's flower?" A pause. "The first King's reign nearly broke the world, Dragan Saedus. And now they call you *DoomBringer*. So I ask you again: will that name continue to bring doom only for your enemies on the battlefield…or will it spell the doom of us all?"

These words brought about a lengthy pause, during which no sound could be heard save the faint crackling of dying flames. There was hardly any wood to speak of out here in the desolation, and what little of it Dragan had managed to find among the ruins earlier he'd fed all at once. Presently he looked up from the coals: "Was I chosen because of my mother, then? If she'd not placed herself in league with the Daemon, would I be nothing more than a common, spoon-fed prince?"

"Perhaps. And maybe even a step further than that. Maybe you wouldn't have even been born…"

This time Dragan's jaw did drop. "Are you saying she saw beforehand what I'd become? That she *planned* it?"

"Perhaps."

"But that makes no sense at all! If it's my fate—as you say—to stand against her…"

"That's not what I said," Erroth cut in again. "I said it was your choice. All your life your mother's groomed you to choose her side. But remember what my master said: *her hold on you is slipping*. This breastplate of yours," he pointed a finger at it, "…is a crutch that should be cast away. As long as that tie remains, you can't hope to defeat her. Why don't you leave it behind when you depart on the morrow? I'll keep it safe until the day you return…until you can look upon it as nothing more than an heirloom."

Yet with these last words the servant had made a terrible mistake. Suspicion arose again in Dragan's mind at the thought of anyone wanting to lay hands on his armor, and he wasn't shy about making this known. "Do you take me for a half-wit, Erroth? Hand over my prized possession to a stranger I've known less than a day—who refuses to show me his face? Suppose I believe some portion of what I've been told here...but still the gaps are enough to keep even a simpleton wary!"

"What else would you know, then?" The steward's voice remained calm, but once more his invisible frown was tangible.

"Well, to begin with: what proof is there that the Father's real? Men hardly speak that name in oaths these days, much less in prayers—though the Daemon's never far from their lips. I've heard as many tales of the Creator as you have, no doubt...yet that's all there seems to be of him. *Myths.* I've witnessed a King's power with my own eyes, and my mother's involvement with dark forces seems evidence enough on that end. But tell me this, steward: if Kamani's so powerful, why does he allow his enemy to exist? How could he let the Daemon murder his own son, unless he's just as cold and cruel himself?"

"It's not our place to question the Father's mind," said Erroth firmly. "Yet if you must know: it's been said that Kamani let his son die as a test for his mortal lover, to see if she'd remain faithful even in suffering...or else would deny him and walk the easier path to evil. Perhaps if she'd not cursed him but continued to call upon him for aid, he would've restored the child to life himself without the Daemon's taint entering the line of Kings...and so much of the world's pain and suffering might've been avoided. Yet you're right about one thing, at least. We're living in an age of pagan gods and unbelievers."

Dragan shook his head slowly as if still unconvinced, yet a great portion of his anger had now faded. "Then you won't gape to find me among them." He took in a deep breath and let out a sigh. "I'm sorry, Erroth, but I can't make the promise you'd drag from me here. I need time to think things through. Away from this place. And away from Mother as well."

PART FOUR

42

She lit a final candle then leaned over the table, holding the glass close to the light and frowning at the single dark spot remaining within. This vial had once been filled to the brim with Tiramas Vendhane's congealed blood: a depository of power from which she'd been carefully rationing since her son first yielded it to her years ago. But at last it had come to this. The day she'd dreaded from the start.

Saedus of Ost let out a sigh before pulling the cork stopper free. Taking up a slender, bladed tool crafted exactly for the task at hand, she inserted this into the vial and began scraping up the last fleck of dried contents. Yet partway through removing the implement she froze, narrowing her eyes to cast an irritated glance over her shoulder.

"Back off, Seela!" she hissed—and the ghostly gray face floating mere inches from her own reacted at once, flying up and away from the table to vanish into the murk beyond her circle of candlelight. Yet Saedus could still sense her pet's presence as surely as she felt the utensil in hand. "Mind the reason I summoned you. You're to guard me against interruption—not cause it with your childish spying!"

As usual, the banshee sent no answer into the witch's thoughts. None of her five ever did so unforced. Theirs was a silent breed of spirit while their leashes were pulled tight. But woe be to any man should the mistress let go...

"Shall I tell you a story, Seela?" spoke Saedus again after a few moments had passed in silence. Her voice was sweet now, like a mother soothing her scolded daughter directly after administering a beating. "Something to pass the time?"

Again no response was received or expected, and another pause lingered as the sorceress went on with her work. If indeed Saedus was about to tell a story, it'd certainly be for her own benefit rather than the banshee's. Her nimble fingers glided easily through the steps of preparing this potion that she'd brewed now so many times before. A pinch of this, a spoonful of that. Stir, remove the cup from the heat or set it back, and so on. She needed something to distract her from the tedium.

"Once there was a princess with lovely white skin and flowing dark hair. An innocent little twit. Full of spunk and laughter. Her father was none other than Banen Israd, the mightiest warlord Ost had ever known; yet he cherished the girl above all the wealth and power in the world. All she needed to do was keep on laughing and dancing and pouting her days away, and she could've lived out her youth in spoiled, ignorant bliss...gossiping with her playmates and mooning at the lads sparring in the castle yard. But alas, that life wasn't to be! Someone she trusted showed her things he shouldn't have shown—and set her down the path to secret knowledge from which there's no return. You know of whom I speak.

And how I both love and despise him for it!"

At this point the witch reached for a nearby coffer and pulled it closer to her, unhooking the tiny latch and opening the ornate lid. Inside was a coarse, white powder: all that remained of the ground bones of the Beast of Thirannon. Taking a pinch from the dwindling pile, she dropped this into her cup and stirred before continuing:

"In those days Poltoros was a young man masquerading as a mere charmer, performing pathetic little illusions and such for the amusement of the court. The great Banen had no need of powerful sorceries, you see — and Poltoros was wise not to reveal himself outright. That surely would've branded him a dangerous rival in my father's eyes. So instead he sought to worm his way into favor over time. And part of that plan was his tutelage of me. He knew well that I had my father's ear: that if he could get me to embrace his arts, Banen would likely place more stock in them as well."

Her cup had begun to steam again over the burner, and Saedus absently took the vessel off and set it aside to cool. Only the fleck of Vendhane's blood still lay before her on the instrument's blade: the final and most potent ingredient to be added. She'd already begun to seal up and segregate the other miscellaneous components for removal from her workspace. And now she rose from the table with an armful of these and a single candle, moving off to the rear of the tent in order to stow them away. Presently her voice came again, intermingled with the sound of clinking glass as she set the containers one by one back in the strongbox from which she'd extracted them earlier.

"At first I simply found Poltoros' lessons amusing: yet enough so to keep me coming back to him. It didn't take long, though, for me to develop a real thirst for the arcane. No longer did my teacher need come searching for me nor scold me for not paying attention to his instruction. Soon he wished that he'd never opened the door to begin with, for I came knocking on it uncalled for, day and night, demanding to be shown more and more. I was no longer satisfied with mere parlor tricks, and whenever I pressed and saw him holding back, I became increasingly angry — eventually threatening to reveal his true nature and power to my father. And thereby threatening his very life."

"It was at this point he finally called my bluff, for he knew if I went through with the boast — and he was either exiled or slain — that I'd be without a teacher; and he knew I'd rather have my learning stifled than ceased entirely. But in this he failed to account for one thing: I had my own plans for continued training. A secret training not even *he'd* be aware of until..."

"...it was far too late," a raspy voice finished for her. The old tutor himself, standing just inside the tent's entrance...

The sound of shattered glass and a sharp curse followed from where Saedus was kneeling over her cache. "Seela! You bitch!" she shouted into the blackness. "I said not *anyone!*"

"Don't be too wroth with her, mistress. I do still have a few *parlor tricks* up my sleeve, after all."

The witch snorted loudly at this, stood, and began a return to the table where her nearly completed potion sat. On the way back she raised her free left hand to rub its thumb against the ring on her index finger, muttering a few words in the process: and instantly the banshee's presence—sensed until that moment by both her and her unwelcome visitor—was gone. "Well, now that you've succeeded in interrupting me, servant, you might as well come in and sit down." She took her own seat as she said this, not bothering to face the steward. Instead she picked up the bladed tool and hastily stirred the dried blood into her cup. "I won't ask how much of that you heard. It's old news now, is it not? No doubt you've run it all through your mind a thousand times more than I have, scourging yourself over and over again for your foolishness."

Lifting her eyes from the cup, she saw that Poltoros had silently taken a seat across the table from her. With his maroon cloak's hood drawn in the dim light, the steward's face was a black pit amidst a shroud of shadows. For the span of a few breaths the pair sat staring at one another...until Saedus raised the potion to her lips at last and drained it dry in a single, slow draught.

"So that was the last of it..." said Poltoros as the empty cup clinked down on the table.

The sorceress nodded. "Enough to see me through the gates of Chalemos, if all goes according to plan. After that..." She let the thought trail off, seeing no need to elaborate. The lich knew how she meant to replenish her stock. They'd discussed it before, after all, and he'd likely be no more receptive to it now than he'd been earlier. Somewhere inside this withered shell before her still lurked the heart and soul of the man Poltoros once was—and that man had been more of a parent to Dragan than she'd ever hoped or cared to be.

It wasn't that she felt devoid of any attachment to her son. She still recalled fond memories from his youth—and he'd served her unquestioningly for several years into his manhood. But those days were long since gone. Dragan was too strong and willful now to be left unfettered any longer. *It's not like I'll be without him,* she told herself again. *It'll be just as it is with Poltoros. No...better than that. As it is with Valreecius.* And as it would likely be with any other who threatened her dominance but was too valuable to simply crush and leave lying in the dust. Dragan would remain her son—and even retain his power, to some extent—but under no circumstances could she allow him to come into his true inheritance.

"I'll never forget the look on Banen's face," mused the lich, "...when he saw the first of the goblins leap down from the wall to the yard. So many times he'd scoffed at my tales of them…sworn they were no more than childhood fancy. I was right there — smiling beside him — when they ran him through. He was too shocked to flee. He drew his blade but only glanced at it like it was some foreign thing he didn't know how to use."

"And now you regret it," said Saedus. "Of course you do! But you couldn't have known it would come to this. Your decision to join me then didn't seal your fate. You had so many years thereafter to change your mind…to run back to that rock you crawled out from under. Does immortality truly chafe you so?"

Poltoros was silent for a moment after this — and when he did speak, it was as if he'd not heard his mistress' rebuttal. "You murdered your father, as surely as if you'd plunged the blade into his guts with your own hand. Dragan is all that's left of your bloodline." Leaning into the candlelight, the steward let his haggard face show. "Who's to say if he sits the throne in Dolras that he won't simply brood upon it? Or perhaps he'll choose to wander the land as a beggar — like Santhû Basoth — or even sail off to the uncharted reaches of the world? One may be a King without possessing your ambition, mistress. I advise you to make peace with your son."

"Make peace with him?" the witch snapped. "You act as if he were already my equal and more! I've had enough of this, Poltoros. What brings you here in the dead of night?"

The lich leaned back into the shadows. "A scout has returned. It seems the rumor's true."

For a long moment the *Spider* remained still and silent, appearing as though she'd retain her composure even in the face of such a detrimental roadblock to her long-laid plans. Then suddenly she stood, backhanding her cup from the table in the process. "Berac! That ignorant, driveling bastard!" she raged at the top of her lungs. "How can this be?" She began stalking the tent as if searching for something else to lay her hands on and destroy. "It wouldn't have shocked me to learn the Sinians were riding south with that dolt's head in a basket — or even that he'd fled so deep into the desert that only vultures might hope to find him. But *this*? Lounging like a dog at his master's feet in Oen's palanquin, spit-shining the man's boots like some goddamned scullery maid? Tell me again, lich, why we chose to suffer him over Argen. Van may have lost his grip on sanity for a moment, yes — but we'd never have seen *him* and Deserus arm-in-arm!"

Poltoros chose to treat this question as rhetorical, whether it was meant to be or not. Silently he allowed Saedus a pause to let the tidings fully register. Then he spoke again: "I'm afraid that's not all the news. The scout claims *Baeldrin* is somehow behind this unlikely alliance."

The sorceress had returned to stand across the table from Poltoros as he was relaying this, and now the look of sheer hatred in her eyes might've withered any living man where he sat. But the steward merely pressed on: "I warned you not to dismiss the man lightly. You could've dealt with him personally — or at least given me the task. But instead you placed faith in that incompetent ambassador from..."

The witch's fist thundered down on the table so hard that it broke more than Poltoros' sentence. A thin crack wandered now through the center of the heavy wood almost end to end, nearly having split the entire table asunder. The effects of Saedus' potion had clearly surfaced.

Again the lich seemed unfazed, but this time it was the sorceress who spoke:

"They're *dead!* As soon as they set foot within my sight, I'll lay waste to them both!" Her frown gave way to a wicked smile. "No, that's too good for them. I'll lash them behind my chariot and drag them within a breath of their pitiful lives. Then I'll cast them in a cell and delight myself each day with their torture!"

"It might not be so simple as that. Remember Zera's claim...that the prince unleashed fell spirits to defend himself..."

Saedus laughed at this like a child over her playthings. "What better excuse for him to concoct for such a failure? The entire city's resources at his fingertips, and he let one unsuspecting man escape his grasp? The most recognizable figure in the city? Ridiculous! Baeldrin could no more command a minion than use his nose to scratch his ass..." Pulling back a chair, she reseated herself at the marred table. "Most likely, Nephos secretly aided Baeldrin's retreat. In any case, he'll pay for his incompetence or lies in due time. Domal is of no concern at present. We have their army, so I care little whether he retains order there or not."

"Yet there were some beyond Zera's men to support his story," said Poltoros, digressing somewhat to drive home his point. "Citizens who claimed the prince miraculously survived a plummet from the tower..."

"And by now they're probably claiming he sprouted wings and flew circles around the palace!" Saedus shook her head in disgust. "How Baeldrin managed to bring about this far-fetched union between Berac and Oen, we'll learn soon enough — assuming they don't turn on each other before they ever come within sight. But as I said: all that other rubbish doesn't matter. What *does* matter is the enemy host descending on us sooner than we expected — and in untold numbers. That's what we must discuss. We've been taking our sweet time pulling supplies upriver, lingering near every village on the path to let the Domalins grow soft on whores and wine. But no more! From here out they'll be glad to get bread and water and an hour's rest to keep their legs beneath them. You hear me, Poltoros? Go. Rouse G'nilbor and tell him to drag Sorec and his captains here by their ears if he must!"

"Perhaps you should summon Valreecius instead, mistress, and let the three of us go over the needed alterations first. I still think it unwise to let Sorec retain command over the Domalin army. What makes you think we can trust the man, especially when you insist on treating him like a common slave? If he were to abandon the field entirely...or worse, go over to Baeldrin..."

"I don't have the time—or the stomach—to inflate the general's ego, steward. I've promised him the governorship of Chalemos. He needs no more persuasion to remain loyal beyond that. Besides...haven't you seen how the fool ogles me? It seems the man's desire for my flesh is as strong as his thirst for power. No, Sorec will do exactly as I say. If not out of greed or lust, then out of *fear*. Fear of what I can do to him should he ever dare betray me."

In response to this, Poltoros simply nodded acquiescence and stood at once to depart. Yet before he could reach the exit, the witch's voice came again:

"You and Valreecius shall take the imps and goblins ahead at dawn. I want every Sinian village you find burned to ashes! Their fighting men slain, their livestock butchered, and their women and children enslaved. Am I clear?"

"As you command."

43

The chill of a sunless dawn kissed Bronwyn's cherry lips as she inhaled her first breath of the morning. Yet even so, her naked body was warm as it pressed against her lover beneath the woolen blankets of their cot. She felt the rhythmic rise and fall of Astelidus' broad chest as he slept beside her. His face appeared peaceful in the dim light. *No dreams of your brother this night, my dear? How long must Ban haunt you?* She freed a hand from the covers to gently brush a lock of stray red hair from his brow. A grin formed on his lips as he stirred slightly, but his slumber wasn't broken.

The two had chosen to ride with Fedrin Rae's host out of Mardotha, leaving behind Crûthior's dust and grime for the pristine, grassy plains of Sinia. The old warrior's fatherly relationship with Bronwyn had been mostly what decided this for her, but Astelidus' reasoning had been that Fedrin was now in command of the army's vanguard. Sinia's champion wouldn't be denied a moment of fighting should they be waylaid before reaching the intended ground. A great battle was soon to be had, for to the west along the river Olendarth, Saedus of Ost marched now with all her strength on their homeland. Astelidus yearned for a chance to prove himself against this new foe—even to face Dragan Saedus himself, should the dog still be nipping at his mother's heels. In fact, Bronwyn had already heard Astelidus boasting before his men when the latter subject had arisen:

"His defeated foes, you ask? Do you mean the ones we witnessed ourselves in Mardotha? Talmar Rû the Heavy-Handed? The Lion of Agrardob? Worthy, I'll admit. But only men—and Mardothan men, at that. What if the witch's son had taken up with the enemy from the start? How would he have faired against you, the stout warriors of Sinia? I say he would've been beaten into the dirt by the same mighty shields that were used to protect him!"

"Or do you mean those foes existing only in the glamorized tales of his own bodyguard: a superstitious gang of mercenaries from some remote land? Are we to sup on the food of fables? Trolls and bear-men and the like? Ha! These are nothing more than fodder for the bard's song. Bedtime stories for children! And the White King? He met his doom, indeed…but does anyone truly know how? Could the witch of Ost not have twisted the minds of common folk to the glory of her ilk?"

"Hear me, men! This dog Dragan feeds on the fear inside men's hearts. Do not let him consume your courage with his false legend…nor heed his boastful tongue when it vomits treacherous lies upon you. Don't cower before the same feet that fled our ranks on the eve of victory. Nay, if you see his disgraceful face, stand tall and take heart, for the son of Ny stands beside you!"

At this his men had cheered and beaten fists upon chests; yet many had left the rally doubting Astelidus' words, for the *DoomBringer's* mighty feats lingered in their minds. Bronwyn too had listened to her lover's boasts with incredulity and feared a confrontation between the two champions. Most of all the Sinians, she knew Dragan was different from other men...although she couldn't explain how or why. After learning that the *GrimHelm* and his Haxûdī had abandoned Gethod, she'd outwardly hoped he'd turned rogue: that he'd decided to seek out some new land and its people to torment with his infamy. This sentiment was shared by King Oen and his council, who surmised that a siege of Gethod — no matter how brief — would've kept the Ithiros occupied during Saedus' invasion of Sinia. Yet already some of their Ithirian allies had trickled back into their ranks, no longer needed in defense of their home. And these few claimed others would soon follow. Something had gone awry with the witch's plans — but to what end exactly, no one knew. And despite what she'd expressed to the council, Bronwyn secretly felt certain she'd not seen the last of Dragan Saedus.

Leaving Astelidus to his sleep, she rose to slip on her undergarments, a ruby tunic, and over that a leather jerkin. Heavy boots were laced from ankle to knee over dark leggings. She pulled her hair into a ponytail, dropped her dagger into its sheath hung about her waist, and exited the tent.

The encampment was coming to life, although the drear morning seemed not to reciprocate. A gray blanket hung low across the dome of the sky, making the Sinians look colorless as they moved about tending their various duties. Some attendants disassembled tents and gathered wood while other servants fetched water and began preparing the morning meals. A few sentries still stood their nightly posts as other warriors began donning their armor for the new day. This camp was a watch post, made high atop a plateau above the main host that had bivouacked in the valley below. Bronwyn espied the army from afar, and from her vantage the men looked like ants crawling along the ground. They too were performing their morning rituals, preparing for another day's march that would lead them inexorably to death or to glory. But before she could contemplate her people's fates any further, she noticed the brothers Rindus and Garenor — Fedrin Rae's young bodyguards — chatting to one another on the plateau's ledge. They rarely left his presence these days.

"Brothers," she hailed the pair, swiftly closing the distance to them. "Where's Fedrin? I don't see him about..."

The elder of the two, Rindus, glanced at his sibling before settling his eyes on Bronwyn. "My lady, the commander yet sleeps."

"Sleeps?" she questioned incredulously. "Who watches his door?"

"No one...presently." Rindus seemed content with divulging nothing more, but as Bronwyn opened her mouth to protest, Garenor interrupted her:

"Something strange happened, Bronwyn. Just before dawn, he stepped out of his tent and commanded us to finish our watch elsewhere. When I asked him why, he looked at Rindus and said: 'Do it—and don't return until I call for you.' Brother was already pulling me away before I could object. We decided to take our position here, where at least we could see his tent from afar."

Bronwyn peered across the camp. Her old mentor's tent looked quiet. Too quiet. "You fools!" she scolded them. "Must I show you the scar on Astelidus' chest? Come!" She waved for the brothers to follow her as she turned and made straightway for Fedrin's tent. "Something's amiss…"

Garenor began to follow at once—but Rindus grabbed his arm, holding him fast.

"She's right, Rin," Garenor responded hastily to the contact. "Remember the sand elf? In the middle of the entire army! Were it not for Ny, Bronwyn would be dead…"

The other paused for a moment then said: "Right. Let's go."

When Bronwyn reached the tent she raised her hand, ready to fling aside the leather flap of the entrance…but something stopped her. *Voices.* Stepping aside, she pressed her ear to the thin canvas of the shelter instead. Seeing Rindus and Garenor approaching, she gestured for them to halt.

"…take more than some dramatic speech of mine to save your hide this time, lad!" came Fedrin's deliberately hushed words from inside. "Daemon! I ought to be screaming for the guards now…while fending you off with a drawn blade!" A long, audible sigh. "But that wouldn't be wise, would it? Only a fool would raise his weapon to threaten you: even one you still claim as your friend. Am I wrong, Dragan? Tell me you wouldn't lay me low then maim half the damned army as you carved your way back out of here…"

Whatever answer Saedus' son was preparing to give to Rae's query, it never came—for on hearing the word *Dragan* leave the old bear's lips, Bronwyn had set her jaw, raised her chin high, and injected herself into the tent. The heavy flap smacked shut behind her on Fedrin's last word, whereupon both men turned on the newcomer with wide eyes.

For a lingering moment Bronwyn merely stood with arms folded under her breasts, returning her lost love's stare with a look that didn't quite portray its intention. Her frown and posture were all bitter hatred and revulsion, indeed: but try though she might, she couldn't hide a sparkle of *anticipation* in her eyes. Finally her mouth opened to break the silence that'd enveloped them all—yet once again words were foiled by an intrusion. First Garenor then Rindus—hot on his sibling's heels—came barreling through the entrance, nearly knocking the king's niece to the floor in their rush to be first at her side. Hands were on hilts even as they reined in…but not till they caught sight of the *DoomBringer* did they consider drawing swords. Garenor pulled his blade out nearly an inch before he thought better of it and slammed it back home. Rindus' hand never moved at all.

Fedrin's words of a few moments ago, although not heard by the brothers, were no doubt swimming in their minds as well: "*...only a fool would raise his weapon to threaten you...*"

"Lord Saedus!" said Garenor, rupturing the muteness at last.

"This man's no lord!" Bronwyn snapped, never taking her gaze off Dragan. "He's a snake in the grass, waiting to sink his fangs into whatever unsuspecting creature crosses his path! How dare you show your face here, you *monster* — with the blood of betrayal still wet on your hands? And you!" It took an effort to peel her eyes away from Dragan and fix them on Rae instead. "You're damned right, you should've called for the guards! But instead I find you closeted in here with the bastard, plotting who knows what heinous scheme with him..."

"That's enough!" roared Fedrin, conjuring a visible flinch from his chastiser. Bronwyn hadn't been expecting such an outburst from her old friend, and he used the moment to his advantage. "Get away from the entrance, all of you, and *keep your voices down!* There's no need to be rash. He's threatened no one here, at least — and I say he deserves a chance to be heard. There's hardly a man in this camp that doesn't owe the *GrimHelm* a life debt — including myself at least thrice over! And you, girl, of all people..." He shook his head to finish.

In answer to their lord's command, the brothers eased around Bronwyn and strode further inside. Garenor took a seat at Fedrin's table, but Rindus opted to lean against a post at the rear of the shelter — his arms crossed, and shadows all but hiding a scowl on his face. Bronwyn still hadn't moved, other than to resume her glare at Dragan:

"Well? Spit it out then, *hero*. I can't wait to laugh at the lies you've prepared to spare you from the headsman. Or have you merely come cowering beneath a white flag, playing errand boy for your infernal mother?"

At this point Dragan — who'd been barely able to hold Bronwyn's gaze out of shame — gave up the ordeal entirely, taking a seat opposite Garenor then resting his skull in the palms of his propped arms. His eyelids closed as if a sudden weariness had taken him, and another moment passed before he could speak:

"If it's my head you want, Bronwyn, then do what you must." Slowly he opened his eyes and cocked his head in her direction. "I can't blame you for it, and I won't resist when they come to lay hands on me. Still, I never swore an oath of service to your king, so there's no treason to be judged. At worst I'm an enemy who'd turn friend against our common foe: no different than Berac and the horde of Mardothans that've joined you. War is all I know. I'm drawn to it like a fly to dung. Perhaps Deserus will choose again to have me with him, just as he did before. In any case, I'm done with Saedus. Soon I'll slay her — or she me — and it seems either outcome will please you."

Perhaps if Bronwyn could yet see the proud, fearless warrior she'd known before in Dragan, she would've indeed raised an alarm by now; but neither his words nor the look of him were the same as they'd once been. The longer she stood staring and listening, the more her emotions became jumbled. On the one hand, she was furious—for the obvious reasons given. But on the other, she could barely control an impulse to throw her arms about her former lover's neck in her excitement to see the man again, old feelings swiftly rekindling against her will. And even as her conflicting thoughts battled with one another, Dragan was continuing to address her with talk of his regret and shame...and of wanting to redeem himself after finally breaking free of the chains that'd so long bound him. Could she really condemn him to execution, if the decision were hers to make? Or would she fall wailing at her uncle's feet to prevent it instead?

"Rin's gone!" said Garenor suddenly, cutting Dragan off in mid-sentence and snapping Bronwyn from her trance. All eyes darted to the support against which the elder sibling had been propped just moments ago. "He must've ducked out back! Shall I go after him, Lord Rae?"

"Well, Dragan," Fedrin sighed again. "It looks like you'll get your audience with the king, whether we like it or not. No, Garenor...let him go. We might as well sit tight."

"I didn't touch Mehdurin or Kalen...or even Irenys," mused Dragan, picking up his monologue right where he'd left it off: as if his impending seizure were of no concern. "But I allowed all but the old man and his servants to perish, so I'm guilty all the same. I'm not here for your forgiveness. I don't deserve it. Just let me take the field against my mother! Only then can we hope to defeat her..."

"We?" posed Bronwyn incredulously. "There's no *we*! Our men won't trust this traitor, Fedrin—especially not the Ithiros! They'll likely attempt to slay him on sight, should even the most cowardly among them lay eyes on him!"

"I'm not sure I agree," said Rae, taking a seat himself at last. "If we can keep our own boys off the Mardothans, then surely we can keep our Ithirian friends off of Dragan. It will take much more than a speech from the likes of me, as I said. But a command from your uncle—well, that's another thing altogether. Besides, sins of the past will be all but forgotten once the killing starts. As long as his blade's pointed in the right direction, they'll follow the *DoomBringer* through hell if need be. He's turned the tide of battle for them time and time before—and they know he can do it again."

"Follow him through hell, you say?" Bronwyn stepped to the table to loom over her subject. "Then on into *betrayal*? Rally them against the witch first, only to turn them against our new allies in the hour of need—or lead them straight into the jaws of a trap? Who's to say he'll even make it to the battle? Suppose he's begged this audience just to put his sword through the king's belly?" Her eyes flicked back to Fedrin. "We have a new champion. Or have you forgotten?

A man loyal as he is strong. *Astelidus* shall lead us where this vagabond failed!"

Even as his name was spoken, the son of Ny appeared unexpectedly before them, pushing his way inside with naked steel in hand; and instantly on seeing her lover standing there with a look of pure hatred aimed at his sworn nemesis, Bronwyn recalled that Rindus was one of those toadies who'd listened to all of Astelidus' vaunts concerning Dragan. The man must've run straight to his idol after slipping from the tent. Still…not enough time had passed for Rin to have stirred the hero and waited for him to dress and arm himself. Astelidus must've already been up and about…likely searching for her.

Panic struck her like a mallet. Astelidus had boasted too loudly and publicly to simply step aside now and let Dragan be on his way — whether to the king for judgment or otherwise. One of these two men she had feelings for would likely die today. All because of her.

"No!" she cried out, rushing at Astelidus to get her face in his line of sight — even daring to grasp and turn his jaw to force his gaze on her instead of Dragan. "Look at me! Calm yourself, my love! Please…*listen*…"

Quick as a cobra's strike, Astelidus' hand darted up and grabbed Bronwyn's wrist, yanking it so forcefully from his face that she gasped in pain as he released it. Immediately both Fedrin and Dragan were on their feet, leaving Garenor the only person still seated in the dwelling. The young man was apparently torn as to which side to take in this blossoming altercation, and both his mouth and his eyes were open wide in surprise and confusion.

"*My love…*" muttered Dragan, moving his eyes from Ny's face to Bronwyn's. "I should've guessed."

Bronwyn winced visibly at these words, and Fedrin turned on Dragan to say: "Now hold on, lad…" Clearly these two were expecting a rage of jealousy from the *GrimHelm*. But instead, keeping his gaze on the woman, Dragan answered:

"It's alright, Fedrin. I abandoned her — and so beautiful a flower mustn't be left to wither from neglect." Then, glancing at Astelidus: "I've no grievance with you, son of Ny. She's all yours. Make her happy, and you have my blessing…"

At this point Astelidus had held his tongue for as long as he possibly could: a near-superhuman effort indeed. The compliment his rival had given Bronwyn — after he himself had just handled her roughly — only served to enrage him more than if Dragan had verbally lashed out at him directly. "She was never yours to give, coward! Nor will she ever return to you now she's known the love of a *real* man. We spit on your worthless *blessing*! You claim no grievance with me out of fear alone — but it matters not, for *I've* a grievance with *you*. One so hot it sets my blood to boiling. Draw your sword, betrayer, and let's settle this matter outside!"

"Careful, Ny," warned Dragan slowly, his volume not rising to the challenge put before him. "My newfound humility isn't without limits."

"*Patience*, Astelidus..." Bronwyn urged again, reinforcing the *DoomBringer's* words. "Deserus will judge Dragan's fate. There's no need to risk your life over this...this *scoundrel*..."

While the king's niece was speaking thus, Rindus and another of Astelidus' sycophants entered the tent to check on their leader; and upon seeing his brother reappear, Garenor finally stood as well. Then it was Fedrin's turn to chime in: "I suggest you listen to her, son. Everyone knows your worth. You've nothing to prove to us by this except your childishness if you press on. Have you lost all your wits, man?" The old bear released a chuckle despite himself. "Challenging the *GrimHelm* to a duel?"

Seemingly ignoring Rae's comments, Ny chose to address Bronwyn instead: "You call him *scoundrel*—but once more I see through your words. Don't try to deny it! Your sickness for the man still festers..." Here he spat forcefully on the ground at Dragan's feet, whereupon Bronwyn swiftly backed away from him in horror. "At least Fedrin speaks plain. Neither of you gives me a chance—but I tell you: I don't care if this bastard's indeed the greatest warrior in all the world. That means nothing to me, and it'll mean even less when we step toward each other out there. Neither his fame nor his lackeys will come to his aid then. It'll be just him against me—and may the best man win!"

A ripe pause followed during which all stood as statues save Dragan alone. Putting one foot forward, he made a display of rubbing Ny's spittle into the dirt with the toe of his boot. "Did you actually believe such bravado would set my knees to shaking, Astelidus? I didn't come here to trade blows with every single man who holds a grudge against me. Your king needs soldiers—not corpses. It would be a shame to snuff the life of one with such confidence in his prowess as you...whether you've truly the skills to back it up or not. No. I won't fight you today. Go now, and leave me to the wisdom of your betters."

To all present except Ny himself, this reply from Dragan was accepted as the final say on the matter: a speech filled with nothing but common sense and cold, hard fact. Rindus even reached out to touch Astelidus gently on the arm as if he were about to escort some elderly woman back to her bedchamber. Ny shrugged the hand off violently but without a verbal rebuke: for his mind was desperately hunting the words that would break the *GrimHelm's* calm—lest he must resort to charging his enemy here and now where they stood. Then suddenly they came to him like a bolt of lightning illuminating the night sky:

"So that's it, then? You mean to give up the sword in favor of wagging your lying tongue in a circle of old men? Whether we fight and I defeat you, or you slink away, you give all the glory to *me*. Astelidus Ny: the man the *DoomBringer* fled from! I'll see those words spread from the Great Ocean to the wastes—and your name will live on only as a footnote in *my* legend. I've already taken your woman…and soon your fame will be mine too. So why don't you go ahead and hand over that fine breastplate you're wearing as well, since you'd deny me the pleasure of stripping it from your mangled hide!"

And with that, Astelidus had at last hit the mark: not with the intended barb concerning stealing Dragan's woman and fame, but rather with the spontaneous afterthought regarding the breastplate. Just as Erroth had lost Dragan's trust in Dolras by urging the champion to give up the armor, just so now the son of Ny had won his argument by evoking that same emotion in his would-be opponent. Suddenly Dragan's sword was in his hand, pointing past Astelidus to the tent's opening. "No man shall ever don this plate but *me*, wretched cur! You've just spoken your dying words!"

"Dragan, no!" cried Bronwyn. "How could you give in to such foolishness?" She took a step forward as if to fling herself upon him — but Fedrin caught her by the arm and reeled her in, squeezing her contorting body against his heavy chest.

Astelidus merely smiled and spun on his heel, leaving the dwelling with Rin and the other warrior in tow — and Dragan followed them immediately as a man possessed, not taking his eyes from the exit for an instant, even with Bronwyn's earsplitting curses flying directly at his skull.

Then lastly Garenor shuffled toward the portal as well, offering an unheard condolence to Torensus' daughter as she collapsed sobbing in Fedrin's arms.

44

A strident clang and scrape of metal shattered the plateau's stillness, and the son of Ny groaned, stumbling back into his bearers' shields. The morning bustle outside Fedrin's tent had faded to nothing just before this first crossing of blades, leaving behind it a field of onlookers with held tongues and bated breaths. Yet now, as Astelidus rebounded from his surprise at Dragan's freakish strength and rushed his enemy again, the yard came alive with intermittent clashes of combat. Sounds whose interval sped and slowed with each burst of aggression, like wind chimes left out in a gathering storm.

The next exchange pierced the gloom: three ringing notes in rapid succession followed by a sharp slap. Ny had planted his left foot and sent his armored right shin smashing into the side of Dragan's knee, buckling the struck leg and causing the *DoomBringer* to stagger. The kick created an instant of vulnerability in his rival on which Astelidus should've capitalized. Any sane man who'd witnessed Dragan fighting before today would've viewed this as a god-given opportunity against a godlike adversary. But whether out of sheer arrogance or raw emotion or both, Astelidus abandoned logic and let the chance pass, wasting the opening in an attempt to incite the gathered crowd.

"You shouldn't have returned to us, deserter!" he spat, lifting his voice next from Dragan to the host: "This man butchered our brethren in Ithiria!"

Unlike during his earlier bout with the *Baneful*, however, Astelidus received no roars nor throbs in answer from the encircling mass. Some may have cursed Dragan under their breaths—but thus far none of them had summoned the nerve to invigorate either combatant with cheers or the drumming of their weapons on shields. The *GrimHelm* had abandoned them and reportedly betrayed them also; yet the day wasn't so long gone when he'd occupied the role Astelidus was now trying so hard to fill. To most observers, no doubt, this contest seemed wrong.

Dragan chose not to bite back with words, flicking his sword out instead as he leapt forward, feinting to one side. The blade's tip drew a crimson line across Ny's shoulder before the Sinian could block, yet still the young man didn't shrink from the sting of first blood. On the contrary, it seemed this shallow wound had actually freed Astelidus from some intangible burden that'd been weighing him down. Perhaps—despite his outward confidence at the onset—he'd been unable to fully shake an inner fear that left him stiffer and warier than his usual martial self. Or perhaps the cut was like a splash of water in a drunkard's face, waking him from his delusion and reminding him that every morsel of his concentration and skill would be required to survive this challenge.

Either way, Astelidus' counterattack sequence was a thing of blinding speed and calculated rage that left Dragan backpedaling toward the ring of shields. *If I can just manage to pin him there...* Astelidus thought, ending his combination with a devastating front kick to Dragan's chest. A normal man would've lost his feet from the sudden force of that impact; but again the *GrimHelm's* aberrant physical attributes came into play. To Astelidus' horror, an instant later he found that *he* was the one who'd fallen on his rear and was gazing up at his towering foe like a red-faced boy struck by an angry father. It felt as though he'd thrown his weight against a rock wall and been brutally repulsed.

Dragan, on the other hand, had hardly taken a step back.

Panic threatened to slay Astelidus at that moment. The *DoomBringer's* blade would've been merely an afterthought to the actual killing: a tool to scrape dead flesh from a spirit ground to dust. Yet he refused to wilt before these people. He would gladly receive the Bastard's blade into his body, if that meant saving him from the life of a craven. No, he wouldn't cringe. He would *fight.*

Regaining his feet, Astelidus barely got his blade up in time to block the next attack from Dragan; yet rather than falling back in defense until he could recover his stance, the red-haired warrior roared back with another lightning barrage of blows. Unfortunately for him, however, all seven strikes in this succession were expertly deflected. Indeed, Dragan's parries appeared effortless: as if the Prince of Ost were merely engaged in a fencing match, his casual motions focused on speed alone with no power behind them. Yet power there was. Astelidus had to put all of his strength and swiftness behind every swing of his own to keep from being thrown back or disarmed. How long could he keep this up? He saw now that he'd tire long before his opponent; and each moment Dragan lasted against him was another moment added to his shame. He needed to end this quickly. It was time to take a risk. A gamble that'd likely end in either a brilliant victory or his sudden death.

Sliding to the ground at Dragan's feet, Astelidus swept his blade in a deadly arc that forced the *GrimHelm* to leap aside. Yet even as Dragan swarmed back in for the kill, Astelidus arose in a blur, planting a perfectly timed spinning backfist on the Bastard's outstretched hand—knocking the sword from his nemesis' grip.

The crowd finally stirred at this, issuing a collective gasp in surprise at Ny's unexpected triumph; and over the top of it came the stifled cry of a woman being forcibly held back from entering the ring. Bronwyn—with one of Fedrin's hands clamped over her mouth and the other latched onto her arm...

Astelidus heard these sounds and exulted as they registered in his mind, but this time he had the sense not to pause and gloat. Taking a step back, he put his entire weight behind a wide slash of his blade: a strike aimed directly at Dragan's neck. A cut to change the world, elevating the son of Ny above even his hated rival's perch amidst the lofty peaks of fame and legend. Never again would he need worry about filling his brother Ban's shoes. No man alive nor dead would overshadow him after this day.

Dragan, momentarily dazed by the loss of his weapon, registered Astelidus' follow-up swing too late. He'd only just begun to throw himself out of reach when Ny's blade struck home with a vengeance, conjuring a muffled shriek from Bronwyn on the tail end of the collision. Yet the sound of the impact itself was not what anyone gathered there — including Dragan — had expected. Instead of a sickening slice and crunch to accompany the *DoomBringer's* head on its flight from his shoulders, the note was a booming metallic clash. A herald to proclaim the breastplate's curse as Astelidus' weapon slammed into Dragan's steel collar and faltered, blade snapping in half.

Shocked and enraged at how close he'd just come to death, Dragan reacted without thinking. Lunging forward, he rammed his skull straight into Astelidus' nose, grabbed the warrior's hand that was still holding the jagged hilt half of the broken bastard sword...

And slid the shard deep into Astelidus' neck.

A dark cloud erupted from Ny's jugular to wash over Dragan, transforming the victor's face into a sadistic mask of blood. Then the *GrimHelm* shoved his foe to the ground and loomed over the body, releasing pent emotions in a sharp roar of anger and relief.

And so arrived the end of Astelidus Ny. In that penultimate moment before his soul slipped free of its mortal shell, the Sinian's eyes met those of his slayer. Yet what he found in them was neither calm blue sky nor angry red flame. What his dying mind imagined there instead were two black ellipses running through orbs of yellowish-green light: the serpentine slits of the Daemon.

Your lack of patience shall be the death of you, she'd foretold of him once in a dream. And now her words came streaking back to Ny like a barrage of searing arrows, their impact waking him in a flash from each and every foolish figment of youthful invincibility he'd ever known. The last thoughts of a doom-struck man. A confrontation with all his life's follies in the blink of an eye.

Then his world went black.

"No!" wailed Bronwyn, having worked her lips free from Fedrin's muffling paw. *"You murderer!"* She writhed wildly as the man-at-arms regained a clamp over her mouth, but Rae's grip held as he swiftly yanked her away from the circle. In another moment the pair was swallowed by the crowd.

But Dragan had heard the woman's accusing scream, and suddenly he reeled back from Ny's corpse, aghast, swinging his head about in a desperate search of the onlookers' faces. Surely there was a pair of eyes in that ring that wouldn't condemn him for what he'd just done? He had to find that one understanding expression. He had to know there was still some shred of humanity draped over the savage monster he'd become.

Yet one-by-one the faces met his pleading gaze and shied away, till it seemed the earth itself had utterly shunned him.

And so, one-by-one, Dragan undid the clasps of his bloodstained breastplate, letting the hated armor fall to the ground.

This time, there'd be no going back for it.

45

A beautiful purple and orange twilight spread the heavens of northern Sinia as if formed by a masterful artist's strokes, the evening sky capped by a cluster of ominous clouds traversing its expanse. A relentless autumn gale drove this dark army east toward the lonely mountain, biting gusts diving to the earth to set banners streaming and the flames of hundreds of fires dancing from close at hand on out to mere pinpricks of light nearing the horizon. Yet, though there was this *motion*, it might've been that time wasn't actually striding forward, and rather the clouds were a chain encircling the globe, the flickering fires deathless as stars of night, and the banners immortal heralds to forever announce the reign of Mother Earth. Yes, with no eyes to mark its passage, this scene indeed might've been an endless cyclical reality, had no *men* been present to insinuate individualism and constant change into the landscape. As it was, however, between one surge of air and the next the camp's silence was broken by the snarling and yelping of dogs fighting over a tossed bone and the ringing of a smith striking metal against anvil. Then the wind rushed in, drowning all sound save its near-deafening roar.

The *DoomBringer* had no cloak nor hood to draw against the gale as it ripped through the unwalled prison cart's bars and stripped away his body's warmth. He was dressed only in the light arming clothes he'd been wearing on that fateful day when he'd struck Astelidus Ny down. Not that it mattered. Dragan Saedus no more felt a chill than the iron and wood caging him, for his thoughts were far away, fixed with his black gaze upon the blacker shadow of Gorm Nadur rising like a cruel spearpoint in the distance. Nearby his four guards sat in a semicircle about their cookfire, passing food and drink back and forth, speaking just loudly enough under the buffeting wind for their captive — had he been listening — to hear their voices but not make out the words.

Was his mother out there, even now, her own gaze spanning the divide to return his stare? Was that her evil shadow cast on the mountain?

Barely a week in this jail, yet already Dragan felt a horrible madness creeping over him. Not from isolation. He could handle that. After all, before his return to the poisonous Sinian bosom, he'd been traveling alone in the wilderness for a month, maybe longer. And not from a fear of whatever awaited him when his sentence behind bars was done. There were indeed things the *GrimHelm* had come to fear since the day he turned his back on these people — but never would he cower at the thought of mere death or inflicted harm. Not even the shame of defeat nor the loss of his legend held top slot in the ranks of his anxiety anymore. *Revenge* and *redemption*. The thought that he might perish without accomplishing these things is what terrified him now: the fear that each day he spent cooped in this cell was one day closer to the witch's imminent victory — or else her defeat at another's hands than his own — depriving him of his day of reckoning. That this was the spot where Oen planned to engage Saedus, the signs about Dragan were plain enough; but other than this obvious fact, he'd no idea how long they had left to wait. The guards were tight-lipped, and part of the king's judgment had been no visitors allowed.

Many had come to stare from a distance, true enough — Fedrin most notably among them, nodding his head in sad greeting whenever he caught the captive's eye — but none had yet dared defy Deserus' order. And likely none would. For a day or two after his incarceration, Dragan had actually hoped to see Bronwyn at Rae's side. Hoped and dreaded all at once. But no...it'd been foolish of him to think she'd want to do anything other than spit in his face and then run him through: for she above all was the victim of his crimes. He realized now that if anything could stave off his madness, it would be to shut her out of his mind completely. So why had his thoughts strayed to her again just now, when he was trying so hard to set fire to that damned mountain with nothing but the fury of his glare? Why couldn't he stay focused on his mother's sickening, unnatural beauty instead of imagining his fingers tangled in Bronwyn's gorgeous golden hair: her head tilted back...those luscious lips eagerly parting...

"Lady Bronwyn!"

Yanked from his reverie, Dragan spun his head to the spot from whence the guard's startled salute had come: and there, across the flames from the semicircle of now risen figures, King Oen's niece indeed stood in the flesh. Her curves were all but hidden beneath the folds of a voluminous gray robe; but even in the dim light, her stunning face shown clear. In one hand she held a shuttered lantern at her side, and a wrapped bundle of some sort was tucked beneath her other arm.

"My lady," the same guard addressed her again, having regained a degree of composure. He bowed low. "Forgive us. We didn't expect to see you here."

"Stand firm, Ellerin," said another of the four, taking a step toward the first as if the closer proximity to his brother-in-arms would add strength to his words. "Remember the king's command! Not even *she's* allowed this near."

"Easy, soldier," Bronwyn returned with a charming smile, setting down the lantern to pluck the bundle from her arm. Thus far she hadn't even glanced at Dragan's cage. "I'm aware of my uncle's orders. But look here: I've brought you something..."

The guards watched her curiously as she began to unwrap layers of fabric to reveal the prize inside. *A bottle.* And not just some jug of water, Dragan saw at once. Its characteristic shape showed it to be a container of the most sought-after drink in all the lands: Tholmian liquor. Immediately the eyes of all four men — even those of the stern one at Ellerin's shoulder — became wide as saucers. It was a wonder foam and drool weren't pouring from their mouths. Despite his own shock at seeing Bronwyn appear so suddenly among these men, Dragan nearly laughed aloud at their reaction.

Likely struggling to fight back her own amusement, Bronwyn grinned as she held out the gift for Ellerin to take. "Do you boys think Deserus cares who talks to Dragan now, on the very eve of war? Surely you've heard the report. Scouts say the witch will move into position under cover of moonlight—and that battle will be had at dawn! This bottle could be your last, friends. Take it, and each of you have a drink for me. I won't be long with him."

"But...my lady..." Ellerin started to protest—yet his voice was so devoid of conviction that the trailing end was hardly audible.

"I've brought him a blanket, you see? A *blanket*. And perhaps a few parting words..." This time Bronwyn feigned a pitiful half-smile in place of the alluring one she'd arrived wearing. Or was it feigned? Either way, it had the desired effect.

Ellerin and the man beside him exchanged a quick look before turning their hungry eyes again on the bottle. Finally the dour man shrugged: "A moment or two won't hurt, I reckon. But we'll be watching you. Just stay clear of the bars."

They accepted the bottle then and turned to reseat themselves at the fire, no doubt to begin immediately passing their gift around. To Dragan, however, they might as well have stepped through a portal to the void—for as soon as Bronwyn picked up her lantern and began to walk his way, it was as if no one else but the two of them existed in all the world. She stopped just shy of arm's length from the cage, unshuttered the lantern, and held it up so she could get a good look at what was inside.

Squinting, Dragan shied away from the sudden light—but Bronwyn merely stood patiently without a word, letting the warrior's eyes adjust. To say that her face was expressionless wouldn't have been quite the truth, for there was a hint of some hybrid emotion in the way she set her jaw and brow. *Grief? Rage? Pity?* How many others fought for supremacy in her mind? One thing was certain, though: there wasn't a trace of the mirth with which she'd greeted the guards.

"You shouldn't have come," said Dragan at last, his sight recovered enough to focus on his visitor. Then, suddenly recalling the soldiers, he nodded toward their cookfire: "That liquor will set at least one tongue wagging, and Deserus will hear about it come dawn—if not before. He'll not be as indifferent as you made him out."

Bronwyn had noticed the cart's external hook and was already in the process of hanging her light there as Dragan finished talking. Then, stepping closer, she shoved one end of her blanket through the bars. "Has fear of my uncle's wrath ever stopped me before? Well...go on. Take it."

Dragan hesitated a moment more then gave in and pulled the blanket into his cell. "Why are you doing this *now*, Bronwyn? Surely you don't expect me to swallow what you told them about *parting words*? No matter what happens here tomorrow, I'm to be dragged to Chalemos and put to trial. Both you and I'd be whisked away from any real danger like infants snatched up in their mothers' arms! This isn't our last goodbye..."

"Tell me why you did it!" Bronwyn started suddenly, her pent anger boiling to the surface at last. "That's the reason I've come. I want to hear you admit the truth. Tell me how you're a heartless bastard who'd murder his own child to retain his vanity! Tell me why you couldn't have just forced the fool to yield!" Here she paused for breath, tears welling in her eyes; but — as Dragan's jaw was clenched tight, teeth grinding in an effort to control his unjustified anger at these well-founded accusations — she immediately carried on. "Everyone knows it was Astelidus who started it. In his mind he'd already fought you and won before you ever set foot in Fedrin's tent. You're a lot of things, Dragan — most of them stomach-turning to dwell on! — but you're no half-wit. Why in Daemon's name did you let him goad you on like that? They all warned me about you from the start, and thus *I'm* the fool for not listening. Now look what's become of me! A sniveling trollop who can't stay away from the poison that's killing her..."

Another gust of air swept down on them, causing Bronwyn's hair — and her trickling tears — to stream across her face. She waited for the wind to subside, then wiped her cheeks with the back of her hand, pushing the loose, wet strands back in the process.

"Do you really think I could've made him yield?" said Dragan at last, staring at her as he draped the blanket about his shoulders. "He'd have struggled to the bitter end. *Gods!* If it wasn't for that cursed armor of mine, it would've been *my* pyre you watched burning afterwards in place of his. Or he'd have stripped my corpse — just as he threatened — and fed it to the dogs!"

"You're right. He'd never have yielded to you *willingly*," admitted Bronwyn after considering his words. "But if you'd given us a blasted moment before you struck him down, perhaps we could've stepped in...dragged him off and bound him till his wits returned!"

"And he'd have laid low the first man — or woman! — to lay a hand on him!" Dragan spat back, his composure slipping again. "He was *fey*. Both of us were. Don't you see? To have gone on living after being beaten by me...wouldn't that have been a fate worse than death for him?"

As the words sank into her skull — and she realized that the truth of them had been lurking in her mind as well, hiding just behind the grief of loss — Oen's daughter jerked a hand up over her face and turned her gaze aside.

Instantly Dragan felt remorseful, wishing he could recall his words...or do or say anything to ease the woman's pain. She was within his reach, but the hateful bars of his cell prevented him from gathering her into a comforting embrace, and speech utterly failed him. He could do no more than stand there, staring at her with his knuckles turning white from a terrible grip on the metal. Could he rip the bars out or bend them — with nothing but bare hands and brute strength — to get to her? Was this iron tougher than the rippling limbs and thick neck of the Beast of Thirannon? But no...he'd thrown the source of that strength aside when he forsook his armor. And despite what Erroth and the Kings would have him believe, he knew now for certain: without the breastplate he was just a common man. A man of great skill, perhaps, but no demigod. It wasn't his skin that had shattered Ny's blade, after all...

"I was so angry when you left me," said Bronwyn, still looking away; but she was noticeably calmer now, the volume of her voice having dropped nearly too low to be heard above the wind. "I didn't know when — or if — you'd ever come back. I felt like a used doll that'd been thrown away. He was there for me when I needed to feel desired again. *Important.*" Now her face returned to the captive. "Yet he never took your place. I still love you, Dragan. I won't deny it. With my mouth I condemn you even now — but my heart's not deceived." Ignoring the guard's warning, she stepped closer and placed both hands atop his on the bars. "I meant most of what I said to you in Fedrin's tent, but I couldn't bear to leave things like that between us — whether this is our final hour together or not. I'm no stranger to being manipulated by family. I'm sure you did what you felt you must do for her, without gaining pleasure from the wicked deeds. Please tell me that's so! Give me something — *anything* — to lift you from the rank of *devil* in my mind..."

As much as he hated to do it, Dragan forced himself to pull his hands away from her touch. "What else is there for me to say? I'm Mother's puppet no more, but that's not enough to earn your forgiveness...much less your love. Yet if your feelings for me truly remain, as you claim — *even against all reason* — then will you not go to your uncle now and plead for my release? Or should he deny you that, then *please!* — beg him to kill me this very night! I can stand this cage no longer. I'd rather die than face the morning locked behind bars, while Saedus struts the field like she owns the damned world! I'll even humble myself and swear fealty to Deserus at last, if that's what it takes! All I need is my armor returned — and a blade with which to cut her down!" His hands returned to their grip on the iron, and he moved his face closer to the bars. "I've not forgotten my feelings for you either, Bronwyn. If only you knew how I yearned for you, hoping against hope that one day you'd be mine again. But there can be no love, no peace, no *life* for me until the witch is slain. Can't you see what must be done?"

"Your armor's been stolen," said the woman, making another effort to wipe tears from her puffy, red eyes. "It was found missing the same day your brother disappeared. We assume he took it for himself."

What? the *DoomBringer* bellowed in his mind — yet the rage was too pure and deep within him to find its way out through his mouth. So instead he just stood there, staring into Bronwyn's eyes but looking through her, his mind frantically searching the plains, the mountain, and the entire known world beyond — as if he could locate and summon his half-brother back to the camp through nothing but sheer force of will. Then all would see whether it was Dragan or the armor that truly held the power…when he latched onto Baeldrin to rip his prize loose from the man's thieving hide! *Keep my secret, keep your head.* That was the threat he'd uttered. And no matter whether Baeldrin had since turned ally against the witch or not, there were now two grievances for which the man would have to answer: the cold-blooded murder of their father being the first…

"Dragan?" said Bronwyn, disturbed by what she found now in the prisoner's face — and at that same moment, a creaking noise issued from above their heads, pulling her eyes to where the bars he gripped were set in the roof of his cage. A trickle of dust shown faintly in the lamplight, and she thought she saw the metal turning…

Another sound. This time a louder *crack*…and Bronwyn took an involuntary step away.

The noise must've broken Dragan's trance as well, for he jerked his hands from the bars and turned his palms up, looking down on them in clear disbelief.

"What's going on over there?" came Ellerin's voice, then all four guards were on their feet with hands on weapons, awaiting only a reply — or recurrence of the noise that'd disturbed them — to set them racing to the cart.

Quick as an adder, Bronwyn shot a hand inside the bars, placed an object in one of Dragan's upturned palms, and — folding his fingers down over it — pushed the fist further into the cage. Then she grabbed her light from the hook and spun away from the cell with it, letting shadows consume the prisoner. "It's nothing," she answered the guards at last. "Snagged my lamp on the hook."

"She hadn't touched it yet!" exclaimed the gruff man to his companions; and just as Bronwyn strode forward he came running up to her with the others on his heels, his suspicious eyes scanning her person and the cage behind. Apparently satisfied that his king's niece was unharmed, this one rudely snatched the lantern from her grasp and held it up to the cart to have a look at his charge.

Two steps closer, then he stopped dead in his tracks with his mouth and eyes wide open. The three men coming up behind were similarly affected when they reached his spot…and there all four stood as if suddenly struck dumb…

Not long after this, the scene's former peace was restored. Two guards were now absent from it, having left to escort Bronwyn back from whence she'd come: but the sounds of the wind and camp had settled back in, and Dragan was left alone in the dark. Moving closer to the front of his cage, he ran a finger down one of the two noticeably curved bars that'd so amazed himself and his captors; then, raising his other hand, he opened it to reveal in faint moonlight the object he'd been gifted by his lost love.

A key to his cell.

He didn't care to guess how she'd come by the thing. All that mattered to him beyond its imminent use was this: she'd planned to give it to him all along.

Grinning to himself, the *DoomBringer* sat down to wait.

46

The pre-dawn plain about Saedus' host was dark as the smoke billowing up from it: a black plume snaking past a red-orange horizon to dissipate in the blue-gray sky overhead. The priests of Ost had dug themselves a sacrificial pit in the deep hours, and now they encircled it, motionless as stone shadows rising from the stygian earth. And although the world behind them was growing ever more impatient for the new day's beginning — with a background of murmured voices, clanging metal, and even the occasional bestial howl issuing from the assembled formations — these devout worshippers of the Daemon appeared oblivious to it all: as if instead of being here amidst the army they were in fact hidden away in some secluded witch's grove, with no sound to break the silence of their conclave except their own ritualistic chanting. Yet presently a dim ray of oncoming light touched naked steel in one shadow's hand — then a frantic bleating began as, digging its hooves into the ground, the victim struggled against another shadow that was dragging it toward the first.

The goat was trembling uncontrollably by the time it passed over to the head priest's grip, but by now his followers' chants had grown so loud that the beast's protests were all but completely inundated. In one swift motion the man ran his blade along the victim's neck, then he raised an ornate bowl and began to fill it with flowing blood.

Two more shadows detached themselves from the circle long enough to hurl the goat's corpse into the flames, returning to their positions at the exact moment their leader presented his sacred vessel to the *Queen of the West*. And at this point the chanting ceased.

Shrugging off the fur-trimmed cloak that'd kept her warm throughout the night, Saedus stepped forth to receive the offering in nothing but the scant battle garb she wore beneath: a studded harness and strap skirt, leather overskirt, and scale bracers and greaves. Her raven hair was pulled back in a tail falling nearly to the small of her back, and the Diadem of the Gazer rested upon her head like a battle crown. Irreverently snatching the vessel of blood from her kneeling priest, she walked to the edge of the pit and held the bowl out over it in one hand:

"Hail, Issalzon! Daughter of Night! She whose name alone strikes fear into the hearts of our foes! Accept this offering of blood I bring thee. May it seep into your dwelling in the bowels of the world to sate your dreadful thirst — and cause you to look upon us here with favor, that we may have the victory!"

"Protect us in battle this day! Curse the heretics who speak your name not in reverence — as we, your beloved servants, ever do! — but in blasphemy. Grant us the power to destroy all those who hate us! Release your blackest daemons from hell, to scour the field of all unbelievers…and let the wombs of their women fall barren with their deaths, so that their lines fail utterly and are wiped clean from this earth!"

Slowly now the sorceress turned her wrist, tipping the bowl sideways to let its contents stream out. Then, drawing back the vessel from the brink, she ran a finger inside it and streaked the collected red blood down her forehead to the tip of her nose. "If this offering has pleased you, Dark Lady, then I beseech thee: let my prayers come to pass! And so shall I sacrifice to you until the end of days!"

These last words seemed to conclude the ritual—or at least Saedus' part in it. Spinning on her heels, she shoved the bowl at the nearest priest and immediately strode off to rejoin her gathered captains.

Valreecius was first to receive her. The lanky, pink-eyed servant had also added some armor to his typical attire; yet, unlike his mistress, it was doubtful he meant to engage in the melee. He may have been learned in the ways of war but was no warrior in his own right. The most noticeable addition to his clothing was a polished steel skullcap whose shine, come daylight, would be even harsher on the eyes than his stark-white baldness. "A fitting ceremony, my Queen," he cooed, stepping into stride beside her. "We'll surely have her blessing."

Saedus didn't bother with a response to this. Valreecius was no priest, and she took his words for what they truly were: a superficial opener to the business at hand. Having reached the others now—Poltoros, Sorec, and his retainers—she chose instead to address them all at once:

"Finally the dawn! I trust all is ready..."

"*Ready*, mistress?" replied the Domalin general, gazing down on her from horseback. His smug face was illuminated by a torch held in his mounted aide's hand. "Why, if I didn't have these men here to tell me otherwise, I might swear this saddle was the cushion of Oen's throne!" At this he threw a smirk over his shoulder—yet not the slightest snicker from his attendants was heard in return. Saedus hadn't laughed, after all: and Saedus held the cards here. This reminder appeared to sober Sorec, and his grin slipped a bit. "Yes, of course we're ready. I await only your command to set these plainsmen running for their broken walls in the north."

"The Sinians aren't renowned for their skill in *fleeing*, general," interjected a raspy, muffled voice coming from Sorec's left. All eyes turned on the speaker: a maroon-cloaked man astride a black warhorse, his face covered by a silver mask. "Especially in their homeland's defense—and not with their Mardothan enemies-turned-allies watching them. They'd rather slit their own throats than let Berac's warriors see them quail. No...I'm afraid they'll stand toe-to-toe with you till the bitter end. So you'd best plan your tactics accordingly."

Sorec nudged his charger to come alongside Poltoros. Coming face-to-face with the lich, he said: "And who are you to school me in the business of war, old man? Or whatever you are..." His face scrunched in disgust as he scrutinized the steward. "Tell me this: did you drag some ancient warlord's spirit up from hell with you when our lovely queen conjured you back? Is he roaming around in that mummy's head of yours right now?" A wry grin touched his lips. "No? Then I'd suggest you leave the *tactics* to me..."

"Shut your mouth, Sorec!" hissed Saedus — and the Domalin angrily clamped his jaw tight, yanking the reins to turn his steed away. "I've one last thing to do. Wait till I mount my chariot — then the field's yours!" Her face turned slightly to the left. "Valreecius, take me to the ghoul."

The moon steward nodded and set off at once, leading his mistress through an ever-widening gap in the ranks. Men and creatures alike fell over themselves in their efforts to clear a path for the sorceress, with most kneeling or bowing or making some other gesture of obeisance to her as soon as they were safely out of reach. The pair didn't have to walk far to reach their destination, however, for already G'nilbor's prison lay just ahead of them. The goblins that Valreecius had placed around this wagon to guard its occupant were visibly relieved to see the ghoul's handler return — with none other than the *Spider* in tow — and they raised their weapons in a redoubled show of mock courage.

The monstrosity glaring down at them from the cart was noticeably larger than he'd been when Saedus first harvested him. Months of gorging on flesh, blood, and bones had not only thickened G'nilbor's body but had also enlarged his frame supernaturally — to the point where, with the platform's height added, he loomed over twice the height of his salivating visitors.

Yes... grins of crazed satisfaction were quite plain on the faces of steward and witch as they stood inspecting their handiwork. For several days now the ghoul had been left chained by his neck and wrists to this wagon, denied the slightest morsel to sate his terrible hunger. And now his mind was so full of rage that not a single thought could rise within him beyond this: what it would take to murder and devour the closest man or beast he could sink his claws into. Presently one overzealous goblin stepped a bit too close to the wagon... and suddenly G'nilbor lunged to the end of his lead with a maniacal roar, straining against the rings that secured his chains to the platform. Black spit flew from his mouth with a rush of his foul breath, and his thick muscles tensed and quivered from his exertion. The offending goblin — utterly forsaking his show of bravery — dropped his spear and fled shrieking into the crowd.

Under other circumstances this would've surely amused the ghoul, and he might've hurled a laugh and a taunt at the fleeing pipsqueak. But now G'nilbor fixed his white, pupilless eyes on Saedus of Ost instead and began to pace back and forth at the edge of the platform like a caged tiger: never taking his glare off her, snarling or growling low in his throat with each pass. He said not a word, however — as if in his present state the power of speech had deserted him and he'd been reduced to a wild animal. Thus it was the sorceress who spoke first:

"Are you famished, ghoul?" Without awaiting a response, she walked to the platform right in front of G'nilbor, carelessly placing herself within harm's reach. "That's good. *Very* good." Her voice had taken on a soothing tone, as one might use to comfort a child or pet. "Come to me..."

In the blink of an eye, the beast halted in mid-pace, spun, and dropped to his knees, slamming his dreadful claws down into a grip on the cart's edge so strong that it ripped huge splinters from the wood. Lowering his head nearly level with Saedus' own, he screamed straight into her upturned face.

Unlike the cowardly goblin, the witch's only reaction to this savagery was a look of annoyance as she wiped a fleck of putrid spittle from her cheek. Then her deranged grin returned — wider even than before. Reaching for the ghoul's chin, she clamped down on it and swiveled his head to her right, forcing him to gaze in the direction of the enemy encampment. "The feast day begins, G'nilbor! Out there stands legion upon legion of meat on which to glut yourself." She released the creature's face then and, extracting a key from her clothing, began to unlock his manacles one by one.

Still the ghoul remained at bay, making no further show of aggression other than to continue producing his low growls of warning: as if in his current animal state he'd forgotten she wasn't omnipotent: like a tame lion recoiling from a puny whip. Or if indeed Saedus was addressing an animal with no trace left of man, perhaps she was now in direct control of the monster, no longer needing to rely on the threat of her minions coming to her aid. After all, the White King's power was yet within her. In any case, she showed not the slightest bit of fear as she let the last shackle drop:

"Just remember what I told you. There's one you mustn't spoil! My son is with them. I've seen it. Find him and slay him if you can. But his flesh is mine!"

Finally free, G'nilbor wasted no time in leaping from the wagon; and as soon as his enormous feet hit ground he swung his head from side to side, searching for a victim on which to break his fast. The remaining goblins scattered like flies: all except an unlucky churl who was shoved down in the chaos. This one felt a vise clamp about his neck before he could stand. Then he felt nothing more.

With her work here completed, the *Spider* fell swiftly into disinterest, just as she'd done following the sacrifice to Issalzon. Turning her back on the grizzly slaughter, she simply strode away, paying no heed to the ghoul's sickening howl of ecstasy that resounded behind. The chariot had now been brought up by her tattooed slaves, and without further delay she mounted it with Valreecius at her side, passing the reins to him. One of the servants handed up her weapon — the slender steel trident she'd selected earlier — while another waved her personal banner high in the air as the signal for Sorec to begin his advance.

Then the sun crested the horizon, met by peals of war horns answering one another along the ranks.

Across the divide, somewhere deep within the mass of Sinian infantry, there stood a nondescript soldier in light armor, a visored helm concealing most of his face. Just one more anonymous warrior on the battlefield. No legendary name riding on his shoulders. No murmurs nor awestruck gazes aimed his way. No spirit-kings to advise him, and no oath-bound guards to shield him in the fray.

And no curse writ about his neck.

47

The ancient peak Gorm Nadur formed an achromatic background for the battle over the realm. The mountain stood alone, segregated from the Seomyr range to the south by a healthy steppe of grass and shrubland. It appeared to hang from the diffused layer of livid clouds above like an iron curtain draped from the sky, inviting opposing armies to entertain the main stage that was the amber plain. A hem of gnarled evergreens and rubble ran anarchical around its base, warming its knees in winter and drinking its cold tears in summer.

The alp donned a veneer of ice that shown steely black in the feeble light of dawn. Stone outcroppings exploded from its facade into cruel, unusual shapes, made all the more prominent by the deep crevasses they contrasted. Some of the outcrops resembled the teeth of dreadful beasts, others the protracted spears of a wary phalanx, and still others the spewed guts of a severed belly. What titan of old had whetted his blade upon this giant? What mob of spirits had flogged this orphan rock with flails of thunder, whips of tempest, and cudgels of quakes? The mountain had persevered the ages to emerge a juggernaut of time. And its apathy was infinite to the events unfolding beneath.

From the west marched the hordes of the sorceress, Saedus of Ost, with her chariot at the head. Her contingent was stationed upon a slight incline of earth at the mountain's base: a comprehensive vantage point except for an area to the northwest where the plateau's rolling edge converged with the tree line and fell from view. There the witch placed a small detachment of warriors to guard her flank; yet should the lightly-armored and ill-trained Ûnathī savages be engaged, they'd likely be annihilated within moments. Guts would vomit from bellies, heads tumble from shoulders, and limbs litter the ground like driftwood. All to alert Saedus. That's what the lives of the men from the dark forest translated to in her mind. Two hundred men for two seconds of warning.

In the valley below, Saedus' main host advanced in loose block formations. The Domalins held the vanguard. Stalwart warriors not easily broken. Pride for their once-great people yet stirred in their hearts, and no longer did it matter to them *why* they were being led to war — only that it was them against those who weren't them. They marched with determined eyes forward, each man wearing the expressionless visage of a professional.

To either side and behind was a motley of the remaining armies of the West: woodsmen from Ûnath, goblins from Gorm Vûdoc, cultists from Ost, and imps from Braured. They advanced warily, as if an invisible force was prodding their backsides. They were raiders, pillagers, thieves, assassins. The grand spectacle of war unfolding before them had set their eyes wandering about the panorama with looks of awestruck stupidity. To the sorceress, they were all bags of meat: no more than a fleshy bulwark to protect the Domalin flanks.

The armies of King Oen and his allies approached from the east, their ranks arranged similarly to their foe's. The Sinian heavy infantry occupied front and center, led by Fedrin Rae himself. His blue banner appeared pallid against the gray sky as it fluttered in the morning wind. The bear had set his men in a saw formation meant to funnel the enemy between opposing rows of spears, swords, and shields—and there be chewed to pulp by steel teeth and ground into the dirt by the advancing army's inexorable force. The light infantry were on Fedrin's flanks. They'd harry the Domalins, control the enemy's position, and force their foes to engage the Sinian front line. If they were pressed, they'd withdraw; and if pursued, they'd lead the witch's forces into a trap between hammer and anvil: for the Mardothans held the extreme flank to the north, and a contingent of Ithirian and Tholmian allies held the south. A few battalions of archers, the king, and his personal guard of cavalry were in the rear.

"Rotate!" Dragan heard his captain shout from behind him, followed by two shrill whistle blows. The men holding the front line systematically stepped aside and retreated to the back of the column while the next warriors in line advanced to take their place. When the whistle blew again, it would be Dragan's time to fight.

Perhaps. On his first tour of the front line, he'd been surprised to learn that not much real fighting took place there. The legion of light infantry was more concerned with taking up certain spaces on the battlefield than killing the enemy. The troops moved this way and that. Advancing, retreating, circling—but never overextending, even when the foe appeared most vulnerable. Every man was a spoke in the wheel. One small component of a greater machine. Wholesale rout and slaughter would never come to his company while the front lines held. But nor would it come to his foes—the soldiers across the line—for the same reasons.

And Dragan didn't like that at all. He understood what they were doing. He was aware of this type of formation fighting, but he'd never paid it much heed in the past. He'd been a champion. He'd chosen for himself the manner, location, and style of his combat—and the fates of nations had wavered on the outcomes of his decisions. *A champion indeed,* he thought. *Now a mere* foot soldier! *Is this worth Bronwyn's shame? Astelidus' death? For me to kill a few Ûnathī goat herders?*

"*Ahhhh!*" screamed the soldier in front of Dragan as the tip of a blood-soaked sword jutted from the small of the man's back. Dragan caught the Sinian as the soldier stumbled against him…and he held the body briefly before letting it fall. In front was the foe who'd done the damage, already on his knees from a thrust taken in the thigh. Dragan drove his spear halfway through the enemy's neck, kicked the body over with a boot to its chest, and took up position on the front line. He was now shoulder-to-shoulder with allies on either side, spears looming menacingly over the tops of wooden round shields. His eyes darted side-to-side. He rolled to the balls of his feet and bounced gingerly. He readjusted his grip on his spear haft. All in the anticipation of…nothing. The ragtag group of untrained Ûnathī and Ostian fighters kept their distance, loosing occasional errant spear thrusts to keep the Sinians honest.

"To hell with this," muttered Dragan, taking a few steps forward. Two spear points came biting hard at his face. He lunged back to dodge then crouched to leap upon his adversaries while they were still exposed. In his mind he saw the sequence play out. His targets were already dead…they just didn't know it yet. Muscles flexed to launch his body forward — only for him to be brought up short. Rough hands had grabbed him under the arms to haul him back in line.

"Are you dense, soldier?" asked one of his allies. "You're gonna get yourself killed. Or worse, *us!*"

Dragan shrugged the soldiers' hands from his person with an angry gesture. "Don't you know who I am?"

"I don't care if you're the *DoomBringer* himself! You won't be breaking rank like that again," answered the bulky, gap-toothed Sinian to his right. The man spat in disgust before turning his attention immediately back to the line.

The son of Saedus felt a stab of rage well in his chest and creep up his neck. "What did you say?" he hissed. "I *am* the *Doom…*" But no, that was wrong. He touched his chest with the inside of his shield arm and felt nothing but a worn leather tunic above a ratty piece of chain mail. The time for proclamations was over. Speeches were finished. Boasting was done. Taunting seemed juvenile. He'd play his role as a normal soldier and be glad of it.

Yet…why did he still *feel* like the *DoomBringer?* Tiramas Vendhane's words returned to him. *That breastplate you wear holds no magic of its own. Your power lies within you…*

"Rotate!" the captain roared, followed by the obligatory whistle blast.

"*Damn!*" Dragan cursed, reluctantly filing to the back of the column. There he found his captain talking with the legion commander and another man. *A runner,* he thought. The newcomer was out of breath, his voice wrought with fear — though at first Dragan couldn't make out the words. The runner pointed southward. All four men mechanically followed the invisible line made by the runner's finger. A great tumult in the distance surrounded Fedrin Rae's banner like a pot of water reaching a roaring boil.

"*How?*" Dragan heard the commander's voice clearly now. "How could they be through the van?"

"Sir…" the runner stammered. "The van's routed! The witch has unleashed a…a monster…upon us. The heavy infantry's falling back in retreat…"

For a single bright moment Fedrin's blue banner stood tall amidst the rabble, like an unshakable oak in a field of storm-blown weeds. Then suddenly the flag teetered, fell, and became instantly consumed by the throng. Dragan vaguely heard the legion commander begin shouting orders—but orders meant nothing to him now. *No, no, no!* he thought, pushing his way through the troops in the direction of the fallen banner.

A hand grabbed his shoulder. "Where the hell do you think you're going?" its owner snarled. Dragan glared at the hand as if it were a piece of smelly dung before locking eyes with the offender. It was the same gap-toothed soldier that'd yelled at him earlier. Meeting Dragan's gaze, the man stumbled backwards, face pale, eyes swimming with fear. "Who *are* you?" he gasped.

A sleeping ember of fury blazed awake for an instant in Dragan's eyes. "I'm the *DoomBringer*."

Fedrin Rae reached down and grabbed his standard bearer under the armpit, jerking the young man back to his feet. "Get up, boy! Don't let the flag fall!" he shouted. "*Do* not *let it fall!*"

The old bear looked around. A mass of bodies, mostly his men, lay strewn about the field before him. The vanguard was broken, ripped apart by Saedus' colossal ghoul. Sinian soldiers ran this way and that, heedless of horn blasts or whistle shrills or pleas for rally. Fedrin knew the battle's outcome depended on the van holding the line, that the enemy was far outmatched on the other fronts, and that, in time, Sinia and its allies would work their way around the invaders' weak flanks to surround them on three of four sides. Then they'd smash their foes or watch them flee, only to ride them down in glorious pursuit. It seemed that the witch knew this all too well, however, and thus she'd sent her hellish champion straight into the mouth of the beast: to smash the teeth from the Sinian army before the jaws could clamp tight. The ghoul had to be dealt with...or all would be lost.

A group of the captain's guard remained behind him—perhaps a score or less whose courage hadn't fully wilted—still holding a loose formation. Yet by the looks on their twisted faces, Fedrin saw what little heart was left in them fading rapidly. "Men!" he shouted again. "Master your fear! To me! Line up!" But only a few took a nervous step forward. "*By god!* Where's your guts? Are you boys or men? Sheep or lions? Would you not rather die than see Sinia's crown on the witch's head? To grovel before her as she rides victorious through the streets of Chalemos with this filth in tow? *Our* streets?" At this last he spat sour spit on the ground, appearing as if he'd wretch at the mere thought.

The old bear's words hit home with the proud warriors. They gave a battle cry and ran to their captain, forming up. And just like that, the decision was made for each man: victory or death in a final charge.

Then, as if on queue, the beast G'nilbor loomed up from the body of corpses in which he'd been wallowing. He spotted Fedrin's guard in a tenuous line: one drastically thinner and shorter than it'd been before he'd cleaved through Sinia's vanguard with all Domal's strength in tow. The ghoul examined his enemy and smiled at the futility of their resolve, revealing a mass of yellow fangs besmeared with blood and grit. More easily would a drop of water extinguish the sun than twenty men lay low the mighty G'nilbor. Without taking his eyes off of Fedrin, he reached down slowly and grabbed the nape of a nearby goblin, picking the smaller creature up and setting it down gently before his feet. Then he guided another in by the shoulder…then another…

"Little ones," he said like a father to his children. "Form the line!" And he laughed in great mockery of the Sinians as he ushered more goblins in: each one more confused and terrified than the last. Across from them — no more than fifty strides away — the opposing soldiers were forming up below a blue banner; and from the looks of it, those warriors had no intentions of falling back like the rest of their brothers.

"Good, good," G'nilbor drawled, inspecting one goblin with an approving pat on the head. "Now go!"

Nothing happened. The goblins looked at each other, bewildered. They were here to pull up the rear, to capture or kill the wounded, to scavenge the dead — not to charge into a score of heavily armed men. G'nilbor's milky eyes opened wide in disbelief. "I...said...charge, you maggots!" And with that he took the nearest goblin by the head and squeezed, sinking his talon-like nails through eyes, ears, nose, and cheek. A sickening crunch followed as the flunky collapsed to the ground. The others got the message: probable death in front, but certain death behind. They raised what sorry excuses for weapons they possessed and charged.

"Here they come, men!" Fedrin cried. "I don't know if that fiend can feel pain or not, but its limbs aren't made of steel. Hack it to pieces! Charge!"

The two lines met with a dull thud of metal. Most of the goblins were cut down in seconds, but that was enough time for G'nilbor to butcher five Sinian warriors. The hulk hovered over one of his victims: as if trying to resist the urge to feast upon the corpse right then and there while there was yet more killing to do. Then another five Sinians grouped up and ran at the ghoul's back. G'nilbor spun, the back of his hand rounding in a massive arch that swept all five men from the earth and sent them flying like leaves in the squall. He dispatched the rest with astonishing precision. A swat here: gnat. A stomp there: beetle. A pick here: itch. Until...

"Ah!" G'nilbor winced, grabbing the back of his right leg. A long gash ran the length of his bloated calf. No blood spilled from the wound. Only a gritty black matter remained on the blade that'd inflicted it. The blade of Fedrin Rae: lone survivor of the Sinian charge.

"Your time's done, old man!" the ghoul growled. Fedrin raised his blade above his head and rushed in—but G'nilbor was too quick. He caught Fedrin's sword hand in one fluid motion, crushing the veteran's fingers, knuckles, and palm to pieces against the weapon's hard hilt. Then the hulk's free hand found the captain's neck and lifted him high into the air.

Fedrin struggled with the iron vise that was constricting the life from him, his good hand feebly pulling at the ghoul's meaty claw. But it would've been easier to tear through stone with his bare hands than to pry open one finger from that grip. His legs kicked, then trembled, then twitched...and finally hung limp.

G'nilbor snorted with pleasure and tossed the body like a pebble through the air. It crashed down in a heap some thirty strides away. Then he turned back to the corpses he'd been mutilating before Rae's intrusion, drool already forming in the corners of his terrible maw.

"Bring me that one!" shouted G'nilbor, pointing with the severed arm held in his right hand as if it were a club. What remained of his goblin retainers scurried about, falling all over themselves to carry out the command. The ghoul laughed wickedly; then, lowering his voice, he went on in a sinister tone: "Yes...I'll feast now on the flesh of their fallen captain. Wear his bones about my neck..."

The colossal pale beast looked about then, as if seeing the battlefield for the first time. A large void had opened up around his location. His goblin lackeys were with him, but the Domalins kept their distance to press their advantage on both sides as the Sinians tried to give ground without breaking rank. Volleys of arrows still flew overhead, back and forth, mixing in the sky, striping the ground with evanescent beams of shadow.

"Why don't the Domalins feast with me, little goblins?" G'nilbor mused. "Do they not enjoy my company? Ha! I'll consume their souls with the rest when I'm done here. The witch also! The whole world shall be devoured!" But the ghoul cut his tirade short then, confused. Something he'd commanded hadn't occurred. *Unthinkable.* He peered around to see who'd be the first to die over the slight— and to his amazement, he found a pair of servants staring at him and shaking with fear. His lip curled in anger. "*Where is it?*" he bellowed, smashing the mighty fist of his free hand down to pulverize the skull of one goblin. "I said *bring me the old chief's body!*" He looked about stupidly, mouth open wide, and saw how the rest of his minions had slinked away behind him. Some were even fleeing now in a full sprint away from the area. "*What's this?*"

"Master," said the remaining servant, voice unsteady with terror. "He won't let us near the body..."

"*He?*" G'nilbor seemed only now to notice the warrior kneeling over Fedrin Rae's broken corpse. "*He?*" The monster took a step forward—yet hesitated as the body's protector raised his head. Two infernos of orange fire met G'nilbor's milky white gaze. "*You...*" the beast cooed, licking his lips in delight.

"Me." Dragan removed his helmet and set it softly on the ground beside his vanquished companion. Then, taking up Fedrin's sword, the *DoomBringer* rose to his feet.

"The witch said you'd come," said G'nilbor, tearing off a bite of the arm he held with his jagged teeth. He chewed the chunk slowly in his massive jaws. "The thought of it made my mouth water, I confess. And now, here you are!" The beast pulled back his lips to reveal a hideous maw full of blood and meat. Spit oozed down his jowls and dripped in slimy lines to the bloodstained earth. He flexed his chest and arms, revealing bulging veins atop misshapen muscles that seemed to pop hard as iron from every nook of his gargantuan frame. "Lost your prize, son of Saedus?" A smile spread over the beast's face as he examined Dragan's gear and found the silver breastplate lacking. "Makes no difference. It was a lie. *Your whole life's a lie!* The only power that armor held was the power to enslave you!"

A roar of laughter burst from G'nilbor's mouth. "But you know it, don't you? Else you wouldn't have come here to die." Another step forward. "You mean to redeem yourself in death, after all you've done? That will never happen! Look around you, Bastard. There's no one to see. No one to know. I'll grind you to pulp! Then the witch will ensure your name lives on in infamy. That all hate directed at her is deflected onto you until the end of time! A traitor, a liar...a murderer!"

And with that, the ghoul crouched and exploded into the air, razor claws itching to sink into Dragan's flesh. But instead of that end actually transpiring, something unexpected occurred.

G'nilbor had miscalculated his leap.

Impossible! Mid-air, he lost his balance and came crashing down a few strides from Dragan's feet. The hulk struggled to gain his footing, but no sooner had he risen than three stray arrows precipitated from the hail of them overhead, piercing him in the back, shoulder, and neck. He groaned at the impacts but paused only long enough to rip the most offensive bolt free of his neck. More furiously than before, he set his back legs to spring again—but in that very moment a sinkhole opened in the ground beneath his right foot, engulfing that entire leg up to the hip and causing his other leg to bend back awkwardly. G'nilbor struggled to loose himself, clawing at the ground; still the harder he fought, the more the earth's grip tightened around his trapped leg like a vise. He looked up, face full of rage and confusion. Dragan Saedus was looming over him.

"You're right about one thing, fiend. *I do know*—and that's why I came. But it's not for redemption. I'm unredeemable. And it's not for glory. I'm infamous. It's for a reason far less noble. For I am the Black King cometh, the *GrimHelm of Ost*. Fate is my dominion, and I bring doom to all my adversaries!"

The Black King lifted Rae's blade and, with one fell slash, severed G'nilbor's head. The massive lump rolled about the ground and came to a stop.

Some would-be meals are poisonous.

48

The Mardothan soldier shrieked uncontrollably as he sat clutching the stump that'd just been freed of his right leg: the result of an unfortunate impact with a scythed chariot blade as the *Spider* came plowing through enemy lines. A jet of crimson blood shot from between his fingers as he lost consciousness — then his companions were leaping over his prone body in their haste to catch and engage the sorceress.

Others had been fleeing before Saedus' wheeled onslaught, but now — as the allied voices from behind called for a rally — most of them turned and stood their ground. Nevertheless, Valreecius saw the wall of spears forming…and at the last instant he yanked the reins to pull the horses aside, avoiding a direct charge that would've left the animals skewered and the car overturned. Spinning axle blades struck again as the chariot passed close to the Mardothan formation, conjuring horrid screams from new amputees as the driver veered to survey the plain for his next lane of attack.

"Run them *all* down!" cried the witch, burying her trident in the unprotected neck of another hapless foe and wrenching it out as she sped past him. Her eyes were bright and feral in her bloodlust, outshining even the gems on her diadem that sparkled in the sunlight.

As the horses began to slow in their circuit, a nearby Mardothan captain saw his opening and shouted for a coordinated strike. A hail of missiles rained down on the chariot just as Valreecius was bringing it about; yet — miraculously, in the eyes of the assailants — no fleshy mark was struck. Not the witch. Not the driver. Not even the horses.

Four of Saedus' banshees were with her, blinking in and out of vision about the chariot like rapidly forming and dissipating clouds — and they'd deflected every single threatening shaft.

But the attackers hadn't waited to see if their aims would prove true. They had rushed forward immediately after hurling their projectiles, most committed to the charge before the marvel had fully registered in their brains. These brave souls drew their swords and mouthed words to their gods as they came on: some praying for a chance at unending glory, some merely begging to live out the day. Others with slower starts or weaker resolves thought it best to disengage instead, and these promptly turned tail and ran.

Weaponless Valreecius hissed like a warning viper as the Mardothans leapt at him, frantically whipping the reins in an attempt to get his mistress clear of danger. The banshees swooped in to spare him and the horses, flinging aside and mentally incapacitating all who came within striking range — yet the chariot was going nowhere. The horses could do nothing but rear and kick at the enemy forming up again before them. And with all four banshees occupied at front and left flank, the queen herself was left temporarily exposed.

"Die!" she squealed with each thrust or blow as the fools waded in, seeming not to notice that her guardians had abandoned her. The augmented speed and strength that Saedus' potion had granted her was too much for these common soldiers to contend with — and either one by one or in pairs they fell before the chariot, quickly dispatched by the trident's prongs or else brutally beaten down by its shaft. Meanwhile, however, one clever warrior had come up behind the car unseen, readying to make good on a clear shot at the witch's lightly-armored back. Grinning, he raised his spear...

...and screamed in agony as his entire body suddenly erupted in flames, his face melting away as he raked at it with char-blackened hands.

Poltoros lowered the tyberwood staff and kicked his steed forward, covering the remaining distance to his mistress; and behind him poured in a band of imps brandishing their hatchets and bucklers with cruel intentions, eager to finish off the remaining Mardothans and strip them clean. Now even the most stalwart foes had seen enough — and a moment later the immediate vicinity of the chariot was devoid of all but Saedus' minions...and fallen corpses.

"You lag behind, servant," was all that Saedus said to the lich as he reined in beside her. Then, still staring at Poltoros, she addressed the moon steward next: "Valreecius! Find more of these *desert rats* for me to slay!" But when no answer came to this — neither in the form of speech nor simply the horses being whipped into motion — the sorceress turned her head to her driver, opening her mouth to chastise him as well. Yet what she saw then gave her pause. Her fifth banshee, Seela, had returned and materialized before the steward.

"Speak!" she yelled at the hovering gray figure.

Your son Dragan has revealed himself on the battlefield, and G'nilbor is slain! Your enemies have been rallied — and now they push forward, seeking you, leaving destruction in their wake...

Saedus screamed in rage at the tidings, her arm flailing out to backhand the dust that was Seela's body. The banshee winked out of existence as her mistress' limb passed through her, only to re-form in a spot just out of reach: unfazed by the violence, calmly awaiting instruction.

"I knew he'd fail me!" the witch spoke of the defeated ghoul, beginning to compose herself. "Yet Dragan's here...just as I divined." A wicked grin came to her lips. "The *DoomBringer's* day is done! Seela — guide us to him. I'll deal with him myself!"

The circle of Domalin soldiers exchanged nervous glances as they timed their constricting attack, spears extended before them like spokes seeking the hub of a wheel. All around this band of six, a heated contest between their company and the advancing Sinian detachment was constantly threatening to wash in and foil their maneuver; yet they paid no heed to any danger from behind. Their sole focus was this deadly adversary they'd managed to single out and were now warily approaching. Apparently they'd recognized Dragan on sight from his earlier days spent in Rardonydd — or else they'd just witnessed the hero make short work of some number of their brethren.

Likely it was both.

The tension that was nearly paralyzing to these six men hadn't infected the *GrimHelm*, however. Although Dragan still wore the frown of mixed sorrow and rage that'd transfixed itself on his face with Fedrin's death, for the moment his raw fury lay dormant. The swift revenge he'd dealt to Rae's slayer had taken some of it out of him, filling the void left behind with a renewed feeling of calm confidence in his prowess: a feeling he'd not enjoyed since the days before his breastplate's worth had been brought into question. Yet no longer could there be any doubt. As surely as he'd sworn Erroth to be wrong when Astelidus' blade snapped upon the armor's collar, he was now absolutely convinced otherwise. *I am what the Kings proclaimed me to be. All that...and more. The power lies within me!*

He was in his element now, after all, reveling in the carnage. The battlefield: his only true home. No matter what land he roamed in...no matter whether his reputation or deeds there caused him to be scorned or shunned...*War* and *Death* were always waiting for him with open arms, longing for his return. His earthly mother hadn't shown him love — or it'd proved but a lie for her gain. Yet the blade in his hand loved him *unconditionally*. Thus he'd return that love, gorging it with the blood it so dearly craved.

Caught up in this emotion, Saedus' son began to casually twirl his sword in an easy stance. The corner of his lip turned up in a smirk, and a wink was ready in his eye as he slowly revolved to scan his assailants' troubled faces. So relaxed did he appear under their pressure, in fact, that one might've assumed he were preparing to instruct some greenhorn retainer rather than take on half a dozen capable veterans. They were almost on him now: at the point where they'd have no choice but to engage or else to break and flee. But just then a succession of urgent cries pierced the din: "The witch! She comes! The witch draws near!"

Dragan's smirk vanished instantly — and his sport with the surrounding men ended with it, forgotten even as he rushed them without warning. Leaping forth with blinding quickness, he barely avoided impaling himself on the nearest shaft as he spun around its point, slashing at the wielder's neck with his sword while simultaneously stripping the offending spear from the doomed warrior's grasp. And just like that he was free of the circle and dashing to intercept his mother's approaching chariot with a weapon in each hand, swiftly dodging or dispatching anyone blocking his path.

Many of the Sinians called out to Dragan as he sped away, eager to continue following their resurrected champion — even on into the dark heart of the contest where their chances of survival were slim at best. Yet the *DoomBringer* paid them no mind. The appearance of his mother had his blood boiling again, and he had neither eyes nor ears for anyone but her. Thus brazenly he pressed forward, far outstripping those who might aid him should he become overwhelmed.

Yet Saedus had done the same. Scores of imps and goblins gushed in behind her, running over one another and howling and foaming at their mouths in their effort to catch up with the careering chariot — but even under the lash their labors were futile.

There! shouted Seela into the witch's mind, her wispy arm extended with one finger pointing directly at Dragan's onrushing form. The *Spider's* sadistic smile grew even wider as she fixed her gaze on the prize, and Valreecius began at once to set the chariot in line for a direct charge. But scarcely had he pulled the reins when Saedus' left arm shot out across his chest to slow him. Her eyes were still locked on her son, but her expression was now dramatically altered from that of a moment before. Apparently she'd just seen something in the hero to give her pause — something she'd not seen in him before — and the resulting dread had swept over her so suddenly and unexpectedly that she was unable to suppress a look of fear and doubt.

"Stop, Dragan!" she cried, thrusting out a warding palm. "Speak with me!"

But it was too late for that. The *GrimHelm* hadn't faltered for an instant, and thus the chariot was still racing forward when he joined with it. Sidestepping an attack from Seela to come at the horses, he severed the closest beast's throat with a backhand swipe of his sword — then hurled himself straight at the car, putting the spear in his other hand clean through the driver's chest before rolling free of the impending wreckage. And narrowly did he avoid the wheel's rotating blade in the process.

Valreecius' mouth flew open in shock as he felt the shaft enter his body, and he dropped the reins to grasp at it just as the horses went down before his eyes. The chariot followed suit an instant later, thrown up in the air to come crashing down hard sideways — then flipping over and over again before finally skidding to a halt, the earth ripped cruelly asunder at each impact point along its path.

Saedus had leapt from the chariot as soon as it went airborne, following her son's lead. But Valreecius was not so fortunate. The ruin of his skewered body lay trapped beneath the overturned car. An arm could be seen poking out of one side — but the limb was motionless and bent at an odd angle, with a white bone jutting out from the pale skin.

"You *bastard!*" screamed Saedus, raising her weapon in one hand as she felt around her head with the other. She'd lost the Diadem in her plunge from the car. "Look what you've done!"

Mother and son had risen together but stood at least ten paces apart, for the moment content with staring at one another. All about them the battle raged on; yet the soldiers in this stretch of the field had been present long before the estranged pair appeared and were locked in their own desperate mortal conflicts, having no desire to interfere in a duel of demigods. And so they gave the area about the chariot's path a wide berth.

As his mother's enraged voice fell upon him, Dragan gripped his blade's hilt tight and fell into a ready stance. A burst of wind streamed by, blowing strands of dark brown hair across his face. "I'm not done yet, *bitch!* You dreamt of this day from the start, didn't you? Why wait so long to be rid of me?"

"*Bitch?*" the *Spider* roared back, murder gleaming in her eyes. Suddenly five gray figures took shape in the air about her, bristling like rabid hounds at the end of intangible leashes. "You've grown out of hand, child. But in the end you'll learn your place!" Leveling her trident on the prey, she addressed her pets next: "Bind him!"

Dragan had launched himself forward again while these last words were still in Saedus' mouth, and now he reared back to hurl his sword at her chest before the banshees could converge on him. Yet as soon as the weapon left his hand it was deflected by a phantasm — and the blade soared harmlessly past the witch to strike nothing but earth.

Seela was the first to connect with the *GrimHelm*, injecting her horrific wail into his skull like a burning hot lance. The sting of it caused Dragan to stumble just as a second and third spirit joined in — then he went down on his knees. With eyes closed and teeth gritted, he fought to suppress a howl of agony as his hands wrenched up clods of grass and earth before him.

Saedus had wisely chosen to hold back her remaining two bodyguards, not wishing to unnecessarily expose herself to errant darts or would-be heroes from the throng about her. Yet as she watched the trio of parasites dance around their crippled host, her earlier fear suddenly redoubled. They were moving faster and faster now, swarming the human...their agitation rising as he struggled against their control. Then Dragan's eyes opened — and as the blue irises locked on his mother, they erupted into crimson infernos. He rose to one knee...

"*Cast him down!*" shrieked the witch.

The final pair of banshees rushed in to join their sisters; yet, to Saedus' terror, the added burden appeared to have no effect. The *DoomBringer's* resulting sharp intake of breath was drowned by the clamor, and this time he held his red gaze fixed on the *Spider*, barely wincing from the pain. He continued to rise...

...then suddenly groaned and fell, clamping his hands over his ears in a vain attempt to shut out the punishing screams.

"You see?" Saedus grinned wide, her panic subsiding. "Here's your answer! Why rush to slay a lion I can so easily cow?" She began a casual stroll toward her son, as if she had all the time in the world to deal with the man. "But your life's become more trouble now than it's worth. Soon I'll drink your blood, and your strength shall be my own!"

On his knees again, Dragan uncovered his ears and made a hoarse sound in his throat before doubling over in agony.

"What's wrong, son?" Saedus laughed at his failed attempt to speak. Raising one hand, she caused the banshees' dance to slow somewhat, visibly alleviating Dragan's strain. "Come on...out with it!"

"Go ahead, Mother," he gasped, meeting her gray eyes. "You may end my life...*but I take the victory!* I've lost all fear of you. Finally I know the truth, and I serve you no longer..."

"*You know nothing!*" She stood within striking range of him now, her trident threatening. "In undeath you'll worship *and* fear me—fawning over every word I say! The truth is what I make it. You'll have no choice but to serve me!"

"No matter what you do, you'll never be one of *us*. I was next in line—not you. Another will come, and you'll grovel in the dust before him!"

"Never!"

The Queen's eyes flashed as she reared back to plunge her weapon straight through Dragan's heart. But just before the prongs tasted leather and flesh, her attack came to an abrupt halt in midair—as if the trident had instead been thrust into a stone wall. Immediately sensing the interferer, Saedus cursed and whirled to face the lich...

Yet it wasn't Poltoros alone who'd intruded on her moment of triumph. The steward was there, indeed...and it was his arcane magic that'd hindered her. But also standing nearby was a tall, dark-haired man with a naked blade in his hand and the recovered Diadem of the Gazer sitting his brow—and Dragan's missing breastplate strapped to his torso.

Baeldrin.

Saedus had kept her mouth open to continue railing as she spun around, but instead the combined shock of her servant's willfulness and the Domalin prince's unexpected showing left her temporarily speechless. No doubt she was torn as to which one of them to set upon first.

"Surprised to see me?" offered Baeldrin, seizing advantage of her hesitation. He wore a strange look on his face: one caught somewhere between exhilaration and wariness. The former was a culmination of his plan to get to this very spot, whereas the latter was a more natural reaction to the odds stacked against him. He believed in the power he wielded...but here were two others with mastery far exceeding his own. Somehow he managed to hold a pretentious grin as his eyes darted back and forth between his sworn enemy and the questionable ally beside him—yet at the same time he was nervously gripping his hilt so tightly that his knuckles went white. His free hand was balled in a fist at his side.

It took only one glance at Poltoros, however, to see that the steward wasn't well. Leaning on his tyberwood staff for support, his hooded and masked head drooping, the lich's appearance was in sharp contrast to Saedus' alert form.

"Taking after your poor dead father, Baeldrin?" returned the witch at last, a broad smile winning over her initial scowl. "Cowards all your lives, only to find some petty courage in your final moments? A surprise indeed!—and a welcome one at that. You've spared me the trouble of hunting you down!"

"As for you, *old fool*," she turned next on Poltoros, not giving Baeldrin time to retort. "You dared stay my hand just now—but look what the strain of rebellion cost you! You know you can't kill me yourself...so you've placed your bet with this dog? Look at him. Somehow he's gotten his hands on Dragan's armor, and he actually believes it will spare him my wrath? How pathetic!" Then, looking to Baeldrin: "Wearing that breastplate no more grants you Dragan's power than donning that crown restores you to the throne! In a moment you'll be dead..." She pointed her trident at him as she said this, then moved it in line with the lich next. "And *you'll* wish you were! Begone from my sight, slave—and perhaps I'll choose to ease your punishment."

Poltoros made no move, however, quietly maintaining his slouch as if he'd not even heard her threat. Not so with Baeldrin. He was livid:

"You lie to save your skin, witch! You'd not have stopped Dragan if he still wore this armor! I'll cut that silver tongue from your mouth and..."

Shouts and clangs from the nearby melee washed over the end of his taunt, followed by a wave of fiercely hacking and thrusting combatants that spilled into the gap between Saedus and her confronters. Nevertheless—with each afraid to lose their chance at the other in the sudden crowd—both she and Baeldrin leapt forth at once, bashing aside all bodies in the lane they were forging.

As soon as he was in range of her, the prince raised his sword as if to dare a straightforward charge, hoping to make it past Saedus' counterattack to embed his blade deep in her skull. But it was only a ruse. As the trident darted out he jumped aside instead, shoving an adjacent off-balanced soldier before him. The expected result of this move was that the *Spider's* fork would become trapped in Baeldrin's meat shield, allowing him a brief window in which to cut her down...

But what he actually found was a prong sprouting from his own bicep. The speed of her thrust had been incredible.

Grunting in pain, Baeldrin opened his left hand and let the stone within fall to the ground. "Defend me!" he croaked, abruptly realizing his folly and mortal peril—and nearly fainted as Saedus wrenched her weapon free.

"There's no one to save you, fool!" the witch laughed. "Join your sires in the abyss!"

Just as she'd planned to finish Dragan moments earlier, Saedus drew back once more to deliver a killing strike. Yet again her attempt was foiled. Baeldrin's minion had heard its master's command—and the gray particles of its shrieking, horribly distorted visage rapidly coalesced now within a foot of the Queen's own face, threatening to consume her mind and soul.

"*Ah!*" she exclaimed in shock as her thrust went wide. Yet her surprise didn't slide into fear. Immediately recovering, she took one step back—then barked an arcane phrase while reaching out with her left hand, forming a sign to seal the banishment of the Domalin's offending phantasm.

Yet for the prince this distraction had proven long enough. Ignoring the pain in his punctured arm, he reacted instantly with the other. His sword flicked out to cut clean through the witch's gesture, removing all four of her fingers with the sweep—and dropping to ground with these digits were three of the ornate rings she used to bind her banshees.

Exulting, Baeldrin planted his feet and followed with a backhand slice aimed at the screaming witch's neck. He slung the blade out in a wide arc, committing every ounce of his adrenaline-fueled strength, aching to feel that beautiful tug of resistance midway that would secure his revenge. "*Domal is mine!*" he cried with the attack, his words joining in chorus with the whistling steel...

And missed his target entirely, losing his balance as the sorceress' unnatural reflexes delivered her from harm's way—and allowed her to smack her spinning weapon's shaft into the base of Baeldrin's skull on his way down.

Shoving her spurting hand against the leather under her right breast, Saedus grimaced in pain and rage. This time there'd be no shout. No boast. Only the orgasmic satisfaction of her trident drinking this stunned cur's blood...

Suddenly Dragan felt a great weight lift from his mind. Like a gust of sweet spring air dispersing autumn leaves, three of Saedus' pets had just departed him. They cackled as they sped off in separate paths over the heads of the soldiers that had spilled into this patch of field, rejoicing over their newly sundered bonds by spreading fear and panic through the ranks. The area about Saedus' overturned chariot began to thin. Fleeing bodies could be seen radiating from its center as if someone had loosed a deadly plague in their midst.

Two spirits yet remained as leeches in the *DoomBringer's* thoughts. But two weren't enough. Leaping to his feet, Dragan was running forward again before he even knew the path, screaming his mother's name to draw her out:

"Saedus!"

Then he saw her. The shaft of her trident was raised high in one hand, fork pointed down and ready to be plunged into his half-brother's exposed neck.

"*Mother!*"

For an instant she paused to glare over her shoulder; then Dragan slammed into her body with the force of a colossus, breaking her grip on the trident and sending them both flying away from Baeldrin's prone figure. Even before they landed, their struggle was underway. Dragan with arms constricting about her torso, squeezing the air from her lungs, threatening to crack her ribs and send the shards knifing into her guts. Saedus with her left arm pinned to her chest where she'd been holding it…but with the right hand free to snake up to his neck and crush his throat.

"*Die!*" she shouted once more as her nails sank deep into her son's flesh; yet the note had fallen now from its earlier height of ecstasy to a pained, guttural cry of desperation. Nevertheless, her attack was succeeding. Unable to draw breath, Dragan was forced to relinquish his own hold, darting both hands to her wrist in an attempt to fend off the viselike clamp.

Strong as her occult concoction had made her, though, the *GrimHelm* proved stronger: especially with his two limbs pitted against her one. A moment longer, and he would've pried the witch's claw away, likely breaking what few fingers were left to her in the process. As it was, however, the digits had barely started to unfurl when Dragan faded again. Choking. His face turning red then purple as he fought to stay awake. The sparkle in Saedus' eye returned as she prodded further into her son's mind, stoking to life the spirits he'd relegated as naughty pupils to some lonely, dark corner. And in answer to their mistress' call, her minions lashed out with renewed purpose and vigor, the pair wailing as if they were all five of the brood yet undone…

"Release him!" blasted a grating voice through the slits of a silver mask: and up stumbled Poltoros behind his words, staff raised before him one last time. A final spell, then, to redeem the foolish choices of his past. To spare a man he'd once treated as a son.

His command had an immediate effect. The remaining banshees were out in a flash, appearing as two storm clouds hovering above Dragan's prostrate body; then, spinning into twisting whirlwinds, they flew at their summoner and were sucked into his skull. Pressing both hands to the red cloth covering his ears, the lich groaned as his staff dropped to the ground. His knees buckled…and he fell face forward, limbs sprawled atop the tyberwood in the grass.

The witch's face turned pure ivory as she trained it on that crumpled mound. Her mouth began to open in disbelief…but instead curled up midway into a tight grimace of pain — then into a wide, shrieking maw of agony — as the bones in her forearm suddenly snapped with two sickening *pops*.

The *GrimHelm's* strength had returned twofold. Still grasping Saedus by the broken limb, his mind cleared now of all daemons, he drew a shuddering breath and proceeded to manhandle her more. Rolling her over with ease, he mounted his mother's chest and rained an elbow down on her face, bursting her nose in a shower of blood. Instantly she went limp, head hitting earth and staying put. The sign of Dragan's victory. She had nothing left to defend her but words.

"O mighty *DoomBringer*," she spoke, hardly above a whisper, then followed it with a ragged breath through her mouth. "Saved by his guardian yet again…"

Dragan had to lean in to hear her over the din; and as he did so, cocking his head slightly to the left, he caught the image of a man approaching with a glint of drawn steel hanging from one side. There was no need to turn further. No need to look his half-brother in the face. He knew what he'd find in those deep blue eyes…and knew that if Baeldrin wanted his life as well as his mother's, the blow would've come already. No…the prince halted a few strides off instead, silently awaiting his turn like a runner anticipating a baton: content to let Saedus speak parting words to her son, yet standing vigil to ensure those words would indeed be her last.

If any gaze *had* been fixed on Baeldrin at that moment, it would've noted him struggling to fight off a swoon. His legs weren't quite beneath him yet, and his sword arm was crossed over his chest as he pressed the weapon's hilt against the hole in his left bicep. Saedus didn't appear aware of his presence, however.

"Have you forgotten who fed and clothed you, son?" she continued, staring up at Dragan's face. "Who succored you all your days? Without me you'd have no feared titles…"

"Without you I'd be free of disgrace! Free of the bloodstained hands I earned through believing your lies! No. Those words fall on deaf ears. I might not have won a great name, but maybe I'd have a real home and family instead. A father I'd have known."

"Your brother's to blame for Acomalath!" And suddenly the witch surprised Dragan by rolling her head to look daggers at Baeldrin. She took another deep, crackling breath. "There he is! The fool who dared steal your armor! You hate him more than me. Slay him now! Take back the plate and crown, and together we can rule these lands side-by-side!"

"You still don't see it," Dragan shook his head in genuine sadness. "To what end? To win nothing but hatred from these nations you'd break with the sword? There's no glory in the whip and shackles. No legend to be forged with nothing left to overcome. No longer will I be the child hiding behind your skirt, Mother. Today I choose my own path!" And with that, he pushed himself up and stood. "Farewell. Perhaps the Daemon will be kind."

"No, son! Wait!" The *Spider's* voice was filled with panic as Dragan turned from her to meet Baeldrin's gaze.

The half-siblings exchanged no words: yet Baeldrin nodded as if in answer to a question posed. Then he stepped in to take Dragan's place, grip tightening on the blade in hand.

"Coward!" the witch cried at her son's back. "You've not the stomach to slay me yourself?"

But the *DoomBringer* was done with her. He barely even heard her shouts as he strode away. All that remained was the broken old man lying face-down before him. Before he could shed the final strip of skin from his former life and pass on into the new, he must say goodbye to the one who'd held the door open. If not for Poltoros, he'd be dead thrice over — and he'd have no inkling of what a true parent should be.

More desperate shouts from his mother hit him in the back and slid futilely to the ground: "Dragan! Protect me!"

He knew time was against him. Any moment now Baeldrin would bring an end to the scourge of these lands — and as Saedus' spirit fled to the netherworld, she'd pull her stewards' souls down with her. Kneeling, he rolled the lich's body over and stripped off both mask and hood, running a supporting hand behind Poltoros' head so they could look level at one another. The blaze in Dragan's eyes had since died and been replaced by their native blue, but the orbs staring back at him remained black.

"Dragan?" scraped the lich's voice. He was clearly exhausted. Disoriented. "Where is she?"

"*Shhh*...listen to me. She's fallen! You're almost free..."

Poltoros smiled as the words slowly registered in his thoughts. "At last! I've waited so long..."

"You rescued me..." Dragan glanced over his shoulder. Baeldrin knelt over Saedus now with his blade held to her throat, apparently finished with whatever it was he needed to say to her. But Dragan wouldn't interfere to buy more time. The Prince of Domal had his own score to settle.

"No, son..."

Dragan whipped his face back to his old tutor and friend. The man's papery eyelids were shut now, but his smile had widened further.

"You delivered yourself. All I did was..."

A stifled cry from behind them cut off Poltoros' speech. Then he spoke no more. His mouth fell open, losing the grin…yet his eyes had reopened in his passing, and the black in them was fading fast. Soon they were clear as the day he was born.

Dragan gazed into those eyes a moment longer, recalling early memories of a shared past. Then he reached out and pulled them shut.

49

"DoomBringer..."

The word hardly left one mouth before it was freed from another just ahead, pummeling the hero from either side of the lane down which he strode. At times the acknowledgement was voiced aloud, aimed directly at him and followed by a nod of greeting; but more often it came to his ears as a low, awestruck murmur of reverence—or even fear. *I've made this walk before,* Dragan mused as he passed the huddled groups of soldiers.

He was in a different realm now, but the faces staring up at him looked the same as on the day he'd defeated the Lion of Agrardob. One might've assumed the warrior who'd all but single-handedly won yesterday's battle would receive some fanfare—and Dragan supposed it was better than his head mounted on a stake for his past transgressions. To be honest, though, there was another man who deserved as much credit for the triumph. *More, actually.* Baeldrin had been the one to orchestrate the alliance between Berac and Oen, after all, thus ensuring enough men were afield to even put up a fight. And if not for his half-brother's unlooked-for appearance at the crucial moment, Dragan's struggle with Saedus might've gone the other way. *Yet he's as unlikely to receive a victory parade as I am. That's one thing we have in common.*

Although Dragan's eyes had hardly strayed from his destination since taking the first step toward it, suddenly he found himself standing before the threshold, momentarily pondering where he was and how he'd arrived there. His reverie had been strong, indeed. *Or maybe my mind's still addled from the banshees' control.* He realized one of the two soldiers maintaining vigil at the tent's entrance had a hand held out. Then the guard's words of a moment earlier registered as well. *He wants my sword.*

"You must disarm before you enter..." the man elaborated, though seeming less sure of himself now since Dragan hadn't immediately complied. His teeth were gritted in a worried frown, and his companion appeared equally distressed. The second guard's free hand inched slowly to his spear's shaft, as if readying to lower its tip on the visitor—but a single glance from Dragan stopped this motion midway. The man swallowed hard instead and let the gloved fist fall to his side.

Still Dragan made no move to acquiesce, merely turning his face away from the pair to consider their demand. His eyes lit upon Gorm Nadur in the distance as he did so, and the peak caught and held his gaze, causing him to rudely ignore the guards for a drawn-out moment. The last time he stared at the mountain had been through the bars of a Sinian prison cart. Would they attempt to return him there as soon as he ceded his sword?

"I'm sorry, lord...but I must insist."

Both guards flinched as Dragan shot a hand to his hilt, the closest man nearly falling into the canvas behind him as he took an involuntary step backwards. Yet instead of finding his head suddenly swept away by the hero's drawn blade, this one soon felt the visitor's weapon, still sheathed and held sideways, shoved into his arms and chest. "See that it's cleaned and oiled before you return it," Dragan spoke at last then shouldered past the slack-jawed sentries and pushed through the entrance's flap. The well-lit interior was in sharp contrast to the fading light outside; and in response to this change he paused just inside the portal, allowing his eyes to adjust.

"And here's our champion, as we speak!" announced Torensus Oen, waving a wrinkled, cup-filled hand in the newcomer's direction. Apparently there'd been some celebrating going on while the tent's occupants waited for Dragan to arrive. The old man's greeting seemed overly enthusiastic, considering the likely nature of this summons...and his words were a bit slurred. "Welcome, Prince of Ost."

Other figures within turned their heads on the object of Torensus' attention now, including King Oen himself — seated on a cushioned throne in all his finery, leaning forward slightly with a goblet cupped in both hands — and several of his attendants. The latter began to scurry from the room immediately, not bothering to wait for dismissal. Likely they'd been instructed to make themselves scarce as soon as their lord's visitor arrived. Dragan hardly noticed them — even as one woman nearly bumped his arm with a tray in her rush to exit behind him. His gaze had just met Bronwyn's own scrutiny, and for the moment all else was lost.

The king's niece had been crying earlier, he discerned. *Over Fedrin's death, no doubt — and perhaps some others she'd held close. She must be upset with her father. His drunken joy was dearly bought...*

Their mutual stare was short-lived, however. As soon as the king addressed his guest, Bronwyn meekly looked away.

"Come in, Dragan, and put yourself at ease." Deserus leaned back casually in his seat and took a sip of wine. "This tent is not a cage."

"We both know that's a lie," said Dragan — yet he came forward all the same, halting within a few paces of Oen's throne. "It's just a different sort of cage. One with invisible bars."

A bark of laughter escaped Torensus' lips. "I doubt our entire army could subdue you by force, man! It's we who should be wary, don't you think?"

"My brother exaggerates, of course," said Deserus, turning a slight grin from Torensus to Dragan. "Still I trust you see his point. Have a seat...and let's start again. More civil this time, perhaps?"

The king motioned to a nearby couch, but Dragan declined by not moving a muscle. "I'm listening," was all he said.

Deserus sighed and ran a hand down his gray beard. "Very well. I owe you an apology for not summoning you yesterday. There was much that needed my immediate attention, as you can imagine. But Torensus reminded me that you're not one to keep waiting — and so we made a point to discuss you this morning at length. First we must offer you our sincere thanks for coming to our aid, despite the circumstances behind..."

"So it's all decided, then?" Dragan rudely cut in, frowning. "My fate's been tossed and pulled between the pair of you — like two old crows squabbling over a worm? Why bother to soften the blow?"

"Dragan, please..." Bronwyn chimed in from her uncle's right side, her voice visibly startling the champion as if he'd forgotten she was present. Yet she got nothing else out beyond this brief plea. Once more she was cowed by the king's words.

This isn't like you, Bronwyn, Dragan considered. *Were you let in on their plans and coached to keep quiet – or are you nervous because they left you in the dark?* These thoughts flashed through Dragan's mind even as Deserus spoke:

"Fine, *DoomBringer*." His eyes narrowed as he fought to maintain patience. "I don't know why I ever allowed such insolence from you...but I might as well save my breath. You tell me, then: what *should* I make of you? Savior? Traitor? Heartbreaker or friend? You think your fame sets you above my judgment — and you're wrong. State your case, if you wish. But you're *not* absolved. Not yet."

"Gods!" cried Torensus, nearly choking on his wine. All this harsh and stern talk was apparently starting to sober him — but not fast enough for him to bother hiding his annoyance at the discoursers. "What happened to '*more civil this time*?' Just let me tell him our proposal, brother, and we can avoid all this."

Deserus sighed again. His cheeks were flushed now; yet after a moment he relented, nodding for his sibling to continue. As he did so, a jewel on the crown of Sinia sparkled in the lamplight.

"Excellent," Torensus grinned, giving Dragan a once-over. "Ah! You must forgive our poor manners! Anden! Some wine for our guest!"

A young man entered with a cup for Dragan, averting his eyes as he held it forth. The Bastard of Domal didn't hesitate to accept; yet he made no move to drink from the vessel, merely standing with it held loosely in hand, still frowning as he waited for Bronwyn's father to get to the point.

"Surely you know how much we're indebted to you," Torensus began. "For all of your heroics in Mardotha — and for your great victory here just yesterday. But you must also acknowledge our grievances. Strictly speaking, you've broken none of our laws: for you never swore an oath to Deserus that would keep you from abandoning us...nor does an assault on our Ithirian allies dictate that we *must* turn you over to them. And your duel with brave Astelidus was begun by him, after all. None of these things demanded your imprisonment." Here he paused, glancing at his brother before taking another drink of wine. "However," he began again with an apologetic note to his voice, "...there's still the matter of you escaping the king's sentence — regardless of how it was my *wicked daughter* here who aided you." He grinned again as he said the last. "And despite the boon we received as a result. Yet we're willing to forgive you all these slights, Dragan — even to the point of risking our alliance with the Ithiros in harboring you — if you'll but agree to one thing. And there's no need to frown, hero, for we believe you'll find it to your liking! It's a thing all eligible Sinian men, young or old, would crawl over themselves like insects to be the first to get at. A thing you yourself nearly died fighting for. What we're offering is my daughter's hand in marriage."

"*What?*" Bronwyn blurted out, her cheeks reddening. Whether it was from anger or embarrassment or both wasn't immediately obvious. She returned her gaze to Dragan, choosing to address him before her father: "You have to believe me! I had no idea..."

"Come now, daughter," Torensus chided amusedly. "Why play coy with us? You can deny it all you like — but I'm no fool. We all know what you want."

Bronwyn's blush deepened. "Apparently it doesn't matter what *I* want! You couldn't have talked to me about this first?"

"And let you sabotage our plan before we could get it out on the table? Ha! Not a chance. Don't you even want to hear what Dragan thinks about the offer before you try to talk him out of it — just because it came from me first rather than him? Honestly, I'm merely doing him a favor. Isn't that right, son?" Torensus' eyes found Dragan's again, and in that moment the cheer in them was gone. The look said: *Don't you dare disagree with me, boy. Only a fool would insult the king's brother. You've no choice but to accept our proposal.* Then the mirth returned. "I'd hurry and say *yes* before the silly girl runs off pouting!"

Yet Dragan said nothing of the sort. Instead he continued to stand in silence, wine unsipped, frowning even deeper than before.

Bronwyn had clearly been expecting such a reaction — or lack thereof — from him. She was so pleased by her correct guess, in fact, that for a moment the urge to say '*I told you so*' won out over anger and embarrassment...and even squashed a growing tingle of excitement at the prospect of her and Dragan sharing a future together. "See, Father?" she smirked. "What did you expect? For him to drop to his knees, praising your generosity? What did you think was different now than in Mardotha — other than all your warnings about him having proved true? You didn't want me with him then. So why now? Not just because you want to see me happy, that's for certain! It's all about you and Uncle instead. A contract to legitimize Dragan, bringing him back into the fold. Some fine plan — *if only you had willing participants!*"

"Hush, girl!" Torensus hissed, appearing stone sober now in his anger. "Let the man speak for himself! You're willing enough, *as I said*." Then he turned to Dragan: "Perhaps you'd like the evening to think on the matter? Marriage isn't a thing to be taken lightly, I know — even considering who we're offering. What say you, Deserus?" He cut his eyes to his brother. "Shall we meet again in the morning? Give them some time to warm to the idea?"

"Agreed. It seems we all need a recess to simmer down." The king looked then to his niece. "Your father and I will retire to his tent now — and give you two a night alone."

Bronwyn held his gaze defiantly for a moment...yet nodded her acceptance just before he turned away.

"But consider this, Dragan, before I depart. A union with Bronwyn needn't leave you idle. With the grievous loss of Fedrin and others of our captains, we're in need of heroes to replenish the ranks. In Mardotha you led a modest band of warriors into battle...yet your prowess and reputation should afford you a loftier position than that. Take my niece's hand and swear fealty to me, and I'll place you in command over *all* the legions of Sinia, answerable to no man but myself. As Torensus said, you won a great victory yesterday — but our safety's not yet secured. Who knows what will happen in the aftermath? Domal lies in chaos, and the need for our alliance with Berac is done. No...war is still on the horizon, I fear: and there's no man better at waging war than the *Bringer of Doom*."

"No matter how much I've longed for it these past months," said Dragan, finally moving to set down his cup, "...an evening in your niece's arms will do nothing to sway my answer. Nor will any other bribe or threat the pair of you can devise. Something happened to me after I left Mardotha. Something I can't explain to myself, much less make you understand. You think I fear idleness? Perhaps that's so. There *are* still trials awaiting me on the horizon: but I don't think they involve your politics or wars." His eyes shifted to Bronwyn as he spoke this last: "I'm leaving tomorrow."

"Bah!" spat Torensus, flinging his not-quite empty cup to the ground in a fit of anger. The boy Anden was there in an instant to grab up the vessel — but only found himself an indiscriminate target of his lord's rage. "Get out!" the elderly man shouted, looking around for something else to throw. But before Torensus could vent any further, the king lashed out with a sharp command, ordering him to compose himself.

Deserus Oen's scowl was as deep as his brother's, however: and not just from the outburst. The indignation in his eyes was palpable. "Where will you run to now, drifter? You had your pleasure with my niece...and slew an irreplaceable champion over her. And now you expect me to simply bid you farewell—while watching you toss her aside again like some common whore?"

"Our relations aren't your business, Uncle!" Bronwyn countered, her earlier meekness gone. "You act as if he forced me into his bed!"

"Silence!" cried Torensus, pushing himself up to stand—and nearly falling in the process. The wine may've loosened its hold on his thoughts somewhat, yet it still loitered unabashedly in his body. Steadying himself, he pointed a gnarled finger at Dragan: "Set this *bastard* in chains, brother! A year in the dungeon will clear the fool's mind!"

"Sit down, Torensus," the king spoke softly but sternly, suddenly relenting. It was as if his sibling's words had reminded him to clear his own mind. To let go of his emotion and focus instead on the logic of the matter at hand. Had they gone entirely mad? Two old goats threatening the deadliest warrior alive—and only a handful of guards within earshot? This man could break both their necks before Deserus even got out an alarm. "We shouldn't be so surprised. It's in his nature to move on after he's left his mark." He shook his head at Dragan then, disapprovingly. "So be it, Prince of Ost. You've made your decision. We'll give you until noon tomorrow to clear out."

"What?" Torensus' jaw dropped in shock. "You mean to let him walk out of here—after we've just threatened him with our wrath?"

"I'm not finished!" Deserus snapped. "Unless you'd like to put the shackles on him yourself?"

Torensus frowned but said nothing.

"I didn't think so. Your earlier jest wasn't far from the truth. Who among our men would dare lift a finger against this hero, whether out of praise or fear? How many of our lives would be spent to subdue him—and to what end? If he'll not join us willingly, what use is he languishing in prison?" He turned again to Dragan. "But know this, *GrimHelm*. After midday tomorrow, you're no longer welcome in my presence or in my lands. If you're found lingering in the camp after noon, I *will* set the entire army against you, no matter the cost. You can't refuse me and still roam among us at your leisure—*and you'll never toy with Bronwyn again!*"

"This is a mistake, Deserus!" Torensus cut in once more before Dragan or his daughter could respond. "Leave him alive and free after *this*, and you'll find him set *against* you next time on the battlefield. Or worse: you could end up like poor Mehdurin, waking one day to find his blade at your neck!"

"That was the witch's doing—not his!" said Bronwyn at last, no longer able to contain herself. "He's free of her now..."

"No, Bronwyn," Dragan spoke, drawing all eyes to him. "Your father's right to distrust me. What have I ever done to prove otherwise?"

"*Give them your word, then,*" she urged, almost a pleading whisper. "Or say anything else but that! *Daemon!* Why can't you just tell them what they want to hear?"

"My word means nothing."

"Enough of this," said the king, rising from his seat and stepping toward his niece to look her square in the face. "My order's been given, Bronwyn. You'll abide by it *this time* or be held in treason." Still meeting her gaze, he placed one hand lightly on her shoulder, and his lips curled up into an apologetic half-smile. He drew in a breath as if he'd say more but sighed and turned instead, motioning for his brother to follow him out of the tent.

Torensus also sucked in air as if he'd continue complaining...but just then servants began to reenter the room, gathering up such goods as would need be moved with Deserus to the adjacent pavilion. He followed their motions for a few blinks of his glazed eyes then shook his head briskly as if to sling all of the *nonsense* away. Anden finally returned his wine cup—now refilled—without incident, and another lad draped a coat about his shoulders, waiting for him to grasp it before stepping aside.

Then, without further delay, the brothers and their retainers headed out into the night, leaving the would-be couple behind.

Neither of the pair rushed to speak. Instead, as if really seeing Bronwyn for the first time that evening, Dragan took a moment to examine her gorgeous coral gown—with its string laces that crisscrossed over her enticing cleavage—before staring again into her luring eyes. In contrast to his relaxed stance, however, she stood with arms folded tightly beneath her breasts, biting her lip as she struggled to fight off her emotion, waiting to see if he'd answer for his foolishness without further scolding to prompt him.

Finally he did so, although his words weren't at all like the ones she'd been expecting. "I should be drowning in torment over this. Over *you*. You've never looked more beautiful than you do tonight. Yet all I feel is numb."

She almost ran to him then, longing to forget everything save the touch of his lips as she melted away in his arms. But the last part held her back. *Numb.* Did the bastard really just say that? *'Oh Bronwyn...you're the most ravishing creature in all the world—yet still less than dirt to a pompous ass like me?'* Had he gone insane? She blinked at the sudden jolt of pain from her bottom lip. Her teeth had nearly drawn blood. "You said you'd find no peace until your mother was slain..." she managed at last, voice quavering. "Well, she's gone! So what's wrong with you now?"

"Bronwyn, I..." Dragan held up his hand in a gesture to soothe her—yet she just barreled on:

"But that was a lie, wasn't it? You'd have told me *anything* to get you out of that cage! All you wanted was to..."

"*Calm yourself!*" he suddenly flung back at her, causing her jaw to clamp shut instantly and her eyes to widen in shock. The words hadn't been shouted, yet they carried all the weight of a bellowed command. "It was no lie. You came to me with the key in hand, remember? Can you honestly tell me you needed to be *persuaded*?"

It took her a few breaths to recover from the unexpected retort; but when she did speak again, she was admirably composed. "No. You're right. The thought of you in there was slowly killing me." She sighed. "I didn't fall in love with a *knee-bender*, Dragan. Like my father said, there were plenty of strong, handsome warriors in this army that I *could've* chosen. Men — like Astelidus — who'd slaver at the very thought of swearing oaths to fulfill my uncle's every whim. Yet I saw in you the rebel I longed to be. You weren't meant to be tied down."

"*Weren't?*" said Dragan, raising an eyebrow. "But now..."

"Maybe now things have changed..." She risked a half-smile. "Just look at us! We should be joining those two in celebration." She jerked her head in the direction her father and uncle had departed. "Yet here we stand arguing instead, you *numb* and me on the verge of tears!"

"I can't stay..."

"Then take me with you! Return the favor, and set me free of this cell!" She waved an arm around her as she said the last, obviously in reference to Dragan's earlier talk of *invisible bars*. Her face had lit up with eagerness as she voiced her true heart's desire — but quickly the expression fell. A hand shot involuntarily to her mouth as if she'd spoken an unladylike curse. "Oh gods! I've done it again. But I don't care!" In an instant she closed the distance between them, throwing herself onto the hero, reaching behind his neck to pull his face down to hers.

Dragan flinched as if to deny the embrace. Yet he gave in as soon as her lips brushed his own, pulling the woman's body tightly against him as he returned the kiss with abandon. It'd been too long since he last held her. He could fend off uncounted hordes of men and beasts, dealing death without rest throughout night and day — but this threefold assault of Bronwyn's touch, scent, and passion dropped him like a heart-shot stag. It took all his strength of will to rise from the killing ground, gripping her by the arms and lightly pushing her away.

She frowned at the break: but only as if it were a mild annoyance. This new surge of excitement and enthusiasm in her was not to be so easily quelled: "We could slip away tonight! Allethion and Bellaroth are in the pens nearby, barely guarded! I need only gather a few supplies..."

"No!" he cut her off, taking a step away. "I'm sorry."

Bronwyn opened her mouth to object but stopped short. At that moment she found the truth in his eyes: nothing she could say or do would persuade him. It was as if in an instant they'd transformed from star-crossed lovers to strangers separated by an impassable gulf. Then the tears came. They streamed down her cheeks as she blinked her lids against them. "What happened to you out there? What happened to *us*?"

The Black King approached Oen's niece as she spoke her words of loss, and once more the young woman found herself wrapped in his arms. Yet this second embrace lacked the passion of the first. This was the hug of a father consoling a crestfallen child. "I *did* find peace in my mother's death, Bronwyn. At least for today. But there's a hollow in me now where her barbs were before. I feel like a smashed lump of clay, waiting to be remolded: but I can't yet see the new person I'm to become. *Peace* isn't enough. I won't truly live again until I've discovered this new man's desires and purpose for being. And I must do that alone, without any distractions…"

Sniffling, Bronwyn turned her face to the side, snuggling deeper against him. "I wouldn't hinder your quest," she spoke, almost in a whisper.

"Not of your own will, perhaps. But who knows what dangers await? The need to protect you from them might lead me astray." Unfolding one arm from around her, Dragan moved a hand to Bronwyn's chin, prompting her to look up and meet his gaze. "When I've found my answers, our paths may cross again." He tried to present her with a hopeful smile. "And if we're meant to be together then, I swear that no decree from your uncle will keep us apart."

She tried to return his smile but failed at the last, unable to summon enough courage. So instead she buried her face into his chest again and wept.

50

"No farewell this time, brother?"

Dragan yanked the leather girth taut then slipped the belt's prong through a hole in the strap and let it clack against the buckle's frame. Allethion snorted at the resulting constriction of his ribcage—or perhaps instead from his annoyance at Baeldrin's unwelcome intrusion. Only the horse knew which it was. Yet there was no such ambiguity in his master's response: "I'd have avoided one, yes…and had thought the same of you." Dragan took a step back from the saddle to gain a better view of his approaching half-sibling. "You take a great risk, seeking me here." Even as he addressed the object of that last statement, however, his gaze shifted from Baeldrin's tall, regally attired form to the slender, dark-robed figure walking two paces behind the man.

A sand elf maiden with flowing silver hair—and sharp amber eyes that were busily sweeping her surroundings as if in search of a hidden threat.

Who's this? the Black King pondered. *His bodyguard?*

Baeldrin didn't miss Dragan's scrutiny of his companion. "Intriguing, isn't she?" he grinned, half-turning to appraise the elf as she came to a halt beside him just inside Allethion's pen. "This is Fashra, Dragan. I trust you don't mind her presence?"

"I've nothing to hide in my words to you. Nor shall this woman spare you my wrath should you wake it."

Baeldrin raised his right hand to pat Allethion's flank. His wounded left arm was in a sling. "Two days ago I might've scoffed at that. But not now. Not since I learned the truth."

"The truth of what?" Dragan frowned.

"That you've ascended," the elf spoke in Baeldrin's stead. Her voice was like a crisp mountain stream that, for all its gentle ripples, held the power and resolve to carve out a massive canyon over time. "We'd be fools indeed to bait you, my lord."

For a moment Dragan met and held the exotic woman's seductive gaze; then, bending to lift a bag near his feet, he returned to packing. "Already handed over your leash to a new mistress, prince? This meeting was her idea, I take it."

Baeldrin loosed a snort of laughter. "There was a bit of convincing involved, to be sure. On both sides. First I had to steal her away from Berac." He moved the hand with which he'd been petting Allethion to the elf's face and ran two fingers softly down her cheek. The action didn't seem to displease the woman. "Fashra claims to owe you a life debt, *DoomBringer*. Though I was hoping you'd absolve us both."

Dragan paused in his work once more to stare at the pair before him. "How do you know of my destiny, elf? And what's this debt he speaks of?"

"You slew Astelidus Ny in single combat! The very same man who took my brother Ashyd's life. That kill should've been mine in revenge. Yet even so, I place myself in your service as repayment." She followed her words with a bow, deep and formal.

Dragan's face revealed nothing of what he thought about having a she-elf at his beck and call—nor how he felt about his killing Astelidus being the deed that had won her allegiance. "And my *ascension,* as you called it?"

"Your people have all but forgotten the lore of Kings—yet not so with mine. Forgive me...but I visited this animal last night. The magic drew me here, surely as a blazing red beacon against a dark horizon."

"Is there no possession of mine left unprofaned?" Dragan mused, eyeing his steed anew as if searching for an injury to the horse that he'd thus far failed to detect. "What did you do to him?"

"No harm, I assure you. Yet as soon as I touched the beast, a vision flooded my mind. I saw a white-robed figure sitting on a throne: face hidden in shadow. I believe you know the man. You've seen him before, haven't you?"

Dragan's frown deepened at this, but he made no other answer.

Thus Fashra went on: "I began to take the steps rising to him, but he lifted a palm to halt me and pointed to a marble statue at my side. I may be a stranger to your eyes, lord—but this isn't the first time I've seen your face. That statue was an exact replica of you, and your name was carved into the pedestal. When at last I turned back to the throne, the man's robes were no longer white..."

"Black," Dragan murmured, casting his eyes to the north.

"Just so."

A moment passed between them in silence. Dragan's thoughts had no doubt drifted back to his own encounter with the steward Erroth at Aldrotherin's Red Castle. "And you?" he finally asked, turning to Baeldrin once more.

"I've come to ask your forgiveness, not to bow and scrape at your feet. Yet I won't deny this: when we led that final charge side-by-side, after defeating your mother and setting her forces on the run...in that hour I felt a bond form between us. One that might've been there all along, had Saedus not cast us as rivals from the start. Tell me you didn't feel it too."

"You *murdered our father*—then stole my armor while I was locked away in a cell! Yet here you stand professing your *brotherly love*?" Dragan shook his head tiredly. "Did you really think one shared victory could erase all your crimes?"

"I can't bring him back from the dead, Dragan...no more than you can bring back all those *you* slew in the witch's name. You needn't bother pretending with me. You had no love for Acomalath." The Domalin paused a moment to reflect. "As for the armor: what use is a magical breastplate — so I thought it — collecting dust in a tent? Would you have lent it to me had I come begging at your cage?" Then, glancing over his shoulder: "Martassin!"

Dragan hadn't noticed the one newcomer remaining outside of Allethion's pen until that moment. A spindly servant started forward in answer to his lord's summons, clearly encumbered by the weight of a cloth-wrapped bundle held in his arms. His robes were so long that he nearly tripped on the hem twice before reaching his master and offering up his burden.

"Not to me, you dolt!" spat Baeldrin, glancing down sharply at his wounded arm to indicate its uselessness. Then, looking to Dragan again: "I had it cleaned and oiled."

Still frowning from his lord's chastisement, Martassin raised the bundle now for Dragan to take.

"Do what you will with it," said the *GrimHelm*, ignoring the servant in favor of returning to his work. "I never want to see that cursed plate again."

Baeldrin caught Martassin's eye and waved the servant aside. Then his gaze returned to Dragan. "As you wish. In that case…perhaps I'll set it on display in Rardonydd, soon as I regain my throne."

Dragan presented his brother with a skeptical look before bending to retrieve his final belongings from the ground. This bundle contained a pair of sheathed blades wrapped in the cloth: one his own unornamented bastard sword, and the other the bejeweled weapon he'd reclaimed for Gavix in Braured Forest. As his eyes passed over the latter, his thoughts lingered on his former retainer. Should he head south this very day to deliver the heirloom to its rightful owner? Did he dare hope to win back the oaths of service from Ûladriss and the Haxûdī horde, now that he was free at last from his mother's spell? To leave all this *Black King* business behind, returning to his life of glory-seeking wandering instead?

Or should he heed Erroth's words, riding north to rejoin the steward without delay? *"You can't give back your power once it's blossomed,"* the man had said to him. *"I chose to embrace my calling. Will you?"* Even now — mere moments from him swinging into the saddle and setting off — Dragan's mind was still torn. And now here was his half-brother and an elfin minx standing before him: two more who'd use him to further their own gains, just as the Oen siblings had tried to yoke him the day before. "Why have you *really* come, Baeldrin? I'm not fool enough to believe you've reformed overnight. What is it you want of me?"

"So you doubt my sincerity…as well as my ability to regain power in Domal. I may never grace the pages of the *Book of Kings* alongside you, Dragan, but that doesn't make me impotent. You saw me wrench the oath from Sorec at sword's tip after we routed his forces! I fled Domal with only Martassin here in tow—yet I'll be returning with an army at my heels."

Dragan shook his head, unconvinced. "An army of questionable loyalty and crushed morale, stripped of their blades and all but the barest provisions. You'll have trouble holding them together long enough to reach the Olendarth...much less to mount an assault on Relinydd." Finished tying down the sword bundle, he stepped away from Allethion and looked his brother in the eye. "And you're lucky Deserus allowed you even that. Anxious as I am to be away, I'd expected you to march before I took my leave. We're both heroes of the hour, Baeldrin— and as soon as the celebrations die down, you may find your new allies have had a change of heart."

"All the more reason for me to have come here," Baeldrin returned without hesitation, his demeanor calm despite Dragan's harsh rebuff. "Who needs scraps from those old fools' table when he can have a powerful young mage-king at his side?" Taking a step forward, the prince reached into his clothing and produced the Sun of Domal, holding it out to Dragan in his unbound hand. "You ask what I want of you? Well here you have it."

Dragan hadn't beheld the triple-rayed disc since his and Baeldrin's stances were reversed: on that day in Ost when he'd thrust the thing upon his brother as if it were a poisonous asp to be quickly rid of. "Did I not make it clear before? I've no use for that symbol."

"Can you still be so sure?" Baeldrin countered with a wry smile. "Back then you were a soldier of fortune; but now you're a rising monarch with claims over several lands. Why sit alone in a deserted keep far to the north—or take up the petty rule of your mother's savages in Ost—when you could live a life of luxury and worthy challenges in Relinydd? Or Rardonydd itself, for that matter. Take your pick!" He raised the Sun of Domal a bit higher and nodded to it, offering it up again. "This may be mine by rights, but Acomalath wanted you to have it. If he'd had his way, no doubt he'd have set you on the throne in my place. Domal is big enough for both of us, brother. Together we can do more than just *retake* the twin cities. We can restore our father's land to its past glory! What do you say?"

Despite his answer being decided before Baeldrin's speech had hardly gotten underway, Dragan didn't rush to reply. It must've been exceedingly difficult for the Domalin prince to concede respect to his formerly-loathed bastard brother, and so Dragan thought at very least he could feign a moment of consideration for the generous offer—however self-serving to Baeldrin it was beneath the surface. "Or I could marry Bronwyn instead," he finally spoke after a long, audible sigh, "...and take command of the armies of Sinia—according to King Oen's proposal to me yesterday. No. I'm sorry. I must find my own path."

Baeldrin didn't bother trying to hide his scowl at the response. Letting fall the hand holding the Sun of Domal, he looked sharply at Fashra for support. "I told you he wouldn't be swayed..."

"And I told *you* what would happen if he wasn't."

Although the woman's face was impassive, Dragan thought he saw the hint of a smile in her eyes. She'd known more so than Baeldrin that this enterprise would fail—yet it seemed she was the one who'd prodded him to it. *This elf's a mystery I might enjoy unraveling*, he thought, more subconsciously than not.

"So that's it, then?" Baeldrin's voice had risen a notch with his displeasure. "You change masters more than a starving whore! Wait...that's just what you are now, isn't it? How foolish of me to dissemble!"

Dragan expected the woman to at least loose a retort if not slap the prince's face outright—or worse. But she did nothing of the kind, ignoring the comment completely as Baeldrin pressed on:

"Yet I've not heard my brother accept your offer. I'm betting he's no more interested in it than he is of mine. Isn't that so, Dragan?"

Indeed that *should* have been the case, and Dragan almost opened his mouth to voice an agreement. But then, meeting the woman's intense amber stare once more, he was suddenly unsure. On the one hand, if he were to take another with him—and a female, at that—should it not be Bronwyn, the woman he loved? Or *did* he love her, truly? At one point he'd thought he did, and he knew his words to her last night had come from the heart. Still...things had changed between them. If he really loved her unconditionally, then wouldn't he have accepted Deserus' offer and stayed with her, regardless of what grand destiny lay waiting for him out there in the wilds?

Still holding the she-elf's gaze, Dragan felt as if time had slowed around him. Vaguely he heard Baeldrin say something else in the background, but the words weren't strong enough to pull his thoughts away. He saw now that taking this elf-woman with him wouldn't be the same as dragging Bronwyn along behind. Fashra could take care of herself...and perhaps even take care of him as well, if her oath held true. Sand elves were rumored to be deadly, efficient fighters, after all. Both sexes alike. And this one claimed to know much of the lore of Kings, not to mention her apparent ability to seek out Allethion and tap into the steed's magic. What better guide could he have on his journey besides Erroth himself? And for the moment his steward was leagues upon leagues away...

Then, just like that, his path was decided: the Red Castle would have to wait.

"Well, brother," he said at last, breaking free of his reverie to look Baeldrin in the face and smile. "You were right about one thing: I *am* a king now, and a king needs subjects. I suppose I'll take Fashra here as the first." Thrusting a foot into

Allethion's stirrup, he swung himself into the saddle then looked back to the elf, holding out a hand for her to join him.

At last the woman's flat expression cracked, replaced by a mischievous grin that lit up her face. Baeldrin watched with reddening cheeks and gritted teeth as she strode forth and doffed her black robes to reveal a tight bodice and divided skirts beneath. Then she took Dragan's hand and let the hero pull her up into the saddle behind him.

"Be warned, Dragan!" Baeldrin blurted suddenly, having held his tongue for long enough. "The elf's treacherous! You'd best hope she doesn't stick a blade in you while you sleep…"

"I won't live out my days seeing daggers in every shadow," Dragan laughed, taking the reins in hand. "If I'm to share the Red King's fate, then so be it." For a moment his eyes found and lingered on the northern horizon; then he began to turn Allethion south instead, causing a startled, encumbered Martassin to trip and nearly fall again as the servant hurried out of the way. "Farewell, brother. I wish you success in the task ahead."

For an instant Baeldrin looked as if he might let wounded pride seep out into his reply; but then he shook his head slightly, and his expression changed as he bit back whatever spiteful words were in his mind. "You should reconsider my offer. I won't hold a throne vacant for you if I retake my own without your aid."

"Domal's your dream, Baeldrin, not mine. But let's hope this new sentiment between us holds."

"Agreed. So what *is* your plan, then? You turn the horse as if you mean to escape your own holdings as well."

"There's something I must see to first." Breaking his gaze with the prince, Dragan glanced now impatiently toward the south. Toward Haxûd.

"Then farewell, Black King. Until we meet again."

Finding his brother's gaze one last time, Dragan nodded then set Allethion in motion, swiftly leaving Baeldrin and the servant far behind. Fashra wrapped her arms tightly around him and leaned in close as the white horse picked up speed, her long silver hair streaming behind them on the wind.

Epilogue

"Drink. Please…you must."

Reluctantly, the slave turned his head to meet the water bearer's pitiful gaze, squinting and raising a hand to shield his own fair elfin eyes from the torturous sun. Having stared too long at the shadowed patch of earth over which he'd been toiling since daybreak, he grimaced in pain at the sudden influx of light.

"Quickly!" the elf-child urged, thrusting a bladder forward before stealing a glance over her shoulder at the nearest gray-robed taskmaster. That gruesome walking corpse stood but a few paces away from them, seemingly boring a hole in the girl's back with its glazed white, pupilless orbs that stared from beneath a drawn, tattered cowl. If the slave hesitated much longer to accept what meager sustenance was offered out here in the unforgiving desert, one of these zombies would surely take note and report him to the overseer.

Then the real hell would begin. Sanisar the Usurper, Lord of Agrigoth, did not allow his valuable elfin thralls to give up on living.

Fighting out of his stupor, the slave grabbed the bladder and began to drink from it slowly, all the while covertly surveying the scene about him with rapidly adjusting sight. The hillside mineshaft opened a short distance off to his left: that gaping black mouth through which a steady stream of his fellow slaves came and went with their baskets, busying themselves with removing quarried rock. Even those working deep within were closely supervised, he knew…just as the elders and children — and known troublemakers like himself — were being observed out here. He'd rather have been slinging a pick in the dark, cool tunnels all day than bent over a mortar in this searing heat; but he was hardly in a position to request a transfer.

"*Enough!*" rasped the taskmaster, taking a step forward and raising its nine-tailed whip threateningly. The minion's voice was like a boot scraping over dry gravel, as if its throat was packed full of the sand at its feet.

Hastily the slave pushed back the bladder and looked away to hide his face, fighting down an almost irresistible urge to assault the foul creature. Not long ago it would've been *him* shouting orders. To servants and priests. To soldiers and slaves of *men*. And when he wasn't issuing commands he would've been idling in luxury like the overseer was just now beneath his erected canopy — not shrinking from this shriveled automaton that smelled as if it'd been rolling in putrid, days-old meat.

Yes, the overseer's condition was markedly better than that of his elfin crew. By the number and quality of attendants and warriors in his entourage alone, not to mention his rich, purple-dyed clothing and lavish jewelry, it was obvious that he was a member of the wealthy ruling caste. There he sat atop cushions spread over an intricately-patterned carpet, enjoying the shade provided for him by the wide awning overhead. A pair of serving girls were waving fronds to fan him, and several others knelt nearby with pitchers and trays of succulent delicacies in hand. He might as well have been Lord Sanisar himself, for all the pomp.

And it didn't stop there. His five assigned bodyguards were a far cry above the common soldiers of this land. One stood vigil at each corner of the canopy, and the last had stationed himself hardly a step from his charge's side. They all wore wicked-looking masks and sheathed, curved swords but little in the way of clothing or armor — for such apparel would only impede their movements. These men were *blademasters*. Members of a sect trained nearly from birth to wield the swords they carried with blinding speed and deadly precision. The slave could attest to their prowess personally, having lost a contest with one of them: despite the fact that in another land he'd been considered a peerless swordsman as well. Perhaps if there'd been only the one nearest the overseer, he would've tried his luck again by now. But five together…and no one to aid him but his wretched kin brandishing mere stones, pickaxes, and hammers?

"Grind!" shrieked the taskmaster, lashing out with its whip to lick the slave's shoulder and arm.

"*Ah!*" the elf flinched in pain, cursing himself for a fool as he plopped down in the sand, snatching up the pestle to resume his work. Why had he let himself get caught up in a flight of fancy? There'd be no rebellion this day. Nor the next. Nor any day to come. He might as well get used to it.

Still… he thought, busying himself so as not to attract further attention. *If I could just get close enough to rip that string of bones from the overseer's neck…*

Another scream filled the air just then, longer and shriller than the slave's cry of a moment before. Disregarding the warning thought that said he'd likely be whipped again for it, the elf straightened his back and craned his neck toward the shout's source.

No! his mind raged, muscles tightening at what he saw. Another taskmaster further away had a familiar elfin female's hair twisted in one hand as it dragged her through the dust, repeatedly striking the maiden with its whip — as if it were actually experiencing some sick pleasure of its own from the torture. *Almari!* the slave shouted again in his mind, feeling his hands ball into fists. He'd known her when they were children…before the easterners had come to carry him back with them beyond the mountains. But now one of these stinking abominations had the innocent woman in its grasp, yanking her along as it strode ever closer to the overseer's canopy.

I won't let them harm you! The slave stood defiantly then, eyes radiating pure hatred in the direction of the awning. It seemed there *would* be a rebellion today, after all. A pitiful insurrection of likely one elf alone, extremely short-lived.

The same taskmaster that'd whipped him caught his motion and raised its ninetail again, preparing to deliver a harder lash than before. The elf shifted his weight, ready to counter the impending blow...

But the whip's crack never came. In the same instant that the minion pulled its arm down from the zenith, the creature's hooded skull nearly exploded before the slave's eyes: crushed like an overripe melon behind the devastating force of a hurled stone!

The man who'd thrown the chunk was just leaping into view from behind one of the nearby outcrops as the slack-jawed elf retraced the stone's trajectory to its source. An imposing figure — tall and muscular with long, dark hair flowing behind a black-armored torso — crossed the distance to his teetering foe in but a few powerful strides and deftly spun, sending a gleaming steel blade soaring in an arc that instantly severed what remained of the minion's ruined head. The gray-robed body dropped to its knees, lingered in that position for a heartbeat, then toppled and slammed hard into the ground.

Several things followed in quick succession while the dazed elf struggled to make sense of it all. Even as the unlooked-for assailant met his wide-eyed gaze, the slave caught sight of several more suddenly-revealed warriors rushing in on the man's heels. Who were these people? And why had they come? Were they savage raiders here to slaughter taskmaster and slave alike in their lust for ore — or might they be looking to acquire the elfin thralls along with it? The first man certainly could've hacked the hesitating slave to pieces before hurling himself at the next undead minion. But he didn't — and it appeared his companions would follow suit.

A rough tally formed in the elf's settling thoughts: about two dozen attackers in total were now weaving through his startled, cowering kin, foolishly targeting the mindless taskmasters first. Their outlandish appearance marked them as foreign invaders instead of native bandits. *They don't know what they're up against — and they've wasted the element of surprise!* He supposed any one *blademaster* was a match for half their number now that the bodyguards had been given a chance to rally. And as for the overseer...

Once more Almari's desperate cry rang out, cutting through the noise of the growing tumult to resound in the slave's ears — and suddenly he had a choice to make. Should he take up the suicidal race to spare a single member of his kin or else gamble with *all* their lives by trying to aid these bizarre foreigners?

Dropping to one knee, he gripped the fallen minion by the arm and flipped the corpse over, tearing aside its robes to reveal the long, curved knife that he'd hoped from experience would be there. "Rise up!" he shouted then, standing to thrust the blade in the air for those about him to see. "Now's your chance!" He made frantic gestures with both arms to indicate them joining him on their feet.

"Arise! Make them pay for your suffering!"

The elf didn't wait to see how many would heed his call. Turning his gaze to the awning, he took off on a mad dash for it, spinning or shoving past anyone in his way. He was nearly upon the threshold without challenge, and his spirits rose at what he saw ahead. The hated overseer was cringing helplessly behind a human shield of serving girls, and even the nearest of his bodyguards had been drawn out and was engaged some distance off! Now was the moment to...

Movement in the corner of one eye...and the slave instinctively rolled to the other side out of harm's path. Yet when he attempted to leap right back up into a ready stance to meet his assailant, he fell flat on his face instead. A terrible pain lanced up his right thigh. Crying out, he involuntarily gripped at the laceration and brought his hand back smeared with blood.

So this is the end, he thought, rolling over in the sand to face his slayer. Was there a grin of triumph behind that hideous mask looming inverted in his line of sight? Time seemed to slow as the *blademaster's* sword rose point-down over his crippled body — and, closing his eyes, the elf awaited the final thrust that would feed his soul to the earth.

Yet it wasn't the slave's own death wail that forced his eyelids back open an instant later: it was a bestial snarl that ripped through the air above, followed by a dark mass that knocked the guard aside like a leaf caught up in a storm wind. Then it was the *blademaster's* turn to scream in agony as the huge, pouncing black tiger sunk its fangs into the man's throat and stole his life away.

Shocked as he was by the sting of his wound and the sight of such an exotic, savage animal coming to his rescue, what the elf saw next eclipsed both. A lean, stunningly beautiful she-elf suddenly appeared at his side, kneeling hurriedly to inspect his spurting thigh with a curious mixture of emotions. Anger? Concern? She was dressed as one of the invaders, not a slave. And surely he would've recalled that striking face had he seen it before. "Who are you?" he managed, grinding his teeth as the woman snatched up his fallen knife and began to cut his pant leg away.

Ignoring the question, she tore a strip from the bloody material, wrapped it around his leg above the gash, then used the knife as a handle to twist it tight.

The slave cried out again at the intense pressure of the application, and for a moment his sight went dim.

The tiger had leapt off of its kill now and was crouched at the she-elf's back, growling low as a warning to any would-be assailant. "You're the one from his vision," the woman spoke as she finished the makeshift tourniquet. "I can't let you die before he's spoken to you..."

"Leave me!" her patient growled, fighting through the shock and pain. "The necromancer…" He jutted his chin at the canopy behind her. "He's controlling them all!"

The she-elf followed his gaze to where the overseer had last been seen hiding behind his servants. A desperate fight had broken out there — and the invaders were incurring losses. With a glance at the cat, the woman made to rise…

"His necklace…" the slave grabbed at her arm, pulling her attention back to him. "Each bone on it binds a minion…and there'll be more coming up from the mine! Strip the thing from his corpse…and stomp it into the ground!"

Nodding understanding, the woman wasted no more time. She leapt to her feet and was off in a flash, a long knife of her own gleaming in hand.

Pushing himself up on his elbows to get a better view, the slave was instantly wracked by another violent wave of pain. He let himself fall back with a groan; and when he finally blinked his eyes open again, he saw black dots swimming in his vision.

Such pretty things, he thought, confusion rapidly setting in.

Then the world faded as he lost consciousness.

"Nine slain. Five crippled." The lean, brow-scarred marshal shook his head following the report, breaking eye contact with Dragan to inspect their remaining men. The few Haxûdî who'd lived through the conflict with only minor wounds were either busily tending less-fortunate companions or dragging corpses to a cleansing pyre. Some of them had fished out crude talismans from beneath their clothing, superstitiously handling them as if they could ward off any curses one might receive from touching the unholy dead.

Dragan frowned at the self-blame written on Ûladriss' face. It had been his own decision to strike immediately with this scouting party rather than wait for their full force to break camp. Not the marshal's. And Fashra had even warned him about the masked guards — yet he'd merely scoffed at the threat.

Were his warriors not the best the world had to offer, after all? That had been his first thought upon hearing her words. But now it seemed this desert realm extending east from Agrardob might be the gateway into a new world all its own. One where the rules were different than they were back home.

One where even the Black King might find himself in over his head.

" Gavix!" Dragan called, choosing his former retainer over Ûladriss to carry out his next commands. He wished the marshal to remain by his side, for he and Fashra were about to question the elf who'd drawn them to this place.

The confident young man who approached at Dragan's summons bore little resemblance to the lad who'd once scraped and stuttered under his lord's hot gaze. The son of Jedan Mûran now had more of his father's bearing than that of a timid youth — as well as the fallen rearguard captain's rank and weapon. There was a soaked red cloth wrapped tightly around Gavix' right triceps as he came into view: yet the wound did nothing to prevent his hand moving involuntarily to the forked pommel of his sword as his sharp eyes met Dragan's own.

Will he unsheathe it against me one day? Dragan thought, recalling the hatred in the youth's gaze on that momentous evening in Gethod not so very long ago. *At least part of him still blames me for his father's death...*

"My lord?" Gavix was standing at attention.

"Gather up their provisions and weapons — and any tools that may be of use to us — and have what can be carried on their donkeys and our horses ready for packing. See to litters for the wounded — then have someone make a sweep of the mine. I don't want anyone left hiding out here who could speak our tale."

"Yes, lord."

Just as the young captain was turning away, Fashra and Erroth strode up to take Gavix' place. The steward's familiar — that same massive black tiger that had fought so ferociously in today's battle — now padded lazily beside the man, happily swishing its tail as if it were no more than an overgrown kitten. Placing a hand on the beast's neck to scratch it behind the ear, Erroth spoke first:

"I've dressed the cut and given him trellin leaf for the pain, but it was your she-elf's quick thinking that saved his life and his leg." He gave an appreciative glance and nod to Fashra. "You should hurry, though. The herb will soon drag him to sleep."

Gone was the dark mask that'd once muffled the steward's speech and hid his cleanly-shaven, angular face from prying eyes. The man was at last "reborn" under a new master's rule...and Dragan was glad to have that strange ceremony ended. Erroth's haunting green eyes never smiled — even in those rare moments when a grin touched his face — yet his words were often as these now had been, belying his appearance of one haughty and unkind.

"What has he told you already?" Dragan looked to Fashra as he started off, leading the pair — with Ûladriss following not far behind — to the spot where the wounded elf lay.

"He thanks us for freeing his people but warns us not to linger here. He says the necromancer may've used his dark art to warn the Usurper before I slew him. Other than that...only that he's agreed to speak with you."

Dragan eyed the woman suspiciously. "You're holding something back."

Fashra frowned and came to a halt, pulling Dragan aside to stop the group's procession. They were in earshot of the prostrate elf now, so she lowered her voice in confidence. "No more than a feeling. He may speak of gratitude and concern for his kin…but mark carefully his words. There's something else lurking behind them. A side of him he doesn't want us to know."

Dragan simply nodded as one satisfied then moved on, halting a few steps from the object of their brief discussion. Another attractive elf woman—this one a member of the liberated slaves—was kneeling over Erroth's patient, tenderly wiping sweat from his brow with a look of concern on her face. She gazed up at the onlookers then down again questioningly, whereupon her kinsman nodded as if to indicate it was acceptable for her to leave him.

As soon as the female stood to depart, Dragan greeted the male: "I'm told you're to thank for today's victory—or at least for saving what's left of my scouts. What's your name?"

"Cirad." The elf's voice came out weakly, and after speaking he gritted his teeth in discomfort.

"*Cirad,*" Dragan repeated the name, pausing a moment as if rolling it over in his mind. "I'm sorry for your hurt. Erroth here…" he indicated the steward with a gesture, "…says you need sleep, so we'll be brief. My name is Dragan Saedus, and these are the foremost of my followers. You must be wondering why we've come."

Cirad's eyes flicked to Fashra as he replied. "She says a vision led you to this land. That you saw me here before departing your home, far to the west. Is this true?"

"It is. I saw you standing before the throne of the one you call the Usurper, whose identity Fashra here helped me decipher. You didn't look very pleased." Dragan showed a wry grin. "But that was at the end. First I beheld you in a different realm: a coastal marshland spreading beneath a wide, clear blue sky. You were standing there alone at the base of a beautiful white tower, deep in thought, slowly running a finger down the metal slab barring entrance. Then time shot forward, and you were replaced in that very spot by another man: lean, dark-haired, with intense eyes. He held a baby in the crook of one arm, and his free hand reached out to touch the door. There were others there to support him, standing close behind; yet I sensed an evil taint on the scene. One that I've felt before." He sighed, glancing to Erroth as if for support. "If that baby's who we think he is, then I must protect him from that evil. No matter the cost."

The elf's eyes and mouth had opened wide as he listened to all of this. There was no need for him to confirm belief with words. The look on his face made it plain for all to see. "What is it you want from me?" he asked instead, eyelids suddenly drooping from the strain of holding them up. Just as quickly he snapped them back open, eyeballs rolling back into focus on Dragan's face. He didn't have much time left, it seemed, before sleep came. "You wish me to lead you to this tower?"

"Why else would the vision have shown me your face? Do you deny having been there before?"

"No. It's there, just as you said—far to the east, in the land of Kagnus." The elf's gaze briefly touched the horizon behind Dragan. "You've marched an army into this desert? You said these men were scouts..."

Dragan nodded.

"Then I shall be your guide: on one condition. Finish what you started here! Help me free the rest of my kin who toil in Sanisar's palace. Lead your warriors against him before he has time to prepare!"

Dragan gave no immediate response to this, only furrowing his brow at the proposal. Thus Cirad pressed on:

"The Usurper sits his throne, not two days' walk from here, preparing to invade the forest realms where you'd have me lead you. He doesn't think of threats at his doorstep and might be taken unaware—just as the overseer was today. A swift victory's within your grasp!" Excitement must've made the elf's muscles tense, for he clenched his jaw again in pain, cutting off any words that might've followed.

"And what would I receive in return for taking such a risk," Dragan replied at last, "...besides your service as guide? There are others beyond the mountains we could find for the task."

Cirad needed no pause to consider his answer. "The debt of my people! We are many...and would be free to join your cause. The vision was of *me*, not some other beyond the mountains. Aren't you afraid that without me you'll fail? The last of his words faded into little more than a mumble as the elf's handsome face sagged to one side. He appeared barely awake now. His eyelids had begun to blink slowly closed and back open, remaining shut a bit longer each time. "I too know of the evil you speak," he continued in a near-whisper. "I know it all too well..."

"And how do I know they'll choose to join me?" Dragan frowned, distracted momentarily in surveying the work of his scouts. "Are you their leader, that you might speak for them without deliberation? Or perhaps you've something quite different in mind for my men once we've finished your dirty work?"

Receiving no response to his question, the Black King looked back to Cirad. Slumber had claimed the weary elf at last. His eyes were closed—and mouth slightly parted—as his chest rose and fell in an easy rhythm.

"They won't," answered Fashra in his place. "And even if they did, what use are a multitude of untrained slaves? More mouths to feed. More corpses to bury on the road."

For a moment Dragan was surprised Fashra didn't share Cirad's desire to see members of their common race rescued from bondage — but then he remembered who he was dealing with. Fashra had sworn an oath of fealty, and like the others who'd crossed over into this new world with him, she'd place that oath above all else. He suddenly felt a wave of pride that was only slightly diminished by what she said next:

"And don't forget what I told you, lord — proven true here today. Sanisar's ruling caste is filled with such powerful sorcerers guarded by elite swordsmen. Whether he's prepared for us or not, such a course of action may likely spell our undoing…before we ever set foot in the land you seek!"

Releasing another sigh, Dragan turned this time to Ûladriss with an impish grin and raised eyebrow. "What say you to that, marshal?"

Shaking off his previous disheartened look, the Haxûdī managed a smile of his own when he saw Dragan's change of expression. "I'd say no matter which path you choose, it looks like we're in danger. Yet again."

"Always, my friend," Dragan laughed aloud. "Always."

www.ingramcontent.com/pod-product-compliance
Lightning Source LLC
Chambersburg PA
CBHW030850030726
47495CB00005B/1466